AS THE BUTTE BURNS

Cover art by Ilia Zuri
Author photo by Carol Hook
Special Thanks to Amy Horowitz for her support and detailed memory
Book design and publishing management by The Publishing World

Johnson, Dr. Norman P.
As the Butte Burns
978-0-9990992-5-4

1. Fiction / General. 2. Fiction / Biographical. 3. Fiction / Political.

Printed in the USA
Distributed by Ingram

First Printing, 2025

As the Butte Burns

DR. NORMAN P. JOHNSON

CONTENTS

DISCLAIMER

This mostly true story is a parody about young kids dropping out of the rat race in the '70s. Trust funders running from responsibilities, low-dollar hustlers on the lamb, artists on the fly, and other non-conformist rebels of the '70s—all running away from Cold-War conformity to personal freedom and an idyllic mountain Camelot. Most were in search of a better, more free, and honest life; some looked to make their fortune in the tourist industry, and some were just ski bums looking for cheap thrills.

Although the time setting of the novel is the late '70s, it draws inspiration from the people, events, and societal issues that occurred in Crested Butte between the years 1968 to 1988. Names have been preserved as much as possible in order to expose the guilty and remember the innocent. All characters, places, names, and specific situations depicted within, should be considered entirely fictional and strictly parodic in nature. It contains explicit adult situations and is not intended for use by anyone below the age of 18...or squares or prudes of any kind.

What happened in Crested Butte during this period qualifies as a very special experience, made so by the spunky, resourceful, and caring people who spat in the face of the extreme living conditions and made Crested Butte into a legendary mountain home for profound growing, thinking, and maturing. All the while, we worshiped at the alter of eternity, enjoying one of the most beautiful places on earth. This book is dedicated to all those innocents who came to the mountains, who sought her solace, who basked in her brilliance, and died in her arms. May they all find heaven as once they did on earth.

~ 1 ~

AS THE BUTTE BURNS

"Rules and laws are just suggestions for the intelligent responsible freeman and only apply to the ignorant, irresponsible, and incompetent masses who need to be kept in line." — Cowboy

"I can usually see trouble coming two, three feet away." — Townes Van Zandt

"Freedom is something that dies unless it's used." — Dr. Hunter Thompson

"Damn, it's getting dark," I finally have to admit to myself, squinting out the windshield into stark darkness surrounding a lonely white line ribbon all too closely appearing out of the black void. "Something's not right," I drunkenly declare.

I'm driving all night taking the usual roads out of the mountains to the eastern flatlands and in this case, a little town just north of Denver: Greeley. I stare at the battery meter on the dashboard, noting its own dimness. Maybe I'm going blind from alcohol. I've been pounding beers all day long and even while driving over the pass I chain drink until I can barely see. I even spin the old girl 360 degrees from alcohol spasms steering on a straight and level road just north of Salida. That scares the shit out of me. I have to get out of the car and run around it in tight circles, burning up some of the debilitating horse piss so I can continue. My new job starts in about four more hours and I'm still three hours out of Denver.

"Oh no! *Et tu?* When's the fun going to stop?" I pound my fists on the oversized '58 Oldsmobile Rocket 88 station wagon steering wheel. I'm being forced out of my home, out of my paradise, out of my life. I've lost everything. I've lost my only home, my best friends, my only true love, my meager fortune, and now, the last of my dignity. I've not only lost the only love of my life but lost my ability to ever love again. There's nothing left to love with. I shamefully wipe away more tears for the umpteenth time this night as I pop another Coors.

I finally admit to myself the battery gauge reads low and I'm slowly discharging the car's battery driving at night with the lights on. The generator just can't keep up. Soon I will be stranded without any hope of making it to my new job starting in about four more hours. Literally after all that's happened, my last chance of surviving this day, my day of retreat, with any trace of self-respect, quickly slips from my weak and desperate grasp, leaving me a hollow crust of burned-out worthlessness.

"SHIT! FUCK! WHORE!" I scream into the empty void, soaking it up and choking it off so fast, it's as if it never happened. Then the old car just slowly dies and I have to steer it slowly to the shoulder, leaving me now in total silence as well as blank darkness. Like my life, everything just comes to a dark end.

"I-I-I-E-E-E-E-E!!!" I scream uncontrollably, while flailing my arms around viciously. Then I abruptly stop. The silent curtain descends immediately, again, along with a lot of foolish feelings. If animals are witnessing this, I bet they just got their thrill for the night and are hopping home as fast as they can.

"Where's my home?" I yell. Silence is all I get. "What the fuck is happening?" I sit for a moment as silence descends again all around me. I think I hear something. Scratching sounds. I don't care. I reach under my seat and pull out the Colt Commander I pull it out of its holster and look hard at it. I cock it, putting a round in the chamber. I look around me at the darkness outside so enveloping and heavy. How can so much nothing be so damned crushing?

*

JULY 9, 1970, MARBLE, Colo. (UPI) – Nets were strung across a turbulent mountain river today while searchers checked the banks for the remaining victims of one of the worst traffic accidents in Colorado history. Nine persons were killed Monday night when a pickup truck carrying 12 people plunged 200 feet down a Colorado mountainside and into the chilly waters of the Crystal River. Bodies of three of the victims still have not been found. The Colorado State Patrol said the mishap on 10,500-foot Schofield Pass in the central Colorado Rockies was the worst in state history, excluding those involving trains.

"Hello?" comes the voice of Kemp over the phone.

"Hello, yourself. I just heard it on the news. What the hell is going on out there? Crested Butte is spread all over the airwaves like a train wreck. You're the marshal there, did you know them?" I demand without waiting for an answer. "Twelve people? Jesus Christ, what kind of truck can hold twelve people?"

"I only know the driver, Doctor Robinson," Kemp replied. "He walked away. The State Police won't let me get near the accident. I just saw the guy a couple of days ago and he told me he was going over to Aspen to pick up his new Blazer and apparently took the Aspen shortcut through Marble, up Crystal Canyon, and through the Devil's Punchbowl to Schofield Pass. He said it started to rain and he got out to engage his hubs and the truck just fell off the road."

"Fell off the road?" I exploded. "Shit, we drove that road all the way over to Marble last year with an antique Dodge pickup and my equally old Harley. It's not that bad."

"He's a university professor and apparently didn't know how to set the brake properly when he got out to throw the hubs. Book smart, but fatally incompetent when it came to four-wheel driving. The sad part is he just retired here from Urbana with his newly pregnant student wife who died along with her entire family of cousins they were visiting in Aspen."

"Don't these people know the wilderness is not a place where you take a Sunday stroll down to the park. It'll bite you in the ass if you're not prepared."

"You're preaching to the choir."

*

Eight hours of non-stop squeezing, sucking, philosophizing, fucking, political discourse, more sucking, some more fucking, a lot of pessimism about the state of affairs and so forth and so on. Between bouts of abundant friction, lubrication, and long gasps of pure pleasure, we analyze, idealize, and fantasize about our lives, the times, changing society, non-conformity, peace and love hippies, long hair, dope smoking, and revolution. We went from stroking, scratching, and squeezing every nook and cranny of each other's body to solving world peace and social unrest. And I still don't know her name.

"C...c...all me...Jane," she stutters between gulps for air as she bounces up and down.

"They...call me...Cowboy," I gasp between bounces, wondering if we should shake hands.

"I hate Nixon!" she growls as she pushes down hard and then pulls up, literally lifting me off the bed. "Hell no, we won't go!"

"DuPont deals death!" I squeal in response. I sound like a little boy at Christmas with a squirming puppy. I try to lower my voice. "Burn bras and draft cards!"

"Ya-HOOOO!" she screams. "Born to be wild!"

"Be wild and free like the sea!" I respond not sure if this is a thing.

"All you need is love, dah di-dah di-dah da," she chants in tune with her hip shoving.

"You have nothing to lose but your chains!" I shout and roll her over on her back.

"Power to the people!" she squeals and puts her legs up over her head.

"Turn on, tune in, drop out!" I yell as I greedily mount her again.

She starts barking like a dog. I start howling like a wolf.

We go into another squirming bout of horizontal calisthenics trying to stay hooked up while doing the dirty dancing. We truly define what it means to get all wrapped up in your work. Finally, we take a much-needed breather.

"What do we do now?" I ask, not feeling particularly consumed yet. Just very wet with sweat and loaded with wanton desire.

"Curl up like kittens and wait," she teases.

"Wait for what?"

"You'll know," she whispers as she goes south looking for something to slap around.

I never had a user's manual for this sort of thing so I still feel like an amateur. I'm making it up as I go along, hoping naked instinct will get me by. So far, so good.

I'm also still new to this *love the one you're with* thing. My coolest friend from high school, Melvin, reminded me that it was a sin against God to turn down a woman's offer. Which might explain why, not too much later, he had a fat wife and four kids. I took his advice seriously though, and, anyway, it's so damned long between hookups, I really can't rationalize saying no under any circumstances anyway. Maybe if they're coyote ugly, but again, that's why we have alcohol.

While most teenage boys were getting their brains bashed out on the football field, losing what little IQ they had to spare, in preparation for a quick marriage and the usual middle-age lobotomy and early unjust death, I did my high school time behind the scenes, running the film projector and hanging out in the chemistry lab with frustrated, brainy, non-cheerleader-type girls—preventing me from having any chance at early sex. Everything I learned about a woman's body was done sparingly, in the dark, and with a lot of guessing.

Undaunted by this marathon loser's party, I figure I only have to keep it together for one, maybe two more days, tops. Tonight, I break all kinds of personal records and all because of Nix-goon, the shit-for-brains street pimp turned douche-bag, winning the presidency, not once, but TWICE! What the fuck is wrong with my fellow Americans? I can't keep sublimating like this, only getting pity sex every four years when my nation makes a bad decision.

I'm not really complaining though. That's a waste of time. I'm just depressed as hell and wondering if I'll ever find a life worth living in a capitalist piggy society. Corporate America is just not the answer for me. I love my dignity and freedom too much and I'm not alone with that feeling.

Like good little scouts, we stock up on supplies as she leads me from Ed's apartment down past the brightly lit street kiosks near the Village that never sleeps, offering whatever we need, including bottled water, a first for me. Then it's back to her large, open-plan apartment on the top floor. Some excellent, straight-off-the-boat, blond Lebanese kief that Ed laid on me right after handing me over to her, makes it all even more exciting and exotic.

"I love weed!" I exclaim. "It massages the soul and renews hope after bitter disappointments."

"I love getting high...and naked!" she says in a low seductive voice.

"That works for me."

I look around during our break, now that the sun is just starting to glow orange over a cold Atlantic, brightening up the large open area. It appears to be a typical SOHO open-plan warehouse filled with artist projects and little living areas replete with mattresses, hot plates, and a few beanbag chairs. Hippie flats are the only reasonable way to afford living in New York and not have to commute to Harlem. Young kids on their way to a career or a life begin here, in groups of like-minded people, sharing space, food, drugs, and sex, growing together, learning how to live humanely in a madding world. I don't see anybody else moving about, so apparently we have the whole place to ourselves. Good, I hate performance critics.

*

I'd spent the whole day yesterday hawking our Warlock Productions 16mm underground film titled, *The Tortoise and the Egg*, to the media producers on 45th Street.

"Unbelievable," I sputtered as I blew out a big cloud of blue smoke in Ed's crowded little apartment. I was tired and sweaty. Our one claim to fame maybe was the screenwriter, Nicholas Pritzker, a billionaire heir to the Chicago Pritzker real estate empire, dabbling in filmmaking, hired me and the Coits as his production crew.

Ed let me stay on his couch whenever I ended up in New York. He and I were classmates in Physics at the Rackham School of Graduate Studies at the University of Michigan. This time, I'm trying to interest someone in the film and TV industry to distribute our little film, or perhaps hire our crew for revolutionary, perhaps edgy film projects. After visiting a few highly corrupted and bigoted New Yorker film producers, I experienced an epiphany: New York isn't ready for the likes of me. I'm way too nice for these vultures. They'd eat me alive. So, I save on the taxi fare and walk all the way from Central Park down Broadway to Twelfth and a couple of blocks over to Ed's fourth floor tiny apartment. There's a crowd of equally pissed-off friends gathered around his little TV when I get back and it's official before they even finish voting out west.

"That douche bag gets elected, again?" I squeal. "He's a cheap-assed liar and a low-class thief and yet I bet my own damn brothers—all traitors—voted for him. I can't believe it!" I rant on with the others as we settle in for a long night of misery, alcohol, drugs, and dejection.

Ed hands me a bong loaded with some Moroccan hash he's been saving up for "just such a day as this," he says. "Everybody's lost their freakin' minds," he yells as he lights it up. "First he drives me out of graduate school with his fucking Vietnam lottery, making me live like a refugee in a slum warehouse, and now, that turd-sandwich wants to put us in some kind of Cuckoo's Nest!"

I take a big hit, cough, and pass it on. He plays a lick of Blues on his prized handmade Spanish guitar he almost always keeps in his lap, then stops to take his turn. He explained to me earlier that after spending each depraved week teaching in the Manhattan school system, he eagerly plays classical guitar on weekends in the village for tips. He's a prodigy of his father, a music teacher in the New Jersey school system.

He consumes massive amounts of gelatin which helps him grow strong fingernails on his right hand, which he sharpens daily into five perfectly shaped guitar picks. Listening to him is like listening to a whole orchestra of guitars performing in perfect sync. He's really good, but he wanted to be a physicist and now that dream is dead. Fuck the government that eats its own children.

"If it wasn't for my guitar and weekend gigs, I don't think I could tolerate living here. I've been robbed three times, accosted in the subway, and had my car looted almost weekly until there's nothing left to drive. And last month, they threw my Rottweiler out the window before cleaning me out for the fifth time. It's down to just my clothes and this guitar, which I take with me everywhere I go." He plays another sad wailing Blues lick.

"Life sucks!" he declares. "What are you going to do if you can't sell your film?" he asks pointedly. I grimace.

"I'm trying to finish my PhD in Atmospheric Research at Space Physics, but after that, I don't know," I admit. "Science research budgets are being slashed by this puss-faced president. The space race is over, and apparently, we won, so everybody packs up and goes home. No more money for physics research and my salary, as pitiful as it is, might disappear at any moment.

"I don't want to end up teaching like you," I say, "no offense, so I'm scouting out some TV producers as well as movie distributors. Maybe I can land a gig doing live Rock & Roll concerts for a TV show or something. But I'm not going to live here. If I went through what you have, I think I would kill someone. I need to find a dirt road to nowhere. Maybe join the rest of my film crew out in the Rocky Mountains where people live free and are not hassled by fucking pigs."

"Good luck with that," he fires right back. "I had to take a job teaching little pissant yuppies at Stuyvesant just to keep from getting drafted. I agree, no future here for sure. Nobody wants to do physics anymore. All those little disrespectful bastards I'm teaching are only interested in making money with their family's influence, quickly, as if it was owed them, the self-entitled little snots!"

I toast him and down the official drink of a roadie, a warm Coke still in the can well-laced with Black Jack, something I picked up recently touring with Joe Walsh, REO, and Grand Funk. The election party quickly turns into an impromptu wake, mourning the passing of our democracy, our freedoms, our rights while consoling ourselves with large amounts of alcohol and pot.

Nix-goon, the shithead California real-estate scammer that somehow hoodwinked a lot of stupid Americans to vote for him, showed himself to be a cheap street thug and a corrupt incompetent government official for decades, and yet here we are again. The liberal progress and enlightenment that John, Robert, and Martin bought with their very lives is now officially pissed away by a bunch of greedy power-mad, war-mongering corrupt business jerks, hell-bent to suppress everything us new-age kids, the boomers, stand for and should vote for. Somewhere America went wrong and the new, new-age seems to be turning into soccer parents and real estate speculators. Ass-licking is now a required resume skill.

The door flies open and in explodes what looks like a girl wearing an oversized Yale sweatshirt like a monk's robe and reminding me of a new literary graduate interviewing with *The New Yorker* poetry editor. She holds a bottle of champagne in one hand and several long stem glasses in the other.

"Here!" she orders while handing out the glasses and splashing some liquid somewhere near each one. "Drink this! It may be the last before we're all sent to re-education centers!" She sniffs the air. "Oh, hash? Don't mind if I do." She drops the bottle and grabs the bong out of Ed's hand.

She's beautiful in an intellectual sort of way, drunk and obviously liberal to a fault. Curly black hair falls over black-rimmed glasses that resemble Coke bottle bottoms. Just my kind of woman, an intellectual and not fussy about what they can't see in the dark.

"Who wants to get laid here?" she pointedly demands, looking directly at Ed. He fakes surprise and looks around the room with a pained face.

"Not again, thank you. How about him?" He points at me. "You two have a lot in common. Products of small liberal artsy-fartsy colleges and obviously both horny as hell and pissed to the max, which makes for hot vengeance sex."

"I need to over indulge in hedonism to compensate for my philosophical loss," she declares. "What do you say?" She turns to me. "Are you a Kierkegaard, Nietzsche, Heidegger or Sartre existentialist?",

I stop looking at her ankles. Old habit I picked up from one of my high school buddies who came back from his first year in the navy swearing he'd learned that a women's ankle size is in direct proportion to her vagina. "Sartre, with some overtones of Heidegger and Kierkegaard. Nietzsche was a Nazi in disguise," I proudly volunteer.

"You'll do, come with me!" she commanded.

She grabs my hand and jerks me out of my depressive malaise and into the next great adventure of my life.

*

I'm trying to be casual even though stark naked in a large, strange, and open space. Windows line all four walls with not a blind or curtain in sight. I look at her gorgeous shapely body in the dim morning twilight and try to relax as if it's all normal, everyday happenings. Secretly I'm carving another notch on my imaginary penis post.

"I don't know what war our fathers fought to save us from tyranny," she expounds, "but in the end, the tyranny they defeated ended up infecting them; like a doctor heroically curing the sick only to die from the sickness. They became the generation of blind obedience to absurd ideas. No sex out of wedlock. No birth control unless married. No peace from war. Can't even smoke weed, for Chrissake, something our forefathers did regularly with no concern, but now, it's banned with absolutely no valid reason other than preventing us from having freedom of thought! It's mental censorship. We're being terrorized and controlled by a bunch of closet Nazi evangelicals out to destroy knowledge and truth, enslaving the world to their absurd beliefs, justifying their inhuman atrocities."

When she gets worked up, I know I'm in for another frantic bout of incensed sexual energy released like a series of small thermo-nuclear explosions. "If you can't take the heat," I remember my professor enjoining us, "then get the hell out of the nuclear accelerator!"

"You know, poor liberal white intellectuals are just as discriminated against as blacks and women," I proclaim. "I can't have a good job unless I cut my hair and join the right fraternity. I have to self-lobotomize in order to put up with corporate bullshit. These bastard capitalist conservative pigs are killing me and my friends just so they can enjoy the freedom to make another dishonest dollar. Graduate students, especially poor ones whose families can't buy them out of the draft, are just like blacks, fighting for their very existence in an oppressive and restrictive society controlled from the top down and whose only purpose is illicit power gain. They want to take away my right to vote and ultimately my right to life, liberty, and the pursuit of profit. We're just fuel for their corporate boiler, fodder for their imperial cannons. Labor and wages are nothing but carrots on a stick to only incentivize the mule, but never truly reward him."

She looks at me quizzically.

"That's right," I add, "I said profit. That's what they wrote in the first draft of the Declaration of Independence. Don't they teach you history at Swarthmore?"

She viciously grabs my now re-erected cock and holds it up to her mouth as if a microphone.

"I'm not from Swarthmore!" she shouts. "I'm from Vassar!" She drops the mic.

"Ouch!" I yell before realizing its not hurting.

As expected, she climbs on with an ugly look in her eyes and away we go again. About fifteen minutes later, our language of love devolves to Latin.

"Cun Nuncio, Quo Perio-o-o-o-o-o-o!" she screams and collapses on me. I relax and light up a cigarette. My mind drifts as I stroke her quivering hips.

I really love the sexual revolution, except for the part afterword where my primordial Methodist upbringing kicks in and I think I owe something to my gracious and merciful partner. Somehow, Anglo-Saxon puritanism imprinted me with the feeling that any women sleeping with me should be paid with a lifelong commitment of love. This is clearly my weak point and surely will cost me dearly someday.

"So, how about coming to Ann Arbor for the weekend? It just so happens I'm heading in that direction. I've got a little red Fiesta convertible and a lid of weed. I'll show you some fun on the Pennsylvania Turnpike."

"You poor clueless bastard. You just got the experience of a lifetime and you expect to keep it going across state lines? Get real. I was just a little depressed and figured sex, drugs, and

Rock & Roll is better than just drinking alone in misery. Besides, I have to get back to my graduate school in Rochester."

"And the troops thank you for your service, my beautiful consolation," I fire back and start crawling back on top of her with a hungry smirk. She still smiles invitingly and I'm not stopping until she begs me. I can take it.

*

I peek from behind my newspaper when Joe and Marty, both wearing dark sunglasses surrounded by messed up long hair and looking a little worse than warmed-over bear shit after a record salmon run, come through the door of the hotel restaurant searching for the usual empty secluded table. The place is filling up so, I hunker down slightly hoping their dark glasses will save me.

Apparently not. Marty spots me, waves, and pushes his way through a knot of clueless suits to my corner table.

"Whas up?" asks Marty, twisting his black handlebar moustache and smiling like a sick puppy. Not waiting for an invitation, he sits down.

"Think it's gonna rain?" he adds.

Joe giggles and sits opposite.

He's referring to the 3 a.m. hotel hallway wastebasket water war, drunkenly but valiantly fought by band and crew after closing the last concert in Minneapolis on the first Barnstorm tour. Joe recently broke with the James Gang and with money from Geffen Enterprises and specifically the little bean counter, Irving Azov, Joe was being bred for a spot with the new Eagles' production formula taking California and the rest of the culture-starved world by storm: Find talent, put 'em in a studio until they produce an album, put 'em on a cheap, fast, cash-generating concert tour, and secretly pocket most of that cash for those all-important monetary transactions that grease the dicks of the vultures as they suck talent dry. Dave Geffen and Irving Azov were looting musicians by storm—hence, Barnstorm.

"I'm an Oregon duck. I can take it," I grunt in reluctant recognition. "You're up a little early for happy hour."

"Marty tells me you're a former NASA scientist now doing Rock & Roll," says Joe. "I didn't know that. What brought you down? Drugs? Women? Running away from home after your dog died?"

"Shithead Nix-goon," I reply without looking up.

"Oh," he says, almost understanding. Our second-term idiot criminal president was cutting research budgets nationwide, throwing scientists and students out on the streets to survive or die. Many were being forced into military industrial research, which made them cringe from obvious moral conflicts. Students were taking a moral stand against the unlawful Vietnam war, winning the political moral high ground, but losing the economic war. Now, one either had to sell out their ethics and grovel for a false sense of security, or go it alone in the desert of freedom and rugged individualism, where the language is cash and only the flexible survive.

"When I was thrown to the street after six years of doing the work of four PhDs, I decided to run away and join a Rock & Roll band," I explain sarcastically. "I thought it would be romantic."

Marty sniggers. A waitress appears and pours coffee for everyone but doesn't seem to notice Joe, the newly anointed rock star.

"The work you did on the four-channel playback effect is working out great," he declares, sipping on his hot brew.

Marty and I had set up a four-channel tape deck where we play back an earlier recorded version of, "I've Got A Ride," which he plays with on stage and we mix the output to a full four-channel surround-sound setup. The spooky effect seems to rotate Joe's guitar around the hall assaulting the ears with his unique sound from all directions.

"Irving just told me he's got twenty more dates booked for a second tour," Joe says. "I want you to come with us and help run the board. We're going to add lights."

"There's not enough cocaine in Palm Beach to keep me going for another month like the one we just finished. I didn't get any sleep or sex for weeks."

"Then you need more of this. Here," Marty says leaning over toward me and holding out a little spoon filled with sparkly snow. I instinctively lean into it and snort it right up. "Bump?"

"Can't fly on one wing," I quip. He dips, offers another, and I oblige.

"So, what are you going to do?" Joe asks.

"I'm going to join some friends of mine and do some film-making, maybe learn to ski."

"And where would that be?"

"Where the fuck do you think? You're the one telling everyone where to go, every damn concert!"

*

"I feel like Wile E. Coyote," I pronounce for no apparent reason. "He keeps trying to catch that little skinny bastard, but no matter how good the plan something always fucks it up."

I'm strung out in the afternoon from a thirty-six-hour non-stop drive from southern California to southeast Michigan, convalescing on Eber's couch, watching my six-foot color TV projector, a one-of-a kind machine made out of old WWII optical bomb sights and radar screens that projects a full-color picture onto a six-foot home movie screen. Old color cartoons look especially impressive on the big screen. I love watching the art work of Chuck Jones and the lunacy of Wile E. Coyote. Can't help but feel sorry for the big dumb bastard. He uses technology to solve all his problems, but they all fail. Maybe he should try something simpler, like a shotgun.

"Crap," I think out loud. "I've got to pack up this giant projector and take it with me. But I don't have room in the truck for the freakin' twelve-foot rear projection screen. I'm going to have to store the screen in your garage for a while. I hope that's okay?"

"What?" Eberbach sputters as he coughs out a blue cloud of smoke. "You know this is not your best stuff." He hands the joint back to me.

"I know, sorry," I apologize, "but it was all we could find in Encinitas when I picked up Margie. It's probably Tijuana ditch weed but at least I made enough off the trip to get back here and cash in my real estate contract. There's nothing holding me here anymore."

"I think you were lucky to find some teenager from Traverse who sells shit weed to rednecks, 'cause this stuff sucks!" Steve declares. He hands the twisted joint back to me, but I wave it off. "Do you know what Margie plans to do with her share of this crap?"

I picked up Margie in Encinitas where she was banging a bunch of horny coke-snorting surfers. I'd taken the summer off after being a roadie for Fanfare Productions all winter, to visit family and friends in Oregon, have my hernia surgery performed in Seattle, and maybe make some contacts in California looking for a film gig or maybe a dope connection.

Margie said she had a contact for weed and wanted a ride to Ann Arbor. I wanted to make a buck on my trip back, so we ganged up for the return drive. She had been married to Tom, a very close friend and owner of a 4WD Chevy truck identical to mine, so she helped with the continuous drive back in my truck.

"Don't know and don't care. After I heard her at full volume doing half the surfers in southern California, I'm almost sorry I brought her back. How's Tom doing?"

"He's all right," Steve says. "I've got him building crossovers for our first run of Time Windows. He's already living with some new chick."

"That's good, but I know how much he loved her and this has got to hurt. How long were they married?" I ask.

"Six years," he replies.

"That's got to be rough," I declare. "I don't understand. They seemed so happy. On the way back here, she told me she felt like she missed something, getting married so early. She didn't miss about fifty well-tanned surfer dudes from the sound of things when I picked her up."

"Sounds like she missed out on being a slut," he quips.

"How would you feel," I continue, "if your high school sweetheart who gives you her virginity and promises forever love, and you work your ass off to provide a home, a ceramic studio, and parties up the yin-yang, up and disappears with the first surfer dude to pass through town, leaving you holding your dick in your hand?"

"Sounds like a typical Ann Arbor soap opera," Steve laments. "They were a model of young love. Then she just hiccups and gets an itch to spread it far and wide, like Johnny Appleseed."

"Exactly! Shabby!" I declare. "That's why I'm getting out of this rat race. It's only designed for failure and great disappointments. I'm going back to the country, the beautiful places, and find my way among similar people."

"You can stay here and help me manufacture the Time Window for a PA application like what you originally designed," Steve offered. "I just think the real money is in the living room. Can't you convince Marty to help you sell it to some big band? Doesn't he work with KISS now?"

"Those no talent hucksters wouldn't know good sound unless it was laced with coke, in which case, they'd snort it all up before the opening act," I declare. "Rock & Roll roadies have no vision outside of pretty flashing lights, blow jobs, a lot of sexy knobs to twiddle, glowing VU meters, and more power to the amplifiers. Rock & Roll makes money by distorting sound beyond reality, not making it nice and pure. Hence, speakers don't have to be better, just louder. He said nobody would believe it was a good speaker anyway if it didn't take up half the stage."

"Image issue. I bet we'll have a similar problem with a new home speaker that looks like a fancy pickle barrel," he predicts. "But sounds like expensive headphones."

"I wish I had the money to stay here and make a prototype that'd blow their minds. But I'm just a poor little farm boy from Oregon without a trust fund. I have to work to feed myself and put gas in the truck. But here, I can't even get a job pumping gas. Over qualified!"

"You can join DCM, but we can't pay a salary. You'll have to work for stock options like the rest of us," he offers. He gets up and goes in the kitchen. "Want another Coors?"

I also brought back ten cases of Coors. Turns out, I can almost make as much money smuggling beer as I do pot. Go wonder.

"Yes, to the beer, and no thanks to working for you," I say. "If I have to work for a living, then I might as well do it in paradise. Working with a bunch of greedy capitalist MBA pigs doesn't sound like much fun anyway. No offense, but business types are basically thieves and assholes. I'd spend all my time convincing them to be smarter than they're capable, and all my money staying high enough to prevent murder charges.

"Actually, though," I continue loudly so he can hear me, "I'd love to build that electronic pipe organ we designed. With these speakers married to the Mauer amp, all we'd need is my design for a fast-Fourier synthesizer and your design for the proportional keyboard. Only our speakers can hope to equal the sound power and purity of a sixty-four-foot cathedral organ. We could rattle gargoyles right off the walls with that puppy."

Steve returns with two yellow cans of Coors. "I'll take four cases. It'll probably be a while before I see any more."

"I'm tired of being poor," I go on. "I need to find something like our speakers where I can make some serious money using my brains. I can't stand working for assholes and idiots."

"Isn't Crested Butte close to Aspen? Maybe you can marry money," he suggests with a big smile.

"Not likely," I respond. "Crested Butte's not like Aspen. It's full of poor young college kids, living in freedom, beauty, and low rent. Instead of me having to follow NASA to fucking Houston or grinding my ass off at a tie-choking engineering job, I'm going to retire to the wilderness while I'm still young enough to enjoy retirement. Jobs are for old people and losers. I don't want to end up like Margie with nothing left but surfer sex and shit weed.

*

When driving non-stop across America with hours of grinding out asphalt miles, one at a time about a minute each, I have plenty of time to think and reflect. I always drive non-stop because poor people like me can't afford to stop and rent a room for the night. I drive and drive until I start nodding out, at which time I pull off the freeway, search for a quiet and hidden parking place where I'm not likely to be surprised by a bored random cop passing by, and grab a couple hours sleep.

Also, when living a life of freedom without the money to support it, then petty, unjust, or plain old oppressive laws are applied to your case, making it hard to be free. If a redneck cop catches someone like me, they give no quarter and fuck with you until they can find a reason to haul your ass in. I was carrying my guns, as I usually do, and so do most of us in the antiwar, Civil Rights, and student rights movement, so I needed to look plain and ordinary, blending in, attracting as little attention as possible. I didn't want to be another fucking statistic. I would not cut my hair though. I drew the line with my hair, as did a lot of us liberal rebels.

A dark blue 4-wheel drive Chevy Carryall truck, slightly dented and dirty, shouts *redneck*. And when I put an NRA lifetime membership sticker on the left rear window, any approaching cop can't help but think I'm one of them. Plus, dressing like a stupid cowboy truck driver with requisite hat, boots, Levi jacket, over-sized silver belt buckle, and turquoise watchband gets my hair through the few random stops I do encounter. I'm not going to be obvious bait for the Nazi cops padding their arrest rates by making sure all traffic stops find a reason or, with cultural profiling, too often a crime. Insane drug laws only exist so cops can arrest anyone they choose and if they're not carrying, that can easily be fixed. Cops make sure that there is always a crime to justify their actions, even if they have to invent one. There's no justice in the organized world of today leaving one more reason to head for the hills and beyond their reach.

"...summer's come and gone, winter's coming on, and I've laid around and played around this ol' town too long, and it feels like I gotta travel on." —Billy Grammer 1959

From Ann Arbor, I follow I-94 across southern Michigan to Chicago and before hitting the Loop, turn left on I-55 heading to St. Louis. I pass Argonne National Lab, where a few years earlier I helped run an experiment that showed the proton has structure called quarks. Since then, I made a short underground film, joined a NASA lab doing satellite atmospheric research, and finally invented a whole new type of audio speaker. I try my hand at live video projections of rock bands in large venue concerts, namely the Allman Brothers, make some art movies, and try my hand at being a college-town drug smuggler investing windfall profits as a student housing slumlord. But now, shit's flying everywhere so time to leave without my hat.

"Whether I'm right or whether I'm wrong. Whether I find a place in this world or never belong. I've gotta be me, I've gotta be me. What else can I be but what I am? I want to live, not merely survive. And I won't give up this dream of life, that keeps me alive. The dream that I see makes me what I am. That faraway prize, a world of success, is waiting for me if I heed the call. I won't settle down or settle for less as long as there's half a chance that I can have it all. I've gotta be me, I've gotta be me!" —Walter Marks, 1967

I soon turn right on I-80 and begin the long straight westward stretch across the flat prairie lands, until eventually I'll run into a wall of mountains. I'm eighteen hours from Denver so my mind has plenty of time to wander all over my world. I call it truck driver self-therapy. The only problem is, I have no fucking idea what I'm going to do next for income. I just know I have to do it in a safe place where I can feel secure and not subject to constant surveillance and threat of punishment for simply being free and exercising my inalienable rights. Maybe my wits, practical skills, and rural background will somehow see me through in a depressed little hideaway, a partial ghost town high up in the Rockies. Besides, my best buddy is the town marshal and he smokes dope and enjoys cocaine just like real people.

I can't ski. My parents, being practical farmers, couldn't afford any sport for their kids requiring anything more expensive than a bat and maybe a jock strap. Expensive sports equipment, like gloves, simply wasn't on the Christmas list. I found it particularly depressing when, not long ago on a boring wintery Sunday, my graduate student friends took me to Whitmore Lake's little pimple-hill ski run. After strapping on a pair of cheap wooden rental skis, I discover I can't even stand up without holding onto a nearby tree. My friends from Minnesota and Wisconsin, all expert skiers, try to help but gravity rules the day. If I stay over the coming winter in Crested Butte, I'm sure I'll have to figure this ski thing out, eventually. I'm up for it, I think. Wintering over in the Rockies is a rite of passage that looms as a personal challenge I must accept if I am to call myself a free mountain man.

On long drives, I often think about my situation, my history, human history, philosophy, science, and why people do the weird fucking things that they do. I'm a keen observer of human foibles, constantly questioning commonly accepted ideas and behavior because, quite frankly, most of it makes no sense. As an accomplished physicist, I figure if I can understand relativity and quantum mechanics, I've got as good a shot as anyone for figuring out the human condition, and hence, mine. I take it on as a long-term challenge.

I reach the I-80 cutoff near Joliet and turn right to begin the long-haul, due west, to the other side of the great continental flat-top prairie. The boringly straight highway allows me to kill huge amounts of time thinking and going over in minute detail every aspect of my conscious being. What's happening? Why? And where am I going to get my next meal? For the poor, economics always sets limits, and for me, the limits have always been tight.

I stop for gas at the border in Davenport and grab a six-pack and a sandwich for the long night run ahead. I climb back on the freeway thinking perhaps I've been operating out of my given social class, hanging with brilliant academics and radical thinking students. My friends at home in Oregon were mostly loggers, mill workers, mechanics, or at best, shopkeepers, accountants and maybe a nurse, but never a doctor. But since going east to college, most of my new friends now come from the upper classes, self-identified as business people, professionals who belong to monied families, providing them a guaranteed income far beyond the eighteen years that I and my kind are lucky to receive at all. They're known as *Trust Funders.*

I'm on my own without a dime, living on my few talents and lesser wits. Like all the historical poor who are lucky enough to break out, I must take advantage of what little leverage I can find. It's a new awakened age of extended brotherhood and un-restricted love. I'm unfortunately too cynical to be a hippie, be-sides most hippies are from wealthy to middle class families who can afford experimenting with communal living amongst strangers. Poor people don't rough it well with rich people. But I'm thinking that a new, organic, perhaps intentionally formed family can exist that doesn't need to be biological.

"Well, they tell me of a pie up in the sky, waiting for me when I die, but between the day you're born and when you die, they never seem to hear even your cry. So as sure as the sun will shine, I'm gonna get my share now, what's mine. And then the harder they come, the harder they fall, one and all. Ooh, the harder they come, the harder they fall, one and all.

Well, the oppressors are trying to keep me down, trying to drive me underground. And they think that they have got the battle won, I say forgive them Lord, they know not what they've done. 'Cause as sure as the sun will shine, I'm gonna get my share now, what's mine. And then the harder they come, the harder they fall, one and all. Ooh, the harder they come, the harder they fall, one and all.

And I keep on fighting for the things I want, though I know that when you're dead you can't. But I'd rather be a free man in my grave, than living as a puppet or a slave..." —Jimmy Cliff, "The Harder They Come," 1972

As soon as I landed at Lake Forest College, fresh off the turnip bus from Oregon, I met Kemp Coit, cousin to the curtain cleaner empire and a low-level trust funder from Martha's Vineyard. When he had it, he generously shared his free money with his friends. But I worked for a living holding down two jobs while in college and many times I bought the Friday night pitchers at the Lantern when his monthly check ran out. We started sharing lots more, as he bought a movie camera for my classes with Manupelli at the U of M film school and I bought him an old Dodge pickup for his first mountain truck in Colorado. I drove a '62 Ford Falcon in college given to me by my dad for commuting home to Oregon. I freely shared it with him and others as most of the trust funders weren't allowed cars on campus. We sort of got used to sharing almost everything we had, like beer, drugs, food, and from time to time, girls, but not motorcycles. I quickly learned that's a sacred male thing, where we share our bikes with nobody. This fact makes the Hells Angels a little easier to understand.

I pass by Des Moines, seeing most of it from the top of concrete overpasses, but I keep right on heading into the setting sun.

Kemp found Crested Butte and he and I spend our Christmas vacation in 1968 staying with his fiancé, Taffy, who rented a little house at the end of Elk Avenue, right next to the old train station. Attending Western State, she found rent in the Butte much lower and more romantic than Gunnison. Besides, the town was full of similar college kids seeking cheap rent, a nearby empty ski area, and walking access to a 3.2 beer joint for eighteen year olds.

Tony's Tavern was famous for its New Year's Eve party which, for 1968, Kemp and I were hired to be the bouncers with free beer and ten bucks each. We only had one rule that night: If someone throws a beer bottle, they get a one-way flight to the nearest snow bank which is right outside the front door. We quickly lose count of how many college kids taste brown snow that night.

Kemp marries Taffy, outside, under a typical Crested Butte spitting June snowstorm in Slavic peasant wedding costumes. I ask him why. He mumbles something about being normal or maybe having kids. They buy the little white house at 640 Elk and his crazy brother Cordley imports his English girlfriend, Sue Anderton, and he buys a single-wide mobile home parked in the low-rent district behind the Elk Mountain Lodge.

Kemp, with a degree in sociology and beer-drinking, hires on with the city as the town marshal. Cordley and Sue open a silkscreen shop/photography studio in the basement of the old Company Store now called the Emporium. Sue earned an MFA from the Manchester School of Art, so she settles into doing pen and ink drawings of all the Rocky Mountain beauty around her and begins a career designing exciting new art posters for the annual Flaushinck celebration commemorating the coming of the slush season and the revealing of the winter stash of frozen dog poop melting out of the snow.

Council Bluffs and Omaha slide by right after sunset. Normally, I stop for dinner when heading west and the sun shoots straight into my face. The fall clouds obscure it, so I blast right on by.

Kemp, the marshal, creates an oasis for young people to live unmolested by state and federal pigs looking for counter-culture victims needing persecution for not being subservient enough. I try to finish graduate school while messing with student politics, ego artists, musicians, and fashion monsters. Besides the local rock promoters and revolutionary communal prophets at the U of M, I hang with Manupelli and his student cadre of abstract movie worshipers all practicing the *do less with more* stagnant film philosophy. I perhaps learn more from the artsy-fartsy European-style orgiastic student parties held pretty continually at his former-church-turned-fashion-altar home located just downriver from campus. Modern ideas and cocaine flow like lies at a New York gallery opening and I feel accepted just because I'm different and practice it openly.

I enjoy hanging with the worthless entitled pricks of the well-educated Ann Arbor intellectuals and other well-to-dos. They're fun to party with. They know how to, without guilt, freely enjoy drugs, sex, Rock & Roll, and liberal philosophy. But they'll sell you out for a gram of coke in a second. My new friends instinctively substitute the manners of the wealthy for the ethics of the poor as required. As my birth ethics are naturally flexible from being poor and demanding better, we at least have something in common. For their personal amusement, they surround themselves with interesting and stimulating people, like a cowboy from Oregon who owns a Craftsman chainsaw, a .357 Ruger Blackhawk, a monster Chevy truck, and a helluva lot of arcane physics and electronics knowledge.

Lincoln creeps by in the darkness. Hardly notice it. But from here on, it's due west for about the next twelve hours. This is the real boring part.

The times are a-changing and conventional families are breaking apart. Not physically, but psychologically, and being reconstituted with more compatible free-thinking, new-age constituents. Something new is happening here. I must find the new way that fits the new me.

There's a revolution going on. The societal cat is out of the bag and can't be put back. Religions and the threat of god, ridiculous examples of human hypocrisies and false pretenses, are no longer fashionable. Yet, they still control a great deal of our human reality, defining without substance what is agreed true beyond verification. It corrupts real truth and kills free thought. It insidiously worms itself into every aspect of the thinking human mind, infecting it with terminal absurd beliefs, making it immune to questioning, analysis, or any critical thinking that might help with error correction. Religion does not allow error correction, and is inherently evil and dehumanizing, meant only to control and enslave adherents with addictive psychological brainwashing, holding them in rigid slave classes so they can be continually bled for the benefit of the religious vultures and the elite-class leeches. Why do we stand for such shit? And yet there it is. I want to live somewhere where religion and mindless social pressure have no sway. I demand to be free of all such nonsense. Those strange immutable mountains are regarded as a source of great inspiration and the yearning for freedom.

Late at night and after a few beers with nothing else to do, I think back to my youth. I sort of naturally grew up outside society because the only society for farmers is the immediate family, where I lived alone with my older parents, and the church which we attend each week. I have a hard time dealing with phony religion, so my pubescent society revolves around milking cows—morning and night—and school, where my quaint country three-room joke has exactly eight kids in each class, one teacher for all, severely limiting any real exposure to a modern education. By the time I get to high school, also a tiny rural school of about a hundred students per grade without resources or effective teaching talent, I lack not only an equitable education compared to my urban counterparts but any real future opportunities, as well. So, I become a scientist, an intellectual, a rebel, and a revolutionary, all proving I was smart enough to understand the universe, but not the people in it. I felt I could make money and get out of my confining poverty if I could just summon up the courage to go out and interact with people and partake in the societal norms of the wealthy practitioners of business, lifting oneself up the ladder of economic class. I deserve to be recognized for my talents, hard work, and diverse skills, and not just abused because of them.

I barely note passing Grand River where the road starts following the Platte River all the way to the divide. I'm halfway across Nebraska and several more hours to sunrise.

In Ann Arbor, I have the chance to befriend the local kids my age by working alongside them at Space Physics and partying with them on Division Street. Most had attended the University High School where the latest ideas in education are tried out on the sons and daughters of the smartest people assembled at a world-class university.

I make it to North Platte where the river splits into the north and south Platte rivers. The South Platte goes to Denver and the North Platte goes to Yellowstone. In the past, I usually followed I-80, which goes straight on to Salt Lake where it branches into north and south versions; I-80S goes to Reno and Sacramento, while I-80N goes to Boise, Portland, and home in rural Oregon. I have a new home now, so I head southwest to the mountains.

My hopes disappeared in a blur of Rock & Roll one-night stands and a vicious cycle of making little money, working my ass off and blowing it all on nose candy just to keep going. I needed something more permanent and less harmful. I discovered the works of Hunter Thompson and the good doctor recommends spending more time in the fresh, free air of the mountains. I felt as if some of my birthright freedoms had been taken away by this repressive government. They forced me to sign a loyalty oath to the federal government, *against all enemies, foreign and domestic.* In the age of Vietnam, we knew that foreign enemies were often not our real enemy and the newly invented term, domestic enemies, meant young people who protest. To us, the domestic enemy was the pigs themselves.

I find myself in a repressive society that doles out rewards for the compliant and complacent. I can't get stupid enough to abstain from sex, obey bad rules, and listen to shithole music. I've already been deprived of any further rewards from the system. I've had enough of Lawrence Welk and the Lemon Sisters. I want loud, rude, freedom-loving Rock & Roll and I'm not waiting for anything, especially love and sex and the right to be me, whoever that might be.

I pass the Colorado state line and soon zoom past Julesburg. There's a glow starting to light up behind me. My eyes feel a little scratchy from being exposed all night to the dry prairie air.

From the bottom of the socio-economic structure, my climb out should depend only on my character, intelligence, and capabilities, not on being a phony suck-up. My mind is integral to my life and I will not change it so some already brain-vacuumed rich bastard can infect me with their who-gives-a-shit attitude in order to become one of them. Unlike my army major brother, I will not justify the morally corrupt rich in order to become one.

The horizon reappears ahead of me and then the blue line of white-capped granite begins to form a castle keep of stone, altitude, and attitude.

"Spent the last year Rocky Mountain Way, couldn't get much higher. Out to pasture, think it's safe to say, time to open fire. And we don't need the ladies cryin' 'cause the story's sad. 'Cause the Rocky Mountain Way is better than the way we had.

Well, he's tellin' us this, and he's tellin' us that, changes it every day, says it doesn't matter. Bases are loaded and Nixon's at bat, playin' it play by play. Time to change the batter." —Joe Walsh, "Rocky Mountain Way"

I made up my mind a long time ago that I would not be victimized by stupid rules or corrupt social conventions, so whenever I travel with my lover and stay overnight at friends' parents' houses, I would not sleep in a separate bed just so they could have the mindless satisfaction of preventing an imaginary sin being conducted under their roof. *What hogwash!* But really strange how many normally intelligent people are doing this. *Piss on them!* I won't assume the false morals of the people hosting me. I cannot respect their insulting demand to conform. It's just not right and they need to know I have values, too. Only mine are right for both of us.

It's late fall and I see flocks of big birds migrating south as the sun rises behind me. The birds turn into billowing pink sheets waving like a giant flag against a dark line of craggy peaks reaching into the western sky and already dusted with snow, anticipating the coming onslaught.

I like to think we live in an egalitarian society where strict social hierarchies are a thing of the past. With modern technology, it's really anachronistic. Talent comes from anywhere now. People should be judged by their character, abilities, and potential without regard to color, age, sex, or family wealth. I demand a level, status-free playing field where the privileged must share their wealth and pay respect to those similarly deserving. If they accept me for my success and potential, then maybe I'll find my true worth in society class, rather than the one I was condemned to at birth.

Seeing the great purple mountains from a distance always swells my soul. From this vantage point, reality is truth and truth is beauty. If nothing else, at least a life lived in beauty is a life well lived. Here, if nothing else, I promise to live in beauty and practice love. This will be my new home. A home to fill my empty soul.

~ 2 ~

THE BARN DAYS

Once upon a time...there is a magic mountain town where everyone's dreams come true. First, they begin by looking for it and if lucky, they accidentally find it, and finally, like fairy-tale romantics, firmly commit to wintering over, making them official residents of a comic book snow-draped Camelot. Testing oneself against the wild elements has always been a noble challenge, but for the Butte, it becomes a trial by fire in so many other ways that few are really prepared for the burn that actually happens.

All the livable houses are full and market pressures force many garage, barn, and woodshed owners to quickly make them over into low-rent livable sheds with beds. They're lucky if they have a stove, running water, a toilet, and maybe some insulation. Many such concoctions have issues their first winter with ice blocking doors and windows, or pipes bursting when hastily built by amateurs and not properly constructed by the tried-and-true traditional methods only known to the tried-and-true natives. For a major part of the winter, thirty-five degrees below zero is a normal nighttime temperature and it separates the seasoned mountain cabin from the improvised bunkhouse real fast.

I arrive this *moon landing* summer with the Coits after making an underground art film with them in Chicago. Taffey moves us all into her one-bedroom rented house at the end of Elk next to the train station. I stay in the loft above the kitchen while Cordley and Susan quickly rent a mobile home in the low-rent district.

Donner, who housed our production team in his deluxe Chicago suburban home during the filming, also follows us to the Butte in his red Z-28. He immediately falls in love with the place and also rents a mobile home for about six months, until he finds out about Mrs. Doc Smith. He makes her an offer she can't refuse and moves into a nice Victorian at 215 Sopris. Great location for Donner, being only about a hundred feet from the back door of Tony's Tavern. He adopts an Alaskan Malamute for an appropriate-image, cold-weather pet and together they became a regular fixture in all the bars, every day until closing.

I am still in graduate school so I have to be back at the scholastic farm by September, but now I consider Crested Butte my new dream home. I pledge to get back as soon as practicable, during or after my degree studies.

I am also on the rebound from a long-fraught college love affair, so I welcome this first mountain adventure to get back in the game. I soon find myself caught up in two very intense love affairs, more than I surely deserve, but that's the allure of the mountains for a young ambitious lad out on his own for the first time.

The first, an estranged young blond wife from Lake Forest and a volunteer on the film production, flies out for a down and dirty two-week mountain vacation with me, a filmmaker, hippie artist, hanging in the picturesque Butte. The other one, a horny little cowgirl/thespian college student from Western

State, is introduced to me by my brother, who at the time is studying for his master's degree in education at Western State summer school. He finds her at the summer college theater.

After getting to know her better at the down and dirty cast party, I temporarily move into her little rental house and together we study all the marathon mountain sex rituals we can devise. Then Donner gets jealous and hunts down our secret love nest trying to horn into some imagined Gunnison *action.*

But my brother goes back to work as a teacher in Alaska and I must return to Michigan. She follows me uninvited to Ann Arbor but, like the summer winds, the lust has blown away with the leaves of fall and I have to send her on to some plan B older guy in Ohio she knows, who breeds quarter horses. Sounds like a winner for everyone.

By the time I return to Crested Butte for my delayed winter-over initiation, my friends have all become well-known Crested Butte figures and some of the first actors in the local small town soap opera just getting started.

During the time I'm absent at graduate school, Kemp's first marriage to Taffy quickly dissolves due to apparent impotence on his part and no baby on hers. She's the person responsible for finding Crested Butte, renting and then buying the little house at the other end of Elk and ironically insisting on a traditional Slavic-costumed outdoor wedding in the adjacent city park under snow-spitting, cloudy June skies. But she drops her enlightened free spirit when it comes to starting a new kind of modern mountain family. To her, apparently, love without children is not love at all.

I consider this nothing more than typical female brainwashing by the ugly fifties' generation. Her mother once threw us out of sleeping over at her house when I insisted on my inalienable right to sleep with whomever I chose, with or without a stinkin' license. Screw her and her generation's moral tyranny demanding solo bed occupancy unless approved by a limp-dick priest. Kemp should have paid better attention to what daughters often end up becoming, after marriage.

He takes it well and rebounds quickly, I think. He somehow inherits 640 Elk from her, finds a much more compatible drinking mate, Linda, who looks like a skinny Wagnerian winged goddess on speed and who seems to have no need for children somehow justifying sex. She makes Crested Butte the *Never-Never Land* experience we all suspect it is and one of the reasons we came, we saw, we loitered, we stayed. Love is in the air and more so, it seems, as the air thins and the temperatures head south.

They settle in at the little white stucco house on the corner and decide to do what every other property owner is trying to do—make money on the side so they can afford to live here. There's an old weathered garage next to the house that begs to be turned into a little back-alley rental unit. The alley between Sopris and Elk is famous for such coal-shed conversions. Kemp is now the full-time paid town Marshal and can't be bothered with doing any real work on his own, so he hires some of the boys in town to do it for him.

They insulate the hell out of the place and add a double entry door and mud room to help keep the ice from breaking through to the inside. He finds an old enameled stand-up parlor coal stove which he places in the middle of the north wall. They punch a stove pipe through the wall and next for the only window. In one corner is a small electric hot water tank feeding a small stall shower and a sink. The wall above the sink has a couple of shelves and next to it is a little apartment-sized two-burner gas range with oven. In the opposite wall from the stove is an alcove bed big enough for two close friends. It's actually an ideal mountain cabin and I'm lucky to have it for my new bachelor pad. It's perfect for what I hope will be a marvelous wintering-over experience.

I build a workbench along the empty east wall with shelves above and below. I unload my truck and fill the bench with all my electronic instruments, professional stereo gear, a pair of Model A DCM speakers, and a 4-track Teac tape deck recently donated by Grand Funk Railroad for unsolicited services rendered. In the middle of the floor, I place the old wooden cable reel I find nearby to act as a coffee table and something to gather around on cushions when entertaining guests and passing joints in a close circle.

When I lie in bed at night and survey my new mountain home, aka womb, I immediately think of David Thoreau and his little cabin he made for himself after being discovered by the literary community of 19th century New England. Through isolation, one can find, and be confronted by, your naked unpretentious self as it ponders its own undefinable existence in the light of its obvious insignificance. Simplify is to analyze, and analyze awakens us to the simplicity of beauty. Only then can one appreciate the wonderfully complex world that gives rise to such simple thoughts.

I jump right in with the required ritual of maintaining a continuous fire in the coal stove. If the fire goes out, all the pipes inside the insulated structure will freeze within hours. It is imperative to keep the fire going even when you're not home. I order a ton of coal from Paonia for $20 cash and marvel, when it arrives, at just how much that is. It's a lot! I have no doubt I will be toasty warm all winter and then some.

The coal comes in shiny black chunks about 6 to 18 inches in diameter and the stove door is only about 8 inches. So, the bigger chunks have to be broken up to fit in the stove. This becomes a weekly chore, busting the big chunks with a hammer and filling the inside coal box behind the stove with enough burnable chunks for seven days. If I work this right and if I'm careful and vigilant, I can keep the same fire going all winter. In case I don't, I lay in a supply of dry kindling and newspaper for quickly starting a new fire. Coal is not easy to light, but practice makes perfect.

Coal stoves must be watched like scheming children. They can go bad at any moment. If they are not going out unexpectedly, then they may run away with themselves at any moment. That's when your stove pipe coming directly out of the stove turns into an orange glow resembling the after burner of an F-15.

I note that Kemp still has an automatic propane heater in the main house that requires no tending or ritual other than a phone call to the gas company scheduling the truck to stop by and refill his lonely white tank. It stands out back in plain view, near where the town map says there is an alley. So far, it's just a bike trail from the town park to the county gravel pile.

The county yard is just an open area with Mount Negace, or *Mount Black,* as we call it. It's a big hill of cinders mined from the accumulated ashes from the old coke ovens and stored here by the county to be spread on road ice in the winter. Every once in a while, a local skier has to give it a try.

Hitch announces in the Grubber one night that he can do it. We quickly start a pool. He finds some old rock skis, carries them to the top, straps them on and actually makes it to the bottom making two legitimate turns along with starting a minor avalanche of cinders right behind him burying his skis. We have to pull him out of his bindings to get him released from the slag. Faude wins the pool.

*

I slip into a simple routine, spending daytimes hanging with Cordley and Susan uptown in their silkscreen print shop, which is now located in the basement of the newly remodeled Company Store. In the evenings, I hang in the bars with Kemp and Cordley, like most everybody else in town. Right across the hallway from their shop is Weasel's record shop, Mountain Records. I spend a lot of time there when he's open and convince him to let me demo my stereo system with my incredible DCM speakers in his private listening room, if he lets me perform repair services out of his back room.

The Company Store is an abandoned warehouse once owned by the big coal and iron company, CF&I, down in Pueblo, that once upon a time pretty much owned Crested Butte lock, stock, and barrel in exchange for all the Anthracite coal it could gouge out underneath it. John Benjamin and Murray Howe dig up the ten grand necessary to convince CF&I to sell it, the only building in town made out of concrete and adobe.

It's over a hundred feet long and fifty wide, making it the largest building in town, as well. It has two floors, which John immediately partitions into shops on the upper main floor, four feet above ground level, and, in the lower floor, four feet below ground level, he builds a new bar with plenty of room for tables, a large dance floor, and a stage. The original stairs from the first floor to the basement are right up front, occupying prime retail space in the front shops. John digs an outside entrance through the foundation right on the corner of Elk and Third, eliminating the internal stairs and giving the bar almost equal status with the Grubstake, Tony's Tavern, the Waystation, and Kochevar's for size and convenience. Not an easy thing to do in a town with many more bars than churches.

Whitey McDuff blows into town with nine kids, a lot of money, and a dream of owning a Rock Bar in a ski resort town that makes him very wealthy. After all, it's the seventies and there is money to be made from loud music and beer, both well known to be demanded by skiers. Benjamin rents the bar to him and he dumps a lot of money fixing it up for the coming season.

He hires me to design his stage lighting and sound system. I find him a pair of DCM PA speakers of which only a dozen or so were ever built. He launches the bar when the ski area opens and then slowly misses his numbers until by the end of the season he finally succumbs to the end of his money and all of his patience. He loses the lease, but instead of running away, he finds an hourly job at the ski area itself, sufficient to support his family. He becomes a regular fixture up there for a long time as the ski area parking lot manager, who looks a lot like Santa Claus. His kids, along with Garcia's, almost double the population of some grades at the local elementary school.

I'm trying everything I can to make a buck, but it's not easy. A new song about bringing in dope through the LA airport gets me thinking. Maybe I can do a t-shirt silkscreen print that will sell to tourists. Maybe have a dope importing message as a joke. I sketch up a picture of a biplane with a funny pilot in goggles, handlebar moustache, and windblown scarf, and his airplane has lumps of white stuff hanging off the wingtips and tail. The caption reads: *Snow is Coming.*

Susan draws the picture and shows me how to set up the silkscreen printing press to copy and print the artwork on t-shirts. I learn a lot about silkscreen printing, but the t-shirts barely fall off the shelves and we don't make much money.

I decide to try what works best from before. I ask Cordley and he turns me onto an artist friend in Albuquerque who might know someone who knows someone who can help me out. We take a trip down to New Mexico in Cord's antique BMW and luck out by scoring a couple pounds of some really nice weed, almost Sinsemilla.

When I offer it for sale in the Butte, the Bump immediately hears about it and drives his new giant GMC 4-wheel drive truck down to my little hovel and demands to see what I've got. I take him inside; he sees my stuff, samples some of the weed while I demo my high-powered stereo, and we hit it off immediately. He wants to buy my entire stash at my street price. I collect some much-needed cash and keep a little stash back for my personal use. I did good and that helps me get through the rest of the winter and encourages me to try it again later.

The Bump turns out to be the biggest dope dealer in town, followed by the Wease, and for a short time the engineering boys over at the solar house on Third Street. I'm interested in solar power and have an advanced degree in physics, so I visit the boys and check out their work.

It's a marvelous design of clever practicality in that the solar collectors are nothing more than fifty-gallon drums split vertically and laid out end to end forming one-half of a long cylinder, oriented east and west. The inside is coated with reflective metalized mylar creating a mirror surface and a copper pipe runs the length down the center of the barrels, at the prime focal point of the reflected sunlight. When the high-altitude sun hits the curved mylar mirror face and bounces to the copper pipe, enough energy is captured from intense high-altitude sunlight to create steam.

They dig a big hole in the ground underneath the house, line it with large high-density rocks and it becomes a combination rock hot tub and solar heat storage unit. I love it and realize how easy it will be to heat and cool using this same design. After all, at night the whole thing reverses and it can chill the water in the pipe by sucking energy away as infrared radiation reflects into deep space. Freezing might be an issue during winter nights so some improvements are still needed. I suggest a few, but engineers never listen to physicists, so it stays a novelty.

Unlike the Bump, Wietzel and the engineering boys specialize in importing coke. Wietzel gets his supply from his California surfing buddies in Encinitas and the engineering boys actually come up with a pretty good original plan to bring it in all the way from the Caribbean. Being rich brats, they find a twelve-meter yacht that they sail from St. Thomas in the Caribbean, straight up the middle of the Atlantic until they damn near reach Greenland, and then steer southwest heading straight for someone's summer home on the coast of Maine.

For a while, Crested Butte is pretty well supplied and everyone gets used to plentiful coke, uncut, at a decent price. Finally, the boys try it too many times and the Coast Guard catches them sailing toward Maine from international waters. Before being boarded, the boys scuttle their boat hoping at least there will be no evidence. The Coast Guard actually spends the millions it takes to dive on the boat and retrieve the goods, in spite of such blatant stupidity and all the better things that could have been done with such money.

The boys get a few years in a tennis club federal prison where rich and important people or their kids can serve time in relative ease and comfort. The supply of coke in Crested Butte suddenly dries to a trickle. When the boys get out, they manage to squirrel away enough cash from the whole enchilada, that they all retire to St. Thomas where they become boat boys for the rich and famous. Meanwhile we mutter on in the Butte.

Some winter skiers take up motocross in the summer as a body abuse substitute, but most of us simply go fishing or sometimes in my case, spelunking for gold. A mechanic from Gunnison decides to open a motorcycle shop in Crested Butte and buys a couple of lots on the south side of Whiterock between third and fourth. He builds a simple cinder block and metal industrial building and adds a couple of rental units on the second floor. It soon becomes a hangout for fast motorcycles, slow sex, and young coke abusers.

All the motorcycle guys love coke, as does just about everybody else in town under the age of forty, and even a few over. So much so, that when the hotshots go off to fight a wildfire, coke prices go down because of a slump in the buying market. When they get back, with cash hanging out their pockets, the local price for coke suddenly doubles and the local stockpiles soon dry up. We call it the after-fire drought and plan accordingly.

During a slump in the weather and tourism, Wietzel challenges everyone to a backgammon elimination tournament. He holds it in the back of the record store with a board on a small table in the middle of the room and just two chairs for the combatants. The rest of us have to stand around in a crowded circle watching the game in silence. I've never seen the game played before and have no idea what the rules are. As a challenge to myself, and pretending I know what's going on, I carefully watch while several contestants eliminate each other until only Cordley and Wietzel are left battling over the prize of one gram of coke or its equivalent in cash. I work out the rules in my head pretty quickly, including some simple strategies that I see them using.

I challenge the winner, Wietzel, by saying I've never played before but will challenge him to a one-game showdown. He accepts and I simply turn some of his strategies against him and add a couple of my own. For a theoretical physicist, the math behind the game is ridiculously simple, but if both sides know this, then it becomes a game of poker: who can bluff whom out of what. There is a different correct strategy for pieces in each quadrant and it's important to read the dice and then apply the different numbers correctly. Miss an opportunity and it will come back to bite you. I, an amateur, beat Wietzel soundly and after that, everyone else loses interest. They play these games for bragging purposes and they can't brag when they can't win. I'm not a bragger so it all goes to hell real fast.

*

When I open the record store each morning, I adjourn to the back room where my repair bench is located and I light a fat one to start the day off right. One day, I finish a small joint and when I reemerge, there, sitting in the middle of the listening room, is the new town Marshal, Don West, wearing the official town marshal uniform, badge and all. He took Kemp's place after the July 4th McLung brawl incident. He's just sitting there lamely pretending to listen to a Led Zeppelin album I had put on earlier.

"What's up?" I ask trying to not panic. He shouldn't be here and he knows it.

"Nothing," he says. "Just enjoying the music."

"What do you want?" I ask outright, about to start putting up a fight because I know that he knows I was just smoking some pot and he can obviously smell it.

"I just want to learn something."

"What?" I respond.

"I want to know what dope smells like."

"I can do you one better, but you need to come back after work."

"No thanks. I just need to know the smell. I never smelled it before and now I have." He gets up and walks out without another word. I take it as a warning that things aren't going to be the same anymore around here.

Donner senses the same thing but he's not a common criminal, even though he pushes the boundaries very hard. He says he spent time in the Boston Hells Angels when a teenage runaway, but I doubt it. They have pretty stringent requirements when it comes to riding bikes and I know for a fact Donner's riding skills are almost zilch. His last project, a 1959 Vincent Black Shadow he bought in Chicago, went exactly a thousand yards before hitting a fence at the end of his driveway.

His story's simple. He was born rich with old Boston money. Parents died or disappeared; he never made it clear. He inherited a modest fortune that was administered by his aunt, also a wealthy indolent. He grows up in Boston, drops out of high school, hangs out with the fringe element including druggies and perhaps biker gangs. He learns the manly arts of motorcycle maintenance, quick-draw gun fights using wax bullets, all-night poker games and general drunken mayhem. After a few scrapes with the police over drugs and underage sex, he, usually being the one underage, ends up learning the biker drug trade as a covering vocation. His first true love though was, "all pistols on the table, cash and gold only, no jokers, and no fancy hands" poker games between friends who didn't mind a little gunfire through the floors while placing their bets.

Donner has a bad habit of sniffing out horny virgins, defiling them, and if he likes it, comes back for more until they're impregnated. He finally gets one of his older-age girlfriends in Boston pregnant, and under pressure from his aunt, they marry and move into the big house in Lake Forest while his wife finishes college there and has the baby far from the prying eyes of Boston society. She tries to live with Donner as a respectable Northshore family but it's just not his style. She divorces him when he starts the process all over again, chasing any girl in sight, and with her baby being an heir to the Hanson fortune, she moves back to Boston and the aunt where she becomes set for life as wards of the Hanson Estate.

One of Donner's favorite pastimes was driving his Z28 to Denver and back in less than one day. One time, I ride along and he does it in five hours flat, both ways. It takes me a couple of hours and a lot of whiskey just to calm down afterward, but he actually did it. Mountain driving is an art of betting. You're betting your life there isn't a car coming around that next blind corner. Oh yeah, and the yellow line in the middle is just a suggestion as to where the road is located.

True to form, Donner, now playing out his *Black Bart* imaginary role in an old west-looking movie-set town, defiles the local shopkeepers Tony and Elenore Stefanic's adventuresome sixteen-year-old virgin daughter, Rose. Of course, she gets pregnant and becomes an early soap opera legend. Rumor headlines run something like, *Local girl does very well, in spite of how it looks.*

Rose marries him for about three months so the kid is born a Hanson and automatically joins the line for a big piece of that Boston fortune. When I meet her at the age of eighteen, she's already legally separated from Donner, so we enjoy a guiltless one-night stand at her mobile home where I tell her all about Donner's first wife. It's not long before she hires a lawyer and moves to a Southern California beach house, retiring with a comfortable life her well-respected and humble Crested Butte parents could only dream for their child.

Donner hosts a lot of poker games at his house on Sopris, which sometimes have very large stakes among the ones who think they can afford it, so, over time, enemies are made. Donner upgrades his local ride to a new Lincoln Continental, more in line with the other rich little trust funder bastards showing up in town, except they all seem to have a penchant for Cadillac Eldorados. When snow starts blowing in the fall, Donner locks up his house, stores the Continental in the back garage of Tony's Conoco station, and drives his Z-28 to Palm Beach for the winter.

Then, about a month later, I get a call.

"Hello, Cowboy?"

I recognize Donner's voice. "Donner. What's up?" I ask wondering why he's calling me.

"I need your help," he declares.

"Then you're in real trouble. What the fuck did you do this time, shoot the neighbor's dog?" I ask lightly.

"It's serious. These bastards machine-gunned my Z-28," he declares.

"What?" I demand. "Who the fuck did you piss off? The Cuban Mafia?"

Now I suspect why he's calling me. I just happen to have come across a machine gun recently when some ex-Vietnam veteran, now hippie, passes through town needing cash. He has some interesting guns in his trunk, which he offers to Cordley for a quick sale. Cordley finds me and together we buy a Colt Commander, a Vietnam Air Force survival knock-down rifle, AR-7 in a .222 caliber, and a good old-fashioned .45 caliber M3 *grease* gun. Apparently, I'm now Donner's go-to friend for armaments.

"I'm not going to sell you a machine gun," I pronounce outright.

"My dog was in the car at the time! It could have been me! It's personal now!" he warns.

Donner's purebred Malamute, a giant fluffy white mutt with stunning blue eyes, is easily his closest confidant. Donner likes to pretend his beloved dog is a killer Doberman, but instead it is really a big lovable panda.

"They killed Bear? What did you do to piss them off?" I demand, in shock with the news.

"It's not my fault. I'm just onto some rich fucking smugglers and doing some surveillance in West Palm. It's a well-known bar on the main drag and I parked out front like I always do and while I'm inside, someone does a drive-by right there on my car. How the hell did they know? It's got to be the bar. They're behind this. I need your help to get them. I need to do a drive-by on them."

"I'd like to help, but my new girlfriend says it's time to go to bed now so...."

"I'll pay you five hundred dollars and a round-trip plane ticket to come down here and just look at my problem. You got to help me. I'm serious."

I cuss to myself under my breath. I can't say no to the money. "I understand. Okay, I'll do it." Just as I say it, I regret it. "No guns!" I add, and hang up.

Two-week paid vacation in Palm Beach? Who could say no when outside it's minus a thousand degrees and snow is piling so high that direct sunlight on north-south streets is cut down to one hour a day. Besides, I need the money. I always need the money.

Donner meets me at the Palm Beach airport in a rental car. His Z28 is still in the shop getting the holes filled. He takes me directly to the bar in question and it's a big disappointment if I'm expecting a den of thieves and smugglers.

"What's the deal?" I ask sitting at the bar and looking out at the busy street in front. The bar has a spaghetti slinger in the back pretending it's an Italian restaurant, as well. A couple of pool tables gives it that roadhouse look, but all in all it didn't appear to be much out of the ordinary.

"Are you sure it wasn't a mistaken identity? Maybe some other gang thought your car belonged to some Latino in town and you got his welcome basket."

"My godfather is the county vice officer. His relatives own this place. I've been following drugs coming into Palm Beach from outside and I think he's involved. This place is where some of the richest kids in Palm Beach come for their drugs."

"And how is that your problem?"

"These people are not nice. Look what they did to Bear," he demands.

"But it's not your business. You're here to enjoy your winters in a nice warm place. Sit back, relax, and stay out of trouble."

"They made it my business."

He takes me to his house. We drive straight down Royal Palm Way to the end, turn left, go about four blocks and turn left again. It's about the fourth house in.

"The Kennedy compound is a couple blocks away," he explains, "and we can use the pubic beach access next to their mansion to get to the beach behind. There's always a lot of young girls hanging out there on weekends." He smiles his normal wicked smile.

"Nice," I respond unimpressed. His house is a little white single-story bungalow with three bedrooms, all with their own bathrooms featuring tiled walk-in showers. Out back is his pool, which has private access from the kitchen or the two bedrooms on either side. I'm impressed. I could be tempted by this kind of living.

"My aunt found this house for me," he explains.

"So, what do you do down here, besides piss people off?"

"The usual. I cruise the bars and find girls who want to do unspeakable things," he volunteers.

"There you go. A man with a hobby."

"What about we find some dynamite and blow that bar all to hell," he suggests seriously.

"I know someone who might be able to do something like that. But I strongly suggest you let it go."

"What's he got?"

"About two pounds of tri-nitro toluene."

"TNT?"

"That's what rookies call it."

"What's it going to take to get it here?"

Next thing I know, I'm calling my friend Bill in Ann Arbor and offering him $500 for some TNT I know he has and his expenses flying it down and showing Donner how to use it.

A couple of years ago when still in Ann Arbor, Bill shows me a lump of white clay he's just acquired in some complicated drug and car deal, and then tells me it's TNT. He breaks off a little chunk about an inch in diameter, wraps it around an electric blasting cap, and places it on a wooden fence post out behind his garage. We retreat to inside the garage and touch it off with a car battery. An intense blue-white light envelopes the top of the post followed by a huge blast of sound that rattles the windows in the shop. When we go back out, the post is missing about two feet of its top and the rest is shredded all the way to the ground.

Deep down, I'm pretty sure Donner will do nothing. He just doesn't have that kind of dedication to anything that would drive him to such extremes. He likes to play the game but he knows it's a game and will do the right thing, eventually. But he likes to dream and we are just helping him come to the right conclusion.

"He says he can be here tomorrow, with the goods," I inform him.

"Great. Let's go out and celebrate."

He takes me on his bar circuit for the well-to-do crowd. Bars in Palm Beach are obviously for the rich and bars in West Palm Beach, not so much. I can smell that coke is the major drug under the table in Palm Beach and West Palm is more conventional with weed and diet pills. We sit at the bar in each place and spend at least one hour or four drinks, watching all the activity in the bar and listening closely. Donner is down to drinking peach schnapps and Kahlúa with cream because of a threatening ulcer.

"I've been having to take it easy on the hard liquor. My stomach can't take it anymore." He pops a couple of Tums just to prove his point.

"All these bars have bartenders that are crooked as hell," he explains. "In fact, they may not even work for the bar. There's talk of an unofficial union that tells the bars who they can hire and when they should work. I'm trying to figure out who's behind it all."

"It's not your business. You can look the other way and stick to what you do best. Fucking young girls on the run from their parents."

"But it's personal now."

"Personal now..." I mimic his whining.

"I'm in contact with the feds and they believe me. But I now have a bigger problem. "

"Bigger than trying to get yourself shot up as a nosy dick?"

"My godfather is the local vice chief and I think he's one of them."

"So, let's see. You've stumbled onto a local drug ring based on bartenders. You're known to have contacts with the cops and your car gets machine gunned. You think the cops are bought off and they know what you're up to."

"That's about right. So, what do you think?"

"I think you should get your ass back to Crested Butte," I implore emphatically, "where you might have a chance of surviving the next few weeks. Crested Butte or maybe Mexico, but you've shit all over this place and it stinks to high heaven."

"You get your friend here with the goods and I'll take care of this," he counters. "In the meantime, let's go pick up a couple of dates for the night. I feel like a pool party."

He takes me on his regular round of about eight bars in total. The last bar is a late-night one in Palm Beach, the Royal Palm. Donner says everyone goes there at the end of the night to pair up if they haven't done so already. I'm not very interested, as I'm technically on the job and I don't want to let my guard down for a little squishy action. But he finds two willing girls and after buying them some drinks, he has to relate his bear hunting story he apparently tells everyone outside of the Butte.

The real story went something like this: Donner decides out of the blue to go bear hunting with his quick-draw pair of pearl-handled, chrome-plated Colt .45s. He buys a tag from Tony's and then starts cruising the high country in hopes of running across one, hopefully near the road. After he scrapes his car's bottom on a few rocks, he decides a Z28 is not a good back country vehicle.

Finally, he gets word that a bear has been spotted up above a friend's cabin near Lake Meridian. He talks me into going with him and we drive up in my truck to the cabin where it was last reported. He gets out and I drive on up to the top of the hill above the cabin and begin to walk back down in his direction. The theory is, if there is a bear, the noise I make will drive him down the hill to where Donner can get a shot at him.

No sooner do I get in place when I hear two quick shots from down below. I walk toward the edge of the ridge and hear the god-awfullest sound I think I've ever heard in the woods. It's like a roller coaster jumping its tracks at 90 mph. I instinctively jump behind a tree just in time to see a huge ugly black bear charging up the hill at an unbelievable speed, crashing through bushes and jumping over logs, scattering rocks as he plows in a straight line through the forest, his blubber flapping in the breeze.

The bear goes by me like a New York subway express and disappears. Later, I find out that Donner had walked right up to him hiding behind a bush and when the bear made a dash for it, it scared the shit out of Donner so bad he almost shot his foot in the excitement of pulling a fast draw under pressure. Later, he swears he would have gotten him, except his finely honed hair triggers went off too soon. *The bear that escaped Quick Draw McGraw* became a nightly joke in the bars for some time.

We bring the two girls back to his place where we quickly doff our clothes and jump in the pool. Before I know it, Donner and his girl are missing and the other one is climbing all over me.

"You want to join us?" Donner calls from the door to his bedroom.

"No thanks, I've got enough on my hands right here." I hate it when I feel like I have to perform flawlessly for some damn reason. I'm damn sure not going to do it in front of Donner, especially after all the women we've competed for in the past. Now he wants to play dirty for some sick reason and on his terms. *No thanks, Bart the bum.* "I think we'll keep it close and personal," I yell back. "And don't come looking for us in a few hours. I'm fucking tired and need some sleep."

"You don't know what you're missing," he says, and closes the door.

"Yeah, I'm missing having to watch your hairy ass." I go to bed with my date and enjoy a very conventional and relaxing experience. I sleep like a baby and wake up eight hours later.

The girl is gone, thank goodness, so I take a shower and go looking for Donner. I find him still asleep in his bed.

Bill calls from the airport, so I wake up Donner and tell him I need to rent a car for Bill. He gives me his credit card and keys to his rental car, then goes back to sleep.

I pick up Bill and take him to the rental agency where he gets a car and follows me back to Donner's house. When we pull up, there's a black Mercedes parked in the front. I caution Bill to stay in his car while I check it out. He parks down the block and watches while I go in.

Inside, I find a balding Jewish-looking squat middle-age guy sitting at the kitchen table drinking a cup of coffee.

"And you are...?" I say as I look around the room but don't see Donner.

"I can say the same thing. Who are you?" he asks directly. He calmly takes a sip from his coffee.

"I'm Donner's friend visiting from Crested Butte. Should I wake him up?" I ask.

"No, not really. He knows what I have to say. When he wakes up and can understand you, tell him George stopped by to make sure you do nothing about your dog problem. Get over it, get a new dog, and stop going around pretending to be a narc informant." With that, he gets up, pours out the rest of his coffee, drops his cup in the sink, and leaves. He seems to be right at home like he's been there many times before. I shudder with fear and loathing.

I signal the all clear to Bill and he moves his car in place of the Mercedes and brings his bag in. I show him the room next to mine, explain the shower to him, and caution him about the untouchable parlor up front. The first day I arrived, Donner showed me around the house and I noticed a very nicely decorated and uncharacteristically clean living room up front near the main entrance. But the hallway to it has a yellow police line tape across it baring the way.

"This is where he entertains his aunt when she visits. It has to be perfectly clean and unused so the old lady feels like Donner's being a good boy. So, after the maid cleans it, he cordons it off so it stays that way just in case the old lady shows up unexpectedly. We're not allowed to go in there."

"Who was the mafia guy?" Bill asks the obvious.

"That's ironic. He's apparently Donner's godfather. He's also the local vice cop or something. Donner sniffs around the drug trade in Palm Beach and apparently finds out the cops know more than they're saying."

"That sounds about right," Bill responds. "When the drug trade exceeds a certain level of activity, it will absolutely corrupt the local cops. They need to have a safe playground. Stay away from those creeps. You don't know what motivates them and they can turn on a dime and fuck their best friend's wife."

"My best friend has a wife?" Donner says, wandering in from his bedroom, yawning.

"Bill, Donner. Donner, Bill," I say, introducing them.

"How do you do?" says Bill, offering his hand.

"Could be better," Donner admits, shakes his hand, and then goes to a cupboard door and pulls out a bottle of aspirin.

"Your godfather was here," I announce.

"George?"

"Yeah, I think that's what he said. He also said to tell you to cut it out."

"Cut what out?" he asks stupidly.

"You know damn good and well. Keep it up and there's a horse head headed for your bed. And I'm not talking about just an ugly woman."

"That son of a bitch is heading for a fall and I'm the one to do it."

"Is this guy related to your family or something?" Bill asks. "How did he get to be your godfather?"

"He was my father's business partner. Enough talk about jerks. Where's the TNT?" Donner asks anxiously.

"It's right here," Bill says, pulling a paper-wrapped package from his bag. He hands the round object to Donner who eagerly unwraps it to reveal a plain-looking white lump of clay-like substance. Pretty innocent looking if you don't know these things. I'm a chemist so I look at it like it's a giant rat trap, cocked and loaded, all ready to go boom. I respect this kind of stuff and don't like to see it handled like cheap cheese.

"Do you have a source of blasting caps?" asks Bill.

"Don't you have any?" he asks right back.

"All I have is one fuse cap, but no fuse," Bill informs him. "You can buy fuses easily, but it's best if you use an electric cap so you can set it off remotely. Lighting a fuse and running is probably not the best idea."

"I'll have Cowboy here whip something up." He looks closely at the white chunk like a lost puppy. I just make eye contact with Bill and wink.

We all go out barhopping again, but this time smooth Bill has some coke with him so we attract willing higher-classed girls than Donner's normal prey. After the bars close, we all go back to Donner's house where he again tries to get us into some kind of group sex thing. Bill and I stick with the pool, where the girls are having fun splashing around naked and being awesome. My puritan background comes to the surface and I find myself missing the Butte where one-night relationships are usually a bit longer than just one night.

The next day, Bill has to leave and I tell Donner I'm going to drop him off at the airport and then I'll have his car for use afterward. I feel bad about lying to him but I had to get out of there and I didn't want Donner trying to force me to stay by some unknown devious means. This caper is way out of my league and I don't feel comfortable sticking it through to the end.

I call him from the airport, telling him I have to leave and good luck with his venture. He tries one more time to convince me I have a future in Palm Beach.

"I know a lot of rich people who live here and I know when they are gone for long periods of time. You could make a helluva lot of money just high-grading their jewelry boxes. It's easy and safe."

"This is boring, Donner. You're messing with some bad dudes and if you don't run like me right now, you'll regret it," and I hang up.

About three weeks later back in Butte on a dark cold night, I'm drinking as usual in the Grubstake when Marshal Don walks in and comes directly to our table. I get nervous.

"You guys were friends of Donner's, right?" he says.

"Yeah. What's up?"

"I just got a call from the police chief in Palm Springs. Donner was found dead in his house yesterday."

Shocked silence. I look at Cordley and he just looks pained as hell.

"What the fuck happened?" I demand. "Pardon the language, but I just visited him a couple of weeks ago and he was fine."

"The chief said he was found in his bath hanging from the showerhead. He called it..." he pauses to check his notebook..."*autoerotic asphyxia.*"

"What the hell is that?" I ask. I'm so naïve in these things. I never heard of it and never even suspected such a thing exists.

"Apparently people get off by masturbating and choking themselves at the same time," Don explains emotionless.

He looks at us dispassionately and simply says, "Sorry for your loss." He turns and leaves. I'm astounded, as is Cordley. I tell him about the recent visit with Donner and what he was up to.

"Sounds like a mafia hit to me," Cordley deduces after a few more beers. "Looks like his godfather needed to stop him from ratting out the family so they make it look like suicide.

"Murdered by your own godfather. Is there nothing sacred anymore?" I quip.

"Not when it comes to old money," he points out wisely.

But that's not the end of the story, even though I'm pretty sure somebody got away with murder. Later that same night, the marshal walks into the bar again and finds us still at the same table.

"You guys know anything about Donner's car?"

"Now what?" I ask in frustration, considering the earlier news.

"Somebody broke into the Conoco and stole it about two hours ago," he explains. "Have you been here all the time since we last talked?"

"What?" we both exclaim in unison.

"Man, talk about a third-act twist," I interject.

"Fuck yeah, we've been here," he tells Don. "We didn't even know his car was there. Who the hell would take Donner's car, anyway?"

"That's what I'm asking you. Did he have any enemies you know of?" he asks point-blank.

"It was Donner. You tell me," I counter.

"I don't know Donner. Who do you know might have had a grudge against him?"

"Anybody who played poker with him or any father of any girl he ever screwed. Does that narrow it down?"

He just gives me a screwy look, turns slowly, and leaves.

Later, we learn the state police get a tip and about 4 a.m. the next morning, they surround John Benjamin's new farm he just bought over in Paonia. By Kebler Pass, it's only a two-hour trip. They find the continental hiding behind a barn and arrest Richard Duckworth, a friend of John's from Connecticut sleeping off a hangover on his couch. He claims he collects old Eldorados and just couldn't resist stealing Donner's car when he heard the news. When pointed out to him that it wasn't a Cadillac, he said he had a change of heart after he broke in and saw it. "Besides," he says, "Donner owes me money."

None of this makes any sense to me. Coincidences just don't happen, especially when it smells like a rotten egg. First his dog is machine-gunned, and then this. I can't help it, but it seems plain to me, Donner was offed by a crooked relative for something he knew and they had to make sure he didn't leave any evidence in the Butte. They probably already searched his house on Sopris because the next day the Marshal put a padlock on the door and a sign saying it was a crime scene investigation and to call the sheriff with any questions.

Money makes people act different from normal society. If there's one thing I'm learning from being around people with too much money, is they can't seem to control it; it controls them. It allows them to do atrocities as if they were on a mission from God. Maybe the real absurdity of wealth is that money makes a person feel innately superior to those without. They adopt a false invincibility feeling that they're too good to fail, they can't lose, and everything they get, they deserve. What a terrible surprise when reality rears its ugly head and deals them the fucking fickle finger of fate.

On the side, and predictably, the asshole I let stay in my cabin while I went to Palm Beach with the sincere promise to keep the coal fire going came home late the first night, drunk, and passed out without stoking the fire. He woke up the next morning to water spraying all over my stuff. He turns the water off but there's still an ice mountain in the center of my cabin when I get back. I curse his black soul but in retrospect, nobody is as good as I am when it comes to being responsible, so what did I really expect? I learn the obvious: never trust a drunk to keep the fire going, or anything else responsible.

After cleaning up the mess, soldering in new copper pipe for the broken section, and melting the impromptu ice sculpture on top of my coffee table, I get back to my old routine. Things are quiet in town and I'm feeling a bit lonely. Thinking back on my trip to Florida, I feel maybe I might have pissed off my Karma with all the debauching I did and now I'm getting the opposite. I sort of feel I'm in a monastery monk's cell and should be copying books with a quill. All things eventually come into balance, physicists say, and if not, just wait a little longer.

*

Late one night, sometime after 3 a.m., I awake to a loud banging on my cabin door. If it was a friend, they would come into the mud room and knock politely on the inner door. I get up immediately, turn on a light, and go into the mud room calling out, "Who is it?" I'm really curious now because not very many people even know I live here. Who the hell could be looking for me at this hour?

"It's Cecelia. I need some help."

I open the door a crack. There she is, all bundled up in her parka with its fur-lined hood up. It's cold as hell out and she's standing at the bottom of the snow trail over the ice mountain between my door and the street, piled high by the passing snowplow.

"Hi! I bet you're surprised," she says demurely. "I was walking down from the ski area with my dog and he got into a skunk up the road and I knew you were close by. I thought you'd still be up. I'm sorry if I woke you."

I just stare at her for a moment while I gather my thoughts. I know her from the Grubstake. She's been the bar waitress there for over a year and she dates boys with good looks or money, including Hitch, I was told. I thought she had sort of a plain face and wasn't all that attractive to me, mostly, to be truthful, because she had too many boyfriends and I don't like competing for favors. I don't like competition because I don't like losing. I like to pick my targets carefully, sneak up on them, and make my move when they're not paying attention. I wasn't moving now, except for some shivering.

"Come in. Come in," and I step aside. She steps down into the doorway dragging a huge black dog behind her. I don't smell any skunk. I close the outside door and turn around in the crowded mudroom opening the door to the inside. She steps in and the dog follows. I still don't smell anything.

"I don't smell anything," I point out mildly, feeling much better. I really didn't want a skunk dog in my little cabin. That stink can last forever.

I go to the stove and throw in a chunk of coal to help warm it up a little. I turn around and she's already out of her coat and sitting on my alcove bed.

"You have a cozy little home here," she comments. "I bet you like it a lot." The dog curls up by the stove and seems quite comfy. I sniff carefully but smell no skunk. Only suspicion.

"Gee, you have a lot of electronics. You must be very smart," she offers with a smile.

"I just finished some research on the upper atmosphere for NASA. But that shithead Nixgoon cancelled our budget and the whole damn lab had to close. So here I am. What about you?"

She pats the bed next to her indicating I should sit down. I check the damper on the stove and go over and sit on the edge next to her. She's wearing a nice tight sweater showing an exquisite outline. She must have been working the bar tonight and was walking the dog after work, I surmise.

"I'm a dropout too. My father is an anthropology professor at Kansas State. I grew up around the campus and just got tired of all its puritan bullshit. I transferred to Western State and now I'm taking a sabbatical studying skiing and waitressing."

"That's nice. I like smart girls who know what they want."

For the second time in my life, I get blindsided by a girl I completely underestimate. The first was the girl who perfunctorily devirginized me before I even knew I had my pants off. Cecelia reaches over and with one hand pulls my shorts down, while, with the other, she pushes me back on my bed. The next thing I know, I have her clothes off and the dog starts snoring. Wise men say, *When it rains after a long drought, drink till you puke.*

No woman had paid me such an honor before. She obviously tracked me down without any encouragement on my part but confident in my need. I loved the idea. And of course, I guiltily think I owe her something the next day, like becoming her full-time defender or assuming we have sexual exclusivity. My puritan upbringing says I must fall in love now that we're doing the nasty. I try to join in her life and participate the way she wants it. I try to make her happy.

She's highly independent. She works and makes her own way, or so it appears. She rents one of the apartments over the motorcycle shop where she lives alone with her big black dog. She works almost full-time as a waitress and on a good night probably pulls in a hundred bucks in tips alone. It dawns on me right away she might be out of my class even though her looks were a little less than what one might expect. She certainly made up for it in so many other ways that she becomes quite intoxicating and very habit forming.

Then the light starts to turn on. She tells me there's a load of cocaine coming to town soon and everyone is lining up with advance-sales commitments. I buy into the premise and know on the side that Wietzel knows who's bringing it in and can get me a better price. I scrape together a hundred dollars, representing two weeks of my normal income, and commit to buy one gram. It's all I can afford.

When it comes in, I pick up my little brown bottle from Wietzel who is dispensing out of the motorcycle shop below, making me think I now know who the importer is.

I meet up with Cecelia when she leaves the Grubstake at closing time and we barely make it the three blocks to her apartment before starting to tear each other's clothes off. I pull out the little bottle and we each take a little hit to get our motors going. But then she takes the bottle and I spend the rest of the night infatuated with what she does with it and how it goes so fast *I hardly knew ye*. The worst part is when she rubs some on my penis, which I guess helps make it stand up harder and work longer to accomplish its duty. I think it's a waste of good coke, trying to numb what I came to enjoy.

It's a night to remember for a young boy, but nothing so special that I haven't done it before. It's fun, we explore our bodily pleasures, and we make no commitments outside of enjoying life together for one splendid though expensive night. I realize my beloved is a coke whore. When we separate the next day, she's quiet and reserved. I sense something's wrong. No idea what it is, but she's clearly different now, unattached.

Over the next few days, she avoids me and finally I discover Tapley, the teenage rogue son of the Dawsons and a little coke whore himself, is now sharing her apartment. When I stop by unannounced to see her, the sixteen-year-old punk kid and passable motocross rider opens the door and delivers a subtle but direct message that the girl is just not that into me anymore and has chosen a different track.

"Good luck, though," he says, as he closes the door in my face.

My heart is broken. The person I love, because she picks me, making me feel special, leaves me because she's using me. The one who loves, never leaves. That's almost the definition of love. It's always the one who's using the relationship to better themselves that when it comes to an end, discards it unemotionally in favor of simply replacing it with the next one. Relationships today have become low-commitment arrangements, nonrepairable, toss it when its broken, objects of selfish pleasure and personal taste alone. I ask Cordley, a self-described Druid priest, to put a curse on her. He lights a candle and recites some strange chants. It isn't long before she leaves town.

*

I continue to work at the theater and the record shop until summer finally comes around once again. Then one day, a strange skinny little cowboy-looking kid rolls into town driving an old rusty Plymouth and pulling an ancient wooden horse trailer containing a mean looking Appaloosa. Tim Reed, apparently, had met Townes at a bar in Austin where he was singing, and told him about Crested Butte. Townes loves the idea, leaves Austin in June, and comes to spend the summer camping with his horse in the high country around Lake Irwin.

But when he actually shows up in town, Tim sends him to me for help. *Could he park his car and trailer at our house at the end of Elk?* Tim doesn't have the parking space at his house on Sopris, while we have all that empty space behind the house and next to the park that is all grass. "It's a good place to pasture the horse," he explains.

As the record shop representative and a recent professional Rock & Roll sound engineer and lover of good music, I immediately want to help the poor looking bastard. Tim says he's a songwriter and folk singer with two albums so far pressed. That's good enough for me.

"That's great," he says when I tell him it's okay. "Let's celebrate by having a drink."

"I don't think the bar is open yet," I observe.

"That's okay," he says brightly. "I got something right here." He whips out a pint of rot gut whiskey and takes a long swig. Then he hands it to me. I can't say no.

"Here's to you," I say, and take a drink that immediately chokes me up. "*Cough! Cough!* And you are?"

"Townes. Townes Van Zandt of the Texas Van Zandts. My great-great-grandfather fought at the battle of San Jacinto. Here's to fucking Texas!" And he finishes the bottle, throwing it to the ground.

~ 3 ~

GRUBSTAKE ON THE 4TH

The Fourth of July is a very important holiday in the mountains. I assure you; it has nothing to do with patriotism or even the universal predilection for partying that mountain folk have, especially in the summer time. Long before I actually move here, I partied many times in the Rockies and they were all special. Even though locals live for the winters and the special status one gets from successfully wintering over, whether for the first time or anytime, the real fun time begins right after the summer solstice and the mud season and goes through to the first snows of September and October. Time for bouncing wildly around those crazy mountains and surviving the onslaught of like-minded low-life flatlander tourists.

It's all about tradition. For several years, young punks from Denver deliberately target Crested Butte for a spontaneous reenactment of some twisted old western myth, namely the bar brawl. What attracts them, I think, are the classic hand-carved wooden backbars that are iconic to the period and which Crested Butte has several. At last count there are five bars in town that look like western movie sets.

With a choice of four bars within one block all having classic backbars and pumping liquor out all day on the Fourth, Elk Avenue between Second and Third becomes a huge open drunken playground for adults (or so they claim). Here, young budding alcoholics come up to altitude with an attitude and get the rush of their lives when alcohol metabolizes slower in a low-oxygen atmosphere. It builds rapidly to dumb-assed male testosterone levels culminating in the inevitable thoughtless insult answered with a punch to the face or a kick to the groin.

From there, it rapidly devolves into a free-for-all with no apparent rules or sides to defend or any clear-cut reason for the need to seek physical superiority through bloody combat or even an eventual winner. In most cases, it ends when the survivors, or the ones too fucked up to disappear when the sirens sound, get captured by the cops and sent to the holding tank in Gunnison until they sober up and pay a fine to cover the cost of transport. The new city leaders, well-educated carpetbaggers from respectable society, fear for Crested Butte's reputation in the burgeoning tourist market at a time when they are trying to attract a new high-priced tourist that spends more and expects less throwing of furniture through windows.

You have to understand something about living in a town at the end of the road. You can't get any further from regular society and coercive living and there's really nowhere else to go beyond that. After all, it's the end of the road. Another thing you have to know about civil law at the end of the road is the application of an ancient English legal tradition known as *Salutary Neglect*. All the trappings of a principled judicial system exist here, except certain laws common to the outside are summarily disregarded and ignored in small localities where they are not desired. For Crested Butte in the '70s, it's drugs and money, mostly cocaine and a lot of pot. Everyone knew it, kept it on the low-key, and went on about their business, seeking their high-altitude ambitions while enjoying a hell of a good time doing it.

So, my best friend from college, freshly graduated with a major in sociology, becomes the town marshal with the explicit understanding that his job is to maintain a low-key status quo, which means enforce the usual and necessary community regulations but ignore any socially repressive outside laws such as victimless crimes involving people freely exercising their constitutional right to the pursuit of happiness. Like freedom of religion, we feel we inalienably have the right to put in, on, or around our bodies what the hell ever we want. It's not anybody's business and especially not the government's. It is a simple matter of personal freedom versus a tyrannical oppressive government. The freedom of the wilderness infects those who live there.

The job requires him to wear a uniform shirt but he wears normal clothes below that and never wears a tie, except when the state or federal pigs are in town and he has to play the role a little more convincingly. Otherwise, he is one of us, having enjoyed the weed and the psychedelics and having a mission to show how a small town can regulate itself and do it responsibly, serving its constituents without suppressing them.

Living at the end of the road also requires a great deal of tolerance. When populations are low and the challenges high, we quickly learn to put our differences aside so we can concentrate on what's important: like survival. The town is full of young well-educated kids all looking for something different from their parents' uptight world. We tolerate all who come to the same community, we join the brotherhood of the mountains and work together to build a wilderness home. We stock it with plenty of wood and coal and maybe an elk or two and hovel together as we share this common love affair.

When people work hard and play hard, they tend to drink hard. The bars of Crested Butte in the '70s are the living rooms of the community. There is little or no TV available anyway, so after dinner every night, most Butte-ers wander downtown for a few drinks and some pleasant daily conversation amongst friends, sharing the local news of the day and helping keep everyone's spirits up during difficult times. July 3rd was no different, except for one topic on everyone's mind.

Cordley, Bleau, and I walk into the Grubstake for the daily after-work happy hour gathering where one can get a beer for twenty-five cents or a pitcher for a buck. Cordley waves around the daily money he just lifted from their cash box at the print shop, from what few postcards and incidentals they sold to tourists that day. He buys a pitcher from Faude and brings it to the table I corner.

Bleau is up for the weekend from Denver where she lives and works but spends every moment she can up here. Cordley introduced us and the two of us consummated it that night in Kemp's garage and sealed our bond as a couple, for a couple of months now.

"Have a beer," he announces, knowing I can't afford one right now. Bleau offers to buy the next round. I haven't found much steady work after being in the Butte for a whole year, wintering over in Kemp's garage. Now I manage the Princess Theatre for a paltry monthly salary of two hundred bucks and I'm helping out Cordley and Susan in their shop by printing T-shirts and custom posters on their big silkscreen printing press. Cordley and I try to get work for our cameras.

Recently, I also started running the local record shop for the owner, Chris Wietzel, aka the Weasel, who is out of town for an extended stay in southern California, pretending to be a surfer/skier bad boy and a successful tropical fish entrepreneur. In reality, he is on the lam for doing a little too much coke dealing in Colorado and is on a break from the local heat. He pays the shop rent and I keep what tiny revenues it generates. All I have to do is keep it open six hours a day or so. I didn't realize he was laundering coke money, so operating at an economic loss shouldn't have made me feel uncomfortable, even by Crested Butte standards.

"Thanks," I reply, "don't mind if I do." I grab a glass, fill it for Bleau, and then fill one for myself and sit back with a sigh. It looks stormy outside and will probably rain tonight.

"You want to join the pool for tomorrow's action?" Cordley asks.

"What pool?"

"Faude's running a pool on how many people will be arrested tomorrow and how many cops it will take to do it," he explains. "It's a tradition."

"I thought Kemp said he has it covered this year," I toss back.

"Yeah, he said that last year and look what happened," Cordley reminds me. "It ended up six and eight, with the local jail being used and later declared unfit for any further human habitation. Seems as though you're supposed to provide a toilet to inmates being held overnight. Kemp was letting them piss off the rear railing into Coal Creek but they had trouble aiming."

"I was here for that one," Bleau adds. "It was a stinking mess the next morning."

"That's what that sign says now, on the door of the jailhouse. It's an official national historic site and can't be used for anything except a museum," I add. "No more pissing allowed."

"Hey, Hitch!" Cordley shouts. Hitch sits at the end of the bar nursing a beer and talking to Faude. "What do you think's going to happen tomorrow?" He follows it with his crazy laugh indicating he's just ripping on him. Hitch turns slowly on his stool to look in our direction.

"I just told Faude to board up the windows now and avoid the insurance claim."

"But then we'll have to go outside to watch the action," Cordley complains. "These are ringside seats!"

"That's all right, they aren't going to enforce the street ban. You can take your beer with you," he adds with a wide grin and holding his mug up in salute.

"Oh, boy. That's going to help maintain order and the rule of law! Hey Jack, put me down for four and four."

"You got it, Cord," Jack responds from behind the bar. He pulls out the card from under the bar, locates the box at 4 and 4, and signs Cordley's name. "That'll be two bucks."

Cordley gets up grabbing two bills out of the stack on the table dedicated to our bar tab for the night and walks over to them. "Here, probably the best investment I've made today." He slams the two bills on the bar laughing maniacally.

Jack takes his money and puts it in the box with the rest of the pool money. I pour the last beer from the pitcher and bang it on the table.

"And another, barkeep!" I yell. Faude hears and signals he's on it.

"I've got this one," announces Bleau, and she pulls out a green wrinkled paper ball which she carefully flattens out on the table into a recognizable five-dollar bill.

"Cut that man off!" Kemp shouts coming through the front door. Some stranger in a marshal's shirt like Kemp's walks in behind him. He's about four foot nine by my estimate, based on the height of my friend Amy, whose head barely comes up to my arm pit. He also looks like a brick shithouse on steroids. His biceps are stretching his shirt sleeves to bursting and he simply has no neck, with shoulders directly connected to his earlobes.

"Who's your bodyguard, Coit?" asks Hitch, turning around in his barstool to get a better look at the stranger. Kemp steps up to the bar next to his brother and the stranger steps up to the next bar stool, leans back against the bar, and scans the room. We meet eye-to-eye.

"This is Rob McClung, the new deputy the town hired just for the Fourth," Kemp announces loud enough for the whole bar to hear. Rob does a three-finger salute to nobody in particular, signifying he must have been a pimply-faced Boy Scout at some time.

"So, you're the football guy I've been hearing about," says Jack, putting my pitcher on the bar. I get up slowly and move to pick it up. Everyone is looking at Kemp and he looks a little down, almost embarrassed.

"The town council thinks I need help with this year's Fourth after what happened last year."

"I was here last year," McClung butts in, "and saw what happened and just had to see if me and my friends might be able to help. I belong to the Denver Sports Club and thought a little muscle might be just what's needed. I'm here with some weight-lifting friends to make sure Marshal Coit can handle the situation without all the fighting."

"That's gonna screw with your fight pool, Jack!" announces Cordley.

"What fight pool?" McClung asks.

"Nothing," counters Jack, "just a local joke."

*

Later, after I close the Princess, I'm sitting at the bar in the Nickel when Kemp walks in alone. He sits next to me with a groan and orders a beer with the wave of his hand.

"It's okay, I'm off duty," he mumbles, more to himself than anyone else at the bar.

"So, who's that guy, anyway?" I ask without looking up.

"McClung? Yeah, I know. It was a surprise to me, too. He apparently made a deal with the mayor and they sprung it on me today."

"Nice. Big city politics comes to the Butte," I declare. "Did anyone bother to tell them that they might as well pour gas on a fire if you use strangers to stop a couple of our drunks from settling their penis-size street argument?"

"I'm getting a divorce," he suddenly adds.

"What?" I respond, mildly shocked.

"Linda didn't come home last night after I left her in the bar drinking with her friends," he painfully explains.

"That's not grounds for divorce in Crested Butte," I counter, trying to add comfort. "Maybe she got too drunk to walk home in the dark and crashed on a couch. It happens all the time."

"She slept with Terry."

"Terry the fat guy?'

He nods his head yes.

"Terry the anthropologist turned baker?" I query in vain.

He just looks down at his beer, and then takes a long slug.

"How do you know?" I quiz him.

"She told me today when she stopped by to pack some things up and move into his house."

"Vicious!" I exclaim slowly. "Bed to bed without even a respectful breakup kiss. Are you going to kill him?"

"*Naw*, I felt there was something missing in our relationship ever since I suggested we try to have children. Let her go...and I might as well go, too."

"What do you mean?"

"I'm going to resign and look for a job somewhere else. I'm tired of this mess."

This is all a shock to me. I try to lighten the mood. "But it's *your* hellhole. You just need to stop marrying every hungover girl that wakes up in your bed."

"I really liked this job. I thought I was doing something unique and worthy. I made Crested Butte a safe home for the marginal and persecuted. I applied proven social mechanisms to get the people to support their local sheriff and make this a safe home for everyone."

"I'm sorry, but you're still a cop. Just a very bad one from a cop standpoint, but damn good for the rest of us." I offer to clink glasses. He reluctantly complies.

"You don't know how many times I've had to pull strings to keep the Colorado DEA from coming here and staging a sting operation."

"Stinking bastards!"

"They arrest college students for possession and then flip them for a lesser charge," he explains. "They then send them to a small town like us where they contact sympathetic drug users, innocent bystanders, trying to help a newcomer score. They bust innocent naïve pot users like us, ruining our lives while the big city drug corporations serving death go untouched."

"Ignorant scum!" I exclaim. "Victimless morality laws should be banned. Every free human should have the final say about what goes in their bodies or not. The fucking government, in trying to regulate morality, which is about the same as supporting a state religion, just creates crime where none exists before. Administrative laws not serving or protecting people need to be expunged. Don't they understand that when a law prohibiting consumable products is enforced, a black market always appears that serves the need being suppressed, creating an artificial crime situation? The only reason the Afghanis are a bunch of primitive religious fanatics controlling a major government is that they are being exclusively funded and fueled by the world-wide illegality of heroin. Legalize heroin world-wide and those sick anti-humanitarian bums would disappear in an instant."

"I'll drink to that!" Kemp agrees, and clicks his glass with mine.

"So where are you going to be a hippie cop now?" I ask.

"Virginia City, Montana," he replies. "Remember *The Missouri Breaks*?"

"Oh yeah, the movie where the guy gets shot inside an outhouse."

"That's it. They filmed it nearby at a Hollywood-built set on an old ranch. But some of the scenes were shot in town. Anyway, they are very similar to Crested Butte, except no ski area."

"*Oooh*, sounds like a town full of alcoholics and wife swappers with no expensive diversions in the winter."

"That's about right. I'm going to rent my house out to Titler. Helene just threw him out and he needs a place to get his shit together."

"Oh shit. It just doesn't let up. Who's the reason?"

"Cloud," he says simply. I shake my head in disbelief.

*

July Fourth dawns cold and grey. Everyone is greeted by a huge explosion from somewhere near town at sunrise, shaking dust from the rafters and waking everybody up way before they prefer. Nobody knows who did it, but I bet it's the guy with dynamite. I know a couple of people like that. Could even be me. Who knows?

A little snow falls overnight and when the Grubstake opens for breakfast, at nine, I find myself with a bunch of hardcore locals in their down coats sitting in the outside beer garden. Our beer glasses sit on the weathered wooden tables in three inches of snow, keeping them properly mountain chilled. Bleau steps in as an impromptu waitress and keeps the mugs full.

Elk Avenue is blocked off at Mehelich's Conoco, so all traffic has to go right or left, around the celebration area, to find parking on the off streets. It's starting to fill up with the usual family-type people milling around and hitting all the souvenir shops. Locals and other young kids from Gunnison, and farther, start to hog the area between bars. They drag chairs from the Grubber out in the street, where they sit, drink, and catch some rays. It's warming up fast.

Gorbett sets up the Grubstake speakers outside and begins playing music for the street crowd. People fill the street and by eleven there is a modest crowd lining both sides of Elk waiting for the festivities to start. At the far end, I can see the Grubstake Marching Girls forming up for the big kazoo band parade. They wear bikinis, but use body paint to decorate themselves like an American flag with stars and bars and blue faces.

Somebody hitches a flatbed trailer to a pickup—I think it's the Verplank brothers—and with a couple of streamers and a few early morning drunks guarding their drinks and throwing firecrackers, follow the kazoo band down the avenue past all the bars and visitors to the Conoco, where the girls simply begin marching backwards, all the way back to the start. By the time they reach Third, however, they begin having trouble holding their formation together.

Dana Atchley is out with his video camera shooting the parade right at the start as it passes by his house. He performs the Ace of Space Roadshow, which he tours around the country in a box van he lives in and uses as a production studio. Little bastard was born with all the advantages in the world I can only imagine, and he spends it all on his weird live performance slideshow about, of all things, living on the road as an artist.

His show consists of projecting color slides on a large, double-wide screen showing major roadside attractions from around the country. He's been eyeing my video projector ever since I brought it to town, and if it could project a brighter picture and not be the size of a small Italian car, he probably would have scarfed it up from me a long time ago. Instead, he hired me to go along on some of his performance tours, which was right up my alley, having retired from the Rock & Roll touring business before it killed me. He loves the romantic and sometimes artistic roadside attractions and spends most of his time taking still pictures and then projecting them at his show along with a terrible impression of a road warrior artist. His favorite saying is, *We don't makes art, we finds art!*

Townes follows the float riding Amigo as our one and only equestrian unit, all dressed up like a Texas toothpick cowboy and hoisting the unofficial town flag representing Crested

Butte's martial participants. The flag, of course, is Coney's gulch flag, *Don't Tread on Me*, a green coiled snake on a yellow background. It normally flies over the gulch cabin, but today it comes to town with Townes. He follows the float to much laughter and shouts from the crowd. Townes whoops and yells like a Texas madman entertaining the crowd with his amazing performance just keeping upright on Amigo and preventing a nervous horse from bolting and running amok from all the firecrackers and loud music. Cindy holds Geraldine on a leash looking on with stern resignation to his usual shenanigans.

Following Townes and holding down the end of the parade is Albert Maun's freshly washed backhoe with a cardboard sign attached to the side saying, *SUPER DOOPER POOPER SCOOPER."*

The float, followed by Townes and the backhoe, make a U-turn in the intersection and follow the backward marching kazoo band back up Elk. When they get as far as the Nickel, somebody in the band trips or runs into something and the whole lot goes down like well-worn dominoes. They reassemble themselves with some help from some shirtless young men in the crowd and together, complete the backward march to more cheers and ovations. Townes gives up trying to keep Amigo calm, dismounts, and takes him to the rear of the Nickel, where he ties him to a tree.

The sunny day creeps forward with much drinking in the streets, some people dancing drunkenly and everyone else wandering around aimlessly enjoying the sun, suds, and music. All the young guy's strip down to their bare chest as the sun heats up the street revelers. I'm hangin' in the Grubber with Bleau and James Griffen, my old friend from Ann Arbor who helped me get my first film gig. His father is U of M's Professor Emeritus of Anthropology and James grew up with some of the smartest people in the world. He's one of the brilliant local kids in Ann Arbor I used to hang with, who all had exceptional parents and the exceptional upbringing I wish I could have had.

We knew each other for over four years while I attended graduate school and neither one of us ever mentioned Crested Butte to each other. But he's a Michigan skier and had some skier friends from Grand Rapids who turn him on to CB's great powder skiing without the ridiculous cost of Aspen. When I finally show up to live in Kemp's garage, James appears out of nowhere, at the Grubstake one night, and surprise, surprise, we have no idea how we ended up in the same place, at the same time.

The magic of Crested Butte often puts strange people together all over the world having only CB in common and, in all cases, it's definitely an excuse to celebrate in CB style. He introduces me to the rest of the Michigan contingency of ski bums and bar owners. Jack Faude and his partner, Derf, the colostomy bagman, buy the decrepit Grubber for about ten grand and make it a central fixture of Crested Butte's new young rebel drinking society.

James is also member of the Hot Shots, as are most of the young guys in town who have to work for a living. It was pretty much free money for doing what we normally do for fun, i.e., run around the wilderness like the wild animals we are and have fucking fun, fishing, peeking into holes in the ground, seeing what's on the other side of the hill, and maybe put out a fire or two. A few of us didn't need to sleep out on the ground for two weeks or more at a time, living in the same clothes, no showers, and constant hard work doing something or another, like digging holes or filling others in. I kind of felt like I didn't need the money that much and somebody had to stay behind and entertain their lonely girlfriends.

"What's Kemp goin' to do with his new deputies?" James asks innocently, with his usual shit-eating grin. He's a master at the *I-know-something-you-don't* smirk.

"I saw them earlier putting up traffic cones," I offer.

"Did you buy into the pool?"

"Can't afford it." I take a sip on my suds. I have to make five dollars last until the theater opens and I can tap the receipts, giving myself a little tip for my exceptional dedication to duty. I hate to take Bleau's charity; I'm poor as hell and the pay from the theater is minimal. I figure Hollywood can afford it if I accidentally underreport a couple of seats sold.

"Have you noticed some beefy flatlanders hanging around?" he asks, looking around the bar.

"Nope."

I look around the crowded bar and notice most of the Hot Shots are here getting plastered as usual and having a damn good time. "Why do you ask?" I ply sarcastically, knowing everyone is expecting something.

The air is electric with tension. Everybody seems to be too happy and in an excessively celebratory mood. James leans in close so only I can hear him.

"Ron Barr says he's going to flatten the first bastard that tries to start a fight," he says. "I believe him. What do you think?"

"Didn't you bastards start a brawl last summer in Grand Junction that got you all permanently banned from the city?"

He just smiles his big shit-eating grin again and looks away with that classic smirk like he still knows something. He doesn't know shit and he's probably a big disappointment to his father. But who cares in Crested Butte? Everyone here is more or less treated equally and without prejudice until proven a chump and found to be unworthy.

Over the sound of the loud music, I hear a commotion of some kind outside. Somebody is yelling or whooping or, what the hell ever, I can't tell the difference. I stand up with everybody else in the bar to get a better look outside. There's movement across the street barely discernible through the thick crowd. Then I spot him. Actually, both of them, and they seem to be pushing people out of the way and heading straight toward us. It's Amigo with a drunken Townes on his back.

Now people start scattering in all directions. Townes urges Amigo under the sidewalk awning, bends over backward in the saddle, and inside they come. People scatter, along with tables and chairs, while Townes fights like hell to control an Amigo not happy it's not a barn full of oats. He flares his nostrils and whinnies loudly for being cheated.

"Whoa! Whoa Amigo!" shouts Townes. Townes is visibly shit-faced and barely staying in the saddle. One thing I know about Amigo is he hates having Townes ride him when he's loaded, which is just about all the time. How he got all the way through the parade without being bucked off earlier is still a mystery to me.

"Barkeep!" he shouts. "A shot of whiskey for me and get Amigo whatever he wants."

"Townes!" Jack yells back. "You can't have your fucking horse in the bar!"

"Why not! He's thirsty. This is America! We're celebrating a birthday! Somebody called Sam!"

About then, Amigo tries to rear up but the low ceiling prevents him from getting it done. He slips instead on the waxed wooden floor, flips sideways a little, and Townes goes flying into the nearest table, collapsing in a pile of wooden splinters, beer foam, and broken glasses.

Amigo scrambles back up and makes a break for the door, where I see Cindy on the other side getting ready to grab his reins. Amigo whirls her around and tries to keep going, but Cindy is a big strong fifteen-year-old Texas cowgirl who knows how to control a rogue horse or a crazy drunken troubadour. She pulls him into running in tight circles onto the street where he calms down from the frustration.

I turn to help Townes off the floor when a stranger rushes him screaming, "You spilled our beer you bastard! I'm gonna kick your ass!"

He slips in the beer and wildly swings, missing everything. He falls into one of the local Hot Shots, who simply pushes him away in the direction of another who is already winding up.

"Townes is our guy. He doesn't dance, but we do," and connects with a fist to the stranger, who crumples to the floor, stunned. The annual July 4th fight officially begins.

"Come on, Townes," I yell. "Time to leave."

James grabs one arm and I the other. Bleau breaks trail and we drag him backwards out the door as the entire bar erupts into a free-for-all. We stop outside and help Townes regain his feet.

"Where's Amigo?" he demands.

"Over here, Townes!" Cindy shouts. She's holding Amigo by the reins in the middle of the intersection. We all head in her direction.

The music stops and everyone is now looking at the Grubstake as the sound of crashing chairs and macho yelling is coming from that direction. People are streaming out of the

Grubstake door and scattering madly. Then the sound of shattering glass is heard as a chair comes flying out the front window, followed by Carson holding some stranger in a headlock. As soon as they hit the street, some bystander blindsides him with a wicked punch to the head.

Up the street, another commotion commences as several beefy weight-lifters led by McClung pour out of the Nickel running toward the Grubber, pushing and knocking aside anyone in their path.

"It's the Bronco rejects, sports fans!" James pronounces calmly, pretending to hold a mic like a sportscaster. "Where's the law?"

We all look around, but see nothing but people and contenders. We can hear Faude screaming from inside the bar, "Get the fuck out of here! If you want to fight, go the fuck outside!"

The mercenary deputies from Denver confront the Hot Shots as they're attempting to drag several of their adversaries out into the street. McClung doesn't even pause to give any orders to stop or break it up. He just KOs the first person he encounters, which happens to be Ron Barr. Ron goes down for a moment, but soon struggles up from all the other bodies now littering the sidewalk.

Cloud and Starr drag out a couple more, but are tackled by two of McClung's boys in what is considered at the time a classic football clipping and should have earned a fifteen-yard penalty. Neither one seems to notice because as they scramble up, they immediately fall back like pro wrestlers, with elbows pointed down at the fat bulging guts squeezing what little thin air they have, out with a loud grunt. As they try to catch their breath, the boys pummel them repeatedly about the head and shoulders.

Carson is holding his own as he fights off two more trying to surround him. He's so drunk they can't predict what he's going to do or which direction he's going to fall. A couple of his wild punches actually connect and he starts getting cocky, dancing around in the middle of Elk Avenue swinging his fists around like Muhammad Ali on steroids. Someone tries to bodyslam him, but he dances out of the way at the last moment and the guy flies by Carson, hitting the pavement like a bag of wet concrete. The loud thump of his breath exploding from his lungs could be heard up and down the street. The crowd went, *Ahhhhhh!*

Then the siren goes off. Apparently, Kemp, sitting at home and drinking quietly alone until the die was cast, gets a call from the county dispatcher. He has to do something. His little Bronco police car can be seen at the far end of Elk heading this way with lights flashing, siren wailing, and kicking up a thick dust cloud behind it. He doesn't even slow down for the traffic cones spread across the street in front of the Conoco. One cone flies clean over the houses on the south side of Elk, landing in the back alley.

Townes and Cindy see him coming and quickly take Amigo and Geraldine up Third and into the alley behind the Nickel, where he normally keeps him tied up.

"Hey Cowboy, stay out of trouble. I'll be right back," Townes yells at me, while rushing Amigo out of sight.

"Don't worry, I can see trouble comin' two three feet away," I yell back. About then, a body or two comes flying by. James makes like a matador, stiffens, steps aside and bows as they flounder through. Bleau hands him her drink and he takes a swig with a flourish.

"We better get out of the way. Here comes the cavalry," James proclaims, as he drags us back towards the sidewalk. I step over a couple of bodies just as Kemp comes roaring up the street behind us. Nobody pays him much attention. The action is just getting good, as blood now marks many of the participants.

The Bronco comes to a skidding stop short of hitting somebody. If Kemp has been dispatched, then for sure the County Mounties are not far behind. Normally, Kemp would wait for backup or at least try to talk everyone down before they arrive.

He climbs out of his Bronco screaming. "Everybody stop!" he yells, as he pushes deep into the combatants, actually attempting to push a few apart.

"Welcome, sports fans!" James yells. "The annual games have begun!"

Over the general shouting and cursing, we hear what sounds like The Face giving odds and taking bets. "Two to one Carson takes the blond guy!"

I spot Carson still standing, mostly, in front of Stefanik's store, weaving and holding onto some slim blond kid who's flinging his arms aimlessly. Somebody gets shoved hard into the two of them and they all go down on the steps of the store. A big *Ahhhhh...Ooooooooo!* comes up from the crowd.

"The god-damned sheriff's deputies are coming and they don't ask nicely," Kemp yells from the middle of the foray. He's shoving people aside and slapping locals on the shoulder to get their attention. "Break it up and go home!"

About that time, somebody throws a haymaker at someone who ducks and Kemp is in the direct line of fire. *Bam!* He takes a full fist in the jaw, knocking his head half off his shoulders.

McClung stops fighting with a couple of dancing Hot Shots, sees what happened to Kemp, and decides he needs to act like the uniform he's wearing.

He steps up on a nearby gas lamp and yells over the crowd. "Everybody stop! You're all under arrest!"

Then we hear the distant sound of more sirens. The sheriff's deputies have been operating a speed trap just a couple of miles down the road near CB South, catching turkeys speeding on the long downhill straight run that invariably yields a good number of fines for those unfamiliar with rural crooked cops and their crooked ways and who won't fight or complain. They just pay it. Cash for the county coffers!

"Run for it!" rings out over the crowd. And they do. Every local, every Hot Shot, every alley dweller and trust funder suddenly drops whatever they're doing and just scatters in every direction.

Cordley comes out of hiding in the Nickel and saunters over to Kemp, still kneeling in the middle of the street trying to get his jaw back in place. "You knew the job was dangerous when you took it," he croons.

James goes back into the Grubstake with a few others left behind. Bleau and I go over to help Cordley get his brother to his feet so he won't have to press charges when the Mounties get here. The street is strangely empty for this time of the early evening, but littered as if after a fucking hurricane.

Kemp goes back to his Bronco to wait for the sheriff deputies, while Cordley, Bleau, and I hide in the Grubber to watch the third act play out through the wide-open, now panoramic window. Jack is already dragging a sheet of plywood out from the back room where he stores it for just these occasions.

Two county sheriff's deputies arrive all pissed off, having given up their lucrative toll collection for this. They are not happy. For the next two hours, one deputy listens to Kemp and the other listens to McClung. McClung screams and yells in their faces about how they need to arrest everyone in the Grubstake. Jack quietly locks the door.

The sheriff deputies trade places and continue. They take notes, compare together apart from the two uniformed town marshals now not talking to one another. They finally get bored, talk to the sheriff on the radio, and then just leave without arresting anybody.

We all heave a sigh of relief when all the sheriff's cars depart Elk and Kemp picks up the cones, opening up the street to normal traffic. The town engineer will get out the sweeper later tonight when the streets are empty and wipe away all evidence anything ever happened.

Everybody left in the Grubber is hunkered down over their drinks, reviewing the events of the afternoon, comparing notes on all the exciting individual highlights. Locals who ran away earlier slowly return to the bars as another legendary Fourth comes to an end.

I show the movie as usual at seven, but it's a small crowd, costing the theater to show it. Good thing I don't own this place and can't make it pay its own way. Rich people can actually operate something at a loss and still make a profit in the long run. If you're a clever, aka, criminal capitalist, then playing the long game is more important than winning every hand.

After a quick vacuum, I close the Princess and head across the still littered street to the darkened Grubber with a major window now blacked out. I spot Cordley and Bleau at the bar talking to James in his usual animated manner of an Irish drunk explaining philosophy to a priest. Otherwise, the place is muted with pockets of locals occupying tables in small groups all going over the details of the day, along with play-by-play criticism.

"Hey, Cord, buy me a beer," I demand. "Nobody showed up at the theater, so no slops."

He turns to the bar and Jack, still standing guard on duty.

"Hey, Jack," Cordley finally breaks the quiet. "Give this thirsty man a beer." He slaps a five-dollar bill on the bar. "By the way, who the hell won the pool?"

Jack pulls a mug out of the freezer under the counter and fills it at the tap. "I forgot all about the pool." He sets the beer in front of me and pauses to think.

"What was the score?" he asks, as he reaches under the counter to retrieve the pool card.

"Nobody got arrested," says Hitch, with his *Red Badge of Courage* head gash, as he saunters over to our group. "Otherwise, it would have been me." He slams his mug down on the bar. "Another!"

"So, zero and..." Jack muses, looking at the card tracing along one line.

"Three," I declare. "Actually, four, if you count McClung."

"Three or four," he asks, "which is it?"

I turn to the rest of the crowd for a consensus. "He's no cop!" someone yells.

"So, do we count McClung and his goons as cops, or what?" Jack demands.

"That could be as many as nine," James pipes up. "I counted."

"Nine to zip, what kind of score is that?" Jack scoffs. "It's off the charts. How can you have nine cops and no arrests? Nobody thought of that possibility. What do we do?"

"How much is in the pot?" asks James, with his damn smirk again.

"Over two hundred dollars," Jack reveals. He smiles with greed.

"Did anyone take three-zip?" I ask pointedly. "If we disregard the football goons and toss them in with the combatants, then who gets it?"

"Let's see," answers Jack. He glances at the chart, tries to focus on it in the bar light, and then announces, "The Rat."

Richard the Rat is sitting at a table with Tim Reed and Townes. I notice Townes is being very quiet and unobtrusive, drinking his whiskey from under the table and not saying much. He turns around when he hears his name and sees everyone looking at him sternly.

"Hey, I didn't even know what square I got," the Rat squeals. "I just bought the last open space."

Townes looks around and realizes he's the center of attention again.

"Now guys," he says, "let's all be nice and do the right thing. How about Richard here buys a round for the bar?" He's greeted with a loud cheer as he pats Richard on the back. Guilt-tripping is legal in the Butte.

Jack serves up a round of well shots and Richard the Rat pockets a couple hundred-dollar bills. Everyone is happy, except for Kemp and McClung.

*

During the following week of finger pointing and accusations, an emergency town meeting cancels McClung's proposal to control the locals with force. He's let go and Kemp's resignation is accepted, leaving Don West, the recently hired new deputy, in charge. Don missed the fun on the Fourth, being on vacation, and has little to go on as far as finding out what truly happened after he takes over. That leaves a sore spot with the locals, as Don is not of our kind. He does not indulge, drink, snort, smoke, or show any compassion for those who do. He will not have a good time here.

The spotlight swings back to our illustrious clean-cut, high school president mayor, Tommy Glass. A harmless guy, more or less, nice enough but truly out-classed by the job. His days are few and we all anticipate re-establishing our fundamental freedoms from an appropriate change in town politics.

Kemp packs up and leaves for his new job in Montana. I move from the guest garage and into the little white house at 640 Elk and begin feeling like a real local. Bleau comes up every weekend in her little red Toyota pickup and sort of moves in, as well.

My beloved Chevy Carryall blows its transmission and I don't have the money to fix it. I sell it to the new local garage behind Whiterock. I consider it tantamount to being so poor as to having to eat your horse. It happens. The next day, Don West stops by my door with a complaint from the buyer that I had somehow snuck back at night and stole my own stereo system out of the truck.

"Sorry, Mr. West," I patiently explain, "but I knew the stereo didn't work and that's why I left it in the truck. You'll have to look somewhere else." I close the door on him.

He always suspects Cloud for most unsolved petty crimes. Cloud was poor like me and therefore our morals had to be somewhat malleable in that we never steal, but when things are left unguarded and owned by someone who can afford it, well, all I can say is, survival is a harsh mistress.

I'm horseless now and have to rely on Bleau's little truck for my wilderness travels. Two-wheel drive wilderness exploring becomes a new challenge for me. Amazingly, it gets us into places we often thought only 4-wheelers could go.

The boys—Frenchy, Face, and the Greek—rent the house across Elk from me and so they have this end of town nailed down for the summer duration. Life is good. Time to go fishing.

~ 4 ~

THE PRINCESS

Most of the young kids I know in Crested Butte are running away from the outside corporate world of crooked capitalism, unjust patronage, and a government hell-bent on persecuting the nonconformist and the free. From draconian paranoid drug laws that only create victimless criminals where none existed before, to the incredibly unjust and criminal war raging for more than six years in Vietnam where fifty thousand young men will eventually become senseless sacrificial victims, butchered for no reason other than profit and international bravado. The huge corporations who own our government destroy lives and environments as if just a nuisance for the entitled.

I dabble in the smuggling business because it's the only small business open to the poor and unconnected. But you have to be smart to lower the risk factors and survive hostile police. From this basic of all businesses, you buy low, transport across artificial barriers, and sell at a ridiculously high price to those who need it. It's about the only way a young ambitious man with no family resources might get a leg up in the money game. When governments pass laws banning certain commodities only because of corrupt politics, then they've lost the moral high ground and mindless compliance no longer can be expected. It's amazing how many big-money families today got their start in smuggling and piracy.

From my earlier profits flying weed from El Paso to Ann Arbor, I bought a house, remodeled it, and sold it for a nice profit. I lived off the proceeds for a few years, but it finally ran out about when I arrived in Crested Butte, for the second and hopefully last time. But a lot of kids, who are drawn here like me, have a few thousand stashed away here or there and so an immediate blossoming of local small businesses and real estate investments occurs. I and my similarly poor friends are left out of the first real estate boom when houses are going for a few thousand dollars each. But a lot of young kids did scrape up the money and now have homes and are looking around to start sustaining businesses and possibly a family to boot.

Basically, there are two kinds of young people moving to town: those with long hair who dress in Levi's and plaid shirts, maybe leather boots, and those with short hair who dress *Friday casual.* Another way to describe it might be fraternity versus independents, or working slobs versus trust-funder trash.

Steve Glazer, a short hair, arrives with a few more than a few thousand, being the only son of a prominent Jewish accountant from Colorado Springs and boasting of a fresh CPA degree from Denver College. He decides to invest in the burgeoning Colorado tourist hospitality industry that he and others know damn well will eventually sweep Crested Butte away to the rich and the white, like Aspen, Vail, or Breckenridge and make them all rich as hell as they enjoy living off their modest but early investments in the burgeoning rich-man paradise business.

He buys the old Princess Theatre building for a measly three thousand dollars, including the projectors, sound system, screen, and a popcorn machine. There are only three channels of snowy TV over the air from low-power repeaters near Almont, so he reasons a big-screen movie theater is just what Crested Butte needs for its young growing and bored population.

The Glaze gains an early reputation in the Butte as our own local Simon Legree, the infamous fictional *tie-a-maiden-to-the-railroad-tracks* villain, who he also eerily resembles: tall, skinny, dark complexion, and a huge hooked nose. But even the devil can be enticing, so when I arrive, broke and unemployed, Cordley puts the word out to the locals introducing me as the new electronic genius in town. I can fix anything electric or electronic and I have a few nice tools to help convince people that I might actually know something about good sound and music as well as the new video tape technology.

I have the best stereo system available anywhere, hand-built including a pair of Model A, DCM speakers. I also have a first-class Collins S-51 shortwave receiver, a four-track 1/4" Teac tape deck and my real find—an RCA 6-foot color TV projector. I also own a four-wheel drive carryall truck sporting a big V-8 and a loud cassette deck stereo system I installed. When I was staying in Kemp's garage, I hung out my sign: *Quantum Mechanic - We fix all your quantums.* Later, I was nicknamed Smokey Circuits and finally, Captain Neutrino.

Anyway, I get a trade-in-kind job at the local bathhouse being built by Sunshine, a recent refugee from San Francisco. I install their stereo system and wire up the big-ass boiler—for which I use the facilities free. I fix a few washers and stereos here and there, but end up depending on help from Cordley and Susan's print shop just to eat. Tough times.

One day in the bar, Cordley introduces me to Steve, who asks me if I can run a 35mm carbon-arc movie projector. I have no direct experience, except for 16mm projectors in high school and a carbon-arc I built for the 4H Club, winning first place at the county fair. It's a weird project for 4H, but as a teenager I had to find ways to stay entertained while restricted to the family farm.

I tell him, "No problem."

He takes me to the Princess Theatre, which he bought recently and refurbished with second-hand cushioned seats, some cheap curtains, and a lot of paint. We step into the lobby where a good-looking girl is down on her knees cleaning out the twenty-year-old mess under the popcorn machine.

"This is Susie," he says in passing. We barely know each other. I say "Hi." She nods and smiles. I'm struck by her cute cheeks. He takes me upstairs to the projection booth. I make a note to myself to get to know her better.

The original 35mm projectors are still in place, just as they had been installed about thirty years earlier. There is even a third projector, a rare 16 mm Bell and Howell carbon-arc projector, also from the pre-World War II era. The booth still has the original RCA tube sound amplifier sporting two 6L6s and a 5U4 rectifier. *Cool,* I think. I like the old power tubes. They glow and give out warmth as they faithfully reproduce mellow sound. It's connected by a 70-volt transmission line to the rear of the stage where an old fifties-era classic Voice of the Theatre speaker stands on a table behind the movie screen.

Steve needs to finish the motorized winch, so the new hand-painted *Venus on the Half Shell* curtain covering the movie screen will go up and down automatically at the beginning and end of every show. Too many times the operator would let it roll too high or too low, screwing up the support ropes or tearing the curtain. He hires me to finish designing and building a small relay logic unit that detects the top and bottom positions, reversing the winch every time a button is pushed in the booth. After a couple of days work, the roll-up goes up and down remotely from the projection booth at the simple push of a big red button. That thing ends up working flawlessly for the entire rest of the Princess's lifetime.

From that moment, I fall in love with the place and become an official Princess Theatre fixture for almost six years. Every night, I occupy the projection booth and from the second story window overlooking the downtown section of Elk, I watch the Butte slowly simmer and boil over the years. I observe it change from cute and rustic, a spiritual refuge for the broken and rejected, to the phony and despoiled Disneyland Playboy Club of rich exclusivity in just a few precious moments of life.

Susie does odd jobs for Steve, but he needs someone full-time and smart enough to do everything without him having to lift a finger. I don't see her much after I took over the day-to-day management, but I figure out a way to at least get to know her better.

My high school friend drives in from Portland to go skiing in the Rockies because now he knows somebody who lives there he can stay with. He damn near kills himself trying to complete the last leg of driving at night in a snowstorm between Montrose and Gunnison near Blue Mesa Pass. Basically, a truck runs over his car's fender, knocking him into the ditch. I have to rescue him, somewhat shaken the next day, borrowing Cordley's BMW and bringing him the rest of the way.

I arrange for Susie to be his ski guide while here, and with the money he saves having a place to live, he hires her to ski the whole week with him. I get to see them each day at the end of their sessions. We all have dinner together the night he leaves and I get a chance to be alone with her in a relaxed atmosphere. We hit it off immediately, talking about movies.

But I'm with Bleau and she's with Russ, one of the local super skiers and spending a lot of time skiing the backcountry with mostly other boys. I don't ski, so I have to find another way to attract her. The theater is our common love. I hire her back as an assistant manager.

It's sad but true that the only good thing Steve ever did, to his credit, is the commissioning of the painting of the Princess's rollup curtain screen. Botticelli's *The Birth of Venus* is borrowed and updated, becoming *Venus on the Half Shell* in a Crested Butte mountain setting. It turns out to be a signature artwork that makes the Princess a significant piece of local culture and pride. This is truly something way beyond Glaze's usual lust for easy money and corrupting power that will surely be the only thing positive that outlives him.

But that's just the movie theater. In order to operate one, Steve next has to find films to show. Small theaters with low attendance numbers and no friends in the big-city film business get cut out of the distribution chain, and recently most rural theaters were being forced to close for just this reason. Steve searches for a sympathetic distributor who can get first-run films into smaller venues without the great expense of house minimums and unrealistic grosses. He searches all over Denver and finally finds the one person who faces the same problem—even more acutely than he—and who is pioneering a solution. He's overjoyed at what Bill Pence ultimately offers.

Bill Pence and his wife, Stella, decided to not run away from the big city, like most of us, but instead tackle the city on its own grounds and implement a novel business idea in tune and in synch with the changing social times. Bill bought a decrepit four-story brick warehouse in the slum industrial area northwest of Denver, gutted it, and built a four-plex movie theater sporting a different theater on every floor. He called it *The Flick*. It's brilliant. It anticipates the malls with multi outlets all under one roof. Now you can go to one location with plenty of parking and have a choice in what you see.

But he still has a problem. He can't negotiate first-run Hollywood films due to the big distributors' corruption and monopolistic practices. They try to dry him out of first-run showings of any mainstream movies, but young audiences, especially in college towns, are waking up to other more meaningful types of movies, something more interesting than the Saturday night horror shows and sanitized fluff that dominate the mainstream movie circuit.

A whole new generation of movie makers can't get decent distribution from the big guys and the pressure is building. But companies like Janus films and New Line Cinema are finding new markets in importing European films that challenge Hollywood's squeaky-clean puritan-censored films with raw movies about real people, young people, people thinking, living in turmoil, struggling with all the nuances of newly freed and redefined lives after a devastating war.

So, many regional theater owners set up their own distribution systems with the burgeoning independent and non-corporate Hollywood films exploding from the new revolution in cinema production technology. Films are becoming cheaper to make, especially using the incredible hand-held 16mm French cameras and Swiss tape recorders. This frees the motion-picture film from the expensive studios and huge rigid cameras, providing an active participant in the plot instead of a rigid window limiting the view. French and Italian films are breaking out of the art house brand and into mainstream cinema market with such films as *Jules et Jim*, *8 1/2*, *Weekend*, and *Belle du Jour*. Award winners such as *A Thousand Clowns*, *Easy Rider*, and *Five Easy Pieces* set the example for a lot of indie films making money, in spite of the studios locking them out of distribution.

Bill loves the idea of *The Show* and considers himself a showman first and a businessman last. He loves the art and history of film and at every opportunity searches out and finds long lost and underappreciated films, bringing them back to the public theater—his theaters. Young audiences are eating it up and as most of the mountain ski towns are loading up with young people, Bill sees an opportunity to tap into this new movie revolution.

Instead of Bill and Stella exploiting their multi-plex art theater by franchising it or growing bigger, they opt to use their money and labor to save the old and sometimes abandoned theaters scattered around the remote Rocky Mountains. These opera houses were beautifully crafted at great expense a long time ago, built with rare and exotic hardwoods, providing an exceptional entertainment experience for the wealthy miners and lowly workers, bringing world-famous live talent to their remote mountain villages. Now they will be resurrected, providing a rich and glorious setting for what Bill calls *The Show*.

They cash out of The Flick and form a local distribution company, Rocky Mountain Cinemas, and begin buying and leasing cheap ski town theaters, forming a small distribution circuit. They quickly acquire such notable theaters as the Wheeler Opera House in Aspen, the Princess in Crested Butte, the Egyptian in Park City, the Chief in Steamboat Springs, and their beloved Sheridan Opera House in Telluride.

They love skiing and horseback riding when not watching movies. Whenever they visit a theater and it's in the wintertime, everybody's going skiing. They build a designer's dream home south of Montrose with a full 35mm theater inside and stables outside. They live temporarily in an old wooden steam-train water tank relocated to their property while the eco-friendly earth and concrete house is under construction. Both are marvels of architectural design and eco-friendly engineering, years ahead of their time.

When Steve can't make a profit from his little theater investment, he gladly gives Bill a long-term lease and I suddenly have a new and much better boss.

The Glaze is well known for his business ethics, or lack thereof. He lets nothing get in the way of his business antics: not friendship, not compassion, not decency, not even societal pressure to be a righteous dude. He has a singular focus when it involves money and pretty much everything of value in his world is equated somehow with money. He is a true classical capitalist wolf/pig in sheep's clothing, pretending to be a responsive contributor to the community, but in reality, he's just an unproductive leech sucking the blood of those with vision and aptitude who fall within his slimy grasp.

One time while managing the theater under his management, I accidentally slip the teller at the bank on Monday morning an extra twenty-dollar bill. I count out the cash receipts in front of her and she does the same in front of me, but somehow it slips by us both and the deposit is short by twenty dollars. Steve, when discovering it later that day, immediately calls me and accuses me of outright stealing the difference and somehow trying to cover it up at the bank. I, of course, am not stupid and take his charge as the insult it is intended to be and tell him so. Later, when the bank teller does her cash drawer reconciliation at the end of the day, she finds the twenty-dollar bill we both missed earlier. Glazer never apologizes for the wrongful accusation and I never forget it.

Under Bill's leadership, however, Susie and I are pretty much left alone to run the Princess any way we please and he provides us with a constant supply of interesting films. He pays us a minimal salary and we figure out how to do our job efficiently, so the pay somewhat works out. I still practice my tip-donation program by double tearing a couple of tickets once in a while, thus collecting the extra ticket sale as excess petty cash, which can be taken out at the end of the daily accounting as cash, helping with our nightly beer tab. Everybody who owns a public shop in town probably does this in some form or another. It's tax-free unreported income and quite necessary for tourist town survival.

I'm still not getting paid enough for all the work and expertise I bring to the game. Believe me, the tiny amount I liberate is more than made up in all the improvements and technical support I provide off the books. Under conventional management, serious technical issues require dispatching expensive crews, usually from Denver, which really drives a hole in the budget. I, on the other hand, can troubleshoot and fix every piece of equipment in the theater including "Old Poppy," the popcorn machine, the real moneymaker and secret behind profitable small-town theaters. Susie and I run a good operation that serves the needs of our community, challenging it with uncustomary film exhibition excellence and good tasting popcorn that earns a whopping 10,000 percent profit.

Then in early spring and out of the blue, Bill invites Susie and me to a Montrose motel to watch the Oscars. They don't have TV at their new wilderness home halfway between Montrose and Ouray and simply cannot miss the Oscars. We're in the same boat, so Susie and I end up driving down from the mountains studying the line of motels lining Highway 50 as it descends the last few miles from the Black Canyon of the Gunnison into Montrose. We spot an ordinary-looking cheap motel he named earlier and we pull in looking for their room number.

Susie knocks on the door and Stella answers.

"Come in, come in," she says. As we step in, Stella moves in for the Hollywood hug and light kiss to the cheek. At first, I'm embarrassed, but I play it real cool for Susie's sake. I don't want to seem like a country bumpkin to the new relaxed social manners of the young and wealthy. Bill gets up from one of the beds and shakes our hands, instead.

"Here's a present from the Princess," I announce, handing him a giant paper bag full of theater popcorn, well-greased with artificially butter-flavored palm oil.

"Wow! Thanks," he says. "I didn't think of that. This is perfect. Now we can watch the show about the shows." He laughs at his own joke.

"We ordered pizza for everybody," Stella adds, pointing to an open box on top of two more on the table. "I hope you like sausage and pepperoni. We can't get pizzas delivered where we live now."

"Neither can we," Susie adds. "That's one of the reasons I visit my sister in Denver."

We all laugh at the irony. When you live at the end of the road, you can't expect convenience. When visiting Denver, we'd often load up on Domino pizzas and McDonald's burgers, smuggling popular fast food like it was heroin.

"Have you been following the buzz about this year's nominations?" he asks in general. We all shake our heads no. We don't get buzz where we live. "Coppola is up for another sweep with *Godfather 2*."

"Yeah, tell me the Oscars are run fairly," I quip. "They just reward their own and prevent all the real talent from any meaningful opportunities. Look at all the old actors and has-beens that keep winning when the new stuff is just ignored. It's all about money, power, and nepotism."

"There's beer in the bathtub. You're going to need a couple to get through tonight." He laughs again.

Bill never has another personality except optimistic, happy, and supportive. He's a great mentor on how the deal is done. I respect the guy just because he's a fair boss and likes all those art films from Europe that I delved into while studying film at Michigan. I like their free cinematic style and wish I could do something like that, but, of course, I can't begin to afford it.

About halfway through the Oscars, Susie and I take over the floor in front of the color TV with leftover pizza crusts and empty Coors cans scattered around our little nest made of blankets and pillows from the other bed. It's okay for Bill and Stella to lie together in one bed, but we feel a little uncomfortable, so we make a G-rated effort at pretending innocence. I think it's right after the award for the best 16mm original dramatic film and my fourth beer, making me very relaxed, when Bill makes his proposal.

"I understand you have a 16mm arc projector at the Princess," he announces offhand. "Do you know if it works?"

I have to think for a second or two. "Sure," I guess. "I think it works. It requires smaller carbon rods than the 35, which we don't have, but other than that, I think it works. Why?"

"As you've heard, we're going to do another film festival in Telluride this fall. And I want to count on you and Susie to join us and help run one of the theaters."

"One of the theaters?" I query. "How many do they have?" I thought all these little mining towns only had one per.

"And who'll run the Princess while we're gone?" asks practical Susie.

"We've got the Sheridan Opera House equipped with 35mm and the Nugget is operational with 35mm," he explains, "but we need a third theater. The town is willing to let us use the Community Center, which is a big basketball court with a screen at one end.

"And you have enough time," he answers Susie, "to train backups for running the Princess while you're out of town."

I already started that process because I want to travel with Susie when she visits family and friends. We're a pair now. It's kind of expected we be together now, wherever we go.

"Are you sure?" I ask. "Feeding two theaters for a festival is six or eight films a day, for, how many days? That's a lot of film cans to be handling."

"Oh, don't worry about that. We have lots of volunteers in Telluride who can handle the logistics. We're even running our own travel agency so we can bring in the best." He smiles satisfyingly.

"I don't know if you know this, but I've been working with Janus Films and now have access to their entire library of 16mm prints." He waits for that to sink in. I know who Janus is as any student of film must know. That's where we get esoteric, educational, historic, and foreign films pretty much free to show and study.

"I've seen a few," I admit.

"Stella and I want to make the Telluride Film Festival different from all the other commercial festivals. We want to make it a grassroots retrospective of great films, filmmakers both old and new, and do non-competitive awards based on bodies of work or impact to the art of film. Our first honor will be to actress Gloria Swanson and directors Francis Ford Coppola and Leni Riefenstahl." He pauses to let it sink in, plus there's another Oscar being awarded on TV, for cinematography. *Surprise, surprise.* Godfather 2, *because of all the money it's making,* I think to myself.

"Not again?" I protest verbally. "There are other films out there you know."

"What do you think?" Bill asks innocently.

I probably should keep my mouth shut more, but I'm in my thirties and feel like I'm old enough to freely express my opinion. "About what?"

"About a third theater showing just 16mm films and Leni Riefenstahl as an honoree. She's still alive and willing to come."

"I understand that she's part of film history now, but isn't it sort of a D. W. Griffith thing? Good art, bad subject? Quite frankly I never saw anything worthwhile in *Birth of a Nation.* It should have been titled *Birth of Bullshit.*"

He looks at me with that quizzical but smiling look that makes you automatically like him and effectively hides whatever he's really thinking. Natural diplomat, no doubt.

"I can put together a 16mm theater using our arc projector, but it's going to cost you a little bit."

"How much?"

"I'll have to look into it but you'll probably have to buy new lenses for whatever the projection distance is at the Community Center."

"Okay. Where do we find some?"

"Do you have a friend in New York? You can get anything you need in New York."

"Turns out Bill Luddy lives in New York. He's one of our co-founders. What do you need?"

"There's a little shop on 48th street, sells old World War II cameras and projector parts. Those particular projectors probably made it halfway across the Pacific before they landed in the Rockies."

"What else?" he asks.

"You're lucky in one respect."

"How's that?"

"The carbon rods are now common parts for welders. We can get them cheap almost anywhere."

"Great! Let's do it!"

*

By the next Labor Day weekend, we have a full-blown large screen 16mm projection system with carbon arcs throwing out probably the brightest movie picture as either of the other two normal theaters. The Community Center could hold up to 400 seats, making it ideal as an always available second choice if festival goers couldn't make it into the main theaters. All total, there are only 140 seats in the Nugget and not quite 200 in the Opera House. With standing room only, we could, and often did, accommodate even more.

I baby the old Bell and Howell projector for most of the first festival, but also provide backup projectionist work at the Nugget and Opera, especially if Bill arranges an impromptu unadvertised late-night screening and the normal crew needs rest.

I almost feel like I'm back in the Rock & Roll touring business, as cocaine is everywhere and prolific. Without it, I doubt we would have had the number of volunteers and workers that we needed to pull this off. Steve demanded a role to play at the first festival, but without any usable talent other than counting money, he was relegated to going around and making sure all our workers are well-laced with cocaine. He had to supply it out of his own pocket. Karma is a bitch. Such is the price of fandom.

In subsequent years, the festival ran under the corporate umbrella of the National Film Preserve, a non-profit organization whose mission corresponds with Luddy and Pence's long-term goals: bring forgotten films back for preservation and presentation. The annual festival gains more press, more visitors, more controversies, more film coups than their newly upstart self-proclaimed competitor, Sundance.

I introduce Dana to the Pence's and he provides video documentary recordings of subsequent festival highlights for several years in a row, and I was right there making sure everything ran smoothly, quietly and efficiently behind the scenes. Bill and Stella had a lot of talented people working for them, but only I provided fundamental electrical and electronic support for all their equipment and facilities as well as the important work of helping document the festival using Dana's new high-tech portable video production van.

For most festivals, I borrow Mitchell's Georgie Boy RV and park it next to the Community Center, where we plug it into Telluride city power. Susie and I make it our Crested Butte headquarters, living and sleeping right on site. The community center theater ends up dealing with the general overflow from the rest of the mainstream festival and as a bonus, Stan Brakhage, who has a standing lifelong invitation to the festival, shies away from the power-rich snobs at the Opera House and ends up hanging with us most of the time he is in town.

Every time I see him, he's either watching a film, standing at the rear of the theater so in case he gets bored he can leave without bothering anybody, or he's wandering around burning raw film in his little Bell & Howell 16mm windup camera. When I first bump into him, somewhere in Northern California during a spiritual festival of acid and fine art, he just seems to be the guy burning as much film as he possibly can without much care for planning or even framing.

When he exposes film, he films everything, all the time. He's not happy unless he's burning film with his little camera plastered to one eye. He didn't remember me when he showed up at the Ann Arbor Film Festival, where I volunteered to screen all submissions and ended up watching about twenty hours of Stan Brakhage films. I complained directly to him at the reception about submitting too much footage. Now he remembers me.

At the festival, he's always hanging around the Community Center asking if I've seen any good films he should watch. During breaks between films, I adjourn to the RV for a quick toke and maybe a beer; if Stan is around, I invite him on board. We're not allowed to have beers or smoke in the Community Center so the only thing left to do safely in the projection booth is coke. With the four-day schedule, coke is just another tool the staff needs to survive the pressure and lack of sleep. Thank goodness many people, including Glazer, contribute to the coke support program and as a direct result, the show goes on, sometimes as planned, usually on time, but definitely on schedule.

I'm alone taking a break in the RV when I spot Stan approaching. He bangs on the door. "Cowboy? You in there?"

I open the door, trying not to allow any smoke to escape, possibly giving us away to the general public. Like nobody knows what's going on in here anyway!

"Come in, quick!" I tell him, holding the door wide open. He climbs aboard.

"I'm glad you're here. I have to talk to a sane person or I might lose it." He sits down at the table opposite my joint rolling kit. I sit down and finish rolling another fat one.

"You know they made me sit on that panel thing in the park."

"Was Jack Nicholson there?" I ask absentmindedly.

"No, thank God. It was bad enough with a bunch of big-time rich bastards complaining they don't have the money to make good films. The fuckers probably don't know which way the film threads in a camera anyway and they demand more money to make more bad movies."

"Rotten spoiled bastards!" I add.

"Most of them are too old. They've had their shot. And the young ones just can't find who to blow in the business that will actually make them a star."

"Yeah, the real movie is one where someone spends four hours driving by a bunch of birch trees shining in the dazzling sunlight. Now that's a movie." I hand him the joint and a Bic lighter.

"That was only shown at the Ann Arbor festival!" he explains, but doesn't wait for an answer. "I've changed." He holds up the joint. "Just what I need. A cool cannabis bath to clean my soul from being over-exposed to evil." He lights it carefully and takes a big hit. He passes it back.

"Where's Susie?" he squeaks out while holding his breath.

"She's inside. I'm on a quick break. The next movie starts in five minutes. It's already cued up and ready to roll." I take a hit and hand it back.

"I want to shoot you two." He savors the joint taking his time. "I think this is a perfect example of what a film festival should be all about. Endless films and getting laid."

"Take away the money and that's only what happens at Cannes," I assert.

For the rest of the festival, Stan is all over the Community Center shooting with his little Bell and Howell camera. Susie and I take a break in the afternoon and adjourn to the RV, where we get high and knock off a fast afternoon *Love Story*. I guess the RV moved in strange and mysterious ways, because when we reemerge ready to go back to work, there's Stan filming us doing the walk of happiness, grabbing each other's ass as we saunter back to the theater in lock-step. The smiles on all the young faces watching are enough to make a lasting literary film statement alone.

*

The weirdest event at the Community Center had to be the shows put on by Les Blank, the brother of Mel Blank, the voice behind Bugs Bunny and Elmer Fudd and all the other Warner Brothers cartoon characters. Les does documentaries, usually inside the film industry, as that is where he has all the best connections. He clearly doesn't make money at filmmaking and again reminds me of the rich bastards who dabble in whatever art they can buy, denying the poor artist a shot at recognition.

Les is here every year, showing his latest work, like the one he made of Verner Herzog eating his shoe. Verner is another permanent invitee to the festival and is known for bringing something new and different each time he attends. Eventually, Les makes it to the Opera House when he shows a documentary of Werner Herzog making his only spectacular cast-of-thousands big-budget film, where the documentary turns out to be seen more than the movie it was documenting.

At noon, we take a short break waiting for the next film to show up. I'm told it's Les's latest project about northern California farmers and healthy living. I'm thinking how neat it would be if he's talking about the dope growers of northern California. I'm about to go out and sample some in the RV when Susie comes stomping up the open staircase to the projection booth.

"Here's the next film," she says coming through the door luging a couple of film cans. "You're not going to believe what they're doing down there." She indicates the auditorium or basketball court where all the medieval torture-inspired folding chairs are set up.

"Huh?"

"Come here, take a look." She holds the door open. I walk over, take a quick look and notice a bunch of tables surrounding the audience and on each table is something looking like a gas burner and a frying pan.

"What the fuck is that?" I ask pointedly.

"Les calls it a total environment experience. He's going to have a bunch of people frying garlic all the way through the movie so we can get the total film message."

"Garlic is a message?" I ask incredulously.

She puts down the film and then I notice she also has two T-shirts in her hand.

"Look," she proudly proclaims. "*Garlic is as Good as Ten Mothers.*" She unfurls one and sure enough it has a picture of a garlic bulb in gold and the message written around the outside. They look kinda cool.

Susie looks around quickly and then pulls off her plain yellow festival T-shirt with just the words *SHOW* and *STAFF* printed on it that we all wear for identifying the guilty and providing a little security, of which we almost never need. I immediately pay her my full attention and before she can re-shirt, I show my deep appreciation for one of the most perfectly gorgeous geometric shapes ever made by nature. She blushes, returns my attentions with a passionate hug and kiss, squeezing up close with hormones flying about. We slowly separate and she slips into her new T-shirt and I follow suit, only she gives me a quick purple-nurple when I'm not looking, followed by her twinkling eyes and polite Connecticut giggle. God I'm in love. I can't believe she's so perfect.

She departs grudgingly and I start the film.

Halfway through the fifty-minute *Smell-o-Rama*, Les comes up to the projection booth.

"Are you Cowboy?" he asks quietly, halfway through the door. A waft of garlic smell spills into the room with its enticing sweetness and unique smell all crying for a Pavlovian drool. "I just want to thank you guys for helping us pull this off." He's got a paper plate in his hand and a jar in the other.

"You've got to try this. We're giving it to volunteers in the audience and it's a big hit."

I look at the plate and it contains a golden pancake with some kind of chunky filling bulging out of the surface.

"Is it what it looks like?" It looked like a pancake with little white grubs buried in it.

"Even better," he boasts. "Try it. It's cooked in butter and here's some maple syrup if you prefer."

"I do love maple syrup," I admit. I take the plastic fork he offers and try a bite.

He walks over to the projector, looks at the film going through it, and then out the tiny window toward the screen. "It's never the same," he comments. "Whenever I watch it, no matter from which perspective, I see something different."

"And I have to watch all films from the worst position," I counter, "looking right down the throat of the projector with a seasoned critical eye. We see everything. Especially the fuck-ups." I make yummy sounds as I enjoy the flavor of a garlic pancake drenched with buttery maple syrup. "This is good. But not better than my mother."

He laughs. "It's a marketing scam. The garlic farmers pay me to develop media, which they slice and dice for a multitude of outlets and I get an art film out of the deal. Just think. Your theater is a first-time smell-a-thon film experience."

"More than that," I eagerly add. "It's now a taste-a-thon as well. I'll tell the Pences tonight we pioneered smell-o-vision and taste-o-vision. Sure to be big hits when theaters merge with restaurants and soup kitchens."

"They're actually doing that. I know a restaurant in the hills that shows classic silent films in the background all the time. This is different. Here, the kitchen becomes part of the performance."

"The Show," I correct him.

*

Pence and were always on the lookout to be the first to find a film archive. Luddy had been following Kevin Brownlow's ten-year restoration project of Abel Gance's famous *Napoleon*. Filmed originally in 1927, it is one of the last great silent film extravaganzas made in France, representing the height of film-making art at the time. Pioneering many aspects of modern cinematography and modern film technique, Abel Gance foretells the wide screen by including a final twenty-minute segment, one projection reel, of three cameras in sync providing a film tryptic or 4:1 widescreen presentation, forty years before it is finally adopted by Hollywood as *Cinerama*.

Napoleon is an unfortunate example of what happens when an independent commercial film is sold to Hollywood. In this case, after its completion in 1928, *butchered* is the nicest term to describe what they did to the original 240 hours of exposed footage. The original is lost and a lot of the film itself was lost. Without a surviving master copy, and losing international control over the raw footage early on, Abel Gance begins a forty-year crusade to reconstruct as best he can his vision for the original film. The film, as finally released in France by Abel the same year, has to be painstakingly reconstructed from damaged and incomplete copies found all over the world.

In the sixties, Kevin Brownlow corroborates with Abel Gance and gets results searching out rare and surviving footage. He finally produces results acceptable to Abel and generates some interest in the film community. Kevin's task is daunting, but Luddy keeps in touch and when he thinks he has a film nearly complete, but still rough in many segments, showing water and heat damage, they agree to bring it to Telluride. Bill promises the aging Abel that we'll show it as it was originally meant to be shown, on a large brilliant screen including the full 3 screens for the final section.

Pence keeps me informed and I help develop a projection plan that depends on looting four carbon arc projectors from somewhere and synching three of their motors. The building of a giant screen in the park, the only place in town big enough to hold them, was a piece of cake, compliments of all the loggers around town. We use sixty-foot spruce poles set in the ground and guyed, to build a triple screen frame, each one thirty by forty, or thirty by one hundred and twenty feet for the full 4:1 screen format. We estimate the maximum capacity of this outdoor theater as over five hundred people on the grass or chairs with most of the western facing windows in the Sheridan Hotel across the street acting as box seats with prime indoor viewing.

I build a high-power extension cord, which I illegally hook up to the main entrance power to the Opera House and string it across the street to the park, ending where we plan to install the projectors. It's all temporary, so no need to have an inspector tell us there's a rule against what we're trying to do. We also have to lay down three big platforms using 3/4-inch plywood so we can mount the projectors to something stable and level.

Again, we send Luddy to that little projector store in New York where he finds the sync motors needed to mount on the front of each of our antique machines; when wired together, each projector will be frame-by-frame in-sync among the three final-reel projectors. The first five reels of the film are simply projected using the center pair of projectors, both focused on the center screen.

We wait until sunset, which is about eight or eight-thirty. At this altitude and time of year, it's not improbable for cold air to sink off the surrounding mountains the minute the sun goes down and there can be a twenty degree drop in air temperature within minutes. And that's what happens. As we wait for total darkness, everybody starts scrambling to find their down coats and bundle up for a very cold screening. A lot of the flatland guests are not so prepared and many have to find a window in the hotel in order to continue watching the show. Abel Gance himself has prime seating in his second-floor hotel room window directly facing the park. He's 87.

About a hundred of the hardcore film addicts stick it out until just before midnight. We switch to the last three reels all cued up in the already smoking and glowing machines. Susie joins me from the Community Center. She doesn't want to miss this either.

Earlier, we tested the setup and are pretty certain it's going to work. But when those three screens light up with one continuous picture spread a hundred and twenty feet across the park, literally spanning a viewer's complete field of vision, an audible *AAAAHHH!* rises from the audience. I'm transfixed. It's incredible. My eyes water from this incredible and auspicious moment in film history. I'm seeing a panorama of France filmed fifty years earlier and I feel like I'm in the middle of it. It's astounding.

I feel like I'm right there in the film, standing next to Napoleon, watching his troops by the thousands march across the horizon. This is what film can do! And that little man watching from the second-floor window did it all and so much more; fifty years ago! I get a tingling feeling all over my body. Susie senses it too and squeezes my arm tighter.

"Look at that!" she whispers. She doesn't have to whisper; it's a silent film and the only sound is the projectors running and some guy playing an electric organ down near the giant screen with standard silent-film music. I think they actually dug up some guy who does it for a living. Anyway, nobody pays any attention as the super wide screen weaves its magical spell, visually sucking us all into a place and time otherwise unimaginable and unattainable, in any other way.

I squeeze Susie in turn and we stare transfixed at the screen. I'm not assigned to a projector during the show so I can sit back and watch without worrying about a carbon arc burning out under my care. "This is worth the effort and the cold," I whisper back. "I just wish more people could see this. This is amazing!"

We stand there awestruck for the next twenty minutes watching history be displayed for the first time in decades as the images move across the plain white sheets strung between poles in a blind Rocky Mountain canyon by a bunch of film-loving freaks freezing their balls off. This modest showing represents tens of millions of dollars in a giant human collective effort spanning continents and dozens of years that finally ends up here. It's downright romantic and probably deserves a film of its own. I should talk to Les.

Unfortunately, it comes to an end and another sound is heard from the audience indicating disappointment that it's over: *Ohhhh!*

Someone hits the park lights, lighting up the whole area, revealing a sad-looking giant sheet stretched between poles with nothing on it and a lot of puffy, down-inflated patrons reluctantly getting up from their blankets or lawn chairs.

"Hey everybody!" someone shouts over the crowd. "Look at the hotel!"

Susie and I unwind ourselves, turn and walk toward the hotel to get out of the bright park lights and see what's going on. People are flashing their flashlights at a window on the second floor where Abel Gance is seen standing up and bowing slightly to the sound of applause and verbal *Hoorays!* from below.

"Is that him?" Susie asks.

"Yeah. He's nearly ninety and this might very well be the last time he sees his film in a public setting."

"That's kind of sad," she responds softly. "But at least he has this. I'm sure he's very happy we did it."

"Can't say no to validation," I conclude. "But think about it. Old films shown in old theaters in old picturesque mining towns with a lot of old filmmakers being honored for simply still being alive. That's Telluride."

I point up to the window where now he's gone from view, and say, "That's what makes this not a festival so much, but more like a temporary museum. I bet he feels very honored and he certainly deserves it. This is a festival of love, not a competition. It's the way we should honor all our creative people. Not by competitions that separate us into camps but festivals of celebration that bring us together to honor and experience what's been accomplished and ponder what's still left to be done."

"Kind of like an art convention," she points out. "Or a science convention where smart people show off their talents and the old and ignored ones that turn out to be right might be honored."

"Sure, why not? And we can hold it in Crested Butte." I laugh, but in truth, it actually happened, in a small way back in the fifties, before ski areas and any rich white privileged winter tourists. Crested Butte hosts a doctor-lawyer convention every summer in August, where the elite medical practitioners of Kansas City and Oklahoma City would converge on Crested Butte for two to three weeks of fishing in the mornings and necessary tax-deductible lectures in the afternoons.

I know, because I found the lantern slides in the old Mason Hall on Second Street where they held their meetings. They discussed things like autopsies and trauma evidence as seen by the legal system and how to bridge the gap between doctors' science and lawyers' ignorance. I examined some of the lantern slides and just gag. They were pretty graphic.

Doctor Smith is a famous Crested Butte summer resident after the mines close and he buys up a good deal of the old Victorian houses downtown, which he maintains and rents out to participants for his forensic medical conventions. Mitchell buys one of his houses, which he turns into a high-tech headquarters for his many public and private endeavors. Mrs. Smith is infamous among young renters and seekers of homes in Crested Butte. She for a time is the largest real estate holder in town during the late sixties after the good doctor dies and young kids start renting from her...and if she likes you, then you might persuade her to sell at a very reasonable price. A lot of young Crested Butte emigrants get their first boost into the burgeoning resort real estate market by the good doctor's efforts in preserving a ghost town for fishing twenty years earlier.

*

There's something strange that happens when people are starved for oxygen and challenged by alcohol poisoning, perhaps also sleep deprived or loaded on any number of other powerful alkaloid drugs, that may make people reflect deeply about their life's pitiful situation. Some people cave and get religion, but most mountain people simply gear up and ask for more.

It's a long day. Fourteen hours of films running through just my projectors alone makes one a little dizzy and disoriented. When I'm getting near the last show of the night and running low on my allotted coke for the day, one of the other projectionists from the Opera House unexpectedly shows up. He doesn't hesitate and takes out his little brown bottle, gives me a hit, and takes one for himself.

"Pence needs you over at the Opera House," he announces, then takes the chair next to the projector.

"What's up?" I have to ask.

"One of our projectors failed and we need it for the next show."

I knew sooner or later we were hanging our ass on the line with these antique projectors. I still have nightmares of film fires when we run nitrate films and I make sure everyone is trained in nitrate procedures.

"What the fuck, this film sucks anyway. Might as well," I mutter to myself, as I grab my coat and leave.

I tell Susie as I pass her downstairs, "Don't wait up for me. I'm off to save the world."

I walk the two blocks to the Sheridan Opera House where I run into Bill pacing the lobby, apparently waiting for me.

"I hope you can help us out," he explains, as he conducts me upstairs to the auditorium and then to the top of the auditorium to the crowded projection booth. I hate this booth and am glad I don't have to run it. It's small, tight, prone to accidents, and full of equipment way too big for the space.

"Number one machine won't start," he says in desperation, "and we need to do a late-night showing. The honoree is here and we can't cancel. Can you fix it?"

"How long to move one from the Nugget?" I ask, as I step into the booth and see they already have the motor cowling off exposing the electric motor driving the machine.

"Too late for that. They told me the motor seems okay, that it hums but doesn't start," Bill adds, looking over my shoulder.

"That's right," I confirm. "Looks like the starter capacitor has failed. Got a spare?"

"If I had a spare, would you even be here?" he responds. "Sorry, but I'm under a lot of pressure here."

"Give me a moment to think about it."

"Is there anything I can get for you?" he offers in all sincerity.

"A hundred-dollar tab at the hotel bar," I jokingly reply.

"Done," he states, and walks away.

I look at my watch and the 1 a.m. start time for the special showing is coming up fast. I look around and find what I need and get to work. On my first try, I turn on the projector and tap the two wires together I had just connected to the motor and it starts up running. As long as they don't turn it off, it will keep running just fine without the starter capacitor. I look at my watch and I've got 15 minutes to spare. I take a quick hit of the rest of my gram du jour I was saving to share with Susie later, but figure, what the hell? It's an emergency.

Pence reappears with a concerned look until he notices the projector is running. He brightens and asks, "What did you do?"

"I had to do a little rewiring," I say mystically. "It's a physics thing. You can get a new capacitor out of Montrose in the morning, but for now, all they have to do is tap these two wires together when you want to start it."

"Thank you, Cowboy! You've saved the festival!" he gushes. "I set up your bar tab already. Don't use it all in one sitting," he smiles, knowing I could probably do worse and still be trusted. He looks at the stage and some waiting dignitaries. "Gotta go."

"Any time," I say. I stick around to show the two projectionists how to work the machine now, and then leave right after they get the film started. It's a full auditorium and stuffy as usual.

I wander outside to get some fresh air and then turn the corner to the hotel entrance where the bar is still open. I'm tired of beer and seek something a little stronger, maybe help me sleep better. Susie and I share the big rear bed in the RV, but both of us have trouble sleeping enough, given our festival schedules and us fooling around as much as possible.

The room is quiet with just a few hard-core drinkers holding down the window end of the bar. I find a barstool with a view of the street, just for the entertainment. All the theaters have finished their schedules for the night except for the special showing in the Opera House, which is probably why nobody is in the bar. I order my favorite drink.

"Double shot of Crown Royal with a soda water back," I say to the bartender. "And put that on Cowboy's tab."

"That's fast," the bartender says, "Bill just called it in." He goes away to make it.

The guy next to me says, "Trying to catch up?"

I don't look up. "How far behind am I?"

"Oh, about two shakes of a lamb's tail. Here's to yah," he says. He lifts his glass in salute.

The bartender brings back way more than a double shot in a rock glass and puts down a tall soda water behind it. He puts a little parachute in the soda.

I lift my glass of whiskey in response. "Wah ha ho tah!" and I take a big swallow as does he. He looks at me with a big smile and suddenly I know him like an old familiar friend. An old friend from the movies. His big eyeballs staring off stage signature look and his big friendly smile drives me crazy. I should have a name to associate with this guy, but I don't. I draw a complete blank. He laughs.

He reaches across with his right hand and I shake it. "Jack...Jack Elam. Nice to meet you."

"I had no idea. I'm sorry. They call me Cowboy. I run the 16mm theater at the Quonset hut."

"Don't worry about it. Happens all the time. I'm the most recognized actor you never heard of. Cheers!"

"Cheers!" I respond, and take a sip of my soda water. "So, what brings you to the end of the road?"

"King Vidor's an old friend of mine so I thought, why not catch one more party before winter."

"Compared to LA, this *is* winter. You have to be serious to party at eight thousand feet in September," I quip.

"It's not really partying. I need my next job. This is cheaper than Sundance and attracts real producers."

"What's a real producer?" I ask innocently.

"Let me handle that," someone interjects behind us. I turn and see two guys sitting at the nearest table. I blink unconsciously as I recognize Roger Ebert immediately, only with bloodshot eyes and lids drooping like a wet sail. Pence's major partner in crime, Bill Luddy, sits next to him.

"A real producer makes new art. Bad producers remake old art. As for Jack here, the classic western is dead," Roger pronounces. "At least the historical ones. Now westerns are disguised as science fiction."

"Great!" Jack yells. "Cowboy hats are out and funny looking plastic helmets are in. I've been pigeon-holed by a costume clash. But I just don't look good in plastic." He gives everyone in the bar his signature smile with eyeballs asunder. He's right.

"I predict in the future, all actors will be paid whenever their likeness is used to construct a film," Roger adds, as he gets up and wanders over to the bar with an empty glass.

"How the hell are they going to do that?" Bill asks from his seated position at the table.

"I don't know!" he says with emphasis. "But they're already doing it. Look at the new animated movies coming out with so much processing they've lost the art of the artist. Haven't you noticed some animated characters look an awful lot like the actors doing the voice." He turns to the bar. "Bartender! Another Jack and soda, if you please."

"Anybody else?" he asks, before getting to work.

"Hit me," I say.

"Same here," says Jack.

Bill orders and gets up from the table and joins the rest of us at the bar. "Another scotch and soda here, please."

"So, what makes you think actors are going to be manufactured and not discovered?" Bill asks.

"Money!" Roger announces loudly. "Films already cost too much and that restricts creativity and innovation. One of the reasons is the anointed actors demanding too much for their so-called guaranteed box office draw. One hit film and they're set for life, but then they hold hostage every tinhorn producer with a decent script that should be made. Eventually, it just drives extreme corruption and nepotism to the top, much like royalty or the mafia."

"Can anybody join your discussion or do I need a ticket?" a female voice asks behind my back. Everyone turns in her direction and I can see by the looks on their faces it's someone surprising. I turn and at first see nothing. Then I look down. Blond hair billows out of a down coat framing the face of Julie Christie.

"By all means," Bill jumps in. "Let me offer you my front row seat at the bar. What can I order for you?"

The New York academic is the only one of us who keeps his cool. I signal the barkeep to put her drink on my tab.

"After that boring special showing, I need a pick me up," she announces. "How about a gin martini?"

"Julie!" Roger interjects, "it's been a while since we last talked. I hope we're still friends."

"Now why wouldn't we be?" she gushes. "You've always been very kind to me and my work."

"That's because you're smart enough to pick good scripts and good directors. How do you do it? What's your secret?" and he winks at her.

"Listen to him, Jack," she points out while poking him in the ribs. "He thinks actors just need good scripts and good directors."

"You should have been here earlier when he was advocating replacing all actors with an animated likeness who don't negotiate contracts." He turns to Christie and they do the Hollywood kissy-cheek, light-huggy greeting. I compare it to Black Panthers doing the arm and fist bump. It's how they and the KKK can identify their own.

"You know these two yahoos!" Jack informs her. "But I don't think you know Mr. Cowboy here."

"Nice to meet ya, ma'am," I respond. I step off my stool and offer her my hand, attempting to be acceptably cool. I'd always had a secret deep and lustful attraction to her from the movies I've seen, especially *Far from the Madding Crowd* and *Doctor Zhivago*. I'm lucky I can even talk coherently.

"Cowboy saved the festival tonight, so now all the drinks are on him," Jack adds.

"How does that work?" she asks. The bartender hands her a big martini. She raises it in salute.

"Thank you, Mister Cowboy, festival saver," she pronounces. "Cheers!".

"Cheers!" everybody responds. And we all throw down our drinks.

A couple of hours later, I carefully unlock the door to the RV and quiet as a mouse I sneak into the bedroom and slowly start to take my clothes off.

"What took you so long?" Susie quietly says without moving. I can see her silhouetted curves under the blanket and it makes me think of the lust I just imagined with Julie Christie a short time ago.

"I saved the festival and they forced me to have drinks with Julie Christie and Roger Ebert," I whisper back.

"That's nice. Come to bed. I miss you."

"Jack Elam introduced me to them."

"Jack who?" she asks. "Never mind."

She reaches out from under the blankets and helps me finish undressing. I'm fumbling around in the dark, still half drunk. Finally, she gives up, pulls me down under the blanket and we make sweet, sweet love, with me thinking what Susie might look like as a blond.

*

Dana hears our stories about the film festival and immediately asks if he can talk to Pence about documenting the next one with video. I anticipate this and have already laid the groundwork by telling Bill about this crazy performance artist, with connections, living in Crested Butte, who has a complete 3/4-inch color VHS production studio built into a custom GMC RV. I tell Bill I helped design and build the mobile studio. Dana and I built a small bunk for him in the back with a full bath and alcove galley. Most of the midsection, however, houses a complete two camera, two tape deck recording and editing studio. There's a small bed in the forward loft where I sleep when we're on the road.

Stella agrees to give him about a grand or two each festival, depending on how many total hours of tape he ends up recording. She asks him to document all of their public events such as lectures, panel discussions, and interviews. This amounts to a few hours of live recording every day for two or three days.

Susie and I are promoted from the Community Center theater and anointed senior staff. Now we float between venues jumping in and helping when we can, but otherwise overseeing the overall program and keeping everything on schedule. I spend my time supporting Dana because I actually know how to run all the electronics in the van, plus know how to interface with all the festival systems like sound and power.

Dana and I have been working together on his various projects since I first arrived in town and started letting some people into the Princess Theatre free when I felt sorry for them. He happened to be broke one night, but wanted to take a girl to the movies. I'm a sucker romantic and invited them in to make out in the back row, which is naturally reserved for such things. By the time we land at the festival together, I'm already well-versed in his custom RV, dubbed *The Space Ship*, and know all the ends and outs of the festival. We kind of have the run of the place for the next few years and are a center of secret fun for a lot of the festival stars.

Dana proclaims himself the *Ace of Space*. The *Space* being generally all the highways and byways between the Atlantic to the Pacific where he glorifies the American road culture, discovering and photographing all those nostalgic picturesque roadside attractions along the way. His one-man story and song performance, backed up by a synchronized big-screen color slideshow, attracts attention from some notable celebrities in LA and elsewhere.

I think Dana is considering breaking into the big time TV production somehow. He's not sure what that might look like, but his performance art is sort of ground-breaking and begs some kind of bigger stage.

Dana is also on a quest to earn his father's respect. The electronic RV monster he builds, mostly with loans from his technical genius and corporate executive father, needs justification by being an economic success of some kind. Dana dabbles in documentaries hoping for a commercial payoff somewhere. He's marketing himself as a production company and one way he sees this happening is developing contacts among celebrities and networking friends and fellow artists. He's already crossed paths and become friends with Larry Hagman and Peter Fonda. He hopes the festival might be a good source of more high-power contacts and some more paying gigs.

First day on the job, we record an outdoor discussion featuring Klaus Kinski, famous from his recent big hit *Operation Thunderbolt* and his new ho-hum release with Werner Herzog, *Nosferatu*. Now they are showing segments of a new film, where they actually move a steamboat over a sizeable hill in a jungle, recreating an historical event where a crazy man moves a steamboat from the Pacific side to the Amazon side of Peru. I knew them from when they were peddling *Aguirre Wrath of the Gods*. Great performance, just poor writing. Story could have used a little more action and a lot less insane soul searching. Although crazy is something Klaus is admittedly good at portraying.

Somehow, he finds out—probably asking anyone associated with the festival—where he can find some dope. Being highly fucking illegal, big-time stars don't dare try to take along their own stash when they travel. They instead, like all of us, rely on word-of-mouth referrals among trusted friends as the way to score in foreign lands.

After the event, I'm rolling up a video cable in front of Klaus and Werner, who are still talking with some leftover attendees.

"That's him," says Werner to Klaus. He speaks up, using his signature German accent, "Pardon me, Cowboy?"

"Yeah, that's what they call me," I respond, looking up. We'd crossed paths for a few festivals, but he had never spoken to me directly before. I figure he should know me anyway, by reputation at least.

"I *vas* told you can help my friend here get high."

Someone in the group sniggers. Klaus looks desperate.

"Sure, follow me." I lead them over to the west side of the park where we have Dana's RV parked for the duration. Dana smokes and snorts and so do I. It doesn't take long until a lot of people also know where to go for a quick hit between movies, if you are connected and you follow the protocol.

I knock on the side of the van first. "It's me. I've got friends." That's code for clean up your act.

I walk in first so I can tidy up some space for sitting. Dana is reviewing the footage we just shot when he looks up and sees Klaus and Werner come through his door.

He stands up. "Hi. I'm Dana. Welcome to our Space Ship," he says politely. "I just saw you outside. Nice to meet you. I can't wait to see your finished film. It must have been hell in that jungle."

"You have no idea," Klaus jumps in, "I thought vee ver going to have to eat grubs and maggots before I could get out of zat hell hole."

I direct them to the short couch opposite the editing table and right behind the swiveling captain's chair which I now oc-cupy, while fishing out the RV stash box from under the seat. We all contribute to the stash box what we have or can afford and share it with friends and guests. We all have our own pri-vate stashes, but that gets shared out just as liberally, so it's al-ways a potlatch affair by the end of the gig. I light up a fat one someone rolled earlier and put away for just such an occasion. Might have been Susie.

"Here," I say handing it to Klaus. I also hand him a lighter.

"Now zat looks more like it," he declares, holding it up to Werner's face.

"I know," he declares. "I know vhat they look like. They joost didn't have zat sort of zing in zi jungle. If you smoke what zey have to offer, you'd just be another statistic. You know I saved your life."

"And I saved your career," Klaus counters, and lights up. Werner doesn't smoke any so Dana pretends to not smoke either and leaves the joint for just me and Klaus to finish. I keep staring at his face. It's so chiseled that it speaks reams of emotion at every contortion. I'm reminded of Lon Chaney, Senior. That man had a face for every emotion and a few more I'm not even sure of. But like Hunter Thompson warned me one time, "...if someone turns down good weed, there's something wrong with their brain."

*

Over the next few festivals, we repeat the rescuing of stars-in-need on many occasions. The most notable is when the festival honors Sterling Hayden for his body of work, and at a special time in his life. Sterling had been a Hollywood staple through the forties and fifties for his devilishly good looks in a swimming suit. He strives to move beyond the grade B movies and finally does when he meets Stanley Kubrick. After his performance in *Dr Strangelove*, his whole career changes and he credits it with the discovery of pot. He won't make any major decisions, he says, until he first runs it through his cannabis computer.

"Hey!' someone outside calls out, knocking on the door to the RV. Dana and I are just hanging out on Saturday afternoon doing nothing, waiting to video the on-stage presentations that tonight. "Anybody home? Hagman sent me." He knocks on the door again.

Dana opens the door and sees an old man with full beard wearing tweed and a matching Ivy cap.

"Hi!" he speaks right up. "Are you Ace of Space?"

"Yeah," Dana responds, still not recognizing him yet. I'm looking over his shoulder and I don't recognize him either. He sort of looks familiar, like a possible mountain man, except for the hat.

"I'm Sterling. Sterling Hayden," he says, and shakes Dana's hand. "I'm one of the honorees here. Larry told me you'd be here."

"Larry Hagman?" asks Dana.

"Yeah, he said you could take care of me."

"Sure, Mister Hayden. I'm sorry I didn't recognize you. Come on in. Watch your head."

"That's the whole point. Thanks. Call me Sterling. Nice to finally meet you."

He sits on the couch with a big sigh. "Boy, am I glad you guys are here. I don't like to go anywhere anymore without my weed. It's getting downright Nazi out there, and I should know."

"Wow," exclaims Dana. "This is great. Can we do an interview with you? Cowboy, get this man a joint."

"Aye, aye, sir," I reply nautically, then turn to Sterling. "Hi. I'm Cowboy, Welcome to the Space Ship." I shake his hand.

He looks around the inside and lingers over the video editing console and the two tape decks. "Wow, look at all this gear. Larry said you have quite the rig. Larry's into RVs and I'm into boats, but we still have a lot in common. This stuff is going to revolutionize Hollywood eventually. I just hope not too soon. I want to do something good first, the old-fashioned way."

I hand him a freshly loaded bong and lighter.

He looks at it, says, "Nice," and lights it right up.

"Oh, let's see," Dana points out, "we have *Godfather*, *Long Goodbye*, *Chinatown*, *Doctor Strangelove*? I'd say you've made a hell of an impact already."

He blows out smoke while saying, "Yeah, ever since I learned how to use my cannabis computer for making decisions, I've been doing a lot better. I just feel like I haven't quite nailed it yet."

"Hang in there," I say, "your best work's usually your last. Look at John Wayne."

Dana goes into a coughing fit, as does Sterling.

"You know what I mean. Artists are never really appreciated until they're gone, leaving all their work to their undeserving offspring."

"And in the meantime, thank God for weed," he declares with a shit-eating grin on his face.

"Another happy customer of the Ace of Space. Yes? No? Maybe?" queries Dana.

*

Our last star who enjoys a joint in the van is Robert Altman. We do the Santa Fe festival. Dana's old buddy Peter Fonda shows up, mostly because Altman is coming and Peter is trying to drum up money for a new film; they all think Santa Fe might have some untapped production money. Robert loosens up before a public presentation by joining us in the RV for a toke. Peter joins us but he's a purist and will only do coke, which Robert turns down.

I'm sitting there with a shit-eating grin, meeting one of my all-time favorite directors, and listening to him complain that he can't find any money for his projects. It gives me a personal inside perspective of just how fucking hard it is to make a movie, even when you're good at it. It's a little depressing for anyone from the outside contemplating a career in the game. I take this as a reason to embark on capitalizing my true skills and not on my romantically desired ones. He changes my perspective a little.

Peter just pisses me off, the weaselly little no-talent coke whore that he is. I met his sister one time at a Vietnam sit-in where she taught a class about women stopping the war, and she is an angel compared to this little worm. Can't help it, have to call it like it is.

~ 5 ~

PARTY 'TIL THE STARS BARF

Mitchell made it clear to everyone attending the party meeting. "There's going to be a bunch of flatlanders here tonight with more damn influence and money than they need. That's what we're here for. To lift them up, out of their malaise of phony Hollywood glory, and give meaning to their shallow existence."

Everyone laughs and gives him a polite round of applause for saying the obvious. Locals always make fun of the tourists—flatlanders and their cute flatlander ways. I give a cat call whistle. He smiles that beautiful crooked burnt lip scrunch punctuated by an obvious burnt eye twinkle, meaning he's part of the crowd and they all adore him.

They have to. He's one of them and more so now, having lost his face and hands while crashing his new motorcycle in Aspen. His skin-grafted face and hands, the only parts of his body exposed to the dousing of fiery gasoline, make him a new person, truly unique and Honda-settlement rich.

But he was severely disfigured to the point that he bore very little resemblance to the thoroughly modern popular playboy he once was. That's when he changed his name to simply W. Mitchell, with the W standing for nothing, and destroyed all photographs showing his prior identity. His lawyers argued he lost his prior life and now carried the weight of *monster* as an identity he never deserved. The jury gobbled it up but his girlfriend didn't. He lost the love of his life, a young beautiful San Francisco Hispanic who he claims left him because she couldn't handle disfigurement. I think it was deeper than that, but being a terminal romantic, he carried a torch for her way too long, even to the point of supporting her mother all of her life. Mitchell came with a permanent mother-in-law based in San Francisco.

Now, he has the sympathy and money to blend with the wealthy Aspen trust funders. But Aspen is rapidly becoming a big expensive pond and his settlement will go a lot farther in the cheaper next-door Butte. He may have been accepted as the curious monster in Aspen, but in Crested Butte, he's damned near a folk hero. The *ski to die, die to ski* Crested Butte attitude seems to fit his image. A well-known rogue, looking like a silent horror film character, just makes him more interesting and worthy of partying with. He can now afford coke on a regular basis and that makes you more of a well-respected local than just another Aspen carpetbagger. Mitchell became very popular very fast in the Butte, especially among the eastern elite with their assumed entitlement, lack of morals, free sex, and lots and lots of coke.

Then he goes and does a silly thing and belly-crashes his new airplane he just learned to fly, with three of the best skiers on the mountain onboard. Seems as though a full load also included two inches of ice on the wings, which just refused to fly, even when he jerks the airplane off the ground in a last-ditch effort to successfully violate physics. Instead, gravity reasserts its dominance and he belly flops back onto the runway, collapsing the gear and everyone's lower spines.

His passengers, being athletes, suffer only severe bruising, while Mitchell becomes a low lumbar paraplegic and must now assume occupancy of a wheelchair for the rest of his life. That's where I come in. I'm his legs and functioning body (sometimes including the brain), wheelchair stairs-lifter, and crazy confidant, enough so, to carry out most any outrageous idea he might come up with.

Now that he's doubly damaged, he gets ten times the sympathy and ten times the recognition. He stumbles on a little-known philosophical theorem that posits you can find nirvana by long and arduous training and meditation, or, you can cut off an arm or a leg and gain immediate enlightenment. Whatever it is, he's now a minor celebrity in a minor ski town with no particular skill or talent other than having stupid accidents and coming out of them stinking like a rose. How's that for a taste of fate? For every little chiseling of his body, his social life grows by a leap. I hope he doesn't run out of parts before gaining the attention he sorely desires.

"We don't need headlines tomorrow," he continues his speech, "of a famous star OD-ing in the Butte. You know what to look for. Members of the Hotshots are about and can administer CPR if necessary. Watch all strangers and take care they don't overdo it. They're here to be fleeced, so let's make sure they have a great time while we unburden their bank accounts."

"And their coke!" yells someone from the back. We all laugh.

He looks straight at me. I look back at Cathy watching with a wary eye from the kitchen doorway. She looks sour, but I know she's one of the professionals like me, helping run this house and this crazy gig. She's got my back and vice versa. She's his official housekeeper, but like me, she brings much more to the table. Between the two of us, we keep Mitchell more or less functioning like a real person and out of trouble, mostly.

"No more than two drinks per hour. No more than two joints per hour, and dispense the good stuff sparingly. A lot of brave pilots and yacht captains have risked everything to make this a special night for our fight against evil big-corporate mining. Don't let it go to waste. Always be closing!"

"You believe all this?" Cathy whispers in my ear, after sneaking up behind me.

"What's to believe?" I whisper back without turning my head. "We've heard it all before. The message changes, just not the snake oil salesman."

She giggles. Mitchell finishes his little speech to the collected townspeople representing the best of our resistance movement. These youthful healthy Nordic types looking for a cause gladly volunteer to act as guides to the guilt-ridden celebrities brought here to lend their voice and money to our efforts. Tracey is here to play her protest song that John Denver just released on one of his big corporate albums. Townes is scheduled to show up later and play if he can stay semi-sober for an hour or two.

"Doctor Cowboy!" Mitchell yells.

"Yes, sir!" I mockingly reply with a boy scout salute.

"Go down in the cellars and bring up five bottles of the good Zinfandel for me and my friends, and five more bottles of cheap Chardonnay for the masses. Bring up a bottle of *Brut* in case we need to celebrate something, like getting a big donation from Redford."

One of my many duties is to climb into the hole under the kitchen repurposed into a well-stocked wine cellar. He and I drive the RV to Denver one semi-sober weekend looking for expensive whores for the disabled and some exotic new dick drugs. While there, we clean out a liquor store of its supply of good California wines and stock his cellar probably better than any restaurant in town or on the hill.

Two places in the house are now beyond his access. One is the tiny wine cellar and the other is the whole second floor. Before he crashed the plane, he has the boys in town rebuild his newly purchased antique house with a bachelor pad second floor containing all the amenities of a second-rate Aspen bachelor pad. He even had a dumbwaiter installed going down to the kitchen for those late-night necessary refreshment runs.

The boys, though, were staying in his house while he was going through nine months of wheelchair training and, of course, they drunkenly pass out forgetting the rekindled fire in the woodstove, which dutifully starts a good old-fashioned 3 a.m. cold-as-hell winter chimney fire. The fire takes off the entire second floor before our ice-encrusted volunteer firefighters have it similarly encrusted.

So, the boys guiltily do a quick rebuild of the entire house, restoring it better than before, and adding a large addition to the rear of the house, which includes a wood-fired sauna with outdoor access for rolling in the snow and a big open-space den for getting high and listening to music. The real purpose, of course, is to provide a place where all the beautiful naked ladies invited to partake of the sauna can relax and be entertained by good liquor, clean drugs, and the best stereo money can buy. It sports a signature shiny nickel-plated potbellied stove in the far corner that when fired up with plenty of good local anthracite keeps the room Hawaiian toasty, alleviating any necessity of wearing clothes, even on the coldest of nights. However, as part of the required mountain survival buddy system, shared bodily warmth is always encouraged.

This is where we plan to contain the artist types in town so they can entertain a well-controlled group of celebrities, passing through a few at a time and hopefully keep the local unpredictable citizens influence to a minimum.

"The artists in town are the more vocal of the protesters and the artists coming from California might be attracted to them," Mitchell warns us. "Celebrities get strange when they get around others of their own kind. We'll need to keep them moving and don't let them bunch up where who knows what thoughts they might be exposed to, let alone uncontrolled substances and other locally grown bad influences."

Now, restricted by wheels, he sleeps in the front room office, now a bedroom, and I inherit the whole second floor for my personal use, except when *Mamacita* might be visiting. All I have to do is hang with this crazy guy and take care of him. Kind of like hiring the fox to watch the chicken house—and I was not complaining. At least maybe now I could get some notice from the rich and famous swirling around him, being the *Gonzo* house boy.

In case Gonzo is unfamiliar, read Hunter Thompson or simply know his definition. Hunter leads the counter-culture movement in Aspen, making sure the rich and famous pay their dues. Gonzo is an adjective describing the proper response for a critical condition of reality. "When everything gets freaky, the freaky turn pro." In this case, a bunch of wild, drug-crazed ski-bums, trust-funder drop-outs, and various other immigrant mountain folk like me are experiencing freaky times where *sober turning professional* is our only option in order to defend our little mountain town and our freedom-loving extreme wilderness lifestyle.

Amax, the world's largest international mining conglomerate, decides to remove one of the mountains overlooking Crested Butte, grind it up into caustic sludge, and fill in a nearby pristine *Bambi-wilderness* valley without shedding a single tear of remorse or regret. They've already done it once, removing Bartlett Mountain near Climax and filling in a nearby valley with a caustic sludge lake that will be a dead-zone, chemical-polluting lake for centuries to come.

So, Mitchell becomes the adopted ambassador of our mountain counter-culture freedom movement, and being the duly elected mayor of an actual real Colorado town, and having invested a large amount of his Honda settlement money in buying nightly rounds at all the bars, he becomes the de facto icon of a David verses Goliath fight to save innocent nature. The image of an activist as a small gnarly knot of a severely damaged person blasting around in a wheelchair like a goat in a go-kart just can't be ignored, disliked, or dismissed.

And Hollywood, always on the lookout for a shooting star, finds the wheelchair mayor of a cute, aka film-set, mountain village an enticing source of free, save-the-world publicity. Now they gather like roaming wolves jockeying for the best position, and I'm in charge of the feeding order.

Climbing out of the hole in the kitchen floor, Cathy grabs the bottles away from me and takes them to be opened. I peek in on Mitchell still working the parlor crowd and this time he's got some big blond babe sitting in his lap wearing a white fur coat, top to bottom, including a little white fur pill-box hat topping it all off.

"I bet the wives of the three council members here don't show up later," Cathy announces gleefully in my ear. I glance back at her looking over my shoulder at the scene around the dining room table. "Tawdry Hollywood has nothing on those bed hoppers."

"Easy girl," I caution, "the night isn't over yet. Where's your brother?"

"Gary's in the den keeping Paul Ehrlich in sight. He's supposed to be hanging with Tim Reed and David Leinsdorf."

"If you see him, tell him to keep the Californicators away from the locals. I heard rumors in the bar today."

"What did you hear?" she demands, always ready to spread new rumors.

Applause from the people surrounding Mitchell drowns us out, so I motion to Cathy that I can't hear her before turning back and working my way around the room until I'm standing in the other corner near the stairs. Mitchell sees me and points me out to the girl in the white fur coat sitting on his lap. She kisses him on the forehead, gets up, and threads her way in my direction. Some other cutey immediately takes her place on his lap from the knot of groupies at his feet. He continues speaking.

"So again, I want to thank you for all your generous donations. I know it's hard for celebrities to deal with the onslaught of good causes and deserving people. Wilderness protection is the highest achievement we as a species can accomplish. By preserving the wild places, like David Thoreau showed us, we not only acknowledge where our spirit came from as an inhabitant of this planet but where we need to go when renewing that spirit."

More applause.

"Hi," says the white-furred woman as she catches hold of my arm. "Mitchell says you have something upstairs to cure my headache."

"What's your name?" I ask. More applause drowns me out. She leans in close to where I feel her warm breath on my neck.

"Dyan. What's yours?"

"Lucky. Follow me."

She's a gorgeous Hollywood blond bombshell celebrity looking very familiar, but I can't quite put my finger on who she is. We push through the crowd sitting on the lower steps of the stairs and slowly make our way up to the empty second floor. I take her into the big bedroom where she flops down on the bed with a big sigh.

"How can you people breath up here? I feel faint half the time." She puts the back of her hand on her forehead in a pose of desperation and I start having feelings. I reach into the bedstand drawer and pull out a little mirror already set up with a few lines laid out. I can't afford a hundred-dollar bill to roll up into a straw, so I use a real straw. She spots me and sits up.

I hand her the preloaded mirror.

"Oh, how quaint," she bubbles. "A McDonald's coke straw. How original!"

"Now I know where I've seen you!" I calmly announce, as she deftly puts the straw to her nose and makes a mighty sucking sound as she eyes me askance. "You were in *Heaven Can Wait.*"

She makes a little finger gun at me, winking, indicating I have it right. Then the door flies open and in stumbles a short bald-headed guy, looking like a little sweating gnome.

"Richard!" she exclaims.

"Where's the coke?" he yells. He lets go of the door to push his finger against the side of his nose. I rush to him and catch him just before the door swings out of his grasp. "Hi Dyan! We're in the mountains! Where's the sn-o-o-o-o-w?"

"Come and get it, big boy," she challenges, and pulls open her fur coat, revealing two well-formed pale breasts in all their glory. I forget what I'm doing for a second and Richard acts startled and staggers backward losing his balance. Before I can react, he tumbles backward down the stairway only cushioned by all the people's bodies sitting on the lower steps listening to Mitchell.

Mitchell's finishing up his speech about the little Colorado mouse that roars when Dreyfuss tumbles out at the bottom of the stairs, none the worse for wear, sporting a surprised look on his face.

"Cut that man off!" Dreyfuss yells as if he were a bouncer at a big casino. Everyone laughs.

I rush down the stairs, pick him up, and help him to a corner where he can find his balance between two walls. Dyan sneaks down behind us and every one looks up at her. She takes a little bow, everyone politely claps, and she proceeds to walk over to help me. I hand Dreyfuss over to her and slip her a couple of tickets to the Princess Theatre for the evening's performance.

"Why don't you take Richard here to the movie theater downtown," I offer. "It's just a couple of blocks away and you two can watch a free movie on me. I think we're showing *Rancho Deluxe* with Jimmy Buffet. It'll give him a chance to sober up a little before the late-night festivities get started."

"There's more?" she asks, acting mildly surprised.

"There's always more," I fatally inform her.

"Do you know who showed up downstairs?" Richard the Rat's voice startles me. He is supposed to be running the entertainment in the den with the artists and musicians.

"As long as it isn't the cops," I pause to look at him. "It isn't, is it?"

"No. But the crowd has separated into two drunken mobs. One is apparently a bunch of California butterfly chasers hanging around Paul."

"Ehrlich is here?" I gasp. "He doesn't have any money."

"He probably thinks he's a local now."

"Yeah, I don't think he can handle the entrance requirements. So, what's wrong?"

"The other group is Cloud, the Wease, Hitch, Barr, and a bunch more of our guys and some other guy from Tucson by the name of Abbey," he explains.

"Edward Abbey?" I shout back. Mitchell stops talking and everyone looks at us.

"That sounds right."

"Oh shit!" I exclaim, and pull the Rat from the room with Mitchell and all the dignitaries watching. "He's the *Monkey Wrench Gang*!"

I grab him and elbow our way through the crowded kitchen and down the long ramp past the sauna. A blue skunk haze surrounds the sauna door and the sound of laughter can be heard from inside. We emerge into the large add-on den crowded to the hilt with young people standing and sitting around, talking and listening to music. Most are in small groups, sharing drinks, pot, and other stuff. Gorbett is in one corner with his turntables and mix board and my speakers. Tracey is sitting on a stool between the speakers, playing her guitar and singing her only hit song and our anthem against the onslaught of mountain destroyers.

"I came here from the city, a thousand miles away
I came just for a little while, you know I never meant to stay
I meant to take my pleasure, have a good time and be gone
But I fell in love with a lady, now I sing a mountain song"
—Tracey Wickland, "Mountain Song," 1975

I turn to Rat. "Where's the problem?"

"It's not here. It's outside," he says, and takes the lead, threading through the crowd past the DJ, past the little pot-belly nickel-plated coal stove, and out the rear door. I spot Dana and his current artist entourage, along with Peter Fonda, sitting in one corner conspicuously passing a little brown bottle around. I don't see the rest of the boys, or Townes. He is supposed to be doing a set with Tracey and he promises to be more or less sober. Rat pushes through the rear door leading to the back lawn and the RV parked in the alley.

There are a few people standing in groups watching the sunset light up the surrounding mountains in pink and gold. Every time I see it, I hesitate and absorb the views like syrup. *Goddamn it's beautiful!* But everyone's looking at the RV. Then I hear Townes pleading from inside the open RV door.

"Now guys, can't we just all get along? Here, have a drink and we'll toast to nature."

I recognize Townes' voice. His speech is only slightly slurred, so I know he isn't falling-down, glassy-eyed drunk, yet.

"Your prissy academic attempt at preservation just turns wilderness areas into giant museums. That's development by anyone's definition. Unrestricted development just for preservation sounds like cancer. It destroys wilderness!"

I don't recognize *that* voice. I walk straight to the RV past Cloud and Wease drinking beers, laughing, and listening to the argument going on inside. I also notice some clean-cut strangers standing off to the side not laughing. Probably some of Paul Erhlich's students staying in their recently acquired township of Gothic, turned exclusive University of California summer camp for the tenured and other academically privileged.

"Overpopulation will eventually overwhelm and destroy all wilderness, just by the numbers," I hear Paul say. "Don't you realize it's better to preserve and protect for the future by keeping the mass of people out?"

I push through to the door and climb onboard. Sure as shit, Paul is sitting opposite some stranger at the crowded dining table. Townes is sitting next to the stranger and Paul seems to have his usual backup surrounding him of fellow professors from UC Berkeley. Locals consider them just summer folks using the phony butterfly research center as their free exclusive luxurious summer vacation homes at the expense of the taxpayer. We'd been butting heads for some time about hunting and fishing in their newly acquired now exclusive *Butterfly* resort.

"What part of no development do you not understand?" the stranger demands.

"Ed, look," Ehrlich asserts, "people cannot be trusted to keep wilderness wild. Look at the Jeep trails and motorcycle trails that tear up the National Forests around Denver."

"So, we're supposed to trust you to manage a wildlife preserve as if it were a zoo! The wild in wilderness precludes a zoo and must include humans on the other side of the fence. Look at our host. Mitchell. How is he supposed to tap into his primal wildness connection without the forbidden vehicle?"

"Tell 'em like it is, Abbey!" Cloud yells from just outside.

"Nature killers!" I'm not sure who that is.

"Fuck you, Californicators!" That sounds like one of us for sure. That's gonna start something.

I step to the door and yell, "They just tapped a new keg in the front yard! Better get it while it's hot!"

Someone mutters, "Shows over," and most begin to move toward the front yard where Bob Starr oversees the suds dispensing. I just hope he still has something left.

I turn back inside to the debate.

"Excuse me, Cowboy," Paul says. "I need another beer. At least now l think I understand where you get your ideas."

"Same right back at ya," I say. Paul brushes past me exiting the RV with his two cohorts.

"I don't have ideas, I hatch them!" I shout after him. Turning back, I see Townes and Ed smiling like two Siamese cats after stealing the goldfish.

"Ehrlich has connections with the Sierra Club and Mitchell wants to get them to commit some serious legal money to our cause. Otherwise, I'd toss the bum out on his ear."

Townes laughs. "Have you met this guy?"

I stick out my hand. "Doctor Abby Normal, I presume."

He laughs. "Monkey Wrench University. Glad to meet you. I've heard a lot about you."

"I bet it's all good, too. I'd love to spend some time with you, but I have to get inside. If you're out and about later, I'll catch up with you, but right now," turning to Townes, "you need to get inside. Tracey has started her set and you're up next."

Townes holds up an empty bottle and wiggles it in my face.

The Rat pats me on the back. "I'll see you back inside," he says. "I'll tell Tracey you're coming."

I step farther into the RV kitchen and open a small cabinet near the front. I pull out the half gallon of Jim Beam and motion for him to give me his bottle. He passes it to me as Rat and Ed leave the RV. I refill it carefully and hand it back.

"Make us proud out there," I tell him sarcastically. "Now get in there and milk those guilt-ridden white-eyes."

"I'll be with you in a Dallas second." He takes a big swig from the pint, grabs his guitar, and I lead him back into the den where Tracey just happens to be talking about him, having run out of mountain music material. As he enters the room, an applause breaks out. He smiles that silly Texas grin of his, waves at the crowd, and sits down on a stool and begins tuning his guitar. Tracey leans into the microphone and speaks.

"I'm proud to introduce the legendary, incomparable songwriter, folk performer, and fellow Crested Butte musician, Townes Van Zandt!"

Everybody applauds again, only louder and more obnoxious. He waves at the crowd and strums a couple of cords. He pulls up the mic and taps it.

"What does corn say when complimented?" He pauses. "Aw shucks, folks!"

Everybody laughs.

"You really shouldn't. I'm just here to help save my summer camping ground. Amigo and I come here every summer to get out of the Texas heat and enjoy the freedom of the mountains. Amigo is my horse and best friend."

Every one laughs again.

"I'd like to sing for you my Mountain Song which I wrote while high somewhere wishing I could be back here in Crested Butte."

Everyone applauds wildly.

I spot Dana still in the far corner with his artist buddies and his Hollywood pal, Peter Fonda. He waves me over.

"My home is Colorado, With their proud mountains tall.
Where the rivers like gypsys, Down her black canyons fall.
I'm a long, long way from Denver, With a long way to go.
So lend an ear to my singing, 'Cause I'll be back no more."

"Hey Cowboy," Dana says as he pulls me closer. "What was going on outside?"

"Just a little run-in between the butterfly chasers and the monkey wrench gang. Townes took care of it." He gives me a dirty look. "You had to be there to believe it."

"I made me some friends, Lord, That I won't soon forget.
Some are down under, And some are rambling yet.
But as for me, I'm headed for home.
Back to high Colorado, Never more for to roam."

"Look what Arin's artist farm has come up with. A comic book in their middle mountain misty style fighting off mountain-eating monsters. Peter here might be interested in producing it as a movie."

He holds up a set of illustrated flip cards with hand-drawn comic strip cells featuring the little mountain gnome people doing something to something. The art is unique, stylish, and colorful. I'd seen most of their work over at Dana's house where they're living for free when not in Boston. It's good, but lacking something, like a compelling story.

"Is there a story?" I innocently inquire.

I spot Peter pocketing what probably I saw him sharing with Dana and Arin a little earlier. The little prick has pulled this shit on me in the past. He coldly calculates if you're worth his attention and if not, then you're on the end of his prissy shit list. What a douche! The only good thing about his one-trick-pony movie is the music. I think that's the real reason Dana puts up with him. He knows a lot of celebrities and attracts them to his Livingston, Montana ranch for the elite and their kiss-asses. Dana currently brags about knowing Jimmy Buffet after meeting him at Peter's ranch. No small coincidence we're showing *Rancho Deluxe* at the Princess.

"So friends, when my time comes, As surely it will.
You just carry my body, Out to some lonesome hill.
And lay me down easy, Where the cool rivers run.
With only my mountains, 'Tween me and the sun."

Every time I hear Townes sing his mountain song, I think of myself and the travels that brought me here. It fits so damn well it's downright spooky. My emotions always surge and tears come to my eyes every time I hear it. I'm a hopeless romantic and in love with a place, a little town, a little thought, a little love, and about walking in beauty for a while on the way to oblivion.

"I gotta go check on Mitchell," I say, and leave quickly.

I pass by the sauna going up the ramp and I'm assaulted by the same sounds and smells still hanging in the air. I bump into Cathy in the kitchen, but now it's nearly empty. She's sitting at the little breakfast nook with a glass of white wine in her hand. She takes a big drink, almost finishing it off.

"Where's everybody?" I ask.

"Who cares? We're all out of food anyway. I think somebody suggested a walking history tour of the downtown area and the next thing I know about four young hussies are wheeling him through the front door." She finishes off the glass and refills it.

I look at my watch. It's about nine. The movie has started. It'll be about another hour until it gets out and the bars get re-stuffed.

"Townes is playing in the back room so this place will be capped for about another hour."

Cathy just stares at me like she's just been through a stampede and a mine explosion.

"I've never seen so many suck-ups in one place. It was like an octopus massage parlor. They can have him. I'm not going out there to wheel that drunk back here. He can put himself to bed."

She takes another slug off the wine and gets up slowly.

"Might as well go listen to Townes," she says gloomily. "Maybe his depressing songs will cheer me up."

"I've heard him before. I've got to go check on Susie at the theater and probably hang out at the Nickel in case Mitchell needs a push home."

"Good luck."

"You, too."

I swing by the upstairs and pick up the little brown bottle and what's left inside. I shake it and look at it in the light. Not much, but enough for a few hits in an emergency. I pocket it and head uptown.

It's a short, two-block walk to the downtown area. I pass through Mitchell's normally pristine white picketed front yard, now looking like a minor battle field with abandoned kegs scattered about drained of their final drops and a last standing tap sitting alone in a watery ice tub. I round the corner behind the fire station and see the lights of Elk Avenue all lit up with their *period appropriate* gas street lamps left behind from a prior G-rated movie production. A few people wander the street, along with some mountain bikers cruising the two-block downtown area on this cool summer night.

I cross Elk in front of the Grubstake and look back at the window. Looks strangely calm and empty for a Saturday night. No Mitchell there. I hit the sidewalk in front of Stefanic's, walk along the empty lot to the Nickel, when I hear from across the street a more usual commotion.

"Hey! Barkeep! Another round of shots for everyone!"

"*Yeeeeaaahhhhhh!*"

Okay. The target is located. He's on the second floor, so at least he doesn't have unrestricted access to the street. The villagers are not yet at risk.

The liquor store is closing up as I pass by heading to the Princess next door. The marquee is lit up with *Rancho Deluxe Jimmy Buffet.* Jimmy is a local hero here, having invented both a song about drinking margaritas, the new cool drink among the hip and famous, and those *crazy mountains* where the people who live in them seem a little weird, but special. I'm not sure if Livingston, Montana actually qualifies as a mountain town like Crested Butte, but actually, I don't care, because we define what it is to be a free mountain town.

I prefer the Hollywood stars and big money live somewhere else. They may seem to have the golden touch, but in Aspen, everything they touch has turned to shit. Now you can't even call it a mountain town anymore. Mountain people can no longer afford to live there. Aspen had by now become a museum for the rich and famous seeking wilderness status while hidden away in a luxurious glass case. I call it an inverted zoo where the people are inhabitants and the animals look on from a distance.

Hardly any self-respecting Rocky Mountain animal would bother to visit Aspen anyway. The stink from all the perfumes and detergents drives them deeper into the woods and across the mountains to our side, the clean air side. Their rich garbage isn't even desirable with all the plastic crap getting in the way.

I pop through the theater's big door to the empty lobby. Susie peeks through the drapes from her seat just inside the auditorium, checking on who entered. She smiles when she sees me and motions me in. I step through the drapes, letting my eyes get used to the dark. It looks like a full house and should be, from all the extra people in town. I get down on my knees and lean into Susie's face to give her a big kiss. She responds, but turns her head a little so she can see the screen. I see the big white coat sitting about halfway down turn and look back at me.

"I'll be next door. Come get me after you clean up," I whisper.

"Sure," she says quietly, while trying to look around me.

I go back out to the lobby and open the lower door to the box office double-door and grab a handful of popcorn out of the big machine behind the tiny candy and drink counter. Then I take the hidden narrow stairs in the corner up to the projection booth. I walk in on Tapley sitting on the stool at one of the projector's little view windows watching the movie. The other projector is already threaded up and ready to go for when he does the cutover. Most films are six reels long so the projectionist must do five precise cutovers and get them right on cue. The running projector top reel shows about half still remaining, so I know he has about ten minutes until the next changeover.

"How's it going?" I ask as I dip my head down to look through the other tiny window at the movie screen.

"Just hunky-dory," he responds. "Full house tonight. Did you see who's in the audience?"

"Yeah. Richard Dreyfuss."

"That doesn't impress you?" he asks.

I pull out the brown bottle and dig out a heaping scoop with my custom silver coke spoon made in the shape of leg bones and a ruby-eyed human skull.

"I think Mitchell and Redford are tearing up Sanchos. Fonda and Dana are not sharing their coke at Mitchell's house, and I think Edward Abbey might be floating around someplace looking for a fight. Here!" I command.

I offer up the spoon to his face and his nostril starts snorting Pavlovian-like. I give myself the second hit, by custom, followed by his second hit in the other nostril, followed by mine completing the ceremony. It's the brotherhood of the powder being expressed in an ageless ritual of sharing and respect.

"Sounds like low-class Montana Hollywood trash for sure," he offers up. "But I wouldn't mind being at one of their parties up there on his ranch."

"Me, too. Just so I can piss on something. He has hundreds of acres of freedom and I still can't afford to rent a hole to shit in."

"You'll figure it out. You're smart. You've got Susie."

"I do, don't I?!"

DING! The projector bell rings on the running machine, warning you've got one minute until the film runs out and to start watching for the dots on the screen telling you when to mechanically switch film from one machine to the other. Things are going to get busy.

"There's the bell. I'll see you later in the bars." I depart having done my duty as the manager. I round the corner at the bottom and the white coat is standing in the middle of the lobby looking around for something.

"Hi, ah, Dyan," I remember.

"Oh. There you are," she says, flashing beautifully sculpted high-priced Hollywood teeth. I spot the curtain open a crack. "I thought you could maybe give me a little bump. I've got to watch the little twerp so he doesn't have a heart attack. Surely that means something."

"Don't call me Shirley and step this way," I mimic a hobble as I lead her by the hand to one of our two unisex bathrooms. She giggles and hobbles along with me. The curtain cracks open again.

Inside, she unbuttons her coat a few inches, confirming her lack of undergarments, and begins waving her hand at her face like a fan.

"For a cold climate, you sure keep a warm theater. I almost wish I wore something less."

I hold out the little skull spoon with ruby eyes and she pauses a second, eyeballing it, before sucking the payload off the spoon end.

"Looks like you've done this stuff before. I bet you keep your girlfriend happy."

I dip another load and offer it to her. "She's delirious."

She holds one side of her nose and sucks up the last of my coke.

"*Ph-f-f-f-t-t!*" she sneezes. "Nice. Do you want to see my tattoo?"

"Where?" I ask innocently, thinking it's a butterfly on her arm.

"Here," she says, pulling her long white coat apart until one leg showing skin from Timbuktu to downtown Denver appears with a brilliantly colored butterfly hovering over a neatly trimmed black flower. "You can touch it if you want to."

"I want to, but I'm sort of taken." I look back to her eyes.

She quickly closes her coat and winces visibly. "I thought so. It's that healthy looking Nordic girl sitting in the back, isn't it?"

I scrape the bottom of the vial with my spoon trying to hide my discomfort. It's not every day you get a chance to fool around with a gorgeous Hollywood star. Especially one this beautiful. They said love isn't going to be easy.

"I'm out of coke and I have to find Edward Abbey before he finds a phony-assed developer. And we have a few of them hanging around here, not that I'm trying to protect them. I just want to make sure he makes it out of town unscathed and I get to pick his brain. I like his writing style."

"Never heard of him. Anyway, if you're ever in Beverly Hills, look me up." She turns, unlocks the door, and sweeps across the lobby and back through the curtain to the auditorium. The curtain parts and Susie looks out at me. I can't see her face clearly, but I feel something not nice. I'm sure she understands. She knew the job was dangerous when we took it. The curtain closes.

I leave the theater, stepping outside now in total darkness, lit only by the phony-assed streetlights and a few bar lights shining out the street-facing windows. There's loud music coming from Kochevors across the road and Tapley is hanging out the projection booth window overlooking everything and humming along with the music.

I duck into the Nickel and wander along the crowded bar checking on who's here and what's happening. Nothing weird so far. Then I scan the darker regions and notice a booth with only one man sitting alone. It's Ed.

I order two shots of Crown Royal from Baggins who's working the bar. He knows me and serves them up promptly. He pours an extra shot and throws it down as I pick up the order. "Wha-ha-ho-te! Put it on Mitchell's tab?" he asks.

"Yeah, and bring two more in a couple minutes," I tell him, and head to the booth.

"Hey, mind if I join yah?"

Ed looks up, recognizes me, and nods. "Help yourself."

I sit down and push one of the shots over next to the beer he's nursing. I salute him with mine, "Wa-ha-ho-tah!" and I slam it down. He looks at his, looks at me, shrugs his shoulders and says, "Why not?" and gulps his shot in one swallow. Clearly a practiced man of letters.

"So, why aren't you across the street whooping it up with the other big Kahunas?"

"I'm not a Kahuna and that's their problem. Always trying to apply political pressure through money and influence for some supposed good, but in the end, it's all just greed and corruption trying to destroy wilderness indiscriminately for corporate gain. Meanwhile, wilderness continues to disappear behind all kinds of self-righteous and cleverly disguised development plans."

"Insidious!" I pronounce. "I know exactly what you mean. Look at that...."

I point out the window through a gap in the buildings and trees at the Mount Crested Butte lights in the distance shining down on us, reminding us of our status as the low-rent district.

"Everyone here thinks they should be the last ones allowed to enter and it will never change as long as they have anything to say about it. They pass all kinds of rules to zone out blatant money development only to drive prices up irrationally as they price themselves out of existence and force development to be guided only by extreme profits. Example: Aspen and Vail. I call it *Aspenitis*, a fatal communal disease. Basically, you sell out to the rich and find another wilderness, somewhere else, or not. It's the American way. Find, steal, promote, sell, and move on."

"Then you understand. That's why we need to put sand and sugar in all earth moving machines found in or near a wilderness. We need more monkey wrench gangs. This is no place for that level of technology. It should be reserved for those who use nothing more than a shovel and an ax."

"I know a guy living on a gold claim just out of town that you should meet. He thinks just like you. He works and lives on a small placer mine with just hand labor and clever ingenuity. He harvests his food from the wilderness, leaving little or no impact. He is in tune with his surroundings and simply uses them to survive well with absolute minimal impact."

"Exactly. It's all about motivation. If you want to restrict access, then you qualify as a developer. Your product becomes the limited access-by-money-only wilderness. That's what national parks are for. But if you build a ski resort or worse, a fucking golf course, it's time for the customary tossing of the sabot."

"You know what's strange?" I ask. "Most of the people living here claim they are not here to make their fortune, but to live in a natural wilderness with beauty and grace, unavailable anywhere else. And yet, they are all scheming in various ways to sell out, in a Dallas second, as Townes would say. From restaurant developers to hotel builders, contractors to accountants, they all think they are keeping it real while they count the free inflated equity money dropping like shit from an elephant. They pass zoning laws restricting competition, only inflating values for what they already own."

Baggins appears with the next two shots. Ed looks me in the eye with a sad look. I feel sorry for the poor guy. His heart is big. He tells us how to treat the desert to get the most back. But I feel he is fighting a losing battle of some kind. We down the shots and I order a couple of beer-backs to help keep it down. He gets serious.

"You know the real reason I'm here?" he asks, not expecting an answer. "I was sent here by my publicist to sell Redford on producing my book as a movie."

"That sounds good. What did he say?"

"He didn't say anything. I told him to go look at John Nichols' book if he wants to make a movie about fighting development."

"Who's John Nichols?" I ask.

"You'll hear about him soon. He's written a trilogy about rural New Mexico communities at the bottom of the social economics taking on moneyed developers in an up-close and personal battle for humanity. I like his writing style. He's much better than me."

"Don't sell yourself short. At least you have set it all down in words that will never die."

"If only," he says dejectedly, and throws down the shot.

$$\sim 6 \sim$$

THERE'S GOLD IN THEM THERE HILLS

For my next summer in the Butte, I go even deeper into the wilderness. I'm an amateur geologist, having had the privilege to attend a college summer school in Geology when I was between Junior and Senior years in high school. The Kennedy administration was pumping bucks into research if research professors would go out of their way and introduce bright high school students to college sciences. I was turned down for a program in physics but at the last minute, they needed students for a hastily put together summer school in geology.

It was my first time away from home on my own. I flew for the first time on a jet airplane to legendary Los Angeles where I lived for 6 weeks in a brand-new dormitory at a new college being built in the vast orange groves of Simi Valley. I lived with about 20 other kids like myself from all over the west coast, on our own in the big city for the first time. Needless to say, I was ecstatic. It was an experience most would kill for. I came back knowing full well, Oregon was too small to hold me.

But while I was having the time of my life, the professors forced some geology into me that has been a great comfort for the rest of my life. Every time I fly, I watch the ground as an ardent observer of nature and lovingly appreciate the forces that create our incredibly sculpted earth. It has been a great comfort to me to know why the hell the earth is in the state I see it.

Besides this, and having a host of other specialties and interests, I also like to collect gemstones and mineral specimens.

When I was a boy in Idaho, my father took us on rock hunting expeditions where we found agates, opals and thundereggs. I can't afford to buy them like most rich bastards who proudly display them, so I have to go out in the mountains and find them on my own.

Cordley introduces me to a bar regular who is definitely not one of the boys. But he knows geology and the mining history of this area like nobody else. Gary Christopher loves to engage anyone in serious dialogue about Colorado mining, Gunnison history, and who owns which claim, and what's left, if anything, in every mine or claim he's been able to visit within the Gunnison National Forest.

He's a big man and wears strong glasses. He's also pushing middle age, has a trick knee, and can use some muscle help with his wilderness explorations. He asks me if I'd like to help him do some prospecting.

"I'd love to go along," I excitedly volunteer. "My truck is laid up, though."

"Don't need it," he says. "My truck is a modified Jeep Wagoneer. It's got a 350 Chevy engine in it and a big-assed PTO winch."

"Good engine, but your body's a little smaller than a carryall," I assert.

"That's why they're in such demand. You'll see. I'm planning on going up to the Silvanite mine next week if you want to see what I'm talking about."

"Isn't there still snow up there?" I ask. "I don't even think hikers are going up that high yet."

"Oh, there's snow all right," he confirms. "That's the whole idea. Go early and use dynamite to move the snow out of the way. The main entrance to the mine will still be snowed in. Sometimes it never melts, unless the owners go in and clear it out. But the owners are in Denver and only go up there to seriously work starting in July. If you're going to high-grade a mine, you have to hit it early before the owners show up and there's still snow."

"It just so happens I have explosives training. Our neighbor back in Oregon worked at the Atlas Powder Company and had a barn full of explosives and various accessories like caps and fuses. I learned how to handle the stuff, prime it, set the charges, tie together multiple charges with Primacord and shoot it off safely. We routinely dug ditches with it, dug postholes in hard clay, blew stumps out of the ground, and I used the electric fuses to make a killer gopher trap."

"You'll do," he says.

I look him in the face. He looks like a big puffy teddy bear, innocent as a kind old bachelor uncle. But he uses words like *dynamite* and *high-grading*. I like it.

"So, what're we going to be looking for?"

"What do you think? There's gold in them there hills." He points out the front window in Tony's Tavern at Gothic Mountain.

*

So, real early in the morning a couple of days later, I climb into his Wagoneer in front of his thirty-foot trailer in the trailer park. The Jeep is already loaded with boxes of equipment and tools.

"Got everything you need to build a railroad?" I ask sarcastically.

"I think so," he responds seriously. "They were out of thirty percent sticks, so I had to get sixty percent, and it wasn't cheap."

"Hope it didn't cost an arm and a leg."

He doesn't laugh. He just concentrates through his Coke-bottle glasses on driving the over-powered Jeep up the Copper Creek trail toward my favorite campground, which is just below the trail over East Maroon Pass to Aspen. There's about a foot of snow left on the road and we easily break trail for the first time this year. The road branches about a mile before the lake and we take the north fork that takes us above timberline and zig-zags following an old mining road and then across a broad slope of dangerously loose scree. The first switchback on the other side is covered in a huge snow drift.

He pulls out a long wooden rod from the back and hands it to me.

"Here, go poke a hole in that pile of snow near the bottom," he instructs. I know what he needs.

He starts by crimping a cap onto about a foot of fuse. He cuts the stick into two equal pieces. He sets one aside and uses a pencil to push a hole into the powder in the open end. He inserts the cap and fuse, wraps it in masking tape so the fuse doesn't fall out and hollers, as is normally required by miners with live powder all primed and ready to go, "Live stick walking!"

I back up instinctively because I think maybe sixty percent might be a bit much. He shoves it down the hole I punched in the snow bank and lights the fuse.

"Fire in the hole!" he yells, as he runs half skipping back behind the truck. I'm watching and he motions for me to join him. I start to walk in his direction when the damn thing goes off.

BOOM!

Suddenly, I'm hit by a sideways avalanche. There's snow everywhere and for a moment it's a complete white-out. I'm blown off my feet into another snowbank.

"*Jees*, what the hell happened?" I yell, getting up and throwing the snow off. Gary laughs his ass off.

"Probably should have used a third of a stick," he admits.

"Ya think?!" I yell, still spitting gravely snow out of my mouth.

He wipes some snow off his windshield and hood, gets in, and starts up the big Chevy engine.

"Let's go. We've got two more to get through before the mine."

We repeat the process with a little less drama this time and end up shoveling the snow on the last switchback. Gary is pretty good at getting his little Jeep through the half-frozen slush that clings to rocks making them slippery as slime on a river rock. He fishtails the last few hundred yards and we end up popping out on top of a flat shoulder of tailings sticking out from an old mine shaft opening. We're parked literally on a man-made pile of rocks removed one by one from the mountain behind us and piled against the mountain below us. It's as big as the pyramids at Giza.

"There's actually three openings to this mine," Gary says as he ponders the snow blocking the entrance. "The original strike is down below near the bottom of this cliff. It got covered up when they tunneled up and opened this entrance. Here they can just throw the tailings over the edge and never worry about it. There's another one about a hundred yards above us."

He points up to the cliff above us, but I don't see any openings.

"It's hard to get to and it's partially blocked, but I've been up there. If you look carefully, you can see a major fault going up this cliff. It's that fault that they were following, finding pure silver in a hard quartz matrix. They hauled heavy machinery up here and mined it extensively for about fifteen years before it petered out and then the silver crash of '93 pretty much killed everything."

"So, it's abandoned?" I ask.

"No. There are owners and they still come up here, usually in July or August. Sometimes they do some work to keep the claim up. It's patented, so it never expires and there are still a lot of valuable mineral specimens in there. I've filed over the top in case it ever defaults."

"You can do that?" I ask.

"Sure. I've over filed on about a dozen claims around here so that if anything happens to the current owners, I'm next in line."

"That sounds a little crooked," I point out.

"It's the law. 1876 mining law states that if a prudent man can make a living off of a ten-acre claim on federal lands, he can take private possession and do so. He just has to renew it every five years. Things happen." He shrugs and starts priming another stick.

I poke a hole in the mountain of snow covering the entrance all the way up the slope, hiding exactly where the actual entrance is located. So, we blast little holes along the base and follow the old ore car tracks leading into the mountain.

"We have to be careful," Gary cautions. "If we cause a rock avalanche from our dynamite, we could seal this entrance forever."

"And us?"

"Only if we're in the way."

I look around gauging all possible paths of escape. There aren't very many.

"Let me do some more shoveling," I volunteer.

It's not long until I punch a hole through the snow big enough to squeeze our bodies through. We load up our backpacks with tools and put on our miner's hats with lights. Gary wears rubber pants and he gives me a pair to wear over my Levi's so we won't mind a little mud. We slide down the snow on the other side of the hole into a wet dark mine shaft.

We move down the shaft slowly, inspecting the overhead pilings and timbers, trying to keep from tripping over loose rocks and the old iron tracks. Soon I make out a big piece of iron equipment in front of us. As I get a closer, I can make out *Patent Pending 1889* imprinted on the side of the giant rusty iron casting. There is a flywheel about four feet in diameter attached to one side and a large galvanized tank overhead with a pipe extending down and stopping just above a strange steel mesh attached to a larger pipe leading down and into the piston housing at the base.

"That's the carburetor," Gary points out. "This is one of the earliest gas engines ever made. Gas drops on that opening, which is stuffed with wool socks, and the piston draws air through it evaporating the gas and pulling it into the engine. It runs about sixty rpm, firing about every second as the flywheel drives a belt to an air compressor. You control the speed with this drip valve on the end of the gas line from the tank above. Damn clever, and it worked great."

"Why is it still here? Man, this would be a great artifact to collect," I suggest.

"They've tried, but it just too heavy. It's a miracle how they got it here in the first place. There were some tired mules that day." He laughs at his joke.

"Let's go deeper," he suggests. "I've never been past the vertical shaft ahead. Too scared to try it alone. With you here, I think we can get over it."

"Okay. Let's see what we got."

We proceed past the wide area in the tunnel where the engine sits. We pass an alcove on the right. Inside is a terribly worn-out shovel rusting away and some rotten cloth on the floor. I think about the last people who left that stuff maybe over eighty years ago.

"Here we go," Gary says, pointing his hat-light down, following the tracks as they continue on unsupported by rock and spanning about a six-foot hole straight down. I approach carefully and point my light down it. I can't see the bottom.

"That's an old hoist shaft where they pulled ore up from below with a winch. It used to have a wooden floor, but it's long gone now. We can walk across on the tracks if we have something to belay against. That's where you come in." He looks at me.

"What?"

"I'll slide along on one track and you'll do the same on the other. We'll face each other and hold hands."

It takes me a second to visualize it. I look at the two steel tracks and they are definitely not going anywhere. I kick at them and they are solidly attached on both sides.

"Just like dancing, except you're not pretty enough," I observe.

"Use your imagination, handsome," he quips.

We sidestep carefully on the tracks over that black hole, looking at each other in the eyes as we use each other to stabilize. Works like a champ. We'll have to do it again coming out.

"I've never been this deep before," Gary points out.

He takes out his Pentax and takes pictures of anything that looks interesting. Unfortunately, things get really boring as far as finding artifacts or exposed mineral veins.

We follow the tracks until they come to an end, then walk a little farther until the shaft ends—not at a wall, but at a huge open cavern. I step up to the edge and shine my light around.

From about fifty feet above us, the rock walls squeeze together in a dark chasm going deep into the mountain above, disappearing into darkness. Below, there's about a hundred-foot diameter open cavern with a jumble of huge boulders strewn across the bottom. A black discolored wooden ladder leads down the rock face below us to the floor.

The black colored wood means it's rotting. I feel it and it's slimy with water and some kind of algae growth on the surface.

"I guess that's it," I observe. "Can't get past here."

Gary leans out over the cliff and inspects the ladder with his light.

"There's only one rung gone and it's near the bottom. Looks good to me."

I look at him quizzically, but he's already climbing onto the ladder and descending carefully.

"Don't step in the middle of a rung," he advises, as he keeps going. "Keep your feet to the outside next to the runners. That's where it's strongest. I'm heavier than you, so if I make it, you can make it."

"Good idea. Somebody has to tell them where to look for the body."

I follow him carefully down the ladder and am mildly surprised it doesn't break. I reach the bottom and Gary is already off exploring around the chamber. He has to crawl over boulders, which makes me think these might have dropped here since it was mined, and not before. I look up again and throw my light beam around, but I see nothing but featureless rock in all directions.

"I don't see any quartz!" I yell out so he can hear. "Where's the vein?"

"I know," he yells back. "I don't see it either."

I look around and there are just no white stripes anywhere. Everything is a dull brownish grey.

"It looks like we made it to the surface of a granitic intrusion and the mineral veins all stop here," he yells out.

He climbs back over a boulder and approaches. "This is one of the granite cores of the Rocky Mountains that pushed up squeezing the metamorphic rock above and around it causing mineralization to occur in fractures and faults. No sign of any mining activity here either, so let's go back. There's a suspicious nodule near the entrance I want to sample."

We carefully climb up the ladder, but one of the rungs breaks away, scaring the shit out of Gary. He yelps, but the other foot holds, so he creeps on up. I, of course, have to climb around it. We both make it up and look back at what could have been our grave if we had fucked up any more.

We scurry across the vertical shaft and get back to the tunnel between the old gas engine and the entrance. There's enough sun coming in the hole we made earlier that we can easily see what we're doing. Gary takes out a large hand chisel and a five-pound hammer then kneels down near the wall on one side where there is a small bulge about a foot in diameter sticking out about four inches from the bottom wall of the tunnel.

"I noticed this the first time I came in here," he explains, while he starts smacking the chisel on the side of the lump.

"The old timers left it here for some reason. If there is something sticking out that anyone could possibly trip on or hit, they usually remove it."

He keeps hitting the chisel as hard as he can but there's not very many shards breaking off. In fact, the chips are so tiny it just looks like dust. That thing is hard, I realize, a lot harder than high-carbon steel apparently.

"Here," he says. "You take a shot at it. I'm getting tired."

I take the hammer and chisel and give it a try. He's right. My wrist starts hurting from the abrupt blows it keeps taking each time I hit the immoveable chisel.

"I give up," I mutter. "Isn't there an easier way? How about explosives?"

"Are you kidding? Look around. We're so close to the entrance, a good sneeze could bring down these old timbers."

I look around and start seeing things I probably should have noticed earlier. There's a broken beam almost dangling. There's a giant rock poking through a couple ceiling rafters.

"Maybe we shouldn't be hammering so hard," I suggest.

"We just have to find its weak point. Every rock has one."

He takes over for a while, hammering like hell while moving the chisel around, testing different spots near the base of the nodule. Sometimes he throws a little chip or two, but mostly it stubbornly resists and just rapidly dulls the chisel.

"Here, take over for a bit while I massage my wrists. Try hitting along this line," he says, pointing with the end of the chisel.

"All right," I say, "but I'm not sure this is going to crack."

I work on it for five minutes and then we switch. We keep this up for about a half hour when suddenly, without any visible warning, a big hunk of the nodule splits off from the wall. Gary screams like a little girl as he picks up the biggest piece, looks at it, and starts dancing around in a circle.

"It's a Silvenite nodule. Look!" he shouts. He holds it out to me and I can clearly make out on the fractured side a spherical surface indicating a possible round nodule at the center.

"So?" I challenge.

"Watch!" he says.

He carefully uses his rock hammer to chip away at the edges of the quartz matrix, leaving just the round grey ball of almost solid squeezed quartz at the center.

"Now. Hold this in that notch and I'll split it open." He puts the chisel in a little indentation in the rock floor.

"Are you sure?" I ask hesitantly. I know what happens when a hammer misses its target and hits whatever's nearby.

"Don't worry," he reassures me. "I don't miss."

I hold it nervously and he strikes the chisel hard, right on the center. I can't believe how easy the two halves just fall apart like a cracked egg. He picks them up and holds them in front of me.

"Have you ever seen anything like this?" he asks gleefully.

I look hard and I'm not sure what I'm seeing. It looks like the bottom of a tiny bird's nest full of grey fibers all tightly balled together like somebody squeezed a long piece of grey thread into a wadded-up ball.

"What the hell is that?" I ask. I'd never seen a mineral specimen like it before.

"It's pure wire silver, just like it was made millions of years ago. It's literally squeezed out from between layers of quartz at very high pressures and temperatures and they sometimes emerge in these hollow nodules as little tangled balls of extruded wire silver. Gold can be found in the same form."

I stare at it and marvel at the process that could have possibly caused such a beautiful and amazing object to form. I'm seriously impressed. Again. With nature.

"We just made our mining wages today. Now you can buy dinner, pay for a room, and do it all again tomorrow."

"Whoopee," I announce flatly, twirling my finger in the air.

*

Two weeks later he asks me to go out with him again. This time he asks for me to drive my Suburban, along with him taking his Jeep.

"What the hell do we need two trucks for?" I stupidly ask without thinking.

"You know, just in case one isn't enough. We need to get as high as we can on an iffy trail and with two trucks, we can help each other get over the rough spots."

I bite again. After all, that silver wire was spectacular and I'm curious to know what else Gary has up his sleeve.

The next day, we head back to Copper Creek, but this time, we turn off the road early and start zigzagging up a steep wooded slope until we pop out at the top in Virginia Basin. Not much of a challenge yet, then Gary gets out of his Jeep, grabs his pack, and indicates for me to follow.

We go along what looks like an old abandoned mining road that soon disappears under a more recent avalanche of basketball-size rocks covering the old road. Thin tire tracks lead on through the trees on one side and up a steep slope, around some narrow gaps in trees and boulders, and finally breaking open at tree line onto a little shoulder of land sticking out from talus slopes on almost all sides. I judge the drivability of the road to be difficult, but doable.

"I've had my Jeep up to here before, but I'd like to go even higher," he says, huffing and puffing from the climb.

"I can get here with my Suburban, but it might take a few tight turns in the woods back there. You should have said something. I could have thrown in my chainsaw."

"That'll take too long. Follow me."

He climbs up the rocks on one side of the major talus slope at the head of the basin. Near the top, I spot a new gouge opening out of the ground from a recent avalanche of snow, mud, and rocks from farther up. We see the broken trees around us at precisely the same height of about six feet. Something like a bulldozer swept through here at snow level, clipping off everything sticking above it.

Gary picks his way across loose boulders to one of the open gouges. It is quite deep and he goes back into it about ten feet. He sits down and looks back and up at the low rock ceiling above him.

"Look," he says, pointing up to what he's looking at.

I squat down and crawl in far enough to look back and see what he's looking at. He shines his light on it.

It's what I can only describe as a huge dinosaur-looking egg-shaped rock, cracked open on the back side and revealing on the inside sparkling purple crystals the size of Coke bottle necks. It's a giant amethyst nodule.

"Wow!" I exclaim. "How did you find this?"

"Every spring, I look around for the big avalanches. I like to check them out before anybody else does because they can expose huge amounts of dirt and rocks, possibly revealing new veins and faults. Like this one."

He points out some other dirty looking crystals just hanging out in the open on the ceiling and one exposed wall. He knocks a big one off the wall and pulls out a bottle of some liquid, which he pours over the pointed end. It bubbles furiously until the brown scum on the surface begins to dissolve away, revealing a deep brownish red crystal inside.

"Garnet," he declares. "If we can find it in a deeper red, it could be alexandrite."

"These crystals are huge," I say. "I've never seen naturally terminated crystals this size before."

"Down in Mexico, there's a cave with crystals the size of Greek columns."

"No!" I say incredulously.

"Yep," he asserts. "And there may be even bigger ones buried so deep we'll never find them with our puny technology."

"So, what's the plan?"

"Simple, we get as many of these amethyst and garnet nodules loaded up and out of here before the rest of the world finds out about it."

"Let's bring the trucks up and get with it. Bleau is coming in from Denver tonight and I need to be ready when she shows up."

"Ready for what? Some strange disease?"

I can see he's not sexually liberated yet. "Yeah, it's called *getting laid*, and I'm not missing out."

The nodules, weighing about a hundred pounds apiece, give or take, are amazingly easy to pry loose from the cavern walls. Some are already broken off and lying around in a jumble of crystals, rocks, and mud. We load up both trucks with about a ton of rocks and get back to town in time for happy hour and Bleau.

His trailer in town is now surrounded by giant amethyst and garnet crystals that are spectacular in size and color. They write an article about him in the *Chronicle* and he becomes a notable local fixture for talking mining and minerals, especially his favorite: gold.

The next time he asks for my help, he shows off his newest acquisition. With all the money he made from the amethyst crystals, he buys a little fat-tired all-terrain scooter. It looks like a toy motorcycle with a single-cylinder Briggs & Stratton 5-horsepower engine driving a rubber belt to the rear wheel.

Gary straddles it, demonstrating he can walk along with it as it crawls over rocks and logs up to a foot in diameter, carrying most of his weight and capable of hauling another 300 pounds on the back rack. It's designed to carry out big carcasses of moose or elk, saving on many old hunter heart attacks.

This time, we tackle an actually scary trail up the side of Treasury Mountain above Yule Lakes to an old gold, silver, and galena mining town called Eureka. The old mule trail is washed out in many places and covered in others by recent avalanches.

There's a thin hiking trail overlaying the original mule trail so Gary saddles up his scooter and starts the three-mile trip across one of the scariest slopes I've ever been on. On one side is Treasury Mountain, blocking the sky, and on the other is nothing until you hit the Slate River about a thousand feet below. And the rocks underfoot are loose and sliding almost every step. It's a good thing he brought the scooter because several times his trick knee kicks out of place and he has to sit down on the trail, massage his lower leg until the knee joint reengages, and then he's good to go for another mile or two of straddle walking on the scooter.

We make it finally, and I'm amazed at how many old buildings are still sort of standing or newly fallen. There's obviously been lots of relatively recent activity, but nothing in the last decade. We scout around the place, but can't find any open shafts we can inspect. Gary takes a long time checking the most recent tailings to see what they were last pulling out.

"Keep your eyes open for galena crystals," he suggests. "They took a lot of lead out of here in the form of galena before it closed right after the war."

"You know, galena is nature's transistor material," I inform him.

"What do you mean?" he asks, as he busts open another big ugly grey rock.

"It has natural semiconductor structures buried in it," I explain. "You know diodes, transistors, and other non-linear electrical properties. Didn't you build a crystal radio when you were a kid? If you did, the crystal they supplied with the kit was probably a little piece of galena."

"I didn't. I got a rock hammer instead."

"You know, some people say that these natural semiconductors can talk."

"Whada ya mean?" he asks skeptically.

"They can naturally demodulate radio signals and maybe vibrate the rock causing sound. Some say they might attract UFOs."

About then, he cracks open an ordinary looking rock and suddenly, inside, some cubic crystals fall apart into little square-edged shiny black facets. They look amazing and almost unreal with the sharp edges and perfectly square corners. He found the galena.

We collect about 50 pounds of ore and head back carrying everything on the scooter. When he hits the avalanche scree field crossing that we slid across earlier, the scooter begins to fishtail backwards down the slope. I rush in and catch it just in time to stop it from sliding over the trail edge. Gary bails off the bike on the mountain side, and I have to hold the scooter by its rear end as it tries to slide farther down the steep scree field.

Gary quickly crawls around to the front of the scooter and grabs the front tire, pulling it back straight and stable.

"Holy shit!" I yell. "Hold on. I need to get better footing."

I'm sliding, he's sliding, and the scooter is sliding. I give up trying to fight it and instead climb on as fast as I can and jam the throttle full on. The scooter actually catches some traction and begins to crawl back up the slope and onto the trail. I balance it between my legs and walk it back to level ground. Gary catches up, puffing and sweating.

"Wow! You saved it. Thanks."

Gary owed me one for the save, for sure. I like the guy, even though he is a professed repugnator. In our trips, when hiking is boring, we debate political philosophy. His view is pretty simple—as all miners and finders of wealth usually hold—and they are quite wrong.

I point out that the difference between finders of wealth and thieves is indeed thin.

"There's only two ways to make money," he says. "You can earn it by working your ass off for money already collected from the ground, or you can work your ass off and maybe find money directly from the ground and cut out the middle man. Lots of it."

I see what he's saying, but I point out that money is no longer based on gold, but printed as needed to control the economy. Resources like gold and oil belong to all humans alive on this earth. We should share in all of earth's treasures because we all own them by default.

"The wealth should go to the one putting in the work to find it, and if they want a share, then grab a shovel," he counters.

"That sounds like Marxism. You might be savable after all," I goad him.

Later in town while sharing a beer at Tony's Tavern, I continue with his education.

"This is just typical Ayn Rand bullshit," I declare, "romanticizing the brave exceptional individual against the supposed oppressive lazy and jealous crowd."

"Don't you think you should own what you create with your own two hands?" he asks.

"Of course, but she got it backwards," I point out. "It's more likely that the oppressive one, the tyrant who ultimately steals all the money by having all the money, is the exceptional individual taking advantage of the gullible crowd or society. That's the problem with you repugnators, the evil you imagine all around you is the same evil you practice as your creed. You're the elitists, suffocating young exceptionals, stealing their creations, and depriving them of their rightful status in society because they don't have your class-based money status to begin with."

He orders another beer and turns a little red from the heat. I continue.

"Ultimately, the game is dominated by one winner depriving everyone else on earth of their true value. That's not fair, and will ultimately always lead to exploitation, instability, violence, and in the extreme, revolution."

"And that's the problem with you idealists. Of course, the world is not fair. It's never been fair. That's just nature. Get used to it."

"It's not fair and that's the problem. People deserve justice without having to pay for it."

We have a couple more beers and change the topic of discussion.

"You want to help me high-grade some placer gold?" he asks quietly.

"Gold? Fuck yeah! Where?"

"Where else, up Washington Gulch," he calmly explains. "The only placer gold found in Gunnison County. Which means that somewhere on Mount Gothic, a gold vein eroded out of the rock a long time ago, washed down the gulch side and got trapped in the gravel and clay along the creek bottom when it flattens out in the valley. The early miners washed whole mountains of dirt off the sides of Washington Gulch, causing a new alluvial fan of mud tailings at that same place. I've spent a lot of time searching this side of Gothic Mountain looking for any remnants of the original vein, but nobody has ever found it. Not a trace."

"I thought that area was all staked out and pretty much washed out years ago. I know Coney has a claim up there where he digs out some placer gold from time to time to keep up the claim where he lives in his cabin."

"Yeah. I know," he mumbles. "That's the washout tailings I was talking about. No, this is farther up the creek to the next big wash out. The old timers ran big water lines down from above to create powerful, high-pressure water jets that could tear down tons of soil and rocks up to boulder size. When they found a hot spot along the creek, they'd wash down the entire hillside into giant sluices. But there are all kinds of little hot spots they left behind where gold gets trapped in small pockets of loose soil and mud bottomed out by dense clay or solid rock. They also left a lot of fine gold directly in the washouts and al-luvial tailings."

"Did you get permission from the claim owners?" I jibe him.

He looks at me with that stupid smirk like he's seeing something naughty for the first time.

"I thought we could quietly carry in some shovels, a small gasoline pump, a jitterbug sluice box, and maybe move a little dirt. I've been sampling holes all along the creek and I have a couple of spots on the Gothic side I'd like to take a harder look at."

"Look, or take?"

"We'll see what ends up in the sluice box."

I meet Gary again at his trailer at sunrise. He loads the sluice box in the back of my truck and he's already packed his Jeep full of crap he thinks he might also need.

"We may only have one shot at this," he explains, "so we need to be prepared for anything."

He seems to be a little more paranoid than usual this time. I follow him up the Gulch past the Peanut Lake local hippy-phony-earth-mother-cabin-development, past the hidden entrance to Coney's cabin, and about two miles farther. He pulls into a side track on the Gothic side and then drives behind some brush and willows. He stops and gets out, flagging me to do the same.

"People driving by won't see us here," he says, indicating the road behind me. "Park on the other side of me and unload. We'll have to pack everything in on our backs. There's barely a trail and I may have to clear some brush."

We make two trips. The first one takes a long time while Gary stops once in a while to cut brush or limbs so we can bring in the big sluice box relatively unobstructed. We make it to the creek and he cuts out a large swath of willows along the bank so he can set up the sluice box and pump.

It takes both of us to carry the sluice box. It has its own little 2-cycle engine used to shake the table, so we bring a couple gallons of premix to keep everything going for a few hours. Along with shovels, picks, and other crap, it starts to look like a minor arctic expedition. I bring a six pack of Coors and wonder if it's going to be enough. It isn't.

Gary shows me how to set up the rig and then he shows me the most important lesson anybody coming into the mountains should know: He pulls a big gold pan out of his pack and sets about making a little spot for himself right next to the water's edge where he can relax, sitting on a rock, while dipping his pan in the water.

"Here's what yah gotta do," he begins. "We need to look around this flat alluvial bank for the hot spots. We'll use the steel rod and a hammer to probe the soil bank. We need to see where the rock bottom is."

"Rock bottom?" I ask, not quite following what he's referring to.

"There's a rock floor to this whole area and it appears near the surface here under the river bottom and extends up this side of the mountain under all this soil. We need to find low places or shallow dips in the rock base, dig it out, and run all the dirt through the sluice box. But first, I need to sample the holes we find to see if we have any color at all."

"Color?" I ask again like a rookie.

"Gold!" he shouts. "I've already been here and found color before and always wanted to come back and do a little more thorough search. This new technology of small portable mining equipment will revolutionize the business."

"The business of high-grading?" I kid him. He flashes me a funny look and just goes about finding the first hole.

I set about driving the probe into the mud at about two-foot intervals. Sure enough, some went deep and some not so much. Soon we had a little underground topo map of where the low spots were in the rock bottom.

For the next four hours we move a lot of dirt. I thought we'd dig posthole-size holes, but he meant backhoe-size holes. He shows me how to dig for a sample, usually a shovel full from as deep as you can go, deposit it in the gold pan, and then do the slow sluicing process that releases the gold from its tiny hiding places in the soil and fine black, iron-rich sand.

As he picks out the big rocks and washes the dirt out carefully by sluicing the water around the pan in a circular motion, he carefully lets the lighter sand overflow the rim, leaving the heavier gold sticking to the bottom of the pan. When he runs low on water, he simply dips his pan back into the creek to partially refill it. The circular motion carefully allows centrifugal force of the water to wash gently over the edge of the pan, carrying the gravel and fine soil away and leaving only a very black fine sand left at the very bottom because of its greater weight.

And then I see it! *GOLD!*

Tiny little sparkling stars begin to shimmer and flash in the fine black sand. What a glorious sight! I get it now. It's truly a beautiful stunning thing to see and I instantly realize why people go crazy chasing this stuff.

I try my hand at it and amaze myself as it only takes a few tries and I'm showing color, too.

"You're right!" I exclaim excitedly. "This is a hot spot!"

"Now you know why I want to keep it a secret. This is the unwritten miner's code of confidentiality."

"What the hell is that?" I demand, annoyed that he's distracting me from panning.

"Partners trust and defend each other, no matter what. I will always be honest with you and you'll always be honest with me. NO LYING! NO CHEATING!"

"Yeah, good luck with that," I respond sarcastically. "Sounds like a marriage contract."

"It really makes a lot of sense. Cheating partners destroy everything for both of them. It's in nobody's interest, therefore, to cheat in the first place."

"Have you ever seen *Treasure of the Sierra Madre?*" I ask smugly.

"Yeah, but that's Hollywood. What's the drama in everybody doing the right thing and going home wealthy at the end of the day? I like to think of it as *honor amongst the ambitious.*"

"More like honor among good old boys. But you've got a point," I admit, and go back to concentrating on producing color.

After we locate the size and shape of the hot area we intend to dig, we begin moving as much of the dirt into the sluice box as we can with the rig running. We crank up the gas pump and the vibrating sluice table. The noise of the little gas engine clobbers the normal silence and gives me a sense of guilt for the loud intrusion.

We don't talk much; can't hear each other anyway. But it's obvious what we have to do.

Every so often, Gary stops the jitterbug and washes out the carpet in the bottom into his gold pan. This is really spectacular because what he pours into his pan is almost pure gold in color already. He does another hand wash to separate it out from the ever present black fine sand. I'm getting strange feelings the more I see that enticing color winking at me from behind a wimpy curtain.

Finally, Gary starts to drag a little. We're both getting tired and the beers and a sandwich just keeps the energy up so far. The sun is getting low, so we finally pack up and remove everything back to our trucks. Gary polices the area very carefully to make sure we don't leave any evidence of who left this little scar.

We dodge a couple of random cars coming down out of North Pole Basin in the late afternoon while crossing the road, but nobody pays us any attention.

Back in town, we drop off Gary's gear from my truck and I go home to wash up before we agree to meet back at Tony's later and split our take. When we both show up, they're just a few locals in the bar. We both have shit-eating grins on our face as

I order a double shot of Crown Royal and Gary orders his usual Coors Light.

We take a table in the darkest corner where Gary subtly pulls a couple of little vials out of his pocket and carefully shows them to me like it's a winning hand at poker that has to be hidden from prying eyes.

"What do you think? The one on the right is yours. It's about 25 grams of pure placer gold from Washington Gulch. I split it one-third and two-thirds. Hope you understand."

"Understand!" I gush. "I love you, you old fart!"

I reach over and before he can react, I kiss him right on top of his balding head. I notice some guys at the bar watching. I'm sure to hear about this later as the Butte telegraph spreads the usual rumors, speculations, and fun fantasies.

I go back to the little white house at 640 where Kemp is visiting from his new job up in Montana. He's picked up a cop friend somewhere along the way and they're celebrating the weekend by drinking from Friday to Monday.

I, of course, have to show off my gold. They marvel at the beauty of the tiny flakes of pure yellow gold flowing like a liquid in my little vial. I think I also see pure greed in their eyes as they admire my day of hard labor.

I hide the vial carefully in my little closet workbench where I have all my test equipment. It wasn't locked because that would be an affront to Kemp and an assertion of mistrust to anyone accepted into the house.

So, they party the weekend away and I hang out with Bleau in the loft. We go out early Sunday for a hike and when we get back later that afternoon, I discover Kemp's friend has suddenly departed, unexpectedly. I get a very bad feeling.

I rush into my little shop and sure as shit, the vial is gone. He probably sobered up Saturday, late night, found it and got the hell out before anybody gets wise. I confront Kemp about his friend and suddenly he doesn't have a clue what his real name is or where he might have gone. He knows almost nothing about the guy, except he seemed to be a good drunk and he liked cops and guns. Kemp is making bad decisions and this one is serious.

The deed is done and I'll probably be kicking myself for the rest of my life because of my trusting stupidity. I learn an expensive lesson today: *there's no such thing as trusted friends when it comes to gold, or love.*

$$\sim 7 \sim$$

TROUT FISHING IN AMERICA

Anybody living in Crested Butte who has to work for a living becomes a handyman or contractor. Just about all of the old-timers, because they stayed, are exactly that. To celebrate another day in paradise and mark the end of a hard day of work at ten thousand feet, they gather in a chosen local bar to have a couple of happy-hour beers before going home to supper, bed, and the same thing tomorrow, hopefully.

Another thing mountain people become is a fisherman. And not just any fisherman, but a fly fisherman. Every stream has trout. Every lake has trout. If you're not fixing something, building something, or celebrating something, you're probably fishing for something. This has been true at every stage of Crested Butte's evolution.

My fondest find while fishing is a *casket* whiskey bottle from circa 1890. Its color is a rich purple from being dyed by the high-altitude sun for so long. But it's flawless, not even chipped after being left in one of the worst environments on earth for grinding rock to sand. But the thought that I'm here and now doing the same thing someone else was doing in exactly the same spot and probably using very similar flies and fishing techniques, over eighty years before. I feel connected to whomever it was, and they may or may not have thought about me. I carefully bury my beer bottle nearby and feel like I've continued a tradition.

Summer without a doubt is still the best time of the year in the Rocky Mountains. Winter is an experience in pure survival, but summer is a time for dancing and partying till you puke. This is the time when the mountains shed their protective snow and open themselves up to life at its fullest. Fields of columbine turn horizons blue and white; marmots come out of their dens and sing to all passersby; the elk and goat climb higher for the tastiest grass; and man goes into the mountains to either steal its gold or catch its fish. Most of the boys brag about their secret lakes where they regularly bring home sixteen- and eighteen-inch native cutthroat trout, without a doubt, the best tasting trout or fish, bar none.

Bleau, who has been visiting me for some time now, finally cinches the deal and we start sleeping together while I'm still living in the garage. She now makes the trip from her job in Denver every weekend to be with me and enjoy guiltless sex. It's comfortable, easy, fun, and I don't have to worry about tomorrow.

Kemp leaves for Montana and I move from the garage to the main house as its new caretaker...and Bleau starts leaving personal stuff and sort of moves in with me. Frenchy, Louie the Greek, and The Face all move into the house across the street at 615 Elk. I slowly work my way into their confidence by now being neighbors and spending time helping them do electrical work on their house—and they share their gourmet fresh-caught fish dishes with us.

I know how to fly fish and put a worm on a hook, but up here, a shiny spoon spinner is a natural killer for the plentiful brown trout in the rivers. So, I do all right and keep fish on our table. Finally, I find one of the boy's secret lakes up above Crested Butte to the south and on the back side of Mt. Axtell. It's an easy hike from town, but far enough that few deliberately go all the way with the proper equipment.

But it's worth the hike, because Green Lake at the end of the trail is full of big cutthroats all anxious to be dazzled by the fatal *Triple Ought* spinner. The water is so clear I can watch the whole drama play out under the surface. The spinner hits the water and the fish all scatter. But as soon as I begin reeling it in with my classic hiccup retrieval, which makes it look alive to the fish, they begin curiously following it as I reel it toward shore. When the water starts getting shallow, the leading (usually the biggest) fish following decides to make its move and then there's a mad dash of many fish to the spinner and invariably one wins the race, grabs the spinner, and he's hooked.

I fight him for a while as he tries every trick he knows to get away. But soon he tires and as I bring him to shore he rolls, showing me his crimson throat, and I know I've caught a beauty. We'll grill it lightly in butter, basil, and garlic, pair it with a nice Pinot Grigio wine and extra-sharp white cheddar cheese later, enjoying an incredible mountain delicacy that can't be matched.

I want to be more like a local: one of the boys. I already have handyman status, so I just need the boys to show me the best fishing areas and I'll consider myself one of them. Of course, *Secret Lake,* the code word for where the trout are big and hungry, is a closely guarded secret. I persist and finally convince them to take me along on one of their fishing expeditions.

I borrow Bleau's Toyota truck and Kemp's little inflatable one-man raft and follow The Face and Louis the Greek on a sunny afternoon float down the Gunnison River between Blue

Mesa Dam and Morrow Point Dam. It's basically a long skinny reservoir boxed in on both sides by sheer five-hundred-foot cliffs. It's part of the Gunnison River Canyon where few fishermen can get to and the fly fishing for big lake trout is exceptional.

They share a canoe and I'm alone in the rubber raft. We do an easy float down the free-flowing part coming out of Blue Mesa until we get to still water indicating we are at the level of the next dam. At this point, I'm committed to make it to the spillway because there is no paddling back up this part of the fast-flowing river. Soon, they outdistance me in their fast canoe and with two people paddling, they quickly disappear around the next bend. They leave me behind paddling like hell and not getting much fishing done. I catch a couple of decent rainbows, but I start to get worried because I thought we were supposed to stick together.

Then the wind comes up. In the late afternoon, the sun shines right down the slot that is the east-west canyon that we're in, and its heat starts moving air. Soon, the canyon, acting like a natural chimney, generates a thirty-mile-an-hour wind straight in my face. Now it becomes obvious I can't possibly make it to the rendezvous at the other end of the reservoir. Halfway down the canyon and I'm stuck, and the boys are nowhere to be seen. The wind becomes so bad at one point I have to hang onto an out-jutting rock with my bare hands to keep from being blown back up the canyon. I finally make it to an opening in the south cliff where a side stream empties into the river. I know this stream from the fact we cross the same stream up on top of the canyon rim when we drive US50 to Montrose.

I paddle to shore and wait what I think is a long time in case the boys come back looking for me. Nobody shows up. The wind gets stronger and I have to assume they've continued down the river without me and I'm now on my own. The sun is rapidly going down. Soon, it will be pitch black. I'm miles from the road and even farther from where I left my truck at the put-in point upriver.

I'm surrounded by cliffs, which are extremely dangerous, especially if I try to climb out in the dark by just going straight up to the highway on the rim. Instead, I decide to follow the creek, which I know will gradually go up and eventually reach the road and be a lot safer ascent out of the canyon. I deflate the raft, roll it up, strap it to my back, and head up a game trail along the creek, hoping it will lead me out of this canyon.

The going is slow and tortuous, with giant boulders constantly blocking my way. It gets darker and darker. I see the headlights of cars on the road above shooting across and lighting up the cliffs on the opposite side. But I can't get to them. Finally, I have to ditch the raft if I'm going to climb out. I'm getting a little scared and desperate. It's very dark, but I feel like I might be past the worst part of the cliffs, and so I begin a blind climb in the dark up the west side. Surprisingly, I make it to a more gradual slope and soon cross a Jeep trail I can barely recognize. I follow it to the highway, but now it's 2 a.m. and there's not much traffic.

I flag down the first truck that comes along and they suspiciously hear my story. If it wasn't for the fact I still have my fishing pole and two fish, they probably would have blown me off. They reluctantly give me a ride to my truck back at Blue Mesa, where I finally head home somewhat relieved.

Then I run out of gas. This is starting to look like a bad day, and night, even for fishing.

I lie down in the front seat to get some much-needed rest and hang my fist out the window with an extended thumb. Some rowdies come along at about 5 a.m. and give me a cold ride in the back of their truck into Gunnison, where the hotel is the only thing open. I call home to let Bleau know where I am. I'm thinking the boys and her would all be crazy with concern over my whereabouts. I could almost hear her yawning.

When I lived in South Fork Colorado as a teenager, my friend and I decided to skip the 30-minute bus ride home from school and catch the early showing of *20 Million Miles to Earth*. He tells some other students on the bus to tell our parents we will hitch a ride home later, don't worry. Of course, they didn't and by the time we get home, the place is crawling with cops and distraught parents. From this early experience, I mistakenly believe that, if missing, someone will mightily care. But, the second lesson of the mountains I learn is: *Don't expect anybody to give a shit! You fuck up; you're on your own, chump!*

Turns out nobody cares because I make them believe I'm a resourceful, smart, and *can always figure something out* kind of guy. They know more about me than apparently I do. That's a good thing, I think, and it's just the beginning of many valuable but hard lessons to be learned from the mountains.

The boys later explain that they were not that far ahead of me on the river and they couldn't make any headway against the wind, either. So, they decided to turn around and let the wind blow them all the way back to the put-in point. They didn't see me because I had already started my hike out. They figured I could get back to the put-in point somehow and left because I had a truck to drive home with, thus making me technically not stranded.

My mistake, in retrospect, is I made a rash decision. If I had tried to paddle back, I would have been eventually found. By striking out on my own, I assumed responsibility for myself because I was no longer following the assumed game plan.

I forgive them and when Frenchy and the Greek come up with another hair-brained fishing expedition, I'm all in. This time the plan is simple: I'll borrow Bleau's blue Toyota pickup again and the three of us will go up Taylor River to the fish ponds.

The fish ponds are strictly private property, but we figure the capitalist pigs who try to own the wilderness need to pay a local tax. Actually, they should just go home and stop using the wilderness as a bribe for doing business with drug-store sportsmen.

This bum buys damn near ten miles of the river bank on both sides and builds a big lodge with breeder ponds at the upstream end. He then tries to restrict all other fishermen from access to the river. Technically, he doesn't own the water or the fish in it and fishermen can legally float from one end to the other any time they want. As long as they don't touch land, they can fish to their hearts content. We don't have that kind of time or equipment, so we do it a little bit different.

The boys keep an eye on things and they notice that the owner is absent and the live-in caretaker is spending most of his time in Almont at the bar. So we get together on a Friday afternoon and I drive them up the river above Almont until we see the lodge off to the left. I drive on and as we pass by the lodge, I slow down and the boys bail out and duck down below the road as I continue on up the road. They sneak through the woods on the high side of the road and nail the ponds right during the afternoon mayfly hatch. Big breeder brown trout are jumping everywhere for the dancing mayflies.

They spend an incredible half hour catching some of the nicest pond trout this side of the state hatchery. I keep cruising up and down the road, keeping an eye out, and making myself available for a fast getaway if needed.

Then the caretaker shows up driving up from Almont to the lodge. I turn around and follow discreetly, knowing if he surprises the boys, things could get dicey. He turns in the driveway to the lodge and I pass by, only to spot the boys down the road signaling me to hurry up. I pass them, whip the little truck around in the middle of the road, and come back by slowly while they throw their poles and a couple bags of fish in the back, and they pile into the front.

Thinking we've made it, I slowly pass by the lodge trying to be unobtrusive, but the little bastard is waiting in the driveway for some reason and pulls out behind us speeding up and honking his horn.

"Shit!" I exclaim, seeing his big red truck fill my rearview mirror.

"What the fuck is he doing?" yells The Greek.

"He can't do nothing but follow us and try to call the cops somewhere," offers Frenchy. "He's got no proof, so fuck him."

"He can't pass us on this road, but when we get to the main highway, he could cause some trouble with that big truck," I point out. "Look, there's the cutoff for the Almont triangle. Watch this!"

I slow down a little and let the truck get close. As we pass the cutoff, I accelerate quickly causing him to do likewise. Then right at the last moment, I faint to the left and turn suddenly to the right, just barely catching the cutoff while the big truck behind can't react fast enough and keeps going straight toward Almont.

We make it over the cutoff to the highway way ahead of him and nobody is waiting for us there, so we know we've got a free ride back to town. All we have to do is sneak into town by turning off on Seventh at the old cinder pile before the Chevron station and go directly to our houses.

Sure as shit, we crest the hill into town and we can see down below the marshal's Bronco sitting at the Chevron station, watching cars entering town. The bastard called the cops on us, and they called the marshal.

Today, one of the new deputies, the redheaded wife of the city engineer, is on duty. I slowly and deliberately turn off the road and hurry to the house where I cut a U-ey into our driveway. The boys grab their gear and most of the fish and head off across the street. I grab the last bag of fish and run inside where I find Bleau making lunch.

I quickly explain what's going on, when someone knocks loudly on the rear door. I answer it and the red-haired deputy stands on the porch looking fine in her clean new uniform, staring at me with a big smile on her freckled face.

"Can I help you?" I ask nonchalantly.

"I got a call from the dispatcher that someone in a blue pickup was trespassing up Taylor River," she explains patiently, while looking at the blue pickup parked a few feet away. "I saw you coming into town and thought I'd stop by to see if you know anything about that."

"Really?" I innocently inquire.

"You haven't been trespassing, have you?" she asks directly.

"Of course not. Wouldn't hear of it."

She turns slightly and points to something on the porch. It's a fourteen-inch brown trout just lying in the middle of the deck, real lonesome-like.

"Oh, wow, where'd that come from?" I quickly step out, pick up the fish, and hand it to Bleau.

"I think you forgot to clean one last night." I hand it to her and she disappears quickly inside.

I turn around fully expecting an argument ending in me getting a ticket or something.

She looks around and says, "They said it was three guys." Then she winks at me. "I don't see three guys, so I guess this isn't the right place."

She turns to leave and I hear her add, "Just don't do it again!"

"Yes sir, madam, your honor, sir. I'll do just that."

She left snickering, and I learned another lesson in the mountains: *A dickhead is a dickhead, and everybody knows it in a small mountain town.*

*

I have new responsibilities now, costing me more money each month just to survive here. I have to pay the electric bill on Kemp's house and the water, sewer, and all that homeowner stuff. I decide to try a second go at importing some good dope. I borrow Schenkle's 1968 Buick station wagon in exchange for him staying in my shed.

I head for Albuquerque again, this time without Cordley. The contact that delivered before just can't find anything. The timing is wrong. I get desperate and take whatever I can find.

I end up buying a couple pounds of Mexican ditch weed, full of stems, seeds, and yellow leaves. I barely get off on it, but it's all that I can find, so I have to figure out how to sell it. I fear that if I take it back to Crested Butte, the quality will ruin what little reputation I have. So, I call Kemp in Montana and ask him how the dope situation is up there in no-man's-land.

"You know you're talking to a law enforcement officer," Kemp informs me, sounding serious.

"Who else would know better what's going on in your territory?"

"Well, now that you mention it, the people are complaining of no weed in town. Being at the end of civilization means we're the last to get it and the first to run out."

"You don't mind if I bring a couple of pounds up for trade?"

"Mind?" he exclaims. "Bring it on. When there's no dope in town, everybody ODs on alcohol and my job gets a lot tougher."

"Great. I'm in Albuquerque now, but I'll start driving north, stop in Denver and pick up Bleau so she can help me with the driving, and we should be there in a couple of days. Hang in there, the easter bunny is on his way."

I make it to Raton, New Mexico around midnight and stop for a taco and some beer refueling. By the time I reach Denver at four in the morning, I'm not feeling well. I go to Bleau's house and as soon as I get inside, I have to adjourn to her bathroom for some blasting from both ends. No matter, can't wait, I give Bleau the keys and crawl in the back of the station wagon to die. She's a trooper, and takes over driving all that day and all night across Colorado and Wyoming.

Unfortunately for me, it's Sunday and no stores are open. We finally find an all-night drug store in Rawlins where I buy a gallon of Pepto-Bismol and a bucket of Tylenol. I crawl into the back again, but now I have hope of making it alive through the miracle of modern medicine.

Finally, we pull into Virginia City from the back way over the mountains and through Yellowstone. We locate Kemp's rental house and find him watching TV and drinking a beer in the dark, just like he used to do in Crested Butte, only now he does it a lot more because it's a much smaller town.

Bleau immediately takes over his only bed and goes to sleep. I try to get to know the new Kemp. We head out to hit the local bars, which passes as his nightly rounds as the marshal. The town has lots of phony, newly added false front building done in the old-west style, making it look like an old western movie town, but quite frankly, our little coal mining town is a lot more authentic.

The people here are also sort of phony. They have no other purpose being here than to drink, bullshit, and maybe kill an elk or two. But no big social issues, nothing controversial, no turkeys to contend with, and nothing to get the blood boiling is ultimately a boring nightmare. What's the point? They don't even ski here.

Kemp puts the word out to the nefarious members of the community, who soon line up with their orders. I want to off it quickly, so I price it low, which works, and it's sold with just a couple of phone calls. I'll make the deliveries in the bars, nice and public, so there is never any disagreement among witnesses as to what happens. Besides, it is all semi-sanctioned by the local cop, so I shouldn't have any problems.

Once Bleau gets rested, she's up bubbling around the house, cooking for us and talking up a storm with Kemp about his new job, which is pretty boring.

"The biggest problem in this burg is alcoholism," Kemp informs us. "I spend most my time stopping drunks from killing each other—if not in bar fights, then in car accidents."

"Don't these people know there are better drugs out there?" I ask jokingly.

"I like it when there's cheap dope in town," he responds. "Most people get mellow and my job gets really boring."

"I wonder if anybody has researched that?" Bleau adds. "Seems like the police would be on the side of legalizing marijuana if it lowers the crime rate."

"Oh, you poor naïve fool," I quip. "Cops aren't about lowering the crime rate. If anything, they want more crime. More crime is more justification for more cops and more money. They don't care about right and wrong, as long as it doesn't impinge on their economics. Their culture is based on alcohol, so that's all they understand. And that's all they take into account when they have to arrest one of their own, one of the good ol' boys."

"What do you mean?" she asks.

"*Oh, he couldn't help it. He was drunk. We've all been there.*" I mockingly mimic the typical good ol' boy excuses.

"That's about right," Kemp adds. "That's what I'm hired to do. I can serve both as a law enforcement and a social worker at the same time. I have the degree and I have the training. I take care of this community as a member of the community and therefore, my job is sometimes easier, like now. It's been a long cold winter and a lot of people here have cabin fever. Good pot helps with stress and helps socialize people. I just look the other way, as long as they keep it together and not flaunt it."

"How does that go?" she asks.

"Not well, lately. Like I said, there's not much in town right now. This will help."

"Wow, I never thought I'd be helping the cops by selling dope," I point out.

"It's strange new times," Bleau says.

Kemp just lets out a moan.

Later, we hit the bars just like everyone else in town who is ambulatory after nine. Most people live in town and so they walk to their favorite bar. The whole damn town is only about four blocks in any direction. Most of the young people we meet seem pretty ordinary, lacking perhaps some of the more colorful character like what we have in Crested Butte. There are no skiers, but there are lots of horse lovers.

While Kemp sits at the bar with Bleau, I sit in the back of the bar delivering the pot to the three people who buy up the whole load. I make a little money, just barely enough to cover my expenses, but at least Bleau and I will be able to get back to the Butte with a little cash in our pockets. Better than nothing.

I know Bleau has known Kemp a couple of years more than she has known me, but still, I wish she'd spend a little less attention to him. I know it's silly, but still, appearances, attitudes, and actions mean things. If she acts this way, it sort of makes people think she's free and looking.

Listen to me, I declare to myself. *I know better than this.* But still, I can't stop thinking about it and when I do, I don't feel good. I need to find some stronger weed. This ditch weed I just offed is not doing it for me.

Later, when we get back to Crested Butte, I score some good Texas weed from the Bump and that changes my mood. Kemp calls, though, and tells me his constituents are not happy with my weed, either.

"What can I say?" I ask. "It was as good as I could find at the time. The price was right, so what do you want me to do?"

"Nothing," he says. "They'll get over it. Just thought you might like to know."

"I know." I change the subject. "Did you hear about Brian Wright?" I ask.

*

Brian arrived last summer in Crested Butte and we got to know him, as he spent a lot of time holding down the end of the bar in the Nickel. Just about every night he'd show up, sit in the same spot, and nurse shots of Black Jack and beer all night long until closing. People got to know him, and I happened to spend one night sitting with him and we talked.

"So why are you in the Butte?" I open. "Are you a skier?"

"Nope," he answers.

I see he's not big on words. "I don't think you're into real estate, so maybe you fish or go camping?" I pry.

"Nope," he simply says. "I like the privacy. I don't have any worries here. It's therapeutic."

"I can see that," I agree. "Did you have a life before this one?"

"Nope. I mean, you might think it was a life, but it wasn't. I don't know what I want to do. All I know is I can't do that anymore."

"I hear ya. Those who can't do, do it here. Are you planning to winter over?" I ask curiously, now that he seems interesting.

"I don't know. I met some friends here and I have a room rented in a house." He pauses. "Maybe."

"I came here for the wilderness," I declare. "I love being out in the mountains, roughing it, at least as rough as the twentieth century allows. Thanks for goose down. If you're going to stay, you'll have to buy one."

"I'll get something when it gets cold," he concedes.

"That won't be long. There's snow up on the passes already. It only takes one good dump and everything shuts down. I was hunting and camping out with some friends up above Keystone last week and it started snowing. We didn't think twice about it. We were packed up and out of there in two hours. And still we were having trouble breaking snow on the way down."

"Yeah, and then it melts," he adds.

"Only down here," I point out. "Up where we were, there's over two feet on the ground and it's not going away until spring. Look, this is a wild place and anything can happen, and when it does, it can often be fatal if you're not aware or prepared. When I go out in the woods, I always take some food, a gun, and a basic sleeping bag just in case I get caught overnight. I learned my lesson not long ago when I got abandoned in the Black Canyon fishing and had to walk out in the dark. I didn't have any survival gear. Damn near could have killed myself by walking off a cliff."

"You should have stayed put and just waited till morning. I won't walk off a cliff."

"That's what that turkey thought last summer when he walked up the ski area road to the top and then hiked on up to the peak. Apparently, he didn't look at the face of the mountain before climbing it, because when he got there, he looked down on the town and figured it looked so close and deceptively easy, like you could just walk down there directly."

"And he fell off the cliff," he concluded flatly.

"It took a National Guard helicopter a couple of days later to fish the body off the mountain."

A couple of weeks later, as the high country slowly shut down for winter, Brian turned up missing. Word began going around town that he had apparently hitched over Kebler to visit a friend in Paonia. He wanted to get back to the Butte the next day, because there was snow in the forecast. His friend drove him up as far as the base of the pass and let him hitch-hike. Normally, one can walk from there to Crested Butte in a couple of hours, or if you're lucky, hitch a ride over in twenty minutes.

He never showed up in town. A snowstorm hit later that night, and the pass closed the next day.

*

"No, what happened to him?" Kemp demanded.

"Pretty much what you would guess. He got about halfway up the pass when he decided to take a nap. They found his body sitting against a tree looking quite peaceful, except his face had been pecked to the bone by birds."

CLOUD'S BENEFIT CONCERT

Some people think Crested Butte attracts a criminal element. Things like shoplifting, car break-ins, missing tools, and general disregard for traditional societal niceties are definitely on the rise. So is the population.

The old-timers say it's just not like what it used to be. I beg to differ, because when I talk to them over a few tongue-loosening beers, they tell me stories of bad boys and loose women in their time, just like ours, only with a little pride. It's all how you look at it. If they're in your generation, you tend to make compensations for them; if not, then it's all their fault.

Not everyone moving in is a trust-funder overflow from Aspen. The town is attracting young people from all backgrounds and social statuses, simply because of it being a cheap place to live, incredibly beautiful, private, and remote. And it's a community that accepts people on their own terms, welcoming new residents simply because of the common ground we all share; surviving on the fringe of civilization, being responsible, competent, self-reliant, fiercely independent, and...we know how to mind our own business. We value our freedoms and therefore we don't impinge on our neighbors'. Here you never know who you may have to depend on someday, so it's best not to make many enemies. The closer you get to nature, the more you have to be flexible and adaptable. The rigid ones are soon eaten.

Among the young newcomers, there springs up a simple solution. Everyone is simply known by only their first names or nicknames. Nobody wants to know last names because inadvertently one could expose a friend to outside nosy people looking for trouble. There is an automatic glass wall between residents and anyone from the outside. If they ask questions, we know nothing. If they want a beer or a good meal, we'll be happy to help.

There's Bump, Face, The Greek, Rat, Verp, Weasel, Frenchy, Cloud, Cotton, and Starr to name a few. We, out of respect, very rarely inquire about anybody's real name, where they come from, or who might be chasing them. It's all in the now and the enjoyment of the now. The outside is the past. You're only judged by your most recent actions here and not by anything before CB. There is no before.

And we really never answer a question from a stranger looking for somebody in town. If they don't know how to find them, then they probably don't need to be found. This is truly what honor amongst thieves is all about. But we're not thieves and the honor is just a simple sacred unwritten trust between people living on the edge. It's truly strange to live somewhere where you're accepted so universally and without question, while not really knowing your name or where you come from. It's like belonging to a secret cult. The CB cult.

We have code words or a local vernacular to show we belong to a special group with our own language. Mostly it involves bastardizing real words, especially if they are politically incorrect. The working stiffs among us refer to our almost slave labor as *nee-gaces*. Tourists are *turkeys* and the best you can hope for is to get a turkey into a local poker game and find out if he's a *chump*, a *rookie*, or just a pitiful *choach*.

After a few years, the wandering tribes start to coalesce and adjustments in living style are often made in different locations. Santa Fe attracts the eastern art nouveau rich. Telluride attracts the young and adventurous westerners. Lake City attracts mother earth hippies, and Silverton attracts the mediocre middle class. Crested Butte still lives in the shadow of Aspen and so has two kinds of residents: skiers rejected or ejected from Aspen and real estate developers trying to be like Aspen. But the word goes out that Crested Butte is something else, something different, something better.

We are affordable, so poor people stop by and decide to stay, even though they may live like bums. Many come, set up some kind of shop, and try to make a living here as if they were still in the bigger world. Most of us adopt new personalities here. It is like a hatchery for lost and wandering identities. We feel a difference, a mutual understanding that something important is going on that needs nurturing.

But we lost our protective and understanding marshal when Kemp moved to Montana and have instead inherited a new one, Don West, who has no clue what's going on, what the community is, or how it works. He's conservative, a practicing Christian, and believes he's a moral man because his hair is short. He takes his job way too seriously. He starts harassing those who appear to be on the margins of legitimate society. He's young, brash, and assumes profiling is a good way to police. Those who are poor are suspects for petty crimes, while the big crimes, well, that's way above his pay grade.

Townes Van Zandt brings Cindy, Geraldine, and Amigo into town, who are poor and barely have money for gas. They try to camp out in the high country, but the summer is wet and there is a rainstorm almost every afternoon. This finally drives them into town, staying either with Tim Reed at his house on First or with me at the end of Elk. Don West hassles them about leaving Amigo running free, grazing in the city park, or up on the CF&I bench and threatens them with fines and confiscation of Amigo. We start hiding Amigo at various places around town to protect him and start looking out for the cop car and where he's lurking.

But when Townes is in town, he drinks from breakfast to midnight snack time. Cindy gets so mad at him for his derelict drinking and partying, she gives him a real dressing down, sometimes in public. He gets drunk and angry one night and tries to ride Amigo all the way back to Texas. But he only gets a couple of miles down the road toward Gunnison when Amigo gets pissed and throws Townes into a ditch. Don finds them and again wants to arrest him, but we show up and while Cindy explains how things work to Don, we spirit away horse and sore rider.

Then he writes a ticket to Cloud for driving an unlicensed car in town. Cloud is always finding abandoned cars, which he fixes up and drives around discreetly on mountain roads and in town while waiting on a replacement title. He isn't hurting anybody. It's how he makes his living.

Finally, we are all sitting in the Nickel on a cold and wet Sunday afternoon when Cloud has an idea. The place is loaded with locals, along with me, Cordley, Amy and many of the Grubstake gang. Don walks in wearing his badge and cowboy hat, so I guess he's on duty on a Sunday afternoon for some reason. He doesn't need to be here and is kind of resented for flaunting his presence among his apparent prey. Crested Butte shouldn't have to be afraid of its own marshal.

I'm minding my own business, as is everybody else. Don goes to the bar and orders a cup of coffee, then proceeds to a corner table, sits, and waits. He's obviously asserting his official position at an odd time and place. Cloud gets up from the bar and comes over to my table.

"Hey, Cowboy, you wouldn't happen to have any acid on you by chance?"

Why he's asking me I haven't a clue. I am not known in town for psychedelics or anything harder than weed or a little coke.

I have to think for a second, but then it hits me. I still have a tab of Owsley acid laid on me by no one other than Ken Kesey himself. He was on the Pranksters bus hanging out at the Rainbow Peoples Party commune in Ann Arbor when I stopped by to video the bus and Ken for their archives. He and I get high on some good pot I happen to have at the time, and he laid four hits of Owsley's best on me. Window pane to be exact. The one that totally dissolves in hot water without a visible trace.

"Yeah. What's up?" I innocently inquire back.

"Do you want to give it to me?" he says, and then looks over his shoulder at West in the opposite corner.

"I'll have to go get it at the house," I reply reluctantly.

"Okay, I'll hold your place." He looks at me with a foolish grin that tells me he's up to something. I know exactly what he's thinking without saying anything further.

"Sure, why not?" I calmly get up, go outside, jump on my klunker, and ride quickly downhill to 640 where I find the acid in an old plastic envelope. I pedaled back uphill to the bar and come in huffing and puffing. Cloud is still at the table with Cordley, and West is still sitting in the corner. I drop it in front of Cloud, he covers it with his hand immediately, and it disappears.

"Thank you, gentlemen," he says politely. "It's been nice doing business with you." He goes back to his seat at the bar.

I sit back down and ponder what's about to happen next.

"Do you think he'll do it?" asks Cordley.

"Do what?" I ask stupidly. I start to turn around to get a better look.

"Don't look," he cautions. "Wait. Cloud is ordering something."

We lock eyes, but his flit back and forth between me and what's going on behind me.

"Looks like it's a cup of coffee," Cordley reports. We wait some more. "He's getting up." Another pause. "He's taking it to West. Oh shit. What did you give him?"

"Acid," I say quietly. "Damn good acid, I might add."

"Oh, man. He's going to..." He stops.

"What?" I demand.

"He took it," Cordley says, and then pauses again. "Cloud picked up Don's old coffee cup and took it back to the bar. He's acting like a goddamned waiter!"

Nobody says or does anything out of the ordinary, but there is so much electricity in the air you could kill an elephant. I've seen it happen many times before and it's delicious how everyone can put up such great acting at trying to be normal.

Then Cordley's jaw drops. "He's drinking it."

"Really?" I gasp. At this point, I swear the whole bar gets really quiet. Nobody looks up, nobody does anything, but the conversations all of a sudden get a little quieter. I shiver from the tense feelings flying around. It's no longer a normal Nickel Sunday.

This goes on for about another five or ten minutes until West gets up and slowly walks out. Immediately, once he's out of sight, Cloud gets up, goes over to the table and picks up the unfinished coffee. He takes it back to the bar where it is shared eagerly with about three or four more friends. Everyone starts getting nervous and slowly we start vacating the bar, heading in all directions. I go to the theater for the evening show and when it's over, I go instead to the Grubstake, where Cordley is hanging with Griff.

"You're just in time," Cordley says, as I sit down.

"What's happening? Did West get high?"

Griff laughs and gets that silly smirk on his face. "I'd say he's having a rainbow moment all right. Doc George called the city manager and told him West will be out of commission for a while. He was at home when he noticed something wasn't right. He called the Doc and told him his symptoms and Doc told him to stop by and he'd check on him."

"Let me tell this part," Cordley interjects.

"Go ahead. It's too funny, anyway," replies Griff, starting to laugh.

"So, he shows up at the Doc's place out at Crested Butte south," continues Cordley, "and the Doc diagnoses him right away. He tells Don, *you might want to just relax for the next four hours or more. You're going to take a little trip.*" Griff and Cordley both break out laughing.

"And he did?" I asked, trying to get to the point.

"The chump opted instead for ipecac and spent the rest of the day driving the porcelain Buick!"

"No!" I exclaim. "All he had to do was ride it out and he'd been fine. He didn't even have that much. What a choach! So now what?"

"Just hang out here for a while and you'll see," Griff suggests. "The state police will be here shortly to probably arrest Cloud and maybe whoever he was with. He's waiting for them in the Nickel."

I sit down and order a beer. "Shit, that could be me." I begin to worry.

"Don't worry," Cordley says. "I talked to Cloud and he said he'll just fess up and take the consequences. He'll never rat on anyone."

About then, we hear sirens in the distance, something pretty rare in Crested Butte. Soon, two state patrol cars pull to a stop right in the middle of Elk Avenue in front of our window.

I order a shot of whiskey to back up the beer. Jack brings it over and is watching out the front window like the rest of us.

The four cops confer in the middle of the street, when someone steps out of the Nickel and hails the cops. It's Cloud.

"Hey, you looking for me?" he yells, and we can hear him inside. The cops look around and aren't sure what to do next. Maybe they thought they were going to have to search the entire town, or maybe it's a clever trap. Two cops approach him and we can't hear what they are saying, but at one point Cloud turns around and offers them his hands behind his back so they can handcuff him.

They put him in one of the patrol cars and then stand around for another half hour consulting on the radio. I'm pounding down shots as fast as Jack can pour them, but finally, the cops get back into their patrol cars and leave town, presumably to take Cloud for booking at the sheriff's office in Gunnison.

"We gotta do something," declares Griff.

"Like what?" Cordley asks.

"Cloud's going to need a good lawyer, which costs money," he reasons. "I think we should put on a fundraiser. Sponsor a concert or something. Set up a defense fund and start getting donations. You know, the usual stuff."

We'd all gone through the sixties and knew all about organizing concerts to protest the war in Vietnam. Then, we had to raise money for the protesters who got arrested. It became an almost endless loop.

"Who should we get to perform?" asks Cordley. "I bet Townes will do it."

"Tracey might also perform," I add. "She does all the local concerts."

Then Helene Teitler, Tim Reed, and Townes walk in. Helene is Cloud's current squeeze and she lets him live at her house on First Street. They walk right up to our table.

"Can you believe those pigs?" Helene declares. "Cloud didn't have any acid. Some weed maybe, but not that."

"It's okay," Townes reassures everyone, "He didn't kill him. In fact, he'll be a better marshal now that he knows what it's like to get high."

"He didn't get high," Cordley informs him. "He spent the last four hours throwing up all that coffee he drank. He's going to be pissed."

We all laugh.

Over the next few hours, we notice nobody else is being hunted by the cops. Everyone agrees that we need to raise enough money so Helene can hire George Garrison, currently the best defense lawyer in Gunnison County. The word goes out and volunteers start showing up willing to do whatever it takes to help Cloud.

Cordley and Susan Anderton agree to make the posters and put them up on every power pole and streetlight in town, including buildings and bridges. Bob Teitler owns a big flatbed truck which we'll use as a stage. Griff applies for a permit from the city to close off First Street from Whiterock to Elk for the concert and they just say: *When you do it, use cones to block off the street. Oh, and by the way, the town shops have all the cones you'll need.*

I volunteer the PA system and Chris Weitzel, better known as the Weazel, or Weaz for short, volunteers to host the concert and inspire the crowd.

*

On the day of the concert, the sun is out and it's another glorious summer day in paradise. We park the flatbed in front of Helene's driveway, hook it up to her power, and let the crowd spread out on First Street all the way back to Whiterock and into Tim Reed's yard on the left and Helene's yard on the right. A big crowd shows up and the Weaz pumps them up for the passing of the bucket.

Tim goes on first. He plays his repertoire of folk and soft rock songs, which everyone has heard many times. He'll play at the drop of a hat and often drops the hat. People love him and he is a solid contributor to the community spirit. The Weaz gets back on the microphone after Tim finishes.

"Are we having a good time in paradise or what?" he yells into the mic.

Y-y-y-y-e-e-e-e-s-s-s-s-s-s! everyone yells back. I can hear an echo from the downtown buildings so I know the whole town can hear us. I estimate about two hundred people are gathered around the truck and another fifty or so out on the nearby lawns, lying on blankets, some on car roofs, and all enjoying the music.

The Grubstake Gang is running the buckets through the crowd collecting money. Helene is near me watching the whole show from near the truck cab. She's got a grin on her face from ear to ear.

The Weaz continues. "One of our own is locked away in a cage because he can't afford justice in this crooked world. Let's show them they can't push us around anymore. Every dollar you give helps make Crested Butte stronger to fight those who want to suppress us. A lifestyle should not be a reason to arrest anyone!"

Everybody screams in agreement. I notice a steady stream of six packs coming from downtown helping elevate the mood even higher than the gorgeous mountains we can see in every direction. There is a sweet smell in the air as well. It's amazing to see so many young people enjoying nature and freedom. All digging on good music. Everybody agrees, this is what life is meant to be.

"Cowboy!?" Helene calls to me. She comes nearer and has to shout in my ear to be heard. "Do you see that?" she asks as she points down Sopris. There are a lot of parked cars and a few people milling about, and then I spot it. The marshal's Bronco is parked down about midblock and I can barely make out that someone is sitting in it.

"Yep, I can see the big white cowboy hat," I respond, "the same as what Don wears when outside and on duty."

"It's West," she declares. "Should we do something?"

"Naw," I declare. "We have a permit. We're legal. I've been around a lot of concerts with cops and if they are going to do something, they would have done it already, and with a lot more cops. He's probably being punished by the town manager, making him just watch over us."

"Let's hear it for another of our own great musicians, Tracey Wickland!" the Weaz announces from the stage.

"Gotta go," I tell Helene, and I get back to adjusting the PA sound levels for Tracey's delicate voice.

Tracey does her extended set, lasting about an hour. The crowd loves her music and she's got Tim backing her up on rhythm guitar and Archie does the drums. When she sings her one great hit, "The Mountain Song," everybody goes nuts. She does an encore, twice. The crowd screams and demands more.

I came here from the city, a thousand miles away,
I came just for a little while, you know I never meant to stay
I meant to take my pleasure, have a good time and be gone
But I fell in love with a lady, now I sing a mountain song
I listened to the music of the night wind in the pines
I saw the quiet splendor of a field of columbine
I skied on crystal pathways to a mountain peak so tall
And I walked the mighty summits with the one who made it all
And I fell in love with a lady, 'cause I've seen her at her best
And I've walked her wild and rugged paths, through her open wilderness
And now I never can betray her, steal her riches and be gone
'Cause when you love a mountain lady, you're gonna sing a mountain song
Now people come from everywhere to see what they can find
And some take lots of pictures and some just take their time
But they're some who take her beauty that can't be bought or sold
And they think of only money while destroying wealth untold

But you fall in love with a lady, when you've slept upon her breast
And I've walked her wild and rugged paths, to her open wilderness
And you never can betray her, steal her riches and be gone
'Cause when you love a mountain lady, you're gonna sing a moun-
tain song.
—Tracey Wickland, "A Mountain Song," 1974

"Thank you! Thank you! We really appreciate you listening to us. My voice is getting dry and I need something to wet it down."

Everybody screams in unison and several people hand her beer cans. She passes them around to others on stage.

The Weaz grabs the mic and yells, "Tracey Wickland, everybody. You can hear her on most weekends at the Ore Bucket Lodge on the hill. We're going to hear a lot from her in the future. I smell a record contract."

She waves him off and jumps off the truck with the help of Tim and me.

"Okay, up next is the wandering Texas troubadour we all love and call our own. He has over three albums out and I'm sure we're all going to say someday, I heard Townes in Crested Butte before he got famous. Let's hear it for Townes ... Van .... Zandt!"

The crowd drunkenly roars and applauds. Townes is struggling to climb up on the stage and I'm pushing him from behind, but he seems a little unsteady. I look around and spot Cindy and Geraldine standing in Tim's yard. She shrugs her shoulders at me, indicating she tried to keep him sober and it's my problem now.

He makes it onto the truck bed and we hand him his guitar. He sits down in front of the two mics and strums a few chords and listens carefully. I adjust his volume.

"Hi ya folks," he says in a charming Texas accent. Everybody screams *Hello* right back.

"Gosh, I didn't know Cloud was so popular." He puts his hand over his eyes to shade them and scans the audience. "I hear he was trying his hand at waitressing and something went wrong!"

Everybody screams with laughter and hoots and whistles.

"I also hear the whole kitchen staff volunteered to lick the cup clean afterwards. Reminds me of a song I wrote when I was in prison for no particular reason...*Living on the road my friend, is gonna keep you free and clean.*"

Everybody starts screaming at the word *free*.

"Now you wear your skin like iron and your breath as hard as kerosene
You weren't your mama's only boy but her favorite one it seems
She began to cry when you said goodbye and sank into your dreams"

Now everybody stands up, holding their drinks in the air, and the crowd starts swaying to the music. A lot of people are mouthing the words. This isn't the first time he's performed it in the Butte.

"Pancho was a bandit boy his horse was fast as polished steel
Wore his gun outside his pants for all the honest world to feel
Pancho met his match you know on the deserts down in Mexico
Nobody heard his dying words, ah but that's the way it goes"
"And all the Federales say"

The crowd screams in response to the word Federales. From here on the crowd begins singing along with Townes.

They could have had him any day
They only let him go so wrong, out of kindness, I suppose"
—"Poncho and Lefty," Townes Van Zandt, 1974

Townes may be drunk, but he's got the crowd wound up and everybody is loving it. At least he's not stumbling on words or forgetting lines, like when he plays for money down in Gunnison and gets so damned drunk by the second set he can barely stay in his chair. But I have to give it to him, he's pretty good at remembering lines, even when he's really plastered. I think he has over fifty songs memorized if he can only remember them, as he would say.

"I want to play a song for you that I'm sure is close to your heart. It's called 'Our Mother the Mountain.' I wrote this when I first saw the mountains above Boulder. When I was in college."

"My home is Colorado, with their proud mountains tall
Where the rivers like gypsies, down her black canyons fall
I'm a long, long way from Denver, with a long way to go
So lend an ear to my singing, 'cause I'll be back no more
   I left as a young man not full seventeen
With nothin' for company but the wind and a dream
'Bout all the fast ladies and livin' I'd find
When I left my proud mountains and rivers behind
   So I rolled and a-rambled, like a leaf in the wind
Well, I found my fast ladies, and some hard livin' men

Well, I sometimes went hungry, with my pockets all bare
Lord, I sometimes had good luck, with money to spare
I made me some friends, Lord, that I won't soon forget
Some are down under, and some are rambling yet
But as for me, I'm headed for home
Back to high Colorado, never more for to roam
So friends, when my time comes, as surely it will
You just carry my body, out to some lonesome hill
And lay me down easy, where the cool rivers run
With only my mountains, 'tween me and the sun
My home is Colorado-o-o-o-o-o!"
—Townes Van Zandt, "Our Mother the Mountain," 1969

The locals really like this song because it reminds them of themselves. They scream their heads off. They can relate to loving a mountain and wanting to never roam anywhere else. This is our mountain home. This could be the theme song of just about everybody here.

"Hey," Townes says close to the mic so it will be heard over the applause. "I hear one of our better citizens is out there and wants to make a big donation. Where's Steve Glazer?"

Everyone looks around for the guy who sort of thinks he belongs here and tries to fit in, but is really pathetic. He can't fish, he doesn't hunt, he barely skis, never shares his coke, and he seems only interested in money. He owns the Princess and gave me my first job here, but I don't work for him anymore since the Princess is long-term leased to Bill Pence. But Steve smells money, and tries to fit in with the Butte money.

A group of locals buy some land at Peanut Lake to build do-it-yourself mountain cabins. Some build conventional structures and some build more interesting homes such as chain-saw-constructed multistory artistically carved log houses. Steve buys one of the lots and builds a geodesic dome house. He hires locals to help him put the kit together, as he can barely turn a screw with a hammer. But he quickly gets a reputation of being hard to work with, or for. For some reason now, Steve complains the dome house always leaks like a sieve and is hard to keep warm in the winter.

He stands up and waves from Helene's yard. Helene runs over to him with a bucket and Steve puts a piece of paper in it. She takes it out, reads it, and brings it back to the stage. Meanwhile Townes is telling his best joke.

"Time flies like an airplane. Fruit flies like a banana!" Everybody laughs because it's such a lame joke.

Helene hands the paper to Townes. "Hold on folks, the money man has just donated one hundred dollars. Let's give him a big hand!"

Everyone applauds politely and we look around for him. He stands up again and waves. I sort of think he's not entirely happy about his new found fame. He looks a little pained for some reason.

*

Helene pulls in well over the six hundred dollars needed to retain a lawyer. Everybody has a great time listening to Townes and Tracey and Tim. It really demonstrates that we are a unique community and we come solidly together to help one of our own.

Now Cloud has a good defense and it seems the coffee cup in question passed between several hands before getting to Don. Also, Don drank two cups that day and one had nothing to do with Cloud. Cloud kept his mouth shut and, in the end, the local prosecutor reduces the charge to a lesser degree; he pleads guilty to criminal mischief and gets 90 days in Gunnison County Jail.

He's pretty much the only occupant and it turns out the jail is run pretty loose and he soon gets to know the jailkeepers, who are paid local citizens, and he ends up getting lots of perks. A nice local mother makes extra money on the side by cooking homemade meals and delivering them to the jail every day. He becomes the chief groundskeeper for the county building, mowing the big lawn and planting flowers around the grounds.

We visit whenever we go to Gunnison and he's usually outside working or just sitting on the courthouse steps watching the people pass by. It doesn't seem like prison at all, as he seems to have the run of the place. He gets good food, lots of exercise, and plenty of sleep not having to hit the bars every night. It kind of turns into a rehab vacation where he cleans up his body, makes new friends, and has a good time doing time. Justice, mountain-style.

Don gets the hint pretty well. He no longer goes looking for crime and instead stands back and only gets involved when he absolutely has to. That's all we can expect. So he keeps his job, but he now has a dream it seems that steers him in a much better direction.

~ 9 ~

MOUNTAIN MEN WITH WHEELS

Things were moving along for the boys and girls of Crested Butte. Not being satisfied with just the best fucking powder skiing anywhere in Colorado, somebody gets a bright idea to push skiing into a new realm or two. There's a picture hanging on the wall of the Nickel showing the snowshoe club of Lake Irwin in 1892. Above the door at the Grubstake is an old wooden ski that looks more like a sled for a fat snake. Inspired by how fucking crazy they were in 1892, our skiers in a drunken and drug-crazed moment decide to ski down a 60-meter ski jump with alpine equipment, just to see how far they can fly. Another group decides to use skinny skis to go up to the top of the mountain and then take the shortcut down by skiing avalanche chutes, trying to stay in one piece. They survive by bringing back the Telemark turn, which they regularly display on black diamond runs, making collisions with *turkeys* almost a certainty.

The testosterone displays of skimanship gets so bad, there is an unofficial contest in town to see who can be the last person to ski the face of Red Lady before it runs each year. The ski area runs are for the wealthy and the faint of heart. All the mountains and wilderness areas around Crested Butte become an instant winter playground for the well-equipped bold and brave. Almost every week, someone organizes a group who don skinny skis for the trip up the mountain and then swap them for the alpine skis they have strapped to their backs for the ride down. Avalanches become a nuisance and some locals, Don Bachman among others, goes back to school studying of all things, snow on a non-horizontal surface.

And when they aren't doing that, because it happens to be summertime, they try their hand at coasting bicycles down long mountain roads. Not just nice mountain roads...after all, what's the fun in going fast on asphalt? Might as well be on a motorcycle. Instead, they choose the numerous dirt roads and hiking trails around the area that have big vertical drops with crooked, rocky, rutty, and slippery conditions, rattling teeth right out of heads, on the way to the bottom. The attraction is obvious if you consider skiers are just practical users of gravity on snow...so why not dirt. too?

Hitchcock takes it to a new level when, because he can't afford one of those new fancy skinny-tired touring bikes, he goes to the local junk yard in Gunnison and finds a couple old Schwinn frames and wide wheels—enough to put together a working '50s bike, coaster brake and all. He adds one refinement, though: high rise BMX handle bars, or Jesus bars, depending on your social background, which makes it a truly awesome and unique machine worthy of attention.

Plus, when you put these homemade babies head-to-head with a skinny-tire consumer bike on a dirt road, the flimsy road bike doesn't have a chance of surviving. Bikes here have to be rugged and wheels have to be beefy to handle the rugged terrain that make up our roads. The old fat-tired bikes of the '50's prove ideal for '70s downhill mountain coasting by bored skiers in the summertime.

When he rides it around town, he sits up high and haughty with the Jesus bars. He can easily pop wheelies, hopping over the curb from street to sidewalk and back. Everybody laughs and makes fun of his clunky mode of transportation, but it proves its worth in bar hopping. It resembles an adult version of the popular kids' bike with small wheels, raised handle bars, and a banana seat. It somehow gets dubbed a *klunker,* and the legend is born.

Hitch has that spark of Butte madness, and just by ignoring everyone's criticism, makes it a Butte thing; something newly invented by one of us, can only be had by scrounging and assembling it yourself, making each one have a unique and one-of-a-kind look, and instantly identifiable as to who owns it. Without a doubt, it becomes a symbol of one's identity and an icon of being Butte-cool. Now everybody has to own one. I put one together and paint it black. Susie buys one from Archie.

It's not long until every last old fat tire bike in the county has been grabbed up, cleaned up, straightened up, and made to look and work more or less like new. For a while, it's hard to find any old fashioned 2-1/2 inch tires and tubes anywhere near Gunnison. Special trips are made to junkyards in Denver and Pueblo, which brings back enough parts to equip about twenty more people. They form themselves into the informal Grubstake Biker Gang and start hauling them in pickups to the top of nearby mountain passes and then coasting them back down to town, or as far as they can get. And nobody ever wears pussy helmets.

The rich Aspen cross-country motorcycle gangs are coming over the mountain passes just to brazenly park their shiny titanium machines in front of the Grubstake, giving it a bad name. They smugly have a beer, piss in our toilets, and go right back to their million-dollar condos making jokes about that quaint little pussy town over the hill.

This insult sets a challenge that can't be ignored. Especially by a bunch of down to earth kids who can't afford fancy shit, but are willing to go up against anybody in a contest of senseless testosterone and alcohol-fueled vain glory. And we always put a freaky spin on it.

So, the Grubstake gang decides to return the favor and ride over to Aspen on klunkers and party down at the Jerome, the Grubber's unofficial sister watering hole in Aspen. In the summertime, the shortest distance from Crested Butte to downtown Aspen is over Pearl Pass at about 11,500 feet altitude and thirty some miles by old mining roads.

Usually by July, the pass is free of snow and walkable. But to the Klunker gang, if it's walkable, it's ridable. By two-lane asphalt, it's about 120 miles, even taking the shortest summer route over Kebler and then north through Redstone to Carbondale and then back south to Aspen. The plan is simple and cooked up over several nights of beer drinking and coke snorting while checking the geological survey map for the region.

We decide to ride our bikes in one day up to the base of the pass to a camping area and then at dawn, cross over the pass and coast about 15 miles into Aspen. *Easy peesy.* After pissing in their toilets, and defiling their gods, we'll all pack into several trucks sent ahead to carry us home, and return conquering heroes.

What actually happens, though, something like this. A lot of bikes broke down just trying to get to the camp ground. The truck that brought some bikes up to the pass without breaking down also brought up a couple kegs of beer. A large fire is built and a typical mountain party commences. After midnight most everyone is passed out or well on their way to unconsciousness only to be broken most rudely by a bright and burning sun coming up at 5AM. People huddle near the fire making do with whatever can be ingested to counter the nights celebrations. A few struggle with their bikes pushing them up the last half mile to the pass where the obligatory mass photo is taken. Then the real fun begins as some kind of horrible retribution for alcohol abuse at high altitudes.

The dirt road descends along Castle Creek along a steep slope of rutted switchbacks paved with rocky rubble and boulders marking the sides of the road that are bigger than the wheels on the bikes. This becomes the real test of the klunker maker. If the frame is strong and the wheels avoid the worst rocks, and if the rider can hold on with all the bouncing and bucking until either you rattle your teeth out or your bike comes apart and you're left pushing it down the mountain in the walk of mechanical shame. Finally, a fortunate few make it to Ashcroft where the road turns to asphalt for the last 11 miles of gradual downhill into Aspen.

Just reaching their destination after all that trouble requires an appropriate celebration to commemorate the occasion. More beer drinking ensues along with consuming anything else of a celebratory nature, until people run out of money and it starts to get dark. It's over a three-hour ride back by roads so they load themselves in the truck, bikes and all, and continue as best they can, keeping the party going.

Crested Butte begins to get a reputation among the Aspenites and a few find their way across the mountains searching for maybe a cheaper and more freedom-loving community than the all-mighty dollar god worshipped in Aspen. Among the new residents is one who immediately makes a big impression on the locals. He roars in with a lot of cocaine and shots on the house until his name is well known to everybody. W Mitchell buys one of Doc Smith's houses on Maroon right behind the new firehouse. It has a white picket fence around it, big shade trees, and a nice full lawn in the summer.

He goes about fixing it up, hiring a lot of the local contractors to help. He befriends and becomes partners with Benjamin and Murray, who are owners of the Company Store. They have been struggling to make the store pay for itself but the Tailings bar had turned into a giant loser the first winter it was open and the rest of the store was having trouble making their rent payments with the low attendance by turkeys spending money.

But he's a good skier and makes friends with a lot of the freaky skiers attracted to the Butte. Cocaine is a local societal lubricant and lures the users and importers to become an ad hoc social class of indeterminate qualifications. But it definitely takes money to belong so I stay in my projection booth watching it all happen from the second floor overlooking downtown Elk Avenue.

The Weaz works his way into Mitchell's circle early, providing both carpentry and cocaine. I work for the Weaz and through him I start to pay attention to this strange guy with only one name and no face. Almost seems like a movie script being written in real-time. And sure enough, it gets even stranger, real quick, when the second act surprise plot twist happens.

He buys a house, buys into the Company Store, and buys some lots behind Whiterock, where he builds a two-story industrial building of workshops and offices. Then he buys an airplane and learns to fly. He has a history in San Francisco, having spent time there just before coming to Aspen and his new destiny. He found his true love there, worked as a trolley conductor on the cable cars, and tried his hand at disk jockeying on FM. He spent time in Vietnam with the Marines and time in Hawaii being a bum on Waikiki Beach. He has everything going for him, except maybe good looks, but at a time when its working in his favor, he goes and does a very silly thing.

Now, I'm a pilot and have a few hundred hours under my belt and I know how airplanes fly, and the one thing they tell you right up front: *wings do not lift when coated with ice.* Apparently, he thinks it's only a suggestion. So, in the dead of winter, he decides to take a little trip to San Francisco, leaving early in the morning and taking a full load of skier friends with him. But instead of taking the time to de-ice his plane, he decides that if he can just get airborne, the ice will evaporate or fall off and everything will be all right.

Now, the runway at Gunnison is over two miles long and large enough to bring in jets, which need a lot longer runway at high altitudes because it takes a lot longer to stop a plane with less air resistance; planes must attain higher velocities for takeoff, as well. He taxies to the end and begins accelerating down the long asphalt trying to get speed up enough to take off. But he can't get it to lift; even in the denser cold morning air, the wings just don't have the right shape and are probably too heavy. But Mitchell is not going to look uncool to his friends or admit he's flirting with incompetency. After a couple of tries at taking off, one of his passengers decides to stay behind and go another day.

On his third attempt, he jerks the airplane into the air hoping that by getting it airborne it will reach flying speed and keep going up. Unfortunately, the laws of physics rear their ugly heads and the plane stalls and falls like a rock at eighty miles per hour, slamming the plane's belly back onto the runway. Everybody receives a broken back, but only Mitchell severs his spine in the lower lumbar region and becomes paraplegic. Off he goes to rehab in Denver for nearly a year while he learns how to live with no feeling below his waist...but more importantly, how to pee and poop and drive a wheelchair over curbs.

The news shoots through Crested Butte like the proverbial shit through a goose. A great friend and good source of happy times, practitioner of youthful sin, instigator of freedom to party, and connoisseur of the wild ambition has just been dealt a severe setback. Close friends move into his house and work hard this time to get it fixed up and make it wheelchair accessible. Then the double whammy hits and the boys staying in the house predictably get drunk one night, fail to deal with a wood fire left burning out of control in the parlor, and the chimney catches fire. Before the volunteer fire department can get it put out, the entire second floor and roof is pretty much gone. Another classic *As the Butte Burns* moment.

I am living in the 640 Elk house and getting along doing the Princess and working at the record store. Bleau comes and goes but has been increasing the times between. I'm having to sell off some of my best test equipment and hi-fi equipment to survive. I struggle along, helping where I can at the print shop, trying to get jobs and helping people set up their stereo equipment or repairing TVs and radios. I get a nice one-night gig at the Grubstake using my television projector to project a TV broadcast of the Super Bowl onto a six-foot screen hung over the pool table. About fifty people crowded in to watch—for the first time ever—a big screen color TV in a Crested Butte bar. Possibly first time in the state or country, for that matter.

After finding Dana, we discover we have a lot in common. He hires me to help wire his slide projectors and show equipment so he can operate them all remotely from his new podium on stage. He's building a podium for his show that reminds one of a big cross-country truck grill coming at you with big rearview mirrors on each side which he performs behind, suggesting a truck driver or truck spirit, not sure which. The whole thing is painted orange and black, which under a stage spotlight looks imposing and garish, just like the harsh neon and overly decorative markings along our highways.

I love the way he's using technology to do art and I want to help. We spend a lot of time together working out how to synchronize two or more 35mm slide projectors that he can control while performing on stage. I build him a little Star Trek-style console into the podium so he can fully remote-control his show equipment while performing on stage. He gets very good at synchronizing pictures between the two screens behind him as he sings songs and entertains with outstanding and imposing color photographic images that illustrate his stories and songs about the iconic American road.

He calls it *The Roadshow* and he's the *Ace of Space*, taking the audience on a whirlwind trip across the more colorful and memorable places that America offers along the way. When his stage screens light up with large colorful and crisp images of strange and faraway places, as he says, of faces and places along the highways and byways, it grabs your imagination and you feel like a child in a playground of trucks, roads, and all-night diners. It's a unique show he takes on self-booked tours and limited engagements all over North America. He sometimes drives thousands of miles between gigs. He tries to earn money with his art and perhaps develop more opportunities to do similar work. I see potential and I'm an amateur filmmaker and ex-roadie; he has a roadshow and uses photography, so the matchup is complete.

He travels around in a box van he slightly modified by adding a bunk bed in the back where he hauls all his stage props. I help him build travel cases so he can safely carry sensitive equipment like his slide projectors, the very famous Carousal projectors that hold 60 slides in a circular container that cycles the preloaded slides down into the projector's lens gate. Now he can fade in, dissolve, and fade out between the projectors, giving him complete control over the brightness in each picture. I added high-power dimmers and he is all set to choreograph his performance slide show like a well-orchestrated movie.

I'm minding my own business in the Grubstake, waiting between happy hour and when the theater opens, when Dana walks in with his puffy red down coat, plastic snow booties, and a thick knitted beanie cap.

"Hey, Cowboy," he calls from the doorway. "I'm glad I found you here. I've got some good news. Hang on, I'll be right there."

He stops off at the bar for two draws then comes over to my table. "I figure you might be ready for another one." He hands one of the beer steins to me.

"What's up?" I ask for the hell of it. I take the beer gratefully, clink glasses with him. "Cheers!" we say in unison, and I take a big gulp.

"I've booked my act at a couple of places back east."

"Great!" I respond. "Only two?"

"For now. I want to do these dates so I can work out the kinks in my presentation."

"Your show, you mean."

"My what?" he asks. "My show? You call it a show, like a vaudevillian?"

"Hey, its got music, costumes, some jokes, a little dancing, and lots of stage props."

"You're right. Here's to *the show*."

We clink glasses again.

"Wanna go on the road with *the show*?" he asks, surprising me a little. "The Roadshow?"

I think about it for a second. "Where would I sleep?" I inquire, knowing from years of roadie-ing that the most important part is sleep.

"You can sleep in the back while we're driving. With you helping with the driving, we can rotate and drive continuously until we arrive. Then I've got friends we can stay with. What do you say?"

"I'd miss out on my theater job. I get paid by the show."

"I'll match it. What do they pay you a night?" he inquires seriously.

I have to think about that for a moment. I usually make at least twenty bucks a night and my management tips make it a little better, before taxes. Like I pay taxes or something.

"How about twenty a day, all expenses, and I'll get the Rat to take over at the Princess while I'm gone. I trained him for Labor Day weekend last year when I went to the Telluride Film Festival." I didn't mind a money wash. At least on the road I'll get fed, have some fun, meet new people, and all that helps me over the edge.

"Don't worry, I'll take care of yah." I have to admit, at least he's better than David Geffen Enterprises, the last promoters I worked for with Joe Walsh.

*

I hear stories about what's going on at Mitchell's house while he's away for rehabilitation. The boys admit they screwed up and they try to spend extra time on the project as penance.

Meanwhile, the migration of more trust funders from Aspen keeps driving up the price of property in town. Most of the early Victorian houses are gone and now empty lots are getting new log houses built on them. The boys are getting plenty of work, so the price of coke doesn't go down, especially now that Mitchell is no longer buying drinks on the house and keeping most of the ski patrol and trust funders noses well laced with the other kind of snow.

The Grubstake Gang just looks on in envy, jumping in where we can to participate in the cocaine brotherhood, but otherwise, we're considered the beer and pot crowd. The next step up, literally to Sanchos and higher social status, involves top-shelf liquor and un-stomped coke. The latest pairing seems to be shots of tequila with lime and salt, followed by a nice line or two of Columbian flake. The rumor is they work together and you can fly high all night long and still have something left over for those early morning pairings. The slogan among the rest of us Butte-ers is: *Take a local to dinner and keep 'em till breakfast.*

I work every night, so I end up checking out the bars before going home just for the hell of it. The bars go through three identifiable cycles a day. First, the cheap working-class happy hour crowd gathers from four to eight, them the post-theater crowd spills out for celebrations from ten to about midnight, where the serious drunks take over from midnight until closing and beyond. In the Butte, bars don't just close empty at the end of the night. There is always a group of hardcore committed partiers who stay intentionally until closing and, if invited, stick around for the unofficial graveyard show.

If you're lucky, someone with more money than sense will haul out a bottle of coke after the doors are locked, the blinds drawn, and the lights turned down low. If you're really lucky, there will be more than one bottle contributing to the lines being laid out on the bar. One time, I do not shit you, there was a single line that went from one end of the bar at the Grubstake to the other, some fifteen feet or so. They dubbed it the I-94 freeway, the freeway that goes through Detroit where a famous cocaine movie was made, *Super Fly*. Also, the Grubstake owners are from Grand Rapids, which straddles I-94 halfway between Detroit and Chicago. I've traveled it many times in the snow. Not pretty.

The road is becoming a synonym for freedom. Celebrated in story and song, the open road expresses our hopes and desires, a distant horizon promising a change and a path leading to a believably brighter future, or just someplace else. Some roads end at places like this, but most roads just go on and on as long as you want to wake up in a different place for whatever reason. *Like a Rolling Stone* or *Keep on Truckin'* are mottos of the youth, and for me it's personal. My truck represents my freedom and traveling is sacred like breathing and growing. Together you learn and become better.

*

"Living on the road my friend, thought would keep you free and clean, now you wear your skin like iron, and your breath's as hard as kerosene." —Townes Van Zandt, *"Poncho and Lefty"*

"On the road again, like a band of gypsies we go down the highway." —Willie Nelson, *"On the Road Again"*

"Looking out at the road rushing under my wheels, looking back at the years gone by like so many summer fields. Running on empty, running blind." — Jackson Brown, *"Runnin' on Empty"*

Dana and I drive all night and all day until we land in Atlanta late at night. He goes straight to the people he knows, who put us up for the weekend while he does his show at the local art museum. I sleep late and when finally through with my morning shit, shower, and shave, I wander downstairs where I hear voices coming from the kitchen.

"Is this where the action is?" I call out in advance of barging in.

"Sure, come on in," somebody yells back.

I walk in and Dana is in the corner setting behind a breakfast nook with his guitar in his lap. A big mug of coffee sits in front of him.

"Want some Java?" he asks me with a big smile.

"Sure, let's try that for a while and see what happens," I quip. I spot the couple that welcomed us last night. The guy is standing next to a strange coffee machine. I presume its some kind of espresso machine, as that seems to be the big rage among the young and hip—to drink espresso and eat hot Mexican, actually bastard Texan, food. I've been eating real Mexican food and drinking strong road café coffee for years, so don't really see the big deal. Oh well, *the times they are a cha-a-a-ngin'.*

"I've been telling my wife how Dana and I spent a dirty summer in Spain when he lived there with his wife and two babies. You know each other long?" the guy with the coffee cup asks, as he hands me a steaming cup of black something.

"Thanks," I mutter, and sit down opposite Dana.

"Dana was trying to find his muse. What else for a young Dartmouth graduate to do but get your girlfriend pregnant and then run away to Spain where your degree in art is worth maybe a cup of coffee. Are you an art major?"

"No," I answer. "Physics."

"Wow," he exclaims. "So how did you end up in that little mountain town where Dana says he lives now."

"Nixgoon the budget slasher." I sip the espresso. It's actually good. Real good.

"Say no more," he agrees. "Our art department barely squeaks by. If it wasn't for our traveling artist grant, we wouldn't have the money to bring people like Dana to our university. Our students need to see real working artists today and what they do."

"Art?!" I ask, looking at Dana.

"I don't makes arts, I finds arts," he repeats again. "You know what? I should print up some degree certificates and award them to deserving people. He sweeps his hand through the air as if making a giant document appear. "Master of Finds Arts!" he proclaims.

We set up in the theater of a downtown art museum reserved by the university for their Travelling Art program. A sign by the door says: *Tonight featuring Dana Atchley and the Ace of Space Roadshow.*

We set up his new props with the remote-controlled slide projectors, the podium-looking truck grill, and two giant screens above and behind his head. We opt not to use the house PA system, as they almost always sound bad and are prone to feedback. I hook up his small PA speakers and connect to it a voice mic and an electronic pickup for his acoustic guitar. I do a simple room flattening with a small 6-channel equalizer and we're all set to go. A decent crowd shows up and we kick off on time.

Dana dresses up like a toy store cowboy with dungarees tucked inside boots, a big belt buckle, a leather vest, and of course a big black cowboy hat. I guess it's the image people have of truck drivers. I happen to have three uncles all in the trucking business and they don't look like that, mostly.

Dana begins showing impressive color photos on the big screens from his apparently many travels around the country seeking out all the stuff we routinely see advertised with big signs along the highways, but are too busy to stop and check out. He checks them all out, takes lots of pictures, and makes up songs using the images to illustrate his stories. He has the giant musky fish building in Michigan, the giant bomber gas station in Portland, the hot dog restaurant in Colorado, the big statue of Paul Bunyan in Minnesota, and his favorite, the Cadillac Ranch just outside Amarillo, Texas.

He blends the pictures with clever dialogue, songs, and the whole stage presentation into a seamless experience that keeps your attention riveted to him and the screens, waiting for the next big impressive picture that is going to blow your mind. His last song about the road is the road he used to take home as a young boy with this family after a long day of skiing in Vermont. His father would drive while singing a song of simple desires:

Show me the way to go home, I'm tired and I wanna go to bed
I had a little drink About an hour ago
*   And it went right To my head*
Where ever I may roam, On land or sea or foam,
*   You can always hear me Singing this song*
Show me the way to go home.

He gets a standing ovation. His show has a certain visceral impact. I have trouble calling it art and prefer the new term, performance artist, with emphasis on the performance part. What he does, he does well, and that alone has my respect. He cares deeply and he desires goodness in what he does. It's why I like all artists. They make things better.

We continue on the road trip up the east coast to New York, where he visits some friends at Columbia. We do a small show there on campus with only maybe twenty or so watching. He still puts on an impressive show and they love it. Someone comes up later and complains the art department didn't do well advertising the event or there would have been more people.

We make it back to an empty Crested Butte as the mud season arrives and that means everyone who can leaves town for warmer places. I sit it out with the rest of the common folk and watch as a whole year of accumulated garbage and mistakes come melting out of the big snow banks around town.

I learn the most important lesson of melting snow besides predicting when an avalanche will run: Snow melts from the ground up, not the top down. Some turkeys wintering over for the first time park their useless two-wheel sedans out back and then when spring comes, the snow melts away from being supported by the ground around the car and now all that heavy snow on top becomes a squashing hammer. Many a car has emerged from backyard snow banks crushed like a pancake.

*

I'm sitting alone in the Grubstake waiting to open the theater for the night's showing when in comes a loud mouth screaming drunk being pushed in a wheelchair by a very good-looking tall woman.

"What the fuck is happening, Captain? The ship is rocking and rolling! Somebody throw out an anchor before we capsize! *Wh-oa-oa-oa!*" He makes it through the door over the door step and wheels on in doing a wheely, showing off his chair skills, finishing with a little pirouette in the middle of the room. He spots me.

"Hey! Hey you!" he shouts, looking directly at me. I look around to see if there's somebody behind me, but no such luck.

"Hey, let me buy this yahoo a drink here. He's setting here without a drink. Bar keep!" he yells.

"What are you drinking?" he asks aside to me.

"I'll take a beer," I answer coyly.

"Bring this alcoholic a shot and a shot with a beer back!"

"Hi, I'm Cowboy," I say to the girl, and hold out my hand. She smiles and shakes it. Before she can say anything, Mitchell starts in again.

"Look out Corinne, this guy's dangerous. He claims to know how to make nuclear bombs."

"Nice to meet you, Cowboy. I'm Corinne. I'm Mitchell's friend from Aspen. Do you have a horse?"

"I'm not that kind of cowboy. Who's your friend in the portable bar stool?"

She laughs.

"This is my friend Corinne!" Mitchell interjects loudly, "who I'm sure you've seen on magazine covers. She's taking care of me. I need all the help I can get." He grabs for her, but she dances out of reach.

"Yeah, I can see that," I observe.

"Are you still working at selling dope out of that Company Store shop that fronts as a record store? What is it? Mountain Records?" he demands. Meanwhile the shots and a beer show up.

"I don't call it work," I argue.

"Don't worry, I didn't. How would you like to do some work for me? Here..." he demands, as he shoves a shot glass in my direction and then grabs the other one with his famous two-handed wrist grip he's making famous locally. He throws it down, slams the shot glass back on the table, upside down. "A-a-a-a-h-h-h-h-h-h-e-e-e!" he gasps in something resembling fine torture.

"Here's to yah," I say. I throw mine back and I slam my shot glass down like his. "Damn!" I declare grimacing. "That tastes like shit. What do you need done?" I momentarily wonder if he knows what I'm capable of. Some of my recent capers have been a little hair-raising.

"I bought an RV and I need it wired for sound and CB and whatever else we can think of. Can you do it?" he asks pointedly.

He leans forward and looks to be about ready to fall out of his chair. I see he isn't strapped in, so it's almost a foregone certainty.

"I fucking built a sound system good enough for Grand Funk. It'll cost you twenty-five dollars an hour, plus supplies and expenses."

"Sounds more than reasonable. So, here's what I'm thinking. I want to be able to listen to the sound system with stereo headphones anywhere in the RV. We'll need a tape deck and some speakers and a citizens band radio so we can talk to all the truckers."

"*Whoopee!*" I blandly declare. "When do I fart? Ah, I mean start."

"Right now, you lightweight. I want to go upstairs to Sanchos. You look like a strong young chump. How about pulling me up and I'll buy you another round. Here. Maybe this will get you going."

He hands me a small bottle of coke with a tiny silver spoon on a chain hanging off the top. I know what to do with it and under the table, out of view, I unscrew it, scoop out a big chunk, bend over near the table edge, and take a big snort. I come up sniffling with eyes watering. He signals for me to take care of Corrine. I dip again and hold it near the table edge and she leans far in and does a dainty sniff and comes up smiling and wiping her nose and gumming what she finds. A pro, I see.

"Oh, what the hell. I've got about a half hour before I have to open the theater. Let's do it. It's not like I've only shown movies sober before."

He navigates his chair out of the bar all by himself and rolls down the sidewalk past the new post office to the long stairway going all the way up to the second-floor bar. I flip his chair around backwards and under his direction, pull him up the twenty or so steps to the top. It's actually not that hard, I think, and stay for one more shot before going to work. I'm thinking this guy might be fun to hang with.

For the next few months, I work on his Georgie Boy 32-foot RV. It has a nice 454 cu in Chevy big block like the engine my friend Bill Smith prefers for his '72 Corvette Stingray. He gets it equipped with hand controls so he can drive it. It has a big bathroom onboard that he can access in his chair, and a bed he can get on and off without any help.

I install the latest auto tape deck, Alpine, and a Motorola citizens band two-way radio. I install new speakers all over the front and rear cabins, putting them all on separate amplifiers and controls so the volume can be individually set. I also run cables throughout and install headphone outlets in the wall so he can be almost anywhere onboard and be within plugin distance for his JBL headphones. It's ready for some Rock & Roll partying on wheels.

I learn more about the man-with-no-face and discover he has some more stories that make him do what he does. His former girlfriend in San Francisco, a Hispanic knock-out I'm told, rejects him after losing his face. But her mother, Beatrice or Bea for short, remains friendly and Mitchell adopts her as his mother and treats her in that manner for the rest of her life. Beatrice always has a room in his house no matter where he lives and she often visits just to get out of San Francisco. I often wonder that if Bea's daughter had inherited her mother's nurturing and loving instincts, she might have stayed with him after the first accident and would have most likely prevented his second one that put him in the chair. Just a fun fact brought to you by a keen observer.

I tell him about my trips on the road with Dana and his weird little custom van. When I finish the wiring, he pays me in cash and then makes another proposal.

"I'm going to take a trip in the RV," he announces. Not surprising, I suppose.

"Bea knows about a priest in Mexico that might be able to cure a broken back," he says, without laughing.

I look at him quizzically.

"Do you want to come with me and help drive? You can sleep in the bunk over the front deck and I'll pay you for your time away from the theater."

"You do realize your condition is sort of permanent? I don't think it's going to be fixed by a lowly Mexican priest doling out crackers and cheap wine. You have a better chance to simply wake up some day and wiggle your toes. That could actually happen, you know."

"Nevertheless," he goes on, "I'm going to San Francisco for a medical follow-up and to visit Bea. She has friends in Encinitas who will introduce me to the miracle priest. I'll make a donation and he'll bless me and we'll see what happens. Can't hurt. We'll at least have some fun in Mexico."

The last time I was in Mexico, it was in Juarez waiting for a ton of weed to be delivered to El Paso, after which I flew it on to Ann Arbor. What a fun night I had, me watching Federales watching Gringos watching Federales.

*

Actually, I don't mind another road trip. The Butte is a little boring in the late spring with a lot of the fun people gone. No turkeys around, no money, so no need to keep the record shop open. Only the hard-core poor like Cordley and Susan keep their shop open, no matter. This trip will be in a full-blown RV with a bed, bathroom, and kitchen. This is pure luxury I'm not used to and we're going to Mexico to boot. What can go wrong?

We take off heading west across the great inland desert on US 50. We follow it across Utah and Nevada, where we finally join up with Interstate 80 in Reno, and then it's a quick jump over the Sierra Madres to Sacramento and San Francisco. Bea has a nice little house not far from Market Street near the hills. We park out front and stay a couple days. While here, Mitchell sees his reconstructive surgeon, the one who built his new hands from literally nothing.

I drive him to the hospital the next day and take him up to the clinic. The old doctor comes out and looks at Mitchell in his chair and just shakes his head.

"Most people slow down after their first brush with death," he comments, as he examines Mitchell's mitten-like hands, testing their grip and holding ability. He marvels at how well the surgery turns out. Mitchell has quite a bit of hand manipulating capability and dexterity for not having fingers.

"What can I say, Doc, it's been a challenge for me to be me."

"Well, just consider that one more like the first two and it might be three strikes, you're out!"

"Thanks, Doc, I'll remember that."

As I wheel him out, I begin to think about being close to someone on the high side of probabilities for having accidents and I'm letting him drive. I decide to offer more of my services and for the rest of the trip, I do most of the driving.

We head straight down I-5 to LA where at a gas stop, I call my former high school girlfriend, Linda Olsen, who now lives in LA working as a professional psychologist. We have been coupling up for a few years, as we both attended eastern colleges and graduate schools. She went to Vassar and the University of Chicago, where we reconnected at a student uprising and anti-war demonstration in '68.

She now lives in a tiny apartment right on Venice Beach, the hottest beach in LA for counter-culture characters and youthful revolutionary spectacles. I tell her about Mitchell and our trip to Mexico. I also warn her I'll try to stop by on the way back after the miracle. She's all up for it.

We finally make it across the border and through Tijuana and all the tourist traps to the coastal highway south. After another couple hours we land in rural Mexico, where we spend more time trying to find the address of Bea's friends he's scheduled to meet up with. We find them finally and camp out at their house until the next day, when Michell meets the local priest in a tiny little plain adobe church. For a miracle worker, he certainly has the humility thing going for him.

Mitchell wheels himself into the little church where the small Mexican priest, dressed in common peasant garb, greets us and takes Mitchell aside for a little talk. Apparently, they discuss things like hope and faith and whether the donation is check or cash. Then he blesses Mitchell with some holy water and a lot of waving of the arms and chanting of some Spanish Latin liturgy. Mitchell slips him a hundred-dollar bill, the priest makes the sign of the cross, and we leave.

We go back to Ensenada, the nearest town, and find a wheelchair accessible bar on main street and move in for the duration. I think he actually had some hope up for a little while and it just got crushed after the disappointing conclusion of a sort of sought-after experience. No magic, no easy way out, this is it. Time to lighten up and get serious. That chair is going to be there for a while.

We settle in with a constant supply of Bohemia beers, shots of tequila, and some great fresh fish straight from the local docks. After a couple of hours, Mitchell hands me a hundred-dollar bill and sends me down the street a couple of blocks to a liquor store. I buy about four cases of Bohemia beer at Mexico prices and hide them in the back closet of the RV.

Looks like Mitchell is into smuggling, just like me. Smuggling laws, I claim, are just corporate corruption, fixing who can profit and who can't. Such laws only inflate prices for someone else's benefit. It's legalized consumer fraud and we're just fighting government criminality.

Anyway, I make a mistake and I let him drive north that night and we hit the border at about midnight. I'm sitting in the right-hand chair, half asleep, when he rolls up to the border guard and hangs his head out the left-hand window.

"Good evening," the guard says, approaching the side of the RV.

"Hi there. Good evening to you," Mitchell responds.

"Where are you coming from?" he asks routinely.

"We've been in Ensenada attending church for the day," he replies. I snigger.

"How many people do you have onboard? Are you all citizens of the United States?"

"Yes," he answers, still trying to keep it friendly. "Two, including me. We're both Americans, I think. No, we are."

I think we have it made at this point. It all sounds routine.

"Did you buy anything while you were in Mexico?" he asks.

I think the answer should be obvious.

"Yes, sir," he politely says. "We have four cases of beer in the rear closet."

I'm shocked, as if taking several hits of acid and they all hit at once and somebody punches the down button. I can't believe what I'm hearing! I make hand movements at him, but he's oblivious, waiting for the guard to respond.

"Pull over there under that roof," he orders. "You're going to be here for a while."

I look at Mitchell when he pulls his head back in and give him the hands up shrug and mouth silently, *"What the fuck!"*

"What's wrong with bringing beer into the US?" he asks innocently.

"It's not a federal law, it's a state law, and it's oppressive, and you are supposed to lie and say we have nothing. He was going to let you go when he saw your gimp plate. *Jeez!*"

Sometimes...you get a big surprise from someone you think you know. Being on the road with someone is an intimate relationship that usually results in a better understanding of each other. I have to watch this guy; he acts cool and has the right values, but clearly, he can be easily led astray from doing what's best. He probably slipped into a former life, Marines no doubt, where uniforms force stupidity and unthinking honesty. I'll have to write this one off to my mistake; I should have been driving and doing the talking.

Of course, it comes down to me to have to move all four cases from the back of the RV out to the big trough running the length of the parking area, just for alcohol transgressors like us. I have to open every bottle and empty it into the trough. Instead of prosecuting the hundred or so a day trying this, they just let you pour out all the offending liquor while they search the RV for *wetbacks* and anything else they can imagine. At least they see he is really in a wheelchair and maybe find something better to do.

An hour later, I finally drive away from the border having put Mitchell to bed after the whole ordeal. I make it to LA about two in the morning and go directly to Linda's apartment. I park the RV on the street, check to make sure he's still breathing, lock it up, and go in for a grateful night of relaxing, no-victim sex and a righteous sleep of the vindicated and innocent.

Next morning, late morning, I finally take Linda out to the RV. I unlock the door from the outside and knock on the wall.

"Hey, hope you're up," I yell. "Coming aboard!"

I open the door and let Linda in first and I follow up the steps to the main cabin.

Mitchell is in the kitchen eating a bowl of cereal without even bothering with a table. He's in his wheelchair, except he's stark naked, with only a towel across his lap to prevent burns if he spills something hot. Cereal is pretty safe, but Linda takes it all in stride, shakes the stubby hand, and looks into the face of something resembling the Phantom of the Opera without the mask. He's clearly just out of the shower and waiting to dry naturally. It's a personal habit we all get used to.

"So, Cowboy here says you have a penchant for accidents," she begins. "How do you feel about that?"

"No more than most," he quips. "It just slows me down a little, so I have to do other things instead of the same thing. I look at it as a growth opportunity for expanding my horizons."

"I wouldn't call it physical growth so much as career guidance," I point out. "At least he's learning what he's not good at, like smuggling for instance."

"You're not going to let me forget that, are you?"

"Probably not."

We make it back to the Butte in record time coming across I-40, old route 66, through Arizona, and then a left turn at Gallup heading up to Shiprock, Farmington, and Durango. Take another left turn and go through Silverton, over Red Mountain Pass into Ouray, Ridgeway, Montrose, right turn on US-50 again, and soon we're back home at nine thousand feet altitude and Crested Butte attitude.

As we drive up Elk Avenue, Susie Fisher rides up next to the RV on her klunker and pounds on the side. I stick my head out the window and she's waving at me and acting really excited about something. I slow down and she rides up next to my window.

"I'm glad to see you're back," she yells. "I want to see you, but I have to go open the theater."

"I'll take Mitchell home," I shout back. "I'll be back at my house in a couple hours."

"I'll come see you after the movie!"

That kind of surprises me. We did have some long talks before I left and we held hands in the bar once, but I figured I'd have to jump back into the game and continue my clever, slow maneuvering if I had any hope of bridging the giant social gap between us. She is way above my station but I can't help the attraction I've had for her over almost two years and two affairs. There's just something about her that I can't shake. She causes me to feel things when she looks at me—strange, exciting, and different things, even though I think I'm well experienced.

I walk home from Mitchell's and start to feel something must be wrong when I see the house. The lights are all on. I open the front door and standing in the middle of the living room is Bob Starr.

"I've got bad news for you," he flatly announces. "I'm just doing a job, but Kemp and Cordley want you out of the house by tomorrow."

"*Wha-a-at?*" I sputter incredulously.

"No point fighting it. They took some of your possessions, so don't go blaming me for anything missing. They left you all your personal belongings, but they say you owe them. I'm just here to protect the house. They're gone and they don't want to talk to you. You can sleep in the loft tonight."

I'm confounded. I'm blindsided. I've been bushwacked. They never gave me a hint anything between us was wrong. My heart is shattered. These were two very close friends for over ten years. We did everything together. We even called ourselves a family, looked out for each other, helped each other and supported each other like brothers. Apparently, someone had a change of heart and is too cowardly to confront me face-to-face. I'm both humiliated and furious. This is wrong and I will not be treated so cravenly and cowardly by someone I so openly trusted. I swear I'll get my justice somehow.

Susie bursts through the front door and rushes to me. I'm surprised momentarily and don't move until she grabs me about the neck and body, pulling herself up to my face just a bit, where she kisses me fully and fruitfully. It goes on for some time. I don't stop and she keeps probing deeper and deeper. My emotions explode in opposite directions and I'm literally fractured into opposing emotional pieces.

"I'm sorry," I say, as I let her loose a little. "I've just had all my belongings stolen by the Coits and I'm in quite a mess right now. They're throwing me out of my house. I have nowhere to live. I'm sorry. My problems shouldn't be yours. Leave me for tonight. I have to get it together and I'm just not going to be able to be with you like the way we deserve."

She just looks at me with a sudden sadness that hurts me a little more than what I am already feeling. I kiss her again, lightly, and take her to the door. She leaves, but I can tell she's hurting now, too. Maybe I did the wrong thing. Chivalry might really be dead or just plain stupid. If we are meant to be together, then do it, no matter what. I become determined to solve this little setback tomorrow and then I give myself to her wholly and mentally intact.

I see Mitchell first thing in the morning and inform him of my predicament. He thinks about it for a bit and says he can give me the upstairs guest bedroom if I take care of the fire in the woodstove and help him get around town.

"You got a deal," I declare. "I'm an expert at wood fires and I'll push you anywhere you want to go."

"Take my truck and pick up your stuff. You're on team Mitchell now."

Mitchell with his ill-gotten gains also bought and restored a couple of antique cars. The first is a '38 International flatbed truck. It's dark brown with all new woodwork on the bed and a shiny coat of varnish. I pick up Susie from her room in old man Dawson's house, kiss her brightly, and tell her I'm okay. I'm working for Mitchell. She smiles happily and kisses me back.

"Good," she says with a twinkle in her eye.

We drive to 640 Elk, where I pick up all they left me and head back up town. I stop at the Conoco station to fill up with gas and while there, Joanie comes up and takes our picture with a camera.

"Thanks," she yells to me, while I'm sitting in the front seat.

"You're welcome," I call back. "What are you going to do with the picture?"

"I'm thinking about doing a Batik."

"What's that?" I ask, not having heard of the word.

"It's like a tie-dye painting, but with a picture instead."

"You mean cloth, like a T-shirt?"

She laughs. "Sort of. Stop by my shop and I'll show you."

Later, I do and I end up buying one of the batiks she makes from the picture of the truck in front of the Conoco, even though I can't really afford it.

Susie and I move what little I have left into Mitchell's upstairs bedroom and we show the movie together that night. She comes up to the projection booth after the movie starts and we make out hot and heavy between the reels, but I don't miss even one changeover.

After it's over, we close up the Princess and walk side-by-side, touching hip-to-hip, all the way back to Mitchell's, where we barely make it to my new upstairs bedroom with our clothes still on. We make mad passionate love all night long that pisses off Mitchell. Next morning, he complains he couldn't get to sleep for some reason. We just stare at each other like we've never really seen each other or anyone else before and ignore him.

~ 10 ~

MITCHELL'S HOUSE OF LOVE,
OR HOW I LE

I hurt tremendously from my best friend's betrayal and theft of my belongings. I vow to not let it go. It is one thing to simply turn away from a close friendship, maybe causing emotional pain, but to steal their belongings, which are pitiful and minimal but personal and some necessary for life in the mountains, well, it's just not right. They took my .22 rifle given as a 16-year-old Christmas present by my father. They took my chainsaw purchased with money from an insurance policy loan paid for by my mother. They took my automotive tools, cameras and photo equipment, and some of my stereo equipment. Now I think maybe they took my placer gold and blamed it on their friend.

Cordley avoids me and is not talking to me and I don't want to confront him anyway, knowing how fucking crazy he can be. It's kind of a relief now that I don't have to deal with him anymore. I miss his crazy but entertaining ideas, and he's a smart guy, but something's wrong that only intense and long-term therapy has a chance of correcting.

Susie and I are sleeping together now every night at Mitchell's. I can't keep my hands off her and she welcomes it wholly, and reciprocates just as fervently. We become a disgusting public spectacle in the bars, usually sitting at a corner table next to each other and glued along one side to the point we only have one arm apiece to feed ourselves while the other two interlock our bodies at the hip. Kissing and snuggling becomes our main public activity, disregarding totally anyone else in the vicinity. More than once, I miss a film reel cutover in the projection booth from being amorously distracted by our number one pastime.

"Practice makes perfect," I whisper in her ear. She giggles her shy little-girl giggle and I'm renewed instantly, buoyed by a force stronger than what makes the plants grow, the sun shine, and the rocks fall.

I immediately assume we have an understanding of exclusivity. She is highly desirable, I think, very popular with lots of friends, both male and female. She says she has just broken up with a skier in town I know who owns a house on Sopris. I didn't realize it while I lusted for her and he seems an ordinary nice guy who likes to ski and can afford it. I'm not threatened by him, knowing his reputation for women passing through his house—often and quickly. Maybe she just needed a place to sleep. I try not to think about such things. She rents a room from Dawson on Elk right now.

I'm always uneasy around strangers, especially ordinary stupid conservative people who haven't a clue about reality or truth or awareness. I communicate and dwell at a fairly high level of intelligence, critical thought, and deep analysis. It usually takes someone of the same caliber to even keep up. I have no patience or motive for validating the ordinary common idiot, full of half-truths, out-and-out lies, and no consistent system of well-founded knowledge for self-guidance. The unaware do not deserve our attention just because they exist.

I'm reading Hunter Thompson's latest book, *Fear and Loathing: On the Campaign Trail '72*, to Mitchell each morning when he has to lie in bed, sometimes for hours, waiting to shit. He can't control it nor feel it, so it all depends on having a very regular food schedule and then a little relaxation and a tickle or two. Out it comes eventually. I sit on a chair just inside the door reading the book, while Corrinne hovers over him with clean towels and a washcloth. I don't even give it a thought. It's just the new ordinary for my friend Mitchell.

What is important, is Hunter understands people and the real politics in this country, as do I, and Mitchell seems to be getting enlightened by it, using his morning ablutions to increase his knowledge. Having been a jarhead and then a player, he might have missed a few important changes in the last few years. He says he gets it, just as any intelligent and aware person would say, but I still think he carries old baggage that pulls and pushes him in confusing directions. He claims he's aware of such things, *but really*? He doesn't have a solid foundation in science and his formal education is minimal. He's gregarious by nature and can bullshit with a straight face, forever about nothing, and keep people listening enthralled. I've got to be careful. Such people can become demigods.

Susie's and my public behavior surely announce to the world of the Burning Butte that we are a mountain couple and all other potential interlopers and naysayers need to back off. I don't know of any in particular, but she does have a lot of loose and free-sex ski buddies, both male and female. Hopefully, they will get the message and leave us to develop our relationship without interference. We're sleeping together every night until, one night, things turn suddenly weird.

I have a night off from the theater, but she has to work. I wait for her to show up after work, but she doesn't come home. By 2 a.m., I'm freaking with hurt and fury, not knowing what to do and feeling totally vulnerable to something fearful. I over-react. I am up all night worrying and wondering, afraid to do anything that might reveal something I dearly do not want to know. I finally go looking for her about sunrise, scared to death of what I might find. My imagination is running wild with the darkest of thoughts, ranging from out-and-out cuckolding to just plain *she doesn't give a shit about me.*

I can sleep with anyone anytime I want, she might say, and then tell me to get lost. I seriously doubt I could handle that. I don't know what I might do. It reminds me of a situation in Ann Arbor where my drug smuggling partner began fucking my girlfriend behind my back while I was away doing research at NCAR in Boulder. They became so blatant I finally caught them in bed together. I held up a loaded revolver and explained to them what a possible fatal mistake they had just made. Then I shot out the ceiling chandelier, leaving them covered in glass shards.

Susie usually hits the bars after work, but then what? I hesitantly go to her place and creep slowly upstairs to her small bedroom on the second floor. Nobody locks their homes at night; they might not be able to get back in if they're too drunk.

She's in bed, alone, with a terrible hangover. I immediately think she must have deliberately chosen her bedroom, because she wanted to be alone with somebody else. Maybe I love her because she's easy, and just as easily as we fell in love, maybe she can fall out to do it with someone else at the moment. We have a new culture with new morals and I'm not sure what they are practicing back in Connecticut.

"What the hell are you doing?" I growl.

She doesn't move for a second and then makes a moaning sound. She tries to turn over.

"Why didn't you come home last night? Is there something I need to know?" My guts are churning. I feel nauseous, hurt, and furious, all at once.

"I got drunk with friends," she mutters out from under a sheet. "I forgot."

"You forgot where we sleep?" I ask incredulously. "How can you do that?"

"I dunno. I just did." She rolls over and opens her blankets revealing her gorgeous naked body. "Shut up and lay down." She looks at me smiling that beautiful innocent smile, just like the one when I first met her.

"I can't. I'm too upset," I blurt out, not sure of what I'm saying. I want to lie down and just cry in her breast, but I'm a man, and men don't cry where I come from. It's a sign of weakness. And that's how I feel: weak, drained, wanting to collapse. I sit down on the bed facing away from her.

"I can't take these feelings," I confess. "Last night, I couldn't sleep because all I could think about all night long was where you were."

She reaches out and touches me on the waist. "I'm sorry. I haven't forgotten us. I want you. I just didn't think...I mean, I thought you wouldn't miss me for one night."

"What?" I turn exasperated. "How can I not miss you for a night?" I turn to her and I'm close to tears, but trying to squeeze them back. "Susie! I love you! Do you know what that means?"

"Yes," she says calmly. "I love you, too. Haven't you been so drunk all you can think about is whether you can make it home without throwing up or walking into the creek?"

"So, you walked all the way down here when you could have come home to me, which is much closer."

"I was on automatic pilot and it took me to the bed I remember the best, mine. Now, lean over here and kiss me before I throw up again."

She lifts up as high as she can in her small bed and I look at her beautiful face and innocent, but sodden eyes. I become overwhelmed by raw feelings again. I want to cry and I want to squeeze her, hard. I still feel pain, but now I feel shame, as well. I want to kiss her and forget the whole thing, but the pain is many hours in the making and can't be so quickly soothed. I kiss her, hard, thrusting my tongue into her accepting mouth.

She grabs onto my body and pulls me towards her. I fall over sideways, facing her.

"Don't ever do that again," I whisper in her ear, and then bite it. I nibble down her neck and kiss her all over her throat. "I just don't know what I would do if I lost you. I've never felt this way with anyone before."

"Me too," she says, "I love you, too." She kisses me hard and this time she's the one probing my mouth. She pulls back and grabs me by the head and says, "I won't forget where your bed is from now on."

She returns to the kissing and she slowly starts undressing me as we dance with our tongues and grope and feel and smooth and hold tight our bodies on a tiny little bed, early in the cold grey dawn of Crested Butte. We hold each other tight and say nothing for the rest of the morning. She falls back to sleep in my arms and I just hold her, wondering who she really is, and if I can survive this kind of love.

*

I can't get it out of my mind, what happened to me that night. I haven't had such strong feelings in my life. I thought I had been in love before, with another Susie. Susie *One* hooked up with me my senior year at Lake Forest College, but her parents didn't approve of my liberal politics and long hair. They tried locking her away from my influence, but after a while, she rebelled and moved in with me in Ann Arbor. We spent a glorious summer together and at the end, I flew home to visit my parents, and while I am gone, she decided that her new sexual freedom included nailing the first horny boy she encountered while I was gone. I was considering asking her to marry me just before she admitted to the frivolous affair, like sex meant nothing.

I felt hurt then, but not like this. Now I feel strange, alien, out of control, basically not me but me anyway, all at the same time. I'm doing and thinking things that I don't understand. I'm judging my lover by my standards of commitment and respect. *Is that wrong?*

She says she got drunk with friends and by habit staggered home to her bed. *She forgot?* I might have believed it if she said she didn't want to wake me. But she knew I was waiting for her and she either forgot or didn't care. *Which?* I am aware of her local reputation for being somewhat of a space case. She says she's sorry and will not do it again. But my fear lingers after the makeup sex.

*

"Cowboy, look what I found," Susie calls out from the attic hatch in the projection room. The little half door on the left side of the room runs the full length of the theater above the auditorium ceiling, all the way to the stage. I suppose at one time somebody might have used it for that purpose, but now it's full of crap from the last fifty years and Susie decides to clean it out. She emerges with a cute little dirt mark on her forehead. I lean in and kiss her and then lick her dirt mark and use my finger to rub it off. She smiles brightly and kisses me right back.

"Look!" she says, holding up a bunch of folded posters. "There must be dozens in here. Let's check 'em out and see what we have."

Her excitement is infectious. I smile at her and marvel again why someone so wonderful even talks to me. I don't feel like I deserve her, but she says she loves me and I'll go with that.

"Wow!" she exclaims, "it's *The Big Sleep* with Bacall and Bogie. Can we put it up in our bedroom? Please? Just look at it. It could be us."

"Sure, Babes, what else you got?" I say with my best Bogart imitation.

"Here's one. What do you think?" I look at it. *The Lost Weekend*

"Fitting, maybe."

"Let's go put them up right now," she says excitedly.

I look into the doorway she just came out and spot something interesting. It looks like a miniature version of the big 35mm projectors we use with bulging carbon arcs attached for producing brilliant white light, but the front end looks more like a conventional high school 16mm projector. I crawl in far enough to get a better look at it. What I see is amazing. It looks really old in that it has a lot of cast iron and good ol' WWII steel. It looks sturdy and I wonder whether it still works.

"Come on, dear, let's go put these up," she calls back to me.

"Coming, sweetheart!"

*

When I went to undergraduate school, I learned just as much from my after-school studies as I did from my formal work. I majored in Physics and Philosophy and Drama, but I also helped break the master lock code system for the entire campus and in so doing, learned a lot about tumbler locks and how they work and how to open them surprisingly fast.

I also studied machine shop practices and metal working techniques. Who says a college degree can't be useful? Give me a well-equipped machine shop and I could make a passable nuclear bomb. As it was, I actually built a polarized proton source for large proton accelerators while an undergraduate, which is what got me a summer internship at the Nuclear Research Institute in Karlsruhe, West Germany and later, a full ride at Michigan's Rackham School of Graduate Physics. I'm a pretty smart guy, but hide it pretty well.

I still practice my skill of lock picking by refining the design of my own lock picking tools. I pick up broken teeth from street cleaners in big cities like Denver and use them to make the pressure key necessary for fast picking. I also collect loose keys, which I examine and determine whether there is a master key system or just ordinary random tumblers. I had one left over from when I worked with Cordley in his print shop. It was for the rear door to the Company Store.

I figure he would have changed the lock to the indoor shop, so the only way to get in would be to pick it. I also know that Cordley keeps his photography equipment and various expensive lenses in the shop, behind the counter in a cabinet.

I watch the weather reports and decide it's a perfect time to take my vengeance. I wake up at three in the morning, a special morning I have been waiting for, for some time. I slip out of bed with Susie still asleep next to me. I hope she doesn't wake while I'm gone, but I'll have to take the chance. This is it. It's now or never.

I put on my clothes and leave by the back door. It's cold and dark. Snow is predicted to start any moment and it feels like it. I work my way around to the back of the Company Store and unlock the back door. I go down the dark hall to their shop door and surprise, surprise, it's unlocked. I quickly go to his hiding place and grab his whole bag of photo equipment.

The illegal guns he recently purchased are also there in a similar gym bag. I shoulder the two bags and leave by the back door, relocking it, and taking the bags across town to the old wooden water tower at the end of Whiterock. I quickly dig a hole and bury the camera bag enough to make it disappear as soon as it starts snowing. I take the guns and one lens with me, the one I bought for the film we made in Lake Forest. It's an Anginous 10:1 zoom lens worth well over a thousand dollars. It's built for the Éclair camera and is much preferred.

I zigzag my way home noting the snow is starting to fall already, right on cue. I'm careful not to leave any visible tracks.

I stash the guns and lens in a nearby abandoned coal shed and go back to Mitchell's. Susie is still asleep and she doesn't wake when I slip back into bed. We wake together, late in the morning, have leisurely morning sex before breakfast, and I act really dumb when the marshal comes knocking on our front door around noon.

"Hi, can I help you?" Susie asks her. It's the redhead female marshal again from my fishing ventures.

"Is Cowboy here?"

I open the door wider so she can see me standing behind Susie.

"We have a report of a robbery at the Company Store. Cordley says all his cameras have been stolen out of their shop."

"Really!" I say acting surprised. "Did he lock his door? He sometimes forgets, you know. I've warned him about that many times."

"The building was locked," she informs us.

I look behind her and point, "It should be easy to track anybody in this snow. Did you check?"

"We didn't find any tracks, so not sure how they got into the building or when."

"You know," I suggest, "maybe he lost track of where he hid the stuff." I tap my head with my forefinger. "You know Cordley."

She stands there for a moment not sure what to say next. She's probably thinking that indeed Cordley has a reputation and this smells like a personal Crested Butte thing. "Okay then, if you hear anything let me know." She turns and leaves.

"Sure will!" I yell after her, and Susie closes the door.

"Who's at the door?" Mitchell yells from the dining room.

"Cordley seems to have lost some stuff and told the cops it's been stolen," I yell back. I walk into the parlor where he's doing his usual ritual, sitting in his chair naked with a towel across his lap, going through his daily mail and smoking a joint.

"I let you yahoos move in and then the cops start stopping by," he jabs. "Not you, Susie; you're welcome here anytime. You and your sister, Connie, are angels and I dearly love you both. But you..." he leaves off.

I quote Hunter: "In a closed society where everybody's guilty, the only crime is getting caught. In a world of thieves, the only final sin is stupidity."

Over the next few days, Kemp and Cordley slowly come to the conclusion that I've got the upper hand and they are going to have to talk to me if they are going to get Cordley's cameras back. Cordley calls me.

"You son of a bitch! I want my cameras back! That's my livelihood. I can't work," he complains.

I have no sympathy for a back-stabbing friend-fucker. Besides, I know for a fact he makes nothing from photography and lives solely on his small trust fund and Susan's work in the print shop. She does pen and ink drawings of all the old buildings and popular local sites, prints them on small postcards and posters, which sell reliably to the turkeys. She pays all the bills.

"Return all my stuff and maybe you'll remember where you lost yours," I calmly suggest and hang up.

Two days later, Kemp shows up in town with all my stuff in the back of his new pickup. The .22 rifle is broken and doesn't work, the chainsaw is missing a chain and in bad shape. The rest of the stuff I just box up and put on Mitchell's flatbed and drive it all back to his place. I feel vindicated because the look of pure hatred on the part of the Coit brothers having been bested by someone they thought they could just run over is priceless. Karma can sometimes be a bitch or an angel depending on your moral position, or lack thereof.

The thing that bothers me the most about our breakup is the realization that there really is a caste system in this society and in this age. We as a community should and *do* know discrimination is wrong and totally counterproductive. It squashes all ambition, opportunity, and hope for the future. Class distinctions create only despair and permanent loss, wasting human life and causing extreme frustrations and eventually bloody revolutions. When only a small segment of our world's society has all the resources, all the opportunities, and all the rewards of life, which they closely guard and keep within their sole confines, then we are left with only the certainty of waiting our turn to be eaten. That's the definition of being a fool, a chump, a *choach* in the local vernacular. Therefore, anytime you can do something to level the justice field, it is both righteous and proper.

I gain from the deal a nice lens that I send to Linda and have her sell in LA for eight hundred bucks. The two guns Cordley got for just about nothing, and I'm sure he won't miss, become my secret private property. In any case, I'm ready for a winter of new and different people for friends, a new lover whom, I hope, will be my last, and a strong desire to make something of myself in the town I love.

I need to make some serious money if I'm ever going to have any hope of overcoming the rich-poor strict segregation here, secure a financial future, and be accepted by Susie's rich relatives and friends. It doesn't skip my attention that when they talk about new people arriving in town, it always goes directly to how much money do they or their family have. Looks come second, and somewhere way down the list is smarts, morals, and awareness.

*

The first big snow comes and I help out at Mitchell's by bringing in a huge amount of seasoned peach tree wood from Paonia to feed his new high-tech stove in the parlor. The dining room area has been opened up to a large parlor room with an alcove behind the stove where Mitchell spends most of his time when he's not in bed or out drinking in the bars. My job is to keep the fire going night and day so we can claim to be some kind of natural renewable energy-efficient house during a big oil and gas crisis.

No fucking problem. I love it. I fed two woodstoves when I was a kid in Oregon, actually logging the timber from our own property, cutting it up myself, and stacking it nicely beside the house. This is old hat for me and it's done with deep satisfaction. I love a warm house in the winter.

The stove Mitchell installed is the first of its kind from a new company called *Vermont Castings.* Murray Howe, an original investor in the Company Store with John Benjamin, sells his share to Mitchell, and reinvests it in a start-up wood stove company back in New England. Damn smart move I think, given the times, and Mitchell throws some money into the venture and as a perk, he gets one of the first new stove models off the assembly line. Now it's mine to play with and report back to the factory how well it does in the high Rockies.

It's pretty simple and uses the old tried-and-true Franklin stove design, which can be opened up like a fireplace for a decorative fire, or in this case, closed and sealed into a high-efficiency wood burning system. The physics is extremely simple seeing as all they did was make a clever air-tight stove so the rate of burning is strictly controlled and a long internal smoke path from the slowly burning wood chamber though a couple of back-and-forth smoke paths across the width of the stove, allowing the hot gases plenty of time to completely burn and transfer most of their heat to the stove surface areas and thus into the room air, rather than going up the chimney.

Every physicist knows that the efficiency of any thermodynamic engine is dependent primarily on the temperature difference between the incoming and outgoing gases. The higher the outgas temperature the less conversion to internal heat or work and therefore the less efficient. There are lots of sealed stoves on the market, including a really simple barrel-looking one by Ashley that only costs a few hundred dollars. Lots of cabin dwellers all over Crested Butte are using them very successfully to heat their homes cheaply. Vermont Castings stoves just looks better...and cost a helluva lot more.

The next job assigned to me by Susie for the winter is to learn to ski. I currently can't even stand up on skis and haven't a clue how they work, or more importantly, how they turn. Long boards tend not to steer all that well when forced to.

One day, Susie just looks me in the eye and says, "Stand up and hold up your hand and bend your wrist down."

I do so, thinking it's the beginning of some new kinky maneuver, but she holds her hand up beside mine and that's it. "Come with me," she commands, and we ride our bikes over to Baggin's house. In his mud room are a bunch of skis. She goes down the line and stops at some silver skis that seem a little fat and long to me.

"Here, stand here and hold your hand up again." I do, and she holds the skis up next to me and says, "These will do."

She grabs a pair of ski poles with a sticker saying they were from Lake Placid Rentals and we take them back home. Apparently, the ski patrol inherits skis all the time and if you know someone, there is always surplus equipment available for those pesky personal emergencies.

We travel to Denver in September and stay with one of Susie's sisters who lives there with her husband. She's surprisingly not a big skier fanatic like most of the rest of the family. Susie takes me to the annual ski equipment tent sale and we find me boots and a down ski jacket. Next, she helps me pick out a complete skinny ski setup with some new Rossignol edged skis, big basket long poles, three pin bindings, three-pin shoes and, of course, gaiters to keep the snow out of my shoes.

It's all strange and expensive for me, but I have to do it. My love depends on it and besides, it's something I always wanted to do, mostly because it was forbidden to our social class of poor who can't afford the equipment or the lift tickets. It's a symbol of escape into a better life. A life where fun and sheer joy of being alive are paramount and fuck the common man worrying about their next measly paycheck. I consider myself an official ski snob now.

Alice, Susie's sister, is really nice and down to earth. I like her right away because she pokes fun at herself for being part of the frugal class and shops at "Tar-jay," the latest white-assed store for the Walmart crowd. She knows she is a part of a very big family with a lot of money, somewhere, but she's proud of not having to rely on it and instead makes her own way with her husband who works to support his responsibilities like the rest of us.

She makes jokes about it and I begin to see the inner workings of the wealthy are not all that straightforward. Some are more inside than others, even in the same family. That seems strange to someone who has lots of relatives and we do a lot of sharing, helping, and pursuing a better life together. We treat everyone the same and we don't play games with our own family members.

It's already December and there's about a foot on the ground at the top of the lifts, but still only a couple of inches at the base area and in town. We are all expecting the big dump that usually occurs right around the middle of November, no later than Thanksgiving. But it comes and goes and around the tenth of December, a little snow falls and we all get excited and then, nothing.

Christmas comes and there's no snow on the ground, just a sprinkling of frost. The ski area is screaming with cancellations. The lodges are all empty. There isn't enough snow at the base area to ski to the lifts. Worse, the kids who are usually skiing every day can't, and people depending on a job based on skiing soon run low on money.

Susie and her friends, including my friend the Griff, have nothing to do. The bars are still full with locals every night, but the working stiffs are being careful how much they spend and the trust funders are buying more of the pitchers. I'm in the Grubstake with the Griff and Susie lamenting our current fate.

"You know, Cowboy," Griff announces to me loud enough for the whole bar to hear, "This might be your lucky winter."

"How so, oh mighty one?" I respond accordingly.

"Well, since you and Susie are a thing now, you're going to have to learn to ski. And I'm the guy who can do it."

"Susie's doing just fine. I can stand up on the skinny skis and we practice a lot up at Lake Irwin."

"*Cheesh!*" he sputters disdainfully, "that's not skiing. That's walking. Look around you...." He leans toward me and points around the room. "All these people in here are the best skiers and ski instructors in the world. They've got nothing better to do right now and I bet they can teach anybody, even you, how to ski in one season."

Somebody at the next table shouts, "Yeah!"

I look around, but don't see who it is.

"I can get you into the official Mt. CB ski class on the hill," Susie says. "They need more students and the instructor is my friend Joanie."

Griff leans into me again and while indicating Susie sitting across from us says, "See that girl you've been following around lately like a sick puppy? She has a twin sister in Aspen who is an advanced ski instructor along with another sister and her husband who work on the ski patrol."

He grins at me in that satisfied Griff look of righteous drunkenness. I guess it is a done deal. I've got to figure this gravity and snow thing out and while doing that, get an formal introduction to the rich ski bums from Greenwich.

First, as an academic, I find an old book in Mitchell's library written by some European blond, Nordic-looking guy with antique-looking skis and bindings, called *How to Ski*. He talks about weighting and unweighting. That explains all the up and down movement I see every one doing. So, the theory is when a ski is unweighted, it is lifted ever so slightly from the snow and then it's easier to turn. Once you have them pointed in the right direction, you apply the weight you had removed before and the skis bite into the snow and go forward in a new direction. That sounds doable, in theory, but what about steep slopes? If I unweight the ski there, I'll be free falling.

The next thing I do is take the official beginners class given by Joanie on the hill. The first day, we don't even go outside but do our workout in the lodge. We practice holding a serving tray in front of us, walking around offering hors d'oeuvres to others. By offering the tray to someone, you shift your weight to the front of your foot and now you can pivot them by lifting the heals off the snow and moving them to the opposite tack. That answers the slope problem, but now it's time to practice on the real thing.

The ski area is spending a lot of money shipping in expensive snow-making equipment and trying to make enough snow for the lower area so they can at least operate the lifts. There is barely enough snow at the top for some limited skiing and the ski patrol has to go around and mark all the exposed rocks with red flag poles. They soon run out of poles and just start spraying any exposed rocks with orange glow paint. Even that is futile as new rocks appear every day. Experienced skiers resort to using only their *rock* skis. A rock ski is any old ski you don't care about, so if it hits a rock, you don't give a shit. Hitting rocks, though, is a real hindrance to speed skiing, so the ski patrol gets more practice at removing broken bodies.

Susie talks me through getting on the lift and bailing out at the top, because of so little snow, there's quite a drop at the top. She has the lift operator slow it down as we approach and I dangle myself over the edge of the seat and wait to bomb myself onto the mountain. Once I untangle myself from the ramp leading off the lift, I follow Susie close behind and try to do everything she is doing.

She has another technique for turning that's even more weird. She skis across the fall line and when she goes up on a little hump or rise in the snow, she uses the fact that at the top of the little hill, her skis are unweighted both in the front and in the rear, thus allowing her to turn them easily, as if they are about a foot long instead of the normal five feet. It requires a good eye and better timing; one fuck up and you're careening off the little mogul with skis going in opposite directions or you're doing a face plant from crossed tips.

On the gradual slopes, I get into the Alpine rhythm from the book and can see where coordination and timing are essential elements, neither of which I have any talent for. But I can see where music may help with the dancing part. I'll have to look into making a tape deck portable enough to carry while skiing and listen to music with headphones.

On the steeper slopes, I discover I have a problem common among anyone riding motorcycles first and skiing second. On a motorcycle, one always leans into the turn and away from the direction of centrifugal force. It's only natural then to try to oppose the direction of falling by leaning into the mountain.

Not by a long shot. It's exactly the opposite of what you're supposed to do. You have to lean away from the mountain and literally put your body over the downhill side of your balance line. But when you do, you naturally turn your skis in such a way that the edge digs into the slope catching the snow and stopping your fall. Now you can hop up and down using your edges to catch the mountain long enough to unweight and turn the skis back and forth rapidly. You're only partially skiing and partially falling. If all goes well and you link a bunch of tight turns and you pop out at the bottom, you live to ski another day.

I'm becoming quite the connoisseur of snow. With all my falls, I'm eating several buckets a day. I quickly develop a taste for the white unskied fluffy stuff and try to stay away from the gritty brown or savory yellow. Don't say it doesn't happen. There are a lot of dogs up there with their masters and I've had to go in the trees once in a while myself. One of my great unexpected experiences came when I watched Susie go behind a tree. She made it look sophisticated and cool. She beams me a big smile while squatting in the snow with her ski pants and long johns down around her ankles. Now if she had done it on skis, I would have been really impressed. Turns out she does that, but only with skinny skis.

I'm skiing, sort of, but I'm missing something very important. I can get on and off the lift without falling and given enough room I can make big sweeping turns and make it down to the bottom. So off we go to Aspen for a weekend of lessons from the rich for the famous.

First, we visit Susie's older sister, Pat, living with another New Englander working on the ski patrol, Dave. He's building a summer home on Martha's Vineyard and has to go to Vermont every spring to help with the family's maple sugar harvest. Poor bastard has to live like a hippie though, just to survive here, so he may be way above me in wealth, but to the average Aspenite, he's still a *day camper*. A day camper is someone who doesn't actually own any property in town, a condo, or live with someone who does.

We camp out on their floor and zip our bags together like we always do when camping, and then spend the night playing tag. It's a little crowded in the apartment because of the high housing costs, forcing many ski professionals to have to bunk together. Susie and I don't care where we are as long as we're together and warm and have a place to shit.

When making love in our bag, we stop in midstride, frozen in place, anytime someone might pass through the room. We quietly giggle with the excruciating pain/pleasure of holding it, and then proceeding with extra fervor when left alone again.

Then Susie takes me to meet Connie. Connie and Susie are identical twins. They don't exactly look very identical to me, but then I'm very close to one of the subjects and can see many differences up close and personal. For one, when I look at Susie, she smiles and I melt with overwhelming love and attraction. When Connie smiles, I just see a pretty girl worldly enough to be dangerous. She looks at me funny, like trying to figure out a crossword puzzle.

"Why are you with my sister?" she jumps right in.

I'm not sure what to say, but Susie steps up. "We both work at the Princess and we fell in love with each other after the show. Mitchell likes him, and we live with Mitchell in his house. I'm teaching him to ski and we need you to let him attend your intermediate class tomorrow while I go skiing with Pat and Dave."

"He doesn't ski?" She looks me up and down.

I'm not sure how twins work, having never known any. I wonder if I'm passing some kind of muster. Do I have to be accepted by both of them to continue?

"Okay," she says simply, and proceeds to show us how to cut up an avocado. *What the fuck is an avocado?*

"This is very healthy," she explains about the unfamiliar green hand grenade-looking fruit. "It's high in vitamin E and C and the good fat. Unsaturated or something."

Susie had warned me that Connie is into healthy living by eating low-calorie veggies and staying skinny. She practices something called Tai Chi; I can only imagine what the fuck it is. Probably something to do with Kung Fu, I think, a big rage on TV.

"Mono unsaturated," I add. "It's the kind of fat that doesn't form cholesterol."

She looks at me funny. "So, this is the nuclear physicist PhD you were talking about last summer?"

"Technically not a PhD yet, but I've done three doctor's degree projects and have published results for all three in peer-reviewed journals. I just can't seem to get them to pay me to write up my final thesis. Fucking Nixgoon cancelled my research budget, so I ran out of money and had to join a rock and roll band."

"You're the roadie, too?" She looks at Susie. "You didn't tell me it was the same guy." She looks back at me and says, "I'm going to have to get to know you better. Want some guacamole?"

"Guaca *what?*"

*

The next day, I show up at the base area to meet up with Connie's class. She goes ahead of us to change in the ski patrol building where she keeps her equipment. She comes out all dressed up in a smart, all blue ski uniform with *Aspen* stapled all over it and finds her class. I kiss goodbye to Susie, who will be finally skiing the whole mountain without having to shepherd me around. Connie herds us onto the ski patrol cut-in gate at the lift avoiding the usual lines, and off we go to the top.

All the ski areas in Colorado have less snow this year. The high elevations are barely open and only the richest areas like Aspen can afford to make snow with giant machines that keep the major runs skiable. Lines are short and the normal crowds are significantly missing. It makes it easier for me to ski without a lot of idiots around to dodge and duck.

There's about ten people in her class, all turkeys except for me. We get off at the top and she takes us to a flat part of the hill nearby and has us ski down below her a little way so she can demonstrate the technique.

"This is all about the hockey stop," she starts off. "When you're going fast, and you will, you can't always stop by making a snow plow or by turning uphill."

"I stop by falling down," I point out. Everybody laughs.

"But that's not recommended when you're at the top of a steep slope.," she adds while laughing with the rest of us.

"So, watch me." She slowly starts downhill gaining speed and then she makes an unweighting that pulls both her skis off the snow just long enough for her to turn them at ninety degrees to her travel and then bring them down, one below the other across the slope digging in her edges and she comes to an abrupt stop spraying clouds of snow out ahead of her. She does it again, only this time, turns them in the opposite direction. You have a choice.

I immediately slap myself upside the head, metaphorically, because now I see how the unweighting actually takes place from a physics standpoint. Skiers take advantage of Newton's first law of motion and realize their center of gravity is high on their body, about lower midriff. So, if you suddenly contract your legs, pulling your feet and the attached skis toward the center of your body, you will not fall right away but continue on in a slightly downward arc of a free-falling body. This gives the skier enough time to reposition their skis off the snow before having to put them back on the snow, arresting their fall and redirecting their momentum in a new direction. If you place the ski edge at right angles to your forward travel, and slide them sideways, you stop. You just have to ride the skis like riding a bucking horse. It jumps and wherever it comes down, you better still be on top of it, literally.

We practice this all the way down the hill, stopping every so often while Connie goes around and critiques each one of us. I get a lot of attention, and before long I'm getting braver and braver, trying my hockey stop at faster speeds and steeper slopes. This was the trick I'd been looking for. Now I can make movements like a seasoned skier. I am starting to feel comfortable on these silly sticks.

After an hour of this, we make it to the base and are given our freedom to ski the rest of the day. Connie takes me back to the top of the hill for another private run. I feel kind of funny being with a girl who looks like Susie, but isn't, and she's seeming way too friendly, like grabbing me around the waist and hugging me once in a while, even kissing me on the cheek. I try to go along, thinking perhaps prematurely that I've been accepted into the family. So far, I'm getting along with her sisters, but then there are about that many brothers still out there somewhere. It's a big family with seven kids, I think.

Anyway, she leads me down the mountain like Susie does, going slow and easy, sticking to the gentle slopes. She seems to be having fun, but I still feel uncomfortable and not a clue why.

At the bottom, I beg off another run and leave Connie to go find Susie and bring them all back to the nearest bar, where I will be waiting. I find several candidate bars, so I select the one nearest the lifts and settle in. Two hours later Susie, Connie, and Pat with her ski patrol boyfriend Dave, walk in, covered in some snow, doing that clunky walk with stiff hard boots and laughing heartily. I hope it isn't about my skiing abilities. I order a pitcher and we all settle in for some après skiing on mahogany ridge.

"Did you hear about the senior captain of the ski patrol?" Connie starts out.

"You mean that new guy from Steamboat?" Dave asks.

"He brought his wife here with him. But he has to get up every day at 3 a.m. to go out and check overnight conditions, run the slopes, and if there's an avalanche issue, he sets the charges."

"I sometimes wish I had that job," commented Dave. "It actually pays a wage you can almost live on."

"Well, while he was out skiing every morning," Connie explains, "someone else was showing up for breakfast, so to speak. Anyway, he came home unannounced last week because there was nothing for him to do with the lack of snow and all. And he caught them in mid coitus delicti."

They all laugh like it's funny to come home and find someone else in your bed fucking your old lady. What are these new age morals all about anyway? We love our new freedoms, but somethings are still the same, like love with sex and vice versa. They think they are just dealing with sex alone with no emotions or responsibilities, but there is way more to it than that.

"There's a new bachelor in town," announces Pat. "You don't know him because he barely skis, but I've had him in my class now for about six weeks. He's very persistent."

"Is that the rich guy from Norway? What's his name? Arnie something?" asks Connie.

"You *have* heard of him," Pat confirms. "I understand he's in the shipping business and owns a cargo ship or two."

"Really?" says Connie with new interest. "So, what's he doing here?"

"Well, he says he always wanted to learn to ski downhill but was too busy running his family business. He bought a garage in town for $50,000 and is fixing it up himself into a small one-bedroom residence."

"You're kidding," Connie says. "Where's his garage? I'll accidentally drop in on him?"

"It's in the alley between 3rd and 2nd."

"Perfect!" she says holding her glass up in salute. "Here's to Norwegians."

*

True to her word, Connie finds Arnie while *accidentally* looking for some place to rent, she tells him. He invites her in and the next thing you know, Connie is bragging about how she's helping him put in a solid wood floor with special tools and so forth. Rich people are always proud of doing actual work. It's that rare for them.

Susie and I go back to the Butte, where I continue my practice skiing. This year's Flaushink celebration becomes a real challenge. There just isn't enough snow for the usual mayhem-on-skis party. So, they decide to use what they have. There is a big-assed mud puddle just up from the base area with a small hill next to it. The snow cats find snow in the trees, dig it out, and haul it down to build a small ski run on the hill leading down to the water. The Flaushink challenge becomes who can ski down the hill, hit the water, and ski all the way across without sinking or falling in the mud.

Nobody makes it, and eventually it just turns into a giant drunken mud fight. It turns out snow is actually optional for mountain people celebrating the coming of spring. Then reality strikes the town and thermodynamics rears its ugly head.

The main water supply for the city that comes from a small inlet off Coal Creek about two miles above town on the Kebler Pass Road suddenly stops flowing. Just about the worst thing that can happen to the Butte in winter time is the loss of water flow. Without flow, the water in all lines below the blockage will quickly begin freezing from end to end. We can lose all the underground water plumbing in the entire town if we don't move fast.

Needless to say, the young clueless real-estate politicians running the town consult the old timers on what to do. They scratch their heads and can barely remember any time in the past with a similar problem. Botsie suggests we build fires in pits above where the water line is buried and hope that over a few days to a week, it might thaw the pipes. He claims that was what was done in the distant past when miners faced similar problems.

Most of the old timers just shake their heads and say they've never seen a year so lacking in snow that the ground freezes down three or four feet. In the old days, municipal water lines were not so necessary, as most homes had small, hand-dug wells under their houses fed off the groundwater from Coal Creek...and so no town-wide freezing problem.

The young people organize themselves and try the fire idea. Meantime, Mitchell's house is without water and Mitchell has big needs for washing all the linens and taking daily baths.

Mitchell and I watch with amusement all the antics that the present town administration goes through trying to fix the problem. They bring in big water trucks and try feeding certain water lines with something warm to keep down any further freezing.

Bottled water is being given away at City Hall, which is just across the road from us. We stock up, but clearly the length of the emergency is getting to people and there's grumbling of incompetence.

It turns out some of the fires lit are in heavy organic layers where old plant life has accumulated over thousands of years, leaving burnable material capable of once being lit on fire, continuing to burn slowly underground for years and sometimes spread for miles before popping out of the ground, surprising everyone. That's what happens here and small smoke holes and fires start popping up all over that section of Kebler Pass for several years afterward. When they did, the hotshots would take a break from drinking and skiing to go up and piss on the surface fires just for fun and practice.

They finally decide to apply the obvious solution nobody wanted to suggest, but it is all they can really do. They lay a new 6-inch pipe on the surface all the way along the underground frozen one. On the surface, they try to insulate it, but with a free-flowing pipe, the water cannot freeze as long as the flow rate is kept high enough. That's also easy. They let it run full blast out the bottom end and just take enough for the town system to stay pressurized. That works, but it is about two weeks later and a lot of houses have burst pipes and the local plumbers, Fritz and Willy Yaklich, are busy for several months cleaning up the mess.

Mitchell and I watch the fiasco with amusement as well as disgust. "Even I could do better than those idiots," he says, and I have to agree with him.

*

Mitchell and I make a couple more trips to Denver, mostly to party with old friends he knows there, but also to get the house equipped for summer. He buys twelve cases of wine, which I store in the little basement hole beneath the kitchen. He stocks up on liquor of every kind a decent bar would carry, and lots of frozen foods like chickens and two-inch-thick T-bone steaks. He's in a partying mood and I know he's on a crusade to get seriously popular and maybe run for town council.

Susie and I keep working at the theater while living with Mitchell. We spend a lot of our free time, though, out in the mountains hiking just about every trail near the town and all the ones between here and Aspen. She shows me where she skis with her friends in the winter and I show her secret lake and how to fish for the wily trout. I buy a collapsible Eagle rod and reel that easily fits in a small backpack and proves to be fatal to the local trout with my trusty Mepps triple-aught gold spinner.

Our favorite hiking ground without a doubt is up Copper Creek to Conundrum Pass where just on the other side is a series of hot springs ranging from boiling to fresh snow melt. People over the years have scooped out and rearranged the rocks to form pools of various temperatures, with the hot water mixing with the cold-water creek nearby. We strip down and splash around for hours naked and free in the wilderness.

What a feeling, being in the middle of a wilderness stripped down to skin and playing like innocent children with no care or worry in the world and nothing to make us feel ashamed or concerned. We're too turned on, tuned in, and dropped out to be bothered by anything. Every time I see Susie naked and playing innocently like a child, careless of worldly realities, I fall in love with her all over again, even deeper and harder. Sometimes my heart feels like it's jumping out of my chest when she just sweetly smiles and flashes her bright eyes at me. I understand the poet's dilemma of trying to put it in words. You can't. You can only feel it and its indescribable.

One day, we're hiking up the south side of Gothic overlooking Washington Gulch and the home of Coney the conehead and his gold claim cabin. Above tree line and about halfway to the top, we stop and have a snack while enjoying the view.

We can see the whole north side of Mt. Emmons, or what we call Red Lady, and suddenly I notice something. There are trucks parked along a new road being built up the north side of the mountain. I look through the binoculars and can make out some earth-moving equipment near the top of the new road just across Wolverine Basin.

"What the hell are they doing over there?" I ask Susie, and pass the binoculars to her. She looks and confirms what I'm suspecting.

"It looks like someone is mining up there." She passes the binoculars back to me.

"I don't know of any old mines in that area that anyone would want to open up," I point out, and study the road more. I can make out wide spots in the road that don't seem to have any purpose outside of providing a level spot for some kind of activity. I take away the binoculars and use my naked eyes now that I know what to look for. Then I see a pattern.

"Look how those gouged out clearings along the road are equally spaced vertically up the side of the mountain," I point out to Susie. "Those are drilling spots where they intend to core drill the mountain. It's how they map out underground ore bodies."

Later in town, I find Gary in the Nickel, sit down next to him, and order a beer.

"How's it going?" I ask.

"Fair. Can't complain," he answers blandly.

"Hey, I was up on Gothic today and we could see somebody building a road up the back side of Mt. Emmons. Do you know what's going on?"

"Oh, yeah. That's Amax," he flatly reveals. "They've been up there for a couple of years now. They have a big claim on the south side of the mountain you already know about."

"You mean that bunch of sheds up there off Kebler Road just above town?" I ask. "I thought that mine was abandoned years ago. There's never anyone there when I've been around."

"Yeah, well they must think there's something there because they're spending a lot of money on security people and gates to keep me out of that area."

"What the hell are they looking for?" I ask.

"Molybdenum," he says simply.

"What the fuck is that?"

"The stuff that dreams are made of."

~ 11 ~

FUCK AMAX

I am extremely proud to be part of the new generation of sexually liberated people. We have been oppressed by the restrictive demigod of banning all sex outside of marriage and not allowing for pure fun at all, too long. How absurd!

Imagine telling a bunch of screaming, drug-laced, Rock & Roll excited youth to not participate in the only thing that actually makes sense in this ugly world. Sex: free, equal, and uninhibited. A celebration of life and essence of sensual wonders. It's time we stand up to the sex-Nazis, who only want to control and direct it to their greedy benefit, and make it clear to everyone. Sex is an absolute human freedom of choice, an individual's choice alone, along with an inviolable veto power, at any time. No restrictions, no condemnation, and no requirements, except do no harm and be responsible. Love and sex are a gift for all to enjoy—while we can, if we can, and where we can. Get used to it.

Get your goddamned government out of my backseat and my bedroom! And that goes for autocratic parents who enforce an unnatural law of not sleeping with your lover in their own home without an official piece of government paper saying you've been licensed to screw. They don't give lessons for the license; they don't even make you pass a test. So why do I have to have one in order to participate in the one human endeavor that should be truly sacrosanct and along with politics and religion, above discrimination? It's clearly un-American to control who a person can or cannot have sex with, assuming of course, we're all consenting adults.

It's also clearly nobody's business but the participants and should be considered as natural and necessary as breathing and pissing. I do not put up with silly rules and often have to gather up my lover in the middle of the night and leave her parents' house because of their ignorant insistence on a formality, violating the trust of their own, when it comes to choosing a bedmate. If they love their son or daughter and respect their choices, then extend that courtesy to their current sex partners. It's only right and natural. Fucking hypocrites.

Dana walks into the Grubstake clearly on a mission. I can tell from his shit-eating grin he's up to something. He walks right up to Susie and me sitting at the bar, enjoying a beer after the nightly show. He pats me on the back then moves to Susie, patting her back as well. It's becoming the age of touchy-feely friendship. I'm not into it except maybe when the lights go off along with the clothes.

"You two are the cutest couple in town right now," he pronounces, as he slips into the seat next to Susie. She giggles her shy girlish laugh, which I know is also a little inebriated, and she adds a blush on cue. "Could I have a draw?" he adds to the bartender.

"You're up to something," I flatly predict. "*Que paso?*"

"Really. I'm happy you two finally got together. I predicted it a long time ago with both of you working the theater together. Just don't forget to buy me a cigar when the time calls for it."

"I'm very lucky to find Cowboy," Susie responds. She pulls my hand around her waist. "He's so different and smart. We work well together." She turns, looks at me with adoration, and kisses me fully upon the lips with a little tongue on the side.

"I still think he's up to something," I joke, as we part labii. "He probably wants to make a porn film, or art film as he would call it."

"Funny you should say that. Wild Bill and I are working on some ideas for later this year when he can come out here and stay for a while. In the meantime, Sunshine Williams has hired me to make a brochure for the bathhouse." He looks queerly at us, quaffs his beer, and proceeds. "I need some photography models. Want to help?"

My brain immediately makes the leap to what he's saying. I have been frequenting the bathhouse since it opened and I have a lifetime free pass for my work getting Sunshine's electrical equipment running. The place is strictly no bathing suits, so he wants us to pose for him in the nude. I don't mind myself, but I have to think about Susie being photographed. On the one hand, it's fucking hot and on the other, it's none of my business, but I also have to consider what message this sends to all the other guys in town, flaunting what I enjoy while they can only lust. It's the old beachmaster walrus syndrome. The old male keeps his females close and well protected, available for his pleasure alone, while chasing away any sniffing Tom, Dick, and Blubber.

"That sounds like fun," Susie pipes up excitedly. She looks to me for my reaction.

Since we've been a pair, we've often gone to the bathhouse, sometimes just to do something different after the show, instead of alcohol. We really enjoy it after a long day of skiing.

Nobody is a prude in the bathhouse, everyone is very adult about the nudity, and as long as I have Susie cornered in the hot tub, I don't mind how many guys imagine what only we know for sure.

"Do I get paid extra for any schlong shots?" I ask seriously.

*

Susie and I walk into the side entrance to the well-lit steamy interior and take our clothes off in the anteroom just off the boiler room and opposite the double-door unisex bathroom. As we step into the business area leading to the showers and the main rock tub off to the left, we see Dana standing stark naked except for his 35mm camera hanging on a strap around his neck. He is talking to Sunshine, who doesn't even have that much on.

Sunshine is a little older than the rest of us, has a little money from a prior life in San Francisco, and cultivates an image of a wise mature woman to be respected and heeded. In this case she brings the message from the ancients stating that a necessity of a healthy and sane society is lounging around a communal bath fully exposed and equally innocent. I think she and the Romans and Vikings might be onto something. Having to see your neighbors all in the same equal state of grim nakedness gives one a level perspective that can't be had anyway else. When pubic hair comes out for air, rank and privilege disappear.

"I thought we could start in the anteroom," Dana begins, "showing the entrance and then follow through the whole experience from sauna to hot tub to cold plunge and then the showers. What do you think?"

"Actually, they need to take the shower first before getting into the hot tub," Sunshine adds with a wink.

Dana looks over and sees us. "There you are! Hi Susie! Do you know Sunshine?"

Everybody knows Sunshine and everybody knows Susie. There isn't much chance that any two women don't know each other in this town. They kind of have their own secret community. It's the new feminist empowering age and they take care of each other just like always, but now with a new more determined and sometimes clandestine purpose. I hope it's just a phase before becoming secure in their new freedoms.

"Hi Sunshine," Susie says, and holds her right hand up about bosom high and waves her hand at her. We haven't adopted the *Hollywood hug* yet when routinely greeting friends. I'm still not sure what *Hollywood friends* even means, except metaphorically. It may assume you're either in the mutual position of love and respect, or stabbing each other in the back. The key is knowing which, and the usual answer is *both.*

"Hi Susie. Hi Cowboy," she says. "I'm glad Dana is using you for my brochure. You are such a great couple. I'm glad you finally got together." This time she goes in for hugs all around and I notice Dana starts taking pictures of our fleshy flounderings.

"Great shots. Guests are greeted by the owner personally," he says for the imagined caption. "Susie, why don't you go into the shower and I'll get some shots of you in there." He indicates the brightly lit and fully tiled shower room just off the atrium.

He later has us both use the big rock tub along with Sunshine and a few other patrons who happen to be here and willing to sign a release. I brought along some water windup toys and he shoots them for fun. He finally puts down his camera and climbs into the tub, joining us.

"Have you tried the cold plunge?" I inquire after he settles into the 104-degree water.

"What's that?" he asks innocently. Susie giggles.

"Come over here," I tell him. I push through the chest high water over to the southeast corner of the hot tub next to the big south-facing picture window eternally fogged, but letting in lots of cold light. "Look," I tell him, pointing to a round hole in the corner of the slate floor about the size of a bicycle wheel. It is filled with crystal clear water.

"When you think you can't take the heat in the tub any-more, just jump in here and your body temperature will be re-set to *Holy cow!* It's quite invigorating."

"Show me," he challenges.

"No problem," I reply. I climb out of the tub, pause as I re-flect on my mortality, and then step into the five-foot-deep hole, plunging quickly to the bottom and covering my head. Immediately, my body goes into a general contraction shock that locks up all muscles as I try to not to scream or suck water. Every square inch of my skin squeezes in on itself tightly shut-ting every pore in my body. I hold it as long as I can as icicles seem to be piercing my skin like a thousand blunt acupuncture needles jabbing at me from every possible direction. I explode back up out of the hole, scrambling as fast as I can to get back into the hot tub. I belly flop the last yard into the pool splash-ing water everywhere. My skin crawls with still more intense tingling, this time soothing and stimulating as each needle is pulled out to exquisite pain and relief.

"That's great! Try it!" I exclaim when I regain the surface and know I've survived.

Everybody gives it a try to a lot of *whoops* and hollers. After Dana tries it, he decides he needs to use the bathroom. When he gets back, he's laughing.

"What's the deal with the bathrooms?" he asks, as he climbs back into the tub.

"According to the health department," Sunshine explains, "we have to provide two toilets with separate gender designated doors. But they didn't say a damn thing about internal walls!"

"Everyone is already naked so what's the point of walls?" Susie points out.

"Not everybody needs to see me at my sometimes worse," Dana points out. "Still, I need to get a picture of it. This is newsworthy."

Before we leave, Susie and I sit on the toilets as Dana shoots some pictures. First, he takes a picture of the two barn-wood doors side by side, each one clearly labeled *Men* and *Women*. We open the two doors and behind each one is a toilet with me sitting on the men's side and Susie sitting on the women's side. Then he moves his camera perspective from head-on to a close-up from the women's doorway. To the right of Susie, there is no wall where one might expect and I can be seen sitting on the men's toilet right next to her.

A couple of months later, Dana shows us a copy of the latest *Playboy* magazine. Inside, in the editorial section, is a small copy of the picture he took of me and Susie in the unisex bathroom under a short news item describing the trend in recent unisex bathrooms in San Francisco and now Colorado. Susie's white skin and pert breasts grab my attention and then I see myself leering from the background. The connection between Susie and me, now published nation-wide, announces to the world what we have sealed in our hearts. I am so lucky to have her as a lover and a friend, and now hopefully a full partner in mind and body and life.

*

I glance over at the red digital alarm clock next to our bed on the second floor of Mitchell's house and see 3:33 glowing in the dark. There's enough light coming through the windows from outside street lights half a block away to see Susie's milk-white naked body stretching out beneath me and arching up like a flower enticing the bee. She's having an orgasm as I feel her body tensing and squeezing my penis. She hooks her arm over my neck and pulls me down, squeezing her breasts to my chest. We kiss long and searchingly. I pull back slightly and look at her eyes, staring intently back into mine as her body twitches uncontrollably violent.

"Okay?" I ask, not expecting an answer. She shakes her head up and down but keeps flinching.

"Yes, everything is definitely okay," she whispers, as she continues to move her hips in sync with mine. "It's really okay. It's not just okay. It's wonderful okay. It's better than okay. It's total love, just you and me, and it's okay!"

I can't keep it back anymore. I give up, losing it, my gonads take over spitting and thrusting as I just give up and experience it. She grabs hold of my back hard, pressing her body into mine as she accepts my little donation with loving passion and glorious glee. I bury my head in the hair over her shoulder, nibbling on her ear and neck. Then I go quiet, feeling spent. I'm still licking her ear and she's gently squeezing her vagina around my penis. Pure raw emotions and tingling feelings slowly subside.

I can feel it getting smaller, anyway, and I'm starting to have trouble holding it in. I push and she squeezes ever so gently, once more, but it pops out.

"Oh, damn," she protests. She gets a pert little hurt look on her face like she just dropped her ice cream and wants daddy to buy her another one. I push up, arching my back while giving her one last wiggle to her crotch. She makes a yummy sound as I slip off to one side still making contact with as much of her skin as I can. I have one leg and one arm draped over her soft well-toned body as I snuggle her neck with more nibbles and kisses.

"What do you really think?" I ask.

"What do you mean?" she asks.

"About us. I feel like even though we come from opposite corners of the world, we belong together," I explain.

"We are together," she declares. "Just like a moment ago when we were one."

"I know about love," I say. "But I'm talking about our cultures. You come from New York high society and I come from the sticks of Oregon. I want to assure you that I'm not a country bumpkin out of water. I went east to go to school where I could enjoy the best of modern American culture, philosophy, music, science, and art."

"We both love movies," she declares, "so we already have more in common than most of my family and friends. That's kind of special. I know you're smart and clever. Mitchell likes you and I like you, too. I just need to explain something."

"You don't need to explain anything to me. We are open to each other and new to the world of love we are creating, with us in it. It's new and fresh and simple. We are new and fresh and innocent. It matters not where you or I come from, or where we've been. It only matters now who we are for each other and where we are going together."

"I'll go anywhere with you," she flatly states seductively and kisses me hard. "But I have to tell you something."

"You're not wanted in Mexico for dancing with a goose, are you?" I quip.

"No," she replies emphatically. "It's my family. I come from a very wealthy family and—"

"I've already been warned," I say interrupting her, "and I don't care."

"You don't understand. My family is very rich and powerful. My uncle just built a music hall at Lincoln Center in New York. My other uncle is the president of the New York Chemical Bank. My family owns half of Greenwich, Connecticut and my dad spends all his time at the yacht club. I want you to know, I don't need money to be happy. I need you to be happy."

"And I'm delirious just knowing you're happy," I assert. "I don't need money to be happy, but it sure is a close second to whatever is first. Just out of curiosity, how much money do you have?"

"I get a small trust fund that pays about two thousand a month, I think. I don't use it, so it just goes into a savings account, somewhere."

"Do all of your brothers and sisters get the same thing?"

"No, my brothers are all into the family business, so it's just me and my sisters that get small trust funds to live on while we wait for some rich boy to marry us and bring more money into the family."

"I take it Alice has been a great disappointment."

"Actually, we all are. My mother still tries to hook me and Connie up with rich little wimps from the yacht club."

I withdraw from her neck and prop myself up on one arm as I look deep in her eyes. I stroke her hair with my free hand as I search for the words.

"Normally, I would stay as far as possible from spoiled rich brats who can't understand why life is serious and how their wealth is an embarrassment to justice and equality. But you're not like that. You support yourself. You're socially blind and you hang out unconcernedly with the common people. You understand us because you honestly live like us and with us. That's just one of the things that makes me love you."

She lies silent, making me think she's thinking about what I just said. Then I hear a soft snore.

*

I look at the clock and it reads *2:22*. I'm groaning from the exertion and the pleasure. She responds with strong body thrusts and her own brand of crying, whining, and moaning all at the same time. She shudders and cries out, rising up to grasp hard onto me hanging over her. I return the thrusts, finally feeling free to let it go, matching her orgasm with mine. I groan a little louder and collapse again on top, holding it in as long as I possibly can.

Suddenly, she announces out of nowhere, "We should go to Denver and buy a car so we can get around without relying on Mitchell all the time."

I know the man of a relationship should be the one with the horse. I lost my truck some time ago when it developed transfer gear issues and I had little to no money for fixing it. I relied on Bleau's little truck when we were living together at Kemp's house, but she left, taking her truck when I had to move into Mitchell's. I now drive around town and sometimes to Gunnison and Denver, when necessary, with his fully restored 1947 Cadillac, equipped with hand controls, or his 1938 International flatbed truck. But Susie and I only own klunkers, which is fine, as it is all we really need for getting around town, going to work, or attempting to find our way home after a night of drinking.

"Your old girlfriend, Bleau, drove a little Japanese pickup," she observes. "I think I'd like that. We can carry stuff like our bikes and go camping. It fits." Her exuberance squeezes it out again. She whimpers in mock consolation and I roll off to my side looking at her in dark profile.

"That was a fun little truck," I comment, remembering my fishing expedition to the Taylor River. "If you really want to, you're in luck. I happen to know how those bastard car dealers work and can save you lots of money. Not that I care, but how much money are you thinking about spending?"

"I don't know," she answers, "I guess however much they cost. Does it matter?"

"Look, you have to understand there's a big difference between the rich and the poor. When the rich decide they want something, they just find what is considered the best and buy it. Story over. On the other hand, if a poor person needs something, they have to figure out how much they can afford and then go about searching as best they can, given the local market for such things, and procure what they need at a price they can afford. Stuff does fall off trucks sometimes. In other words, I know how to make do with what we have. So how much do we have?"

"How about ten thousand dollars?" she suggests.

I almost gag. What I could do right now with ten grand boggles the mind. But I don't dare show any obvious interest. Susie is my lover and that's all I want her to be. I don't care about her money, only her love and respect. I'm here to take care of her the best I can under the circumstances, regardless of her money.

"You have to understand that the big shiny rip-off car dealers warn you in advance by having a shiny expensive building, clearly unnecessary to the basic job of supplying cars to the public, but pointing out how profitable it is for them. Their awesome glass and steel buildings are designed to deceive and make you think they know what they are doing. What they are doing is making unconscionable profits off an ignorant consumer by fraud and collusion. Let me look around and see if I can find the right car at the right price. It's something I do well."

"Whatever you say," she submits. "It's the first car I've ever owned, so I'll take all the help I can get."

"You got that from Mitchell," I point out.

"What?" she asks.

"*Take all the help I can get*," I quote. "No matter your position in life, always accept help if it is honestly offered. It helps you and it helps the giver. Don't be proud, accept graciously, and be thankful."

"He should write a book about that stuff," she suggests.

The next day, I check the *Denver Post* Sunday classifieds and find only two trucks in the whole town in our price range of ten thousand dollars. Susie says she can just write a check for about that amount, so I call them and bend them over the barrel, offering cash at a time when cash is king. I dicker between the Toyota and the Nissan dealers, who are relatively new to town and have some of last year's models still in stock. Finally, the Nissan dealer cuts me a deal on the phone and I jump on it. Besides, it's my favorite truck color: blue.

Susie has Alice go to the dealer and give them the check. We fly to Denver a week later and pick up our first toy together. Alice hands the keys to Susie and she hands them to me. I separate them and give one set back to her. She beams with pride of ownership. I tell her to get in and give it a shot.

It is small and pretty basic with a gear shift on the floor, but we both love it and immediately name it *Blue Columbine*. We drive it back to the Butte, stopping in Bailey at the famous Hot Dog stand built in the shape of a hot dog, where I discover a character selling—out of the back of his old pickup—little hand-held twelve-volt grinders for sharpening chainsaws.

As anybody knows living off the wilderness, the hardest part of using a chainsaw is keeping the damn teeth sharp on the chain using only round files. It's a hard and difficult sharpening procedure and takes a lot of time and effort to do it right. This little tool suddenly makes it simple and easy to have a sharp chain all the time. I feel like I have hit the triple jackpot in a day. I have true love, I have new wheels, sort of, and I have a way to make a lot of firewood, the means to easily keep a home warm all winter. I'm back in self-reliant heaven again.

*

The first trip in our little Blue Columbine comes quickly when several telemark skiers put together a Crested Butte ski team and sign us up for a tour of telemark slalom races at nearby ski areas. The first one is in Breckenridge. On the way over, I give Susie a lesson in mountain driving. Driving on two-lane roads in the mountains is a challenge because of all the trucks slowing down when climbing hills. You have to develop a second sense for predicting oncoming cars or you'll be sucking diesel fumes all your life.

I teach her how to use the naturally winding roads as a viewing platform over longer distances so you can spot traffic ahead for opportunities to pass. I search far ahead for oncoming gaps that allow blind passing of slow trucks. The key to the trick is knowing what to do if you get halfway around and an oncoming car appears unexpectedly. Either you accelerate and quickly get past the truck, diving in front of it as a blasting horn blows by, or you slam on the brakes and dive behind the truck just before being wiped off the highway by an eighteen wheeler. In any case, it takes the boredom out of mountain driving and makes the trip all that more exciting.

We stay at some friends' cabin along with about a dozen other skiers. The next day, I load my cameras with film and head up the mountain with Susie and her teammates. I'm only recently capable of skiing blue runs, so I leave Susie and the others all gathered around the top starting hutch and ski down to about mid-course, where I take up a position right opposite a tight turn after a steep part of the course.

I spend the next couple of hours watching carefully and taking shots of all the members of our team as they come down the course. Finally, I spot Susie making tight turns around the flags using a classic deep-knee telemark turn. Her Rosignol skinny skies have edges and she knows how to use them when down and dirty in a cranking turn. She has a technique of pushing out of a telemark turn with a little tail edge catch on the downhill ski kicking her up and around ready for the next turn. She bears down on the turns and her strong legs hold her steady in tight turns. She kicks from one turn and into the next with a solid rhythm. She's good and she knows it.

Finally, there are no more skiers and some guy comes down the course slide-slipping some of the bigger gouges on the outside turn of every gate. He recognizes me from the early morning racers meeting we attended and motions for me to join him also slide-slipping the course and repacking some turns. When I make it to the bottom, nobody from Crested Butte is in sight. I stand in the open area between lifts looking lost with a bunch of cameras. I'm getting a little pissed for being left behind again and no clue where anybody went. A brightly blue dressed hospitality girl takes pity on me and skis over.

"You from Crested Butte?" she asks, wondering why I didn't look more at ease on skis and being alone.

"Yeah," I reply, "I'm the photographer. Any idea where they went?"

"They're having lunch at one of the campsites in the woods over there," she says, while pointing with her ski pole. The tree line nearby is peppered with trails going off in all directions.

"Which one?" I ask looking back at her.

"I'll show you," and she takes off with the skier's ice-skating technique for propelling skis forward without pushing on poles. Flat land traversing with Alpine equipment is not a well-honed skill yet for me. I struggle to keep up, but she disappears into the woods and I mark the spot, following as fast as I can. I quickly get lost in the many interconnecting trails I encounter. The tracks are narrow and some sharply go up little hills where I have to stop and reposition myself for sidestepping as I'm clearly crippled with my long fat skis.

I get frustrated and tired. I make my signature loud whistling sound Susie is familiar with, followed by our own

Crested Butte high mountain yodeling call, "*TEE YODEL LAY HEE WHOO!*"

Some nearby skiers stare at me, but I don't care. I'm pissed. I whistle again, longer this time, and follow it with the yodel. Then I hear another yodel in response and soon Susie emerges from the woods, walking.

"What's the matter, get lost?" she asks.

"I'm not lost. I'm just tired of taking the road less traveled," I respond hotly. "You know I don't know this place. Why didn't you wait for me?"

"Why do you still have your skis on?" she asks simply, pointing down to my 212-centimeter Rossis. I look around and then notice all the trails are packed down pretty solid and perfectly walkable. I sheepishly pole my release levers and pop out of my bindings.

"Still," I add, "I wish you wouldn't just leave me stranded when you know I'm not a part of your ski crowd and dependent on you for inclusion. If there is one thing I really hate, it's feeling excluded."

*

"Hell yes, include me!" I shout. "I wouldn't miss this for the world." It's a typical after-hours party at the Grubstake with most of the hard core still in attendance after a long day of drinking and celebrating something.

Frenchy turns to me and asks, "Are you sure? The ski back down will be in the dark."

"I've got a headlamp. We skied to Lake Irwin in the dark and that was three miles. What's this? One mile or two at the most?"

"And all downhill. It's your neck," declares Israel with a nasty grin.

"All right! Now," Coney says, "where do we get that many flares? If you just want to drop an avalanche on their heads, I've got the dynamite. Just not enough flares to spell out my inner most feelings."

"If we hit every hardware store and gas station in the county, I doubt if we could come up with a hundred," Dennis interjects. Dennis Hall is the pessimist of our gang, always predicting failure or doom.

"I've got a dozen flares in my truck," Cotton offers. "How many do you all have in your trucks?"

"We need about three hundred flares to make fifty-foot-high letters," the Weaz adds. "I've worked it out." He passes around a diagram with a bunch of numbers on it. "And we'll need about twenty or twenty-five skiers to put them in place just before sunset, then light them off." He makes a quick finger count of everyone present.

Basically, it's mostly the Grubstake gang, with a few Gulchers and CB Southers thrown in on the side, just about every klunker-owner in town who skis both alpine and Nordic, a lot of Hotshots, and then me, just a guy who couldn't miss out on such an historic occasion. Susie is up for it, as are two of her close girlfriends who also do a lot of backcountry skiing and hang out at the Grubber.

Dennis suggests we all swear to normal Crested Butte security standards declaring we'll never reveal any names or details, ever. That goes without saying, as we practice this mind-your-own-business philosophy every day anyway. With the Forest Service enforcing Amax's no trespass declaration on Mount Emmons, our actions might be technically against the law and cause trouble for those of us who have similar private mining claims under Forest Service control.

So, the deed is set. We know the time and place and the word goes out quietly to donate as many flares to the cause as we can locate. For two days, the town is a buzz of expectation because something is in the air. It's electric, palpable, but enticingly lacking any details. Something is afoot, but all we allow is to let Dennis warn Sandra over at the Pilot to keep her camera close by Sunday night and loaded with Tri-X. She'll need the film speed.

*

Susie comes in second at the race in Breckenridge and wins a pair of Rossignol skinny skis with edges exactly like the pair she already owns. She gives me her old pair and she adopts the new pair. Together, with romantically matching skis, we try them out on a moonlight run up to Lake Irwin Lodge, where I spend the day with Dan Thurman consulting on a solar electric system he wants for augmenting their expensive diesel generator.

We are supposed to take the official snow cat from the end of the plowed Kebler Pass road to the lodge like all his other guests, but it is too full of turkeys so we eagerly volunteer to make the two-hour run, skiing in the moonlight. I splurge and buy some nice skins and learn how to ski both uphill and downhill on both powder and groomed slopes. Basically, it just takes muscle and balance, which over time is hopefully replaced by technique. I'm young and strong so muscle is my only current solution.

I also have some pointers given to me when I was learning basic backcountry skiing from one of our best, BC. "If you can't ski down something too steep or fast, sit down between your skis and slide on your ass, scooping snow with your hands to break your speed. And try not to hit any trees."

At about one in the afternoon, Susie and I throw our backpacks in the Blue Columbine and head up to Peanut Lake, where we meet with everyone else. There's about fifty people milling around the little parking area on the Slate, drinking beers and whatever's in the bota bags. While we're waiting, I light up a doobie and send it out into the growing crowd.

Ron, Weaz, Dennis, Conehead, and Israel are hunkered over a topo map spread out on the hood of Weaz's new Chevy pickup. Finally, Dennis crawls into the bed of the truck, stands up, and whistles for attention. Tapley lets out a loud yodel. It's his trademark.

"Listen up everybody," Dennis continues. "We've got twenty-five skiers who need to swing by the truck here and load up with flares. We're going to go up the eastern ridge trail right above us to the bottom of the bowl and set the flares out in the avalanche run where we have a good view of the whole valley. There are twenty-four lines making up the message and you will be assigned to one of those legs or strokes. Each one will place flares every six feet for however long their leg is. Is that clear?"

"Like shit in mud," somebody yells back. Everybody laughs, except Dennis.

"What's the chance of the bowl sliding?" Hitch yells out from the crowd. "I don't care, really, just as long as I'm the last one down."

Everybody laughs.

"Too late in the day to slide now," Ron adds. "Besides, Carson just skied it yesterday and assures us it's solid."

There's a lot of laughter this time. Everybody knows you can't predict the annual running of the snow in the bowl and the boys each year compete to see who's the last one to ski it before the mountain shrugs it off for another year. It's usually in April, and it's still March.

"Bring your folding shovels so we can dig out trenches and cut steps. Bring your own supplies in and carry everything out. We don't want to leave any trace of our ever being there."

"Tell them about the shuttle," Weaz shouts.

"Oh yeah," Dennis adds, "we will be coming down the fastest trail out, which goes straight down to Kebler. Extras here, not skiing, will be taking our vehicles back to town and meet us on the road after dark for the trip back to town."

"Remember to keep your mouths shut and this will be just a little mystery in life. A mountain that fights back!"

We take the trail up the west side of the Slate through the trees along the ridge bordering the east side of Red Lady Basin. We skirt the open basin sticking to the trees so we are not exposed to any nosy Amax guards. It's springtime and the snow melting underneath leaves gaps between the surface snow sheets and the warmer rocks below. When our group crosses expanses of open snow near the bottom of the basin, we hear ominous *whomping* sounds as large sheets of snow collapse a few inches under our added weight. I look around at all the old hands and nobody seems too concerned, but nobody talks about it either. If it runs, it runs. We're committed.

"Do you think we'll get in trouble for this?" asks Susie. She always takes the lead when we're on skis and I'm used to following her gorgeous butt all over the mountain as I try to learn what she knows. It's truly a carrot on a stick situation and I love it.

"Unfortunately, my dear, this is what's called a grand but futile gesture," I pronounce. "But the medium is the message. Here, the medium is the mountain and the message is simple. By just performing an act of defiance to the powers that be is enough to change minds. People feel better about resisting if they see big things supporting it. It's actually protected free speech and where better to practice it than at the scene of the coming crime."

"But aren't we breaking the law?" she counters. "Aren't we trespassing?"

"Poor people, disenfranchised people, people's whose homes are under threat from bulldozers, are all, by definition, law breakers. In a capitalist country, being poor is literally against the law. From vagrancy to trespassing, poor people can always be arrested for something. So, we learn that crime and punishment is just a fact of life to be avoided at all cost, and justice is just an empty dream unless you can afford it. In this case, we can afford the flares."

"Isn't it considered pornography? Maybe AMAX might sue us for defamation. Someone might find out who did it."

"Who?" I ask. "Who really gives a shit one way or the other. No damage is going to be done, except to a few phony uptight sensibilities. But when a bunch of local citizens man the pitchforks and firebrands, believe me, Frankenstein gets the message. They'll soon forget the actors, but never the act. It will be a brand on their heads forever. You simply can't buy this kind of historic publicity."

Finally, after a grueling two-hour climb through the cold shaded forest, we break out onto the exposed bowl about a few hundred yards above the bottom tree line. From this height, we can clearly see both Crested Butte and Mount Crested Butte, plus the whole upper Slate River Valley all the way to Almont. Everyone takes off their skis, sticks them tails down standing up in the snow as a sort of wind break, and then we quickly begin laying out the letters above us on the slope by stomping paths spelling out the message, letter by letter.

"Let's put the M right above us," suggests the Weaz, holding up his diagram, "and then lay out the other letters on a hundred foot high by fifty-foot-wide rectangles. Flares should be placed about every ten feet apart vertically and six feet apart horizontally. That'll compensate for the slope of the mountain being seen in perspective from below."

The sun is shining and we quickly work up a sweat, but the letters get stamped out with snow paths pretty quickly. Soon, everyone takes a break and relaxes around the trench enjoying the view while eating our lunches and drinking some beer, or in our case, wine.

I finish doing my part of the M and then carve a lounge chair out of the snow right at the bottom of the whole thing. I kick back in the sun wearing nothing above my waist except my signature Varnet mountaineering goggles and a bota bag of wine. I marvel at the incredible view while smoking a nice fat one I brought along for good measure. You can't properly observe an historical event without some kind of awareness augmentation.

"We've got the first line already stamped out," announces Coney. "I brought premeasured strings."

"And some politicians and lawyers in town," announces Dennis, "who wish to remain anonymous have provided some incentive for the effort. Gather round!"

Susie has her shirt off enjoying the sun lying next to me in our snow lounge. Dennis hands out several bottles to his Hotshot friends and then brings one over to us. Susie eagerly takes it and starts dumping out small patches of white powder on the skin between her thumb and forefinger where one normally puts the Tequila salt and snorts one up each nose. She offers me one and I take her hand up to my lips as if kissing it but instead I snort it. She offers one to Dennis and he happily complies. I don't like the way several male friends of Susie seem to still be bird-dogging her. Maybe it's just my imagination.

"What do you think is going to happen?" he seriously asks. "Do you think it will make a difference?"

"Oh, you quaint unwashed ignorant peasants are all alike," I sarcastically begin. "The world will most definitely and very soon forget what we have so bravely done this day. But, for a brief shining moment, we have made our collective voices and spirits heard as one and that's all that counts. Today, we stand up and say together: Fuck you Amax! Not here! Not now! Not ever! And curse your greedy soulless stockholders to everlasting hell!"

Many others lounging around within hearing range respond in agreement. "Yeah!"

"Here's to the Crested Butte Monkey Wrench Gang!" Coney yells out for no particular reason, holding his beer can in the air.

"Hell yes!" everyone shouts back, holding up their beers.

"What do we want?!" he shouts again.

"We wanna fuck!" is the group response.

"Who do we wanna fuck?!" he screams.

Everybody starts mumbling about all the different things they would like to fuck. Nobody says Amax. After all, we are here to damn them, not to praise them.

What a glorious afternoon. The view is outrageous. Everybody kicks back and relaxes, waiting for sunset like a bunch of desperadoes waiting for the train. We can see about six different thirteen-thousand-foot snow-clad peaks from this vantage point dwarfing Crested Butte Mountain down below us.

We're high on life, high on cocaine, and high on the mountain a community of friends now defends. How perfect for the cause. This proves we are united and determined with the stuff that binds people together into impregnable bastions of purpose. We don't need a job at the expense of the wilderness. Not with a view like this.

When the sun finally dips behind the Ohio Peaks to the west, we set about our business. We gather up the last of the flares and position ourselves above our assigned line of flares in the snow that we will light as we run down the path from the top of the letters to the bottom. The lighting goes quickly and professionally with all the flares lit in record time. We all gather together at the bottom, admiring our work from close up and excitedly putting on our skis before we make our final escape.

"Awesome!" someone says, obviously impressed by the size of the letters spread out on the mountain in front of us with bright white flares that can be seen for hundreds of miles.

"Magnificent!" pronounces Weaz. "Incredible!"

"You know where the trail is!" he shouts to the first departures. "Rides are waiting at the road!"

"You go ahead, Susie," I tell her. "I'm going to have to side slip myself down from here so it might take some time. I'll meet you in town later."

Susie kisses me good bye, puts on her skis, and starts down the mountain. I watch her ski down the bowl below us holding a flare over her head to light up the slope. Just as she disappears over a ridge of snow, the light suddenly disappears into darkness. She fell.

"Oh-oh," I mutter to myself. "This is not a good sign."

I strap on my headlamp, take a last marveling look at our work again, and begin a slow decent down the bowl to the tree line on the west side. Everyone else has already left me behind and they are in the trees following the trail out. I see a couple of lights disappearing in the woods and follow them.

It's too narrow for me to use any ski turning techniques I know, so I resort to my desperate situation by sitting down on the back of my skis, letting my poles dangle behind me loose on their straps and scooping snow with my hands in order to control my speed and not run into anything. I can barely see where I'm going as my head lamp is not that strong. I ski down a long fairly straight section of trail and then it turns abruptly, descending along another long run to the next switch back. I'm just getting worried I might miss a switchback in the dark with heavy snow in the trees, when I spot a couple of lights ahead of me.

"*Jeeze*, Cowboy," Dennis says, as I slide down beside them waiting at another sharp turn in the trail. "We thought you might have already gotten lost. Man, you look a mess."

"We thought we might have to climb back up tonight to recover the body," Frenchy says jokingly, and they both laugh. I'm sweating from the exertion and covered in snow. One of my poles is missing from my wrist strap.

"I'm glad somebody gives a shit to help a poor bastard like me," I inform them. I kind of expected to get the same treatment I got when abandoned in the canyon a couple years earlier, so I really am happy to see them stay behind and help me get down safely.

They both have much brighter headlamps than I do, so I can see a little better with them surrounding me. From this point it becomes sort of fun as I slide down the trail on my ass guarded by two Nordic types. I swear I will learn this art of skiing steep trails and not be such a burden again.

Soon, we pop out of the trees and in front of me is the road with a parked pickup running with its lights off. We throw our gear in the back and pack five people into the front seat. They drop me off in front of Penelope's, where upon walking in I'm greeted by a round of applause from most of the participants from this afternoon's hike. Susie waves at me from a nearby table. I raise my arms in victory as I dance around in the middle of the room, showing plainly a giant rip in my snow pants bottom revealing layers of insulation ripped to shreds by my unconventional trip down the mountain in the dark. I take a giant bow with a flourish and sit down next to Susie.

"Everyone made it back to town," she says. "We've been waiting for you." She hands me a giant glass of beer. "The whole world knows about us now. We're all heroes."

She grabs me and kisses me with drunken passion. I finally feel like a fully accepted member of the coveted community of Butte-ers. I feel I've finally passed the initiation and now belong to something bigger and better than myself. I've been allowed to contribute to the common good. Setting a record for outdoor graffiti.

The next day is a normal Monday, except when Susie and I meet up with Dennis in the Nickel later, he pulls out an 8x10 black and white photo, taken from in front of the Pilot building, of our work on the mountain last night.

"Can you believe it?" he gushes. "Look at the size of those letters, and not a single dark flare." He high-fives both of us. The bartender, Baggins, sets down three beers and three shots of Crown Royal in front of us.

"On the house for the troops. We thank you for your service." Baggins pours himself a shot and we all do them together, slamming the upside-down shot glasses on the bar.

"This is publicity you can't buy with money," says Dana, sneaking up behind us.

"Dana," I gush, "did you see this last night?" I hold the picture up for him to see better.

"You bad boys and girls didn't tell me," he complains, while smiling wickedly. "I could have recorded it on tape. Maybe take a better picture than that. But nobody warned me. Why?"

Susie and I just point at Dennis and say, "Ask him."

"I didn't want the word to get out to the cops!" he complains.

"But you told Sandy!" we all reply in unison.

*

Later, we learn that Dana somehow gets his hands on a copy of the picture and sends it to his friend at *Playboy* who has just written an article about the Ace of Space and his Road Show. I see it in the news section on the editorial page as a tiny picture clearly showing our message written on the side of a mountain: *FUCK AMAX*. It is cited as possibly a world record for outdoor graffiti. Since coming to the Butte, I made the pages of *Playboy* twice. I'm beginning to feel a serious Gonzo phase coming into my life.

~ 12 ~

A LITTLE LOVE CABIN ON A CREEK

Life gets crowded at Mitchell's house. He hires a full-time live-in maid and then announces he is going to get married to his shockingly beautiful twenty-two-year-old therapy nurse from his stay at Paraplegic University, aka old PU at Craig Hospital. His current live-in maid is a recent model escaped from London, who of course attracts every drooling male dog in town creating unique dramas parallel with ours. The Grubstake boys are spending a lot of time hanging around the Vermont Castings parlor stove in the, of all places, the parlor, or the optional swimsuit sauna out in the office/entertainment room.

I discover a new book by Hunter Thompson detailing his experiences of being an assigned political reporter for *Rolling Stone* magazine, a rock rag with a strong liberal bent, as were all of us. While Mitchell waits in bed each morning for his daily doo-doo to show up on schedule, and after I get up early to rekindle the stove and get it warming up the entire house for Mitchell's half-naked performance, I read to him the entire book. It is during a particularly cold spell when we are burning through a cord of peach wood from Paonia every month.

I don't mind taking care of the fire. It's a sacred ancient job well fit for a physicist. I take on the running of the Vermont

320

Castings stove as if it were a temperamental nuclear reactor, needing fine tuning and constant adjustment for premium performance. My background in thermodynamics makes me appreciate the design and function this new stove provides.

I nurse it into unheard of burning efficiencies by carefully loading the wood for maximizing combustion surfaces while controlling the amount of outside air getting to it. Nobody wants to burn the nice warm air already inside the house causing it to be replaced by cold air being sucked in from outside. I use that new stuff, PVC pipe, to bring outside air directly into the stove, bypassing this issue.

The wood never actually burns with an open flame, but rather consumes itself at high temperatures over a period of hours as it smolders from the inside out. The hot vapors continue to combust in an after-burner chamber where more air is introduced, which further slows and controls the burning process so very little heat is lost up the chimney. Cold smoke is finally emitted having left most, if not all, of its calorie heat inside the house.

"You're not going to believe this one," I announce, walking into his bedroom. He's spread out naked on several white towels lying on his side waiting for an inevitable present from his ass.

"The theory is," Mitchell instructs, "that if I eat enough fiber every day at the same time, this can get predictable as clockwork."

"Yeah, I see how your clock works," I pipe right back. "But dig this. He ends up taking a piss next to Nixon at a rally and keeps his cool. He doesn't piss on him. Boy, I would! But listen how he describes the bastard: 'He was a swine of a man and a jabbering dupe of a president. Nixon was so crooked that he needed servants to help him screw his pants on every morning.'"

"Good morning," Susie announces herself, walking into the room with just panties and a crew neck short enough to reveal her flat belly and the cutest navel ever.

"It is now," Mitchell responds, "with one half of the Fisher twins brightening up my day already with such beauty and grace."

"And skin," I pipe in. She walks right up to me, grabs me by the head, and kisses me hard on the mouth with a hint of a minty tongue.

"*Whoa-ho-ho* you two love birds. It's too early for my blood pressure stress test. As much as it's not in my best interests, but you two really need to get your own place."

"I heard you talking about Hunter Thompson," Susie says. "My sister in Aspen says he may become sheriff. They want to change the drug laws and limit growth, so the town doesn't price all its old residents out of their homes."

"Shit, it's all but over," I counter. "In fact, I define it as the Aspen Syndrome. When the property values are so inflated, the middle and lower classes have to leave. Aspenitis has won when the hired help all have to commute to work from a less expensive area; an *across-the-tracks* situation so to speak. When it happens in Oregon, we call it the invasion of the Californicators. People have to sell out their inflated-value homes in southern California when they can no longer afford the interest and taxes. They have to move to Oregon, bidding up the prices there, and finally driving out a lot of natives from places like Portland, Eugene, and Medford. It'll happen here, too, sooner than you might think."

"Crested Butte's not Aspen," Susie pleads. "We'll never sell out, right Mitchell?"

"Anything you say, my lovely chickadee. When is your sister going to brighten us even further with a visit?"

"She's still in Aspen," Susie explains, "ski instructing and partying with the rich and famous. NBC sent a camera crew to report on the sheriff's election. Connie says she smoked dope with Hunter at the wrap party after the interview and then picked up a sound man for the night. She says he's got a good chance of winning."

"People are naturally crazy in Aspen," Mitchell says. "Look what I did when I lived there."

"You should do like Hunter," I suggest, "and run for mayor against Tommy right here. He's unopposed again. Apparently, his real estate cadre trust him to continue allowing anything money can corrupt. The only thing he wants to preserve about Crested Butte is its movie-set qualities, which he gladly lets out to the highest bidder. All power to the Hollywood producer!"

"I'm too busy trying to pay all my bills right now. I've got two lawsuits still to be settled over the plane crash. Why don't you run? I'll donate the first hundred dollars to your campaign fund."

"Give me a hundred dollars and it'll probably go right up my and my darlin's nose," I declare. Susie laughs.

"No seriously, you two should get a home. Susie here has a cousin in the real estate business. I bet he can find you a deal or something."

"That myopic little twerp would love to sell us one of his chainsaw-construction log piles for another boat in the Caribbean. I want to find a patented mining claim and build an integrated environment living space off the grid. I've got ideas how to use algae to produce methane and provide a primary food source by establishing an eco-chain of protein production. You know, where the algae feed the worms and the worms feed the fish and so on."

"Well, in the meantime," Mitchell announces, "I think it's best for all of us to take a break. I'm bringing in my new fiancé and she needs her space."

"I know what's going on," I pronounce. "Two beautiful women cannot coexist in the same house without causing some kind of trouble. How the Mormon's get away with it is truly a mystery."

Susie slaps me on the shoulder. "Oh Cowboy!"

*

I get an invitation to go up to Dan Thurman's new lodge at Lake Irwin in December, just before the big tourist invasion at the end of the month. He has some paying guests arriving early, so we can ride with them in the snow cat from the end of the plowed section of Kebler Road. He uses the snow cat for as long as the roads are blocked with snow—six to eight months a year. The lodge is situated on a high ridge to the east of the lake, about five miles for the cat on his annually compacted snow-cat road.

It's a cold and cloudless night with a brilliant, white full moon illuminating clean bright bluish-white snow fields, bordered on all sides by indiscernible dark forests. The snow glistens from a million tiny mirrors reflecting bluish moonlight and to some extent our headlamps, which we don't really need.

We clamp on our skinny skis and turn down the ride in the snow cat. Shit, now I can ski, and it's only three miles by overland backtrack trail. You couldn't ask for a more beautiful night. The snow crackles like broken glass as we set out across a fantasy world few ever get to experience, up close and personal.

Both of us hike these mountains every summer, so I sort of know where to go. We cut across the open area near the Forest Queen mine turnoff, follow the road up to the buildings, and then follow the pipeline that brings water down from a small lake up above in the basin. By following this route, we're able to ski over the intervening ridges and sort of head right down to the lodge from an upper basin. Susie, of course, takes off at a good clip and I have to hoof it to catch up.

"Slow down and enjoy the view!" I yell. I'm momentarily shocked by my voice breaking the blanket of mountain silence.

"Make me!" she yells back, and wiggles her butt in my direction indicating how that might be accomplished.

"You know what's going to happen if I catch you," I threaten right back.

"Promises, promises..." she shouts back, and takes off again at a nasty pace.

I put it in high gear. It's just power *schussing* now as we follow the long pipeline carved along the face of a steep tree-covered mountain. I'm taking long kick strides and soon the distance between us shrinks.

She finally disappears over the edge as we emerge from the trees and onto the flat basin. I risk a tuck and head straight down the side toward the exit from the basin on the trail to the lodge. She sees me too late and does the same, but by then I've got a little lead. We both head for the same spot and just as I make the trail edge and stop, she comes up too fast and just uses me as a backstop. We end up in a tangled mess of sticks, poles, clothing, and bodies covered in the lightest most powdery snow you can imagine. It sticks to everything warm and from our exertions, we are soon thoroughly dusted in powder.

She starts laughing and throwing snow at me and I let her, enjoying every second. I move in closer to make it harder for her to swing her arms and then they stop throwing snow and instead wrap themselves around my neck. Her powdery face mixes with snow from mine and we kiss deeply and thoroughly as we hold each other tightly, slowly melting ourselves into the snow, burying ourselves in pillow down.

After a while, we stop to catch our breath in the crisp cold high-altitude air and sit quietly holding each other, staring at the silvery glowing vista below us. We can hear the generator at the lodge breaking the silence.

"God, I love this!" she says. "I can't get enough. Don't you?"

"Yes," I respond quietly. "It's what I came to find." I reach over and kiss her again. "Thank you for teaching me to ski. I thought I was too uncoordinated to learn, but here I am."

"Maybe Mitchell's right," she says. "Maybe we should buy a house where we can have more privacy."

"You know I don't have the money to buy anything. I'm not from a rich family like most of your friends, so we'll have to figure something else out. Maybe I can build something if we can find some land somewhere. I'd love to live out in the wilderness like the Conehead up the gulch, but just not there."

"They're selling lots here in Irwin. My friend just bought one and is going to build a cabin this summer. Maybe we could do the same."

"Where can I get the money? Our salaries at the theater barely cover our bar tab. I've been working with Dana on his roadshow, but there's no money there. His father keeps bailing him out with bigger and bigger business loans whenever he wants a new camera or a new van. But he knows a lot of Hollywood celebrities. Maybe I can make a connection and get some movie work."

"That would be fun. Making movies might be as much fun as showing them."

"Believe me, it is. I just don't have a silver spoon in my mouth or have celebrities for relatives. On my own, I haven't a chance. You need to know someone before you can be someone in Hollywood."

"I'm someone," she says simply.

"I know you are and that's why I love you. One of the many reasons I love you. You don't care about money or how it separates people. You're just like me and all the other poor bastards here who would rather spend one day freezing in paradise than giving million-dollar blow jobs on Wall Street."

"But what if I have the money anyway? Shouldn't we use it? Especially if it supports our love and allows us to live together here permanently."

"What are you trying to say?"

"You know how I said I don't use my trust fund and live on my own? And that it's been going into a savings account for the last few years? I think it's built up to something useful."

I look at her, searching for a sign that maybe she isn't the same person I fell in love with. I've known rich women. I don't want to know rich women any more. They're too demanding and usually spoiled brats with high-maintenance issues. I suddenly have a vision of Connie's face in place of Susie's.

"What are you saying?" I cautiously ask.

"I don't want it to affect our relationship, but I want to share with you what I have. I know you would do the same if it were reversed. I love you and trust you. Let me supply the money and you supply the brains and let's buy a house here. We can share the expenses and maybe rent out bedrooms to our friends. What do you think?"

I can clearly make out her face now in the bright moonlight and there it is. That spark of innocence and truth just seems to jump out at me. I stand up and stare out at the incredible land-scape around us. She gets up and side steps next to me where she puts her arm around my waist, leaning on me and looking out at the same scene.

"There're the lights of the snow cat just approaching the lodge. Guess it's time to go. We don't want to worry anybody."

I look at her and I can see a tear in her eye. She looks away quickly, makes a jump step, and heads down the slope toward the lodge. I side-step turn and follow in her tracks.

Dan is standing next to the snow cat helping unload the guest luggage and supplies when we ski up out of the darkness.

"There you are. Good thing you know what the hell you're doing, otherwise I'd be worried."

"No sweat. I've got one of the best backcountry skiers here as my guide." I slap her on the butt while she's bent over un-doing her bindings. She gives me a dirty look, now that we're under artificial light, there's not much magic anymore.

"I can't help but notice how freakin' loud your generator is. We could hear it clear up at the basin. If anybody needs solar energy, it's definitely you."

"Come on inside where it's quieter and we can talk."

He leads us inside the lodge, which is still not finished in many ways and a smell of fresh-cut wood is still in the air.

"We have twenty-four rooms and can handle up to a hun-dred people," he says as he leads us into the fireplace room.

A roaring fire blazes in the wall-size river rock fireplace along one whole wall. The boys in the Butte built this place and left some signature pieces such as these giant rock fireplaces that you can literally walk into and roast the marshmallows off your prick real close and personal. Exposed log beams are another feature. Chainsaw construction on display at its best.

"I'll bet bringing fuel up here, especially in the winter, is a major hassle. How much do you spend on generating electricity?"

"Let's just say it's way too much. So, what can solar do for me? What do you need to know to give me an estimate?"

"I've done some digging after our talk in town and it turns out the biggest source for photo-voltaic arrays right now is in Australia. Seems, though, they have a lot of outback and no copper mines for cheap wires. Some towns down there are nearly 100 percent solar-generated electricity. In your case, and in Australia, you don't need it as a source of heat. I see you have a big coal-fired furnace outdoors with hot water heating."

"It's state-of-the-art and will efficiently burn just about anything, so I'm sort of sustainable in that respect. My guests often ask me if I'm polluting the environment by being here and proudly, I can say no. This lodge is made out of trees we harvested on site. It's heated by the surrounding deadwood, naturally helping with preventing forest fires, and the sewage is treated to a standard better than the water we bring in from the glacial lakes above. Solar would give me a big boost in not having to burn diesel for our electricity."

"I'm an ethicist," I assert, "when it comes to engineering designs, and photo-voltaic is the way to go. But I have to ask, do you think this lodge is something that is good for the wilderness environment surrounding it? Is this what we need? Easy access and luxury camping for the rich and indolent?"

"What, you don't think they deserve to be here? Kind of sounds like exclusivity for the young and clueless."

"Touché," I say with a wide grin. "Who am I to advocate no wheelchair accessibility to paradise? I say, more wheels. More chairs, motorcycles, 4-wheel drive trucks and so forth. If you want to protect something, then throw them all out or let them all in. Wilderness dwellers should be the first to consider when preserving the wilderness."

"I think in a few years," Dan ruminates, "Ruby will become a little mountain town again and we'll have a year-round population living here. I think this place will be fine for a wilderness lodge and we will do a lot to protect the environment because we are good residents."

"I hope you're right but, on the side, I think grandfathering yourself into this area while you can is a brilliant business move. Now, let's see if everyone else agrees."

Susie and I stay in one of the guest rooms for the night but are so wound up from the ski trip, we stay awake and play doctor 'til dawn. As the sun rises like an atom bomb over the Ruby Peaks to the east, Susie and I stand in the window holding tight to one another naked under a thick Pendleton wool blanket wrapped around us.

"So, what do you think?" she asks.

"About what?"

"Us buying a house together."

"Okay," I say quietly, and then look her right in the eye. "But we split everything. I don't want to be accused of living off your money. I'll figure it out somehow, but we split everything, right down to doing the dishes and keeping the plumbing unfrozen."

She spits in her hand and holds it out for me to shake.

"Done," I declare, and grasp it eagerly.

I let go of the blanket to take her hand and it falls to the floor. We stand for a moment shaking hands, but then I grab her around the waist and bend her backwards while kissing her deeply. She struggles a little to keep from falling and then straightens up without letting go, dragging me back to bed.

The next day I spend with Dan looking over the place and taking measurements. I use an exposure meter to judge the solar light intensity and record all the roof angles, such as pitch and orientation, with the solar arc. By lunchtime, I have a pretty good idea of what it is going to take to build a system that will take care of his needs.

"Fifteen dollars a watt," I conclude as we pack up our gear for the cat ride back to Kebler.

"My generator is twenty kilowatts!" Dan exclaims. "That's about...three hundred grand!"

"Yeah, the problem is that you need high-efficiency silicon cells made in Germany and they are not cheap. The batteries are just conventional golf cart batteries, so that's not an issue, but the high-current controllers to keep the batteries from overcharging are made in Australia. I figure it will pay for itself compared to a diesel generator in about ten years."

"I may not even be here in ten years. So, no way you can do it for thirty thousand, cause that's about all I can afford."

"Mass production hasn't kicked in yet, so unfortunately solar electricity is very expensive. Now, if you just want to heat a hot tub or swimming pool, the boys in town have a solar reflector that can generate steam. Maybe they can hook you up with one that can run a steam turbine driving an alternator."

"No thanks," he says despondently. "I have enough machines up here demanding my constant attention. Thanks, anyway. I hope you had a good time, anyway."

Susie and I look at each other and just smile that secret smile we have.

"Better than I hoped," I say as I follow Susie out to the waiting cat belching black smoke.

After we get back to town, Susie informs me that she's heard from her cousin Lynn Faulkner's husband, Peter Hagen, that Tommy Glass, our esteemed clean-cut ski patrol/real-estate salesman/mayor, is moving to Keystone to take a real real-estate job where there's more stable condo-money action. He's had enough living like a poor broke hippie in a log cabin in paradise. He has a three-year-old little girl and his wife is expecting.

He owns the little log cabin on the creek at the end of Sopris at 105, right across from Tim's house, cattycorner to the Teitler's, just across the creek from Sunshine's Paradise Bath & Sauna, and due south of Dana's house on Elk. It's two blocks from downtown, and Tommy put in a second-floor gable bedroom that looks east down Sopris, or along the creek flowing into town with the backs of several three-story Elk Avenue establishments clearly in view.

We're in Peter's office waiting for him to find the keys.

"You'll get more commissions," Susie says consoling me. She pats me on the arm. She knows how much time I'd spent working on Dan Thurman's solar project, even though knowing full well from the start it was a long shot.

"Here they are," Peter says as he reemerges from the paper-strewn backroom. "It's just a couple of blocks, so we can walk." We follow him out the door and up to Second Avenue, where we pass the fire station and the old abandoned marshal's office. On the way he explains how a job came up suddenly and Tommy had to resign his mayor position and so wants a quick sale on the house.

When we arrive, I note it has a little picket fence out front and a side lawn along Coal Creek which forms the north-side boundary to the property.

"Nice," I say to Susie. "We can have picnics on our own little creek-side park." She squeezes my arm in agreement.

"You're lucky," Peter says, as he unlocks the front door and goes in. "Tommy just packed up a couple days ago, so the plumbing and electricity are still on."

Susie and I walk in and immediately are astounded by the beautifully finished oiled wainscoting on the walls and ceiling. It immediately feels cozy and warm just like a little mountain cabin should. A full-size stand-up brown enameled Ashley coal stove dominates the front room. I'm a little hesitant about dealing with coal, its reputation and all, but there's plenty of cheap coal available and I can buy a year's worth for about forty bucks. I can make it work, I figure.

"The stove is practically new, and check out the grating," he says as he opens the door. I look in and sure enough, the grating looks good with no burn holes or missing parts as so many older coal stoves get just before they cause a fire. "You got to watch these things. They can get out of control sometimes and set your chimney on fire."

Crested Butte usually loses a house or two damned near every year to such stoves. It takes constant attention and is not recommended for the unreliable or lazy. If you're going to be independent of the oil industry, then wood is usually the way to go for low-rent wilderness dwellers, but you have to be dependable and hardworking, two things most rich kids are arrogantly lacking.

I walk into the next room, which is obviously designed to be a little dining room between the front living room and the back add-on kitchen. Tommy put in a metal spiral staircase in one corner leading up to the second-floor attic bedroom.

The old log cabin at the core of the house was originally just three rooms and an outdoor commode next to the creek. When domestic water came to town in the forties, someone added a conventional stick-built house on the back with a second chimney, adding a kitchen, indoor bathroom, and a utility room. Heat for the rear part is provided by a thermostatic, top-loading, Ashley barrel stove. This stove model is very popular around town because it's cheap, about $200, and it works damn well. You feed it wood and it converts it to heat. The thermostat controls it, so no muss, no fuss, no run-away fires.

There is another, unheated structure added onto this part of the house, allowing the indoor storage of a year's worth of wood and coal accessible from inside so no need to go slugging through the snow for fuel. *Cool!* I like this place.

"Don't worry sweetheart," I whisper to Susie, "I've got a chainsaw and know how to use it. I'm more of an Oregon logger than a cowboy anyway. I can easily keep us warm this winter. I know where there's a lot of standing dead up the gulch. Coney showed me."

"I know you will. That's just one of the reasons I love you. You're so smart and self-reliant. You don't need anyone to do anything for you. That's refreshing."

"How much?" I ask Peter. He consults his paperwork.

"It's listed at twenty thousand," he reports. "But I know he wants a quick sale, so just make an offer."

"We'll take it," Susie pipes up.

I grab her and pull her aside so Peter can't hear. He politely pretends he's distracted.

"We can't afford that on our salaries," I caution her, "and other houses farther south are still going for ten grand or thereabouts."

"I don't care," she firmly replies, "I like it and I can afford it."

I stare at her for a moment, wondering. Has she been honest with me about her money and being an honest, ethical person, unpolluted by savage greed or intolerant entitlement?

"Great. You're getting a great deal. I'll draw up the papers. How do you want to make the down payment?" he asks.

"I'll write a check. How much should I make it out for?" she asks, while taking a check book out of her back pocket with such ease, like she carried one around there all the time. She doesn't, but she seems indifferent with spending large sums of money. At least they're large sums for me.

This isn't what I like. I feel strange, like something ominous is happening. But I want to put down roots, even if it is with the help of a trust funder girlfriend. I want to be accepted by my chosen community and be a good citizen. I want to make this our home, our nest, our fortress as we adopt our new lives now.

*

We move our meager belongings into the house in one trip. I go to work right away getting a heated water bed installed in the attic bedroom. I order up a couple tons of coal to be delivered from Paonia. The truck backs up, barely clearing the house to the south, and dumps some big black glistening rocks of beautiful Anthracite that actually look more like giant mineral specimens than burnable fuel. I shovel it all into our coal bin, which fills it close to the roof.

I go to work with my chainsaw cutting up scrap wood for kindling and scouting out a couple of dead trees up the gulch that will make great firewood, all seasoned and cured naturally. I cut a couple trees and buck them up, bringing in several loads of wood in the Blue Columbine. We stack up a couple of cords inside next to the coal and a couple more outside. I'll burn the outside stuff first, but if it snows early, I can always do a tunnel under the snow to the buried wood pile later. Otherwise, when the snow is deep, which is most of the winter, I'll use the wood stored inside.

I know some craftsmen in town making rustic homemade furniture out of hand-made wood frames and big stuffed pillows. It's perfect for that young modern cabin look. Everything outside is old and weathered, whereas inside it's all color and brightness. Our couch is plaid red and I add a big carved wooden rocking chair to the mix...and we have a comfortable home ready for entertaining guests. I set up my stereo system and play "Rocky Mountain Way" at glass-shattering levels, announcing to the neighborhood that a drug-crazed rocker has just moved in next door.

Tim lives right across the road and he loves music so we get along fine. It's kind of the party end of town anyway, with several renowned artists and unique characters living within drunken staggering distances.

It's late summer when we move in, so I immediately find a usable cheap plastic lounge chair that I put on the lawn right next to the creek and in full view of anyone driving along First Street. I put on my signature Vuarnet mountaineering sunglasses with leather side shades, strip to my shorts, and relax with a book while working on my high-altitude tan. I'm a fixture and I enjoy it. I feel like I'm finally at home where I belong. I can now have friends and relatives come visit without being embarrassed about my lifestyle or living conditions.

Townes and Cindy finally pack up their campsite after being rained out for most of July and move in with Tim for the rest of the summer. The monsoons come almost every afternoon now, so camping in the high western Rockies just isn't the romantic getaway some Texans imagine.

They stake Amigo out on the CF&I land a couple blocks away and we begin hearing them yell at each other almost every day. I'm trying to sleep in on a Saturday morning while Susie is in Denver visiting her sister, Alice. She's picking out linens and stuff for the house and bringing it all back in the Blue Columbine. I expect her later today, because there's a big Mango party going on tomorrow we don't want to miss.

"You're going to kill yourself, Townes!" Cindy screams.

I can hear them through my open bedroom window. I roll over and try to go back to dreamland where moments before, I swear, I saw Susie, but knew down deep that she was somehow also Connie. Like a quantum superposition of states, her image makes me feel she's Susie, but her words and mannerisms seem to be Connie. I'm curious where the hell this is coming from.

"Ah darlin', you know I need a little slug once in a while to steady my hand. Gimme my bottle back. Please darlin'!"

"No way! I'm not going to let you commit suicide."

"Now darlin', you know I wouldn't do that. I have friends who need me."

"Like who, besides me?"

"Well, darlin', Geraldine and Amigo for starters. Everybody down at the Grubstake."

"That's 'cause you spend every dime you have in there. Of course, you think you have friends. But real friends don't let each other drink themselves to death."

"Ah darlin'."

"I'm tired. I'm going to bed."

Good, I think. Maybe I can get back to sleep now. I just about start to see Susie's bright and curious face in my mind's eye, all wrapped up in scarves and stocking hats. Her cheeks are a bright pink, almost doll like. Her eyes sparkle with delight. Her happiness is infectious.

BANG! BANG! BANG! I'm startled out of my daze by the sound of our custom wrought iron door knocker that came with the house. I consider it an epitome of metallic overkill.

"Hey Cowboy? You awake?" Townes shouts loud enough for the whole neighborhood to hear. Fortunately, 7 a.m. traffic on this end of town on a Sunday is severely limited and besides, all the boys were on a fire out of town, making it quieter than usual.

Everybody in town knows Townes is here for the summer and grant him a lot of space. He is our adopted superstar, even though he's going through a little dry spell right now, like a lot of us. The Butte is a natural haven for sensitive and creative rebels and mavericks. And we like it that way. That's what creates our unique community.

"Hey, you got any whiskey in there?"

"I'm awake. You don't have to yell. Come on in. I'll be down in a minute. I gotta find my pants." Nobody locks their doors in the Butte. It would be an insult to our neighbors.

I hear the big thick solid wood door with hand-carved grape vines surrounding the iron door knocker, open and close. Some local craftsman made it for Tommy a couple of years earlier.

There are a lot of little works of art like this all over town. We don't just construct with chainsaws; we craft with axes, knives, and any other sharp objects.

"Don't mind me, I'll be really quiet. Where do you keep the hooch?"

"First kitchen cabinet to the right," I call down the spiral staircase. "Glasses are in the cupboard above the sink. Make yourself at home, I'll be right down. Don't pour me one!"

I dress quickly and do the two-bounce ski jump down the spiral stairs, causing the whole house to shake a little. I step into the kitchen where Townes is pouring himself a second shot, standing in front of the open cabinet where I keep a bottle of Crown Royal for emergencies: like neighbors being out of whiskey.

"I see you're up bright and early. What's the occasion?" I don't wait for an answer and head immediately for the bathroom where I continue yelling through the door while taking a piss. "Where's Cindy?"

"She's in bed and won't let me have my wallet. Where's Susie?" I hear more clinking of glass to bottle.

"She's visiting her sister in Denver, buying curtains." I flush the toilet, zip up, and go back out to the kitchen. He's sitting at the table now with just a glass and the Crown bottle keeping him company.

I need to get something in my stomach before I can function. Coffee and toast usually do the trick in an emergency. Looks like that's what's going to happen now. I pour a slug of Crown into my coffee cup, add some coffee crystals from a jar, pour in some hot water from the pot on the Ashley stove, and put some bread in the toaster. I finally sit down opposite him at our little kitchen table overlooking our small side lawn and

Coal Creek just twenty feet away. It's running low in the late summer so we can hardly hear it.

"You want some toast?"

"No thanks," Townes declares. "It might make me throw up."

"*Jeez* Townes, don't you think all this drinking is going to come home to roost some day?"

"You sound like Cindy. I'm okay. I've been worse."

"That's hard to believe. I'm a good drunk, but if I drank what you do, I don't think I could function, if you know what I mean."

"Functioning isn't all it's cracked up to be. Hell, back in sixty-nine, I had a monkey on my back to the tune of five hundred dollars a day. All I wanted to do was cop a spoonful, sit around, and listen to music."

"And write songs. Coke?"

He just looks at me funny. "I was hanging with musicians, not pimps, although I knew a couple. No amigo, heroin. Smack. Skag. Horse. I damn near died several times from bad doses."

"Shit! That sucks."

"Now, I think my manager was keeping me hooked so I wouldn't pay attention as he stole me blind."

"Stole your music? How the hell can you do that?"

"With a pen, like all the real thieves these days. He had me under contract for six albums, but I apparently put up my songs as a guarantee, which he made sure he collected."

"The bastards!" I yell. I take a stiff drink of my sweetened coffee. Townes refills his glass and drinks half in one gulp. "That sucks! I've heard of music thieves, but didn't think they preyed on simple folk singers. Did Dylan have this kind of problem?"

"Fuck Dylan. He's a sellout anyway. And fuck the so-called business managers who don't care about anything except what you're worth to them, dead or alive."

"True," I agree sadly. "I still wish I could have a technical talent manager, someone to find me gigs and gets a reasonable commission for keeping me in work. I don't see why people can't be honest and still make money. It's almost like greed and graft are expected from all who do business, like they all know it's a crooked capitalist world and they need to be the crookedest and most greedy bastards to survive."

"Aw, shucks. I'm just happy to be alive. I try to keep a positive attitude. I can't change it. But I think I've found someone who will really help me."

"Not another New York pimp, I hope."

"No. He's the grandson of Nashville's famous music historian, John Lomax. His grandfather documented all the delta blues and cornhusker country music back when recorders were direct to vinyl. He's helping me get my royalties straightened out. He's even trying to get Merle Haggard to record some of my songs."

"This time, make the bastards pay. You've done something extraordinary and should righteously profit from it. Get tough like your Texas ancestors."

"Okay, Cowboy, but Cindy won't give me my wallet. She says I'm irresponsible with money."

"No."

"You got to help me. I need to buy a pint at Yelenik's when they open. What time is it?"

I look up at the kitchen clock. "It's eight thirty."

"Loan me ten bucks until I can get it back from her. I'll get my BMI royalty check and can pay you back with interest. I'll tell you what. I'll leave my shotgun with you for collateral."

"You know you don't have to do that. I'll spot you a pint. Hell, let me fill up my pocket flask." I go to the cabinet, take out my silver flask and carefully fill it from what's left in the half gallon bottle of Crown. "So, what happened to all the money from all your albums?" I screw on the lid and hand him the flask.

"I gave them to my manager, apparently, to pay for drugs. Actually, he paid for the drugs and I lost my songs." He immediately unscrews the top and takes a pull on the flask, recaps it, and puts it away in his front coat pocket. "Cindy is just trying to look out for me while I'm going through a little rough spot. I love her dearly, but she's a Texas cowgirl and can get Dallas mean when she wants to."

"I was going to say, she looks more like a redheaded bull wrestler from Amarillo than the innocent virgin teenager from Austin."

"I'll drink to that! But she's really from Fort Worth. She loves horses, dogs, and guitar pickers, so I had to take her home, feed her, and give her a name. I think Amigo likes her more than he does me. I know Geraldine does."

"I can see Fort Worth gals coming from two, three feet away," I reply, mimicking one of Townes favorite sayings where he claims he can usually recognize *trouble coming from two, three feet away.* He also invents a measure of time wherein everything can go to shit-in-a-handbag in *a Dallas second.*

"But seriously, Cowboy, I really want that black powder rifle you have. It'll look great over my fireplace in Tennessee. I gotta have it. How about I trade you my shotgun, straight across for it?"

"What kind is it?" My brother in Alaska tells me of the sacred duty of all gun owners to be open to swaps. It's a gun thing.

"It's a Charles Dailey, engraved, over and under. I inherited it from my uncle. It's supposed to be worth some money, even though it was made in Japan. Did you know that a Van Zandt fought with Sam Houston?"

"Never had the need to know. Does it have dual triggers?"

"There's even a Van Zandt county. And they're adjustable."

"I'm glad to see you've overcome it. I haven't liked most Texans, especially since Dallas killed Kennedy and my entire future."

"I'm sorry if my Texanness offends you. I didn't have a lot to say about it." He salutes with his glass and finishes it off. I take a sip from my coffee and put the toast on a plate.

"No, on the contrary, you're the best damned Texan I can imagine and you make me want to go to Austin just to see all the musician friends you've talked about." I salute him with my coffee mug.

"I got nothing against Oregonians." He thinks about it for a moment. "Actually, I don't know anyone from Oregon. Except, of course, you."

"Actually, I was born in Idaho. My parents came from Oklahoma. My father was trying to make it to Yakima, Washington to pick fruit during the Depression, but his car broke down near Boise and he ended up staying another twenty years and raising four boys."

"I'll drink to that. Happens to me all the time." He pauses. "Car breakdowns." He holds out his glass and I slowly refill it from the last of my half gallon.

"I can understand that, given that surplus demolition derby car you drive. What is it, a Mercury Marquis?"

"I'm not sure. The guy who sold it to me said it was a Texas horse car with a hitch for a trailer. That and the price was all I needed. Poor boys with horses can't be choosy."

I reach out and offer him my hand. He reaches back and we shake hands over the table, then do a black pride hand clasp, and finally a fist bump. It's just what we do these days to be different. But he knows from the years he's been coming to the Butte that I, and all the rest of town, consider him a valued member of our infamous gang and will do anything we can for him. Butte-ers look after artists and other fragile contributors to artistic freedom, and Townes is obviously an artist, a free artist, and needing to be looked after. I kind of feel sorry for Cindy. That big, strong handsome Texas redhead has a bigger job handling Townes than any ornery Texas pony she might otherwise prefer.

"I gotta piss," he announces.

"In there...." I point to the far door at the back of the kitchen. Townes gets up unsteady and heads in that direction.

"If Cindy shows up, Amigo, tell her I'm not here." He pats me on the shoulder.

"You got it, Amigo." I check the *refer-dator,* local vernacular for the cold box, for something to put in my stomach besides toast. If I'm going to hang with Townes today, I better grease up the insides and be prepared for an epic drunken adventure. I pull out the half-eaten hamburger I had last night at the Nickel and brought home just for the hangover. Too late for that.

Bang! Bang! Bang! It's the door knocker again. I walk slowly to the front room, peek out the window, and then open the door. Cindy stands there with a mean look and Geraldine crouches slightly behind her looking worried.

"Where's Townes?" she demands. Her green eyes and red hair blindingly blaze at me. I point toward the back of the house. She steps past me and stomps into the kitchen. "Come Geraldine!" Geraldine sheepishly eyes me and steps past, following her timidly. She gets to the kitchen, sees the empty glasses, glances at the closed door to the bathroom and yells, "Townes Van Zandt! What the fuck are you doing in there?"

He timidly opens the door to make sure she's not winding up to get physical. "Now darlin', it's not what you think. Cowboy is just fixing me some breakfast." She looks at the hamburger and leftover toast. She softens slightly.

"I can fix some eggs if you want to stick around," I say, walking in behind her. Townes gives me a dirty look. I shrug. He should know I can't handle female pressure.

"No thanks, Cowboy," she says. "I just want to make sure Townes stays sober, more or less. I've got him a paying gig down in Gunnison next weekend and he can't screw up. We need the money if we're going to get back to Austin on time."

"Yeah, Cowboy. I was going to ask you. Can you do the sound for me again?"

I'm the only person in town with a little Shure M68 mixer, a couple of condenser mics, stands and cables, a fifty-watt home-brew NASA chip power amp, and a pair of DCM Drum speakers, serial number 0002. It's my roadie kit for helping poor, broke musicians by providing a decent sound system at a reasonable cost, usually drinks and tips. I've used it in the Grubstake several times until Gary Gorbett showed up recently with his disco

DJ sound system he bought off a defunct college radio station in Fort Worth.

"I'd love to," I agree. "What's the pay?"

"Free drinks during the breaks and a third of the tips," Cindy announced.

"Figures."

*

"Connie's coming over for the mango party," Susie announces while boiling a morning egg. Connie's boyfriend, Arnie, who built an Aspen cottage out of an old barnwood alley garage, made a bundle off it and moved over here after hiring the boys to build him a deluxe two-story log house just off Whiterock near the old water tower.

"Flying or walking?" I ask. In the summer, nobody drives between here and Aspen, as it takes longer than walking and costs more than flying.

"Walking, as usual," she points out while scooping out a soft-boiled egg. "She wants us to pick her up at Gothic and we'll all go to the party together."

When the day comes, we pick up Connie right on schedule with four other friends of Arnie who walk over, all here for the same thing. Connie crowds up front in the cab with me and Susie, while her friends climb in the back and hunker down for the dusty ride back up the hill to Mt. Crested Butte, where we hit asphalt for the rest of the trip into town.

"So, what's the deal with mangos?" I casually enquire.

"That's how he makes money," Connie replies. "He rents a whole cargo ship and imports fruit from Central America to Los Angeles. He just made a big killing on a ship full of mangos from southern Mexico. He wants to introduce us to the tropical fruit, so he had a crate of mangos flown up here from LA."

"I bet that's not all he flew up from LA."

Connie frowns, but knows exactly what I mean.

"That's what attracts you to him, isn't it?" says Susie.

"Most of the people I know in Aspen never had to work for their money," Connie explains. "This guy actually comes from a humble little village in Norway and now makes millions in the shipping business. He really is self-made. He's smart, clever, inquisitive, nice body, and sort of cute. I may be moving to Crested Butte now that my sister and my boyfriend are living here." She admittedly does a lot of slumming in Crested Butte these days and makes no bones about it.

"Sort of cute? That's your standard for looks?"

"It's more important that they're successful. Not too many cousins in Greenwich actually qualify. I like men who go after the gold and then know how to spend it."

"Do you agree, Susie?" I ask pointedly. She's looking out the window in her usual daze.

"What? I wasn't listening."

"He asked if you like men who are successful and make lots of money," Connie repeated.

"Sure," she says, then looks at me. "I like successful men with or without money. We can always make money."

I smile. I love that girl, but her sister couldn't be more opposite. Or so I think.

We arrive at Arnie's house just when the Black Canyon Gang starts playing on the back lawn. It looks like everyone in town is here. *Why not?* Most of us have never seen a mango, let alone eaten one. Arnie spots Connie and separates himself from the crowd. She runs up to him and jumps into his arms, wrapping her legs around his waist. She clamps her lips firmly on his as he struggles to stay standing. This struggle for balance goes on for a while, so we casually pass them by and go to the drink table. As we pass by, Susie leans over and tells Connie, "Get a room, sleaze ball!"

The bar is a long table with orange-colored drinks already pre-mixed and ready to go. On one side is a bunch of blenders and on the other is a box of green mangos. Several people are cutting up the mangoes and passing them to the people blending, who mix the drinks. Others just crowd around a bowl of cut-up mangos, spearing chunks with their plastic forks or hunting knives. The menu calls for Mango Screwdrivers and Mango Margaritas. I notice a line of vodka and tequila bottles and Bob Starr, of course, hovering at the center of the action, bartending as usual.

"Hey, Starr!" I yell loudly so he'll hear me over the band. "Two of whatever that is!" I point at a line of orange filled glasses near the tequila bottles. He sees me and nods smiling that big shit-eating overly-mustached grin he gets when he's loaded. He brings over two Mango Margaritas with little umbrellas sticking out the top. I immediately see that's a bad idea for Butte drunks. The umbrella stick is long and pointed. It isn't long until little sword fights break out all over the place and someone inevitably gets poked in the ass.

We're drinking this strange concoction and listening to the Black Canyon Gang from Montrose playing stuff like Jerry Jeff Walker and Willie Nelson when Connie and Arnie approach. Connie grabs Susie's hand and begins dragging her along with them. I feel obligated to follow. I grab Susie's other hand and we go inside like a bunch of little kids looking for trouble.

Inside, I marvel at the two-story open beam ceiling and deck surrounding a big open living area. The kitchen is off this huge open area to one side and an office balances it on the other side. He already has it well-loaded with beautiful leather chairs and Danish modern furniture, shipped in from LA like the mangos, I figure.

I notice a small well-worn book lying on his immense coffee table. *Maritime Contract Time Sharing* is the title. While Arnie is showing his house to Connie and Susie, I glance through it quickly. Basically, I discern it's a legal book explaining the international laws for renting out ships that go to sea and haul things for contract. It's all about the *Bill of Lading*. I have a feeling this is his money bible. I pocket it for later perusal.

When they return, Arnie leads us up to the second-floor deck overlooking the living room, which has two bedrooms off it. He leads us through what is obviously his bedroom and onto an outside deck overlooking his backyard party and Keystone Ridge. He assumes the lotus position and produces a little mirror and several lines of white powder. Connie's eyes get bigger as he offers her the first hit.

We each in turn hunch down over the mirror sucking up a line apiece so the people down below can't see what we're doing. But who's kidding whom? They all know what's going on, as it's quite common for all Butte parties, especially if the host is rich. They also know we have been favored with a deck visit, and therefore one of the accepted anointed. It's all part of the cocaine social status ritual of the wealthy and famous, separating those with and without the requisite coke for sharing, resulting in coolness.

Susie and I settle back in our box seats on the little balcony, enjoying the music and the buzz, when I notice Arnie and Connie have disappeared. Susie looks at the door to the bedroom, which is now closed with curtains drawn.

"Looks like we're going to be stuck here for a while," she points out.

"Why?" I ask stupidly.

"Listen," she commands, and cocks an ear toward the door. Now I hear something. It sounds like low moans of either a sick dog or...? Then it hits me. They adjourned to do the nasty in the immediate bedroom, trapping us out here as their unwitting audience and unwilling victims.

"That's typical Connie. She used to do this to me all the time when we stayed together in Aspen. I couldn't take the constant stream of ski patrol studs and desperate rich kids she paraded through our apartment. It was like a Disney attraction. Long wait times for a short ride."

I gave her my best flabbergasted look. "You're kidding! I hope for Arnie's sake, she has an epiphany. I think he's like me. We're raised strict protestants who learn that sex equals love equals marriage, and the man must be responsible for the woman."

"Oh god, no!" she exclaims. "Sex is for fun and husbands are for security. Winter's coming and it's time for mountain girls to find a warm cabin. Arnie's seems pretty warm. I told her she could work part time at the Princess if she stays here with Arnie. She'll maybe do some ski instructing with me on the hill."

"What's love for?"

"What do you mean?" she asks.

"Sex is for fun. What's love for?"

She laughs, moves close to me, and grabs my crotch in a playful squeeze, "For not saying you're sorry, stupid. Didn't you see the movie?"

"Unfortunately, yes." I grab her right back and we sit there in a sort of Mexican groin-hold standoff, eyeing each other and waiting for the next one to move. She starts gently stroking my groin area. I start doing the same. We kiss.

"Get a room!" shouts Bob from down below.

I look over her shoulder and the railing and see a bunch of people holding their mango drinks in the air saluting us and vocally urging us on. I wave at them meekly as we sink down below the railing and out of sight.

*

Saturday night in Gunnison Colorado can be a real brain-twister. Here we are at the Alamo Bar, the most famous redneck bar hereabouts, with vomit-stained pool tables in the back and so much smoke you can't see the walls. When you walk around, there's an unsettling crunch every once in a while, that just begs you to look, but most are wiser not to.

We do the first gig and get about a hundred bucks in tips, just enough to keep Townes in whiskey for a few days. Cindy pockets the lot of it and tells me to see her later. I wasn't doing it for the money, but then neither is Townes. He loves to play and he loves to drink. When he can do both in front of an appreciative audience, he fairly beams with pride, sparkles with down-home humility, and bubbles with fun.

He's sitting on a wooden chair, with two mics on stands in front of him. One is for his beat-up Martin and the other for his voice. He's checking the tuning on his guitar after doing

"Lungs." I always thought this song a little biting if not ironic, considering how Townes probably smokes more than he drinks, which is not easy in his case.

"You know folks, time flies like an airplane." He pauses slightly with his tuning for effect, then finishes it. "Fruit flies like a banana." There's huge laughter and whistles. "Do you know the difference between an apple and my car?" He pauses for effect. Strums some more. "You can't drive my car!" he shouts. Then he quietly adds, "You can drive my apple." More laughs and sniggers. Makes them think.

"Ah, folks. You shouldn't. I don't deserve it. I'm just glad I can be with y'all and have a few drinks together and sing a couple of songs." He hoists his glass and is greeted with more screams of approval. "I hope you like it. I'd like to sing for you now a medley of my hit song, "Poncho and Lefty."

A drunk yells out from the back, "Yeah! Tell it like it is!"

"Thanks folks," he says right back, laughing. "I appreciate that under-whelming response. Here't goes."

"Livin' on the road my friend, thought would keep you clean and free.

Now you wear your skin like iron and your breath's as hard as kerosene."

The crowd goes wild. It's mostly college kids and their dates. The place is packed and boisterous. I keep smelling pot, but can't make out where it's coming from.

During our breaks, I take Townes outside and we sit in my truck while he has a few slugs off his pint and I smoke a joint. Cindy stays inside and pumps the crowd for tips.

*

I honestly never heard of Townes before I actually met him in the Company Store early one summer morning. He came riding Amigo into town, soaking wet from an overnight mountain gusher, found the Company Store the only thing open at that hour, and me, just opening up the record shop I was running for the Weaz. He asked if he could hang out and warm up. I took him in, dried him off, bought him a pint of whiskey next door when Yelenik's opened at 9, for which he said he would pay me back next week. We became instant friends, forever.

It isn't until Tim introduces me to one of his early albums that I realize how my gut feelings about him are more than spot-on. It doesn't take me long before I convince him to play for us in the Grubstake or the Nickel, at least for tips. I do the sound, and everyone in town shows up. I become an instant super fan of the guy. Somehow, the times and the place just conspire and extraordinary people emerge.

Townes becomes a regular fixture of the Crested Butte summer community for the next five or so years. He does fund raising concerts and participates in just about all the goings on, both legal and otherwise. Summer parties just aren't worth going to if Townes isn't there to help us celebrate life and all its twisted wonders.

*

Just before Townes takes the last break of the night, Cindy approaches and pulls me off to the side.

"How's Townes?" she asks pointedly.

I look over at him as he finishes up "The Silver Ships of Andilar," my personal favorite. I look back at Cindy. "He's still in the saddle. Why?" Townes has been known to fall off his stool while singing.

"There's a couple up front who want to meet Townes."

"So? Send 'em back just before the next break. I'll warn him."

"You don't understand. They're fanatics, and apparently, they accidentally found us tonight while driving through town from North Carolina to California."

"Wow! What a coincidence. That'll be a story for their grandkids."

"Anyway, they say that back in North Carolina, where they're from, Townes is somewhat of an underground hero and people are bidding up his albums now that they are out of print. God, I wish I had that box of albums Townes has in his trailer."

She goes back up front, Townes finishes, and the crowd erupts again in more loud drunken applause, replete with redneck hoots and howls. Townes puts his guitar down and gets up to leave for the truck. Cindy reappears with the young couple in tow wearing thin lowland winter gear, letting us know they're not from around here and are probably freezing their asses off.

"Hello, Townes!" the man says, reaching out to shake his hand. Townes looks a little dazed as he always does near the end of a long night of performing, but smiles big, shakes his hand, and says how happy he is to be able to play for them.

"You can't imagine our surprise when we were just getting some gas and saw your poster. We just love your songs. We have all five of your albums and can't wait for more."

"*Aw*, shucks. I don't deserve it. Thanks for stopping in. I hope you have a safe trip to California."

"Could I get your autograph?" The man produces one of the handouts that were stacked near the door. Townes signs it barely legibly, saying how much he likes North Carolina.

I look at the pure adoration on their faces and look back at my old familiar friend and get a whole new level of insight about this ordinary human with an extraordinary soul, exquisite talent, a good sense of the human condition, and living his life to the fullest. He could be just another one of the good old boys of Crested Butte, except this weathered mountain man, out of seemingly nowhere, produces meaningful words for a common folk, a philosopher and lover, fighter and forgiver, victim and reluctant hero, all wrapped up in such simple phrases and melodies, it all seems so close, so guttural, so comfortably suitable, not at all the exceptional emotional scalpel that it really is. In Townes' case, his truth makes us all free.

*

Susie and I settle into our new home nicely. We have our first Thanksgiving and I do a big turkey with all the stuffing and trimmings. We invite our friends over who don't have homes like ours and we share the day, eating turkey and listening to good music. The TV only gets snowy pictures from the major networks, so entertaining becomes necessary to fill the empty times. I have a pretty good collection of rock albums and a damned good stereo, so when people visit they bring their blank cassette tapes for me to record their favorite artists. Now that I have Townes' studio tapes from the *Live from the Old Quarter Houston* recordings, I play them a lot for anyone stopping by.

The big dump this year comes on the same day as Thanksgiving and by the time every one goes home, there's at least a foot on the ground and visibility is nil. Nobody pays any attention other than to remark, *it's about time.* From here on for the next two weeks, we finally get the necessary two to three feet of snow at the ski area, sufficient to open the runs.

Susie and I stay very busy with both of us running the Princess in the evenings and during the day, she offers private ski lessons while I work in my little shop at Mitchell's cinder block building, fixing peoples stereos, maintaining sound systems for the bars, and trying to get commissions for my considerable technical talents.

I already spend a lot of time helping Dana wire his van and keep his video and projector equipment repaired and ready for the Ace of Space Road Show. Even though, like most of us, he has no cash to pay for an assistant, I volunteer anyway, traveling with him on most of his road trips and performances, acting in the role of road manager, stage manager, cameraman, diver, electrician, gaffer, and creative consultant all rolled up into one...and who sleeps in the bunk over the cab. When I'm not on the road with Dana, I'm working on any kind of electronic project that makes me some money.

One night in the Grubstake, Susie and I are unwinding after the show when David Leinsdorf approaches and unceremoniously sits down at our table.

"Hi Susie, Norm," he says, like this happens all the time. David moved here to enjoy this incredible town and immediately assumed the position of the biggest fish in a tiny pond, and pays for it by working in Denver where high-priced lawyers with famous last names can make more money than they would otherwise dare to deserve if depending on their own talents. He makes so much he buys a twin-engine Cessna 210, which he uses to commute here from Denver on weekends in only about an hour's flight time, instead of the five hours on a good day by road.

Socially, he's the top banana, yet he doesn't even own a restaurant or condominium. As the top dog, for those who care about such things, he decides who is in and out of CB upper crusty New Yorkish snob social status. If you're not invited to one of his parties, then you're nobody. The newspaper people assume he can do no wrong and might be the second coming. I just get nauseated.

"Hi David," I answer. "Please, sit down." I beckon him to the empty chair.

He yells toward the bar. "Hey Baggins! Bring me a beer, please." Baggins waves back. He turns back to us and sits down.

"I love to see you together. I think you two are a really good fit." He turns to Susie, and asks, "How's your mother?"

"She's fine," she answers. I look at her quizzically.

"Your mother has always been a great supporter of the arts in New York. My father respects your family greatly."

Susie giggles a little. "They do get involved."

He turns to me. "Cowboy...."

"My mother doesn't give a dime."

"Mitchell says you have a pilot's license."

"Who's asking?"

"Maybe you can appreciate what I think we need down at the airport. Ron Rouse and I both agree we'd like a marker beacon on top of Smith Hill just south of the runway. Do you know what I'm talking about?"

"I've shot the approach with Mitchell a couple of times. You clear the hill by a few hundred feet and then dive fast to make the end of the runway. What's the problem?"

"Landing at night with snow conditions. I can't see the terrain very well, especially on moonless nights."

"I just priced some solar panels for Dan Thurman, but he couldn't afford the eighty or so that he needs. This will probably take just two or three, so a lot cheaper. What's your budget?"

"This is Crested Butte, son. Nobody has a budget. Tell us what it's going to cost, mindful that it's got to be cheap. Ron and I will figure out how to pay for it. I already have permission from the Forest Service to put it in under a temporary safety lighting agreement with the FAA."

"I'm not your son, and I'll need at least some cash to get the parts." I grab a napkin and pen from a passing waitress. "I know Heathkit has a twenty-four-volt strobe light I can get for less than a hundred bucks." I start drawing boxes and lines on the napkin as I block out the circuitry for a solar strobe light.

"I'll need an insulated box for the batteries, about four twelve-volt deep cycle batteries and a little tower section to mount the strobe and panels up above the snow line." I finish drawing the block diagram, look up, and neither David or Susie is paying any attention to my doodling.

"So, what do you think?" David asks, looking back from studying a couple of young female tourists at the bar.

"Five hundred bucks for the parts and five hundred for my labor."

"Sounds doable," he says to me. "I'll check with Ron and get back to you." He turns to Susie. "Give your mother my best."

"Sure," she says, and he gets up smiling and walks casually over to the bar right behind the two tourists.

"You could have held out for more," she says, after he's out of earshot.

"I know, but I want to get in with the in-crowd and maybe get back into flying. Wouldn't it be fun to have a plane and go flying like I did back in Ann Arbor?"

"Sure," she replies, but notably without much enthusiasm.

*

The threat of a big mine opening right next door to the town begins to heat up. More trucks are seen going through town on White Rock, the truck route to Kebler Road and the Oh Be Joyful mine. We had all seen it coming and now it's getting serious. The old timers and developers all duck the conflict saying jobs are good. But the jobs would bring an entirely different class of people than those who live here now: people without concern for the environment, the wilderness, or resource development.

It's all about money, and the cheapest way to get to the ore today is to not mine it at all. Why bother, when modern mining companies have the technology to literally chew up a mountain, reducing the entire skyline to mud, adding caustic chemicals, and spewing it all out again filling up a nearby verdant valley with poisonous muck that kills life forever?

We all seem to agree, even those who could sell out their mothers in a heartbeat, that this concept of tearing up and destroying wilderness for military industrial profit should be stopped. We talk among ourselves and it becomes obvious we need a leader who reflects our values and who has the balls to stand up to these monsters. We nominate crazy Mitchell.

He asks for it by surreptitiously becoming a big donor to the Sierra Club and generating press for the cause. Why not? We all see a little bit of ourselves in him. He's mysterious, he takes chances, he loves to party, and he seems to make friends with everyone. He can talk to different classes of people without having to be one of them. A modern hippie diplomat with a compelling story and a hopeful resurrection. He's in many ways the epitome of an all-American success story. He takes a lickin' and keeps on ticking. Who wouldn't vote for that?

*

He's overwhelmingly swept into the mayor's office and the town hall is modified to become wheelchair accessible. People start going to the town meetings and actual debates and local characters begin showing up in public, making the local newspapers actually go to work spending more time making up myths about it.

Meanwhile, the Butte burns on. Townes leaves for the winter, going back to Austin where he has fairly regular gigs at local college bars. Dana and I spend time getting his props and van put together for a winter tour he has lined up. I put together the solar strobe light and deploy it to the top of Smith Hill right in line with the runway below it. It's snowing the day I set it up and figure I won't be back until next spring. The first night it kicks on at dusk, and suddenly the sheriff's office phone lights up with reports of UFOs landing on Smith Hill.

They finally track down Ron, who tells them about the new marker light. Several ranchers living nearby claim it bothers them and keeps them up at night, but basically, we can't do anything until spring, so it slowly becomes a new fixture of the valley.

*

I'm asleep in our upstairs bedroom with Susie. I may be dreaming about flashing lights in the sky when I wake up. I can see dim flashing lights coming through the window. I quietly roll out of bed and stand up. Susie stays asleep.

I look out on the snowy buildings and see blue and red flashing lights strobing the buildings near the old firehouse. That's a strange place for cops and firetrucks, especially because there's no smoke, and thus, fire can't be the cause. I check the alarm clock and it's 2:30 a.m. The bars should be closed, so what the hell?

I put on my pants, shirt, and down coat, silently descend the staircase, and proceed to walk downtown. When I round the corner at Second Street, I see a big crowd with the marshal's truck, the CB Medics, and our local firetruck all blocking the intersection. People are holding up flashlights all aimed at something on the bridge over Coal Creek. When I get to the back of the crowd, the center of interest comes into view. It's an old blue Chevy four-door sedan. There's the sound of metal grinders and sparks flying around near the driver's door.

I recognize the car as belonging to a resident of the mobile home park. I think her name is Sheryl, or Sherrie. I've shared bar space with her a few times and about all I know is she's running from something, like all of us, and is looking for a life, like all of us, and she likes to drink and party and hang out in the Grubstake most nights until closing, just like most of us. She didn't have very many friends, but she seemed to be having a good time, always happy and smiling a lot.

I spot the Rat standing off to one side and walk over to him. "What happened?"

"Oh man. Bad ju ju." He looks away from the scene and then up to me. "She got speared by the bridge railing. They're trying to cut her out of the car, but it's taking forever."

I look back and now I see that the car is leaning over the edge of the bridge where normally there's a large steel pipe guard rail preventing such things. Then I almost lose my guts when I spot the pipe railing poking out the front of the car at a point where if I follow the remembered length and the position of the car, it puts the end of the pipe somewhere in the trunk. It seems to be lined up to pass straight through the driver's side.

Too many people are at the side of the car to see inside, but nearby women are sobbing or screaming and men are seriously acting sober. Finally, I see someone near the car hold his hand up in a fist and he twists it fiercely. Everyone goes silent. A medic soon appears with a sheet and the crowd lets out a wail. The sheet disappears inside the car. The sparks from cutting steel resume, but now people start meandering away, some tightly holding onto others who are clearly more hysteric or shell-shocked.

I walk back home with a group of neighbors and when I climb into bed, Susie wakes up.

"What's going on?" she asks, while blinking rapidly to clear her eyes. When I tell her who just died, she goes silent for a moment.

"My liver can't take any more wakes!" she announces, matter-of-fact.

I agree and slip into bed, where we hug each other the rest of the night.

The next day, everyone in town has a somber day after all the gruesome details emerge. She lived for about an hour after speeding off from the Grubstake with a new man she just picked up. She must have lost control of the car, which impaled itself onto the Coal Creek homemade steel pipe railing, ramming all the way through the car from grill to trunk, puncturing her gut, and pinning her inside the car like a shish kebab.

Many people valiantly tried like hell to cut the extra-strong, mine certified drilling pipe that was used to make the bridge, so they could remove her. During the whole ordeal, she was conscious and talking to her fervent and encouraging rescuers. They just weren't fast enough. They didn't have the right big-city tools that might have helped. The lack of a *Jaws of Life* for our medics is mentioned many times that day.

~ 13 ~

ON THE TOAD AGAIN

If you have to be born rich and still want a shot at having a human conscience and a clean heart, you literally need to become an artist. This is a great solution to the age-old question, *what the fuck am I going to do, now that I don't have to do anything?* I never had this choice, but when I hit the Butte, art is the only redeeming value left for a poor, broke physicist disguised as a homeless nerd. I like art. It's fun. My art is drama and movies, and I know the new video technology will eventually replace film, but I just can't afford any of that for now.

Fortunately, I'm not the only proclaimed artist with a bent for high technology. I make a few amateur Super 8- and 16-millimeter films while a graduate student at the University of Michigan and take a film class from the great Manupelli. I get the bug when my friend Kemp and I convince Nicky Pritzker, heir to the Chicago Pritzker real estate family and fellow Lake Forest College alum, to remake his underground Super 8 art film as a well-produced 16mm color version with a cast of hundreds.

We make the film in Lake Forest while I am doing a particle experiment at the zero-gradient synchrotron at Argonne National Laboratories just southwest of Chicago. My physics professor did not understand that art supersedes science and took a dim view when I had to leave the experiment near the end in order to honor my artistic commitment to my friends. The experiment was not impacted in any way by my departure, as we had already collected more data than we could possibly use. He just didn't like the fact I had a higher calling than him. Professional jealousy does exist, and is petty. It's one of the things that keeps me from an academic career.

When it's all over, I end up changing my major from accelerators to satellites and join a NASA lab in Ann Arbor while I finish my degree, this time doing research writing programs for large-scale computer simulations of the upper atmosphere. My friends from the film, Kemp and Cordley Coit, Taffy Gray, and Susan Anderton all end up in Crested Butte. I, on the other hand, regularly commute back and forth between Ann Arbor and the National Center for Atmospheric Research in Boulder, where I run my simulation programs on the fastest super computer in the world.

But in reality, I'm hiding out in Crested Butte, smoking dope, playing cop with Kemp, now the town marshal, and pretending to be a film artist and social rebel hanging with Cordley. From the moment I meet Don Bachman at Tony's Tavern, where he hires me and Kemp to be his bouncers on New Years Eve, 1968, I fatally fall in love with the Butte and begin considering it my home to be.

Then Nixon's elected, my lab gets its funding cut, and physics throws me out on the streets again, just two months away from defending my third research thesis. I complete three PhD research projects in five years at the U of M, all leading to peer-reviewed publications, but no final parchment. Instead of running away to the circus like traditional graduate school failures, I go on the road with a rock and roll band, providing the loudest state-of-the-art public address system, or PA, on the market. It can damage eardrums in the rear seats of thousand-seat arena theaters. But within a year, I burn out on cocaine and sleeplessness and have to give up on the world of high-powered musical road tours. I join my semi-artistic friends in Crested Butte, seeking refuge from an ugly world of cutthroat business and lying hustlers everywhere. I'm looking for an escape from Cold War conformity. I'm looking for a new challenging home of beauty and peace, hopefully with a heaping helping of love and life thrown in for good measure.

Right after I arrive in town permanently and settle into Kemp's garage, Cordley drags me out of the Grubstake and up Elk Avenue past the Coal Creek bridge and firehouse, which marks the downtown area from the uptown area. When I first visited Crested Butte, most if not all of the buildings in the uptown area were either abandoned and falling down from the repeated snow load every winter or boarded up and fading rapidly to a dark grey, barnwood color in the intense, unfiltered high-altitude sunlight.

"You gotta meet this street artist," Cordley huffs out between gulps of breath. "He just bought one of the abandoned homes up here on Elk for five grand right next to the old whorehouse."

"You mean the big old house where I shot that Super 8 short with Kemp for Manupelli's class? *The Man-With-No-Name Visits Crested Butte?*"

"He calls himself Ace of Space and has a lot of electronic gizwhizery in his van. He even lives in it while traveling on the road."

"On the road?" I respond. Being a trucker of sorts and a recent roadie, my curiosity is piqued.

"Yeah. He does a weird performance with a giant slide show and sound effects, and colored lights. And he sings. You'll probably recognize all the stuff he has. I just know he takes a lot of color slide pictures of weird road art or exotic highway scenery while driving between gigs. I figure an old roadie like yourself should check this guy out. Who knows, maybe he'll hire you."

"*Jeez*, if he's a performance artist, he can't be making much, especially if he lives in a van."

"His daddy has money. I don't know anything more about him except he has a fine arts degree from Dartmouth."

"Dartmouth, the *pretend to be better than you probably deserve* university for the American *nouveau bourgeoisie*," I recite.

"Of course," Cordley agrees, taking a sudden left turn from the middle of the street and walking up a driveway with a plain delivery box van parked out front. He walks through the rear porch door and starts making himself known.

"Hello! Anybody home? Don't shoot!" he shouts, and then laughs at the shoot part. "It's Cordley! With a friend!"

A door swings open and a short sandy-haired smiling cherub sticks his head out. "Oh, hi Cordley. Que paso?"

"I'm just stopping by to bring my friend to meet you. He's into electronic shit just like you so maybe you have something in common. His name is Cowboy."

I hold my hand out to Dana and he shakes it. "Cowboy, huh? Just call me Ace of Space. Come on in."

We walk into his kitchen and on into the main room, which is cluttered from floor to ceiling with all kinds of weird crap. I spot movie screens, a tape deck, some colorfully painted boxes, a wooden saxophone painted with leopard spots and mirrors, and lot and lots of truck mirrors. I'm not certain what kind of artist this guy is, but it isn't exactly what one might expect.

"Cordley says you were a roadie for a rock band."

"Among other things. I'm actually a pre-doctoral physicist with an electrical engineering degree on the side. I developed a new kind of low distortion speaker and helped build a super PA for Grand Funk Railroad. But I can't take the cocaine lifestyle every day, so I retired here to enjoy my young idle years in the mountains. So, exactly what kind of medium do you work with?"

"Electrons and photons. I do a performance using pictures and stories gathered from my years on the road and all the art that I find out there. Hence, *Finds Arts*. You want one?"

"Go ahead, Cowboy," says Cordley. "I got mine some time ago and I've been finding arts ever since." Then he lets go with his signature maniacal laugh that he normally only uses to alleviate tense situations.

Ace goes to a box sitting on top of more boxes in the corner and pulls out a piece of paper. He comes back and lays it on the table so everyone can see it.

"Let's see: C-O-W-B-O-Y," he spells out loud as he pens it onto the diploma-looking document. "It's nineteen hundred and seventy-four and done. There you go. You are now officially a graduate of the Ace of Space University with a Finds Arts degree and all the privileges and honors that go with it. Congratulations!"

He rolls it up, ties a purple ribbon around it, and hands it to me.

"Gee, thanks," I say, not really knowing if the guy is for real or not. Then he hauls out some of his ganja and we commence to get so fucking high I could leave footprints on the moon.

That's when we get this idea for a movie. Ace, or Dana, as I later learn, has just bought a VHS video recorder and a professional Japanese portable color video camera. He's only been taking still pictures up to now and his show consists of putting on a multimedia live performance with stage props, live action, music, and of course the *coup de grâce*, two big movie screens for a backdrop where he projects 35mm color slides illustrating his stories and songs.

I am impressed. I had been doing somewhat the same thing in the *Ann Arbor Summer '70* film I directed. By using the new Sony handheld video camera, I recorded live events like rock bands in bars and music festivals. I also did closed-circuit video projections at the Ann Arbor Blues and Jazz festival, where we projected live video from the stage to a big screen hanging above the stage. For the first time ever, concert attendees were able to see closeups of their favorite Blues artists, all the way from the back of the park.

We both think video is where it's all going and the game is one of trying to figure out how to make enough money to support such an expensive hobby, or as he calls it, *Finds Arts*. Someone suggests we actually use guns to shoot a boob tube and record it on tape. We can have Kemp arrest a TV set for crimes against humanity and Cordley can execute it with high-caliber weapons.

"So, we get my brother to break into Ace's house," Cordley proposes. "He serves an arrest warrant on a TV set and then we show him taking it away in the marshal's truck. Whereupon, we take it out to the dump and blast away at it with massive firepower."

"I like it!" Dana exclaims. "Where can we find the victim? I don't have a TV, at least not one we can shoot."

"Gustafson's!" I propose. "That's where I found a cheap TV I fixed up for my garage. He's got lots of junkers and klunkers."

They were also the source of a lot of recycled furniture for us poor *negaces* trying to live in Butte garages, and, of course, the first fat tire frames for building klunkers.

"Okay, the next time one of us goes to Gunnison, stop by Gustafson's and pick up a nice cabinet TV suitable for the part," Dana says. "Now, where can we find some guns?"

Cordley looks at me and I look back. We both break up laughing.

*

Finding guns in Crested Butte is only slightly easier than finding a free drink at happy hour. One of the things that first attracts me and others to this wilderness town is the locally accepted practice of packing heat in public as long as you check it with the bartender before being served. Donner wears his pearl-handled .45s almost every day he lives in Crested Butte, commensurate with his image as "Black Bart," and he makes sure they are displayed prominently in whatever bar he happens to be occupying.

Cordley and I agree the crux of this drama will hinge on the firepower we can muster. But after only one night of talking it up in the bars, we have more than enough volunteers for the firing squad. We ask them to bring their most esoteric weapons still safe to shoot.

Cordley finds an old stand-up twenty-one-inch Dumont TV, which he brings back from Gustafson's crammed in the trunk of his BMW. It's heavy and has a big picture tube. It'll make a great target.

All we need now is a location. Most western towns have either an old garbage dump or gravel pit nearby that gets unofficially designated as the local gun range. There's just such a place up the Slate River near Peanut Lake.

Dana and I work together for the first time, shooting the interiors where Kemp reads the arrest warrant to the TV.

"In the name of humanity and decency," he reads from some papers while standing over the TV set in Dana's living room, "the people of Crested Butte do hereby find you guilty of wasting time, lowering intellectual standards, and assaulting good taste. We therefore condemn you to a fiery demise befitting your crimes." He looks directly at the camera and says, "Lock 'em up boys!" Two deputies step in, pick up the TV, and carry it out.

We grab a quick shot of the TV inside the one cell in the old marshal's office. We spread the word that night in the bars, and the next morning at the gravel pit about a dozen good citizens show up with every kind of weird gun they could find. Townes has the .50-caliber black powder rifle I traded to him. Donner, of course, has his antique Sharps .50-caliber buffalo rifle. I help with the taping, so Cordley uses my Smith & Wesson model 29 .44 magnum, the Dirty Harry model.

I fear for the microphone I'm using and stuff a couple of socks over it to help protect it from the gun explosions. The TV is tied to a post and blindfolded. The guys line up and at a signal from Dana, all begin shooting at the TV. Needless to say, the big tube immediately implodes showering the cliff behind it with shards of silvery glass. They keep shooting as long as they have ammo and Dana gets a lot of neat close-up shots of the total decimation of a once respectable piece of family furniture.

He edits it up into a little, two-minute clip which he works into his show. I like what he does and gladly join him in his efforts to find art and bring it to culturally starved audiences.

What he is doing with video as an artform is fresh, new, provocative, and challenging. What I like about it is that it is portable and it's cheaper than film, putting it in the hands of a greater swath of artists than ever before.

No more huge film cameras with crews of thousands. Here is a way to capture real happenings by almost anybody, anywhere. With this technology making cameras cheaper, television will become a visual art and Dana is showing his fellow artists that just like pigments, it's okay to get your hands dirty with the technical details.

The following year at the annual Fourth of July gulch party, Coney makes a catapult that launches TV sets over the heads of all us party goers. Those with shotguns line up and yell, *Pull!* Coney lets go of the device and a portable TV arcs out over the heads of everyone and into the gulch. Shots are heard from all directions as the TV becomes pulverized sort of in slow motion as it comes apart in midflight, maintaining the same general arc, and finally disappearing in the trees down below. Just another way we entertain ourselves without pretension.

*

Without much warning, Dana talks me into going with him to Dallas for a show he has booked at some civic arts center or something. I hate Dallas from some old presidential murder and I want to stay in CB because I'm still getting our house ready for our first winter on Sopris—and the local city politics is heating up with the mayor's election.

The mayor's race is a joke, with no opposition against the business-as-usual incumbent, Tommy Glass. The town is frozen in fear with the implied threat that at any moment, a super corporation like Amax could make a move on the town, say for instance, buying up all the available living spaces, loading them with obedient redneck Republican miners and boom, just that easy, take over the town. Next thing you know, there's DEA agents everywhere. As I pack for the trip, I talk to Mitchell on the phone.

"If I wasn't going to Dallas with Dana," I rant, "I'd run against that fat little cherub myself. Nobody should be unopposed in an election."

"If you do, I said I'll donate a hundred dollars to your campaign," he counters.

"Listen, you little whiny bitch, put your money and wheels where your mouth is. Take over the town in the name of the people. Then we'll find a way to pass a law against Amax and all new development."

"I'll think about it," is all he can say.

No doubt he'll consult his other rich friends because, as we all know, politics is not cheap but easily affordable for a bright new face. Seeing how he doesn't have one, I figure he's a shoe-in with the sympathy vote. But, contrary to my best advice, he barters his soul by bringing new power people into his circle of friends as influencers that he thinks he needs in order to be a proper upstanding Crested Butte politician. I remind myself to get him a copy of *All the Kings Men.*

While I'm gone with Dana, Mitchell quietly files for one of the open council seats and gets elected by a landslide as he has no opponent. I note that he likes to slip in quietly and get close for the killing thrust. Good Machiavellian tactic.

We drive all night in Dana's new GMC 32-foot motor home/ production van, switching the wheel about every four hours or two hundred miles. When I take a break, I try to get some sleep, but when Dana is not driving, he's in his cabin at the back writing notes and making drawings. I admire an artist who clearly can't do much of anything else but at least what he does do, he does a lot of it. Numbers legitimize. Check out Picasso.

Outside of Dallas just before rush hour, we pull in at a truck stop where he makes his daily phone calls. I'm waiting for him in the van after refueling the beast and hitting the gleaming chrome head these new truck stops are famous for, and scanning all their proudly purely *American* stuff for sale that just shouts, *Here's another dumbass thing for the unwashed masses to be falsely proud of.* Often, Dana finds things at these cultural deserts that he can sarcastically use in his show, like porno mud flaps. Suddenly, the door swings open with its characteristic sound of grinding metal on metal and Dana climbs aboard with a shit-eating grin on his face.

"You're going to like this," he says, fairly beaming with pride.

"You think so?" I respond, not wanting to give him any opening in case it's some kind of prank. He's always playing pranks. His favorite is to poke you in the stomach and when you look down like a sucker, he lifts his finger up catching you in the nose. He laughs hardily at your displeasure, while you contemplate punching him in the mouth.

"I've got a friend in town working on a pilot for a new TV series."

"Who?"

"You'll see."

"What's the show about?" I ask.

"Dallas," he answers simply.

"You're kidding," I respond skeptically. "Who the fuck would want to watch that?"

Dana threads through downtown Dallas with crowded streets, sort of owning the place. Who's going to push around a 32-foot motor home—a Texas pickup? He finds the location, outside a large restaurant and dance club, now turned into a temporary movie set. There are trailers, RVs, and cables going everywhere. We're directed to park near a row of other motor homes belonging to the production company.

We make our way past all the cabling and lighting crap to the middle of the club, which has been decked out as a disco with lasers, mirror balls, and ugly costumes. Some guy with a walkie talkie asks what we're doing on his set and Dana tells him who we're here to see. The guy wanders off and about a minute later, a tall dark-haired guy comes pushing out of the crowd of dancers rehearsing their next shot.

"Ace of Space!" he yells, "How the hell are you? You made it here. Good to see you again."

They hug and cheek-kiss as I try to place his face. He looks damned familiar, but maybe older or more alcoholic or something.

"Cowboy," Dana commands, "I'd like you to meet Larry Hagman. Larry, meet my friend and co-conspirator, Cowboy."

"How do you do?" he asks while holding out his hand. I take it, smile, and shake his hand pretending I'm cool, but still wondering where the hell I've seen this guy before.

"I thought we could go have dinner. These guys won't be needing me here for another three or four hours. There's a nice restaurant just around the corner. I sort of have a permanent table reservation going with them."

He slaps Dana on the back and the two of them lead me through the labyrinth of obsessive lighting equipment clogging up the set. I think I see now who has a stranglehold on Hollywood, and it's not the snot-nosed kids of spoiled film executives and over-paid celebrities. It's the lighting union.

When we arrive, the manager spots Larry right off and leads us to a table in an alcove where we won't be seen by most of the other patrons. We sit down and drinks show up immediately.

"You'd think that after several years of no work," Larry laments, "my fans would begin to forget me, or I age enough to not be recognized so well."

I just study his face and sure as tootin', he looks a lot older than the cherry-cheeked role he played for many years on TV. The handsome young bungling astronaut has turned into a middle-aged executive with wrinkles and a gut.

"That's one of the reasons I don't fly," he explains. "Even in first class it's a constant bother. Besides, I don't like to be cooped up like that in a flying coffin. They scare the crap out of me."

"That's how we met in LA last year," adds Dana. "I met Peter Fonda at my LA show and he knew Larry only travels in motor homes between locations, so he got us together. Fellow citizens of the road." They clink glasses and then clink mine.

"So, what do you do?" Larry asks point-blank. It catches me off guard. I've never had to talk to a big-time celebrity before. I feel a little out of place and self-conscious.

"I'm a physicist from the University of Michigan. I invented a new low-distortion speaker and built a giant PA for Grand Funk. I'm trying to break into the film business, so I'm helping Ace here transition from still pictures to video." I immediately feel like I said way too much. Nobody cares what I want in life. It's like I'm spilling my guts in the presence of a superstar for some dumb reason. I stop and look at them.

"We're all trying to break into the film business," he commiserates. "I hope this TV show takes off. I really need this job. My motor home needs a new set of tires."

Like an idiot on drugs, I have to say it. "Boy, if I were you, I wouldn't be counting on a show about, of all things, *Dal-ass*. Who cares about this fucking president-killing redneck hellhole?"

The grim look on his face tells me immediately I hit a sore spot. Maybe big stars aren't as big and above it all like I thought. A shroud descends on our little dinner. After this, the conversation turns light and shallow. I start to feel like shit.

*

"Cheer up, Cowboy," Dana tells me next day while we're driving to Austin to do the show. "He agreed with you but he can't afford to turn down the work. I bet you think that all big stars are millionaires. Most are just like us. Not sure where their next job will come from and running out of money from the last one. Anyway, you'll be among friends in Austin."

We're booked into the Moody Theater, one of the oldest theaters in town, as an opening act for a band I'm familiar with. Austin is the home of the Austin sound, which literally takes the Nashville whine out of country music and adds full-blown Rock & Roll. Young country rock musicians are converting from alcohol to marijuana as their source of inspiration, and they need a place where it is tolerated. Moody is the haven and Austin is the exception to Texas—and the opposite of Dallas.

I learn we'll be opening for the *Lost Planet Airmen*, where I'm sure we'll go through some serious snow just catching up with old friends. George Frayne, aka *Commander Cody*, and his band, got started in my basement in Ann Arbor with their hit song, "Lost in the Ozone Again." I used to party with Andy Stein, Bill Kirchen, and Lance Dickerson, who are all Ann Arborites, spending lots of time with them at our place on Division Street, listening to the best stereo in town.

They moved to Austin for a recording contract, performing country songs with a rock twist, where Commander Cody's kind of old-style Rock & Roll is taking off again. Willie Nelson is making the Austin sound famous, as well as the likes of Guy Clark, Jerry Jeff Walker, and Terry Allen.

After the show, we'll go find Townes wherever he's playing. I called him earlier and he volunteered to let us park overnight at the home where he's crashing. He invites us to Seymour Washington's Friday night neighborhood chicken barbecue and Blues guitar picking. Most of his Austin musician friends will be there, he adds. Dana wants to take some pictures of Townes without a guitar in his hand, so what can go wrong?

Seymour Washington's house in south Austin is the unofficial open mic backyard stage held every weekend. Musicians from all around Austin, and sometimes farther, gather at his backyard barbecues

where a substantial number of chickens are slow roasted on open grills to the music of old, and new, Blues and country. Neighbors and passersby are always welcome to stop in for some delicious chicken and hear all kinds of musicians sitting around sharing songs and stories late into the night. It's an Austin institution, we hear.

We show up about midnight just as Townes ends his last set at a nearby bar. We're pretty high from another good Roadshow performance, with an audience equally high after experiencing Dana's super wide-screen brilliant color images of

America's favorite myth, the open highway and the whimsical artist sometimes trucker who dwells there. My Lost Planet Airmen friends lay some righteous coke on us, and Dana and I are feeling no pain.

Townes plays a few licks at the barbeque and then joins a couple of old black guys doing a guitar / harmonica Blues riff. After a couple of Blues songs, they keep playing and Townes and I adjourn to the kitchen where it's quieter and he can refill his pint. Dana, who is taking pictures all this time, follows inside clicking away with his Nikon.

"What the hell is Dana up to?" Townes asks, just before he joins us inside.

"It's okay," I say patting him on the back. "He just wants to add you to our list of spaces and places that make America great. You do know you're great, don't you?"

"Yeah," he says slightly slurred, "if they would only pay me what I'm worth."

"So, how's it going?" I ask innocently, not having spoken with him in quite a while.

"Cindy's gone."

"Oh no, that's a shame." We all knew it was inevitable.

"Not really, she used to beat me up."

"Yeah, I know. Where's Geraldine and Amigo?"

"Cindy insisted on keeping Amigo and I had to agree. My days of camping out in the mountains with Amigo have run their course. Geraldine is staying at my cabin in Tennessee. I just bought it and my cousin is there taking care of her and keeping the stove going while I finish playing this gig."

"Bummer," I say. "Cindy was probably a little much for you anyway. She could pick up a horse with one hand while shoveling shit with the other."

"Good news is, I think Emmy Lou Harris is going to record one of my songs." He takes a celebratory slug from his pint.

"That'll help. But that's Nashville. I thought they were screwing you. Maybe you should find a producer here in Austin."

"I don't know. It's hard even to just get a job in this town."

"Yeah, but this is a new sound outside the mainstream. Dana knows Terry Allen, who's been compared to you and Guy Clark."

"Guy Clark's an old buddy. He's been helping me a lot. Don't worry, Cowboy. I've got something going that might work." He looks at Dana who is still taking pictures. "Who the hell is this guy?"

"You know Dana, from Crested Butte. The Roadshow artist?"

"Hi Townes," Dana says, waving at us. "You don't mind if I take a few pictures? I never got the chance in Crested Butte."

"Just be careful you don't get splashed."

"Splashed? Be careful." He looks around the kitchen and spots a bottle of liquid pink soap on the sink. Townes is holding a can of Coke now to chase his frequent pulls on his ever-present pint. I don't like the way this is going.

Dana picks up the soap bottle and half-heartedly aims it at Townes. Townes reacts by putting his thumb over the can opening, gives it a couple of quick shakes, and let goes a spray of Coke all over the kitchen, nailing Dana and his camera. Dana reacts instantly and squeezes the soap bottle at Townes, hitting him in the chest with a stream of pink sticky liquid.

"*WHOA, GUYS!*" I yell, and grab the soap bottle out of Dana's hand. "Townes, put down the can!"

Dana frantically tries to dry off his camera.

"Ah gosh," Townes repents, "look at what I done. Here, let me help you dry that thing off. Let's go in the bathroom and get you cleaned up. And me. No more fighting. Honest."

The two go off and I wonder what I just saw. Two of my real-life heroes getting into it for a brief second and then going off like nothing happened.

"Artists," I mutter, as I go back outside to listen to the music.

*

"So, I talked to my dad yesterday. You know, he lent me the money to build this production van and he thinks he knows someone who might be able to hire me. I need more jobs if I'm going to pay him back."

"I don't know. I tried to go commercial in Ann Arbor and I just couldn't find enough commercial work to make it pay. I figure video production is just like film production: you never make money and it's all just a labor of love. Only the rich and famous seem to make money at this and they probably make money no matter what they do, being rich and all. I thought your dad made microwave equipment for the military industrial complex and now they make money selling radar guns to the pigs."

"Yeah, he says he's going to send us a Gunnplexer link to play with. They've got the patent on the Gunn diode and have built one as small as a radar gun that transports video signals over line of sight. But another product they're making is a microwave satellite video receiver. People are putting up microwave dishes and tuning into the geosynchronous satellites carrying television signals. So far there is just HBO, WTBS from Atlanta, and a couple of *god channels*, but my dad says the market for TVROs is heating up and they are manufacturing a low-cost receiver for the retail market."

"What's a TVRO?" I ask, not wanting to be ignorant of any new *technical-ese*.

"Television Receive Only. Community antenna systems all over the country are hooking these up so they can deliver premium channels besides just the over-the-hill local channels. My dad has turned me on to a guy who publishes a magazine for the satellite dish industry. It's called *CATJ* and he operates out of his house near Tulsa."

"Oh god, not Tulsa, too!"

"He says he might have some work for us. So, I'm going to swing by his place on our way to Arizona and see what it's all about."

"Wake me up when we get to Arizona."

*

Dana beams as he shows the van to Frank Jackson, the owner and managing editor of *CATJ*.

"We can bring in at least two cameras," Dana explains, "and if we rent more cameras, we can handle up to four. Right now, we just put everything we shoot on VHS tape with single camera shots and edit it all together later, dubbing from one tape machine to another."

"The reason I asked your dad to have you stop by is, I'm working on a big project for next summer. I've got a deal with HBO to broadcast live sessions from our annual convention over their satellite transponder. I need an origination facility like this van and a dish big enough to uplink to the satellite.

That's what I'm working on now with some Canadians who own a fifty-foot portable dish antenna."

"Fifty-foot diameter parabolic dish that's portable?" I ask incredulously. "I gotta see that."

"It was made for the Canadian military so they can set up a satellite station," Frank explains, "literally anywhere a truck can tow it. It's got wheels and it's self-erecting. It's really something to see."

"My dad said you have a personal satellite dish in your backyard," pokes Dana.

"If I'm going to be advocating satellite TV, I figure I better have one to back up what I say. Follow me."

He leads us across his front lawn from where we parked on the street. He lives out in the open prairie with nothing on the horizon except more horizon blocked by more cracker boxes like his dotting it. I look down just as we enter his house and see a partially squashed scorpion. I hate nasty little desert stingers. I wonder if Frank is the squasher.

We pass through his ranch house and he points out his office where it looks like he does everything necessary to publish a glossy, except without the presses. Through his kitchen and out the back porch we go, when suddenly there it is: a large parabolic dish is sitting in his backyard like a kids' monkey bar contraption gone nuts. It's about fifteen feet in diameter and tilted on a frame holding it up at about a forty-degree angle roughly pointing south. There are three legs sticking out in front of the dish with a little disc shaped box mounted presumably at the focal point of the reflector.

"Oh wow!" I exclaim. "What's the secret to how it works?"

"It's pretty simple, really. The antenna is that box sticking out in front. It contains a five-degree Kelvin low noise amplifier. The dish just concentrates the signal like a magnifying mirror. Those five-degree LNAs are the heart of the technology. Up to now, the only thing that worked was an amplifier actually cooled to five degrees above absolute zero with liquid helium. Tunnel diodes and FETs are revolutionizing the satellite business. Now, antennae don't have to be bigger than a house and have tons of support equipment. A five-meter dish, like this one, concentrates the signal just enough above the noise level and then the amplifier captures it and amplifies it up to a usable signal. Anybody can own one of these. I watch HBO every night with a signal quality exceeding most studio productions."

"Cool," says Dana, as he looks it over with his covetous *Finds Arts* eye wishing he could afford one. I'm thinking about watching movies at home, making the movie theater obsolete.

"I'm going to have to do a little research on this, but I think you've got something here," I muse, thinking this would sure look nice in my backyard, now that I have a backyard.

"Anyway, your dad said you're looking for any kind of production work you can get."

He's turning business-like now. *Beware*, I think to myself, as I watch Dana listen raptly to Frank's proposal.

"I want to generate some material for the show and you can maybe go out and do some short documentaries on some of the industry pioneers. I understand you're on your way to Arizona, and it so happens, there's someone out there that needs his story told. *The Bisbee Antenna Farm*."

"I'm all ears," Dana declares.

*

We follow the romantic, or infamous, Route 66 all the way to Flagstaff and then turn south to Phoenix and Scottsdale. The show is outdoors at night and goes well for Ace of Space's visual presentation. Later, the local rock band gets a little help from me when I get on the intercom at one point and tell the lighting guys how to cue a proper Rock & Roll performance. They don't say thanks, afterwards.

The next day, we drive down through the deserts, then over a small mountain range near the border, following the directions Dana got the previous day talking to the *Antenna Man* on the phone. He sounds very excited and offers to have us stay as long as we need.

I'm driving while Dana sits in the passenger seat making notes. It's where he claims he comes up with his best ideas—rolling down some highway almost in a trance from the monotony of the road. The stereo is blasting out the Austin sound and a lot of Townes' songs.

"What do you think our angle should be for this?" he asks out of the blue. He usually likes to make all the artistic decisions, so I'm caught off guard.

"Wadaya mean?" I demand.

"I don't want to shoot a bunch of different setups over days in order to tell his story. Can we do it in one setting? You're the experienced live action filmmaker." He stares at me with a look of actual respect, which I don't often see. I look back at the road and ponder a bit.

"I'm a physicist and I have a basic understanding of antenna theory. I can ask the right questions for getting him to explain his work in a way that brings out whatever he thinks he is doing better."

"And I just follow the two of you around with the portable camera, capturing a sort of tour of his farm and a quickie documentary for Frank. I like it. I might be able to use it for the *What's Up America* show." He flashes his rare but recognizable delight-of-the-devil smile, always accompanied by a wink. He thinks it's a sign of super coolness. Probably left over from his years hanging out at Costa del Sol in southern Spain in the '60s. Basically, it's gay, but I don't bother to straighten him out.

We arrive at an old farm house way the hell out and gone in a little green valley between the border, a military reservation, and a dry flat desert surrounding everything. We pull up in front of a lonely looking white-washed two-story house hiding behind a semi-circle of old and dying cottonwood trees; which is pretty much what you would see if Norman Rockwell painted it. Out back is a big red barn looking old and rundown, and of course the requisite amount of old rusty farm implements, old appliances, and abandoned vehicles scattered about in a sort of giant child's abandoned playground.

"That's quite the rig y'all got there!" he yells, approaching us before we can even get the van stopped. He looks to be about seventy or more and wears a pair of old bib-style overalls, western shirt, and greasy Stetson. Dana whispers "Perfect," to me as we exit.

"Howdy! I'm Ed, the Antenna Man. Welcome to the Antenna Farm." He extends his hand and grabs each of us in turn as we step down from the van. I look at the roof of his house and don't see any TV antenna. In fact, I don't see anything within eyeshot that could possibly be construed as an antenna.

"So, tell me Ed, what kind of antennas do you make and why are they so damned good?" Dana blurts out without any pleasantries. Ed looks a little startled. I step in quickly.

"Dana is going to be our cameraman and I'm going to play the moderator. I have a degree in physics and should be able to understand or translate what you have to say. He'll focus on you and anything you want to show us. I'll be behind the camera and most of what I say will be edited out or dubbed over. We just want to get your story as only you can tell it."

He seems to be listening raptly.

"Imagine you have a favorite nephew," I continue, "who comes to visit for the first time. He's interested in what you do and you're happy to tell him all about your work. Does that sound like something you can do?"

Ed looks a little confused, but shakes his head *yes*.

Dana says, "Frank said you have invented a new kind of antenna that picks up TV signals from over the horizon, hundreds of miles away where no TV signal should be detectable."

He starts to speak, but I interrupt holding up my finger. "Now, hold that thought while we get the camera rolling."

Dana goes back on board, where he takes one of his cameras out of the special sponge-lined storage cabinet he built to hold the cameras safely while travelling on American backroads. He grabs a roll of tape, comes back out, and shoulders the camera while passing me the cassette. I load it in the camera while Dana frames up and focuses on Ed.

"Rolling," Dana announces for the audio as he points the camera at Ed, adjusts the focus again on the fly, and starts asking questions.

In less than four hours, Ed shows us his workshop in the old barn, where, using aluminum rods and tubes, all welded together, he built from scratch a very long Yagi single-channel TV antenna. A Yagi antenna looks like a long horizontal mast with lots of rods sticking out on both sides. These rods are finely tuned to detect faint signals from only one TV channel and deliver a summed signal of what is usually undetectable.

He brags that the first community antenna system in the US, in Astoria, Oregon, used his antennas to pick up Portland stations over a hundred miles away and behind mountains. His *Super Yagi* antennas, as he called them, are placed in opportune locations where they take advantage of an optics phenomena called knife-edge diffraction. Basically, all electromagnetic waves, depending on their frequency and wavelength, when launched at earth's horizon, will bend slightly downward after passing over the edge of a knife across its path, or in this case, the mountain ridges. TV radio waves, which normally go in straight lines, can in fact bend downward slightly by mountain ridges, and be received over the horizon.

But in this case, here in Bisbee, he needs even bigger antennas to detect signals from Phoenix, which is over two hundred miles away and behind some even taller mountains. He ups the ante and designs a ground-based parabolic reflector of such huge proportions that it focuses extremely weak TV signals into a focal point out front, where he uses his Super Yagi antennas to pick up the already magnified signal. It sets a world record by picking up usable TV signals from over three hundred miles away and behind two mountain ranges.

The giant reflector is a marvel of do-it-yourself inventiveness. It is simply a very large chicken-wire fence about twenty feet high and some eighty feet wide. It's supported by steel pipe ribs that are tensioned with wire to form a framework for two large curves, one vertical and one horizontal. If you use your imagination, the chicken-wire fence takes the form of a small rectangular piece cut out of the side of a giant donut. About a hundred feet out in front of this concave reflector fence stands five of his Super Yagi antennas, all pointed back at the middle of the reflector. Ed explains that each antenna is located at a precise location where that TV station's transmitter is individually focused due to its physical location in Phoenix. Optics at long wavelengths. Simple but elegant. Dana and I are impressed.

"I really hope Frank can drum up some business for me with this film you're making."

"It's video. Television," I correct him.

"I know. I really appreciate it. It's been hard keeping things going. If I didn't have cables running to all my nearest neighbors and them pitching in money every month, I don't think I could keep this up."

"No problem," Dana says. "This is just the kind of community enterprise that brings high technology resources to rural and remote areas. You shouldn't have to be isolated from the world just because you want to live in isolation."

"You boys are all right," he compliments. "I won't let you leave until you've had dinner with us. Come on into the kitchen and we'll talk some more."

I have a vision of roast beef with mountains of potatoes and gravy, just what an old farm house might imply. When we get inside and seated around a large circular farm table with a nice hand-crocheted doily table cloth, an old woman comes out with a bowl full of canned fruit cocktail, which she hands off to Ed. He dips in with his spoon and puts a heaping pile on his plate and hands it to Dana. Dana and I catch each other's eyes as he scoops out a few candied colored fruit-like chunks onto his plate. I can see he is just as surprised as I am. I have never seen someone call fruit cocktail a dinner before. She hands out cans of RC cola, which immediately tells me something isn't quite right in Denmark.

We make our hasty farewells after a decent amount of time talking about antennas and how much he wishes he could sell more. I feel sorry for the old man as the world is rapidly changing and he's doing his best to hang on, but it doesn't look like a good outcome ahead. Where there's money, there's wolves.

Later, as we drive all night past the Four Corners and back into Colorado, Dana asks, "Do you suppose that the antennas that Ed makes might work in Crested Butte? Do you think they could pick up signals from Denver?"

"I've been thinking about that myself," I respond. "I don't think so, because of a lot of topographical issues with what's between Denver and Crested Butte. It's not just one set of mountain ridges. but many. Arizona is flat except for small mountain ranges separating huge flat areas."

"Then what about the satellite dish like Frank has in his backyard?"

"Right now, there's only HBO, Atlanta's UHF station, and two god stations. I don't think that's what Crested Butte needs right now, although I wouldn't say no to watching studio-quality first-run movies in my living room. Especially since I happen to have a six-foot color projector to watch them on."

"I wonder how much a color projector might cost for my show?"

"Fifty grand and your first born for starters, and another truck to haul it around in."

He frowns.

*

We get back to the Butte just in time for the annual Pearl Pass bicycle race to Aspen. This year, Neil Murdoch takes over the organization, if you can imagine anything organized in Crested Butte, and invites a bunch of his new biker buddies from San Marin County to participate with the usual local rowdies. They call it a tour, but some bikers will want to be touring faster than others. We know what it really is: a chance to do some serious bar hopping and to perform the local requisite overnight drunken campout on a mountain top, testing bodily limits for alcohol and dope consumption under severe oxygen and temperature deprivation. It's a thing we do for fun.

"So, here's my plan," Dana begins, after assembling Tapley and I in the Grubstake, buying us a round of beers. "We need a way to get the camera over the pass with the bikers. Vehicles are not practical. We don't want to run over a biker on these roads. So, how about this idea? Cowboy will shoot off the back of your dirt bike, Tap, and you two will have to cover the race from the campground to the beginning of the asphalt road in Ashcroft."

"Aren't you going to shoot the party?" Tapley asks.

"I'll have to leave that up to you. And don't you two bad boys get so drunk you can't function the next morning."

"Don't worry, I'm a well-trained professional. We get the shot no matter the circumstances. Right Tap?" and I hold up my beer for clinking.

"I've borrowed a pickup so I can cover the first part of the race from town to the campground. We can haul your bike and gear up there while we're at it. I'll leave you guys there and drive all night around the mountains so I can be in Ashcroft when you and the racers show up the next morning. What do you think?"

Tapley is young and full of piss and vinegar so he just smiles and shouts, "Fuck yeah! Let's do it!" He clinks my beer with his Coke.

Tapley is only about seventeen, but quickly becomes the town mascot. Everyone lets him cruise the bars as long as he doesn't actually buy any liquor. He is kept well-lubricated anyway by the gang and he fits right in with the local cocaine, sex, Rock & Roll, ski-to-die, die-to-ski crowd (and now, motocross).

We take care of our kids the mountain way. They have to survive out there just like the rest of us. So, we let them get all the experience they want, as long as they mind the basics, like making decisions according to mountain wilderness priorities. They are, in proper order: maintain your personal freedom, all the time; party hard when you can; and always be pushing your limits.

*

"That's as much as I need for this part," Dana announces, after packing up his camera. "I'll leave it up to you two until we meet in Ashcroft. I should be there by around nine tomorrow morning. I've got to get moving though if I'm going to make it on time." He climbs into the borrowed pickup.

"No problem, boss," Tapley assures him, slapping the truck on the tail as it heads back down the trail. He turns to me and says, "Weather looks good. No rain predicted for the night."

I pick up the camera while Tap walks his bike toward the sound of music and the cloud of smoke. Gary has already set up a stereo in the back of Cotton's truck. It's kicking out the jams for all the mountain critters to hear and provides a homing signal for any who might get lost in their drunken wanderings.

"How many cassettes have we got?" I ask, just to make sure my count is right.

"I've got three," Tap reports. "I checked my backpack."

"And I've got two. That's about a hundred minutes total. Good."

As we get closer, I scan the campground. Doesn't look much different from the ones in the past when we were just a rowdy gang of drunks from the low-rent side of the mountain, invading stuffy Aspen sanctity with our rude, crude, in-your-face brand of bar hopping. Bar hopping with some altitude. And everyone knows: with altitude comes attitude.

When someone says something like, *Hey, let's all ride our bikes over to Jerome's and tear the place up!* it actually sounds like a good idea, for a short while. Wiser voices should at this point prevail, except in the Butte, the Grubstake Gang can't let it go until it's actually a done deal, no matter how difficult, and we collect the merit badge.

"Hey! Cowboy!" Starr yells. He comes running up to us with his clipboard of authority. "I've got you guys camping up there on the bench overlooking the firepit area and the trail to the summit. Thought it might be a good place to catch some shots of the action tonight and it'll give you a clear path for the summit in the morning. Don't want to get caught in the traffic jam just before they start dropping on the other side." He laughs heartily from his own joke.

"Who are all these shiny bike people?" I ask, pointing to a group of expensively dressed riders all grouped together with titanium fat tire bikes and low-slung handle bars. I knew earlier from shooting an interview with Neil that this year was going to be an informal *macho-e-macho* race between the high-tech mountain bikes from the laser machine shops of Northern California and the second generation of klunkers with brakes that some of the local boys were turning out of their living rooms. When the boys are up to something, it's as obvious as an albino in a snowstorm because of all the shit-eating grins on their faces.

"Those are Murdoch's friends from California. Those shiny bikes are worth five-hundred bucks apiece, so be careful if you knock one over." He walks away laughing again.

"So, what do you want to do, Tap?" I ask, as he mounts his bike.

"Same old same old," he mutters smiling. "I'll race you to the bench." He does his slam-kick bike start. It roars and he accelerates away, standing up as it bucks it way over rocks and brush. I follow him up the short distance on foot. Once there, I sort out our gear, roll out my bag, and go looking for some fresh boughs before everyone else thinks of it. If it's anything like most of the past Pearl Pass parties, most won't even sack out but stay up all night drinking, smoking dope, and taunting each other for what's about to happen to them tomorrow.

It's important, when mass camping, to pick the best spot and make your bed early, while you can still see. Sure, there's light from the fire and flashlights, but after what is about to be consumed, seeing becomes a real challenge. And not in a moderate manner, but boldly excessive, especially for this altitude. There are going to be a lot of drunks tonight and a lot of craziness. I intend to see if I can stay sober enough to record some of it on tape.

"Want a toot?" Tap asks while leaning on his bike watching all the pedal bikers and supply trucks come straggling in. The sun is about to dip below the peaks to the west and Bob and some of the boys are busy building up the fire, which will be kept going all night. They've already collected a ten-foot pile of dead trees for fueling it.

Tapley loves to watch the mountains, especially when the sun lights them up from low angles. He doesn't take his eyes off them as he does the well-practiced quick motion of surreptitiously single-handedly snorting off his single-shot coke bottle cap. All without looking, he turns the little handle filling the chamber and hands it to me. I take the hit, he motions to do it again, I flip the knob, shake it good, and take the customary second hit.

"Are you thinking what I'm thinking?" he asks, smiling deviously.

"What?" I ask, passing his bottle back.

"The boys are in a party mood tonight and Archie has brought up an awful lot of beer. I saw a Tequila bottle being passed around a little while ago."

"You don't think the boys are trying to bait the lowlanders into a drinking contest in the middle of a race?"

"And Dana would want us to get it all on tape. We've got plenty for tomorrow, don't we?"

"Of course. I made sure of that."

He takes a second look at me as it dawns on him I was thinking the same thing, except for a day or two earlier. I know what the boys are like. I've seen choaches and chumps before and these look ripe for the taking. The bikers from clean California are about to get introduced to power camping, mountain style.

Tap and I try to keep up with everything well past midnight, but I finally creep across sprawling bodies to find my bag in the dark, where I crawl inside, fold myself up into a bundle, and wait for the dancing lights to dim and the boat to stop rocking.

As expected, a lot of beer is consumed by everyone, including all the fans from town who don't have bikes but like to attend all-night mountain picnics. And, sure as shit, Bob builds up the bonfire and then someone might have challenged someone else to jump the fire on their bike.

"You're all a bunch of pussies!" screams Gallagher, kicking some sparks out of the red coals. "I can jump that fire, no fucking sweat. Who says I can't?" He looks around viciously.

"There's no ramp!" someone yells.

"Sit down, Gallagher, before you hurt yourself!" someone else adds.

"I don't need no stinking ramp!" he shouts back, and proceeds to unsteadily mount his bike and ride up the hill aways where he turns around and with a mighty yell, heads back down breakneck for the fire.

He catches me a little off guard, but I grab the camera, which I always keep close, and fire it up. I make a dash for the fire and flop down next to it for a belly shot at Gallagher's bike, now hurdling down the hill toward me.

Every one scatters out of the way. Just as he gets to the bonfire, he pulls a mighty wheelie raising his front wheel over the larger flaming logs and attempts to throw his body over the fire, bike and all. I'm twisting my head with the camera trying to follow the action when I see through the viewfinder a bike and rider pausing in mid-air just before dropping like a bomb into a forest fire.

Sparks fly everywhere! Gallagher starts screaming in a weird falsetto voice that probably scares elk out of their sleep two to three miles away. I scramble to get the camera out of the way of any flames. Gallagher is now dancing around the fire screaming and jumping up and down trying to knock the flames from his clothes and retrieve his bike from the flames.

Several guys run forward and pour their beers on Gallagher, who gets mad and picks up a firebrand to hold them off. Finally, Starr comes running up with a shovel, which we think he is going to beat on Gallagher's smoking parts, but at the last moment he uses it to hook the bike and pull it from the fire, tires melting and all. Gallagher stops beating his smoking pants and picks up his bike.

"I'd 'uv made it if the damned logs hadn't caught my bike stand!" He holds the smoldering bike up, showing the offending protrusion that did him in. Finally, Freckles throws a coat over his shoulders, whispers in his ear, and gently guides him over to one of the trucks where the first-aid kits are kept.

"Did you get that?" Tap asks, helping me up from the ground. "That was nuts!"

"I got something," I said hopefully. "We'll see."

*

The sun is threatening to rise any second. I'm sitting up looking over the carnage, still in my bag sucking on a flat beer I found nearby in an attempt to drown whatever had taken up residence in my mouth overnight. It's a scene right out of some apocalyptic movie where the last people on earth go out in an ecstasy of drugs, dance, and excessive risk-taking, leaving only scorched earth and the living dead behind. I crawl out of my bag, roll it up, and put on my boots.

"Hey, Tap," I yell, as I kick his bag. "Some are already pushing their bikes to the pass. We gotta go."

"Uh umh a mooka gau." *Cough!* "Geez...."

"What?"

"Be right there boss!" he yells back. "Ouch!"

He crawls out fully clothed, including boots. He gargles with beer like everyone else, spits, wipes his face with his sleeve, and announces, "Let's do this thing!"

And away we go. I sit backward on the back of his bike with the camera while he fights the rocks, the ruts, and the racers pushing their bikes to get us to the top. One of the Californicators admonishes us for leaving visible motorcycle tracks in the wilderness. I give him the old single-finger Crested Butte salute as we pass by in a cloud of smoke. Tap accelerates, throwing a few rocks his way. It's our wilderness; we know how to treat it. Ruts up here never last through the winter. Even the old mining roads and trails are all disappearing due to all the ice and snow eventually scouring the mountains to molehills, every year.

It's not far to the top and we set up the camera at the spot for the requisite group photos where they spread out with their bikes side-by-side, filling the gap in the cliffs making up Pearl Pass. A few joints are passed around, pictures are taken, and some take a swig or two from flasks. Then the real fun begins.

From here it's all downhill, some twenty miles, all the way to Aspen. Piece of cake, you might think, for a little bike cruising. Only one slight problem. For the next six miles, the road is almost vertical sometimes, always twisting, hanging over sheer cliffs, and clinging to vertical rock walls. The road is tortuously covered from side to side with rocks—big rocks! It looks more like a ragged, rocky crack in the cliffs then it does an actual usable road. One false move and you could win the annual Robertson award for the most killed in the mountains at one time.

"Okay, Tap," I instruct, "here's the plan. We'll rush ahead as far as we can, get out in front of the best riders, find an ugly spot, and record what happens. I know a couple of switchbacks that should give some good action."

"Hang on then," he cautions, "it might get a little hairy."

And it does. I have to hold on for dear life as we bounce from boulder to boulder, screaming down the rocky road as fast as seemingly possible. Fortunately, we are both motocross riders and know how to balance and lean with the bumps and forces. My teeth, though, are chattering from the constant vibrations as I hold tight to a two-thousand-dollar video camera and Tapley. Hopefully he's holding onto the bike.

We finally stop at a spot where I find a nearby tree for steadying the hand-held camera and we wait for the action. It isn't long until the first bikes show up, bouncing hard as the riders hang on applying constant brake pressure and wrestling the front wheel between rocks and ruts big enough to trip an elephant. One guy goes by me with a jaw-grinding, pure-pain look that means he's fading fast.

Then more appear, one using a ski technique of going back and forth across the trail to help control speed and allow more careful track selection. I look again and sure enough, it's Hitch, one of our guys, a damn good skier and one of the first-ever Klunker builders. I'm impressed—until he flips. He jumps right back up, kicks the rim on his front tire back into somewhat circular shape, and keeps right on going. A true mountain man never gives up on his ride.

After a few more stops and recording a bunch more spills and broken bikes being nursed along, we make it to the asphalt road in Ashcroft. Dana is already there with a camera on a tripod recording all the bikes making it this far. We hang there, relaxing from a grueling ride until the racers dwindle and the sweep truck shows up carrying all the busted bikes that didn't make it, including many of their broken riders.

We load the motorcycle in the back of the sweep truck, where it will be taken along with most of the bikes, back to the Butte later today. By the time we get to the Jerome, all the bikers have arrived and it's overflowing with tired, hungover, and beat-to-death commuters. It's a somewhat subdued crowd compared to previous years. I think the boys' tactic worked too well. Running the worst part of the race with a hangover separates the true bar hoppers from the also-rans. Tap and I do up the last of the coke and get loud and rowdy with the rest of the CB gang, proving once again that Aspen better watch its back. We're just a friendly bike ride away and not afraid to use it.

*

Tapley and I stand behind Dana as he watches the video monitor showing the footage we shot at the fire jump.

"Is this all you could get from the party?" Dana asks, looking up from the monitor.

"You had to be there to understand," I quip. "It was dark."

He rewinds and runs it again. It starts with a nice shot of the campground with lots of people milling around listening to the music. Then, after dark, the footage gets erratic, jumping around from scene to scene. But it is mostly too dark to make out what's going on, with occasional shots of the fire blinding the camera because of its sensitivity to infrared. I can barely make out the one scene where Gallagher's bike is plummeting toward the camera and then the scene explodes into blinding white streaks with some jostling shadows. That's it. No incriminating evidence to expose the debauchery of a world-class bicycle race. Damn!

"Too bad," he says, after looking at it again. We'll just have to skip the party and keep it a secret, like it's always been. What happens on Pearl Pass stays on Pearl Pass."

"It's kind of a shame, though," says Tapley. "Now that we've opened the doors to bicycle turkeys and have to get respectable, we'll lose a tradition."

~ 14 ~

MORE ON THE TOAD

Dana is working with an independent television producer out in LA who's trying to put together a weekly travel magazine show called *What's Up America.* He wants to feature short clips of colorful characters or interesting locations, as well as those roadside works of art that Dana loves to feature in his performance road show. Dana shows him the one about the antenna guy in Arizona, which he likes, and asks if we can come up with more.

John Hahn appears in Crested Butte every summer from June to October to work the Forest Queen mine in Ruby. Colonel Hahn has been retired from the Army since 1959, widowed, and left an energetic bachelor with an undying love of the mountains. On one of his many expeditions into the mountains, he finds and buys the old mining claim for a song and a dance. He then proceeds to become a one-man mining machine, working wonders every summer getting all the old machinery at the mine working again and trying to figure out how to drain the mine of a hundred years of water accumulation so he can get at the prize, the rare and beautiful Ruby Silver.

I know John and have spoken with him many times when he comes to town for supplies and a stop at the bar for some well-deserved R&R. Gary and I often question him in detail about the prospect of getting the mine drained and then work some side veins, maybe find some more of that beautiful red silver ore known as Ruby Silver, or Pyrargyrite. But from all Gary was able to dig up, the mine had run out of paydirt a long time ago and is not about to be rescued by any easy discovery. Literally, silver is almost worthless in the metallurgic sense, as it is too cheaply obtained as a byproduct of other large-scale mining operations like the many open-pit copper mines in Arizona.

But John is a beloved Crested Butte character along with all the other old-timers, whether they live here year-round or just during the summertime. What especially endears him to us is the fact that his cabin at the mine is fully stocked, weatherproof, clean, never locked, and full of little notes welcoming strangers, explaining how things work and where to find what you need for a warm and comfortable stay. It is a perfect stopover on long ski treks or just a place to go and spend the night, leaving it the way you find it, enjoying a once-in-a-lifetime chance to spend a night in an authentic hundred-year-old miner's cabin. Many cross-country skiers have taken advantage of his cabin and they leave notes in the guest book thanking John for the trust, rest, and warmth his cabin provides.

It is even rumored that sometimes in the summer, girls from town will visit him just to hear his stories and spend a night with him, perhaps partially alleviating the dreaded loneliness of the wilderness. Having been treated in a similar fashion during my first winter in town, I have no doubt as to its accuracy.

Dana and I decide he'd be great for the *What's Up America* show. We spend the next week planning it out and then three days shooting it at the mine. It is a gorgeous sunny September day with lingering warmth and flowers that are still being fooled into lavish bloom. The Forest Queen mine is on the north side of Scarp Ridge overlooking the old town site of Ruby, which is next door to Lake Irwin. Susie and I have skied all over that area and taken the route to the Irwin Lodge following the old waterline along Scarpe Ridge that feeds the mine.

John is 73 years old and resembles a thin brown weathered stick. While Dana is shooting him doing his different tasks at mining, he asks him questions about what he thinks and why he picked this as his way to joust with windmills in his retirement.

His answer is simple: He's happy. It may take him twenty years at the rate he's going to complete his work, but that doesn't matter. What he is doing right now makes him very happy and he will continue to do it for as long as he can. Enough said.

I look down from his mountain perch overlooking the valley around Irwin and I instantly understand why I'm here, too. Like John, I'm an ad hoc volunteer member of a community that consists of strange but like-minded people. We love the mountains, we love the wilderness, but more than that, we love the challenge and the freedom. We come here just to be here where we probably shouldn't be, with prudence, but we come anyway. We dig, we fish, we ski, we drink, we sing, we dance, we hug, and above all, we look up every day and see the works of eternity and feel so privileged to be humbled by it and yet be an intimate part of it. It is our anchor; it is our soul, it's what gives us meaning.

*

"You're not going to believe this guy," Dana announces.

Susie and I are having an after-work beer at the Nickel when Dana walks in, spots us, and immediately invades our solitude. It's the Butte. The Nickel's our living room. What are you going to do?

"You've heard of Father Guido Sarducci, right?" he asks excitedly, and sits down at our table.

"Yeah, sure, who the hell hasn't?" I quip. "*Saturday Night Live.*"

"My friend, Wild Will, the video artist from Berkely, is coming for a visit and he wants to do something up here with us," he announces excitedly. "Wild Will is the guy who got Novello to do that underground video about Father Sarducci on TV, nonchalantly climbing up out of the shot of him at his desk in the Vatican, presumably into a young lady who is straddling the TV set in some living room."

"Oh, of course, that one," I agree, not having a clue. Susie just laughs.

"Anyway, I've got this idea for a short film starring Wild Will in one of his absurd journeys into the wilderness. So, he meets this old weird guy, played by Botsie, who's a strange local guide that takes Wild Will to a secret lake where he supposedly can catch freshwater mermaids."

"Freshwater mermaids," I repeat.

"Yeah. I already talked Botsie into it. We'll shoot it at Nicholson Lake. I borrowed a canoe and Will is bringing the props. That's where I'll need your help, Susie."

"Freshwater mermaids," I say again. "Which end is female and which end is fish? Are we talking rainbow trout mermaids or cutthroats?"

"Can you get about three or four of your friends to play the part of the mermaids?" he asks her, ignoring me.

"What?" she asks. "You want a bunch of us to go swimming in Nicholson Lake?"

"Yeah. Nude. Whadaya say?"

He beams his phony innocent New England grin at us like it's a forgone conclusion. Of course it is, especially with a description like that. Who could say no? Besides, if Botsie's involved, that cinches it. He's just a dirty little old Butte-er, but a great character actor. Susie looks at me with her cute innocent smile and I pucker my lips right back at her.

"I'll get Jan and Freckles. They'll be up for it," she adds.

"Water temperature this time of the year is around 45 degrees," I offer.

"Won't be like something we haven't done before," she says smiling wickedly.

*

A week later, we all get up before dawn and converge on Nicholson Lake. The night before, we shoot some lead-in footage starring Wild Bill and Botsie, negotiating the fishing trip and a scene where some weird bearded guy with long red hair and a banjo, Dan Peha, is standing next to an old open-bed truck with dozens of flesh-colored legs sticking out the back. The props Wild Will brought up from Berkeley are about a dozen blow-up porn dolls, all with blonde hair and a surprised look on their faces.

When we shoot video for high quality productions, we have to connect the camera to the big 3/4-inch tape decks in the van by a long coaxial cable. But now, for the first time, we are going to send this video signal to the van wirelessly, using Microwave Associates' new *Gunnplexer* video link. It looks like two handheld police radar guns that, when pointed at each other and as long as they maintain line of sight, effectively replaces the cable. This is just what I need for the shots from the canoe in the middle of the lake.

We set up quickly and shoot all the shore locations with Botsie and Wild Will preparing the canoe and blowing up the dolls. Botsie ties a rope to the canoe with Wild Will in it and a dozen or so blow-up dolls floating around it like duck decoys. He gives them all a shove out into the lake, then sits down on a folding chair, playing the end of the rope like it's a baited fishing line. He ties it to his foot so he can play a little tune on his accordion.

When Dana gets into the canoe to shoot closeups from out in the lake, I set up the Gunnplexers, one in the boat and one on the roof of the van. The girls have taken over the rear of the van and I can hear a lot of giggling and laughing as they get ready.

We catch some shots with just Wild Will thrashing around in the canoe still surrounded by floating flesh-colored dolls. Then Dana waves to me.

"We're ready!" he shouts from the boat. "Send out the mermaids!"

I go inside and knock on the rear compartment door. "Susie! He's ready for you."

"What the hell!" I hear one of them shout. "Here we go!" says another. I hear the clinking of glasses.

The door bursts open and a thunderous herd of mountain girls wrapped tightly in beach blankets make a mad dash for the lake. I look into the cabin and see a half-drained bottle of Black Jack and six empty shot glasses. They whoop and holler running down to the shore bank, where they suddenly hold up next to Botsie, waiting for instructions.

"It shouldn't take more than five minutes," Dana shouts from the boat. "Just swim around the floats and maybe grab a couple and then attack Wild Will in the canoe. Don't worry about sound, as we'll dub all that later. Everybody ready?"

About that moment, one of the girls on shore casts off her blanket, might be Connie, and makes a wild belly flop dive from shore, accompanied by screaming and much flailing of arms and legs. Susie and the rest follow with the apparent philosophy of *quicker is better*. Botsie, still in character, watches intently from his folding chair nearby.

I run inside the van and start the tape deck and then climb back up on the roof with the Gunnplexer to watch the action from a balcony seat. When I get there, I can see the girls are spread out swimming around the canoe with Wild Will acting the part of an outrageously incompetent mermaid catcher, and Dana shooting it all in one continuous recording. I take in the grand view from horizon to horizon and can't believe what I am witnessing. This is what running away to the mountains and finding oneself making movies is all about. This is the message in a bottle waiting for someone to read it.

Six naked beautiful girls are swimming around a canoe with a bunch of floating sex dolls scattered about with a dirty old man in a safari suit slobbering all over himself, while in the background, the early solar rays are lighting up the mountain peaks in a surrealistic pinkish red scene straight out of *Oz*. Then there's Botsie, playing the rope attached to the canoe like it's a fishing line, only now he begins to reel in his catch. The last scene is Wild Will being pulled out of the canoe by freshwater mermaids and disappearing among flesh-colored plastic dolls. Botsie keeps reeling in his catch having sacrificed his client as bait.

"Cut!" Dana shouts. At that command, the girls make a mad swim for shore where I wait holding out blankets for them as they emerge from the water. "You made history today!" I tell them. "This will be remembered throughout the Old West with the likes of the Donner Party and Custer's Last Stand!"

Susie is the last to emerge and I quickly wrap her with a blanket and rub her violently to help dry her and get her blood flowing again. In fact, all the girls are a bit whitish from the blood being sucked from the skin to keep heat loss down. They all rush into the van where it's warmer while I bring up Susie holding her tightly, listening to her teeth chatter all the way.

I go back down to the shore and help Dana get the equipment off the boat. Wild Will is all wet and shivering as well.

"Dana!" I announce. "This is as good as anything on *SNL*! You've got to show it to those guys at *What's Up America* and pitch to them a video absurdist comedy series. This is the kind of stuff that can get us regular work."

"We'll see. Hollywood is a fickle bitch. The guy I've been working with has lost his job, so it's back to square one. Here, take this camera." I grab the heavy camera and he helps Wild Will out of the canoe, sopping wet. "Go up to the van and warm up. I'll be right up."

"Oh, great!" I say. "Now what are we going to do?"

"I still have my dad and that job down in Oklahoma next month, the satellite TV convention."

Then he leans into me with his big devious grin and a twinkle in his eye, and says privately, "I can't wait to edit these shots. You won't believe how big their nipples got."

*

Another all-night drive out of the mountains and this time we land in Tulsa at a giant Hilton Hotel on the southeast side near the university. They have a big backyard with lots of parking lots and a facility big enough to house the convention.

"This is a real professional gig, so I hope you can keep it together," Dana pops at me out of nowhere.

"Hey, you know my motto: *When the going gets weird, the weird turn pro!*"

He laughs. "You know what I mean. You Rock & Roll roadies tend to take advantage of the squares and we're going to be in a mess of them. Frank tells me he has a volunteer studio camera crew with a pair of antique color cameras from the local god station that happens to produce content for a satellite feed."

"I got everything against god people. I just think they should stick with carving their messages in stone like their archaic gods prefer and leave modern television to artists and filmmakers. Television should serve the people by making their lives better, be both entertaining and informative, and not just a whorehouse for prurient consumerism and parasitic mind control."

"Yeah, anyway, we have to be the control room, direct the cameras inside, and provide the uplink feed to the earth station they are setting up for the uplink. It's all going to be going through this van and your hands."

"Maybe I didn't tell you, but I served as a production manager at the U of M television center where we did studio tape productions of live interviews and academic discussions. I have all the hand signals down and know how to manage cameras and talent on a live set."

"I'm going to be running the mobile camera outside the van and, when necessary, I'll add it to the studio lineup with a tripod, which means you'll have to be here in the van all the time coordinating the shots and switching the video."

"I've put on major rock productions and shot clips for major motion pictures. These pumpkins better step aside cause the Cowboy is in town and Rock & Roll madness is about to happen!"

"I've got a new name for you, too. I'm the Ace of Space and Captain Video. I think I'm going to call you Captain Neutrino, master of electrons and ruler of the quantum."

I think about that, and reason there's no reasoning with an artist, so I just agree.

"Another thing. My dad's going to be there with a sales delegation from his company."

"Is this the same dad that paid for all this?"

"Only one I have for now. Anyway, he's kind of an old nerd, like you. He studied engineering at MIT and worked at the Lincoln Labs helping develop radar as a graduate student during the war."

"I've heard of them. They pioneered the klystron. I like that word, *klystron!*"

"Anyway, I just want to warn you that he and the whole lot of them probably are amateur radio nerds. They talk amateur radio stuff all day long, so don't be surprised if they ask you."

"What?"

"Do you have an amateur radio license? If yes, they will talk your leg off; if not, well, they might do it anyway. Just warning you."

"So, if your old man is an engineer, what happened to you? Why did you become an artist? Or better yet, how did you get away with becoming an artist?"

"My grandfather, he was the first Dana Atchley. My dad is Dana Atchley, Junior. That means that road is already well traveled and I'm the next generation, so why not be different and strike out in another direction? Besides, he can afford it."

"That's what I thought. The oldest generation works, the next becomes the shopkeeper, the next becomes the academic, and the last becomes the artist. You just skipped a generation, you little entitled bitch."

He laughs nervously.

When we arrive at the hotel, we pick a spot near a transformer substation serving electricity to the convention center. I have just made up a special portable power tap for Dana that, given access to a power panel, can connect his van to a raw unfused power bus, bypassing the need for plugging into possibly unreliable breaker-fed electrical connections. I provide for all that in our internal van power distribution. I even designed and built him an automatic power switch for his van where his generator onboard is tied together with the external power plug so if power fails, the generator takes over and when it returns, it switches back. But our power needs are 240 volts AC split phase and the hotel power is strictly 3-phase 208. Fuck!

After tying in the power feed, I measure the voltage at 209. I only need one of the phases, but the low voltage is death for our sensitive electronic processing and recording equipment. I need 240 or at least 220. I debate with Dana the possibility of running on generator power for the whole weekend. Then Frank shows up to our van, and I quickly explain our dilemma.

"What you need is a power transformer to convert the voltage?" he asks, getting right to the point. "How much voltage and how much power?"

I tell him what I need and he says he'll find something. "This damned uplink is going to happen and it looks like I'm going to have to do a hell of a lot of minor miracles to make it happen. This is just a little power transformer."

"What do you mean?" asks Dana.

"They erected the dish this morning and discovered the transmitter power amp failed when they tried to power it up."

"What are you going to do without a power amp?" I ask.

"We can't uplink without it and we're scheduled to go live tomorrow at noon."

"Sounds like Rock & Roll to me," I add, "The show must go on."

"Fortunately, Ted Turner is here, and he donated his jet plane to go get another one tonight."

"Ted Turner, the TV guy from Atlanta?"

"Yep, in fact I have to go see him right now and make sure his pilot gets met at the airport with the parts. I think your dad is the one who found a replacement amp. When Dana Atchley, Jr. and Ted Turner team up, it's fucking chaos, but I'll take it. I'll look for a transformer at the local Christian university that's providing us cameras. They also tell me that their cameras have old kinescope tubes and that one of them has a cantankerous red tube that could go out anytime. Good luck!"

And he's gone.

I lean over and ask Dana, "Don't you just love it when a plan comes together?"

*

The next 24 hours are a blur. About two hours after Frank leaves, a pimply young kid knocks on our van and delivers a power transformer. I wire it into our power tap and finally get the van on shore power. Then we string video cables from the van into the main conference hall where most of the action will originate.

We watch the activity around the giant 50-foot dish they just erected in the next-door parking lot. Once erected, it's an imposing three-story structure one can see from blocks away. Soon, gawkers show up, and people start asking questions, like "Is this a secret weapons test?" or "Are you calling for aliens to invade?" We run a single cable to it for the uplink feed.

Finally, Friday morning, we get the word that the power amp has arrived and the uplink is accomplished. All they have to do is coordinate with HBO to have them shut down their feed in New York and we fire this one up here. The satellite just repeats back towards earth whatever it receives, so strongest signal wins. Dana grabs his Panasonic handheld camera and joins the studio cameras in the conference room, and I settle in all alone at the video controls in the production van switching the camera signals onto our tape machines and the uplink. I'm tied to the camera operators with an intercom so at least I can direct the shots and make it sort of professional.

Just before air time, one of the god-camera operators reports losing his red kinescope just like Frank warned. Dana points his camera at him so I can watch what's going on. He removes the expensive and fragile tube from the giant pedestal camera and then he cuddles the tube lovingly in his cupped hand and gets on his knees, stroking the tube and loudly praying to god to please fix the tube one more time. He gets up, puts the tube back in the camera, whereupon powering it up the red tube suddenly begins working. I shake my head in disbelief. It's well known among old tube-type engineers that weak tubes can sometimes be revived temporarily by cleaning or simply exercising the socket contacts. I wonder though, when it finally fails, is he going to blame god?

We work our asses off trying to keep the feed going even between the live convention events. Sometimes we throw in some of Dana's art tapes and suddenly we start getting phone calls from people living in the remote parts of Montana and Idaho who have satellite dishes behind their cabins and are watching us. They begin calling in to say how much they enjoy the filler material. I'm back in my element, having a blast broadcasting to my people.

On the last day, Ted Turner is scheduled to give a talk on the future of satellite television and especially what he envisions for his station, WTBS. Just before he goes on, Frank brings him by the van to show him how the uplink is being done.

"This is pretty impressive technology you've got here," he comments. "I think one day, you'll be able to put all this equipment into one camera that you can carry around in a shirt pocket."

"That's going to be tough considering the amount of bandwidth it takes to record full motion video," counters Dana. "Five megacycle signals are not easy to record and process without a lot of specialized equipment."

"I hear you're related to Mr. Atchley from Microwave Associates? Great guy. He sees a future in this just like I do. Unfortunately, the idiots who run commercial television all have their heads up their asses."

We laugh. We've all said worse. It's great to hear it from someone famous or infamous depending on which side you're on. Capitalist honesty is a rare thing, indeed.

"Here I'm showing them how to broadcast nationwide, hell, worldwide, reaching millions of people, but I can't get Coca Cola to advertise on our station. If I could just get the same treatment that the other networks get from Ford and Camel, I could afford to open up hundreds of stations all over the country and uplink them all to the satellite and broadcast hundreds of channels to an entire world!"

"That means that little country cable systems," added Frank, "can now easily afford to carry distant stations and networks with studio quality signals and with many more programming choices than just the big three."

I look at Dana and he looks at me and it's obvious we are both thinking the same thing. It might be within our means to build a satellite dish for Crested Butte and bring this new world of private cable TV to our humble mountain hideaway. Imagine the best of both worlds, living in privacy and isolation, but with world-class connectivity and entertainment. No more having to watch *SNL* with a snowy picture, and the boys will love to bet on their Sunday afternoon football games with a picture clear enough to know which side is which.

We do an uplink every day for three days from 9 a.m. to 5 p.m. After the uplink on Saturday, Dana Junior invites me and Dana Three out to dinner with his entourage of sales weenies he brought with him to the convention. Artists never turn down a free dinner, especially if some big evil company is paying for it.

I'll take all the help I can get, Mitchell always says. My corollary is *I'm not so proud as to turn down a free meal.*

We pack everyone into their two Ford LTD rental cars and off we go on an expedition to find a locally recommended country restaurant that newcomers simply cannot miss. Dana warns me earlier, but I am unprepared for how much these big corporate executives are actually tied up with amateur radio. First thing they do is pull out a walkie talkie in each vehicle and start talking to each other while driving.

I did some amateur radio in high school just to get out of boring math classes. Instead of cutting up in class, I'd spend time talking to other ham operators all over the world. I was stuck in a little rural high school in Bumfuck, Oregon which could barely afford a Bunsen burner in the chemistry lab. I taught myself science and math, but during the time I was required by law to be in a classroom, my teachers realized quickly I was better off not in the class and prone to asking too many embarrassing questions, ultimately challenging their credentials for being a teacher in the first place. As a result, I was banished to the ham shack on the top floor of our school building, or the projection booth in the auditorium, showing free movies during the lunch hour to lure the thugs from roaming the hallways beating up kids for their lunch money.

But these guys are at a whole different level. They have handheld walkie talkie radios that can connect through repeaters and communicate over hundreds of miles. In this case, it was just a few feet between cars. They're jabbering all the time we're looking for the mythic rural restaurant. At one point, I notice their walkie talkies are more than just wireless intercoms. They have twelve-button touchtone pads and can send touch tones to activate automatic phone operators that provide a dial tone on their radios. All free and compliments of the local amateur radio clubs who maintain these private repeaters all over the country.

"Now that is going to be handy, someday," Dana Three says. "When everyone can have a wireless telephone in their hands.

Imagine making calls from the van without stopping for a pay phone."

"New solid-state electronics will change everything," I interject. "We're going to see computers in homes and satellite dishes on every roof."

"I sure hope so," says Dana Junior. "I've got a lot invested in the Gunnplexer diode. Imagine a tiny little cheap diode that all you have to do is send current through it and out comes microwaves."

"Yeah, thanks for that, by the way. Every speeding ticket now is going to generate another person who hates technology. Some people should not be allowed to use technology and the oppressive pigs are one."

"Are you an amateur?" he asks pointedly.

"I've been there, done it, but never bothered with getting the full license. I had a novice license, KN7WON, and the school had the general license, W7ROU."

"A novice, huh?" he concludes. "Too bad. Real amateurs are a special breed."

"Yeah, I know, they like to dazzle us with Morse code which is just old technology and will probably never be used again, except for exhibitionists like, well...like you engineer amateurs. Don't you think it's an artificial barrier to becoming an amateur by enforcing a stupid twenty-three words-a-minute copy rate for something never to be used again? I have a First-Class Radiotelephone license from the FCC. I think that should trump amateur licenses."

He gave up trying to impress me with his amateur status, but what the hell. I like amateurs, it's just they're kind of elitist dicks.

Apparently, they're also lost in Oklahoma and can't find the restaurant they're looking for. At this point, Dana Three and I are hungry enough to simply stop at a burger joint. But instead, he directs the driver to head for the nearest interstate and a truck stop restaurant where Dana Three gets to show Dana Junior the chrome and plastic culture of the American truck driver. A city on wheels that never stops moving.

"Look at the latest citizens band radios," Dana Three points out. "They're making a culture of the road with its own language and manners."

"Garbage bands," Dana Junior points out. "We hate those things. They're screwing up the ten-meter band for nothing else but jabber and trucker talk."

"Yeah, but you don't need a restricted license and if you need help on the road, they sure come in handy."

Dana had Dana there. I sense a lifelong struggle between these two, one wanting another amateur radio operator in the family, and perhaps disappointed with an artist. So, whenever Dana Three would ask Dana Junior for more money to buy his expensive art tools, it was always disguised as a technical business venture for a video producer renting out a portable production van looking for commercial television work. I don't know if the old man knows how hard his son tries to make it a financial success, but art just doesn't work that way. At least the art that comes from the heart.

After a two-hour ride through the wilds of Oklahoma with a bunch of lost Boston nerds, we finally get fed country-fried steaks with mashed potatoes and brown gravy by a waitress named Bernice and to the tune of Merle Haggard in the background and the smell of unburned diesel in the air. Clearly the epitome of *Haute Cuisine America*!

*

It's a shame the work Dana does on his three-minute *Postcards From America* clips, and these longer human-interest documentaries, doesn't catch hold with any commercial producers. Lots of celebrities like his show, and his artistic work, but he just can't get traction with the big media executives. No wonder; at this time, rebels and edgy art are considered passé because, one, nobody understands it so you can't predict success, and two, there are enough celebrity rebels and edgy popular artists already because of the societal generational thing, like *Sleazy Rider*. In short, there's too much competition in his chosen field. He has to get either edgier or switch over to National Geographic.

"What the hell?" Dana finishes. "I thought with the opportunity here, why not take a shot at it."

I'm in his van looking at some of his edited work he did for *Postcards*. One of his favorite *Postcards* pieces features the building in Telluride that is totally covered in old automobile license plates. He finds several more such buildings among the old towns in rural America and features them in a short colorful piece about this odd, American-only, use of old, expired license plates.

"Roy Smith knows some wilderness magazine people who want him to do a demo ice climbing piece," he remarks out of nowhere.

Roy just published a book about his Alaskan adventures and needs a promotional video to help with the sales. He promises to get it into somebody's hands at National Geographic and Dana agrees to shoot it for him on speculation. I hope it gets us more business, as this could be a great way to support my Crested Butte habits and my new home.

"And he asked you to do it?" I question him.

"Well, I might have suggested it to him when he was telling me about how he's considered one of the best winter mountaineering experts in the world. He led a National Geographic expedition that made the first winter crossing of the Alaskan Brooks Range on skis, a formidable 400-mile, forty-day journey pulling sleds and sleeping in snow caves."

I had listened to some of his stories in the bars. Roy is a skinny, wiry little Brit with a charming accent and a gnarly leathery look from too much sun, cocaine, and raw Arctic winds. He is a consummate back-country skier and snow expert. He helped start the Outward Bound schools, where city kids in trouble are taught self-esteem by learning how to survive in the wilderness on their own. He buys the little green cottage across the street from Dana's house and soon ensconces himself in Crested Butte society as the modern version of a Victorian Arctic explorer.

"And we're going to shoot him," I summarize, "doing an ice climb up some frozen ice wall. What do you plan to do for the closeups? Where are you going to plant your tripod?"

"Don't need a tripod. I'll do a handheld right alongside him all the way up."

"And how are you going to do that? Hire Otis the elevator guy?"

"I'm going to hire Lou Dawson."

Lou is Tapley's little brother and not well known among the rest of us, as he's only 15 and still in high school. But, unbeknownst to most of us, he's been going out alone for years in the winter wilderness around Crested Butte, learning the art of winter survival from the snow up, so to speak.

Don Bachman is perhaps the first of us to take a greater interest in snow than just skiing on it or pissing in it. He and Adele get a divorce, sell Tony's Tavern, and he goes back to school studying avalanches. He becomes a world expert and moves to Silverton, Colorado, where there are more avalanches per year off of Red Mountain than just about anywhere else in the Rockies. Red Mountain Pass is famous for its regular killer avalanches. It's constantly patrolled and monitored for dangerous avalanche conditions every winter.

Three days later, we pull off the infamous pass road where Mill Creek crosses the Million Dollar Highway and Ohio Peak right across the valley blocks the sky like a giant outdoor drive-in movie screen. Dana and I suit up in our best winter gear and drop cables over the edge to the base of the waterfall right below us.

It's late March and the ice has been melting a bit, making it a little soft for supporting pitons. Lou says not to worry, and he goes about stringing several ropes from the top to the bottom that can be used as belays for hoisting the camera as Roy climbs the ice fall. I just stand back in awe at how easy Lou makes it look as he smoothly moves around the giant ice fall like it's a walk in the park. He's smiling all the time and seems to be having a hell of a good time climbing circles around the solid but stagnant star.

Right in the middle of the taping, with Roy and Dana still on the ice, I hear a bunch of noise outside the van and look out the window. I can't believe what I see.

It's a cannon on wheels. Really! It's a military surplus 105mm howitzer being set up right next to us in the same turnout. Before I can get to the door, someone bangs on it. I open it, looking straight at a Forest Service officer, or what we refer to as a *Smokey* because of their funny Smokey Bear hats.

"We're going to be doing avalanche control. Is there anybody else with you?"

"Yeah, I've got a crew filming on Mill Creek ice fall right below us. What are you going to do with that cannon?"

"This is where we always set up to shoot the runs above the highway. We'll be here for about an hour, so you might want to get your crew up here while we're shooting. There's a chance that the noise can trigger small avalanches nearby."

I think of how soft the ice is and how the entire ice fall could come loose from the cliff and fall over like a Champagne-glass tower, shattering into millions of shards on its way down the mountain. I call Dana on the intercom and give him the bad news. They reluctantly retreat off the ice fall and join me in the van.

Then the Forest Service men open up with their little toy and begin blowing big holes in the ice runs on the face of Ohio Peak just above the highway on the other side of the valley. The highway is closed from both directions and the explosions on the mountain from each shot bring some snow movement, but none of them make it to the road so no clearing is required before opening the pass back up.

Meanwhile, we enjoy the entertainment and marvel at how much fun these snow experts have playing with explosives and big guns. Boys and their toys are hard to separate. When they finally finish rearranging the mountain to their satisfaction, we get back to work and finish shooting the ice climb.

I find it highly ironic, though, considering the star of the show is telling everyone how hard it is to climb ice when he is showing us quite the opposite. It makes me appreciate the National Geographic shows where the impossible is accomplished every day, just like us, by very talented filmmakers and their support people. I really hope this hits and gives Dana a way to do more professional documentaries and maybe start paying me what I'm worth. So far, it's been pretty much a labor of love.

*

My real labor of love for the cause comes when the town—actually, Mitchell—commissions Dana to do a five-minute piece concerning the fight to save Red Lady Mountain from Amax, the mindless international ecological disaster conglomerate. Everyone in town is geared up for the David and Goliath fight and it goes on for some time as we gather media exposure and political pressure to stop the wholesale destruction of an entire mountain overlooking the Butte. I, like most, do what we can to fight this real threat to our beloved wilderness skyline.

Tracey Wickland, a local musician and regular performer at the lodges on the hill, writes a protest song that gets John Denver's attention, who then records it on one of his albums. Meanwhile, Dana and I record her doing her song alone, which we use as the background music to a documentary of the people's struggle. Gary finds us some old CB pictures and we shoot some more, which we then animate onto video while Dana does the voice-over. This work is one of the finest examples of the films we are doing while trying to break into the big time.

At one point, someone in Hollywood wrote a short film script starring Ace of Space in an artistic adventure of some kind, mirroring his life on the road. I read it and found it superficial and shallow, missing the whole essence of Dana's search, driving him toward a new video art form. It's clearly non-commercial for now. Innovators are always way ahead of their time, misunderstood, and unappreciated.

Bottom line, he's a people's artist, working with ordinary ideas with a twist, using the Finds Arts concept without all the snobbery or pandering. He likes to just play with technology creating visual stories, like a da Vinci might spend time filling a sketchbook. It's hard to concentrate on making money when all you want to do is have fun and do something that's never been done before. Dana and I are pioneers of sorts, using expensive toys in new, weird, and wonderful ways that may become commonplace in the future.

*

About a year later, Dana finally finds some work for us that pays nicely and gives us a chance to hang out in Aspen with the stars. Peter Fonda becomes Dana's primary contact into the exclusive world of newly anointed celebrities. He meets Peter at a show he does in LA and later gets invited to Peter's ranch in Livingston, Montana, where he experiences a Hollywood three-day party of locals and a new enclave of young rebel stars and Hollywood bad boys. Everybody does a lot of beer, weed, coke and barbecue, marveling at the quaintness of the mountains and the crazy people living there.

They say that one of these parties sparked writing a film script based on the location. They conceive and shoot *Rancho Deluxe* here and hire a newcomer to the music business to do the soundtrack. Peter discovers Jimmy Buffett on one of his many sorties to Key West where Jimmy plays regularly in the beach bars. He brings him to Montana for the parties, and later for the movie, where he pretty much scores the whole thing. It wins a Grammy and the legend starts.

Then "Margaritaville" sends him to Mars.

Meanwhile, the Eagles are making a shitload of money and are lured by the Aspen rugged wilderness image, just like all of us, so they buy a ten-acre parcel along one of Snowmass Creek's little tributaries not far from Woody Creek. Don Henley and Glenn Frey have already built cabins along the creek, and now Jimmy buys the remaining building lot right in the middle of the property and builds a nice two-story modern log house for him, his new wife, and baby girl.

Dana spreads the word among his friends and shortly we get calls from a couple of people in Aspen who want to improve their television experience while hanging in the wilderness. Dana's father's company has released to the public the first commercial satellite receiver for the paltry sum of five thousand dollars, putting it in range of high-end users. With the addition of a low-cost, low-noise amplifier and a ten-foot diameter dish antenna, anyone with money can now watch studio-quality sports and movies in damn near any place in North America that has a view of the southern sky. We pop a price tag on the whole enchilada of ten grand installed, and Jack Nicholson and Jimmy Buffett bite.

I'm back into flying, taking mountain flying lessons from Mike Pilert in Ron's little Piper Colt with the big engine. I fly over on the following weekend and meet Dana, who is already hanging out in Aspen trying to drum up even more business. Thanks to me, he now knows Bill and Stela Pence from the Telluride Film Festival and can use their contacts to further his networking efforts.

I have to visit both sites to make an initial assessment for installing the dish antenna. Nicholson is not in town, so the property manager takes us into his home, which is on the first ridge north of town and overlooking the valley between his house and John Denver's on the opposite side. The house doesn't exude any vibes of the owner's character, sort of looking like a large hotel suite in a cracker box of a building made to look antiquey, as is the way with the phony local zoning board. I call it *Aspen cracker construction*, which says way more about the real estate corruption than the preservation of anything.

I pace out the distances for cables and such and locate a place to put the antenna. These antennas are not small and require a 4-inch steel pipe set in concrete to support it. I make a little drawing and Dana uses it to make up a written proposal.

Next, we drive out of town up near Woody Creek where Hunter lives, and where it's far enough away from Aspen to actually make you feel like you're back in reality. I've been wanting to meet Hunter ever since moving to the mountains. I feel we have a lot in common: like guns, sex, politics, drugs, Rock & Roll, and whiskey. Oh yeah, and existential philosophy.

From the air, the area north of town looks more like a sea of clear-cut condo crap surrounding a few last vestiges of green spots. Aspenitis at its worse. The wilderness is dying in every direction as the tentacles of high-dollar developments strip the land of all its dignity and natural purity. We follow the directions given to us and find ourselves on a little back road paralleling Brush Creek up a narrow valley behind Snowmass. Dana pulls the van into a plain-looking parking area next to the creek, where all we can see is a quaint covered footbridge. We get out and approach the bridge.

"Hi! Are you Ace?" someone calls from the other side.

"Yeah," Dana yells back. "I'm with Captain Neutrino, and we're here to measure you for a satellite dish."

"That's what I hoped," he yells back. "Come on over and I'll take you to my house."

When we get across, a sandy-haired smiling fool stands beside the center cabin of three in a row along the creek and greets us as we come off the bridge.

"Hi, I'm Jimmy," he says, shaking my hand and wearing a smile from ear to ear. "Welcome to Margaritaville, Aspen branch."

He takes us inside his newly built two-story cabin and we sit in his open living room where band equipment takes up half the space. Typical ploy, I guess, writing off your second home as a rehearsal studio.

"I just got married and have a new little girl, so I want this place to be the best for them. Besides, these guys I call neighbors are chipping in for half the cost, so *why not*, I said. How did you two freaks get into this weird business anyway?"

"You can say..." Dana explains, with his own mischievous smile, "I have close relations in the satellite receiver business."

"Nice," he says, handing us both a Corona. He looks at me. "And you?"

"I'm the physicist in charge of all quantums and microwaves. I make the electrons do their thing so we can have music and movies."

"That sounds wild. I'm looking forward to learning all about this new technology. Anybody like a little toot before we get started?"

*

A couple of weeks later, the equipment shows up for Jimmy's dish. Nicholson decides to opt out, saying he doesn't spend enough time in Aspen to make it worthwhile. I don't blame him. The price will only get cheaper with time.

Dana has his father ship us a receiver and LNA, which I will take with me when I go back for the installation. The dish shows up from some small company making them not too far from Frank's place in Oklahoma. Apparently, entrepreneurs all over the country are turning their garages into machine shops, cranking out ten-foot mesh dishes and cashing in on this new wild industry.

We hire some laborers from Carbondale to dig the hole and cement the mast into the ground, then mount the dish on top. I get a call from Jimmy saying the antenna is in and I can come over anytime to finish. I load up the equipment and my tools and drive to the airport where I transfer it to the little Colt. I quickly take off for the short flight to Aspen.

I fly the usual path to Gothic and then up along Copper Creek, which goes over the East Maroon Bells pass and then straight down the valley with a hard left at the end to the airport. As per usual mountain procedures, I fly next to one side of the canyon climbing up to the pass until I can see over the ridge and make sure there are no planes on the other side. Then I make a right turn down the valley and keep my eyes peeled for traffic all the way to Aspen airport. I call Aspen Tower, warning them I'm coming down the canyon. They okay a left turn and direct approach, so I'm back on the ground in less than a half hour.

Jimmy meets me at the private terminal and helps me load the stuff into his car.

"Hey, Neutrino, you hungry? I haven't had my breakfast yet. Maybe we could stop in Aspen for brunch and you can explain how this stuff is supposed to work."

"As long as I can get your dish working before sunset. I don't like flying back in the dark. Too many big airplanes out there, assuming I'm not."

"You can always stay over if you need. I heard of a good lunch place that's not supposed to be crowded. Let's go check it out."

He drives into Aspen and parks on the main drag. It's the off season, so you can actually drive around town and not feel you're in a parade. We go into something pretentiously called *Chez* this or another. It's fairly empty so we seat ourselves and look over the menu.

"Sometimes, it's amazing who you run into in this town. I'm always bumping into people from Key West who seem to think if they saw me in a bar there, then I must remember them."

Then I glance over at the only other table occupied this early in an Aspen day and surprisingly spot someone I know from a former life.

"Hang on, Jimmy," I caution, "I see someone I need to give my regards to."

I get up and walk over to the other table, approaching from behind a short balding guy entertaining several beautiful women. I slap him on the back.

"Hey Irving! How's it hanging?"

He almost falls out of his seat while abruptly turning around to see who it is.

"You!" he exclaims. "Cowboy! What are you doing here?"

I ignore him and look straight at his lady friends.

"I used to feel sorry for this lame lug and feed him fried chicken, back stage at Joe Walsh concerts. That's not all I used to give him. Nice to see you again, Irving! I'm with Jimmy over there," and I point at him. "Just having a little lunch and had to say hi." I pat him on the back again and saunter back to my table with everyone staring after me.

When I sit down, I explain to Jimmy. "If you don't already know, that's Irving Azoff, the little sleazy sidekick of Dave Geffen. Nasty little New York Jew bean counter who sucks blood from rock stars, plus sucks up all our coke when on the road. Sort of a coked-out vampire money-laundering zombie."

"Can't say that I've met him, yet," says Jimmy cautiously eyeing him. Irving is hustling his girls out of the restaurant and looking back at me with fear and loathing in his eyes.

"You will. If you make money in the rock business, and I think you do, he'll find you."

He looks at me, puzzled. He must be thinking: *For Chrissake, this guy is a satellite technician?*

We finish our lunch and go outside. Before we get ten feet, we hear someone yelling.

"Hey! Jimmy! Stop right there!"

We look behind us and spot a brilliant, pale blue '64 Cadillac convertible has pulled up next to us from behind and some tall guy with sunglasses and a floppy white hat gets out and comes running around the car, yelling all the way.

"I thought that was you. Jimmy Buffet, my favorite musician. Hi! I'm Doctor Thompson. Someone told me you were moving in with the Henley gang over on Bear Creek. You can call me Hunter." He starts pumping Jimmy's hand as he looks over at me. "And who's this?"

"Captain Neutrino," Jimmy answers. "Or is it Cowboy? He's here to install my new satellite dish."

"Satellite dish. Wow! I've heard about those. New secret way to spy on people. What do you need one for?"

"Television," he says flatly. "Haven't you noticed how lousy the TV reception is here? The satellite broadcasts high-quality TV signals from outer space to the entire country and all you need is the right antenna and receiver."

"You don't say. Sounds like I need to learn more about this satellite thing. Get in. I've got something to show you and you can tell me all about it." He put his finger on the side of his nose and makes a sucking sound.

I look at Jimmy and he looks at me. We shrug and mutually decide to acquiesce. After all, it's Hunter.

"As your doctor, I insist!" He pushes us toward his Cadillac, now with several cars stopped behind it, waiting impatiently. One guy politely taps his horn.

I jump in the back seat and Jimmy takes the shotgun. "I suppose we can go along for a while," he offers.

"Keep your shorts on!" yells Hunter at the waiting cars.

He climbs in and with a mighty roar replete with smoke, we make our getaway.

"You know they don't make cars like this anymore," he instructs, while not watching the road ahead. "More horsepower than any other production car. There's enough metal in this beast to stop a fifty caliber." He screeches around a corner heading south toward the upper bench and all the newest expensive housing. People don't even look at us. It must be a common sight in Aspen these days, with Hunter here, fighting the status quo. He slows and turns into an alley. He goes slow for a while and then yells, "There she blows!"

He stops the car, reaches over to the glove box, and takes out a pint of what looks like peppermint schnapps. "I gotta do something. I'll be right back."

He gets out of the car and cautiously approaches a couple of cars parked outside a big modern-looking cracker box. He looks around and proceeds to open the gas cap on one of the cars and begins pouring the schnapps into the gas tank.

"Get away from my car, you Gonzo douche bag!" I look up and someone is shaking their fist and yelling out a second-floor window.

"What's the matter, Judas? Not enough millionaires to buy your repugnant rag?" Hunter yells up to him.

"I'm calling the cops!" he yells back.

Hunter screams shaking his fist, "Hayduke lives!" and makes a hasty retreat to the Cadillac, emptying the last of the bottle's contents in his mouth. He throws it against a dumpster, where it shatters into a thousand pieces. He screams "*Wahooo!*" as he gets back in the driver's seat and takes off throwing gravel all over the alley.

"I had to do that. As a doctor of journalism, I'm empowered to discipline our own. I'm on a mission from god."

"Who was that?" Jimmy asks.

"Bill Dunaway, the local publisher of the Aspen rag. I don't even think he has a degree in journalism, and certainly not in ethics or truth."

"I'll have to remember that," Jimmy responds half-heartedly.

He takes the main road through town while I'm half expecting to see a cop car with its lights on coming for us. Jimmy is no longer smiling and just seems to be hanging on with a grim look of a willing hostage. Hunter leans over without watching the road and fishes something else from the glove box. He looks up just in time to avoid hitting a pedestrian walking their Chihuahua. He unscrews the cap on a silver pocket flask and takes a big swig. He hands it to Jimmy who takes it tepidly, studying it carefully. Hunter makes the sign of taking a drink as he careens around another corner, throwing me across the back seat to the tune of squealing tires.

"We've been fighting the eastern carpetbagger developers for decades as they destroy this town and the surrounding wilderness, turning it into a Disneyland for the arrogant and repugnant wealthy. Bill runs a paper that promotes this destruction, all in the name of preservation and progress. The only thing they preserve is their insane profits. Their progress is putting more people on the streets and putting more money in his pocket and the carpetbaggers as Rome burns." He looks sternly at Jimmy. Jimmy takes a small sip from the flask, wrinkles his nose, and hands it back to me.

Hunter accelerates past Jerome's, heading north out of town. I realize with delight that I'm going to get my wish. I have been bugging Dana for years to introduce me to one of my literary heroes. I decided a long time ago; I wanted to spend just one hour at his place in Woody Creek so I can die worthy. I take a swig from the silver flask, gag, and immediately recognize Wild Turkey. "I see we'll be flying on premium today," I quip.

"Ah, premium airlines. I like it," he says.

Soon we get to Woody Creek's only store and intersection where he turns right and then makes a couple more turns and we arrive at two nondescript small log cabins on the corner of a gravel road heading back to a ranch near the foothills. We pile out of the Cadillac, happy to be back on firm ground again. He leads us into the house on the right, as he explains, pointing to the other one, "That house belongs to Bob Dylan's sound guy, I don't remember his name. He's not here much."

Once inside, he leads us through a small, but well-cluttered living area and into the equally small kitchen on the left. He indicates a little white table with four chairs. We sit down and Hunter opens a cupboard door and pulls out a pint-sized, wide-mouth decanter with about an inch of white powder in the bottom. He lifts up a towel laying on the table and underneath is a mirror, already well-scratched and coated with a thin film of white scratches.

"The guy next door said this is Peruvian flake he picked up on a concert tour to South America. God, I love Rock & Roll!" He dumps out a goodly amount on the mirror as my eyes begin to water from just watching. I begin to feel giddy, maybe like a virgin about to be ravished, in a philosophical manner.

"I'm glad I caught you today, Jimmy. Welcome to Pitkin County, with the only jail in America that lets a serial killer escape by opening a window for him."

"I don't know how much time we'll actually be staying here," Jimmy explains. "We have a home in Florida, and I don't ski."

"Neither do I," he retorts, "but that's not the point. We need to make sure the local sheriff doesn't turn into a paid assassin. With all the money behind development, you either toe the line or they send the mafia enforcers after you." He deftly uses an old-fashioned one-edge razor blade to chop, sift, pull out six-lines and then chop them to fluffy perfection. This guy clearly has experience. "You got to watch your back around here, and I can help you do that."

He shoves the mirror over to Jimmy. "Here, Jimmy," he proudly offers, "take your pick."

"That's why as Americans and Rock & Roll freaks," he goes on, "we all must obey the second amendment and participate in a local militia for the maintenance of security, peace, and freedom. That's why I'm running for sheriff of Pitkin County. Only I can fairly administer justice, equally and blindfolded."

"Isn't that the justice department?" I ask, as Jimmy finally makes his choice and slurps up two lines like a shark sucks up the white meat. He's grinning again and rubbing his nose as he hands me the straw.

"It starts with the people, and as the sheriff, I would stop enforcing the pharmacy laws that protect big business from the freedom of self-medication. We'd all be a lot healthier, happier, and wealthier if we could supply our own drugs instead of relying on the huge bloodthirsty pharmacy industry. An industry, I might add, that makes a profit from your desperation. As long as you are desperate and miserable, they make money. Guess what they try to maximize?"

"That sounds about right," I agree, after suppressing a couple of explosive sneezes. I hand the straw back to Hunter. I stare in wonder as his giant nose suddenly sucks up the last two lines and every other pale powdery smear on the mirror. He grabs his nose and snorts a couple of times, gets watery eyed, and finally heaves a big sigh of relief.

"Hey, Jimmy," he says, patting Jimmy on the back. "Do you like guns?"

Jimmy nods his head a little.

"I bet you've never seen anything like this." He gets up and goes to a room behind the kitchen, which I presume is his bedroom. He comes back immediately with a very shiny hunk of metal in the shape of a giant automatic pistol. He's right. I've never seen anything like it.

"It's Israeli," he announces, ".357 magnum semi-automatic." He hands it to Jimmy, who immediately almost drops it from the unexpected weight. Hunter steps behind him and shows him how to hold it with two hands. It's obviously heavy, with a long barrel and a heavy-duty frame hanging out in front. It shines like a finely polished mirror, which doesn't appear very useful for camouflage in a sunny desert situation.

"That's real nice," Jimmy says, pretending to admire the object. "Here, Cowboy, what do you think?" He passes it to me with both hands. Hunter is beaming with pride and then thinks of something and starts looking in several drawers.

I look it over carefully. It has all the recognizable features of a Colt .45, some in slightly different places. I first drop the clip and open the breach, locking it in place. Then I feel for the secret button that releases the slide and barrel from the frame. I lay out the pieces on the table. A fully disassembled Desert Eagle ready for cleaning and inspection. Hunter finds a plastic bag and looks up to see his gun scattered in pieces. He looks at me with surprise.

"Captain Neutrino!" he exclaims, "I see you have talents. Ever been in the military?"

"Nope. I just like guns for their intrinsic fun. They are finely machined tools, crafted from steel whose purpose is to augments man's only real talent over nature: throwing rocks. When we came down out of the trees, we had to throw something at the lions to get their attention. Rocks first, then sharpened rocks on sticks, followed by a machine to throw the stick rocks even faster and harder, and then gunpowder shows up trumping everybody."

"It's a curiosity to you?" he asks incredulously.

"That's what physicists are all about. We study the universe and figure out how it works. Guns are a simple tool, just like nuclear energy and particle beams. Why do you like guns? I don't see an NRA sticker in your window."

"I have guns because the other side is well-armed and dangerous. We lost three of the greatest leaders of our time to supposedly random events of gunfire. *Preposterous*, I say! The right-wing nazi crazies are armed and dangerous and all Americans need to be vigilant and ready to prevent takeovers from the right. I think that's what Jefferson had in mind."

I pick up the pieces and quickly reverse the procedure and put it all back together. I leave the clip out and lay them both back on the table.

"Wanna see what this bad boy can do?" he asks with a wink.

I look at Jimmy who just looks glassy-eyed. "Sure, but where can we fire it?"

"Right out back," Hunter eagerly offers, and slams the clip back into the gun as he leads us to the back of the house and out to a small patio with a table and some chairs lined up on one side. It looks like a bench rest for firing rifles, I'm guessing.

"Grab another chair inside there and bring it out here," he commands.

I spot a small stool and bring it out and set it near the other two chairs. We all sit down. Hunter rests his elbows on the table, cocks the automatic, and takes aim.

"Look out there," Hunter directs, pointing at a rise of dirt behind his house about fifty feet away. The mound extends for some distance in both directions, which may have been part of an old railroad grade that once went through here. Directly opposite from us, up against the mound, are some wooden frames with remains of old targets and various other shot-up junk and crap. I spot the remains of several kitchen appliances, including table lamps, and curiously, a typewriter. It looks like he has been executing more than just TVs.

Jimmy covers his ears instinctively. I look at where he's pointing to see if I can identify what he's shooting at.

KABLOOYEE!

The thing explodes with the sound of a small tactical nuclear weapon. My eardrums hit the end of their travel and lock in place, leaving me momentarily deaf. One of the wooden boards on the mound blows off splinters, and dirt behind it explodes in a brown cloud of dust. Hunter turns around with the widest grin I've ever seen. He offers it to Jimmy, but he's still holding his ears and just shakes his head. He offers it to me.

"Careful," Hunter says, "it's ready to rock and roll."

I stand up and take a stance next to the table. Holding it with both hands, I lean into it expecting recoil. I squeeze off one shot at the same target Hunter hit and note the recoil isn't as bad as my .44-magnum revolver, the Dirty Hairy gun. So, I go for it. I rapidly fire repeatedly, emptying the clip in about three seconds. Dirt and rocks are flying so furiously that we lose sight of the mound. I still can't hear a damn thing for all the ringing in my ears, but it's clear, this is a really fine toy for rearranging mountain sides. *Better we shoot at them or leave skid marks on them, then tear them down completely,* I'm thinking.

Hunter takes the gun and reloads it. He does some fancy shooting from the hip and also while running. After not much time, he's emptied a box of ammo, feels exhausted, and sits back down at the table. He takes out a big red bandanna and begins wiping down the gun.

"You've got that mayor in a wheelchair over there," he changes the subject. "I think he's the darling of Hollywood, or something like that. You might want to mention to him that the enemy of your enemy is not necessarily your friend. He's playing with one devil to defeat another. It's not going to go well if he keeps that up." I took it as a Gonzo word to the wise.

"I can do that," I assert, "now where's that Turkey bottle?"

I promise myself to look back on this day as one of the finest days of my life. Unfortunately, Jimmy maybe doesn't feel the same. After shooting up all his spare ammo and running out of Wild Turkey, Hunter decides to venture back to town where he drops us off where Jimmy left his car.

As he roars out of sight, we can hear him yelling back at us, "Remember the Alamo!"

Jimmy says I should stay over tonight with him and fly back tomorrow after installing his new satellite dish. I can't agree with him more and sleep on his couch that night, listening to Bear Creek burble just like Coal Creek back home.

~ 15 ~

HELICOPTERS, SKIERS, AND SATELLITE TV

"Why don't you and Susie buy the cable company and do it yourselves?" Dana demands, staring at me seriously. I look at Susie and she looks at me. We're enjoying hippie hour at the Grubber and discussing what we had been thinking about for months now, the idea of building a satellite dish and wire the town for cable TV. Maybe even do a community radio station on it and make it a community network.

"How can we afford that?" she asks.

"I checked with Miles, and the present cable contract is held by some woman from south Texas whose husband owns a bunch of rural cable systems down there. They are regular skiers here and they approached the town last year with a contract to build and operate a cable company. The town granted them the use of public right-of-way's and they strung some cables around town."

"They feed their system with a single antenna," I add, "getting the same exact picture quality from the Almont repeater as everyone else in town, which is pretty bad. The town is getting screwed by Texans again. Who could have guessed? Listen, I'd really rather build a community radio station which can help glue this town together better than having happy hour all night long. I'd love to watch satellite TV too, but that means doing business with lawyers and accountants, the two lowest forms of human depravity known. You know how I hate being a capitalist pig." I mockingly spit sideways in disgust.

"I do, too," he agrees. "But someone is going to do it and it might as well be you. All I ask is if you guys get something going, just give me one share of stock. I don't want to own more than I can afford to hang on the wall."

"But you do business all the time! Why don't you do it? I'm a licensed radio engineer. I can wire a studio and run the transmitter. Your dad can help us get the FCC license. The community will love it, with volunteers for DJ slots and live broadcasts of community events. It could be a whole new focus for the town's arts efforts. We could make a little money, support ourselves, and have a place to broadcast all your Finds Arts. It'll be a blast!"

"Wouldn't you rather broadcast video, too? We could call it ColoRadio. It'd be like old time radio dramas with a picture to go along with it. That would be perfect for my Finds Arts."

"Seriously, you deal with money and lawyers all the time. You were raised around them. If you did it here, I'd gladly work with you. I can do all the technical stuff and you can collect the money and pay the bills."

"Business with friends only makes enemies," he points out. "I don't want to be involved in politics I can't control. I just do art with friends and I like it that way."

"How about making it a non-profit?" Susie asks, jumping in.

"Then it's run by a board of directors," I counter, "appointed by some commission or whatever. Then you play politics! I did some homework and apparently the key to starting a cable company is to negotiate an exclusive agreement to occupy a town's right-of-ways, you know, streets and alleys. They then sign a second agreement with the power company who owns all the power poles in those alleys. Turns out these poles only have three kinds of wires that they can hold. The top, of course, is power lines and below that are telephone lines. But there is one more layer below that where coaxial RF cable can be attached. When a cable company rents that pole space with a blanket agreement over a large area, they effectively block anyone else from using power poles because there's no room on the poles left. Hence, a cable agreement is the same as a monopoly. A license to steal, I believe, is the technical term."

"Yeah, so that's why we have to find someone to buy it from them," Dana adds, "so Crested Butte can have a cable system that actually works."

"How much?" Susie asks pointedly.

"Miles contacted the owner and she admits it's been a big loser for her. She has to pay for a full-time technician here to manage the system according to the contract. They are losing about a thousand a month and have no plans to expand any time soon. Maybe ten grand, he said."

"I can afford that," she pipes up with a bright smile.

"Unfortunately, my sweetie, that's just the beginning. I put together a little back of an envelope business plan while on the road and at a minimum we would have to install a satellite dish. That's about thirty grand right now for a big enough one to serve the whole town. Next, we have to figure out a way to bypass the Almont relay and find better over-the-air Denver channels."

"Got any ideas how that can be done?" asks Dana.

"Of course," I respond. "Susie and I hiked up to Gibson Ridge last summer with my little battery-powered Sony TV to search for signals. From Gibson Ridge, just a couple of miles from town, you can clearly see all the way to Gunnison down the Ohio Creek valley. The TV pictures we could pick up direct from Gunnison were clearly much better than Almont."

"Yeah," Susie adds. "They looked as good as what my sister gets in Denver."

"How would you go about building a TV antenna site up there?" Dana asks. "Don't you need special permission to put up an antenna site on forest service land?"

"Shit, they allow mining, don't they? And they let the airport put a strobe on Smith Hill. I don't see how they can say no to an entire city's need for modern communications."

"How about if I get you a partner that can help with the money and running the business side?" Dana proffers.

"Like who?" I'm thinking Mitchell, but he's too embroiled with his Hollywood friends and the Sierra Club playing town defender for little things like community TV and radio stations. Like most, nobody wants to do the work to make it happen, but they all want to be first in line to use it for their own self-promotion.

"Steve Glazer says he's interested," Dana declares.

"He's a slimy vulture and you know it," I declare. "Look how he ruined the Princess. He says he wants to preserve it as a theater, but if it wasn't for Bill Pence, he probably would have turned it into another Company Store by now, destroying a community legacy." I pause and then ask, "Why not sell stock to everyone in town and make it a community thing? There's plenty of trust funders out there with extra gambling and coke money."

"Are you willing to do that kind of organizational work?" Dana counters. "You'll need a business manager, accountants, bankers, lawyers, and the whole nine yards unless you're willing to do that yourself. I told him about the satellite technology and he's willing to put up the money and business expertise in order to keep it in the Butte. There's a Gunnison cable company looking at maybe buying the system as well. At least you can hear him out."

I look at Dana with a slightly new feeling toward him. If he trusts Steve, then should I?

*

The next day, Susie comes up to the projection booth with Glazer behind her. "Steve wants to talk to us," she says.

"I'm busy prepping tonight's film. What do you want?" I keep working and he sits down on the stool next to projector #1.

"I want to build the cable system Dana told me about. I can't do it on my own. I need your help."

"I want to build it too, but I don't trust greedy business types." I study him carefully and he actually seems somewhat humble. "What do you propose?"

"A partnership. I'll do the business side and you do all the technical stuff. I'm thinking we need to capitalize with about twenty grand so we have enough to buy the current company for the right-of-ways. From there, we should be able to obtain leases for equipment and loans for construction. If we can get the satellite dish installed before winter, we can sign up lots of new customers and should become profitable fairly quickly."

I finish rewinding the film and turn around to look at him. Susie steps over next to me and puts her arm around my waist.

"What do you think, Susie?" I ask, while wrapping my arm around her.

"I can put up half of that. What do you think?" she whispers.

"I don't want you to have to pay for everything. I want to do it, but I'm not sure about..." I glance over at Steve and then look back at her.

"It will give you the chance to build a radio station," she explains. "It'll be fun. We're partners. You do what you do best. Let me put up the money." She flashes that Fisher smile that melts my heart, once again. I still have a sinking feeling though when I look back at Steve.

Every time I see his gaunt look with his long thin nose, I'm reminded of Shakespeare's quote describing those jealous of Caesar: "Yond Cassius has a lean and hungry look!" But what can I do? He's the only one to express any serious financial interest. I can't do it alone and I don't have the resources to compete if he decides to do it without me. I'm screwed if I do and screwed if I don't.

"Okay, but we'll have to sign an agreement so our investment is protected and we build it to my design." I'm thinking ten grand is a helluva lot of money for me and I can't afford to even be playing in this game, but if I do, I've got to be in charge.

"That's fine," he agrees. "We'll form a new company and hire a lawyer to draw up the partnership agreement."

Susie squeezes me around the waist and flashes a big smile at me and then to Steve. She gleefully adds, "We'll call it Crested Butte Cable. I'll design the logo for you."

I feel sort of numb, but excited. This is going to be a challenge, but I think I can do this. I want to do it. I want to do it right.

*

Things start moving quickly. Winter is coming, snow is on the ground, and we have to get construction underway for the new antennas to be put on Gibson Ridge. I have to figure out how to string a one-inch coaxial cable from the antenna site all the way to town, which is about four miles. We'll have to lay it on the snow for now and after that melts in the spring, bury it in the ground next summer.

Steve sets a meeting with some new young lawyer in Gunnison whom I never heard of, but then I don't care. I write up a list of conditions I require in the agreement and give it to the lawyer at our initial meeting with instructions to include it in the partnership agreement. Steve agrees and says we have to get moving and can't afford to wait for the formal agreement. He takes Susie's check, opens a bank account, and rents the little yellow house at 340 Elk.

"Should we get a lawyer?" Susie asks, after I tell her about the meeting in Gunnison.

"Who? Leinsdorf? He'd probably charge us five hundred bucks just to look at it. The lawyer we hired represents the company and we are owners, so he has to do what we tell him to do. My list of conditions includes me having absolute authority for all technical decisions, all business and financial agreements must be approved by both of us, and the radio station is a separate non-profit community channel."

"Then I guess this is it," she says profoundly. "We're in the cable business. What happens next?"

"We're all going down to the new office tomorrow and do a little painting. You're welcome to help out. We're encouraging murals from anyone so inclined. The upstairs bedroom in the back is perfect for the community radio station. Gorbett is going to hang a giant wallpaper picture of the earth as seen from the moon. I'm designing the studio layout now. It's going to be a really cool place for a sound studio, live radio, and even video."

"Neat!" she exclaims, and I swear I see a sparkle in her eye that makes my heart skip a beat.

"I'll hire Tapley and the Rat as line techs. We'll set up an electronics bench in the dining room where we can start building some of the equipment we'll need. I've ordered some Heathkit walkie talkies tuned to the 2-meter amateur band. We bought a used twin track Ski-Doo for accessing our remote antenna site on Gibson's Ridge. And a four-wheel-drive Ford pickup, jacked six inches off the ground with skinny tractor treads that when chained on all four, becomes the next best thing to a snow cat. We named it Sherman, after the famous tank."

"Wow!" she says admiringly. She steps back a bit. "I've never seen you so happy before. Even the Telluride Film Festival doesn't get this much attention."

"I'm happy because you're happy." I declare. "Look at you. The beam in your eyes is blinding. We're doing something good, for us, for the town, and our friends. I really want to make this work."

She steps in, grabs me around the shoulders, and kisses me, hard, and we hold on to it for a very long time. I don't want to let her go. Suddenly, I know why they call it heaven. It's like no other feeling in life, because it's not *in life* but *above life*.

It's so strange and new for me. I've never ventured this deep into another's spirit. Never have I been buoyed to such a level of super-euphoria. It's not just physical or mental. It's something more absolute; more real without restraint, more sharing without exposing, more respecting while changing; her for me and me for her, without bounds in space and time. This must be all that schmaltzy purity crap that love songs brag about, and now....

"It's our time."

"What?" she asks.

I do my best WC Fields imitation, while flicking an imaginary cigar in my mouth with my fingers, saying, "This is going to be something big, I tell yah. Yeah. Like a pimple on a buffalo butt."

*

The next few weeks are a blur. It's getting into November and the upper country already has a few feet of snow on the ground. The only way we're going to build a remote antenna site in the snow and string 20,000 feet of aluminum cable down the mountain is with damn good skiers. Fortunately for us, Crested Butte is overloaded with macho types on skis who'll do almost anything for money. And I emphasize the *anything*.

People are showing up at the little house we call an office every day as we prepare for the big build out. The front room becomes Steve's office and reception area while the technical staff occupies the rest of the building. My office is in one of the back bedrooms and already has a black light and some ultra-violet posters. Susie even did a little mountain scene on the wall with glow paint.

"Here's the phone number of a flying service in Fort Collins," I tell Steve sitting at his desk as I hand him a slip of paper. "Call them, ask for Mitch, and make arrangements to pay them for the helicopter I booked. It's under Crested Butte Cable."

"And how much is that going to be?" he asks slightly irritated.

We're spending a lot of money, but it's still a hell of a lot cheaper with me figuring things out and engineering it ourselves than hiring a bunch of city weenie professionals who do a whole lot less for a shitload more.

"Don't know. I think we can do it all in one day, but if it doesn't, we may have to hold him over a day or two. Nobody has used helicopters to install an antenna tower at ten thousand feet in the snow and then thread a giant cable between trees four miles down a mountainside."

He just stares at me and I can see him break out in a visible sweat contemplating what I just described.

"Also, rent a hangar from Ron for a month so we can use it as a lay-down yard for all the cable reels, equipment, and support cradles we'll have to build. I've designed a simple cable reel frame that has a built-in brake so when the helicopter pulls the cable out, we pull on the brake lever, stopping the cable from auto-spooling down the mountain."

"Anything else?" he asks sarcastically.

"Yeah. Our friend in Tulsa turned me on to the best little satellite dish maker in Oklahoma. We can get a five-meter dish, heavy duty for snow loads and higher off the ground to prevent snow backup. Ice and snow can block the signal so it's important to keep it clean all winter. I can get it turnkey installed for thirty grand. Find thirty grand so I can get it ordered. Maybe five grand will at least get them started."

"Just like that. Find thirty grand. Where am I supposed to find that kind of cash? We don't have a cent left of our investment money."

"Lease it."

"Lease it?"

"Yeah, he said all the rural cable companies buying dishes are all leasing them. Lease to buy. It gets them around the usuary laws. But for 5 percent down, they'll pay for the dish and we pay for it with new customers. Remember, the cable business is like a drug dispensing vending machine. People just keep paying monthly to stare at the boob tube. Money comes in from the addicted community and therefore, we need to spend some of that drug money supporting the community like all popular drug dealers do. In the cable business, we buy the pieces, screw them together, and out comes money. Think of Las Vegas if you need a model."

He flashes that knowingly greedy smile again. I'm beginning to think it's not so cute anymore.

"I gotta go hire some skiers. Has the lawyer drawn up our contract yet?" I ask reminding him again.

"I don't know. I'll check on it." And there's that smile. Is he trying to be friendly in some awkward manner? Or... Anyway, I've got a lot of shit to do before the big snow dump comes and possibly shuts down, or makes damn difficult, a lot of our coming work.

*

I walk up to the Grub and immediately spot Rick Borkovic sitting at a table watching snowy TV.

"Need a refill?" I ask.

"Sure," he says without looking up.

"Baggins! Bring us a pitcher." I see a hand come up from behind the bar waving at me. Must be slogging it out again with the eternally backed up drain. Boy, I do not want to know what goes down that thing that makes it keep throwing it back up. I turn back to Rick and sit down.

"Wanna job?" I pop.

"Doing what?" he asks snidely. "I don't know anything about electronics."

"I need what you do best. Extreme skiing."

"How extreme?"

"Have you ever been towed on skis behind a helicopter?" I smile, knowingly.

He looks blank while he thinks about it. Baggins fills up his glass and gives me a fresh one, which he also fills.

"I see you're fatally entranced. Let me explain."

About a week later, a Bell helicopter fights its way below low clouds over Monarch Pass just a hundred or so feet above the road. The whole area is locked in clouds almost down to the ground. By following the highway, like a low-flying car, the pilot is able to make it to town on schedule. He lands in the city park and walks uptown to the Nickel where most of the action seems centered. He asks for me and the bartender tells him to wait a minute while they send someone down to the office to let me know there's a stranger in town claiming to be a helicopter pilot running up a tab at the Nickel under my name. I jump on my klunker and head uptown.

His name is Charley and he, of course, got his training in Vietnam and feels damned lucky to not only have survived that fiasco, but to still be doing what he loves: flying an eggbeater. When I tell him I'm a veteran too, he brightens up slightly, until

I add that I was on the winning side. I explain I was an anti-Vietnam protester in college and marched on the Pentagon. He brightens up again.

"Here's to you. I was too much of a coward to stay and fight. I figured if I only flew evac missions, maybe I could live with myself." He holds up his shot glass, I clink it with mine, and we seal our Vietnam-era brotherhood. Surviving without a grudge is the only requirement for admission.

We put him up in the Forest Queen and I have to put him to bed after closing, as he can't follow directions in his condition. I begin to wonder if my plan tomorrow is going to end up some kind of mountain fiasco that goes down in the history books as the weirdest helicopter accident ever.

Next morning, I find Charley having breakfast at the Forest Queen looking not too bad for the wear.

"Where'd you go to college?" I ask.

"Arizona State," is his calm reply.

"Figures," I say, sitting down opposite. I begin sketching out the day's plan on one of their giant napkins, showing a stick figure on skis with a reel of cable next to him. Then I draw a helicopter with a line going from the reel to the chopper showing how he's going to pull the cable out and thread it between the trees, laying it along a trail.

"All the equipment is staged at the airport, so after breakfast I'll meet you down there and we'll start hauling all the gear up to the ridge. It's only three miles from there and about a thousand-foot climb. We have to ferry ten cable reels and three antenna tower sections."

"No problem."

"And a chest freezer."

"A what?" he asks looking up.

"We're using a chest freezer to hold the electronic equipment at the antenna site so we don't have to build an actual building. It's cheap, very well insulated, sealed, and waterproof."

"Clever." He takes another big bite out his stack of pancakes hiding under a waterfall of maple syrup.

"Also, we have a couple of techs who will bolt the antenna site together and a couple more skiers who will be guiding the cable down the trail as you pull it out. We have walkie talkies tuned to your aircraft frequency. We'll have one skier directly below you marking the trail and the other one behind helping guide the cable down through the tree branches. You just have to get us all up there and then pull out the cables. We'll all ski down to the road just for the fun except for the Rat."

"The Rat?" he repeats.

"He'll be the only one you take back to the airport so he can use the truck to pick us up at the bottom." I look up at him and he's looking at a couple of tourist chicks at the next table. "Questions?"

"Nope. I've got it. Rat goes back. I pick up check at the bar tonight."

I shudder a little. Either it's going to work, or this is the craziest helicopter pilot I've ever had to work with, which is exactly one at this point.

We gather the team at the airport just before taking off for the site. We've staged all the cable reels on their wooden frames so they can be lifted into place along the trail. The plan calls for the helicopter to connect to the cable and pull it off the reel, threading it through the trees and down the trail with the help of some expert skinny skiers, Rick, B.C., and Blumel.

"I'll be on the first flight up with Tap and a tower section. We'll start tamping out an area big enough to work around and dig the three holes through the snow so the three tower sections will rest on solid ground. The second trip will bring Rick and his crew and another section. We'll start assembling the sections in place as the helicopter brings up the freezer and cable reels already on their stands. Rat will stay down here to help load the helicopter and to come get us when we ski out later this afternoon. Any questions?" I spot a joint making the rounds and step in for a quick toke.

"What do we do if the cable gets caught in a tree and we can't get it on the ground?"

I look at Rick. "Rick?" I blow out a cloud of smoke and pass it on.

"We have a chainsaw," Rick says. "It's a big forest. Things happen."

"Whatever we do, do it professionally and safely. I don't want to have to fly one of you to Gunnison because you jogged when you should have jigged. I want you to know that I won't ask any of you to do anything I wouldn't do. That's why I'll be with you all the way down the mountain."

Everybody laughs, knowing I'm not a very good skier and I'll probably spend a lot of time sliding on my butt. That's okay. At least I try.

"Okay, let's do this thing!"

Tap and I grab our gear and climb into the helicopter. Charley lifts off and hovers while Richard hooks up the first tower section. Charley leans over and taps me to put on the headphones. When I do, he asks, "Want to see how we flew in Vietnam?"

"Sure," I eagerly agree. This is my first flight in an eggbeater, so why not enjoy it? Besides, I'm paying for it.

"Watch this," he says with a grinning smirk.

He puts on full power and climbs steeply out of the airport, but as soon as he clears the buildings, he dives again for the ground and we accelerate until our blades are pulling us forward and we're literally looking straight out the front at the ground passing under us at a hundred miles an hour. Soon we're flying across the snowy ranchland just clearing the fences with our load and following the flow of the landscape as we blow across the highway about twenty feet above a Volvo. Then he starts climbing steeply as we approach the north slopes of White Rock and head upslope inside Baxter Gulch.

I love the power this thing has and am hanging on for dear life as he pours the kerosene into dual thousand-horse turbines turning twenty-foot wing-blades, beating mercilessly the thin air into abject submission. This is what life should be all about. Taking a helicopter to work in the wilderness, in the winter, on skis. That's a job to die for.

"Okay, where do you want to put it?" he asks over the intercom. I study the landscape below and immediately spot the opening in the woods right at the edge of the cliff. I point it out to him and he positions us over the clearing where he gently drops the tower section, swings around and hovers nearby right at snow level.

"Want to give it a try to see how deep it is?" Charley asks, looking back at us. I turn to Tapley and he gets a grin on his face, steps out on the skids and jumps off. He only sinks up to his waist, so we get lucky. Any deeper and we might be struggling way too hard to clear holes for the tower legs.

I join him in the snow and Charley wheels the helicopter over the cliff and falls away below us, heading back at top speed for the second load. We quickly stamp out an area big enough to land the next section and crew. Soon the place is crawling with our guys digging out snow for the tower legs and bolting them together. The antennas are already mounted and all we have to do is string coax cable from them to the freezer box setting underneath in the snow.

I prewire the equipment in the freezer so it's fairly simple to just connect the antennas and the big coax going down the mountain. I get with Rick and make contact with Charley using the walkie talkies. He drops a line with a Chinese finger cuff that grips the big coaxial cable by the end and then he slowly begins pulling out the cable as he flies along precisely above the trail. Rick sends Blumel, wearing an orange hunter's vest for visibility, down the trail below us showing Charley where to thread the cable as it unwinds from the reel.

Rick mans the cable reel and the mechanical brake we built into each one, which hopefully will control how fast the cable unreels. When we get to the end of the two-thousand-foot spool of cable, Rick slows the reel down with the hand brake and I radio Charley to lower his end down as low as he can and then drop it on the trail.

After dropping the cable, Charley goes back to the top where he picks up the next reel and brings it to the place where he just dropped the end of the last cable. By that time, Rick and I ski down to the new spot, where we repeat the procedure again, unwinding the next cable reel.

"I can't believe it's going so smoothly," I comment to Rick while taking a breather between cable reels.

"Me neither," he says, which makes me a little unsettled.

For the next run, we are following the steepest part of the mountain trail. When we get to the end of the cable on the reel, Rick applies the brake, but the cable keeps coming off the reel at a good clip. I radio Charley to slow it down, but then the end comes off the reel and with a sinking feeling I see it moving rapidly away from us.

Rick rapidly ice skates on skis and catches the end of the cable before it can disappear down the trail. He grabs onto it good and then pulls hard. I'm still yelling through the radio for Charley to stop and reverse when I see Rick suddenly lift off the ground and fly about twenty feet in the air.

"Hang on Rick!" I yell as he slowly descends back to earth. But before the cable can get fully back on the ground and become impossible to move, even on snow, Rick hauls it with all his strength and his skinny skis can handle, back up the slope about fifty feet to where it can be properly connected to the last cable above us.

"Cowboy!" I hear over the radio. "What the hell is going on down there? I'm being pulled back toward the mountain."

"It's okay. Just go with it."

I can't believe it. Rick gets in a tug of war with a helicopter, and wins. It turns out that helicopters are easy to pull sideways when they are just hovering, but it's still impressive. I'm going to have Steve bonus these skiers for their outstanding work today.

About four in the afternoon, the helicopter pulls the last cable across Coal Creek and we meet up with Rat in the Sherman and our cable tech, Chris, who we inherited from the Texas owners and who can climb power poles with hooks. They attach the cable to the aerial cable we placed on the power poles earlier, which carries the signal the remaining mile or so into town and the new headend equipment shed we build up by the town reservoir.

Charley has become an honorary Butte-er overnight and now parks his helicopter with impunity in the vacant lot across Second Street from the Elks Lodge. We all congregate at the Nickel in a couple of hours in a sort of closing night cast party. Rick and the skiers are here with all my guys and Charley, who offers rides in the helicopter to any girl wanting one, and Steve.

I'm trading shots at the end of the bar with Tap and the Rat recalling all the great things we did today. It's not often a bunch of ordinary chumps can come together and make something greater than themselves, actually proving there are no great people, just ordinary people who rise to occasion when needed. Or, in the words of Doctor Gonzo, "When things turn weird, the weird turn pro."

"I hear you're the new hero in town," Susie whispers in my ear from behind. I turn around and she's standing with Dana, who's busy ordering drinks.

"You should have been there," I burbled. "We were skiing down the mountain dropping cable from a helicopter and performing minor miracles in the wilderness. I sure hope everything works when we turn on the power tomorrow."

She kisses me and flashes her biggest smile. "It will. I know you. It will." Dana hands her a beer and she sits on the stool next to me. Dana hovers over the two of us.

"Well, Captain Neutrino, tamer of the electron, how goes it? I hear you were playing with helicopters all afternoon. Nice work if you can get it." He clinks my glass. "When are you and Steve going to build us a satellite dish? Now that the sports fans can watch football on Sunday, you have to get HBO for the rest of us."

"No sweat. It's all scheduled. The install crew is supposed to show up next week, if the pass stays open. They're friends of Frank from Oklahoma and they're building it to our specific latitude. They'll be bringing it up in a truck with a crew to erect it."

"That sounds expensive," he says. "Why not do it yourself?"

"Turns out the cost of just shipping it here is enough to pay them to erect it. Why not, I said, seeing how it's all handled under one lease? Besides, the bank likes to think it's worth more if guaranteed by the builders and so did our timid Steve, the penny pincher."

"I'm really looking forward to seeing high quality video in this town. How's the community radio station coming?"

"Great. The radio station at Western State just upgraded its transmitter so we can buy the old one for damned near nothing. I don't need the last stage of power amplification for going over the air, so I'll just tap the signal at low power and add it to our RF spectrum at the cable headend. We'll run an RF cable from the studio here in town to the headend up at the reservoir so we can broadcast downstream to all our customers. They'll have to hook up their FM radio to the cable to get us, but we can do it for free with every new cable install."

"That reminds me," Dana says, setting his drink down on the counter. He fishes in a coat pocket and pulls out some pictures. "Look at what I took yesterday when Tapley was working on a telephone pole out in the middle of a snow field."

He lays them one at a time on the bar. The first one shows Tap skiing across a snow field with tops of fence posts barely sticking through the snow. There is a telephone pole in the distance that looks short because of the snow depth. The next shot shows him straddling the pole still with his skinny skis on.

Then the next one shows him about six feet up the pole working on the cable amplifier, still wearing his skis, but this time, I realize he also has his hooks on and he just climbed the pole, skis and all. An undoubted first, anywhere.

"I'll bet Chris, that Texas turkey tech we got with the business, can't do that," I exclaim. "Now that's mountain man talent!"

*

"So, what do you want to bet they can't find the satellite?" I ask Richard the Rat standing next to me and the Sherman I've adopted as my private vehicle during our construction phase.

"I thought they're the experts," he responds. "Why? Now what's wrong?"

There are about four rednecks from Muscovy, Oklahoma, who smoke cigarettes like movie tough guys and scatter tools around like duck decoys, putting on an impromptu three stooges plus one live act. Rat and I are hard pressed to not break out laughing while watching their clumsy amateurish antics.

They've been working all day assembling a giant erector set of beams and plates, all forming a shallow dish fifteen feet in diameter, with a tripod of twelve-foot angle iron extending out in front to the focal point where the low noise amplifiers mount. Then there's this separate tripod of big steel beams forming a tetrahedron with one vertical edge oriented south forming the pivot points for two bearings, one at the top and one at the bottom, supporting the dish like a cradle. The geometry calls for the angle of the pivot shaft to equal the latitude of where we are on earth so the antenna can be steered from east to west following the belt of geosynchronous satellites along the celestial equator. Any amateur astronomer can align a polar mount telescope with just a simple angle measurement. It's basic Star Gazing 101, something any physicist can do in his sleep.

"We're ready to start searching for the satellite!" calls out their boss, Bubba, from our little equipment shed where they have a satellite receiver hooked up to the dish and a portable TV set. Rat and I walk over and watch over their shoulders while Bubba stares at the screen and tells his boys to move the dish back and forth slowly looking for any signs of a signal. The TV just shows a snowstorm, as most of us who live in the Butte are already very used to.

"Go slower!" he calls out from inside the shed. "I can't see anything."

We watch for about ten more minutes as they slowly turn the dish back and forth looking vainly for a picture to pop up. I tap Rat and we retreat to the Ford. We climb inside and I take out a joint and light it up. When I offer it to the Rat, he turns it down. "You know I get too paranoid," he explains again.

"Oh yeah, sorry. But you know, there's probably a reason for that. With a little pot therapy, we could maybe clear that psychotic condition and then you can maybe use it as a crutch to stop smoking."

"No thanks, but it looks like you're right. They're having trouble finding the satellite. What are they doing wrong?"

"Assuming they know how to operate a directional compass and they oriented it correctly south facing, I'm betting they made a rookie mistake in the ascension angle." I dig into my backpack and pull out a little five-cent clear plastic compass for drawing angles. I've already attached a short string to the center of the compass and a small lead fishing weight dangles from the other end. "Come with me."

We get out of the truck and go over to the dish where one of the Bubba Boys, presumably the lowest ranking, still swings it back and forth while the rest stare at the little TV, still seeing nothing. How long will they keep repeating something, each time expecting different results, but not getting them? I shake my head in disbelief.

I find a straight surface along the shaft supporting the dish. I place my homemade ascension meter on the flat part of the dish and let the lead weight dangle along the compass showing an angle of about 37 degrees.

"What's our latitude here?" I ask Rat.

"How the fuck would I know?" he barks back.

"I think I have a Gunnison Forest Service map in the glovebox. It should say."

We wander back to Sherman and fish out a badly folded map from the glove box. I study the borders and find a latitudinal line nearest Crested Butte labelled 38.9.

"What did I tell you? They're two degrees off. Should I tell them?"

Rat gets his mischievous look and I smile in agreement. "We're not getting paid for this job," I point out. "Let's see how long it takes them to figure it out."

*

"Did you know about this?" Steve asks me after Bubba delivers the bad news the next morning in our company office and leaves to presumably work on fixing the problem.

"Of course," I respond. "Who do you think you're dealing with? The Rat and I checked out the ascension angle after they erected it and then couldn't find the satellite. I'm guessing the mount is designed for Dallas."

"Dallas?" he exclaims. "How can they be that far off?"

"I'm guessing their designer probably figured the difference in latitude as being about two and a half degrees, which someone screwed up and instead of adding, subtracted from their standard design at Oklahoma City, where they make these things. Now they have to add a shim on one end that increases it by four degrees to make up the difference. I figure the shim will be about eight inches long, so they will have to make it in their machine shop and ship it up here. Probably take them a few more days and a lot more money."

"Bastards!" he blurts out. "That means our official debut is going to be put back a week and now I look like an incompetent fool. I invited both town councils and managers and was planning on winning some new friends in high places. Damn!"

"We've already got the Denver stations on our system better than what anybody can get over the air. That makes all the sports fans happy. All we can get off the satellite is HBO and TBS. Believe me, I want them on our system, I love movies, but I'm more interested in launching our radio station.

But first I need to change the frequency on the surplus transmitter we got from Western State. We can't interfere with their station, so I did a survey and found a frequency that's open for use. I expect the crystal I ordered for retuning it will show up any day."

"I'm going to call their boss in Oklahoma," Steve declares, "and see if I can get a discount because of their screw-up."

I leave shaking my head. If that's what it's like doing business, I'm glad he's doing it and not me. I don't want anyone to think I concur with his greedy ethics. I need to make sure this stays a *Crested Butte Cable* company and not a *Steven Glazer Cable* company. I remind myself the next time I'm in Gunnison to check on the lawyer drawing up our partnership agreement. It's been long enough.

*

The Denver Post runs a small article announcing that a little forward-looking ski town in the high Rockies is the first cable system in Colorado to add a satellite dish to their TV lineup. They go on to say how satellites will be able to bring television from around the world into small isolated communities, like Crested Butte, making them less isolated, better educated, and more connected.

I, on the other hand, with all the resources, toys, and tools that I now have at my disposal, have an idea: I install a two-way VHF business radio in our truck, which talks to a base station at our office. When we are out of sight of town, we have to switch frequencies and quietly use the amateur repeater to relay our signals back to our base station.

Then, I find a cheap device that's even more cool. It's an automatic telephone operator interface box, controlled just like a real phone, with touch tones generated by a touch pad, only this one is on the back of the two-way radio microphone. It connects the radio to a phone line, giving me a dial tone in the truck. I can dial any number in the world from my two-way radio and connect just like a telephone. I call my brother in Alaska from Sherman parked halfway up the hill to the ski are—and I, perhaps, carried out the first cellular wireless phone conversation in town.

We finish installing the studio on the second floor of our office building where we have a mix board and two industrial-grade turntables, compliments of Gary Gorbett, just like the big time. Gary and Cotton volunteer to DJ every evening, to begin with, and bring their extensive album collections to the station so we have a basic current library of music. Someone does the news, and pretty soon there's a continuous stream of people coming and going through the rear door to work a time slot or just party and hang with whomever is on the air.

Sandy Cortner from the *Pilot* shows up at the office one day when I'm out actually doing the real work and takes a few pictures and writes up a blurb about what apparently only Steve and Gary had just accomplished. But for some reason, she completely misses giving me or any of my crew any credit for everything that we are doing. I've been ostracized for some time by the local press, probably because I'm not popular or rich enough to make it worth taking any notice. I'm not part of the moneyed crowd, or the suck-up popularity crowd so can't possibly be interesting. I don't care. I know the truth and so does anybody who bothers to look. Hunter is right, though. Journalists need watching.

*

R-r-r-i-i-i-n-n-g-g! sounds the phone next to our bed. I know it's not time to get up; the angle of the light coming in from outside isn't right. As I roll over to grab the handset, I notice the nixie tube digital clock next to our bed glows fiendishly red with *7:45.*

"Wha?" I mumble into the handset, wondering who has the balls to be calling me at this ungodly hour.

"Cowboy," says Steve, "you awake?"

"No, I'm sleepwalking and answered the phone. Waddya want?" I feel Susie roll over toward me, causing a small water wave to pass under me.

"The antenna farm is down."

"Dead?"

"Gone. Nothing"

"I'll be right there." I hang up.

I roll back facing Susie and she opens her eyes just long enough to find my lips, then closes them again kissing me hungrily.

Should I stay or should I go? I think. The basic question of all life. Doom definitely follows those who decide wrongly.

"Gotta go. That's Steve. The antenna farm up on Gibson Ridge has failed, apparently. I designed it, so, I have to fix it."

"No," she pleads. "Stay a while longer and keep me warm." She wraps her arms around me and pulls me into her.

"I'm mildly surprised it's lasted all through the winter. Now it's March and the snow is melting and things are moving around up there. I'll probably have to take the twin track Ski-Doo snowmobile loaded with tools and parts and just beat my way to the top, ski if I have to, find the problem, and fix it if I can."

"Oh no. The weather doesn't look good for back-country trekking. A storm is coming through later today. Don't take any chances up there." She pulls on my waist until we're touching our tummies. We kiss again.

"Don't worry. I'll be okay. I just hope I can make it all the way to the antennas. Who knows what treacherous snow conditions I might find up there? Nobody has been there since we installed it." I reluctantly roll off the bed and stand up.

"Come back to me!" she orders with a pout and pulls the down comforter over her head.

*

"You know the trail," Tapley instructs me, as I warm up the twin track. "Just follow the Green Lake trail from the bench until it crosses the cable running along Wildcat trail and then follow the cable all the way to the top."

"I know," I reply. "I just hope this beast can stay on top of the snow and not get stuck. The more it sinks, the harder it becomes to keep moving forward."

"Yeah, the worst part is the last hundred feet to the ridge. It gets pretty steep and deep in there so watch it. You may have to ski in if the Ski-Doo craps out."

"Again, I was there. I'll call you on the radio as soon as I get up there or get stuck. Stay with it in case I need you."

"No problem. Be safe!"

I take off with a mighty roar from the rear of our office building and cross town to the CF&I bench just above town, trying to stay on as much snow as possible and not screw up the tracks. Finally, I climb up the unused road to the bench where there is virgin snow and just an opening in the trees marking the Green Lake trailhead.

It's about noon when I finally get moving, so I only have about four to five hours to get there, fix whatever is wrong, and get back before dark. Although, I suppose, as long as it isn't snowing, I can easily follow my own tracks back out using my headlights, if they work. Having been on a few night-time ventures in the snow, I'm not worried about my safety, just how much trouble this whole little venture is going to cost me, personally.

The Ski-Doo is sinking about a foot in this powder, which for most snowmobiles, would soon grind them to a halt from pushing too much snow and not having the raw power to climb over it. Not this beast. It seems to have the necessary horsepower to simply claw its double-wide track through the light snow, compressing it, and constantly climbing out of its hole-in-the-snow as it burrows its way along like a snow worm.

All I have to do is hang on, stay warm, and keep my balance. The worst that can happen is that I fall off sideways on a steep vertical climb and then roll the beast all the way to the bottom, probably causing a minor avalanche, which will neatly bury all the guilty parties until the summer melt.

All this, and more, is going through my head as I plow my way up the mountain trail. I finally see an opening ahead where this trail crosses the Wildcat trail we pulled our cable along several months ago. The cable was spliced and tied off to trees right after we installed it, so I'm pretty sure the problem isn't with it or any of the amplifiers we have stationed along the way.

In any case, I stop at each beer cooler we use to protect the amplifiers from the elements and check for power. They all look and test good, so I'm led higher and higher along the cable until I break out in the meadow just below where the slope suddenly gets steeper for the last short climb up to the ridge itself and our antenna farm.

The snow is a lot deeper now, having accumulated in this protected circle of trees and being forced over a low point in the ridge where the snow loses momentum and simply falls out of the slipstream. I realize that if I fell off this thing right now, I could end up buried in snow way above my head. If I get bucked off, I might not be able to get back on. Not a good thought for a guy named Cowboy.

At this point, I've probably bought too many risk factors, resulting in some kind of conspiracy of natural forces which will jump out and bite me by the balls at any moment. I feel vulnerable. But this machine is being quite impressive for a snow machine, so I dumbly press on. The trail takes a slant up the slope, still steeper than anything I've climbed so far, but now with another slope of windblown snow bearing off the side of the trail and falling down a steep grade, it doubles the challenge. I don't like the feel as I start climbing, adding more power and then feeling the back end make a sickening sinking sideways slip towards the downslope. I counter by turning the skis back toward the trail, hoping my power will keep me moving forward, albeit at an angle to the slope and the trail.

I'm sinking deeper in the snow and it starts to give way as big chunks come loose and start rolling down the hill to my right. I keep rolling on the power and stand up leaning forward and toward the slope trying to get more weight over the front left ski hopefully bringing my rear tracks up and over the snow that keeps falling sideways. It sort of starts working and I stand on the power and the Ski-Doo digs its way across that steep trail, finally busting through the trees at the top and into the little opening on the ridge itself where we put our antennas and the chest freezer holding our equipment.

With a big sigh of relief, I shut down the Ski-Doo, get out the radio, and call Tapley.

"Hey Tap, you there?" I shout into the walkie talkie while holding the transmit button. "Over."

Static. "Hey Tap. Pick up!" I wait. Then I say, "Over."

More static. I pull off my gloves and fish for my little joint tin I carry emergency stash in. My hand is shaking from my exertions as I try to light the joint. Then the radio barks to life.

"Cowboy. Are you there? Over."

"Yeah. I made it. Tricky, but doable." Static. "I think I see what's wrong already. Over."

"What's that?" Tapley asks. "Over."

"The freezer has melted its way down through the snow and now it's stretching all the cables going up to the antennas. It looks like one of them might be broken." I forget again. "Over."

"Okay. I'll monitor the signals here and let you know when you have them back on. Over."

"Over, over," I say just to be certain.

I get to work and make a bunch of extension cables I can screw onto the antenna cables. Now they have enough length to make it to the freezer, even when it melts the rest of the way to the ground, which may not be much longer judging from the water content of the snow now. As powder snow melts, it gets wet and heavy, and melts from the ground up, often leaving tons of frozen water unsupported except by what man has left behind, usually crushing it like a stomped-on bug.

"Tapley to Cowboy," sputters the radio. "Over."

"I'm here. Are they back up?"

"Yeah, looks good. Better head back down. They say it's going to snow tonight. Over."

"I'm on my way."

I pack up my tools and turn the big Ski-Doo around, which takes a little room, and head back down my already broken trail. When I come to the steep part just behind the ridge, I decide to do the stupid thing, which is what ski bums often do: I turn the Ski-Doo straight down the slope and give it the gun. I lean way back to keep the machine from nosing completely over on the steep part. I crash immediately into some deep powder, almost burying me, but my momentum carries me up and away as the whole slope behind me comes loose and starts rolling down the hill right behind me.

I jam the Ski-Doo on high and stand up so I can spot the trail leading out at the bottom and into the trees. I feel the tail of the Ski-Doo starting to lose it and slide sideways as the snow begins to flow around me like water. I'm cussing myself for being so brash when I spot my track from earlier. I head for it as fast as I can.

Just as I blow past the first trees, snow comes blasting over my head covering me and the snowmobile with about a foot of the stuff before the trees break it up and we outrun it. I slow down and look back, but my original track is gone and the snow is about a foot deeper than when I last came through.

"*Ya Hoo! Yippee ki-yi-yay!*" I scream as I ride that yellow horse out of the woods and down the mountain. I'm going to celebrate tonight. Surviving a self-inflicted life-threatening wilderness experience is always a reason to celebrate.

*

"Good evening, Crested Butte!" Dana says, talking into the microphone mounted over the mix board of our community radio station. "This is the first episode of what we call *Color-radio*. I'm the Ace of Space here with Captain Neutrino, and we will be here for the next four hours playing records and tapes you may not have heard before."

"Okay Ace, the camera is on. You're now live on TV channel 3 and FM stereo at 92.5 megahertz," I whisper out loud, so everyone in the studio can hear me, and maybe the audience hears me in the background. I don't care. This is live, raw, person-to-person TV, like it should be. I bet this is the first FM station to be broadcasting simultaneously on TV and stereo FM from a live studio. I love it when we're in strange new territory.

"I'll bring back nostalgic radio shows of the forties and fifties, with a little esoteric music in between and some nostalgic comedy on the side. The camera is on, but I can't look into it just yet and deal with this board at the same time."

"Turn on your lavalier," I tell him, from across the tiny room. "It's the fourth knob." I point at the antique Gates mix board Gorbett stole

from some Texas radio station, when they upgraded to something more modern with slide pots instead of this monster with its row of six giant knobs spread across a vertical front panel. They control two turntables, an endless 8-track tape player for short commercials and spots, the fixed mic above the board that he's talking into now and a guest mic, in this case, a miniature lapel mic clipped to his collar.

"There we go," he says, and turns to look at the camera. He wears a giant stereo headphone so he can clearly hear what's going out over the air, but muffle the inside studio noise from all the people gathering up here and downstairs.

"Randy the banjo player is going to drop by later tonight and I'm told a local jug band is downstairs right now rehearsing a song they're going to play for us in the second hour. We give an open invitation to anybody who wants to perform or say something to come on down for our inaugural broadcast. We want to hear you. This is your televised radio station for the town and all its members far and wide. We're being brought to you by Crested Butte Cable, the inspiration of Captain Neutrino here, for one, and another Crested Butte entrepreneur, Steve Glazer."

"*Booo!*" Everyone hears that and looks up at the camera to see Cotton Harris standing behind it. He shrugs his shoulders like he doesn't know what we're looking at.

Dana smiles knowingly and turns back to the left turntable and cues the tone arm.

"This first piece I want to play is one about 'Downeast Humor,' which to the people of New England, downeast, or as far as you can go east, is Maine. This is Marshall Dodge's recording of his character Bernie, all dressed in yellow slicker and hat, telling stories about the folks in quaint rural Maine. Here it goes: Bernie and I explain inflation."

He cuts his mic and lavaliere while bringing up the turntable level. The camera is fixed and can only be focused and pointed just so much. It's a small room and it's crowded. The listeners at home see the studio with Dana and I scrambling around setting up mics and wiring in another little mix board for any music groups that might stop by requiring more than one mic.

"Hey, Cowboy!" calls out Cotton. He volunteers to watch the camera even though it can't be moved much. "You're showing us a new version of the Grand Canyon. I think it's called the white crack of no return."

I glance up at the monitor above the mix board and sure enough, my sweater has worked its way up my back, exposing a plumber's badge of courage crack. I sheepishly step to the side, out of sight of the camera and tuck it in tighter.

"We're back in the studio again," Dana picks up after the record ends. "That's Bert and I by Marshall Dodge, a real Downeaster. Stick around tonight, we plan on showing a video later with Wild Will on safari in Africa. We also have the very first episode of the Lone Ranger radio show where the legend begins. And we'll be showing our latest documentary about executing a television set for crimes against humanity."

There's applause in the studio.

"But first, I want to thank Captain Neutrino for building this cable system in the dead of winter using helicopters and our own home-grown skiers. He installed the first satellite dish in western Colorado and now we're the only ski town with a community radio and television station. Clearly nobody else here in the Butte could have pulled off such a feat of technical engineering and daring construction under such harsh conditions than you. We bow our heads in honor of your works. What do you plan to do next?"

"I'm glad you asked me that, Ace," I'm heard off camera. "I think, now, if I can just get a government grant, I will rule the world! *Mwah ha ha ha ha!*" I cackle like a madman.

"Very nice, Captain. Be sure and let us know how that goes. Up next is a gang of musicians that Neutrino and I know very well, having opened for their show in Austin a while back. Here is Asleep at the Wheel, something you really don't want to be caught doing."

*

I'm finally in heaven. I have accomplished something of importance. I can now be a part of the core Crested Butte society where my efforts are contributing to the overall well-being of all who choose to live here. Susie and I are so close you can poke one of us and the other will twitch. I buy a Baja modified Volkswagen bug from Cloud so I have my own wheels and we spend a lot of time entertaining friends who stop by for a visit to our beautiful home on Sopris.

My brother and his whole brood of kids in junior high show up and I give them the tour of the Rockies they never forget. I even sneak them into a show at the Princess while we have dinner at the Grubstake. But when their mother checks on them in the middle of the show, *Rancho Deluxe*, she just happens to walk in during the scene of a guy wearing a dog mask having sex with a cowgirl out looking for horses in the Montana wilderness. Something we in the Butte can relate to.

The kids get an eyeful before being unceremoniously dragged out of the theater by their shocked Catholic mother just when things were getting interesting. Of course, I take the blame, but I feel kids need to know what they're dealing with without hysterical mothers just saying *No!*

My parents also stop by unannounced and ask about me in a bar, only to be given the normal clueless look reserved for strangers seeking locals. I am notified immediately, though, and caught up with them before they left town, thinking I had given directions to the wrong place.

And then Connie shows up with her nightly boy du jour. I try to ignore her total lack of integrity when it comes to relationships and thank fate for Susie being so much more down to earth, loyal to her lover with normal desires of mutual care and kindness.

Eberbach from Ann Arbor even stops by for a two-week visit. I recently bought a new Husqvarna dirt bike with an automatic transmission, something unheard of for a motorcycle.

The reason for the design is for the Swedish Army to be able to ride one-handed, freeing up the other hand to hold a rifle and shoot.

He rides my old Bultaco Matador 250 and we hit the trails around the Butte like back in the old days in Ann Arbor when we all hung with the bikers and the cool gang. I brag to him that even though he cut me out of my fair share of the DCM speaker business, I hold no grudge and have finally found my own way for making some serious money in the cable TV business.

To celebrate my new success, I decide to take a little draw from all the money I had earned over the winter working for no salary while building the company. There is a new toy being sold as an alternative for cooking food. Microwave ovens are being offered for about $600 down in Gunnison at the TV store. I ask Steve for a draw of $600 and buy the microwave oven for Susie's birthday.

Susie and I both love it. It's great for our hectic schedules where both she and I work days and nights at two jobs and find it hard to spend enough time home to actually cook a meal.

But I have to take it to one more level. I hear that you can't do a hard-boiled egg in a microwave. The egg tends to blow up from the steam generated inside the perfect shape for containing high pressures. I reason that all I have to do is immerse the egg in some salt water so the now conductive water will absorb the microwaves before entering the egg and just heat up the water, boiling the egg more or less normally.

I decide to try it out one morning while Susie is still asleep upstairs and I'm rekindling the Ashley from overnight. I mix up some salt and water, put the egg in it, and place it in the microwave. I put it on three minutes and go into the front room to add coal to the parlor stove.

Suddenly, there is a tremendous explosion from the kitchen, far greater than I could have ever imagined. I run back in and find the room full of steam and a yellow haze of egg particles drifting in the air. The door is completely blown off its hinges and lying in the middle of the floor. The glass holding the egg is embedded in the opposite wall. When I carefully remove the glass, it brings with it a perfect round hole cut in the wall by the glass. If I had been standing in front of it, like I usually do, it would have buried itself in my chest carving a hole the size of a gerbil.

My mistake was in estimating the numbers. If I had done the calculations earlier, I would have found out that it takes a lot of salt water to absorb microwaves. I would have needed a full gallon jug of about a kilo of dissolved salt in order to protect the egg from direct exposure to the microwaves. Boiling a gallon of water to get just one boiled egg is simply not efficient. I learn that with every great advance in technology, there is usually a price to be paid in inconvenience and complexity that often negates the advantage being sought. Eggs and microwaves do not mix, like greedy people and trusting friends. Only destructive explosions can result.

~ 16 ~

CONNECTICUT STATE OF MIND

"What are you thinking?" she asks quietly. It's late spring and we're lying in bed enjoying each other's bodily warmth and gentle touches. Her head is lying on my chest. I'm stroking her hair with one hand while I read to her from our monthly *New Yorker* magazine. For some reason only rich people can justify, her mother thinks that a monthly subscription to the *New Yorker* is a proper discharge of her nurturing obligation to celebrate the birthday of one of her own children. She has six, but I can safely bet she doesn't stop with a simple magazine subscription for her boys. I lay it down for a second.

"Why do you ask?" I inquire.

"Oh, I don't know. I just like to know what you're thinking and especially, I like to know if you're happy."

"Any time I'm with you, I'm happy. I don't need anything else." I lean down and kiss her on the forehead.

"I understand your desire to make some serious money so you can have the freedom of doing art like Dana for the rest of your life," she asserts.

"I don't mind working. If it's fun work, all the better. I just need to be free, not worried about where my next meal comes from, or where I'm going to lay my head at night. I'd like to make movies someday, or at least write stories. Now *that's* fun work. But when you're born poor, you don't have the freedom to choose your work. You're lucky to have any work at all, and count yourself really fortunate if it's decent and honest."

"I understand you see wealth as a handicap. That's why I don't rely on my trust fund for my daily expenses. I make it on my own. I do what I want to do."

"I hope you keep on doing me, my dear!" I mimic Groucho wiggling a cigar and raising my eyebrows. "But wouldn't you like to make a movie sometime?"

"I don't know, I've never made one. Except for you and Dana filming us naked in Nicholson Lake, that was fun," she pauses and then shouts, "for about two minutes!" She pulls hard on my penis.

"*Ow!*" I complain. "If you want it to stand up and salute, you have to talk nicer and pet it like you mean it."

"I'll show you '*pet it*'." She squeezes it hard. I stoically take it without my normal little girl squeal she likes so much.

"But seriously," she says, as she loosens her grip and gives it a little pat, "you've accomplished something big here and you seem happy," she says, turning back on her side. "I think this satellite thing is growing all over the country and it might be a way for you to start a business that could do very well."

"I did get a letter from the town attorney in Ouray wanting me to stop by and see if we can build a system for them. He says they're desperate for good TV like everybody else up here in the mountains. All these flatlanders are coming up here to get away from it all, and yet wanting all their flatlander conveniences."

"I got a letter from my mother today," she announces flatly, changing the subject.

"If she wants to come for a visit, she'll have to stay on the couch." I respond jokingly.

Susie giggles. "Be serious. She wants us to come home for my little brother's graduation from Syracuse. He's studying to be an engineer. You might hit it off with him."

"What she really wants is to see who's sleeping with her daughter so she can give a good description to her hired assassins."

This time she hits me in the stomach. "Oh you!"

"*Oooff!*" I burp out. It doesn't hurt, but she reacts with a pout of remorse and kisses me on the spot she just hit.

"I went to a rich kid's college," I explain, "that caters to Ivy League dropouts who pay cash for an easy degree, hence their big endowment fund. I, on the other hand, receive a full scholarship in order to satisfy their need to claim diversity. I guess Oregon qualifies for being far enough away from civilization to make me diverse enough. Like they said in their cute little recruitment film, *Challenge of Change*, which I happen to star in with Richard Widmark, '...we *wish we could afford more like him.*' I, unlike rich kids, actually have to work harder, a lot harder, to get ahead.

I watch them at Lake Forest and they either do nothing, or the bare minimum, knowing they'll eventually get cushy jobs on Wall Street or sit on corporate boards earning big salaries for accomplishing, again, nothing. While you and your sisters get degrees from exclusive finishing schools that train rich daughters for marriage to the highest *old money* bidder, your brothers are sent to the finest schools money can buy. If I were you, I'd be mad as hell. You're being treated like inferior property."

"Oh, I don't think it's that bad. The boys have to carry on the name and that's important to the family. They have to further the fortunes of the family's businesses and quite frankly, my sisters and I don't really want anything to do with it. I'm happy being right here, living with you, skiing the high country, and managing the Princess. I couldn't be happier."

"And I told you from the very beginning that I don't care about your money or where you come from. What's important is who you are right now with me."

"And that's one of the million reasons I love you. Unlike all of my boyfriends before, you don't care if I come from Greenwich."

"I'm sorry, but I generally don't get along well with privileged people. They're usually hypocritical, arrogant, tyrannical narcissists with superegos that feed on degrading and oppressing those they consider less worthy. To counter this, they adopt exquisitely proper manners so they can do their dirty work under a phony cloak of respectability. They think they deserve, and should expect, what others are routinely denied, simply by chance of birth. Rich and poor don't come from the same world and don't speak the same language. But you're different."

"If I'm different, then will you learn to speak my language?" she taunts, as her lips brush past mine to land on an ear for nibbling.

"How's this for a translation?" I respond, and I roll over on top of her, looking her directly in the eyes. "I just need to know one thing. It seems like everything that happens with your family comes from your mother, Elsie. Where's your father in all this? I thought these old New York-money families were always patriarchs led by the eldest male, until they die, and then the wives take over during their *widow-witch old age*."

She laughs and wraps her legs around me and begins stroking my neck and back like a big ol' kitty cat. "Okay, calm down pussycat.... But seriously, there's something I never told you about my family. *Um*, my father is..." she hesitates and I think I see some pain in her eyes. "My father, Ben, is considered a high-functioning mentally disabled person."

I'm not sure how to respond to such news so I wait a respectable amount of time to let it soak in. "What does that mean, exactly?" I ask automatically, knowing right away that it's not the most sensitive thing I can probably say.

"He takes care of himself okay. He just can't handle complex tasks," she painfully explains. "He spends most of his time at the yacht club working on various projects that keep him busy. He likes to draw detailed depth charts of Long Island Sound. The family businesses are mostly run by my uncles, who all live nearby."

"There's more of you?"

"My grandfather invested in banking and chemicals during the Depression. He had three sons, Ben being the oldest. My mother was recruited by my grandfather to marry him, handle his affairs, occupy the ancestral estate, and make babies. She's the one pretty much in charge of my immediate family."

"I get it. If he were penniless, he'd be spit-shining BMW windshields down on Wall Street. Instead, he gets a high-priced, high-class caretaker wife that produces kids like a bunny rabbit and protects the family's reputation, while the corporate facade continues to loot, rape, and pillage its way through our lives. She should come up for air once in a while and see what's going on. Is she Catholic?"

"We're solid Episcopalians and I can't help what family I'm born to. I don't want the money or the crap that goes along with it. If you don't want to meet my family, I understand." Her eyes flashed with defiance. I smile at her and pat her on the cheek.

"And that's just another reason among the million or so that makes me love you. If it's really that important to you, I'll go along. We'll make a road trip out of it and visit some friends along the way. Maybe spend some time in New York hitting the museums."

"Are you sure?"

"Do we get to sleep in the same bed at your mother's house?"

"I don't think so. But the house has thirteen bedrooms. Sometimes people get lost in the middle of the night."

*

Susie and I have never taken a long trip together. We go to Denver often to shop while staying with her sister Alice, who owns a house there. Susie went back to New York one time without me and got to see the Tall Ships parade from the top of the Trade Center. I was a little jealous she got to see that and I swore to not miss it next time. Besides, I'm anxious to show her one of my life's specialties: the road trip.

With me, the basic rules for road trips are simple. First, no motels or hotels if you can help it. If you have to stay somewhere, stop off at a convenient friend's house or relative where usually there is at least a couch or a floor to crash on. If not, then for the long hauls, drive until you're falling asleep at the wheel, then pull off and sack out in the back seat, continuing on after getting whatever rest you can. Stop often to stretch and look at the land you happen to be crossing. Road trips are for reflection, observing, and basically planning the rest of your life.

However, if I'm traveling with my old lady, any host I stay with can't order us to pretend we're not sleeping together. That's absurd, considering what we're obviously doing every other night. This whole repressive idea of *no conjugal visits while sleeping in my house* is an outright insult to our personal integrity and a condemnation of our freely chosen non-oppressive life style, ethics, and morals. Why do your morals supersede mine, just because you own the bed? We simply don't think we have to be formally married to enjoy our sexual freedom, and nobody is the sex police, so kindly keep your prying, voyeuristic hypocrisy out of our sleeping bags.

I haven't earned much more money this year than what I normally make at the Princess and what I make on the side repairing stereos and TVs...and smuggling a little weed now and then. I've been horseless for some time now, since my 4-wheel drive Chevy Carryall had to be sold off for food money. We have the little Nissan pickup and, like everyone else in town, we both have klunker bikes which we built ourselves from scrap. They are absolutely necessary for getting around town in style.

I also acquire, through some bartering, an old, used Bultaco Matador 250cc motorbike for scooting around the trails in the summertime and getting to those secret lakes a little faster. But then I'm offered store credit to buy a new Husqvarna 550cc automatic dirt bike. I have no credit, so why not. It's the first new vehicle of any kind I've owned, and a great machine for running with the boys on wilderness trails at speeds like antelopes on steroids. I'm having so much fun this summer, I think I'm making a movie. The plot has lots of action and adventure with twists anticipated. Good twists, hopefully.

Then, just before we leave for the trip to Greenwich and the Fisher family estate, I'm offered a nice little Volkswagen bug with a Baja modified engine that cranks out about 90 horsepower, which is way above the ordinary 40-horse versions. I snap it up, thinking it will be a good vehicle for long distance travel at higher speeds and affordable gas rates. Plus, it fits our current lifestyle of a young couple: freedom, frugality, and humility, even if it's almost a Porsche.

We finally pack up the VW with our things, leave the house in the hands of Susie's new friend and our downstairs roommate, Texas Jane, and we hit the road. Tap and Rat promise to run the theater and the cable system while I'm gone. Things are calm at the cable company with all the new condos wired and everyone in town signing up for service. Gorbett is running the radio station about twelve hours a day with himself and about four DJs he can count on to keep a schedule. The Weazel and Cotton are two of them, so the schedule thing takes a nose dive right out the gate, as these two cannot be organized. That's the Butte. You have to be on Butte time if you're going to sync with the Butte lifestyle. The party starts when you arrive and so forth.

It's a beautiful sunny warm day and I feel great, getting back on the road again after being cooped up all winter working my ass off building the cable system. On the long climbing straight stretch of US 50 east of Gunnison, I unwind the VW, cranking it up to eighty miles per hour thinking I'm finally enjoying some fruits of my labor when, *BANG! Rattle, rattle, rattle. BANG! Screech!*

Something explodes from the rear. I look in the rearview mirror, only to see a bunch of metal parts bouncing down the road behind me, along with a big black cloud of smoke above it all. The engine freezes, I slam in the clutch and coast to the side of the road.

"*Ahh*, man!" I yell. "This sucks the mighty one!"

"What's happening?" Susie yells back.

"The fucking engine just blew." I know this because I had been with Bill Smith in a newly rebuilt 454 cu in Buick Riviera he had done for a friend when he took it for a test drive. It exploded all over Interstate 75 after hitting an honest 140 miles per hour. This was spectacularly less impressive, but plainly recognizable. This kills our trip for today, and we have to hitch a ride back to Gunnison, where I call the Rat. He comes and picks us up in his Rat-mobile, a normal under-powered dirty grey Volkswagen with two large headlights stapled to the roof, making it look like ears on a big rat, and takes us back to the Butte.

Later that afternoon, Cloud and I pick up the broken VW and tow it back to town. He explains to me on the way that I suffered the most common failure for Volkswagens, especially at high rpms and hot temperatures and now, even worse, high altitudes with lower air pressure and less air cooling. It's called *sucking the number three valve.*

"The result of all that heat stress impacts the number three cylinder more than all the others. It gets the least amount of air cooling from its position far from the cooling fan. With the Baja conversion and the speed and air temperature yesterday, I'd safely predict you've sucked a valve on number three."

"*Jeez*," I bitch, "you'd think that a conversion named *Baja* implies it would work better in hot conditions!"

*

We decide to try to rough it in the tight little Nissan truck all the way to the east coast. It might be rough in such a tiny cab, but doable, I figure. But when Steve hears of our predicament, he finds us and offers to loan us his little Fiat. It's a four door, so has a lot more room, as well as being good on gas. I can't believe he's offering it to us. It just doesn't fit his normal tendency to be a selfish prick, but we eagerly take him up on the offer, swap him the Nissan, and get back on the road the next day.

This time, I take it easy, after my experience with the Baja, but then a Fiat is the definition of taking it easy, or taking it anyway you can. We make it to Denver, uneventfully, and on to Chicago where we stop off at Bob's, the other half of our Warlock Productions film crew, who recently got married and moved into his wife's flat overlooking Evanston's North Shore and Lincoln Park Zoo. Nice. We spend the night together in their spare bedroom and have a wine and cheese party the next day, when several of our mutual Lake Forest friends show up.

Susie and I go out shopping early and bring back a nice, medium-priced bottle of Old Vine Zinfandel for our hosts. Thinking they will be hospitable and serve the bottle while we're visiting, I expect some praise from my friends for being so urbane and knowledgeable with wine. Instead, they put the bottle in their pantry and haul out the cheap stuff for the party. I'm very disappointed in how my friends had gone all low-class greedy. They might as well be back in New York with that kind of attitude. Bob's actually from upper -class Manhattan, so it figures.

We drive to Ann Arbor the next day and stay in my old room on Division Street where Eberbach and all us NASA Space Physics crazies had once lived, played, invented the DCM speakers, and had a few other wild adventures while putting on giant rock concerts and pioneering the live video stage projection. Steve is living alone and wanting to get out of his old hovel, now that he's working with money people at developing a high-end speaker business in the cut-throat electronic consumer market. He seems much subdued from the old times and almost embarrassed to even have to put up with us for a day. But he shows me his new Tandy computer and I immediately see that I have to get one. I know how to program in Fortran and Basic, and there are no computers in Crested Butte. A small computer company might be another way to make some money in these changing times.

We sleep in my old waterbed in the second bedroom on the second floor. Not much has changed in the room in the five years I've been gone. It feels a bit spooky now, being back here, sharing my old bed with Susie, knowing all the weird things that happened to me here. Susie has no notion about Ann Arbor's youth counterculture in the time of protest and revolution at a large and important university. I lived a drama in a place where people made waves.

Susie just puts up with Steve and I, as we reminisce about our Rock & Roll days, putting on first-run concerts of the great artists and touring with some of the greatest rock bands ever. But it was all over now. The explosion of talent that happened here had spread far and wide, leaving a vacuum behind.

On to Connecticut the next day, which brings us within striking distance, so we spend the night in a motel in Pennsylvania, enjoying some private time together before making it to the *Greenwich castle* and putting ourselves under her mother's feudal rules of bed assignments. We arrive finally, at 9 Sabine Farm Road, Saturday around noon.

"I'm lost. We've made so many turns I'm getting dizzy. Are we there yet?" I beg Susie, as she guides me through the forest surrounding the giant estates in an area called Round Hill.

"Just about. Look for an opening in the ivy-covered wall on your right."

"Hole in the wall? Where the hell are we going, a monastery? Is this still America?"

"Stop your whining. We're there. Turn right."

I do and we emerge on the other side of the wall in an open pasture big enough for a whole herd of cattle and a few horses to graze. We proceed up a straight narrow asphalt road to a giant three-story house built in the English Countryside manner, prudently and plainly. After all, they don't need to flaunt their English superiority, they just need a big enough place to ostentatiously decorate the inside with all the heads of their victims. I feel a cold chill descend my spine.

"Just pull up in front of the main entrance and park on the right. Connie and I may want to visit some friends later, so let's leave the car here for now."

A large woman appears in the doorway wearing a full-scale apron, almost looking like Julia Childs.

"Hello! Hello Susan! Welcome home. Come let me hug you," she shouts, beckoning us to come closer.

I discreetly follow Susie as she saunters to Elsie, her mother, and gives her a proper but cursory hug. I don't think their bodies actually touch.

"And who is this big hairy mountain man you've found?" she asks, still smiling like a hungry coyote. She looks plain and maybe on the large side, which explains why most of the Fisher girls are tall and athletic.

"This is Cowboy. I've already told you everything," Susie answers. Susie's imposing mother holds out her hand limply and I obligingly touch it.

"How nice to finally meet you," she says. "Susan tells me you're from Oregon. My, my, that's about as far away as you can get from Connecticut and still be in America. Get your bags and come on in. I'm cooking dinner for all of us tonight, so I won't be much of a host for a while. You're welcome to make yourself at home. The drinks and snacks are in the back porch pantry coolers. Susie can show you. I have to get back to my roast."

We land in a sort of receiving room, or so it looks. Just fancy high-back chairs, coffee tables, and knickknacks all over the place. I spot a couple of paintings on the wall that seem familiar. Susie guides me through a maze of rooms. A greeting room, dining room, sewing room, map room, library, and God knows what other rooms. She opens the door to the map room carefully and looks in.

"Hi Daddy," she says, and enters holding my hand. He's sitting at a desk with magnifying goggles hunched over a colorful chart laid out before him. She walks up to him before he even notices her, kisses him on the forehead, hugs him, and he finally pulls up his goggles, looks up at her smiling blandly.

"Oh. Hello dear," he responds softly. "Nice to see you. I'm working on Narragansett Point. See?"

"That's very nice, Daddy. I want you to meet my friend, Cowboy."

"Oh, hello," he says, noticing me for the first time. He holds out a limp hand, which I sort of shake. "Are you a sailor?"

"Not really," I answer. "More of a sailor in the sky." He looks at me blankly.

"I fly airplanes. You know, wings are like sails, except we hold them horizontally and sailors hold theirs vertically." I demonstrate by holding my hands like a sail in both directions. He continues blankly looking at me with no sign of recognition or understanding.

"Gotta go, Daddy," Susie says, stepping between us. "We'll see you later at dinner." He waves his hand slowly in goodbye and turns back to his work. I'm told later by one of the sons-in-law that he has been working on the same chart for about ten years. I'm thinking, *Nice work if you can get it.*

We finally walk through the large kitchen just off the equally huge dining room with its fourteen-chair dining table, where mamma and a maid are cooking up a storm, to the back porch and pantry where all the food and goodies are stored. I wonder what the kids did living here as teenagers, knowing there's a well-stocked cooler, probably carelessly guarded by the hired help and within easy reach. I guess they start them early learning self-control and alcohol tolerance for the eventual boardroom and their ultimate job, stealing with a grin and a pen.

"Looks like all they have is Budweiser," Susie warns me.

"No!" I strongly object. "Not Butt-wiper! I knew we should have put a case of Bohemia in the car before coming out here."

Hunter warned me not too long ago that people who drink bad beer are similarly bad, and those who drink good beer are good. *Check out any bar,* he adds for proof, then suggests, *Think about it.*

I'm in the home of one of the wealthiest families in America and I'm from one of the meekest. I drink good craft beer, or at least something with flavor and the full fruit of the fermentation process. Whereas these elite drink something that very well may be identified someday as the source of all cancer in the world.

"For you my dear, I'll make do," I say patronizingly, "Grab me one. Better make it two."

"Hey! You got here," Connie yells, as she hurries up to us. She gives me the obligatory kiss on the cheek, which she knows makes me blush, and then gives Susie the *twin* hug. You have to watch carefully, but the *twin* hug has little body nuances that make it unique and theirs to own. I likened it to the KKK secret handshake.

"We have to get going. Is Cowboy going to get along here on his own?"

"I'm not intimidated, yet, just appalled."

"Okay then," she says. "Good luck with that. Let's get going sis. Do you have the keys?" I hand them to Susie as Connie drags her from the room. Susie looks back at me over her shoulder with what I think might be pity or maybe just fear. I'm beginning to feel more and more like Hunter being high as a kite at a cop convention in Las Vegas. I too am having feelings of fear and loathing.

I look at my new digital watch I bought from an airline magazine on my trip back from Florida, just so I could say I did such a stupid thing, and note it's a few minutes past noon. The sun must be over the yardarm somewhere, so I pop the tab on one of the Bud cans and take a long swig, gag a little, and force myself to swallow some more. I wander back into the kitchen with a beer in each hand where Momma is busy giving instructions to the maid helping her. I try to loiter as inconspicuously as I can, but she notices me anyway.

"Have you been to Greenwich before?" she asks politely, as she continues to concentrate on her work.

"Been through a few times on my way to and from Martha's Vineyard and New York."

"Oh my," she responds. "Do you have family on the Vineyard?"

"My roommate from college grew up in the Vineyard. He and I have spent weeks hanging out with his *Haven* buddies."

"How interesting. You know my oldest daughter is building a house on Martha's Vineyard with her boyfriend."

"Good luck. The prices for real estate on the Vinyard are skyrocketing. You have to be a millionaire just to get a building permit." I realize who I'm talking to and shut up. I finish the first beer and look for a trash can. Finding nothing, I slip it in a drawer full of silver utensils when nobody is watching.

"Her boyfriend comes from an old well-propertied Vermont family who have been making maple syrup for a hundred years. Tell me, Mister Cowboy, what does your family do where you come from...Oregon, I believe?"

"My family makes a living," I say without further details. She looks at me queerly. I take another drink.

"I mean does your family have a ranch or something? You do seem to fit the part with your cowboy boots and quaint denim jacket. I just presumed your family is the reason."

"Why I dress funny? It's more of a cultural thing than a legacy thing. My mother grew up on a real cattle ranch in Oklahoma and my dad was a real cowboy working as a hired hand on a big cattle ranch nearby."

"Fascinating. So, your parents got together on horseback, I take it?"

"You can try to take it, but I hear it's damn near impossible to hold."

"What?" she responds, looking up with confusion.

"Actually, my mother's brothers are all in the cattle trucking business down in the Southwest and they dress western trucker style. I like trucks, so I find their style fits my style."

"Fascinating." She looks around for the maid but she's nowhere to be seen.

"So, who made all the money to buy this ranch?" I innocently ask.

"That's charming, but we call it an estate. Susie's grandfather invested wisely in the twenties and did well during the Depression, owning an investment bank and several publishing firms. We are very proud of our heritage and work hard to keep it going for the next generation of Fishers."

"Or hardly working," I mutter under my breath.

"What's that?"

"That hardly sounds like work. At least the work I'm familiar with."

"Well, I assure you, it is definitely no walk in the park. There are board meetings and stockholders' meetings, lawyers, and accountants. I have a bachelor's degree in economics but it is still a challenge keeping up with it all. But I do it willingly for my children. They will hopefully have better lives than I had and Susie and her siblings can enjoy all the efforts of her family."

"I had a friend in college who came from a privileged family like yours. Ever hear of the Pritzker's, of Chicago?"

She briefly scowls at me then smiles grimly. "I'm afraid I only keep track of the New York families. Chicago is more your side of the country." She looks around for help. She looks back to me and asks, "So you ski?"

"No. Susie taught me." She briefly scowls again and quickly brightens.

"Susie also said you have an advanced degree in physics. It must be very fascinating how you ended up in Crested Butte running a movie theater."

"Funny thing. I almost finished my PhD developing atmospheric computer simulations when a rich Republican president cancels my fellowship, leaving me broke without a final degree or a job, and out on the streets with just my truck and a sleeping bag."

She wrinkles her ample nose. "Well, we're all here to celebrate my son's graduation from Syracuse and support him as he starts out his career and life."

"I'm sure he'll do well without Nixon kicking us around anymore." I shake my can and note it is empty. "Excuse me, but I seem to have run out. I'll be right back."

I get up and leave the kitchen just as the maid returns from outside. She flashes me a goofy grin as we pass. By the time I find another Bud and return, both of them are gone. *Good,* I tell myself, *Julia, the six-foot matriarch can easily squash more than a duck breast,* and wander into the hallway looking for another room with more action.

"Hi there. You're with Susie, right?" Some older guy sitting in the library just starts talking to me.

"Ah, yeah, I think."

"*Jeez,* why are you drinking that mama's milk? Here, grab a glass and help me appreciate some scotch old enough to have legal sex with." I take the offered rock glass as he pours a good three-shot pour. I look at the deep amber color and smell the smokey peat bogs where it came from.

"Nice. Been here long?" I inquire.

"Is that in the literal sense or the heritage one?" he answers.

"I'll bite. How are you related to the Fishers?" I continue.

"Let's just say I'm the non-skiing cousin they barely tolerate."

"So, what are you doing here?"

He smiles and holds out his glass, clinks mine, and says, "Cheers!" He sloshes his whiskey and takes a big swig. "I could ask the same thing."

"Why am I here? To support my old lady. She has to be here for some reason and she wants me to be with her, to support her."

"*Oooooh,*" he says, "the sacrificial lamb brought to the feast. How delicious."

"That sounds ominous. Care to enlighten me on my plight?" I take a sip of the whiskey and have to admit it's better than anything I've had. *So, this is what money is good for.*

"It's just that mother bear likes to know what her cubs are up to. She keeps a tight rein on this family, even though the kids may say otherwise. To be honest, nobody marries a Fisher without Momma's blessing."

"I'm not interested in getting married. I'm not a gold digger, except for real gold."

"Oh yeah, you're the mountain man she's rumored to have moved in with. Where is that place? Aspen?"

"Crested Butte."

"Never heard of it. Anyway, you do know the old man is a little loose on the goose and is the family's not-so-well-hidden fact of life. Momma takes her job seriously and the graduate is her boy who will carry on the name."

"Whoop-de-do," I say while twirling my index finger pointed up. "I really feel for them."

"By the way, where's your coat and tie?" he asks, while patting his pockets for something. "Ah, there it is."

"What coat and tie?" I demand. "I thought this was a celebration, not a funeral."

"I see you're not from Connecticut. A coat and tie in the world of money means you subscribe to their hierarchy and you are showing proper respect to your betters."

"I don't wear uniforms, I don't put a noose around my neck, and I don't dress to impress. I dress for practical reasons, like warmth and covering my ugly parts, and maybe making an art statement, nothing else. I don't dress to deceive or to be subservient."

"If you are here with Susie, she must think you have a chance to get along with Momma. I'm surprised she didn't prepare you more for this inspection."

"Inspection?"

"I assume you want to get along with Momma for Susie's sake. Right?"

"I guess. I am here against my better judgement."

"No problem. I'll see what I can dig up for you before dinner. There's a few of us here also against our better judgement, and yet, here we are."

Two other guys walk in and one is carrying a bottle of champagne. He just automatically pours some in each of our glasses on top of the scotch. I taste mine and don't mind it that bad. That's how you think when you're on this stuff.

"This here is Cowboy, what Susie dragged in from the mountains. Be nice to him, he's out of his habitat."

He wanders out of the room, but the champagne guy stays, edging up to me and stating, "You do know you can't sleep with Susie here."

"Yeah, she mentioned that."

"It's all right, it's a big house. Things happen. As long as Momma is happy, we're happy." He takes a big slug directly from the bottle and immediately lets out a huge belch.

So, this is how the rich live, I think to myself. *Not a human value within sight. Is this what Susie needs or is she running away from it?*

*

When my family celebrates with a big meal, we don't sit at a giant table with doilies everywhere wondering why there's more than one fork to play with. Any dinner party with more than four people usually results in a potluck smorgasbord with all kinds of great homemade food and the guests spread out all over the backyard with overloaded paper plates about to dump their contents into the expectant mouths of all the attendant pets and barn animals.

Pretentious bullshit defines the aristocracy because they take a nice thing and turn it into a monstrous demonstration of patronage and mock superiority. It's one thing to try and impress a foreign dignitary with an audacious display of douchebaggery feeding frenzy, but for a single supposedly loving family, I have to ask, what's the point of putting the people you love through such rigid and unnatural nonsense?

Susie returns with her sister and we're waiting to go into the dining room. She whispers, "Now, when we go into the dining room, you have to find your place card. Stand behind your seat until Momma comes in with Daddy. Once he is seated, she'll make a sign for all the girls to sit with the men next to them holding their chair for them. Then you sit down. Got it?"

"I'll just follow your lead. I don't do rituals very well."

About fifteen or so people are gathered in the library, all holding drinks and talking in little groups. Susie and Connie are next to me, along with Alice and her husband.

"She probably won't sit us next to each other. She segregates married from unmarried as a reminder of your status."

"Status?" I respond. "How about we strip off our clothes and make love in the middle of the table. Would that indicate our status?"

"*Shshhhh!*" Susie says. "Someone will hear you."

"Look at this monkey suit. I look like a choach!"

"They all do," piped in Connie. "You look nice. Let me adjust your tie."

She steps in real close so her tits are brushing my chest. I look at Susie, but she's talking to Alice and not noticing.

"Now, see how this looks." She turns me around so I can see myself in a mirror on the other side of the room.

"I still feel like a choach."

A gong sounds nearby, formally demanding our attention.

"Okay everyone, time to move into the dining room," declares someone I can't see.

Everybody starts moving in the direction of the dining room and as they go in, they leave their drinks outside on a table. Before I get to it, I empty my fifth round of scotch on the rocks and slam the glass upside down on the table.

Susie guides me into the room and walks me around the table until she finds my name on a place setting.

"Here," she says. She looks at both sides of my chair and notes there is no woman's name on either one. "Looks good. You don't have to hold the seat for anyone. Just stand until all the men sit."

"Okay, Emily Post."

"I'll see you after dinner." She turns and rejoins Connie on the other side of the table.

I'm not liking the obvious insult to me. I'm not good enough to sit with my lover. But when in Rome.... I sit stiff and buzzing, wondering how long this torture is going to last.

"I want to thank you all for coming tonight," announces Elsie, now dressed in a bulging evening gown. "I know it is hard with everybody's busy schedule."

Daddy perks up, holds his wine glass up, and says, "Cheers!"

"Not now, Father," Elsie quietly warns him. He looks embarrassed for a second then resumes his goofy smile, putting his wine glass carefully back on the table. "Please be seated," she adds, and everybody sits down.

"Larry is graduating from Syracuse tomorrow and we all are here to celebrate his accomplishment and to wish him a wonderful future and a world of success."

Polite applause.

I spot some goofy looking kid on the other side of Elsie, all polished up shiningly with a proper haircut, immaculate suit and tie, shaved to glistening, and looking like a bump on a log, or something equally useful. He smiles and waves politely like a little girl.

"Tell us what your plans are now that you have your degree." She looks at him expectantly.

"Ah, well, I don't know exactly what to do next. I have offers to join high-tech ventures here, and maybe out in California at a place called Silicon Valley."

Silicon Valley is just an alias for the area around San Jose where spinoff high-tech companies have been building campuses on nearby cheap desert land. Hewlett Packard has been there for years. Funny he has all these opportunities when most of the recent graduates have been having trouble landing good jobs. Like me.

"Your uncles tell me they need someone in the bank who can advise them on high-tech investments. Perhaps you can consider working for the family."

"Perhaps," he says in a muted voice.

I'm feeling a little tension in the room, but then what do I know about this weird family? I'm glad Susie chose to extricate herself from this environment and put herself in mine. I'm beginning to feel somewhat uncomfortable myself. One thing I learned from visiting other rich families like this, they all have impeccable manners and etiquette, no matter the circumstances. Decorum and respect must be maintained at all cost, until the moment of any backstabbing, which there are plenty. But before the actual whacking, they are like Mother Theresa. But something tells me, Elsie is no Mother Theresa.

Susie's sisters talk about their various prestigious jobs skiing in Aspen. They describe their various boyfriends in terms of the New England families they came from and how much money they are probably worth. Alice talks about fixing up her home in Denver. When she comes to Susie, she talks about our house and how we've been fixing it up. She also mentions we own a partnership in the new cable TV company where I built a new dish antenna to get TV from the satellites.

"That sounds very important for a place like where you live, but how big did you say this Crested Butte is?"

"About five hundred," Susie says.

"I took a class in satellite communications," pipes in Larry, "and they say very soon we will have portable telephones we can carry around on our back that can talk to the satellites and connect anywhere in the world. Imagine making a phone call from the top of Mount Everest."

I stifle a giggle. I recently did some phone calls over the satellites when we were linked to HBO in New York from Oklahoma. It was damned near impossible to carry on a conversation because of the half-second delay between speaking and hearing. You wait until you think the other end is not responding, you start talking, and then you hear the other end responding to your previous sentence. We had to go back to using a simplex protocol like short wave radio, saying "over" every time you finished talking and wanted the other end to respond. Basically, to make portable phones work, they have to move the satellites a lot closer to earth. But if you do, they're no longer geosynchronous and go flying across the sky at pretty good clips, making it necessary to have a belt full of satellites in order to have at least one overhead at any given time. So far, there are only two or three commercial satellites and they only carry FM modulated video signals.

"Wouldn't you like to be on the side that funds such projects rather than have to actually build them?" Elsie says. "It just seems easier and more lucrative."

"Of course, Mother," he says, submitting to her sound logic.

"Mr. Cowboy, I understand you have a degree in physics. What do you plan to do with that? Teach?"

"Actually, a physicist can do almost anything technical. I figure smart people seek out the hardest subjects just to prove that they can handle anything less. I know nothing more difficult than physics, so I know I can do damn near anything. I just don't get the opportunities that some have."

"How interesting. I'm sure you find plenty of things to keep you busy in Crested Butte. Don't you run the projector at the local movie theater? That doesn't seem like a very good use of your talents."

"I have to make a living at whatever I can wherever I am. I'm not rich like your family, so I have to feed myself before I can do what I really want to do. I'm the chief engineer at Crested Butte Cable and with Susie's help, we also own half the company."

"My goodness. Susan didn't tell me that. How much did you invest in this company, Susan?"

"Ah, we paid Steve about four thousand dollars."

Elsie laughs condescendingly as she realizes it's nothing. "I forgot how small that town is. Your investment sounds like a safe start to your business education."

"Why did you send your daughters to small eastern elite colleges when they could have gone to something much better like the University of Michigan, where I went? You have the money and they could have easily gotten accepted. I had to earn a full scholarship, but you could clearly afford the tuition."

"Excuse me?" Elsie growls, and suddenly turns on me.

I'm not sure what she means, but it quickly dawns on me she thinks she has been insulted. The room goes deathly silent with forks in midair as she glares at me with a sudden hate in her eyes. I'm taken aback.

"How dare you question me about where I sent my daughters to school. I spent a great deal of time and effort making sure they got the best education they need to succeed in our world."

"Those schools are nothing more than marriage brokers for the rich and famous," I blurt out. I know I should shut up. Now I can't even apologize.

There is no response. The silence is crushing. I immediately regret saying that last thing, but still, she has no right to react this way to me. I don't like being belittled and patronized by arrogant pseudo-aristocratic douchebags, even if she is Susie's mother. I'm sure she was raised to be a decent person, even hospitable, as wealth insulates one absolutely from having to be genuine. If you're rich, you have no right to be angry at anyone, especially someone who actually works hard to get ahead, instead of having to fuck for it.

Suddenly, dinner is over. Elsie and Daddy and Larry exit quickly. Everyone gets up and files out to the library for after dinner cocktails and divvying up the bedroom assignments. The awful realization hits me that I just failed the family test. I did not integrate well. Susie comes up to me with a serious look. Connie is right behind, barely suppressing a sneaky smile.

"What happened?" she asks quietly.

Someone passes by and pats me on the shoulder.

"I don't know. I wanted to promote myself a little and maybe I said something I was thinking, but not intending to actually say. She's kind of touchy, isn't she?"

"Nice job," Connie says. "Wave a red flag with a bull in the room." She smiles at me and squeezes my arm. I look at her, but all I can feel is that I let Susie down.

"We've got to get out of here," I say to Susie. "I can't stay here and face her in the morning. I'm sorry, but I'm not going to be treated this way. Where can we go?"

"I don't know. It's kind of late to call around."

"Get your bags and come back here. We'll find something." Connie grabs her hand and leads her away. I think I see Connie taking a quick glance back at me showing admiration.

I look around while doffing my lent monkey suit and spot a simple thing. A humble thimble sitting on a small doily in the windowsill draws my Southwestern artistic eye. It's spotless silver decorated with tiny identical turquoise stones inlaid around it. Clearly it has never seen actual employment as a thimble, but now it's a brazen example of those who work, using the thimble for what it is meant to do, while the indolent simply see it as quaint knickknack they would never seriously have to use.

I pick it up, look hard at its simple purity. I remember my mother's humble thimble, made from cheap pot metal; it had no decoration other than the scratches, nicks, and dents from supporting a family of six for forty years, keeping them loved and clothed at minimal cost and maximum love.

"This mocking symbol of our oppression," I solemnly pronounce while holding it on high, "shall be confiscated in the name of humanity, equality, and the American way!" I put it in my pocket.

Susie sneaks up on me and tugs on my sleeve. "Let's go," she says. "It's not too late to find a motel somewhere." She marches me out of the house of horror and into the little Fiat. I hadn't unloaded my bags yet so we were on our way quickly, noticing Connie waving goodbye to us as we turn around in the courtyard.

*

The next four days are a whirlwind of New York experiences. Susie knows some friends from her high school who are now remodeling high-end apartments on the Upper East Side. One third-floor walk-up is nearing completion, so she gets permission for us to stay there while we are in town, alleviating the need for an expensive hotel. I hope Momma is getting the message that we don't have to succumb to her mean and mindless rules to have fun in New York.

We spend our days just walking around Central Park enjoying springtime and visiting the major museums. We stay almost all day at the Museum of Natural History, where I find the mineral specimen room particularly interesting. With my spelunking experience back in the Butte, I marvel at the finest and biggest mineral specimens collected from over the world. I find their wire-silver specimen and am gratified to discover that the size isn't much bigger than the one we dug out of the Sylvenite mine. I wonder if there might be a record-busting specimen still in that mountain waiting to be discovered.

Susie didn't get much of a formal education, especially in the sciences. So, I spend a lot of time pointing out to her the significance of each exhibit and try to give her an appreciation of our rich natural history. She seems interested and asks many questions. It's a shame she was raised to be a concubine instead of a real human. I actually feel sorry for her situation and hope she has the strength to break free from the many shackles that are trying to confine her.

At night, we find cheap clubs in the Village and enjoy some really wild and creative musicians and poets. We actually get into The Bitter End and Café Wha?, but prefer the little underground clubs that spring up overnight and disappear just as rapidly. There is cutting edge stuff going on here that even challenges my sense of good taste. Susie just thinks it's all cute. The White Anglo-Saxon princess slumming syndrome. I give her a quick catch up by taking her to a Fugs concert at an uptown bar. Now she can say she's experienced.

We go to the top of the World Trade Center to do the turkey thing and see the city from the side that actually looks nice.

Again, I'm appalled by the extravagant wealth tied up with just trading money, something Jesus had a serious hard-on for, kicking over stacks of money wherever he found them. All the good that could be done with all this money is exactly why it is a sham and a crime to concentrate it all in one place, while the rest of the us scramble hard for just our daily bread or a chance to survive. No good will come of this monster called money.

Finally, after spending most of the money we brought with us, we head home. But, first we have to stop by Cornell University to attend Larry's actual graduation. I cringe through the whole affair, knowing how much I secretly desire to be a participant of such rituals of passage, wearing the robes in the color of my major and congratulating students I guide from stupid to barely intelligible. I swear to myself to finish my doctorate degree as soon as I can.

Again, Momma has to embarrass me by demanding Susie and I attend a dinner at the fraternity alumni club. Again, they have to dress me up with a coat and tie, while I grit my teeth in submission. I sit through the whole ordeal keeping my mouth shut and making no expression whatsoever, while Momma at every opportunity gives me the steely stare of a vicious lioness eyeing her recently killed prey.

Before we leave, I pass by her and stop to offer my sincere gratitude for her hospitality.

"Thank you, Mrs. Fisher, I really appreciate you having us as guests. You know, you don't have to be so serious, and maybe you can lighten up and give me a chance. I'm a pretty nice guy once you get to know me."

Her glower sizzled. Susie pushes me aside so she can say goodbye and we leave. Not in a huff, but a Fiat, which is almost the opposite.

*

Somewhere in the middle of the night, on Interstate 70 in Kansas, Susie asks the question.

"Why did you piss off my mother? You were supposed to make her like you so I don't have to choose."

"Choose what?"

"To be with you and piss off my mother or try to change her mind."

"I understand. Parents are not used to taking criticism from their children. Don't worry. Mothers never give up on their children. She'll come around in time and see all the wonderful qualities in me that you do."

"I sure hope so. I don't need them, but they are my family. I don't want to feel unpleasant around them."

"Look, we are the children of a new revolutionary age. We are demanding our basic rights to sexual and intellectual freedom. We must reject the restrictive, phony ethics of our parents. You almost have to kill your parents, in a metaphorical sense, before you can gain the individual freedom you so desperately need to be yourself."

"She is very numbing sometimes."

"After the old oppressive parents are mentally annihilated, they can be reborn into the wise and supportive advisers, the older friends we really need. Your father seems nice."

She slaps me on the knee, pauses, and then leans over and kisses me long and hard, blocking my view of the highway. The Fiat weaves a little on the freeway and someone in the next lane honks their horn.

We get back to our little mountain love cabin in record time. We just keep swapping out the driving about every two hundred miles or so, usually timed to gas stops, and keep it up until we finally arrive, exhausted, and turn off the engine. Blessed mountain silence descends on us for the first time in weeks.

It's early in the morning and we walk in with Texas Jane strung out with another bad hangover, trying to light a fire in the Ashley. She, of course, let the fire go out while bar hopping, comes home, crashes and then wakes up freezing. The house is cold, but fortunately not cold enough to freeze the pipes, and she looks something like the Wicked Witch of the East just after being squashed by Dorothy's house.

We shove past her huddled over the Ashley as she lights more paper under some wood chunks she found, and go straight upstairs to our heated waterbed and crash for the next twelve hours.

*

The summer is upon us and it's truly glorious, as always. Every day is just another typical day in paradise. Susie and I pick up our normal schedule, running the Princess at night while hiking in the day, fly fishing on the fly, riding my new Husqy up and down every trail within reach, and working with Ace, making video documentaries and art films.

But above all, our collective dreams come true with the ability now to broadcast on our own Community Cable TV channel, which allows many in town, especially Gary Gorbett, to live out their dream of being a DJ, one way or the other. Dana and I do the inaugural show, which he dubs *ColoRadio.* It's a shotgun blast of nostalgia radio from the past, and innocent, where we showcase our latest video creations hoping some are revolutionary for the times. Plowing new experiences out of old media is right at the top of a Finds Arts creation.

Eberbach takes his summer vacation and visits us. I throw him on my old Bultaco and I lead him on a merry mountain bike chase that blows that little flatlander's mind. I take him up to Keystone Basin and then we climb a trail that goes over a ridge with a view down Slate River valley that's to die for. We park the bikes, enjoying the gorgeous sunny day from on top of the world, and rest up for the equally grueling ride back down. I light up a joint while Eber takes a swig off his bota bag.

"You know you kind of pissed me off for not letting me participate in DCM. It's been a struggle out here trying to leverage my skills into some serious money."

"You said so yourself. And I quote, 'I don't want to have to do the business thing. I just want to live in the mountains and learn to ski,' unquote."

I laugh. He's right. "I know. But it kinda hurt when you said you had to do business with money people, and due to the fact that I had none, it automatically makes me ineligible. You might be right, but what you did to Munsell, though, was heartless. He had a lot to do with our initial design and could actually get things done, like building your crazy cross-over and making it work on a production line."

"There was more to it than just that. You know I gave him a chance. He just couldn't keep up."

"He's a lot happier working at the School of Music recording lab, I suppose, where he plays with some of the best audio equipment and music recordings known to man. And I'm a lot happier now having built this cable system. It looks like I'll finally be able to break out of my abject poverty and start making some serious money."

"I hope it does," he says between puffs. "But take it from a friend, doing business is not at all like what it's cracked up to be. There are scum dogs hiding around every corner. Be careful."

"But you're an engineer," I argue, "so business is just as strange to you as it is for me. You made it, and now I'm finally going to get mine."

"I wouldn't say I've made it, yet. I'm hocked-up to the heels, and I have money partners who have to be watched carefully or they do dumb things. Everybody looks for a weakness to exploit to their benefit and, if that's not enough, I spend every waking hour thinking how the fuck am I going to sell more speakers. It's a rat-infested, nasty, cruel world and you have to get mean or it'll eat you alive."

His words echo in my brain as we ride back to town. This is Crested Butte. These people are basically honest, trustworthy, and with good values. Those who stray are brought into line with social pressure, or sent packing to more unethical parts of the world. Crested Butte and my friends are different. We have something special here. Trust and respect.

$$\sim 17 \sim$$

THE BETRAYAL

"**S**o, how did it go back in Connecticut?" Steve asks without hesitation when I walk into his office on Monday morning.

I look at him mildly startled, then give in. "I found the people there a bit wanting in basic hospitality and good manners. Other than that, the beer was cheap, the conversation boring, and we had to pull a late-night escape to keep from being consumed by the beast. Why do you ask?"

"Oh, no reason. There's just this rumor going around town that you insulted the queen and have been banished back to the wilderness from whence you came."

"Fuck that old bitch!" I spit out. "Quite frankly, I don't know what I said that set the old witch off. Apparently, she thought I insulted her choice in colleges for her daughters, which I didn't. But then I guess I didn't grovel enough afterwards to gain forgiveness. Fuck 'em if they can't take a joke." I sit down on the couch and pull out my morning doobie.

"Where'd you hear that?" I inquire. "It wasn't Susie or her cousins, was it?"

"I can't say it was definitely her cousin, but I think it started before you two even got back."

"Ancient history. I don't need them. We've got this." I indicate the ground I'm standing on and light up the joint, take a small hit to get it burning properly, then politely pass it to him. "Which reminds me, what's on the agenda today? I'm back and ready to work."

"Let's see," he says, as he takes a big hit and passes it back. He stares at the scheduling blackboard on the wall. *Cough! Cough!* he belches out, while releasing a cloud of smoke. "G-g-gh-ary says he can't gh-et one of the mic inputs on the, *HACK!* board to work. He, *cough! cough!* says you wired it and, *cough!* he doesn't know anything about it."

"If he wants to be a DJ, he should learn his instrument." I put what's left of the joint away for later. "Okay, that's easy."

"Richard and Tapley are up the hill today, *Che-e-e-eze*, that's good stuff," he wheezes, "doing an install at some rich guy's new house. I've been up for days working on our accounts and getting all our tax papers ready for filing. I usually go out-of-town for the mud season, but this year I have to pay attention to all this business accounting."

"What are you whining about, we've been doing all the hard work? You just answer the phone and sign the checks. Which by the way, has been done very well. Why don't you take a vacation? We can handle this ship." I wonder if he's going to respond in kind and break out his coke.

"I could sure use some time in a warm place. Frenchy and several others regularly go to St. Thomas for the mud season. I've been checking on travel to the Caribbean and they've got some good deals on hotels and flights to the Caymans."

"Isn't that the island where international criminals do their banking?"

He looks at me funny, like he didn't expect me to know that.

"It has international banks that aren't required to share information with the IRS, that's all."

"Whatever gets your sunburn on," I quip. "I had my spring vacation, why not you? Go ahead. Have fun while you can. Things might be heating up with the new satellite receiver Dana's father is manufacturing. We might want to expand our business—installing satellite dishes for rich people who want and can afford expensive toys."

"You and Dana have been doing a lot of stuff lately, with the radio station and those weird videos you're making. Any chance you can turn that into something more commercial?"

"We turned this into something commercial. We were the ones who found out about rural cable TV and satellite antennas that make this possible. Dana doesn't want to do business, just art. I just hope he can find some way to support it better than one-night stands."

"I'm glad to see you trying to improve your earning power," he casually adds.

This sounds patronizing, but I choose to ignore such pricks now. "That's something we're going to have to talk about when you get back."

"What's that?" he asks, suddenly perking up.

"Money. We've done what I said we could do. It's time to reap some well-deserved rewards. Consider your Caribbean vacation the first, but hopefully not the last of many more to come."

I give him my best, warmest smile. I really do wish him well. Maybe working together this winter with me and our trusted Crested Butte friends has softened his selfish and greedy ways. "We did it together and it worked. We're winners and everyone likes a winner."

He doesn't seem to respond similarly, remaining elusive when it comes to reading his face. He seems to think business is a zero-sum poker game and therefore requires a blank face of concealment. I wonder why.

*

"Put on a long cut and we'll go down to the office and do a pick-me-up," I whisper to Dana as he turns down his microphone knob after introducing an album. He and I are doing a late night ColoRadio show in the upstairs studio. There's always a bunch of people hanging around during broadcasts, so we have to excuse ourselves so we can go downstairs and find a private place to share what little coke we can usually scrounge between us.

I head downstairs and Dana follows, into Steve's office. I've been using it lately while Steve is off on his spring vacation. If you can afford it, Butte-ers avoid the mud season by going somewhere warm, which is just about anything south of the border.

I sit down at the desk and Dana pulls up a chair to the corner of it.

"I wonder if he has anything in here we can use," I mention to Dana, and start rummaging through the bottom drawers looking for the necessary drug paraphernalia. "Here it is." I pull out a little mirror holding a razor blade and two short straws. I hand them to Dana and he pulls out a little brown bottle and dumps what's left in it onto the mirror. He starts chopping it up with a razor blade.

"What do you think we should play next?" he asks, while still working the snow.

"I don't know. How about some Terry Allen?" I suggest. I'm looking down at the open drawer where I found the mirror and notice a small journal book, one of those plain vinyl-covered books you can buy at the dime store for keeping accounts.

"That's a good idea. We haven't played him in a couple of days. We can do a lead-in with the Fugs."

"I like the Fugs," I add, and pick up the book. "Little known fact. I actually saw the Fugs perform at the '67 March on the Pentagon as featured in Norman Mailer's book, *Armies of the Night*. I was a news photographer for the U of M *Daily News*. I covered the four-day event with friends from Ann Arbor, and we damn near got ourselves arrested for stealing my own car."

I'm absentmindedly paging through the journal while telling my story and waiting for Dana to lay out the lines. I notice one column labeled *S. Fisher & C*.

He makes the final *tap, tap, tap* of the blade on the glass, shaking off any last tiny crystals sticking to the blade. "How'd that happen?" he asks.

I look up and he's already holding out a straw to me.

"I parked my car at a DC dealership near Dupont Circle Saturday night where a police riot was going on." I take the straw in one hand and hold the mirror in my other while I snort up a skinny but sparkly line. It burns a little.

"After we avoid a beating by local off-duty cops, and get some great shots of hippies being beaten and then occupying the fountain waving flags, we get back to the car and were comparing notes when the real cops arrive with real cop cars and flashing lights, surrounding us. We get prepared for some kind of ugly confrontation, when the cops ask me for my license and registration. They have a report from someone in the neighborhood that a gang was trying to steal a car off the lot."

I finish up the line and hand it all back to Dana.

"The cops take time off from a riot," he says, "to actually protect a car dealer during a giant anti-Vietnam march? That's weird. The Fugs were supposed to raise the Pentagon off the ground at the event and it would all float away in the wind."

"Yeah, but just about all the marchers were high as a kite on pot so it was debatable who was actually floating in the wind. I took pictures of them playing to a small crowd in the middle of a Pentagon parking lot littered with stomped-on flowers and piles of burning trash."

Dana pauses to catch up with me. I squeeze my nose tight and sneeze a couple of times. Sneezes are so satisfying. I enjoy them after snorting up. It's a mark of good coke. Then my eye catches something familiar in the journal. The last entry at the bottom shows a six-hundred-dollar subtraction from the amount we paid for our share of the partnership. I received six hundred dollars recently, which should have been a draw on all the unpaid labor I provided all winter.

"Hey, look at this." I hold out the journal so he can see what I'm seeing. "He's apparently diluting our ownership by making illegal deductions in our investment money. He can't do that!"

"Are you sure? Maybe you don't understand what it means. What is that?"

"You look at it," I say, and pass it over to him, "and tell me what you think it is."

He puts down the mirror and takes the journal. I note, almost ironically, that the journal is not vinyl, but leatherbound. What the hell is so important it has to be done up like a bible or an ancient text?

"It does appear to be an accounting of your ownership percentages. It doesn't appear to be fifty-fifty, according to this."

He looks up at me with a serious face. Dana is not one to ever be that serious, unless deciding who is going to be the camera-man on shoots.

"I warned him not to do exactly *this*. We had an agreement. He promised."

There's a knock at the door. Dana calls out, "Come in!"

Cotton pokes his head in, sees too much, and puts on his ear-to-ear grin. "What's that?"

"You tell me. You want a hit?" offers Dana.

"Of course. Does a bear shit in the woods?" He laughs loud and long at his joke while at the same time he's sucking up whatever white there is left on the little mirror. "By the way, the Fugs album is almost over and nothing else is cued up."

Dana declares, "I've got it," and rushes out of the room.

Cotton turns to me. "So, Cowboy, how's the business been doing?"

*

I call a meeting of my cohorts in all this: Susie, Tapley, and Richard. I'm sitting in the Grubstake, sipping on a beer and reading the little leather-bound journal over and over again, when they enter together.

"What's up? You don't look high enough," says Tapley, always getting right to the point.

"Sit down," I instruct with a straight face. They pick right up on it.

"What's wrong?" asks Susie, sitting down beside me and giving me a little kiss, which I return.

"What's that?" asks Richard, keying in on the little book on the table. They sit down looking at me to respond.

"I found this journal in Steve's desk. It appears to be an accounting of our investment in the company and ownership percentages. To make a long story short, he's fixing the books so he gains ownership illegally. We have a partnership agreement that we wrote down and gave to the lawyer to write up in a contract."

Tapley picks up the journal and begins leafing through it.

"Did the lawyer get the agreement written up and signed by you and Steve?" Susie asks. "I thought that was done a long time ago, last fall actually. What happened?"

"I don't know," I admit. "He kept telling me it was okay and it was being done. I gave up reminding him."

"This doesn't look like any agreement," says Tapley. "This looks like a simple bank account, like a savings account, except for no interest payments. What's this six-hundred-dollar draw last month?"

"That's Susie's birthday present," I say. "A microwave oven."

"It looks like you sold him six hundred dollars' worth of stock ownership. Why would you do that?" Tapley looks at me like I might be stupider than I appear.

"I didn't. I took a draw on all the money I earned doing my work last winter getting this company started. We were both going to delay taking a salary for a while until we could afford it. We can obviously afford it now, but he seems to be thinking he's the only owner and Susie and I are just providing a no-interest loan."

"The bastard!" exclaims Richard. He stands up and yells at the bartender, "Bring us four shots of tequila. *Por favor!*"

Dana walks in about that moment and adds, "Make that five!" He walks up to our table and sits down. "You showed everyone the journal?"

"Yes," I answer, without looking up. Susie hands it to him. He looks at it again for a minute, turns a couple of pages, and then looks back up at us. Richard shows up with a plate of cut-up lime wedges and a shaker of salt.

"Maybe this is just a reminder of where money goes or some kind of accounting thing," he suggests.

Richard goes back for the shots.

"Would an accountant keep personal notes in a leather-bound journal?" I inquire.

He looks at the fancy embossed cover and then back at me. "Knowing Steve, it does look incriminating. What are you going to do?"

"I don't know. I'm overwhelmed by the stupidity of this. I thought among all his faults, that being an accountant would at least make him appreciate that screwing a partner who is crucial for his success is not a particularly wise move. Kind of like killing the goose that lays the golden eggs. It was a simple deal. All he had to do was keep his word and his rewards would have been great. This business model has the power to be duplicated, not only all over the Rockies, but all over the west. Anywhere a small rural community is located below the sites of the big rip-off cable companies, they can form their own community cable company, like a co-op maybe, but with us doing the engineering and accounting, we could get a big fat management fee for a virtual monopoly by owning the basic pole contracts."

I slam my fist down on the table. I don't judge my own strength and two lime wedges fly off. Fortunately, Tapley catches one and Susie the other.

"This sucks!" Tapley declares, throwing his back on the plate. "I had hopes!"

"Me too," adds the Rat. He shows up and sets out the shots adding a wedge on each one. I couldn't follow which one was the one manhandled by Tapley. The Rat begins by putting some salt on his thumb web and passes the shaker to the left. We stop our talking, take the shaker, make a pile alongside our thumbs, and pass it on. When it gets back to the Rat, he licks the salt off his hand and everyone follows suit. He holds up his glass and shouts, "*Salud!*"

"Salud!" we all repeat, and down it goes. Everyone grimaces, but we continue.

"This is why," Dana jumps in, "I only ask for one token share of stock from my friends' business ventures. Anything more is just a reason to lose your reason and your friends."

"What are we going to do when he comes back tomorrow?" asks Susie, rubbing my back in sympathy.

"I can't believe it. I specifically told him not to try and pull something like this because I knew from past experience working for him that he turns into a little bitch-whore when it comes to money."

"Maybe you can talk to him and get this straightened out," suggests the Rat. "Maybe he just forgot something."

"Yeah," Tapley adds, "he forgot to lock his desk."

*

The word comes flying through town the next day when Steve is seen driving in from his home out at Peanut Lake. I'm working at the Princess and hear it from three people before I can take a break and ride my klunker down to the office.

When I arrive, he's sitting at his desk opening mail. I walk right in and casually drop the leather journal on his desk. He slowly looks up and gets an ugly scowl. I hear him mutter, *"Shit!"*

"Do you want to explain this?" I bluntly inquire.

"I don't think I have to," he says slowly. "You have no right going through my desk. That's theft. I could fire you for this." He waves the book at me and puts it back into his desk drawer and loudly slams it shut.

"What the fuck are you talking about?" I demand. "We're partners, you can't fire me. Susie and I paid for half ownership of this company, just like you agreed to. You agreed not to dilute or sell or otherwise encumber our investment. And I'm due some money for all the damned work I did last winter. Obviously, we can afford it. How much was your trip to the Caribbean?"

"You asked me for money and the only money you have here legally is your company investment account."

"What the fuck are you babbling about? There's no 'company investment account!' You know damned well what you agreed to. We wrote it down and gave it to the lawyer. That's our agreement. Where the fuck is it and I'll read it to you!"

"I have no idea what you're talking about. The only agreement we have is you and Susie investing money and labor to start Crested Butte Cable and now you want some of it back. Simple accounting."

"You're not *GIVING* anything back! You're stealing it, you fucking jerk! What did our lawyer do with the contract we gave him?"

"What do you mean 'our lawyer?' I have *my lawyer.* You chose not to have one. I instruct my lawyer for what I need, not you. If you don't like it, then I suggest you obtain proper legal representation because I'm not giving away my company under duress to you or anybody else. Now get out of my office! You're fired! Get your stuff out of here by the end of the day or I'll throw it away!"

"Why you lying piece of shit! I ought to jump over this desk and tear your head off so I can shit down your neck!" Tapley hears us from the back room and comes running in as I make a lunge for the little bastard's head, about to smash it into goo. Tapley takes one look and shouts.

"Don't do it!" He catches my upraised arm in mid-swing. Steve dives under his desk as Tapley drags me by the arm out of the room and back to the engineering room.

"Let me go!" I shout, and shrug off his hold. "I need to rip his head off. It's rotten to the core. I'll be doing that miserable thing a favor."

"Calm down!" he orders, as I start seeing normal colors again.

"Did you hear that shit!" turning my attention to him. "He denies we are even partners! He knows that's a lie! Everybody knows it's a lie! What the fuck is he doing?"

"I take it didn't go well. I agree. He is a shithead. We knew that before we started. I thought you had him tied up under contract."

"So did I. The bastard lied to me and said our lawyer was working on it. Now he says *WE* never had a lawyer. Now he claims it's his personal lawyer, while all along I'm thinking he represents the partnership."

"That's low. What are you going to do? You can't kill him. You would not do well in prison. For sure you'd lose Susie. So don't try and whip a little western justice on the bastard."

"I hate to say it, but it's forcing me to have an *Atlas Shrugged* moment. He can't just take what I created. I'm going to have to find a goddamn lawyer!"

*

"Why don't we just sue him?" Susie asks, looking at me with blank emotion. I'm wondering why she isn't angrier, like I am.

She's leaning across the counter at the theater. The movie is started and I've got fifteen minutes before the next reel change. I finally tamed the carbon arcs on the two projectors and when I carefully align them and have their burn rate calibrated, I can count on them holding their brightest output for long periods of time without constant adjustment. Enough time for me to go downstairs and hang with Susie, eat a little popcorn dipped directly out of the machine, and once in a while, share a little treat, like a joint or a line or two. Tonight, we only share our predicament.

"I tracked down Leinsdorf and asked him what I can do. He says without any written contract, it's going to be hard to prove a verbal agreement. It's just my word against his and he has an advantage, being a big property owner and an upstanding member of the inner circle of business owners and real estate developers. It might cost tens of thousands of dollars and take maybe years, if ever, to get justice."

"Then what are we going to do?" she asks plainly.

"I don't know. Tapley and Richard quit in protest today, and so we're all officially on strike. Let's see if he can run a highly technical cable company without any knowledge or ability. Hopefully, the community will step in and force him to honor his word. If he can't provide reliable service, maybe our customers will force him to come to his senses."

"Exactly!" she perks up. "You're right. He doesn't know how to do anything. He's got to settle with us as soon as he realizes he's made a mistake. Besides, we're friends with the Pence's, and they can maybe help put some pressure on him, as well."

"I hope so."

Ding! goes the warning bell on projector number two. I lean over and quickly kiss her and run upstairs to do the changeover.

*

"Wow, that was exhilarating," Tapley loudly whispers as we enter the Wooden Nickel after making a little midnight visit to the cable headend at the town reservoir.

If you just keep walking up the hill at the west end of Elk, going past the old dairy/Bachman house on the left and onto the western bench overlooking town, you arrive at the reservoir. The location, about eighty feet above town, gives a nice pressure for all the faucets down below. The water comes from Coal Creek, a couple of miles up Kebler Road. We have our satellite dish installed here and a little garden shed holding the electronics necessary to feed the cable system.

Tap, Rat, and I pay a little visit to the head-in earlier and sure enough, we find our keys don't work. Steve has already changed the locks, anticipating this. I whip out my homemade lock-picking tools and open the padlock in about ten seconds. Both Tap and Rat are impressed. Once inside, we scramble a few plug-in modules, so somebody will have to be able to read a schematic diagram in order to put them all back in the right places. We calmly lock up the shed and walk back to Elk.

Rat gets a pitcher from the bar and we find a corner table where we debrief our adventure. People at the bar are bitching about the cable being out again and how it's run by an incompetent clown. They know who we are and know we are on strike. Everybody knows what's going on, but most pretend ignorance as an excuse not to get involved.

"I had no idea you were so talented," Tapley continues gushing. "Where did you learn to pick locks?"

"Where else than college?" I reply with a smile. "It's a long story, but basically, I had friends who were rich bad boys and secretly had guns, a private well-stocked liquor cabinet, and lock-picking tools in their freshman dorm rooms. As I knew a little about guns and whiskey, we became friends. They taught me all about locks and lock picking, which they learned by taking apart all the locks at the local exclusive prep school they all attended."

"What do you think Steve is going to do now?" the Rat asks.

"If he is smart like he says he is..." I ponder, "then he'll give back the six hundred dollars in stock ownership, knowing in the long haul it'll be chump change, and sign the partnership agreement that he negotiated last fall."

"Did he make all the right decisions when he started the Princess?" asks Tap.

"The idea to make the Princess an artsy movie theater in the mountains was, perhaps, great. The way he ran it was abysmal. He knew nothing about film rental, distribution contracts, distribution associations, and, as a result, his film venue sucked and with that, revenues. He damned near lost the building until Pence came along and took over management. Now he's doing the same thing with Crested Butte Cable." I take a big swig on my beer.

"That doesn't sound encouraging," comments the Rat.

"Yeah, he could be stupidly stubborn, but if he is, he will lose more in the long run than he possibly thinks he is winning in the short run. I hope he realizes that, for all of our sakes. We have to get out the message and maybe the jungle drums will get it back to him. We need public support if we are going to preserve this community asset."

"Good luck with that," declares Tap. "Haven't you noticed how many New York Jew-types control our town government and even the county?"

"I don't keep track of them that way," I respond simply. "But you're right, they are big city rich bastards looking to milk Crested Butte for all it's worth. I wouldn't trust the lot of them, Jew, WASP, Slobbovian, or whatever. They're all carpetbaggers dancing to the preservation tune while cranking up taxes and real estate values until they take everybody's money and only their kind will be able to afford to live here. Big city corruption has arrived right on time and they're hiding behind liberal environmental politics to pull off a classic capitalist heist. Read Edward Abbey!"

*

We're having a late breakfast at our little kitchen table overlooking Coal Creek.

"Did you see the *Pilot*?" Susie asks, holding a copy in front of my face. "Sandy says here that Steve is blaming disgruntled employees for all the disruptions in service."

"Did she happen to mention that he outright stole our stock ownership and our labor? Did she mention he's a fucking thief and a greedy prick? Did she perhaps consider that a former half-assed advertiser doesn't automatically deserve mindless promotion? But that would impact her philosophy of all the news that fits to print."

"What about the *Chronicle*?"

"Even worse. He's just another one of the eastern carpetbaggers out here taking advantage of our paradise so they can make a dollar off of pimping beauty to the turkeys. As soon as they satisfy themselves raping the Butte, they'll abandon her to live in another equally bad place where even more wealthy people fuck each other, just like them. They'll take all their ill-gotten gains to the new Eastern snob center, Santa Fe or Taos, where they brag over wine and cheese about all the suckers they've cleaned."

"You're talking about a lot of our friends," Susie protests.

"Friends? Friends are honest with each other. Friends support each other. I know who my friends are. Do you? Really?"

"I have many friends who support me."

"That's your mountain girlfriends and a few sniffing male dogs. All they protect you from is having happiness when they have none. Be careful of people who claim to be only interested in protecting you, often from yourself. They secretly don't like one of their own being happy in a relationship. They need justification for their miserable life by dragging everyone down to their miserable level."

"Not my friends. We don't do that to each other. We just support and help as best we can. I've been getting a lot of encouragement on our difficulties with Steve. What are we going to do now that we've lost the cable company?"

"I haven't lost it yet. He'll have to admit sometime that he needs me and he'll come to an agreement. That's what real businessmen do, and he claims to be one, so let's just let him stew for a while. In the meantime, I met the new director of the Community Theater. Seems as though that narcissist Eric Ross got his ass kicked out for being such an elitist snob not letting others into his private little theater club. So fucking typical of no-talent entitled twerps! Anyway, Mike Schultz has taken over and he's asking me to direct the fall play."

"Wow! Really?" Susie says. "That sounds like fun. He's the Austrian skier who just moved to town with that gorgeous blonde model. I think her name is Brenda."

"So I've heard." Everybody has heard. "Anyway, I have to find something to occupy my mind during this shit-works. I have to get my creative juices flowing again, now that I'm free from the vulture."

"I thought you might want to start a computer company," adds Susie, "like what you discussed with your friend from Ann Arbor."

"I've been looking into that, too," I say. "It turns out Heath Kit has an LSI-11 minicomputer for sale in kit form. I can build it in our home and maybe rent an office somewhere in town where we can operate it as a business."

"Cool. How much will that cost?"

"I think I can get all the parts we need for around $1200. I don't want your money for this. I'm really sorry your money was stolen by Steve. I tried my best to do an honest deal, but he hasn't a clue what honest even means. I'll sell my motorcycle or get some more gigs with Dana installing satellite dishes. I'll figure something out."

"Go ahead and order it," she says with glee. "I think it will be fun to have the first computer in town."

"Really?" I ask. She nods her head *yes*. I lean over the table and kiss her. "I love you. You are so understanding and supportive. I won't ever let you down again."

*

Mike asks what I want to do for the fall play during our meeting in the newly renovated upstairs at the old firehouse, and I reply simply, *Ten Little Indians*.

"Good choice," he says. "Surefire winner for a town like this."

"Why is that?" Susie asks.

"Everybody gets their rocks off as community members see their beloved comrades slowly and gruesomely get knocked off, until...." His eyes twinkle. Susie laughs. I take another sip off my beer. "'til none are left." He makes a fake evil intonation with his heavily Austrian-accented English for the last bit. I'm beginning to wonder if he has the background for running an American community theater, but what the heck, I'm all for diversity, even for good-looking blond skiers with accents, fancy ski clothes, and blonde models hanging off their arms.

Connie has already announced her intent to go after what she describes to Susie as her *European Christmas Present*.

*

I'm sitting on the edge of the stage at the little theater above the firehouse. The only access to this pocket theater is by the backdoor stairway to the second floor, but otherwise it is a cute little forty-seat theater with very close seating, yielding an un-intended, yet cozy intimate atmosphere. If one person laughs or cries, they all have to.

"Welcome to Crested Butte Community Theater. I'm grati-fied that we have a lot of talented people in town who care about the *Muses*. It's going to be a great show."

"For casting purposes, Gloria Cunningham will take the lead role of Inspector. It's a modern world and even old British in-spectors can be a woman. Give a wave out there, Gloria." She giggles and waves.

"So, let's get started. I want you all to read this one-page monologue written by Pushkin where Salieri contemplates his uncontrollable jealousy and hatred of Mozart, whom he ulti-mately destroys with deceit and malevolency. Read through it first and then assume a mental state or mood of the character. Then read it to us with that motivation in mind, conveying it with your delivery."

I look at them and am mildly surprised they're all paying rapt attention. *This might work*, I think with a warm feeling.

After rehearsal, I decide to take the long way home by going up Elk to First, and then over the bridge to Sopris and a hard left turn into our house. I think about the little cable TV system I put in the creek, serving several homes of my friends along First Street who refuse to pay Steve.

Of course, the little douchebag immediately disconnected our house from my cable TV system that I built. So I had to go underground and do a tap off the nextdoor cable drop where it was buried alongside the house to the rear entrance. I put in an underground splitter, an amplifier in my back shed, and then strung cables under the water in the creek bed across First and then from backyard to backyard to houses like Helene and Cloud's, Sunshine's and Pat Dawson's.

The snow has come and there's about a foot or two everywhere off the streets. I pass the trail that goes up behind Bachman's house to the reservoir and note only a couple of sets of tracks from recent hikers. I'm thinking about my personal issues and how great the play will be when I notice a pickup about three blocks away pointing in my direction, but parked on the wrong side of the street. A lot of us do that just because we're lazy and we can, but this one looks like the CB Cable pickup, *Sherman*, and it's in the wrong place.

That's odd, I think. There's no reason it should be there at this time of night.

I continue on across the bridge, turn left, and left again into our front door. As I step inside, I pause and look back towards south First and notice the pickup has moved forward somewhat. Somebody is inside driving it slowly with lights out. I step inside but don't turn on the lights. I turn and look out the front window and see the truck lights come on and it moves slowly past, heading for town. I wonder if they are looking for my little cable system or is some new employee of Steve's just up to no good.

I turn on the lights and turn on the TV, but snow just comes up. Great! He's causing the system to fail just like I predicted. I don't need to give it a nudge.

I don't give it any more thought and instead decide to do a little work on assembling my new computer before Susie gets home from the Princess. I'm really happy, even after all the shit at the cable company. I'm directing a play and building a computer. Maybe something good will come out of all this crap eventually.

I work as I sing along with Jimmy Cliff. *"...as sure as the sun will shine, I'm going to get my share now, what's mine, and then the harder they come, the harder they fall, one and all."*

*

The next morning, I'm having my first coffee with Susie when there's a loud knocking at our front door. Susie walks out to the front room and peeks out the window. She audibly gasps and comes running back.

"It's the marshal. Both of them. What should we do?"

I take a quick peek and see Fran the man and Don standing on our front steps dressed in full marshal regalia, including the dime-store plastic badges.

Knock, knock, knock! "Hello! It's the town marshals and we need to see Cowboy."

I run back into the kitchen and ask Susie, "Do we have any drugs in the house?"

She looks panicky. I grab her by the waist, firmly. "It's okay." I kiss her and she calms. "Do you have any drugs?"

She shakes her head no.

"Really?" I ask again, amazed. "Neither do I. Weird."

She giggles and lightens up.

"Listen, it can't be much. Let's see what they want and deal with it. Okay?"

She nods her head *yes*.

"Come on." I take her by the hand and we walk to the front door, open it, and I say, "What's up, Docs?"

"I'm sorry to have to bother you this early, but we weren't given a choice," announces Fran. "I have an arrest warrant against Cowboy, for breaking and entering private property and damaging equipment last night. We also have a search warrant we have to execute on your house. Sorry, again, but the judge seemed to be riding on a butt boil."

"I was here all night last night, working on my computer," I protest. "Who the hell is telling you otherwise?"

"I said it's not us. We're just obeying orders. Did anybody visit you or was Susie here between ten p.m. and midnight?"

"No, it was just me. Susie didn't get home until one or two. I was so busy, I lost track of time."

"Well, anyway, you're going to have to go with Don here to the Gunnison County Courthouse and post bail." She turns to Susie and says, "I'll need to see your bedroom where you keep all your clothes."

Susie looks at me and I mouth silently, *It's okay.*

Don gets between me and Susie and starts edging me out of the house.

"I'll be at the courthouse," I yell back at Susie. "Bring my checkbook and come down as soon as Fran gets through inspecting my underwear for prints. Bye! Love you!"

"Get in the front seat," he orders when we get to the marshal's Bronco. I get in and he climbs in beside me and calls us in to dispatch.

"Don West here with transport to county. Over."

"See you in about a half hour, Don. The judge is having lunch but he should be here when you arrive."

"Ten four."

I have trouble stifling a laugh.

*

When we get to Almont, I can't hold it in any longer. "So, Don?" I inquire. "I bet this is making your day."

"What do you mean?"

"You know," I reply. "From the coffee incident a couple of years ago. Haven't you been trying to get even with those you thought were involved? I feel the tension between us. Ever since you came into my shop and smelled some of the best weed this side of the Pecos, you've kind of had it in for the free-spirited people here. And when they told you to lighten up by sending you a not-so-subtle message from Mr. Mescalito, I thought you sort of flipped."

"Oh, that. I got over that a long time ago. I really don't like this job. I just have to do it for now until I can get my ranch put together."

"Ranch?"

"I put some money down on about eighty acres just outside of Montrose. I want to raise horses."

"Raise horses?"

He looks directly at me for the first time today. "After experiencing the acid poisoning, I thought about it a lot. I realized nobody wanted to hurt me, just make me become aware."

"Aware?"

"Yeah, if it hadn't been for the doping, I probably would have ended up a bitter isolated old cop. No thanks."

I stare at him blankly, wondering how I could have been so wrong about someone.

"Thank you, by the way, if you had anything to do with it. You did me a favor." He looks over and smiles at me, honestly, for the first time ever. I'm astounded. Crested Butte does work its magic somehow.

*

"So, what's the local bad boy been up to lately?" Dana says, as he approaches our table at the Grubber with a beer in his hand. Susie, Tapley, and Richard are with me celebrating my release from the hard-rock county jail. "It's all over town. Seems Steve caught you breaking in at the head-in and he claims he followed you to town and saw you go into your house wearing gloves and snow booties."

"He saw me all right. He was watching the house last night and must have known I'd go there right after rehearsal and be alone until Susie came home after the show. Then he knocks down the cable system and plants boot prints coming down the hill. He calls it in and the cops buy it."

"Did you do it?" he asks pointedly.

"Actually, no. I was working on my computer and was a good little boy for once."

"And all that Fran found," added Susie, "was a pair of yellow gloves in the wood shed. But she looked through everything. All my clothes and some private stuff. I don't like it."

"Better her than anyone else," Dana points out, and pulls up a chair from the next-door table. "I think she's on your side. At least most of the town is sympathetic. Except for Rademan and his crowd, which includes Glazer, that is."

"And all the other phony carpetbagging, thieving bastards ripping off the town," I add.

"Well, that kinda takes care of our ColoRadio," he laments. "Gorbett will kiss up to Steve just to glory in the spotlight, but most everybody else won't want to screw with it. But more importantly, what are you going to do?"

"Well, one thing, I'm going to finally hire a lawyer. I don't know how I'll pay him, but I need real legal help now. I'm going to fight for what's right, no matter what."

"Sic 'em, Cowboy," Tapley says with a straight face hoisting his beer in salute.

Rat follows with, "Hear, hear!" and everyone takes a drink.

"I'm guessing that means George Gunderson," Dana says.

"The best damn defense lawyer in Gunnison County," I proclaim, "and president of the Gunnison good ol' boys club."

We all take another hit off our beers.

"How do you know that?" asks Dana.

"Leinsdorf approached me in the Grub last night and whispered his name in my ear saying, *'don't tell anybody I said so, but he knows what's going on in Gunnison County and he can pull strings.'*"

"You're going to trust Leinsdorf? Isn't he one of them?" Dana says.

"Maybe even he can recognize a rat, two or three feet away. I don't know. But I already decided to hire him on Cloud's recommendation. He's the guy who got Cloud off, so to speak, so I really have no better choice."

"Well, here's to a successful conclusion to this mess and next time, Cowboy, what are we going to do?"

I grumble, "Hire a lawyer when it comes to money." Then I add, "What a shitty world we live in, that requires them."

"Hear! Hear!" they all yell in unison. We take another drink.

*

"Before we get started with tonight's rehearsal, I want to say a few words. Please, everybody, take a seat."

I'm sitting on the edge of the stage at the firehouse two days after the arrest. I hear people talking and looking furtively at me as soon as I arrive for rehearsal.

"I'm sure you all know I was given a free ride to Gunnison courtesy of the town marshals a couple days ago." I switch into a Jimmy Cagney imitation and continue. "They couldn't keep me, you see. The filthy coppers! But I'll get them, *ha ha ha ha*, you'll see. I'll get them all!"

Everybody bursts out in applause.

"I just want to remind you that the truth is always deeper than the simple story. It's truth that motivates what people do, not purely ideas. Dig down and find the truth. Only when you know the truth, can you properly bring the story to life." I pause and notice many begin to relax and talk. "Any questions?"

I hear someone say, "Does the play still go on if you're in jail?"

"The show will go on no matter where I end up, and I intend to end up right here doing with you what I like doing. That's all that can be expected from anybody. Okay now, we have a show to put on!"

*

"That was a great show!" Mike yells at me above the loud music. "We had standing room only for all performances. Here, have some more champagne." He tops off my glass again. I sorta rather have a shot of Crown Royal and a line, but it's a lame cast party and champagne is expected.

"What do you want to do for the Christmas show? It looks like a good snow year and there's always a bunch of turkeys in town for the holidays. You got anything G-rated?"

"How about *Little Mary Sunshine?*" I propose.

"What's that?" he asks. "Never heard of it."

"It's an old standby hoofer musical with young girls in bosom-exposing dresses playing footsy with a bunch of gay Canadian Mounties, all decked out in fancy red uniforms and jack boots. You closet Nazis will love it."

He laughs nervously. "How's your battle with...ah. What's his name?"

"Glazer. It appears I had to sign over my share of Crested Butte Cable just like my idiot partner intended. Only problem is, he lost his share, too. He ran it into the ground without my expertise and had to sell it or declare bankruptcy, where if he did, the banks would go after the Princess. He sold it to Gunnison Cable for about what everybody owed in debt and lawyer fees. Everything in, nothing out."

"What happened to your arrest?"

"They dropped the charges. My lawyer found some flaws in the original complaint and warrants. Seems as though he lied his ass off to the cops so I would be arrested and he could blame his bad performance on sabotage. But he had no evidence or proof whatsoever. My lawyer also found evidence that Glazer had planned from the very beginning to screw me."

"No!"

"Does a bear shit in the woods? Right after I think the corporate lawyer has been instructed to draw up the partnership agreement and we leave his office, Glazer turns around and hires the same lawyer as his personal attorney and instructs him to put our share purchase money in the corporate agreement as a simple loan. They conveniently don't tell me for over six months, while I work my ass off for nothing. Then I find out by accident."

"*Jeez*, what dicks!" he declares.

"My attorney filed a complaint with the Bar Association against his crooked lawyer and he has been reprimanded. I think he moved back to Texas."

"I hate cops, lawyers, and car salesmen, in that order. More champagne?"

"Are you sure you're Austrian?"

"Nobility, if you don't mind. My great-great-grandfather killed a bunch of Turks, I think." He refilled my glass and clinked it. "Salud!"

*

"Hi Faude! Bar's a little empty for 1 a.m.!" I yell over the noise, sitting at the last open stool.

"What can I get you?" he responds in kind, leaning over the bar cupping his ears.

"The usual. Anybody in here I know?"

"Not unless you and Mitchell are into line dancing. By the way, I haven't seen you two in here for a long time. Did you violate some Yuppie New England code or something?"

"He's been busy with his new friends over at Hiccup."

He laughs and heads to get me my usual.

Hiccup is the slang word for HCCA, or High Country Citizens' Alliance. A bunch of Eastern carpetbagger business owners well invested in the tourist trade and supposedly concerned about saving the environment and the Red Lady for future generations. They have part of it right. What they're saving will be future generations of rich people making this an exclusive, expensive tourist trap, just like Aspen. Anybody can be against tearing down a mountain and not be a radical environmentalist, but if you want to save it, then get it out of the hands of the profiteers and money mongers. They just perform the job of pimp for the raping and looting of our chosen home, the wilderness.

Somebody slaps me on the shoulder. I turn and Leinsdorf is sitting down next to me. Faude sets down a neat shot of Crown and a tall soda water back. Leinsdorf salutes him and shouts out, "Same as he's having," and points at me. Jack nods his head and leaves. I take a quick sip from each glass.

"I hear you won your criminal case," he says, leaning into me.

"Dropped and squelched. It never happened."

He grins and tries to fist bump me. We miss awkwardly and laugh.

"Did you get anything out of the company sale?"

"As usual, you guys got it all."

"I'm not a practicing attorney," he protests.

"Still. Trees and apples. Or is it apples and worms?"

"What? Guilt by association?" he protests. Faude sets down his drink. He throws a twenty down on the bar, picks up the shot glass and says, "L'chayim!" He throws it down and goes for the chaser.

"By the way," he adds, "the rumor mill is mentioning your name a lot. You might want to consider leaving town for a while."

"Why? Everyone I know knows the truth about Glazer and his dealings in town. He's a crook and everyone knows it. You know it, right?"

"What we know and what gets written are two different things."

"Yeah, I know what the two rag sheets did to me and never published an apology. So what? Fuck 'em, I'll never buy an ad with them again." I take another sip of my whiskey.

He chuckles. "I just hope you can survive this. I always liked your free spirit."

"I'm doing okay. Haven't you seen my latest hit show at the Mountain Theater? You like musicals, don't you?"

"Not funny. But seriously, there's talk and it's not good, so look out. Your country lawyer embarrassed some powerful people. They're not necessarily friends of Glazer, but defenders of the almighty buck. Glaze has some bucks, so they listen to him. Maybe Susie can help you with her friends, but they probably follow the money people, too, just like all the other yuppies in this town."

I suddenly feel a cold shudder. Must be the soda water. Leinsdorf finishes his soda and stands up. Again, he slaps me on the shoulder and this time he just says, "Good luck," and leaves.

I finish my drink, leave a twenty on the bar, and go outside to where I parked my klunker. I climb on and jump the curb to the street and began riding up the middle of Elk. I immediately spot a commotion on the steps going up to Sancho's. Several drunks are trying to pull a wheelchair, Mitchell in it, up the narrow stairway.

"Let's go, you overpaid Hot Shots, show me what you got!" he yells waving a bottle of wine around in two hands, barely able to hang onto it with his stubby rebuilds.

"You need some help?" I yell to him. He cups one hand over his eyes, shading them from the movie-prop, fake gas streetlights he bought as mayor, and spots me.

"Hey! Cowboy! How the hell did you get out of prison? I hear the marshals finally hunted you down and dragged you to Gunnison for long-term incarceration. You should have your partner, what's his name, Glazer?, loan you his lawyer."

"Thanks, but you don't borrow lawyers, you buy them. Are you sure these drunken yahoos are going to get you up those stairs? I could give you a hand."

"No thanks, they just need to drink some more. This, I'm told, is a two-drink minimum hill and may take the same to go down. How's the Fisher twins? I hear they're hanging out together at your house, you lucky slobbering dog."

"With the two halves together, I finally get the full experience, chump." And I ride on up Elk and turn left on Second. I hear Mitchell yelling epithets all the way.

~ 18 ~

NEVER ASSUME ANYTHING

The last performance of *Little Mary Sunshine* just finishes its second curtain call and I'm coming out from the dark projection booth in the back of the auditorium. The bright room lights blind me for a minute as I make my way through the crowd to backstage and my actors and crew. Mike stood in for one of the Mounties for this last week and he wooed the girls with his athletic, long blond hair rendition of purity and modesty. That got more than a few laughs from the locals. Since Mike's long blonde Swedish girlfriend went back to Europe, Mike's been on the open market and doing all right, according to him.

"Nice work, Mike," I tell him, while pumping his hand. "You actually made me believe in goodness and purity." He laughs and goes back to cleaning off all the rouge he packed on earlier.

Just as I reemerge into the auditorium, I run smack into Sandy Cortner, owner of the *Pilot*. She has always been a bit stand-offish from the mainstream of CB life, preferring the business and professional classes and often spurning the actions of our more famous members and the true Crested Butte youth culture. I attribute her behavior to good old-fashioned bad upbringing, probably with a religious side-guilt against having fun. For general purposes, we just assume she has a stick up her butt and prefers it that way.

Crested Butte has a few fat cracker daughters from the Springs who may spurn the super wealthy Aspen class, but still stampede to the Broadmoor Hotel, where once upon a time in the old west, Cordley and I were kicked out for not adhering to some irrelevant dress or manners code. This was only the third or fourth time Cordley and I had been asked to leave an establishment, including the Newport Yacht Club for camping on their exclusive beach. Or that time at Lake Forest graduation ceremonies where something about him wearing a chrome-plated Nazi helmet set off the athletic director and they got into a slapping contest at the back of the auditorium while his brother was being awarded a diploma up front.

"Cowboy!" she yells directly at me. "I've been looking for you." I'm a little taken aback, as I'm not sure she has ever recognized me in the past with more than two words.

"You found me."

"I just wanted to say, I'm very surprised."

"So am I. About what?"

"Well, you know, I just didn't expect this from you. It was a great show. I loved it. I'm sorry, but I had no idea you're so creative."

"I'm glad you liked it. And there's a lot about me you may also be surprised about. Maybe you need to look beyond the superficial and find the truth." I step past her before she can say anything further. Actually, I don't think she had anything more to say. I hit a nerve. Hunter would be proud of me.

*

A couple of weeks after our unusual theatrical success, the governing board for the Mountain Theater is up for its annual election of officers and we are set to give a solid presentation of our two productions that actually brought money into the budget from our ticket sales. Another record for us. We feel we have a solid case that they will recognize as the best future for the theater. You can argue about art, but you can't dispute box office numbers.

The meeting is held in the theater and I present our case to the board, sitting in the front row, about our year of stellar productions and the paying audience we attracted. I outline what we have planned for the coming year, which we predict will also generate sold-out performances and absolutely fit the small-town theater genre, taking advantage of our unique social conditions and youth culture. My pick for the fall musical is *The Fantasticks,* the highly acclaimed Off-Broadway play in which I had the privilege of starring in the first Chicago performance in 1966, as the girl's father.

Eric Ross gets up and gives his pitch for the coming year, but all I can follow is his claim to have the only legitimate qualifications for being a theater director, and only he should have the power to set Crested Butte's creative arts agenda. I try to rise above his obvious bigotry, arrogance, and intolerance. He never really fit in with our crowd or real people, anyway. He has no wilderness skills, couldn't heat his house without blowing it up, and doesn't seem to have any worthy goals outside of skiing and hanging with the snob art crowd as a sort of Truman Capote of CB society. I think he's an idiot wuss.

I'm standing in the back of the auditorium while he rambles on about himself when Mike comes up and taps me on the shoulder.

"You see that?"

"What?" I ask innocently.

"The Wilsons from up on the hill are here," he points out. "They are known friends of Eric. Then I looked at all the rest. It looks like he stuffed the meeting with his friends. The goddamned bylaws say all the people who are residents and show up at the annual meeting can vote for the director."

"What? That's the first time I'm hearing that!" I think for moment. "What the fuck! And you didn't think of stuffing it with our friends?"

"I didn't think he would go this far. I thought we had him bested when we did such a great job. It looks like nobody gives a shit about reality, the theater, or its success. All they want is their fragile egos stroked and, in this case, shabby vengeance."

"Crested Butte people can still make the obvious choice. They are intelligent individuals with free thinking. They are basically honest and will vote responsibly according to the facts."

He looks at me with furrowed brows. "You poor naïve son of a bitch. You're just asking for it."

He goes back to the stage after Eric finishes his elaborate proposal for a super-duper community theater that only strokes his ego, one that will not so much entertain but showcase.

"Thanks, Eric, for your presentation. I'd like to call for the vote now. You've heard the two sides seeking your approval. All for Mike Schultz hold up their hand." He makes a quick count and announces. "I count five in favor with us. All for Eric Ross, hold up their hand. It's a lot more than five. He hesitates, but announces, "Eric Ross wins. Thanks for coming and all your support this year."

He drops the mike and walks off the stage and out of the building. I can't believe what just happened. Blatant bullshit cultism over professionalism. What the hell is wrong with these people? These are not the people I know who live here. I study the crowd this time as they leave the theater and sure enough, I know very few of them. From their fancy mountaineering clothing, I realize they aren't Crested Butte people at all. They are mostly condo owners from up on the hill or down the valley and don't even mix with us townies.

I go back to the sound booth in the back and pick up all the equipment I had loaned to the theater. I grab my audio equipment and an old lantern projector used as a spotlight. Tapley shows up to help me remove the stuff. He and I take it all back to my house and then go to the bars to announce the cultural travesty and drown our sorrows.

*

I wake up and check the clock. It shows 3:30 a.m. and I realize I have fallen asleep waiting for Susie to come home and here it is, long after the bars are all closed and she's not here. I know some of her girlfriends have rented a large apartment on the second floor of a newly remodeled house on Third, so I get up, put on my clothes, and go out in the night looking for her.

My stomach churns from the dark feelings rearing up inside that make my blood run cold. Did she get picked up by one of her feel-good, psycho-California-New-Age babble boys touting some New Age bullshit awareness cult? Connie's been hanging out with a lot of the California hipsters who come here to open weird food restaurants serving a lot of brown rice and seaweed.

I walk around the empty town streets checking on several places where I might find her klunker. When I get to her friends' house, sure enough, the bike is lying haphazard on the back lawn. I boldly go up to the kitchen door and bang on it. Nothing happens. I start to pound again and the lights come on in the kitchen. Kathie comes to the door, looks out, sees me, opens the door, and says, "What the hell do you want?"

"Where's Susie? Her bike's outside." I start to push past her to the front room when Susie appears in her underwear.

"What's up? Oh, it's you."

"I got worried when you didn't come home. Why are you sleeping here?"

"I got really drunk and we came here after the bars closed to do some coke and listen to some music. I got tired and must have passed out."

"Grab your clothes. Let's go home." Then I see someone else watching from the dark front room behind Susie. It looks like a guy, but I don't recognize him. Three girls live here, so it's not unlikely some dogs will be hanging around.

"Okay. Give me a second." She goes back into the dark room and soon returns wearing her clothes. We leave without saying much else. I grab her bike and walk it home behind her all the way. When we get home, she immediately goes upstairs, and by the time I can get up there, she's in bed and not moving.

My stomach learns a couple more Boy Scout knots and radiates stormy waves of sucking pain. Susie can't be having an affair behind my back. She is just not that kind of girl. Her sister, though, is that kind. I feel confused and fearful. My sense of well-being, my feelings of acceptance, my love for Susie are being assaulted. I refuse to let my natural tendency for being overly protective affect my sincere love for Susie. I will not succumb to my insecurities again, like I did with my first Susie back in Ann Arbor. I know I'm honest and so does anybody who knows me. I don't cheat and I don't lie. I will not roll over either. We mean something to each other. We share our lives and an honest, pure kind of love. We are a model of Crested Butte life. We naturally fit together. She can't just walk away from all this.

*

Connie shows up for the Christmas holidays and stays with us in the downstairs bedroom. Without warning, Mike and Connie become a thing. Connie no longer stays in our spare bedroom, spending most nights at his place, yet still coming and going at all hours.

I'm back to running the projectors at the Princess every night, mostly so I can be with Susie when we close up the theater. We usually do what we always did—have a big juicy burger at the Nickel and visit with the midnight crowd gathering for one last rush before closing.

Mike and Connie come strolling into the Nickel while we're waiting for our burgers after the show.

"Hey guys," Mike greets us. "This is my new squeeze, Connie." He grins a big shit-eating grin. Connie is smirking, but hanging onto the muscular Greek god that he portrays, like a young smitten schoolgirl.

"How do you do?" I ask flatly. "Never mind, I know how you do."

"You wish," she taunts me, while giving us a big smile. "Mike is having an authentic Austrian Tannenbaum celebration. A lighting of the tree when all they had was candles. It'll be fun.

He tells me his family has been doing it for three hundred years. I'm making wassail."

"You realize that dry, dead evergreens don't get along very well with candles," I point out, "especially lit candles."

"Nothing the volunteer fire department can't handle," Susie quips. When we get to the party the next night, it turns out to be not so much a party as an intimate group of strange attractions. Mike is renting the downstairs of one of the big houses on the other side of the creek behind the Grubber, and as most do in the Butte, he goes out in the woods and collects a Christmas tree from the wilderness. He also makes some lebkuchen, like what Eberbach and I used to make in Ann Arbor, and of course, something called wassail.

Connie, as usual, makes no bones about who she is sleeping with. Connie tells Susie everything, and I've heard probably too much already. Mike is swarming all over Connie, helping her light her candle and hold it in such a way as to not burn herself with hot wax. Susie and I have no problem handling candles and soon all four of us are in a dark room with just our four candles lighting up the room and a scraggly pine tree.

A lot of stuff is going on between them, while Susie and I stand idle on the other side of the six-foot tree, trying to figure out what they're cooing and laughing about. Mike and I are good friends having done theater work together, bonding us in a way, but now he's being inscrutable. I guess I'm witnessing the modern mating ritual of young European aristocracy, which I thought I was familiar with from watching Jean-Luc Godard movies of the sixties.

"Okay, we all circle the tree to the right while singing "Silent Night," in German." He starts leading a procession around the tree while I struggle with the German version. Susie is just humming it, but Connie seems to have memorized it.

"...Schlaf in himmlischer Ruh! Schlaf in himmlischer Ruh!" he and Connie sing, and we mouth along.

"So, now we stop and turn to the tree," he instructs, "and light the nearest candle. This is where you have to be careful and not light the tree on fire." He proceeds to demonstrate. Connie follows suit.

"We can light any one we want?" asks Susie.

"Whatever your heart desires, will be my command," he spouts theatrically, while bowing slightly.

I just about regurgitate my last meal from the lameness exploding all around me. Susie and Connie giggle like little girls with a secret.

"Now we circle in the opposite direction while we sing "Joy to the World."

I mutter "In German..." under my breath, while he finishes his sentence, "in Deutsch."

I look at Susie and she seems entranced with Mike and his performance. Connie is just being disgusting. It's almost like she's mocking him and he's too stupid to see it.

He starts singing, "Freude dich Welt, der Herr ist da..." Connie joins in while Susie and I give up and start singing it in English.

"Let earth receive her King!" we blurt out. It goes on like this for a while until Mike finishes and lights another candle. Connie and Susie do the same and then I try to light the tree.

"Hey!" Mike yells, "don't set the damn tree on fire! Knowing the volunteer fire department at this hour, they'd probably end up on the wrong side of town!"

"No problem," I say backing away from the tree. Both Susie and Connie give me a dirty look. Mike swats out the smoking tree branch I had been working on.

Another fifteen minutes of German torture-caroling reminds me again there is something basically flawed with the Germanic people. Anybody who has relatives who voted for Hitler can't be all good.

We finally light all the candles on the tree without losing a branch and we all hold hands while we sing "Oh Christmas Tree," in German.

"O Tannenbaum, o Tannenbaum, wie treu sind deine Blätter!" We all circle the tree now, fully lit up with candles and throwing a warm glow over all of us.

I'm holding on to Connie's hand with my left and Susie's with my right. I shudder uncontrollably as I feel the same tingle from both hands. It scares me for a moment, realizing I was feeling strong sexual attraction to both. Only for an instant. I shake it off with a little embarrassment. I'm 100 percent connected to Susie. I don't even *like* Connie. But there is no denying something strange is afoot.

While we admire our work, Mike goes off and comes back with four glasses of a clear liquid. I guess vodka, but realize it's Steinhäger when the smell hits me. The double-thump liquor that attacks two organs at once, the liver with alcohol and the pancreas with sugar. No wonder the Nazis lost the war.

Then he brings out the coke and we start to really celebrate the holiday. Soon Connie and Mike are curled up on the couch across the room with lots of squirming and giggling going on, while Susie and I are lying on a bean bag, fooling around a little ourselves. Mike gets up and holding Connie's hand, pulls her up and they walk over, hand-in-hand, to where we're parked.

"We're going to take this up a notch. Want to join us?" he asks flatly. Connie giggles.

That came out of nowhere. The last thing on my mind right now is to join a foursome where two of them are related. The complications rise in my mind like Godzilla from the deep.

"What?" I ask without wanting an answer. I look at Susie and she doesn't seem as repelled by the idea as I obviously am. Sort of neutral looking as usual, but Connie is smiling wickedly from ear to ear. Not sure why, but I'll assume it's not about watching her sister.

"You heard me," he says. "Make up your mind. I'm not waiting all night for an answer."

I look at Susie and she appears a little drunk and very high. "I think we should be heading home."

"Suit yourselves," he responds. "You could be missing something historic."

"Thanks, but I get seasick easy." I stand up, pull Susie up, and we kiss passionately in front of them. They leave the room with their respective hands on each other's butt and Connie still wearing that evil smile like she's about to eat the cake and have it too.

Susie and I find our coats and walk out the front door in silence, heading for the bridge across the creek at Third. We hold hands all the way home, humming carols.

*

It's really been challenging for me to put together a computer for the first time in my life. I spent time programming them while in graduate school and learned then that this new computer technology thing may be the most frustrating endeavor man has ever inflicted upon himself. No instructions, no how-to demonstrations, not even any rules for guidance, just some vague descriptions with hand-drawn pictures and a new language that I still have to fully learn.

The core of the computer is a box loaded with plug-in cards containing 120 kilobytes of memory and an LSI processor running about 25 megahertz. Then there's a standup Teletype terminal keyboard with a dot-matrix printer using fanfold tractor paper, which is used to communicate with the computer inputting character data and printing output text.

I build a paper punch tape reader, which is really archaic, but the only way to input the boot loader and operating system for the LSI. Once up and running, it has a separate dual-slot magnetic floppy disk recorder capable of holding up to 360 kilobytes per 8-inch disc. I also build a video display with built-in keyboard so I don't have to waste paper using the teletype terminal all the time. Altogether, the equipment occupies a fair share of a standard business office, so I have to get it out of our house if I am going to make a serious business out of it.

Patty has just taken over the Alpineer building from a divorce settlement and is renting out offices at a somewhat reasonable rate. She rents the back office to an engineering company working for some condo developers on the hill and rents the smaller front office to me, where I install my computer. Immediately, it gets around town that crazy Cowboy has a functioning computer in the Alpineer and is looking for business. What the nature of the business is, no one is entirely sure. I load it with a line compiler called Basic and immediately start writing programs for fun, and hopefully, profit.

Meanwhile, many of the boys have been lately claiming they can make money at casinos by playing Black Jack and counting cards. Frenchy and the Face both approach me to set up a Black Jack training program on the computer so they can use it for practice. Apparently, it deals hands faster and the players never have to touch real cards. Who knew?

I take on the challenge of programming the computer to show the face of the cards by printing normal characters in a line-by-line rendition of what the card looks like. Computer programming takes a great deal of concentrated thinking time, so I put a couch along one wall where I can grab a nap while working late into the wee hours of the morning. I add a hot pot for making tea to help keep me awake. Susie and I are having trouble finding *us* time with her work at the ski area and the Princess, and mine delivering high technology to the unwashed masses.

"Hey! Cowboy! Wake up!" Face shouts through the closed door. I swing off the couch and open the door.

"Whadaya want at this hour?" I ask. I check. It's ten in the morning.

"I wanna play Black Jack on your computer. I need to try out something." He steps past me and goes straight to the video keyboard and sits down.

"How do you make this thing work?" He looks around for a switch.

"It's not that simple, and I was doing some commission work for the guys next door."

"Don't worry," he says, while fishing out a wad of money. "I'm a paying customer," and he lays down a stack of twenties. "Now, show me how to set up the game for dealing from two decks instead of just one."

"I'll have to make some modifications to the program. Move over and let me do it."

We switch places and I wake up the computer, load the basic program I wrote with the little graphic routine, and display the code. I have to use a copy, edit, write command to make the changes. It takes a little while.

"Man, you should have seen us in Vegas. At first, we worked together so we could increase our take from one setting. They caught on to that pretty fast. The security goons kept searching us for wires or something. They couldn't figure out why we were playing a long game and winning ever so slightly. We decided to split up and bounce around more so they can't identify us so easy."

"How does your so-called method work, exactly? You know you can fool me and you can even fool mother, but you can't fool Mother Nature."

"Smart ass! You should know this stuff, being a mathematician and all."

"Physicist."

"Whatever. It's really simple. As a dealer uses up the cards in his deck, there may have been one kind of card or another dealt more, so they can be counted, and then you take advantage of that in predicting the next cards. If done properly, you should know what the last two cards have to be."

"Who the hell has the memory for that, especially when drinking?"

"We use tricks like counting fingers under the table or a simple up-down count of number cards vs picture cards. We don't drink, actually, and I think that's what gives us away. Dealers see us acting professionally for too long, while slowly winning. We tried tipping, but the little slimes will rat you out anyway if they get a chance. Now, we look for newbie dealers or women who might be a little easier to con."

"I take it they're increasing the number of decks they deal from to even out the odds for any disparity to arise."

"Doesn't matter. As long as we keep a running up and down count, all we do is wait for a disparity to show up and then take advantage of it. I just want to practice it for a while to see if it works. Your dealer is stupid and doesn't care."

"So, you might want more than just two decks?"

"Of course. Can you do that?

"Sure. Just have to define a new variable and let it range over, say 1 to 10, and I'll assign that value to the incremental size of the number of decks."

"Jesus, Cowboy, how did you get to be so damn smart and still be a dumb-ass."

"Good looks, talent, and clean living. What did you think?"

*

"My boy is driving me crazy," complains Linda Powers on the phone. "He's interested in computers and secret codes and games, but he doesn't know anything about them and we can't afford a two-thousand-dollar toy right now."

"How is the toy shop?" I ask innocently, not expecting a full business analysis.

"Actually, quite good. People are responding to my organic toys that are safe and educational."

Linda rents the downstairs storefront in the new building just erected where the old post office used to be. Her husband, Dennis Powers, is well-known in town for being the best card counter around. As he bragged to me one time, "I've been thrown out of so many casinos between Vegas and Monte Carlo that I now have to wear makeup and disguises."

"Can you maybe teach him computer lessons or something?" she asks. "I'll pay for your time."

"Sure, why not? I can teach him programming and he'll be a step ahead of everybody when he hits college."

"Oh, that would be wonderful and he can have somewhere to go after school instead of hanging out at the bars."

I laugh. It's not that bad, but in the off-season, kids in town have a tough time keeping themselves busy. But with all the high-achieving parents in town, kids here enjoy adult freedoms and some strange advantages, like mountaineering, wilderness survival, and self- reliance training. Learning computer programming might as well be one of them.

I think about some of the new families in town. Dennis and Linda are a good example. He is a world traveler and professional gambler, she a small toy shop owner in the best little toy town in America, and their son, well on his way to a bright future in a technological world. I wonder if they are as happy as I am, with Susie. I wonder about our future being like them.

*

It's Christmas Eve. We close the theater after showing *It's a Wonderful Life* and hit the bars for a quicky, but they are emptying fast. We walk home with a little snow falling. I stoke up the fires while Susie makes us some hot chocolate. We're relaxing in a spooner position on the overstuffed pillow couch watching illegal cable TV with the Mormon Tabernacle Choir performing its annual concert, when I have the strangest desire to touch her, spiritually, and make a deeper connection than what we already have.

"I think it's time we talk about getting married and starting a family," I whisper in her ear.

At first, I expect her to turn to me with her beautiful smile and maybe hug me or kiss me, showing her total agreement. Instead, I feel her body go rigid. She doesn't move or make a sound. Something is wrong.

Then I heard a quiet word. "No."

It seems like an abyss of black emptiness opens under my feet. I'm falling. I want to scream, but I can't. The blackness is blocking all rational thought or reason. All I can feel is sudden emptiness, a draining of my spirit. I'm being sucked into a hole bigger than the entire universe. I'm mentally flailing without any possible hope of finding purchase.

"What?!" I finally respond.

"I don't want to marry you. I don't want children."

I'm so stunned; I can't think of any possible words of polite conversation to follow. I never in my wildest imagination or paranoia ever anticipated being in this place. Not with Susie. We're ...special!

I hold her face in front of mine. I stare into her eyes. "After all we have done. After all we've said to each other. That's it?"

"No," she says, and starts to cry. "I love you. I just don't want to be married or have children."

"You do realize that family is the natural progression of lovers. Without a goal, how can we build a life together?"

"I can't explain it. I just can't be married and be a mother."

I stare at her for a long time searching for what I have so often been pleased to see before. I no longer see it. Strangely, she seems almost like a blank slate. It's time for action when words don't suffice.

I get up from the couch, turn around, and scoop her up in my arms. She goes along with it. I carry her to the spiral staircase and actually manage to struggle up the straining contraption to our bedroom, where I dump her on the waterbed, causing a small tsunami against the opposite wall. She's smiling her little wicked look, making me horny as hell. I jump on her, making even more waves, and start wrestling her clothes off. She responds by taking off mine and we have hot Christmas sex, which I'm not sure is good or bad, it's just an explosion of raw feelings and animal desires pent up between two passionate people. All I can think of is how I can't let her settle for a lesser man. True love just doesn't walk away unconcerned with the first bump in the road. I love her and she loves me. That should still mean something, even in these sexual revolutionary times, I just need to find her again like we did in the first place. I have to do it. I can't let this die.

"I ... have ... to ... do ... it ... do ... it ... do ..." I catch myself grunting.

"It's okay dear! You did it!"

She wraps her arms around me and holds me tight until I seem to calm. I feel intense foreboding like the calm before a storm. I can't sleep.

*

The next night, after being busy during the daytime working at the computer shop, I show up at the theater about showtime, only to find Kathy handling the box office, with Susie nowhere in sight. Kathy isn't talking, and I have to show the movie.

An hour and a half later, I rush home on my klunker only to note upon arriving that hers is not in its usual spot on the front lawn. I go inside and sure enough, my worst nightmare begins to unfold predictably like a cheap horror film at a drive-in movie. Right in front of me, as I slowly walk around the house noting all the empty spots where her belongings used to be, I'm witnessing a new reality. With every discovery, a piece of me cries out with intolerable pain and loss. For every image I conjure, another knife slices keenly through my heart.

I run away from the scene of the murder as fast as my klunker will take me. I hit the nearest bar running and begin a spiral of sanity into alcoholic-riddled levels of abject paranoia, along with elaborate schemes of self-righteous redemption.

*

I can't sleep. I work in the daytime, show the movie at night, and haunt the bars till closing and then begin suffering the long lonely depressing hours of the deep night. I watch TV or listen to music. Nothing soothes my aching pain. I often go out walking just before dawn, usually landing at my favorite site for watching the sun rise: the CF&I bench park.

The roofs of the town are still in dark with an orange glow flowing overhead, slowly creeping downward until the whole valley lights up with shimmering golds and ambers. The peaks are still there, lit up like an impressionist painting, looming quietly overhead, reminding me of my well-defined insignificance.

Susie is staying with her friends, Jan Runge and Kathy Joyce. She is seen drinking a lot though with Texas Jane, the last person we had as a renter. Jane always has nothing nice to say about men and has a Texas-sized hard-on for some slight she must have endured by some equally dumb Texan.

I feel like one of the fools that Cathy Sporcich is always talking about. She can be counted on for knowing who is surreptitiously visiting whom late at night, and who might be headed for the next Butte Burns divorce. People who escape to the Butte come here mostly to find themselves and when they think they do, they often have to change partners, if they have one, just to prove their newfound freedom. My love for Susie was never that shallow. I can't believe her love for me was just another Aspen affair.

I try to make sure I know about all the parties in town that she gets invited to and make it a point to show up. I'm mostly drunk all the time and she is surrounded by male dogs sniffing her like a bitch in heat.

I lose it a couple of times, but never in a public way. One night, I slide the little Nissan off the CB Mountain Road, landing in the pasture on the other side of a barbed wire fence. I walk into town, catch the bars still open, and recruit several friends who help me retrieve the car, leaving nothing for the morning commuters to see but skid marks through an unbroken fence going nowhere.

*

RING! RING!

I rush to answer the phone because the downstairs door to the projection booth is open for air circulation, making it possible for the audience to hear it.

"Hello," I whisper, pulling the door closed. "Princess Theater."

"Hi Cowboy," comes the voice of Connie. "How's it going?"

"Just hunky-dory," I answer. "What's up with you?"

"I know about you and Susie. She can be stubborn sometimes."

"I'm sorry, when does stubborn turn to cuckolding?"

"Now Cowboy, you know about freedom and respect. It's her choice who to sleep with and it's her choice who to love. Don't confuse the two."

"I'm sorry for my conventional feelings, but I can tell the difference and there isn't any."

"That's too bad. I called to see if you want to come to our end-of-season ski instructors' party this Saturday. Susie is coming. Maybe she'll come over with you and you can get a chance to talk to her."

"I'd love to come. I'm planning on doing some flying this weekend, so maybe I'll fly over to Aspen. I'll see if I can get Susie to go with me."

"There you go. Keep a positive attitude. Things will work out, eventually."

"You know, you could help. Maybe tell her that I'm not as bad as some people are saying."

"I'll see what I can do. Let me know when you plan to land and I'll pick you up at the airport."

"Thanks Connie. I'll be there at one sharp. By the way, I never believed all those stories about you, if that makes any difference."

"What do you mean?"

"Gotta go, changeover's coming."

I hang up.

*

It's a beautiful sunny day and I'm way early. I decide to ride my klunker to the airport for some exercise and fresh air. I've been cooped up lately, feeling sorry for myself. Susie is going to miss a wonderful flight over to Aspen just because she's stubborn.

I get to the airport, winded but still on schedule. I pull the plane out, preflight it, and start it up. The runway has a down slope to the south, so when I can I take off downhill, which gets me in the air just a little bit faster. I need all the runway I can get at this altitude.

I leave the pattern, do a big circle around Crested Butte Mountain, gaining altitude from the southerly slopes and their updrafts from the direct heat of the sun. When I get to the north, I peel off and follow the river to Gothic and then turn right into Copper Creek Canyon.

It's a stunning day and I see hikers and tents below on the trails between Copper Creek and Conundrum. I fly the side of the canyon like all good bush pilots so I have the benefit of room to turn around if I get in trouble and a position to see over the pass for traffic on the other side before venturing over. Once safely over the pass, it's a straight shot down the Maroon Bells trail to Aspen and the airport north of town.

I call the tower and let them know I'm coming and set it down right on schedule. I taxi up to the public ramp and spot Connie standing next to a station wagon in the parking lot through the fence. I shut the Piper off and give it a quick tie-down before joining Connie outside.

"Hi darlin'," I greet her. I hold out my hand, but she brushes it aside and comes in for a kiss—yeah, fully on the lips. I'm startled and feel pleasantly rewarded at the same time.

"I know how you must be feeling. I'm truly sorry." She kisses me again and this time it's with tongue. She hangs on to my neck, pulling me down into her web of entwining arms and grasping hands.

For the first time in months, I feel welcoming warmth and deep desires welling up inside me. *This is Connie, you fool,* I tell myself. *It's not going to help get Susie back.*

"I know what you need," she declares, after coming up for air. "Get in the car. I know where we can go."

I'm having trouble talking, so I just nod my head and get in.

"I don't understand why Susie didn't fly over with you today. I would have. I like flying."

"Yeah, it's fun. Where's the party?"

"Susie and the hikers won't be here for a while. I thought we could stop by a friend's house before meeting up at the party. I know where he keeps his coke."

"Really?"

"It looks like you need some emergency happiness. Does it hurt much?"

"What?"

"Susie. Does it hurt?"

"Unbearable. I wish I could just kill my feelings and wake up without fear of an empty future."

"Maybe this will help." She leans over and grabs me by the crotch with her right hand, unerringly finding its mark.

"Oh!" I blurt out.

I'm wondering if this is a new morality among the wealthy and useless. Separating love and sex so you can have as much as you want of the latter, while keeping faith with the former. Does Susie still love me while fucking every tom, dick, and harry that hits town? Somehow the thought is not comforting.

"Here we are. Come on upstairs and relax before the big show."

What we do is anything but relaxing. She has her clothes off and mine within minutes of entering the apartment. She grabs some paraphernalia from the coffee table and leads me into the one bedroom and a king size waterbed. Before I realize what is happening, I find myself making cool and generous love to Connie...the other Susie. I want to make a good impression, to thank her for her thoughtfulness, so I play my *A game.*

I go down on her in earnest and suck, lick, and chew my darndest on all her best parts, massaging with ardor all the parts needing that sort of attention. And she reciprocates. Oh, how she reciprocates. I can't believe she is from the same family I knew so well back in Connecticut. Again, I'm wondering if the morals of this generation are getting to such a liberal state that I can only imagine them. No jealousy. No possessiveness. No feelings of being taken for granted. Just pure sex for the pleasure and love for the long haul. I don't know if I can handle that. But I'm willing to try if it's that important to Susie.

We alternate between sessions of pure sensual delight with moments of motivational replenishment for our bodies. After an hour of showing off all my best moves and welcoming her warm advances, we end up in a tangle of naked limbs and well-licked flesh slowly squirming in the middle of a wave machine. I can't help it. I like it. After all, am I not a man with manly needs?

But soon, my thoughts are back on Susie and how much I want to see her now. I feel a new energy that Connie gives me, knowing it will only be redirected at my true love. I don't feel guilty of anything. I'm loved and am capable of loving and still know who I love. That's all that is important.

We finally get dressed and go to the party. There are a lot of people I don't know, so I hang out near the bar waiting for Susie to show.

When she does, she is so busy with her friends and family I can't get much of a chance to even say hi. She seems happy, but I can tell she is faking a lot of it. Her laughter is forced. She puts up a good front that works for most people, but not me. I know her inner being.

After a while, I ask Connie to take me back to the airport. I'm not going to get a chance to talk to Susie. I'll have to hope that Connie can put in a good word for me and maybe make her re-think the path she's now on.

I get back to Crested Butte airport just before sunset. As I'm putting the plane away in the hangar, another plane lands. It's a Cessna 310 like Leinsdorf's, but a different color. He lands in the wrong direction. He zooms by the hanger about another thousand feet before turning it around and taxiing back up to the hangars.

I get on my klunker and start to ride back to town, when I hear someone shout.

"Hey there!" yells a bearded long-haired guy from the Cessna. "Can you help me push my plane back into the hangar?"

"Sure!" I yell back and turn around. When I get back, he's out of the plane fixing a push rod on the front wheel.

"My name is Robert. Robert Pimentel."

"Cowboy," I answer, and shake his hand. "I've heard of you."

"Same here. You run the Princess, right?"

"And you dish out the cocaine to girls like it's ice cream."

"Guilty as charged. I do like the ladies. You ski?"

"Sometimes. Nice plane. I've always liked the looks of these. Too bad they're underpowered."

"Not this baby. Twin turbo-charged Lycoming 540s. What are you flying?"

I push on a leading edge while he pushes and steers with the T-hook.

"Non turbo 180 horse Piper Colt. Belongs to Ron. I get to fly off the money they owe me from building that beacon on Smith Hill." I point to the south.

"Nice. So, you did that? Works great, especially on moonless nights."

He parks the plane, chocks a wheel, and we leave the hangar.

"You know, you really shouldn't land in the wrong direction here, especially doing a straight-in approach. You can't see the opposite end very well and someone could be taking off."

"Two planes using the runway at the same time? Hardly likely." He points at my klunker. "What did you do? Ride your bike out here?"

"You didn't?" I joke. "It's too damned far to walk."

"I'll give you a ride back to town. I can throw your bike in the back of my station wagon over there."

"Cool. Thanks."

On the way back to town, Robert mentions he knows Mitchell and admires his motivation to keep on flying with hand controls after crashing his Cessna and ending up a paraplegic. I agree and have a moment of dark dread, imagining Mitchell crashing his plane again. Secretly, I'm afraid of flying but do it because it's the manly thing to do for a guy like me. It's a step on the way to manhood that I choose to include with my other manly skills. I also ski and fly fish, but they're not nearly as dangerous.

*

I see very little of Susie after the party. She shows up for work most nights, but stays elusive and soon disappears at the end of the movie, sometimes before I can even rewind the film and lock up the booth. She's not seen in the normal bars and instead spends a lot of time hitting the new haute-cuisine, organic-swamp-moss eateries that are going up in every little quaint barnwood garage in the alleys of Crested Butte, the same buildings that just a couple of years ago were used to house four or five kids needing a cheap place to crash. Young kids escaping society are not coming here anymore. They can't afford it. I wonder what happened to the sleepy little village of yore that beckoned us here.

I finish another day of pretending to do productive work at the computer office. I have one client that pays the bills, but I turn down Amax when they call wanting to sign up as a client. They like the computer printout paper for their accounting reports. It makes it look so much more high techie and official.

I honestly feel I can't take their money in all good conscience, as my community is fighting their efforts to tear down a beautiful mountain and I feel obliged to aid in that fight any way I can. After all, I am one of the *FUCK AMAX* gang. I probably will regret this move because without more high-paying clients like them, I'm not likely to be successful enough to support living here. I'm about to try making a presentation to the ski area management to do their bookkeeping when I learn they bought an accounting computer at high cost and plan to do it all in-house.

The phone rings. I'm at home watching late-night HBO.

I answer. "Yeah?"

"Cowboy?" asks Susie.

I perk up. "Who else?" I pause to get my breath. "Que paso?"

"I need your help," she adds slowly.

I think she's drunk. "What's going on?"

"I'm down at the Nickel and some guys are buying me drinks and they want me to go home with them."

"I'll get my gun and be right down there." I wait for the laugh but it doesn't come.

"I don't want to go with them again. Can you come down here and be my boyfriend so I can escape?"

I'm stunned. I don't know what to say. She tears a new hole in my heart every time I hear of her sex exploits. I'm feeling psychopathic numb as we speak. My hands are shaking.

"You want me to rescue you from another man?"

"Please. I can't keep fighting him off and he has friends."

Oh, shit is my only thought. *What the hell is she doing? This is not my Susie. Do I need to help her, or is she just taunting me?*

"Okay," I give in. "I'll be right down."

"Hurry," she says, and hangs up.

I walk into the Nickel at around 1 a.m. I see a couple of my friends drinking at the bar. I look down the bar and spot Susie at the other end talking to a large man wearing casual golf clothes with short hair. *What has she sunk to?* I ask myself. As I pass by my friends, I tap them lightly on the back and when they turn, I just point down the bar and give them the signal to watch my back. I slowly approach the pair and notice a few more turkeys dressed for the yacht club, sitting at a nearby table.

I deliberately push myself up to the bar between them. I hold up a twenty and wave it around.

"Hey! Starr! How about a shot and a shot."

"Sure thing, Cowboy!"

I turn toward Susie and ask, "And how about you? Can I get you anything?"

She looks nervously behind me and says, "No, I'm just finishing mine."

"Pardon me," the big guy behind me says. "The lady is with me and I'll be buying her drinks here."

"I didn't offer you one," I say without turning away from Susie.

Starr shows up with a double shot of Crown and a tall soda water back. "Here you go, Cowboy," he says, then looks at the guy behind me. Turning back to me, he asks, "Is there a problem here?"

That's local bar code talk meaning, say the word and I'll come over this bar with a baseball bat swinging.

"No," I say calmly. "Susie is just finishing up her drink and needs to go home. Don't ya girl?" I lean over to pat her on the back and whisper in her ear that now is the time to walk out.

"Hey, wait a minute," says the golf turkey. "You were going home with me! And who the hell are you?"

He stands up, but the bar stools are mounted on a riser foot beam running the length of the bar and when he steps over it, I hook his ankle with my foot and he slips off the rail and falls backwards onto the table of his friends. I push Susie off her bar stool and aim her at the door. "Go! I'll talk to you tomorrow."

Meanwhile, my friends at the bar get up and come back, helping me and Starr surround the broken table and the three drunk turkeys demanding somebody replace their spilled drinks. We help them up and individually run them to the door and give them the old heave-ho as we kick them out for breaking glasses.

They're standing in the street yelling shit at the bar when Hitchcock walks across from the Grubstake, takes one look, and says, "Goddamnit. I missed the fun again. Can we invite them in again for a rematch?"

*

The next day I look around for Susie but can't find her anywhere. A couple days later, Dennis Hall is in the Grubstake, so I ask if he's seen her.

"I think she left town with some guy who hired her last winter for ski instruction. He's from Nashville, or somewhere back there in the woods. Had a lot of money he flashed around last winter buying her a lot of coke. Had some myself. Wasn't bad."

"She left town with a coke dealer?"

"He's not a coke dealer if he pays retail for it. I think he made his money in real estate or something."

"She's with a coked-up real estate salesman from Nashville? How much more am I going to have to endure? Something is definitely wrong with that girl."

"Don't be a fool, Cowboy. There's nothing you can do, and if you do, it will only be taken badly."

"But I have to do something," I whine. "I can't stand to see her like this."

"Why don't you take a trip somewhere? Get your attention on other things. You need to heal and this place is just a big emotional grinding machine when it comes to star-crossed love affairs. Why do you think they call it, *As the Butte Burns?*"

As much as I don't like his arrogance, this time Dennis nails it. I need to get out of town and rebuild my self-respect. I call Bill Smith, my old friend and a major dealer from Ann Arbor.

~ 19 ~

LIFE, LOVE, AND DEATH

"**H**ey Cowboy! What's up?" Bill asks after finally picking up the phone and hearing me growl *'Finally!'*

"Not me. I'm sorry to have to report that I had everything and lost it. I built a cable TV company only to have my partner steal it from me. Now my honest-to-god true love has gone off with a real estate salesman from Nashville. I'm strung so tight I may have to shoot something. Just to watch it die."

"You don't waste time getting on the roller coaster, but don't shoot anybody. I was actually just thinking of you yesterday. I've got a problem down here I think you just might be able to help me with."

"Like what?"

"It's kind of complicated, but my business requires me to monitor a Coast Guard marine VHF radio channel, but the damned thing is too close to a local time broadcast station, which interferes with it here at my house."

"Got it. No problem. Where's your house?"

"Pine Key."

"Fly me down there for a week and I'll fix your problem."

"That's the confident Cowboy I once knew. I'll get you tickets. Where the hell is your nearest airport?"

"Gunnison."

"Never heard of it. I'll call the airlines and see if they've heard of it. Meantime, what do you think we need to fix this?"

"Custom notch filter. Just get me the exact frequency of the offending signal and I'll order a notch filter to remove it from your receiver."

"What else you going to need?"

"A lot of cocaine and weed. I've got a lot of forgetting to do."

"Been there, done that, collected the T-shirt. Can't wait to see you ol' buddy."

"I'm dying to see you, too. Literally."

I fly to Miami where Bill and his latest squeeze, Jeanette, pick me up at the airport. It's bright and sunny as we cross the bridge to the Keys. He bought a little two-story cabin inland and is surrounded by palm trees on Pine Key. It's very secluded and private, just like Bill prefers. I deposit my bag in the spare room on the first floor, where nobody lives because it's hard to keep the insects out. We go upstairs on an outside stairway and enter the main living area, settling around the kitchen table where Bill does all his business and holds daily cocaine court.

"Good to see you man. It's been a while. Remember that crazy dude in Palm Beach? Danny...?"

"Donner. Yeah, he's dead."

"*Whoa!* What happened? He didn't blow himself up with that plastique I gave him?"

"No. Nothing that interesting. He choked to death hanging himself in a closet and masturbating."

"Man! You know how to find them."

"Not really. They find me and I like to observe the fringe. That's why I like you so much. You're interesting fringe."

"Fringe this!" he says, flipping me the bird. He laughs and pulls out a giant joint rolled with fresh Columbian weed. "This is my new business down here. Like everyone else, we're in the import-export business. Check this out. We fish for the square groupers."

He opens a cabinet door behind him and pulls out a giant brick of tightly packed something, wrapped up in what looks like shrink wrap and duct tape.

"Ever see one of these? It's a ten-kilo bale of weed direct from Columbia."

"Actually, I have. Remember my airplane trip to El Paso?"

"Oh, yeah. Anyway, when the South American fishing boats approach the coast at night to meet smaller speedboats that bring the shit ashore, they sometimes get popped by the Coast Guard. They'll dump their load in the ocean to try and frustrate the Coast Guard and that's when I show up with a hook and a faster boat."

"You've got a boat?"

"When I first came down here in the Winnebago, I worked at a marina learning all about marine engines. You know me, I like to be the fastest fish in the pond, and with two 250-horse Merc engines on the back of a 16-foot open fiberglass hull, I can get lost in these mango swamps with a load of pot real fast."

"Except every once in a while," Jeanette points out, "he zigs when he should zag and ends up hitting a mango tree at sixty miles an hour."

"You're kidding!" I exclaim. "What happened?"

"Ah, it was nothing. I was going too fast and couldn't quite make the turn. My boat hit the bank sideways and I was thrown out and broke an arm."

"Or two! He was laid up for six months," Jeanette added. "I had to feed him in bed."

"If something happens while you're down here, maybe you can go out with me and see how it's done."

"How do you know when to go out?" I ask the obvious.

"Simple, I have one of those Radio Shack VHF scanners. I listen to the Coast Guard marine bands and when they show activity launching a bunch of boats without any emergencies going on, I know something is up. By going out and using the marine radio to listen to the boats talk to each other, I can figure out how to intercept them. Then it's just a matter of standing back to watch the action and wait for a bail to go floating by. It's kind of like fishing, I'm told."

"And if they see you?"

"They don't, but you know me. I love to bait 'em and then lead them into the mango swamps around here where I know the territory and can find water paths where their big boats can't follow."

"You know, there are just so many times you can break a leg and still have it work right."

"Believe me, you haven't lived until you've driven a speedboat through these swamps, at night, with no lights."

"Thanks, but I'm pretty sure I'll live longer without the experience."

"So, my problem is, there's a local high-power VHF station nearby that transmits weather and time information to ships in the Caribbean. It's so powerful, it interferes with my monitoring the Coast Guard bands right next door."

"Yeah, that's always a problem when living near a high-power transmitter. It overdrives the front end of all sensitive receivers, which then creates side bands that cause interference and noise for any weak signals nearby. Here's your solution...." I pull out a folded piece of paper from my briefcase and hand it to him. It's an invoice for a custom-made notch filter at the same frequency as the high-power signal. "This will remove it from the front end of the receiver, which kills the interference and lets the low-power signals get through, unaffected."

"Great! Where is it?"

"It's coming COD by US Mail. Should be here tomorrow or the next day. In the meantime, I want to see Hemingway's house and the bar where Jimmy Buffet plays. I want the full Key West experience. I have a broken heart that needs mending or blending or something."

"Maybe this will make you feel better," he says with a wicked smile. He pulls out a mirror from another kitchen cabinet and it has about a dozen fat lines already laid out. Looks like he was expecting me.

*

I get the whirlwind tour of Key West over the next few days. We see the Hemingway house and wander the beaches and bars where nobody wears long pants or long-sleeved shirts. If I wasn't such a mountain lover, I could get into this place. It's no big challenge staying warm here, but there's nothing on the horizon to climb except water—lots and lots of water.

Bill shows me his boat which he keeps discreetly at a small private dock owned by one of the biggest promoters in the Keys. He has 24-hour access and can drive right up to the boat for that late-night secure transfer of their evening's catch. We go out for a nice day of cruising around the Keys in the bright sunshine while smoking fresh reefer straight off the boat, so to speak.

Jeanette and I enjoy a beer or a margarita, while Bill doesn't understand why we use such gutter drugs when we can have coke. He has a little methadone left over from the good ol' days back in Ann Arbor, where he once proudly showed me an entire cabinet full of liter bottles of the stuff. All super-good American pharmaceutical grade. But all it ever did for me was make me nauseous. So, I stick to alcohol and weed with a little cocaine when I can afford it.

The RF filter shows up and I have to pick it up from the post office, paying cash at the window, counting out a lot of used twenties. Nothing suspicious here and nothing they haven't seen before.

We go back to his house and I spend the rest of the day hooking it up to the VHF antenna on his roof and his little scanner. This time when he tunes to the Coast Guard channel, the interfering signal is gone. It's clean and clear as if it didn't even exist. Bill's face lights up and he begins messing with the radio controls, scanning all the channels he was blocked from before. I figure I've earned my keep for the day, so Jeanette and I mix up a pitcher of margaritas to celebrate and roll up a couple of fat doobies.

"Bill tells me you just broke up with your girlfriend," she gently broaches the subject. "I'm so sorry for you. I know what it's like to lose a lover and best friend. Fortunately for me, Bill came along just at the right time to take me away from all my troubles."

"Yeah, he has unerring timing when it comes to finding broken birds."

"What?" she asks, handing me a burning joint from behind the cloud of smoke surrounding her head.

"I'm glad you two found each other. He was pretty broke up when his last love of eight years ran away with the local DJ to some Rock & Roll hideout in Texas."

"Texas?" she says while coughing out more smoke.

"Oh, yeah, he crashed pretty hard. Lost his house, lost his business, and pretty much got run out of town for being too good at his job. Ah, the punishments we suffer from our impertinent successes."

"So, how are you feeling?" she inquires seriously. "From what Bill was telling me, you're taking this pretty hard. Have you tried to make up with her? Are you still talking to each other?"

"I'm trying to maintain a connection. I'm hoping she'll see that I'm the only one who truly loves her without reservation. I love her with all my heart and with all my brain, which is considerable. I want to see the future with her. I want to buy her diamonds from an Egyptian souk. I want to hike the Victoria Falls with her. We are so good together. We run theaters and festivals together. We might even make movies together. We could become a legend if she would just see again what she originally saw."

"That's so romantic. If she has any feeling at all, she'll see that you are the one for her, for always. You just need to be brave, true, and patient. When you get home, call her. Tell her what you're telling me. Be honest and sincere. She'd have to have a hollow soul and a cold heart not to be with the one fighting the most for her."

*

A couple of nights later, I'm pretending to sleep while lying on the downstairs spare folding bed listening to the tiny scratching and tippy-tapping sounds that insects, spiders and other creepy-crawlers make while stomping around in the dark, looking for easy blood.

"Cowboy?" Jeanette calls from outside my door. "You awake?"

"No, I was just dreaming of my true love. What's up?"

"Yeah, I bet," she jokes, opening the door and barging into who knows what. "Put some clothes on and take a jacket. Bill has a possible fish run going on. He's leaving for the boat soon. Wants you to come with him."

"Might as well take the guided tour while staying *Chez Smythe.*"

I climb out of bed and find my clothes. She immediately turns and goes back outside, where I hear Bill's voice.

"Is he coming?" he asks.

"I think so."

"I'm coming. I'm coming. Like the ocean won't be there when we get there?'

"It's not that," he answers back. "We just don't want to be at the back of the line when we get there."

"Back of the line?!" I ask outside, and climb into the front seat of his '74 455 ci Riviera convertible. Bill likes this model because it can do what Mercedes brags about: going 140 miles per hour. His dogs have liked them too, eating a few in the past. *No dogs in Florida*, I notice. I wonder if that means something.

"You'll see." He kisses Jeanette on the cheek, jumps in, and cranks up the big-block Buick aluminum engine. I close my eyes. In a short time, we're on his boat.

"As we go out on a heading of 270," he explains, "I watch those lights on the left and the lights to the north. I can navigate pretty good on a clear night and follow the chart here...." He indicates with his headlamp the folded-up chart showing the area around where we're heading. He points to a spot about in the middle.

"They're reported to be heading to this location for a boat interception by the immigration cops. I think that's code for import violations. They're careful not to mention the DEA, but who else would scramble at this hour of the night?"

"You got me," I admit.

"It's good there's no wind. The water won't be very choppy if we have to make a run for it."

"Run for it?" I repeat. "Where do we run to?" I look around and we look pretty lonesome and exposed out here, even though he has no lights on. I can't see other boats or anything else except the lights from shore.

"Don't worry," he responds confidently, "They can't see us on their radar. Not enough metal to get a signal to bounce. All we have to do is stay ahead of their spotlights."

We cruise along at a good clip for about a half an hour when he suddenly pulls the power and we drift to a stop, I'm guessing about ten miles from shore. I can hardly see any lights at all now.

"Now we wait. I think I saw a light over there just before stopping." Even though it's dark as hell without a moon, he scans the horizon with his binoculars.

"So, what kind of a girl is this Susie you speak of?" He lowers the binoculars and looks at me.

"Now I know what you went through with Patty. I love this girl without any reservations or hesitations. She's a natural, helping me when she can, me helping her always. There was literally nothing I wouldn't have done for her except, maybe, knocking off her old lady, who deserves it."

"She's from a rich family I take it."

"One of the richest, I'm told. I don't care. She doesn't care. I thought we had way more together than just sex. We fit together in so many other ways. We could have done things together. Important things."

"Reminds me of a girl I knew from Dearborn Heights. Before Patty, there was Barbara. She hated her daddy and ran away with me to my garage in Ann Arbor when I used to live in the attic. Somedays, we didn't bother to see the daylight."

"Tell me about it," I concur. "Sometimes you couldn't tell where my skin left off and hers began, we were so...in tune."

"You must be about terminally suicidal by now," he guesses. "Don't do it while you're visiting. I can't explain such things very well and would have to just dump you out here for the sharks and bottom fish to eat."

"Jeanette seems to think I should try to win her back with charm and persistence. What do you think?"

"I hate to tell you, but Jeanette is a terminal optimist. I've found it more likely they'll take charm for harassment and persistence for stalking."

"I just want our happy life back."

"You're a smart guy," he reassures me. "You'll find someone who really deserves you. Remember, the one who leaves is the one using the other. You've been used and abused and abandoned. What do you think rich people do for laughs anyway?"

Damn, he can be brutal sometimes, but honest. Then he looks past me.

"There it is!" he suddenly shouts. "Look!" He points off our port bow to what I see now are some spotlights on the horizon. One is moving rapidly. He turns on the hand-held scanner and listens to some traffic going back and forth on two channels. Then he tunes it to the weather report and writes down the winds and tide information. He makes some notes on the chart and draws a line across it.

"This is the heading reported for the bogey fishing boat by the Coast Guard. I've extended it according to the currents and winds. Somewhere along this line we should be able to find anything they might have dumped when the pigs showed up. Now we have to sneak in there close to the action while we're looking for bales."

He grabs the wheel and starts the engines up and begins slowly moving toward the lights. He pulls out a long police flashlight with a paper tube wrapped around the front lens so the light can't be seen from the side. He sweeps it back and forth on the water as he tries to follow the path of the fishing boat, now closer, which we can see is flanked by two other boats with bright lights aimed at her. Bill moves slowly at a tangent to a downwind position. Pretty soon, we spot something bobbing in the water. It's low and dark-colored, really hard to see if we weren't actually looking for something.

"Bingo!" he shouts, and heads for it. I man the boat hook and standby at the side of the boat. He brings her about on my side and I hook it solidly, pulling it up to the side of the boat. Bill helps me haul it aboard. It weighs enough to make it hard for the two of us to lift it. My mind does the math and I come up with about a fifty-kilo bale worth close to twenty grand.

"Let's get out of here," he whispers, and I shake my head in agreement as I watch the lights still surrounding the fishing boat move off in the distance. I finally calm the uncontrollable shaking in my legs as Bill gives the gas to the two Mercs and we roar off into the darkness.

*

"You know, with your flying skills, I could introduce you to some very interesting characters down here," Bill offers over a breakfast of cocaine, coffee, orange juice, and a dozen Pop-tarts. Jeanette puts a bottle of cheap bourbon on the table for those wishing to add a little sweetener to their coffee. I add two fingers to mine.

"I don't know about flying low and slow over water," I respond, after taking a sip of the coffee. "I'm kind of specializing on mountain flying."

"Why do you want to do that? Hell, just add turbo and anyone can fly the mountains. *Over* the mountains." He laughs at his own joke, takes a hit off one of the lines on the ever-present mirror, and hands it over to me. "But seriously, they'll get you the airplane you need. All you have to do is fly it to an island in the Caribbean and back to some dirt road out in the swamp. Easiest twenty grand you'll ever make."

"The movie plot runs like this: *I run out of gas and have to land it on a freeway where I get hit by an eighteen-wheeler hauling weed.* Irony sells these days."

"In any case, if you ever get tired of shoveling snow out of your ass, come on down. At least we can go fishing together." He fist bumps me.

"I have to go back and fix my life. I can't think about leaving my home and my love all at the same time."

"Good luck with that. Be sure and send me a card if you get work."

Bill pays me five hundred bucks for my help and takes me back to the airport. With this money, I can survive the summer at least, and maybe turn Susie around. I can't think about anything else.

Of course, when I hit Stapleton, the last connecting flight to Gunnison has been cancelled, stranding me in Denver for the night. I decide to go all out and boldly call Susie's sister to see if I can stop by, maybe stay for the night. I find a pay phone and dial the number.

"Hello?" I recognize Alice's voice.

"Alice. It's Cowboy. I'm sorry to bother you, but I'm stuck at the airport and wondered if I could come over for the night."

"Oh. It's you." She lowers her voice level. "I don't think that would be a good idea. She's here and she doesn't want to see you. Not tonight. Not here."

"But we need to talk. I can do whatever she wants me to do. I love her!"

"I know. I'm sorry. I like you, but I can't help you. Sorry. Good-bye." She hangs up.

Just like that. So simple. So final. So disturbing. So painful. So deep. So black. I suddenly have a need to get very, very drunk. I hail a cab, tell him to take me to the nearest liquor store, where I buy a fifth of Crown. He then takes me to the cheapest hotel near the airport, where I check in, find my room, and start pounding down shots with soda water in a can. I draw a hot bath and crawl in, waiting for the alcohol to numb me to the point of not caring anymore.

I'm lying in the bed, getting seriously dizzy and having trouble standing up or moving without holding onto something.

I'm crying and listening to late-night FM from Boulder. I try to stand up and go piss in the bathroom, but just at the door, it all goes black for a couple of seconds and I go down, hard. My forehead hits the porcelain sink causing a gash that starts to bleed, but no blessed unconsciousness yet. I lie on the cold floor feeling disgust, pain, and rising vomit all together. I can't even punish myself for any relief from the thought of what I am losing. I've gone from the very top to the very bottom and I swear, I did nothing to deserve it.

*

I drag myself back to the airport in plenty of time to catch the first flight out at 5 a.m. I have a big band-aid on my forehead and feel like some jungle animal's diarrheal shit freshly scraped off a rock. I'm still alive. I'm still alive and I'll probably never see my Susie again.

As soon as I'm back home, though, and back at my two jobs, my desperation again turns to denial and false hope. Then all hell breaks loose in Crested Butte: our simple little pristine paradise hits the national news again.

ASPEN TIMES, June 18, 1980: Nine Aspen area residents were among the 10 persons killed in two plane crashes near the summit of East Maroon Pass. Authorities are not certain whether the two planes found near the summit of the pass at the head of East Maroon Creek, 13 miles south-southwest of Aspen, collided in mid-air or crashed separately. The two privately owned planes, a six-passenger Cessna 310 and a four-passenger Cessna 182, were found by a search plane sent out from Sardy Field to find the Cessna 182. The six aboard the Cessna 310 were returning from a birthday party in Crested Butte given for one of the plane's passengers, Brenda Boyd. The party was held at a restaurant belonging to another passenger, Michael Pokress. The Cessna 182 had left Sardy Field at 11:10 a.m. bound for Gunnison and was found 50 feet from the summit of the 11,820-foot pass. ...Aboard the Cessna 182 bound for Gunnison were pilot Jeff Kest, Pat Palangi, Tom Spillane and Rudy Csadenyi. Aboard the Cessna 310 bound for Aspen were pilot Robert Pimentel of Crested Butte, Brenda Boyd, Michael Pokress, Ellen Pokress, Betsy Hube and David Freeman.

"Did you hear what happened?" asks the Rat, as I sit down beside him at the Grubstake.

"Somebody stole one of Mitchell's wheels and he's stuck turning in a circle out in front of Sancho's."

"Good one, but no. Two planes collided over Maroon Pass. Ten people are dead. Pimentel's plane is one of them and the other is from Aspen. Tap and Lou went up there to take a look."

It's too crazy to be real. Ten people from this area is a *Titanic* kind of catastrophe. I just talked to Robert a couple weeks ago. I look at Rat and he looks at me. We both turn back to the bar and call out for a shot and a shot. Faude is at the other end of the bar talking to others about the same subject, no doubt. This is about as bad as it can get around here. It's like, we don't deserve such tragedies. We're the good people.

I guess I haven't been paying attention to the Butte social life these days. I have been so wrapped up with my work and living with Susie and all her friends, that I have sort of been out of the ever-changing local scene for a while. Pimentel had come over from Aspen only a couple of years ago and is very well-known for his generosity and kindness, especially to the ladies.

As I walk around town this week, I can't help but notice that most of the young girls are all teary-eyed and huggie-prone. When the Bump died a few years ago, we just had a simple wake, got stinking high and drunk, and told stories about his many escapades. This sadness has a different poignancy to it.

When a young person full of life is suddenly struck down by a fickle twist of fate, well, we just feel something is seriously wrong with the world and it needs to go back to the way we were. Psychologists say we are just feeling bad for ourselves, out of the guilt knowing that we continue on while someone close has ceased to exist in an arbitrary and senseless manner. It could happen to anyone, anytime. Sleep well tonight, for who knows what the morrow will bring?

Connie calls me at the theater the next night and mentions that she and Susie are going to attend the wake next week to be held at Pimmy's house on Third Street.

"If you want to crash at our house, tell Susie I won't attack her. I'll be respectful. I just want to talk."

"We'll see, but I think we are staying with Lynn. You'll be able to see Susie at the wake. Just BYO with something we can tolerate."

"What can you tolerate?"

"About six feet and a lot of muscle. Oh, you mean liquor. Surprise us."

*

End of the week finally comes amid a flurry of stories and rumors concerning the accident. I use my computer to actually connect it to the outside world, using a new thing that I built, called a voice modem, *Pennywhistle*, that has a handset cradle and can send and receive data over an ordinary phone. I dial the number and when a modem at the other end answers with a whistle, I set the handset on the modem cradle and it starts talking over the phone in beeps and whistles. Next thing I know, my terminal prints out a "?" and returns waiting for input. I type "?notam" and my printer comes alive printing out the FAA NOTAMS, or notices to airmen, for the day.

I'm searching for the report on Maroon Bells because rescuers have been up there working in the snow all week getting the bodies out, along with major pieces of wreckage. Helicopters from the National Guard are being used and the FAA has that whole area closed to air traffic until they are done with the ground investigation. I read through all the fluff and finally find some notes from investigators on the ground. One statement catches my eye:

The 182 has evidence of propellor strikes across the main cabin slicing deep enough to break the main fuselage in half.

That pretty much explains what happened. All I have to do is put together Pimmy's penchant for making fast, direct flights between Crested Butte and Aspen, often clearing the pass at full speed with little more than a hundred feet of ground clearance. He probably never even saw the 182 until he hit something hard and it was all over in an instant.

Likewise, the 182 probably only saw the belly of the 310 at the last second as it cleared the pass in front of them, too low and too fast to avoid colliding. I've been over that pass many times, both in airplanes and on foot. I never once thought something like this would happen, even though I'm very cautious about flying low over passes for this very reason.

Why did Pimmy take the chance? He probably took it every time he flew the pass, knowing full well, as I do, that the chances of another airplane lurking out of sight right there at the same time and altitude are pretty slim and close to zero. This time it wasn't. What changed? *Simple*, I think. First, we build a ski area. Then the population increases with high-income people who own airplanes. Then we build an airport and start flying regularly to Aspen. The chances rise to one.

Five years ago, the chances for a collision were probably so low that it was almost an acceptable risk. Prudence and proper safety concerns, however, should guide our actions, anyway. But when you're young, cocky, and invincibly wealthy, and you like to show off your mountaineering skills, living in the extreme and enjoying the spotlight of being an interesting character, then hotshotting it across East Maroon Pass at fifty-foot altitudes becomes a macho habit that unfortunately one day proves fatal.

And it did. In a way, it was predictable, even though it never received the proper respect for its eventual occurrence. Pimentel was just plain foolish and dangerous. He killed ten people and a fetus; some his dearest and closest friends. But the people of the Butte treat him like an innocent victim or martyr, or some kind of an exceptional hero, someone to be remembered and idolized. For what?

I shake my head thinking about this oxymoron. How can people be so stupid and in clear conflict with reality and responsible behavior? Ten innocent full of life people went out on a beautiful day for a pleasant plane ride in the Rockies and died needlessly and tragically, all because of one man's decision to act recklessly. Is this something that should be remembered and held up for admiration?

While the funeral is being held in one of our picturesque churches that rarely gets used these days, except for weddings and occasions like this, most of the Grubstake Gang are getting a head start on the drinking part. Now that I'm sort of single, I find myself hanging again with the likes of the Rat, Coney the conehead, and the Weazel. We all knew Pimmy, as he was called, because at some point or another, we all passed him or vice versa at a party in town or on the slopes or in the bars, after hours. He was generous with the coke and so we counted him as one of us, even though he probably didn't think the same way. It really doesn't matter anymore. We have to give one of us a proper send-off no matter the circumstances, and that include a lot of public intoxication and laughing memories retold.

At the appointed hour, we all leave the bar and cross the Coal Creek bridge to the north side where new money is building National Preservation-compliant houses worth hundreds of thousands of dollars. We join people already coming from the church walking in the same direction.

"I just heard they're planning to scatter his ashes in the stream at the wake," Rat tells me as he catches up to our group.

I'm looking around for Susie and Connie, hoping I can find them and join them at the wake. Everybody will be there and it's important I put on a positive image, showing the laid-back lover, still available, is working things out.

"I would think he would want his ashes in some more auspicious place like the top of a snow-clad mountain or a glacier," I point out. "Also, I kind of wonder why someone that young and active would even have a will or have made a conscious decision whether to have his body rot or go up in flames. I know I haven't done it. You all would have to make it up on the fly."

"Fuck you," Coney responds. "I'd just as soon as have my body thrown in Blue Mesa so the trout can eat me."

"They won't touch your worthless carcass," cracks the Weasel. "Not enough meat on the bones to interest even a starving coyote."

We approach the large two-story house on the corner with a cute white picket fence around a highly out of place patch of green lawn, where I first spot Connie and then Susie sitting in the corner all by themselves. I break free from the boys and head straight for them. I pick some columbines near the house, and now I boldly walk straight up to Susie, who is lying on the ground in front of Connie in her usual cross-legged yoga position, and present them to her.

"Hi Susie," I greet her respectfully. I check them both and they don't look like they have been crying, like most of the rest of the women standing or grouped in support circles. Some are holding hands and some are dabbing their noses with dainty handkerchiefs. "How're you doing?"

"I'm fine," she says back without much emotion. She avoids eye contact, looking away fast.

"How are you doing, Connie?" I pull one columbine out of the bunch and hand it to her. The rest I give to Susie and when she lets me get close, handing them to her, I go in for a kiss on the cheek.

She rears back and looks at me like I'm a baby raper. "Don't do that."

She wipes her cheek with the back of her hand. She takes the columbines, however, and holds them up to her face while making a curled upper lip grimace. Connie laughs.

"Nice, Cowboy," Connie cracks. "You move right in using funerals and flowers to score." She smiles at me. "Sit down here and we'll watch how other people show their feelings about love, life, and death."

I sit down next to Susie, who is now looking out over the growing crowd and acknowledging friends whenever they see her by waving or saying 'Hi.'

I begin recalling the words to the flying poem. I learned it some time ago when I first ran into it and I was flying a lot, but I need to concentrate on remembering the exact words. When I finally work it out, I give a little recital for the Fisher twins:

"Oh! I have slipped the surly bonds of Earth, and danced the skies on laughter-silvered wings...."

*

I feel the obvious tension from Susie. She doesn't know how to handle my advances. She suspects Connie had something to do with it, but says nothing. Finally, after many long and awkward moments, the crowd gathers around some guy wearing a simple frock or vestment of some kind.

"We have come here to honor our friend and neighbor, Robert Pimentel, taken from us so very, very soon and without warning. We must all accept God's will and feel blessed with the life he has given."

I don't feel very blessed. But Pimmy should feel even worse, killing ten. All I've lost is my love, my fortune, and now, probably my dignity. I'm trying to grovel in repentance for Susie and getting no traction at all. It's like we never touched each other, ever. Our love is as nonexistent as Pimentel is right now, and we ain't getting either one back. I can't wrap my head around the lover who is now dead but sitting in front of me alive and uncaring. It's like she got nailed by a Zombie or something.

The frocked guy keeps talking and leads us out of the yard and down the street to where a ditch from the adjoining ranch is running full of spring runoff along a city street before joining Coal Creek and later the Slate River. He has everybody hold hands and sing "Amazing Grace," in which I fail to see the relevance. He then carefully lifts the silver urn over his head and slowly pours the contents into the ditch. I can't help it, but I snigger a little bit from the existential scene unfolding before me. Sartre would have laughed his ass off.

One of the girls in the loud-weeping group, a little blonde we all know as a coke freak and a good party animal, breaks loose and starts chasing the trail of ashes as they are carried downstream. She gets ahead of them, drops on her knees, and reaches out frantically as the white debris floats by, grabbing at some of the bigger pieces and pocketing them in a plastic bag she has brought along just for this occasion.

When she gets back to the crowd, I hear her say, "Look what I have!" and she holds out proudly the Ziploc bag with some bleached, white bone fragments in it. "Now I will have him with me forever!"

I'm slowly becoming appalled. There is so much going wrong here it's hard to keep track of it all. Suffice it to say, I see a different kind of person in this crowd from the people I first met here ten years ago.

The rugged, self-reliant, freedom-loving adventurer has been replaced by the entitled, rich snobs with their indolent and arrogant demands to be treated special, even better, than the rest of us chumps. We came here to find a safe and sane home in the wilderness where we can be self-reliant and nobody gets uptight about our freedoms. The new young crowd are now here to exploit a little bit of paradise for a grand, old-time profit. An era seems to be coming to an end. The Butte has lost her innocence and freedom, and like a slave, is being sold to the highest bidder.

*

Bam, bam, bam comes from the front door. It's early morning; the sun is up and so am I.

"Cowboy! Wake up! It's Townes!"

I'm in the kitchen having my second whiskey-coffee in order to keep the buzz going. I've been up all night just thinking and crying and generally beating myself to a pulp over my loss.

"I'm awake! In the kitchen! The door's open!" I yell back. He walks in carrying a big box, which he puts on the table.

"Hold on," he says, and runs back outside. Momentarily, he comes back huffing with a rifle case.

"Check this out," he invites, and opens the gun case. Inside is a nice looking engraved over-under shotgun. He takes it out, holds it up to me, and points to some printing on the breach. *Chas. DAILY Commander* is engraved on one side of the breach. "My uncle gave it to me for Christmas a few years ago. I told you I would trade it to you for the .20 gauge you gave me."

I pick it up and take a look at it.

"Wow, this is a nice presentation grade .12 gauge, over-under. It's got a fully selectable trigger with a modified top barrel and full choke bottom. Perfect all-around skeet or bird gun. This has to be worth at least four or five hundred dollars, maybe more."

"I'll trade it straight across for the .20 gauge."

"That old thing. I think it cost me fifty bucks, or was it a friendly bet? Don't remember. It's just an old side-by-side exposed hammer, two-trigger shotgun. I gave it to you without expecting anything in return."

"That .20 gauge fits me perfectly and is exactly what I need for my new home in Tennessee. Did I tell you? I found a little ten-acre farm with a cabin and lots of trees. Cindy took Amigo and I kept Geraldine. The shotgun is just what I need hanging over the fireplace with Geraldine sleeping in front of the fire."

"And you sucking on whiskey and singing songs about the blues and the grass. I think you're crazy, but I'll do it. But to be fair, you have to take my .50-caliber black powder to make it even."

"If you insist. Let's drink on it."

"Coffee?"

"On the side. I don't believe in mixing my drinks."

I pour him a cup of coffee from the drip pot on the stove and get a rocks glass from the cupboard, which I fill with Crown.

"I'm sorry about you and Susie. You were so happy together."

"Right back at yah, with you and Cindy."

We clink cups, but he drinks the whiskey instead.

"Don't worry, Cowboy. You'll get over her, eventually."

"I don't want to."

"I hear yah, amigo, but you will. It's like our love affair with the mountains. At first, we are so impressed it takes our breath away, but soon the storms come and we become jaded and hardened. We eventually leave, feeling betrayed by a harsh but beautiful mistress we cannot tame nor permanently hold."

I refill his glass and add some more to my coffee. Nothing like being a wide-awake drunk at eight in the morning.

"I've got a box here," Townes says, changing the subject, "that I don't want to take back to Texas. I want you to have it."

"What's in it? Ten thousand dollars?"

"Oh, shucks, just some extra stuff I don't need and I thought you could use it."

I look in the box and pull out a 7-inch boxed reel of audio tape. There are about six reels all labeled with *Townes at the Old Quarter, 1974.*

"Those are dubs from the original master recording. I don't even have a reel-to-reel tape recorder. You do, so I thought you should have them."

"That's amazing! Of course I'll take them. I'll take very good care of them and if you want them back anytime, maybe when you get a tape recorder, just let me know."

"Here's a picture of me and Geraldine they did recently for publicity. And this is my Song book that John Lomax just published. I'll autograph it for you. Give me a pen."

I look around and find a ballpoint. I hand it to him and he opens the first page and looks at me mischievously.

"Let's play Tic-Tac-Toe!" he declares, and draws out the playing field. He initials the first box and hands me the pen.

"Are you X or O?" I ask, not knowing what *TVZ* stands for.

"Oh, I'll be *X*. X for Texas."

"Perfect. I'll be *O* for Oregon."

He doesn't play fair and deliberately loses, and then writes below it: *Cowboy, you jerk, you beat me playing Tic-Tac-Toe.* He writes some more on the page that shows him holding the .20 gauge.

"I've been listening a lot to your music, more since Susie's gone. I thought it might help with the pain. I think sometimes it just makes it worse."

"Do I need to explain the Blues to you? It's not about feeling better. It's about sharing the pain to help make it tolerable."

"I don't think it's tolerable."

"And that's why you sing the Blues. I've been beyond tolerable and it's no fun. No sense hurting yourself any more than you have to. Now I just sing like a nightingale and they throw birdseed at me. I don't care. As long as I have a home to share and music to play with my friends, I'm happy."

I start to sing his tune, "To Live Is To Fly." *Everything is not enough, and nothin' is too much to bear.* I pause and Townes picks it up: *Where you been is good and gone.* He points to me and we half-ass harmonize singing together: *All you keep is the getting there.* He laughs to himself and empties his glass.

I start to tear-up, thinking this is a big fucking change in my life, again, and all my fervent mountain dreams just went up in smoke, like a fucking runaway chimney fire. It's obvious I need a new set of pointless dreams to replace the ashes. But dreams that do not include my mountain home are inconceivable. How can I live with myself anywhere else?

"You're a good man, Cowboy, I don't care what they all say about you," he gibes me out of my daze. "But really, you need to brighten up. You've got every reason to be happy. As happy as me, at least. But you're smart and young with a lot of future ahead of you. This town is for incubating, not maturing. Time to move on and do some real growing."

We all got holes to fill, he sings again.

I join in: *Them holes are all that's real. Some fall on you like a storm, sometimes you dig your own!*

"Fuck! You're fucking right! If you can do it, then I can do it," I declare.

"I'll drink to that!" he responds.

"Here's to growing!" I down the last of my sweetened coffee. Townes empties his glass and then looks deeply at its emptiness.

"Is it nine o'clock yet?" he asks, looking up with a grin. "I think we can just catch Mary opening the liquor store if we leave right now. Come on, Cowboy. I'll buy."

~ 20 ~

THE DREAM EXPIRES

The summer is here again in its full glory. But now, the sunny mornings with big beautiful snowcapped mountains standing guard on all sides become a sad mockery of happier past summers. I can't get up the energy to go out in the wilderness without my usual friends and our weird motivations.

Normally, I would be seeking out the latest *Secret Lake*, where cutthroats and browns fight over who'll be the first to commit suicide on my killer fly. Or, I'd be hiking the high country looking for mineral specimens, or just enjoying the sights and sounds of being twelve thousand feet above sea level and part of a forbidding world only known to those who walk there, sleep there, eat there, fuck there, and silently experience every raw emotion there. It's a place of birth, growth, and death. It's a place of challenges, victories, and defeats. But above all, it's my home and I'm not going to be chased out of my home.

*

The town is planning all sorts of festivities this summer for its centennial celebration. The Fourth is loaded with special events, historic tours, parties, and of course, the giant town photograph. I'm running the Princess, showing 16mm docu-

603

mentary films about the history of many Colorado mountain towns. Gary Christopher puts together a slide presentation with pictures made by and about the early miners and the mines who made the Butte the rebel mining town that it still is to this day. Bill Pence even finds an early 16mm film made by the first ski area owners in the sixties showing the two-man enclosed gondola lift in operation and people with stiff skis and leather bindings.

In the afternoon, Mitchell gets on the stage in the middle of Elk Avenue and makes all the stupid proclamations, as most of the townspeople pour out of the bars and congregate for the commemorative group photo. Some guy with a big box camera gets on a stepladder and faces the crowd. I'm riding my klunker around, as are most of the locals on such a nice sunny day, so when we line up for the photo, all the cool townies are sitting on their Klunkers in the back. Just so the solemnity of the occasion is preserved for posterity, I make sure I hold two fingers up behind Susie's head just as the picture is taken.

*

"Hola!" comes the familiar nasal voice of Mitchell over the phone.

"Mitchell. I'm glad I caught you at home," I respond.

"Oh my God!" he feigns excitement. "Have they let you out of that treatment facility for the strange and indifferent? I thought you had to wear orange and pick up trash along I-70 for another three years."

"Funny," I respond emotionlessly. "I'll talk in code so the FBI listening won't be able to figure out what you're up to. What are you up to?"

"I hear you still been hanging out with those Fisher twins. I don't know why they haven't called the cops on you yet. Must be due to some misplaced feelings of caring for a wounded animal or something."

"Yeah, I need some more salt ground into the wound. But seriously, it kinda looks like I'm going to be forced to evacuate my home. Another case of not getting it in writing again."

"Gotta pay for protection in this world. I thought you knew this little Mafia fact."

"Yeah, next time. In the meantime, I need a place to live for a while until I can get things sorted out. Can I move into the upstairs spare bedroom for a while?"

"You know I'd love to, but I don't think that's a good idea. I want to stay friends with the Fisher twins and everyone else you've pissed off in this town. Besides, with all the celebrities I have coming to help us in our fight, I need that room for them."

"Okay. Never mind. Sorry I asked." I start to hang up.

"But stop by anytime. I can use your help with these yahoos. At least you can outdrink most of them so I don't have to put them to bed."

"Thanks, I'll think about it."

But I don't.

*

"Have you ever thought about getting a job?" Dana asks over beers at happy hour.

"What the hell do you think I was doing for the last three years?" I reply. "I run the Princess, own the only computer in town, and built the latest state-of-the-art satellite cable TV system, AND I keep your road show running."

"You know what I mean. This town is just too small for your talents. You do great things here with little reward or even acknowledgment. That's a problem with small towns. They take the exceptional for granted."

"Yeah, thanks, by the way, for intervening with Susie and helping her overcome a lot of my bad publicity."

"Cowboy, Cowboy, Cowboy," he repeats cynically. "You knew the job was dangerous when you took it."

"I thought she was above all the big money bigotry. I thought she was different. I thought she was one of us."

"Often, they can't help it," he counters. "They're brainwashed with old money entitlement."

"I know," I continue, "old money uses good manners and good looks to cover their criminal lies while new money is scorned for its impertinent innocence. Nobody cares what you, the lowly commoner wants, only what you, the lowly slave, can do for them. You're right. I feel terribly used and abused with little or no respect. I'm just another CB version of Rodney Dangerfield. The people I loved and respected are now just screwing with me."

"You're getting some perspective now." He grins at me.

"I just don't want to leave. This is my home. This is where my true inner spirit came to life. This is where my joy and life's meaning come from. If I leave, I will have to become somebody else, somebody I may not want to be."

"Think of it as a sabbatical. Leave for a few years and see the world. Find other work and explore flatter regions. Who knows, maybe you'll become a beach bum like Weitzel. But you can come back anytime. You have friends here for life. Go. Live. Be fruitful elsewhere. There are other people out there deserving of your inspiration and leadership."

"Yah think so, oh mighty captain?" I mockingly mutter.

"I know so. And if you need a place to store some of your stuff until you can get settled somewhere, you can use my garage."

"Can I move into your garage if I stay?"

"No. But here, let me pour you another beer."

*

"Goddamn motherfucker!" I spit out between clenched teeth. "How fucking dare she do this to me! What the fuck is she trying to do?"

"It's okay," Dennis says, trying to calm me. "They've gone. The show's over."

"Goddamn motherfucker sonofabitch, bastards!" I dance around contorting in anger like Joe Cocker. "I can't believe they did this to me. I should have smacked the son of a bitch." I make a couple of false swings with my prop staff to demonstrate. "Why would she do it?!"

"Don't be a fool," Dennis says, trying to calm me down. "She's just testing you. Don't fall for it. Be aloof. Ignore them."

"I can't help it. I try to do something nice for the town this summer. Barbara asked me to be in her little musical review for CB, and I'm trying to do the right thing. But this is a cold-blooded insult and pure mockery of our relationship. It takes cuckolding to a whole new level. She isn't just collecting my cajónes with a rusty knife, but putting them on a flagpole for people to see and marvel at her treachery." I turn to the empty tent now that everyone is gone and yell, "Fuck you, you fucking rat bastard and rich bitch from hell!"

Someone turns the lights out. Dennis pats me on the back again.

"Come on, Cowboy," he says quietly, while steering me to the parking lot. "I need to buy you a drink and explain how Butte dating works these days."

*

I'm seriously considering murder. Not the ugly kind with blood and guts all over the place. I'm thinking it should be clever with a Hitchcock movie twist maybe, for fun. I'm contemplating how I can sabotage a klunker then get the chump to take it coasting down, say Schofield Pass to Slate River. Halfway down on a fast curve, the front brake locks up and he does a double flip over a thousand-foot cliff. Rock & Roll justice!

"Hey, Cowboy." A voice interrupts my dream. I take a look and it's Cloud. He slips into the seat next to me at the Grubstake.

"Hey, buddy. How's it going? Can I buy you a drink?"

"Hey. Got one."

"So, I hear you almost did a cop thing. What's happening?"

"Nothing. She brought her new fuck boy to my tent theater performance up on the hill. I have to do a scene in the audience where I wield a long stick in a threatening manner."

"You didn't."

"I almost did. I saw them laughing at me and I could barely control myself."

"And?"

"I pulled up short before hitting the little rat bastard. But he knew what was happening. He almost fell to the floor, expecting the blow."

"Did anyone else know?"

"Only Susie and the rest of the fucking audience. I can't go back."

"Go back?"

"Do another performance. I can't do it. I feel like shit. I've lost my dignity and I've lost my self-respect, my very reason for living."

"Living here?"

"What?"

"You mean, you have no more reason for living here. I agree. You need to go on a road trip with me."

"Road trip?"

"Yeah, some guy in Albuquerque owes me money so I need to go down there on a collection trip and I need somebody to keep me company. You're gonna love it. I found a junker car in a farmer's field over in Montrose and I just got it running good. It's a '58 Oldsmobile hardtop station wagon. I thought we could drive it down there on a test run."

"I really don't want to be around here with that rat bastard parading my Susie around town like a ten-dollar whore."

"You still have your guns?"

"Yeah, so what?"

"You might want to give them to someone for safekeeping while you're under this much stress."

"Don't worry. If I shot him, it'd mean I'd have to get rid of the gun. I like my guns too much right now to give one up. I'd have to find a Saturday night special for that and that takes a visit to the big city."

"Albuquerque is a big town with lots of cheap pawn shops. Maybe we can find something disposable."

"I was thinking a Harrington and Richardson snub-nosed special would be nice. You know, .32-caliber, which hurts like hell, but rarely fatal."

"So, what about it? Do you want to go?"

"I'll have to find someone to take my place in the show now. Maybe I can get Dennis to do it. He knows my lines. He just can't sing worth shit."

"See, that can work."

"This is a little strange. We haven't been all that close. Can I trust you to not get me in trouble?"

"We're just taking a little vacation to help clear our heads and make some attitude and altitude adjustments. What can go wrong?"

"Compared to here, not much evidently. Okay, I'll go."

"Great. Bring cash, stash, and a sleeping bag. I'll pick you up in the morning."

*

I also bring my backpack. It has all I need for surviving an overnight in the wilderness or a night out in Denver, so it should be just what I need for a Cloud road trip. I get no sleep as usual, but I put it to good use, packing and organizing myself like a modern hippie Boy Scout, prepared for anything cool. Cloud shows up around nine driving a giant Detroit fifties car I don't immediately recognize. On the side written in chrome is *Eighty-Eight* with the rest of the chrome outlining a rocket, or at least a rocket tail fin with red taillights imitating a fiery tail and labeled *Fiesta*.

"It's a 1958 Oldsmobile 88 Fiesta station wagon," announces Cloud anticipating my question. "They only made about three thousand of these babies and this one is still running great. Get in."

I immediately recognize a wonderful work of art, a prime example of *Finds Arts*. Only problem is, the paint has faded from something simply unrecognizable to something looking not unlike a rusty barnacle-encrusted submarine. The paint has mostly broken down to just basic baked-on leftover polymers. This makes it appear ugly. But I think her beauty is only masked by the ravages of age. I'm intrigued. I hope it makes the trip. It does look a little worn.

"Don't worry," Cloud says, "you just have to pump the brakes a little on the steep hills and we have to add about a quart of oil every time we fill up. Did you bring some gas money?"

I climb in the passenger side noting the door works pretty well and closes solidly like a bank vault. I like that in these old battleships.

"Get me out of this burg, Jeeves! We gotta beat the posse to the pass!" I make the cavalry signal to go forward as I slouch down in a blanket-covered bench seat that pokes at your butt with hidden metal springs.

"Gung Ho!" Cloud yells, and peels out in front of the house heading down Sopris and over to White Rock, then past the Chevron station and on up the hill to the outside world.

We follow the usual route south out of the Gunnison Valley by taking the Saguache turnoff just a few miles east of Gunnison. Colorado Highway 114 goes over the Continental Divide at Cochetopa Pass and then down to San Luis Valley where it hooks up with US Highway 285 in Saguache that takes you all the way to Santa Fe and Interstate 25.

"You know, this is where Teitler moved to," I say offhand, as we come out on top of a broad, level treeless plateau area that is the flattest pass, I think, in Colorado.

One expects to have big mountains surrounding a pass, but in this case the giant igneous rocks, granite in composition and white in color, push up what had once been the bottom of a large shallow inland sea, raising some of it intact to Rocky Mountain altitudes. This particular high-altitude ancient sea bottom is loaded with giant ammonite fossils left over from the Mesozoic age. What a strange place to find ancient sea creatures just scattered around on the ground. I know, because I've collected a few.

"Yeah, I know," Cloud answers blandly. "We don't have any animosity. We still speak. They broke up long before I moved in with Helene. It's just how the Butte burns."

"Susie and I were not like that," I flatly state.

He looks at me with skepticism. I sink back into my depression du jour and just stare out the window imagining the bottom of an ocean going by with monsters of the past swirling around expecting a feast. We drive for a while without speaking.

Finally, I break open. "I wasn't a leech. I paid my fair share. We were partners in everything we did."

"You can keep telling yourself that, but does it really make any difference now? I think you're a realist. You know people. You also must have known she was way out of your league."

"We had no league," I insist. "We existed outside of the world of class and bigotry and prejudice. We loved each other for who we are, when we're together, and not for any phony-assed chance of advancement in some silly-assed game of one-upmanship."

"And you believe that?"

I'm getting angry again with that sinking feeling of something controlling me against my own will.

"I don't know what I believe anymore. I came to the mountains to find freedom and like-minded people who love to have fun, love living in remote and hostile environments. Above all, I love this unique town representing shared values of survival through ingenuity, strength through planning and persistence. I gained awareness through living with astonishing natural beauty every day. I just wanted to be a part of it."

"You should be a writer. But you need to get over this rich bitch and get on with your life. Maybe get a job. Go back to the big city for a while."

"I love my home. I shouldn't have to leave it for any reason. Fuck those capitalist pigs."

"Well, just consider for a moment, that Susie is a capitalist pig. She bought you at a low price. She showed off her unique find to her friends. She took advantage of your talents and skills. When the investment no longer pays out enough perks to justify continuing, she trades you in for the latest model, newly rich bachelor turkeys out to celebrate their fortune with snow at a rebel ski area."

My god, I realize he is describing Connie. Susie is the opposite of Connie when it comes to commitment and love. Connie was just in it for the cheap thrills. She had no intention of being someone else's dream partner. Is Susie the same, only a little slower? Or did she mean it when she said she was not like Connie, and loved me truly and sincerely. I can't believe the Susie I knew could now be so shallow. I sink into an even deeper, more despondent depression and stop talking to Cloud about my love life.

"Let's stop in Saguache," I suggest. "I need some more beer and need to take a piss. Did you bring any weed?"

Of course, being late summer, the new crop isn't in yet and last year's supply is getting thin. I ran out some time ago and Cloud can't afford the high-priced crap that has taken over the town's taste.

"I know a guy in Taos," Cloud offers. "We can stop there on the way to Santa Fe and check him out."

"Good. I need something other than beer to keep me from flipping off the world."

San Luis Valley is a great open flat area made from the surrounding mountain erosion over the ages, forming a perfectly flat rich soil area where although the winters are brutal, can grow some amazing crops in the high mountain sun. There are artesian wells everywhere so that in the winter, mountains of ice can build around the continuous water shooting out of the ground. This area is so fertile, old man Coors bought up a lot of it so he would have a stable and cheap source of grain and hops for his outrageously badly made, but highly profitable regional beer.

We pass through the triple towns of Del Norte, Monte Vista, and Alamosa when we cross US highway 160. I recall my time as a teenager living in nearby Wagon Wheel Gap for a year when I first came to the mountains as a young boy of 13 and exposing myself to bigger things outside of my life for the first time. It was then I found a very big world up here in the mountains just waiting for me to discover. I couldn't get enough of it. And yet here I am, being told by fate, I can't stay.

It's dark by the time we get to Taos. We stop at a gas station and Cloud calls his connection. He comes back to the car smiling.

"Good news," he says, climbing back into the driver's seat. "My friends say some good shit just showed up and he can let us have some. Plus, we can spend the night there, couching it. How much money have you got?"

We find this guy's house in a new development area just west of town, along with a new pickup in the driveway and a sailboat. Probably from Texas, where boats are a status symbol. Here, it just means you're willing to spend money on an idea where it produces little of either.

Inside, George and his beautiful girlfriend, Jennie, welcome Cloud like a long-lost brother. There is much hugging and patting of backs. I look around and sure enough, there's a stack of audio equipment in the corner with all the big names in expensive sound. This guy deals more than just pot.

"Here," he says holding up a joint. "Jen twisted up a fat one for you right after you called." He hands it to Cloud along with a Bic lighter. "So, you still living up there in the snow country?"

Cloud takes a big hit and hands it to me. They go on talking while I contemplate the joint, smell its smoke, take a hit, suck in some air, take another longer hit, suck in some more air, and hold it. I look around while I'm holding it in and see they're all in animated conversation about Los Angeles and making movies or something. Cloud originally showed up in Crested Butte with some friends claiming they were members of a biker gang that had been hired by some movie producers to do stunts. Most of the others drifted away at the end of that first summer, but Cloud stayed as our very own stranger in a strange land or local rebel without a cause.

"Sorry guys, but I don't have enough to sell you right here. But you're in luck. Tomorrow there's a party at the farm where the rest is being stored. Why don't you follow us out there and we'll get you taken care of and you can hang out and party in the sun? There'll be kegs and god knows what. There might even be a band."

I'm feeling measurably better after having some sweet-tasting weed. "Sure," I agree. "Let's party."

*

I don't sleep anymore. I just sort of drink myself into a stupor and then lie down for a few hours to recuperate. I get the couch, so when the sun rises at five a.m., I get up and wander around the quiet house feeling its vibe. I take note of all the impertinent Southwest decorations like Navajo rugs hanging on the walls and decorated clay pots in every nook and cranny. Baskets are stacked everywhere. They have plastic vigas overhead and a phony kiva fireplace in one corner.

Everything glaring and out of place marks this decorative Southwest style as being image only. Young cool people who have no culture of their own, when attracted to a region, always overdo their adoption of the local cultural symbols, bastardizing them by abstracting a plasticized New York pop art genre as some kind of cool legitimate successor to actual art. I find it insulting to a *Finds Arts* artist.

"Good morning," Jennie says, walking into the kitchen wearing almost nothing. "Want some tea?"

"That would be nice," I say slowly.

That's another thing I have a beef about with the modern young politically correct crowd. They consider it okay to trigger my pre-wired deterministic animal desires at will, while I have the legal obligation to ignore it, suppress it, or at best, figure out how to enjoy the view without being too weird. I opt for the later and let my eyes have some enjoyment while suppressing my libido. It's a trap to me that screams *DUCK!* Or, as Cloud would say, *Suck it up and be a eunuch.* Somehow, I don't believe that the male is designed to be able to do such things. After all, sex is about a two-hundred-million-year-old evolutionary force molding our bodies and minds, while morals are a much more recent invention by man alone.

"Is Earl Grey, okay?"

"Sure," I reply. "You have a lovely house here. I like the adobe parts. It's so earthy. I'm a big fan of the desert."

"Thank you. Aren't you sweet. It cost us a lot, but the property values are rising so we look at it as an investment. Have you been here before? Taos, I mean."

"I've been through a couple of times. There's a ski area here where we raced Gelande back when alpine skiers thought they were flyers. Bad snow if I remember."

"You race?"

"No. My girlfriend raced telemark. I just take the pictures."

"Oh. Wow. Is she the one Cloud mentioned, who's driving you crazy?"

"I'm not crazy. Yet. But when she brings her new boyfriend to town, and throws him in my face, I have to prevent a murder by getting out of town for some R&R."

"That doesn't sound good. But good for you." She hands me a cup of hot tea. "They'll be some girls at the party this afternoon. I'm sure somebody with the name *Cowboy* will be able to get right back on the horse, so to speak. Isn't that what cowboys do?" She pats me on the shoulder and leaves with two more cups in her hand.

"Yeah. That's what we do."

*

We have to drive through Santa Fe and get on I-25 headed back toward Denver, then take the exit for Las Vegas, New Mexico. We drive up into the desert foothills north of the highway overlooking the flat part of New Mexico to the east and south, all the way to Texas and beyond.

Finally, after a couple miles of dirt roads, we pull into a rustic-looking ranch tucked into some rolling hills behind, with an adobe hacienda and some old barnwood buildings scattered about, baked as dark as mud in the brutal eastern New Mexico sun. Even the corral fences are sunburned to a matching shade. The place looks old and well-used with a somewhat dilapidated look, except there's no sign of any animals or other productive farm activity. There are lots of cars, mostly pickups, already parked among the sagebrush around the main house. Music can be heard coming from the direction of the biggest barn.

"George said this guy made some serious money," explains Cloud, "on a Santa Fe real estate deal and just bought this six-hundred-acre cattle ranch to develop a solar energy housing project."

"He picked the right spot for solar. But where is he going to get water?" I pose.

"If they had cattle, they must have had water. Maybe there are springs up in the hills above us."

We walk to the hacienda where we catch up with George and Jennie. George already sports a paper bag and a big smile.

"Here you go boys. Have a nice trip. But you might as well stick around this afternoon and enjoy some tunes and free beer."

We can see dozens of people milling about outside the barn and the sound of some Texas swing band can be heard from inside. It is already getting hot and the men all wear cowboy hats and no shirts, while the girls wear shorts and halter tops. Everybody has their signature sunglasses on, but nobody has my style, Vuarnet Glaciers. These are a bunch of Willie Nelson-type C&W addicts. Drugs, dirty cowboy hats, slim denims, and cowboy boots but no socks mark these southern Rocky Mountain cousins. There's an awful lot of turquoise set in silver flashing about, and I like that. Jewelry always makes the person, and turquoise looks good on anyone.

"I'm not into that kind of music," I say, "but I'll have a beer or two."

I follow Cloud and his friends up to the barn, where we find the kegs. I fill up two big cups so I can limit the number of times I have to get a refill and begin to wander around to the side of the noisy crowded barn and out back to the only green area I've seen so far, with a big cottonwood tree shading one end of a small watered pasture.

Cloud is right. I can see a pipe coming out of the ground and hanging over a big cattle tank up the side of the hill. A green area spreads out on the downhill side all the way across the pasture area to the barn. I head for the only shade around, the tree.

"Cowboy?"

I turn around suddenly, hearing her familiar Brooklyn accent.

"Amy!"

She comes running up and we immediately hug each other tightly. We have history.

"What are you doing here?" I ask, as we continue to walk together across the pasture to the tree.

"I could ask the same of you."

"I'm on a road trip with Cloud. What's your excuse?"

"Is Cloud here, too?"

"Back in the barn with all the other country-music freaks. I thought you were in Farmington working your art."

"Like everyone else, I'm not a trust-funder and need a better source of income than art allows. I'm working on my real estate license and moving to Albuquerque. The guy throwing the party is helping me break into the business. How do you know him?"

"We're just here to pick up some weed for our trip. We're on our way to Albuquerque, too. Cloud needs to make a collection or something and I had to get out of town to prevent a murder."

"Should I ask who? No, let me guess. Is it Glazer?"

"No, I'm over that cheap fucking crook. It's Susie's new lover."

She stops and doesn't speak until it sinks in. "Oh! Cowboy, I am so sorry. You must be devastated!" She hugs me again, only harder. I need all the solace I can get so I welcome her embrace. It's comforting, coming from a woman I respect.

"Jesus, I guess the Butte burns another couple. I thought you and Susie were different. Here, let's sit down and you can tell me all about it. Hand me your bag and I'll roll you up one like the good old days."

"Yeah, thanks, so did I. It was kind of a surprise. I didn't see it coming until apparently it was too late."

"You know Susan and Cordley broke up," she flatly announced.

"No! I mean, finally? I always thought she didn't really fit in with our little weird group, although she's a great artist, in her own way. I liked her a lot, but she's way too serious for me."

"You're not going to believe who she took up with." She pauses for effect, but can't wait. "Kirk the Jerk!"

"What? Gallagher? The drunken shirtless pugilist? That makes no sense. She's got to be smarter than that. I can't imagine what they have in common." I start giggling to myself.

She just smiles brightly, realizing I have temporarily forgotten all about my problems, contemplating something even more absurd, maybe, than my own situation. She takes my bag and finds the Zig-Zags.

"My god," I continue, "what is it about the Butte that lovers can't stay lovers very long? *Geez*, just about everybody I know who came to town with a partner, or found one there, splits up within a year or two. What does Crested Butte have against good old-fashioned loyalty and love?"

"In a place where love and freedom coexist," she says, while crushing up a bud, "love gets reexamined every day one exercises their freedoms. What do you think is going to happen? The Butte is basically a seething pile of young, virile, testosterone-poisoned and estrogen-addicted skiers all mixed up with cocaine and alcohol, while crucially lacking about half the oxygen normally required for rational thought. If you really love her, you should have gotten her out of there and somewhere saner, sooner." She spreads her clean mixture on the paper.

"But Crested Butte is our saner place," I protest. "We fit. We belonged. We were so good together. We ran the Princess, skied together, fished, camped, sailed, and built a home together. I could have been rich except for Glazer, but that proved my ability. I can do so much more than just about anyone else, why didn't she see that and stay loyal?"

"You're damn near a dying breed, Cowboy. You fall in love with a woman, then you're unfailingly loyal to her. You don't feel the need to go sniffing around and trying to put as many notches in your bedpost as you can. That's pretty rare, and it's one of the things I love about you." She produces a recognizable joint and holds it up by one end. "*Voila!*"

"I should have hooked up with you in the beginning, but with Bill and everything, I didn't think that was what you wanted or needed."

"I don't know. I could have imagined it, maybe, back then. But it all works out. I chose my life and I thank you for giving me the opportunity to be here. But, if you and I had been a Crested Butte couple, we would have probably ended up getting the burn just like everyone else."

"For old times' sake," I propose, "let's smoke this joint and just watch the dust settle on the plain. I feel like being happy again."

*

Around late afternoon when the sun lowers behind the mountains and the heat turns to desert chill, I kiss Amy reluctantly goodbye with a promise to visit her in Albuquerque someday, then drive away in the '58 Olds. I have to drive because Cloud is too drunk to drive. We fill up just outside Albuquerque and Cloud wakes up, makes a phone call, and takes over driving.

Next thing I know, we're at a big downtown dance bar with a live band playing about the same music as I heard all afternoon at the hacienda. These people seem to have a broken record that keeps playing the same tunes, over and over. Boring.

I figure I'm along just to watch Cloud's back, so inside, I order a beer in a can and wander around in the shadows while Cloud looks for his contact. I notice a couple different colors on denim jackets, so there must be more than one biker gang in here tonight. That's not reassuring. I don't like these redneck bars because of the chance of offending someone just by the length of your hair. But like this afternoon, I noticed that a lot of these drugstore cowboys now have hair as long as mine. Did I miss something?

I noticed most men's hair length in New York is pleasantly longer than the Nazi '50s, but here in the outlands, they seem to have gone Rock & Roll on us with something they call the Austin sound, and now they smoke dope and grow long hair just like the best Village hippie. Looks like Muskogee, Oklahoma lost the war on drugs and even their kids are expressing their new sense of freedom to look and imbibe whatever silly way they want. I just wish they displayed more artistic taste, but I'll settle for any display of freedom as long as it's honest.

I also notice a new liquor has hit the bar world. Cloud hears about it and buys a pint of *Yukon Jack* just because it sports an alcohol content of 150 proof. I try it and discover what most alcoholics already knew: drinking mouthwash is never a good substitute for plain old American corn whiskey.

"I'm looking for an old friend," Cloud explains when the loud country band stops playing for a minute, "who was the main dealer here. He recently moved to some farm up north of Taos and I'm trying to find out the location." He looks at his shot glass and grimaces. "This candy tastes nasty."

He moves around the crowd, fitting right in with the desert western dirty look. It all starts with the well-worn, sweat-banded truck-squashed Stetson or something resembling it, the more unrecognizable, the more individualistic and desirable...feathers optional. I prefer my open-top leather tennis sunshade resembling what Hunter wears.

Cloud seems to know some people and speaks easily with even the most unwashed. I, on the other hand, am left alone and given hardly any notice by the crazed and sweaty dancing natives. I check out a few of the women present, but none resemble anything close to attractive. I wonder what they use for pheromones down here and then look at the Yukon Jack bottle and it all begins to make sense. I guess that's how you think when you're on this stuff.

*

I'm trying to keep from looking outside my down bag. I can't bear to see bright sunshine what with the raging drums beating my brains to death. I can handle only one catastrophe at a time.

"Hey! Cowboy! You awake?" Cloud yells from somewhere outside. He pounds on the car. I'm now guessing I'm shacked up in the back of the '58 Olds and Cloud spent the night with some girl he picked up at the bar.

"No!" I yell back. "Dave's not here! Go away."

"Gotta go," he yells back, and I hear a door open and feel the car move as his full weight hits the driver's seat. "I got the location of the farm. It's up near Questa."

"Take me to coffee or I'll die and stink up this hunk of steel forever." I peek out and immediately suffer retinal searing. I fumble around and remember where I stashed my Vuarnet's. Once on, I look again and thank my fortune for having *number-nine-welding-goggles* for just these sunny desert hangovers.

Cloud finds a good ol' American diner near Route 66 and I cure my hangover the old-fashioned way: chicken-fried steak smothered in white gravy, a side order of hash browns sliding around a greasy plate, and two eggs sunny-side up, staring you down and winning.

We head back to Santa Fe, on to Taos, and then up the inland valley on the east side to the little town of Questa. There's a line of mountains on the east running north-south. Cloud explains that we are heading for an old Mormon farm tucked away in one of the west-facing canyons that was used recently as a hippie commune.

Several families shared the property and tried to build a self-sustainable organic farm that was a paradise on earth, for them and their children. That was ten years ago, and now Cloud's wealthy dope-dealer friend from Albuquerque just bought the farm from the bank. It was in foreclosure and the families had vacated their little piece of rural hippie heaven and apparently retreated back to capitalist hell to dwell among the shirts and ties.

We arrive near sunset and while Cloud is inside the main house with his friend, conducting his business, I wander around the property. I find it fascinating. I can identify the old buildings and barns belonging to the Mormon days and then the new stuff the hippies had built creating their concept of how a farm should be organized and run.

There are little shacks, multi-roomed and multi-storied, that sort of look like a village for elves and hobbits. The structures are free-form with rooms hanging off the side of other rooms, sort of like a random stack of blocks. Another structure is a delightful combination of an old travel trailer forming the heart of the house and sporting rustic barnwood additions, artistically designed, providing two-story bedrooms with incredible views. I am impressed with the amount of work they obviously did to create a little tribal village, where no doubt the usual conventions of society may not have applied. Now it's in sad disrepair and suffering abuse by invading desert creatures.

They also built an irrigation system based on running black plastic pipe everywhere and then planted vegetables in little raised garden areas that were heavily composted and symbiotically designed to resist pests and be free of insecticides. Clearly, they had been growing big-vine plants that do well in the sun, like watermelons and cantaloupes. I'm guessing they probably tried to sell their produce to the new fancy restaurants in Taos and Santa Fe. I even find a bunch of roughly built enclosures probably used for small animals like goats or sheep. It really looks like they worked very hard to make it a nice place to live. I wonder what went wrong.

*

"Apparently, it was jealousy," Alex says, after I ask him about what happened here. Alex is Cloud's friend who bought the place and is living here now doing some serious remodeling. When I return from my walk around, Cloud motions me into the house where he introduces me to Alex. Alex is pouring some shots of whiskey and looks like most young people today, long hair, some well-trimmed facial hair, and wearing the appropriately soiled Stetson with well-worn Levi's jacket. "They borrowed a bunch of money to improve their operation and when it was spent, they got into a fight about the mortgage payments. They defaulted and I bought it from the bank for about half the amount they paid for it."

"Tell him about the wife swapping," says Cloud, puffing on a joint that he now hands to me.

"Yeah, the two main families, the ones with kids and some money, ended up having a double affair. They were cheating on each other at the same time and when they all figured it out, the women end up switching husbands and addresses."

"See, Cowboy," Cloud points out, "you're not the only one finding that it's hard for paradise and true love to coexist."

"Given all this natural beauty around here," I point out between puffs on the joint, "and the life they were attempting, why would anyone jeopardize it all just for a little nasty nookie?" I pass the joint back to Alex.

"I don't know either," says Alex, "but their natural inclinations have turned into my lucky fortune. I'm going to develop this into five-acre ranchettes that will go for several hundred thousand apiece. I have enough land and water to build ten of them. Here's to hippie nastiness!" he proclaims, holding his shot glass up in a toast.

"To nasty sex and those who pursue it!" Cloud responds.

"Fuck 'em all!" I add, and we all down our shots.

*

On the way back to the Butte the next day, we stop for supplies in Alamosa, where Cloud stocks up on beer and sandwiches for the trip over the pass. Cloud must be feeling pretty good from his business dealings with Alex because he pulls out a big bottle of cocaine and offers me a healthy snort just before handing the car over to me for driving. Once I'm relaxed from the road and the buzz, he starts in on me.

"You know, Cowboy," he begins. "You really are too good for Crested Butte. They don't appreciate intellectuals with advanced degrees. Crested Butte has been taken over by New York trust funders and they are all out to turn it into an exclusive resort for the rich and famous. You just don't fit in unless you have money. Do you have money?"

I look dumbfounded at him. "Are you kidding?"

"I thought so. That would make you their boy toy at best or a hired slave at worst. Knowing you, I'd guess you were a curious toy for a while, someone different from their average victim."

"Susie wasn't like that," I protest.

"Sure, and tigers without stripes eat grass. Listen, chump, you have to get over this bitch and get on with an exciting and wildly interesting life. What she saw in you is your intelligence and potential. But you can't play their privileged game of one upmanship so she dumps you for failing to keep them righteously entertained. She was using you. And when they realize you can't be tamed, she and her kind simply go on to the next one."

"Maybe Connie and some of her friends are like that, but Susie is different. I know I can get her back if I can just get her away from those jealous rich bitches she hangs out with who couldn't stand our happiness."

"Well, believe that if you want, but for now, you need to move past these small people. Maybe you can get a high-paying job in Denver for a while. You'll still be within commuting distance on weekends and can eventually maybe move back."

"I've been thinking I might have to try that. I just don't know what I can do down there. Nobody is hiring physics graduate students and my computer skills are limited to Fortran and some Unix."

"What about that satellite TV work you do? I heard you brag about installing satellite dishes for rock stars."

"They're still too expensive. Someday, everyone will have a satellite dish on their roof, but in the meantime, the price has to come way down before I can do anything with it."

"I heard on the news that Denver is building out a big cable TV system, one of the biggest in the country. Maybe you can show them what you did in the Butte and get a job with them."

"Maybe. I've been thinking about it. If I leave, though, I'm going to have to get a bigger car than my stupid Volkswagen. Susie wants the Nissan back and that means no truck for hauling my stuff."

"Then you need to buy this car," he says bluntly.

"This car?" I look around me at the seats all torn up, and the old cushioned part of the dashboard completely missing. The paint is almost nonexistent and the engine makes funny knocking noises at speeds above sixty. The headliner is actually in good shape as it is solid compressed board instead of cloth. The chrome and Rocket 88 design, though, give it style, and I do like style. It's clearly unique, having never really seen one like it before, and I probably would never see another one again. "How much?"

"For you," he says with a twinkle in his eye, "I'll make you a deal you can't refuse."

"Watch me."

"How about, nothing? I'll trade you straight across for the Volkswagen, sight unseen."

"You've seen it. You helped me repair the engine."

"Nevertheless, I'll stick to my offer. What do you say?"

When I get back to the Butte, I settle on a plan and as part of the retreat, I will spend my days working on my high-altitude tan al fresco, relaxing in my lounge chair in the backyard next to the little burbling creek, with a view to kill for. At least I'll look good for the summer flatlanders.

I get up the courage to call Mile Hi Cablevision in Denver and ask them point blank: "I'm calling about a job as an engineer. Who do I need to talk to?" I say to the female receptionist on the other end.

"VP of Engineering is Brian Owens. I'll see if he's in." Then the elevator music starts. I drop the handset to my side while I take a puff on some of the dynamite weed we brought back from Taos.

"Oh God," I mutter to myself, listening to the canned noise. "I can just imagine these yuppie clowns with their starched shirts and skinny ties."

"Hello, Brian here."

"I have a First-Class FCC License and need a job. Do you have anything?"

"Okay. First of all, who are you?"

"I go by the name of Cowboy and I just built the cable system and satellite dish in Crested Butte. Maybe you saw the article in the *Rocky Mountain News* last year."

"As a matter of fact, I did," he says. "So, you're the ones who put up antennas on forest service land with helicopters and skiers in the dead of winter?"

"That's about it. I need a job. Do you have anything?"

"Why don't you come in next week and I'll introduce you to Bill Daniels and see what we can do for you. How about Wednesday, eleven a.m., so we can go to lunch right afterwards?"

"I'll be there. Where is there?"

"Sheila will give you the address. Hang on and I'll send you back to her. See you Wednesday."

I copy the address and hang up. I think for a moment and decide: *goddamn it, if I have to go back to work for the man, I need to go out in style.* I decide to fly to Denver instead of driving. It's summer and the weather is great. Why not? Denver is only the fourth busiest airport in the country.

*

I climb to twelve thousand feet and dodge the major Collegiate Peaks as I make my way over the Rockies and into the Denver airspace. I'm nervous as hell after all that Pimentel shit we all went through last month, so I keep my eyes peeled for other aircraft and hardly get a chance to admire the incredible views.

I call area control after starting my descent and they vector me all over the Arapahoe Basin in a sort of sightseer's tour, until finally lining me up with one of their service runways and I finally make it on the ground. I grab a taxi that dumps me off in front of a large granite-covered three-story office building in downtown Denver with a huge sign over the entrance announcing *Mile Hi Cablevision* with a big red "C." I shudder for what I am about to have to endure, but charge right in anyway.

There's a nice-looking blonde girl manning the big desk in the foyer with a name plate announcing: *Sheila.*

"Hi, Sheila," I greet her. "I'm Cowboy, and I'm here to see Brian."

"I bet you are. Have a seat and he'll be right down."

I give her a big smile and she throws it right back. She looks like her looks are her only attributes, *but what attributes!* These cable people are into beautiful people. I smell money.

"Hey, Cowboy!" Some guy in a polo shirt and tan jeans yells at me and approaches holding out his hand. "Brian. Glad you could make it. How was the flight in from...where's the nearest airport? Oh yeah, Gunnison."

"I flew a little Piper Colt direct from Crested Butte."

"Impressive. Come on up to my office and we'll talk before meeting Bill for lunch. You know he was a pilot in the Korean War...."

I follow him up the broad marble stairs to the second floor and down a glassed-in hallway to various modern offices. Obviously, from the views of trees and mountains in the distance, these are the executive suites. He's talking all the time about Cablevision and all the great things they are doing like sponsoring Denver sports teams and getting involved in community affairs. When we get to his office, it's decked out in family pictures, company pictures of antennas and telephone poles, and of course, all kinds of sports paraphernalia. I'm getting bored real fast and wondering, even if they don't wear ties here, can I fit with a bunch of Aqua Velva sports nuts? I bet they play golf. *Ugh!*

"Do you ski?" he asks.

"Enough to hurt myself."

"Then you probably wouldn't mind a little blow?"

"Blow?" Then it dawns on me. "Oh, snow! Ah, sure." I'm surprised and look around to make sure there are no cameras or hidden cops.

He pulls a little mirror out from a drawer in his desk and offers me a rolled-up hundred-dollar bill. *What the fuck*, I figure, *when in Rome.* I pull the mirror closer and go to work on a couple of the longer lines.

"I like what I heard about your little system up there. Too bad about your partner. There's a lot of that kind of shit going on. The cable business is an orphan without any family morals or credit and the sharks we have to deal with for construction capital are pretty scary sometimes. For instance, we're having to raise money for the Denver build by offering short-term, high-yield real estate asset investment contracts. I think you'll find Bill runs a different kind of show here. He's honest and open. A great guy to work for. As a company, we are one of a kind with aggressive internal advancement, great benefits, and liberal stock options."

"And apparently, perks," I squeeze out between little sneezes and snorts. It burns like hell, so I reason it's cheap, stomped-on street shit. But it sorta works and I gum a little for a bump.

"What about a job?" I remind him. Before he answers, his phone rings and he picks up the handset instead.

"Brian here." ... "That's a shame." ... "I'll tell him." ... "That's what I thought." ... "Have a good flight."

"That was Bill. He can't make it. He has to catch a flight to Chicago for some investment meeting that suddenly came up. But Bob Thomas will be joining us. He's our pole attachment specialist and helps us coordinate with the utilities for hanging our cables."

"Terrific," I say.

"Bill said you might be perfect for our Greeley build. We just hired our management team to start construction there and they need a chief engineer to get started designing and installing the headend. When can you start?"

*

I almost wish they had been a big disappointment and no job. This is too easy. I tend to be suspicious of things that seem too easy. There might be a hidden reason that if known, would change everything. In this case, I can't think of one, except for their total lack of any style when it came to clothing, hair, and music. I'll just have to be tolerant and adapt.

I fly back in the late afternoon with the glorious sun lighting up all the bare peaks of late summer. The white rocks making up the core of the Rockies are prominent from this vantage and stand out like sentinels holding up the sky. I also think about how this might be the last time I fly into the Butte for a while. Sadness returns and I sink into a deep depression, as I now have to force myself to do something I never thought in my wildest dreams I would have to do: leave my mountain home.

*

It's a normally cold gray September day when I finally box everything up and pack most of the big stuff into Dana's garage.

"Now don't leave this stuff here too long. I might need the space," Dana warns me. "Don't be a bad boy."

"Don't worry. I don't want to leave it here, anyway. As soon as I can rent a house, I'll find a trailer and come get it. Maybe over Thanksgiving. Is that what everyone thinks? I'm a bad boy?"

"Bad in a good way," he backtracks with his big Dartmouth grin. "So, you're going to be running the cable system in Greeley?"

"Chief engineer. They're building a production studio and I might have some cameras I can use for some of your projects. The company I work for is weird. They don't wear ties, they play golf and ski with helmets, and apparently do a lot of coke."

"It's the new generation of money wranglers. They're called Yuppies. Young, Upwardly-mobile Pragmatists."

"Young Upwardly-mobile Pricks is more like it."

"They want the money now and they're willing to play the game. Don't worry, they wear ties when they need to. They take a very practical approach to success: something like, whatever works, works. Be careful."

"I've had my lesson in practical business. Screw everyone just like they want to screw you."

"That should work in Denver. But honestly, don't leave your stuff here forever."

*

The last thing I have to do is stop by the theater and pick up my final check. Susie is working there tonight and I don't want her to see me forced to slink out of town in the dead of night with barely a shred of self-respect left. I am pretty drunk because it takes a lot of booze to numb the feelings just enough so I can do what I have to do.

"Hey! Rat! Open the window!" I yell up from the sidewalk in front of the Princess. The lights are out and nobody is in the lobby while the movie is still going on in the auditorium. I throw a rock up and bounce it off the window. Then Rat opens it.

"Who's there?" he yells, sticking his head out.

"Hey! It's me." I wave my arms.

"Oh, it's you. Good thing you dropped by. I thought you might have left already. I've got your check. Stay there and I'll bring it down."

He disappears and pops out the front door shortly, holding an envelope in his hand.

"Here," he says and he hands it to me. "So, you headed for Greeley tonight?"

"Is he in there with her?"

"Don't go down that road," he cautions. "She's made her choice."

"Why is it always the woman's choice? But if that rotten shit rat bastard thinks he can just slide into my life, and steal my girl—"

"That sounds about right," Rat adds.

"He's lucky I don't stick his head in the popcorn machine while it's full of hot cancer-producing palm seed oil."

"Real clever. Not to change the subject, but do you think this Cloud contraption is going to make it to Denver tonight?"

"It got us to Albuquerque and back. It'll get to Denver, no problem." I have a flash of not making it.

"Well, write if you get work." We hear the bell ring from the running projector upstairs indicating it's close to a changeover. "Gotta go. Take care!"

I slide into the driver's side, start the old car with a sigh, and pull out from the curb on my last sad ride down Elk Avenue and out of town for...for what? I don't know. I pop a beer as I accelerate up the hill, losing sight of the town in my rearview mirror.

*

"Damn, it's getting dark," I finally have to admit to myself, squinting out the windshield into stark darkness surrounding a lonely white line ribbon all too closely appearing out of the black void. "Something's not right," I drunkenly declare.

I'm driving all night taking the usual roads out of the mountains to the eastern flatlands and in this case, a little town just north of Denver: Greeley. I stare at the battery meter on the dashboard, noting its own dimness. Maybe I'm going blind from alcohol. I've been pounding beers all day long and even while driving over the pass I chain drink until I can barely see. I even spin the old girl 360 degrees from alcohol spasms steering on a straight and level road just north of Salida. That scares the shit out of me. I have to get out of the car and run around it in tight circles, burning up some of the debilitating horse piss so I can continue. My new job starts in about four more hours and I'm still three hours out of Denver.

"Oh no! Et tu? When's the fun going to stop?" I pound my fists on the oversized '58 Oldsmobile's steering wheel. I'm being forced out of my home, out of my paradise, out of my life. I've lost everything. I've lost my only home, my best friends, my only true love, my meager fortune, and now, the last of my dignity. I've not only lost the only love of my life but lost my ability to ever love again. There's nothing left to love with. I shamefully wipe away more tears for the umpteenth time this night as I pop another Coors.

I finally admit to myself that the battery meter reads low and I'm slowly discharging the car's battery driving at night with the lights on. The generator just can't keep up. Soon, I will be stranded without any hope of making it to my new job on time. Literally, after all that's happened, my last chance of surviving today with any trace of self-esteem intact, quickly slips from my weak and desperate grasp, leaving me a hollow crust of burned-out worthlessness.

"SHIT! FUCK! WHORE!" I scream into the empty void, soaking it up and choking it off so fast, it's as if it never happened. Then the old car just slowly dies and I have to steer it slowly to the shoulder, leaving me now in total silence as well as absolute darkness.

"I-I-I-E-E-E-E-E!!!" I scream uncontrollably, jumping around in the front seat flailing my arms and legs and then, I abruptly stop. The silent curtain descends like a stone wall along with a lot of foolish feelings. If there are any animals around, I bet they just got their thrill for the night and are hopping home seeking safety and security.

"Where's my home?" I yell. Silence is all I hear. "What the fuck is happening?" I sit for a moment as silence descends again all around me. I think I hear something. Scratching sounds. I don't care. I reach under my seat and pull out the Colt Commander. I pull it out of its holster and look hard at it. I cock it, putting a round in the chamber. I look around me at the darkness outside so enveloping and heavy. How can so much nothing be so soul crushing?

After some more crying like a baby from burning raw emotions and stretched-to-the-breaking point frustration, my eyes get used to the dark and I spot a building not far off the road behind some trees with a truck parked out front. My past nefarious history of overcoming odds at all costs kicks in and with a quick decision, I become calm and determined. I get my miners headlamp out of the back where all my other tools and supplies are stored for the move, grab a crescent wrench, and go about removing my dead battery.

I slip easily into stealth mode and quickly carry my battery over to the nearby parked truck. There, I quietly open the hood, remove the battery, and leave a twenty-dollar bill tucked behind the loose battery cable. Soon, I'm back on the road, my conscience shamed a bit, but what the hell? It's been so badly beaten up and strangled lately, I can barely recognize it as mine and a little more bruising is just, well, unimportant in the great scheme of things. All the activity swapping batteries partially sobers me up and my spirits begin to brighten with the eastern sky.

I find myself on a freeway heading north from Denver, arriving at the Greeley exit just about the time I'm supposed to report to work. I find the little metal building without much trouble just west of downtown by looking for an antenna farm of satellite dishes. They have several already built and two more under construction. I park my Olds out front, conspicuously next to the new white Cablevision trucks and official-looking cars all sporting the corporate logo.

I walk inside, looking a little disheveled from the all-night emotionally devastating trip. A beautiful young blonde woman without a wedding ring is sitting at the reception desk.

"Hello! Can I help you?"

"You sure can, darlin'! I'm Cowboy, your new chief engineer reporting for duty. Where's my office? I need to take a nap."

Dr. Norman P. Johnson splits his home between a horse farm in Lake Stevens, Washington and an off-grid paradise in Hawaii. He is divorced, retired, and has two grown daughters. Some of his many former lives include working under the AEC performing high-energy particle experiments at Argonne National Laboratory and at NASA, launching science satellites and developing large-scale upper-atmospheric computer simulations that became the basis for all computer weather forecasting today. He later became one of the "Higgs Hunters" at the short-lived Superconducting Super Collider in Waxahachie, Texas, where he received his PhD in Theoretical Particle Physics. During the '70s, he spent time touring with major rock bands, gets involved with shady Rock & Roll intrigue and witnesses the backstory on one of Rock's greatest songs, *We're an American Band.* With Fanfare Productions, Ann Arbor, Michigan, he designs and builds a new speaker system that delivered the loudest, clearest PA in the industry and was marketed under the name DCM. He escapes the Nixon oppression by moving to Crested Butte, Colorado, where he designs and builds the first satellite cable TV system in the Rockies. Dr. Johnson later helped design, deploy, and manage large-scale cellular and satellite digital telecommunications systems worldwide for companies such as Daniels Cablevision, Aramco, MCI, Qualcomm and Advanced Radio Telecom. After the internet crash of 1998, he found himself free to start Accel Net, a high-speed wireless internet provider in Seattle, which he grew into a multi-million-dollar business. He enjoys movies and has spent thousands of hours in obscure projection booths showing vintage 35 and 16mm films. He's an accomplished pilot with over two thousand hours in a rebuilt Turbo Mooney he restored from scratch. He has penned several books and screenplays, with more written works in progress. In his off hours, he makes and sells a traditional craft Hash, *Yeti Scat Trails*, enjoys the fruit of his labors, fishes for the wily salmon, skis the flats, restores old things, flies when he can and hangs with animals and other friends at his personal *Rancho Deluxe.*

Wa-ha-ho-te'!

9 780999 099254